To Philip

In Gratitude
For A Job Well Done

Bruce E. Carlson
MAR 01

MW01193295

Red Bird Down

A NOVEL ABOUT AIR CAVALRY
AND AERO-SCOUTS IN VIETNAM

BY
BRUCE E. CARLSON M. DIV.

Copyright © 2000
Bruce E. Carlson

All rights reserves. No part of this book may be reproduced
in any form or media except for the inclusion of brief
quotations in a review, without permission in writing from the
author or publisher.

ISBN 0-9701560-0-6

LOC: 00-91651

First Printing May 2000

Additional Copies of this book are available by mail

Redbird Publications
1600 Grafton Drive
Lexington, NE 68850

Printed in the United States by
Morris Publishing
3212 East Highway 30
Kearney, NE
68847
1-800-650-7888

Dedicated in loving Memory

TO
SARGENT E-5
SCOTT NEAL STANTON
FRIEND, MENTOR, & SUPER-SCOUT
DIED OF WOUNDS 8, SEPT., 1969

THE LITTLE PUPPY

Shriveled, wrinkled and badly worn from a cruel and hard life, old momasan squatted down. With a deep sigh of resignation, she began washing the pilot's bright green flight suit. Looking up from her work, she immediately recognized him. Her recognition came as natural to her as her poverty. She had been working for foreign soldiers most of her life. Reflecting upon her life, she muttered to her self.

"First, he spoke French. Then, for a few years, he spoke Japanese." Shaking her head at a world that she could not understand, she continued. "Suddenly, he became a French speaker again. Today, this one speaks English with a distinctive New England twang." The old woman found the ever-changing world difficult to understand. However, it remained timelessly the same.

Her current charge was the "new guy." One didn't need to be a rocket scientist nor a five-star general to recognize his status within his new world of Vietnam. Just a quick glance loudly broadcast his "NEWBE" status to the veterans. The new guy's freshly issued, bright green jungle fatigues stood out like a Maine pine tree in the midst of the leafless forest's winter snow. Furthermore, his bright eyes and eager energy made him appear as if he were an excited young pup. Like most of his kind, the new guy looked like the young pup who had quietly slipped unwanted and unappreciated into a busy downtown office.

Within the detached Cav Troop, no one wanted to hurt the youngster's feelings. In truth, no one cared a great deal about his feelings either. However, he was becoming a pest. Somehow he was always getting underfoot with his incessant demands for attention. This young man, was just another newly minted Army aviator. Reluctantly, he was beginning to understand his place. His job was to stay out of everyone's way. Despite that humble understanding, he was eager and his steps bounced about with unbridled enthusiasm. Yet, if someone took the time to look deeply into his eyes, what they saw might have surprised them. Bafflement, bewilderment, and the quiet hurt of a rejected puppy filled the youthful depths of his rich brown eyes.

In sad solitude, he stood on the side of the little hill which overlooked the flightline. His quarters, reflecting his emotional world, were bleak, bland, and barren. The nondescript quarters silently stood fifty feet behind him. The Captain, who commanded the Aero-Scouts, had promised the eager new guy that he would begin his "in-country" training soon. However, "soon" was not happening quickly enough. Deeply frustrated, he was growing genuinely impatient at the seemingly endless delays in his training. Like so many who had preceded him, his greatest fear, as he gazed upon the military activity, was that he would spend the duration of "his war" as an unwanted and passive observer to the great adventure.

Just beyond his reach, he looked wistfully upon the varied activities of the busy Army heliport. What greeted his wide eyes was a strikingly beautiful picture slowly unfolding panoramically below him. With little else to do, he continued his quiet and lonely observation. The unrecognized young man stood silently with his hands uselessly jammed into his jungle fatigue's pockets. Reflecting his perceived value, he noted that he wasn't wearing a flight suit. The unspoken message was clear. He was a new guy and yet to be accepted as a Cav pilot.

Suddenly startling him from his musings, he heard several voices stridently repeating a strange and scary sounding refrain. In his previous year of flight school, he had never heard that harsh or urgent refrain.

"Red Bird Down!" And again he heard the refrain. **"Red Bird Down!"**

No other words were spoken. Yet, all about him, the members of the Cav exploded into action. Not understanding, he was bewildered by the suddenness of it all. Confused, he witnesses agitated activity all about the heliport. Just out of his reach, pilots, mechanics, crew chiefs, and door gunners were running about in a frantic military ballet of carefully controlled confusion.

Biting his tongue, he only asked himself, "Good Lord, what's going on?"Everyone, except him that is, was running toward the three flight lines. Dramatically unfolding before his uncomprehending eyes, all the Cav aircraft were being prepared for flight. Everywhere he looked, crewmen were swinging rotor blades and gas turbine engines were whining up to speed. Listening carefully, he could distinctly hear the engines lighting off with their gentle woof. Dancing their individual parts of the ballet, the crews scrambled into their aircraft. While the fast-moving ballet played on, yearning to be one of the dancers, he stood in the wings of the drama.

The eager young pup was avidly devouring the frantic military activities. With eyes wide with awe, he watched the small nimble OH-6A's Loachs, the Red Birds, scrambling out of their revetments. These little birds were the aircraft that he wanted to fly more than he wanted to live. Larger, and far more ungainly were the UH-1H's, commonly called Hueys. He had learned that the Cav called them the Blue Birds. It mattered little what someone called them. Kev knew what they were. Speaking to himself, he muttered. "There go the work horses of the Army's helicopter fleet." They too were cranking up their engines. As their rotor blades slowly began to turn, the Hueys were loading infantry and preparing to takeoff. Far to the other side of the heliport were the slender shark-like AH-1G's. Called Cobras or Snakes by most, the Cav called them the White Birds. They too were trundling with their unique, overloaded ungainly waddle to their takeoff lane.

In what he believed to be his greatest Ernest Hemingway style, he softly and ironically mused.

"This is my war and my greatest story."

The unfolding situation was becoming more painfully difficult for him by the moment. Here he stood, the newly minted Warrant Officer-One, with nothing to do. Kevin Paul Johnson stood forlornly with his hands thrust deeply into his fatigue pants pockets. He was feeling more useless than he had ever felt in his whole terribly uneventful life.

It seemed to him that everybody around him, except for himself, knew exactly what they were doing and where they were going. In his fertile imagination, the dramatic event unfolding before his eyes was just as dashing as a full-color John Wayne movie. It could have been the "Sands of Iwo Jima" or "The Green Berets"

"Wow," the awe struck young man thought to himself.

"The Cav is mounting up and racing off into the sunset. I can't believe what I am seeing. The Cav is stepping out, with the brightly colored pennants and flags of nationhood rippling in the wind."

Unfolding before his bright puppy like eyes, the Cav apparently was heading out on another of its countless and glorious rescue missions. Or, so it seemed to him.

If one looked deeply inside Kev, one would see a star-struck romantic. Most likely, one didn't need to look very deeply. For his whole life he had wanted nothing more than to be in the Cavalry. He had spent years and years dreaming about wearing golden crossed sabers on his collar. As silly as it may seem to the more mature and cynical by nature, Kev had a great dream. In some fantastic and dashing manner, he truly needed to save the world. Or, at the very least, he needed to save a small part of the world. Maybe, if he lived up to his most sacred dreams, he would save the world with a glorious charge into the jaws of death. If he trusted you, young Kev might have told you of his special dream. However, he told no one. He was afraid of being laughed at.

In his imaginative and romantic young eyes, man's highest expression of honor and glory was unfolding before him.

"Gawd, it is beautiful! — It is truly beautiful!"

As the Officers and men of the Cav mounted up, it could easily have been the Light Brigade from decades past. Kev did not need to close his eyes to see his romantic heros beginning their last charge. Looking closely through the cannon smoke and dust, he could see their brightly colored unit pennants rippling purposely in the wind. He could clearly see the brave horsemen with their lances lowered and flashing in the sunlight. Looking to the front of the troops, he saw the officers with their sabers drawn, charging the massed Russian cannon.

Be assured. The romantic Kev was not an ignorant young man. In fact, Kev was a semi-serious student of military history. He was sufficiently well-read to know that the Light Brigade's charge was unbelievably futile. Speaking with a friend one day, while at flight school, he appropriately observed.

"That glorious charge was a militarily moronic mix up of orders compounded by a blind obedience to stupidity."

Nevertheless, being present on that epic battlefield would have been a glorious sight for the romantic fool. He admitted, only to himself, to being such an idealistic and romantic fool. Thinking about it, Kev realistically muttered to the surrounding air.

"Lord, if some of the guys here knew how I felt about being with the Cav, they would laugh me right off the airfield."

Instead of partaking in the glorious event unfolding before him, Kev quietly pouted. Alone, he stood dejectedly on the sidelines. To him, his situation combined both the comical and the cruel. The young man was so close to all that was happening about him. His heightened senses could smell the great production of military history. He could even taste the fever of the moment. Just out of reach, he could see the high drama of men at war unfolding before his unbelieving eyes. Right there, before his dreaming eyes, the Cav of his never-ending romantic dreams was mounting up and setting off on high adventure. The dust, thundering rotors and engines, and the shouting of men was the stereo soundtrack of all his cherished hopes and aspirations. Kev stood forlorn and all the Cav's aircraft were loading, starting, trundling, and waddling their way to their takeoff positions. Again, softly speaking to the unconcerned air, he muttered.

"I wish someone would tell me what is going on!"

Hopelessly lost in his deep longings, he closed his eyes for a moment and allowed himself to dream. To his childish romantic eyes, the scene before him was a reenactment of Britain's Royal Air Force scrambling their Spitfire and Hurricane fighter planes. The cream of British manhood was rising to challenge the onslaught of the German Air Armada. As if magic had transported him through time, he could see them offering their lives to protect their nation. With his eyes closed and a dreamy look on his seamless face, he could almost hear the soul-stirring oration of Sir Winston Churchill. The thundering words were resounding and reverberating in his ears.

"Never in the history of mankind have so many owed so much to so few . . ."

The reality of Kev was that he needed to be one of Churchill's few! Strangely enough, the silly young pup's daydreams continued. For him, it could have been the spring of 1942 serving with the starving Regulars at Bataan in the Philippines. In his youth, he had marveled at the guts and glory of their selflessness. They were buying time, with the most precious commodity of all creation, their lives. In his heart, he could see and feel their heroic and righteously angry sacrifice so American could mobilize the reserves to fight the hated Japanese invaders.

"Darn it! I know why I'm here! Why won't they let me fly?"

Unfortunately, and to his great personal distress, he was not in the middle of military history's great events. Reinforcing his personal horror, he knew that he was only a distant spectator in life's great drama. The events unfolding on the flightline were all powerfully melodramatic, romantic, and so fearfully beautiful to his childish eyes. Deeply distressed, he felt completely useless. Being a passive observer, serving as a mere spectator to the great drama playing out before him was an emotional hell. Passivity was never the part he had envisioned for himself. Rather, Kev saw himself as playing an important part in some magnificent conflict. Regretfully, he acknowledged that the drama of this, once in a lifetime, historic moment, was passing just outside his grasping fingers. Unseen and unknown to him, two sad tears slowly formed in the corners of his brown eyes.

Like the sad-eyed puppy that he resembled, the young man found himself balefully brooding. He felt like a well-trained and well-conditioned young athlete whom the coach has made sit on the bench during the state championship game. Being left out of the frantic preparations made him both frustrated and angry. Muttering to himself, half aloud, he spat his feelings of deep frustration upon the dirt and dust at his feet.

"All the 'glorious' flying that I have done since coming to Viet Nam was to 'fly down' to the administration shack via the old shank's mare. That is, I 'flew down' on my own two big feet and processed several useless reams of the ever-present Army paperwork."

Though, he was forced to begrudgingly admit that he had ridden in the dump truck like cargo bay of an Air Force C-130 cargo plane. However, this kind of flying gave him no satisfaction. He knew that he had been "flying" as another nameless piece of olive-drab cargo, awaiting delivery at the base camp.

"This is not the reason that the Army has trained me!"

With his inner distress mounting, he again angerly kicked at the dust and dirt. Correcting himself, he remembered that he had been in a helicopter. Since arriving in the Republic of Viet Nam, he had spent a grand total of one hour flying the ever-present Huey. Sadly enough, the Huey was a helicopter for which he had no great love. In flight school, he had found the UH-1 to be ungainly. Speaking unkindly, he sometimes called it a duce-and-a-half on skids. Then he remembered that he had also spent another hour as the passenger in the front seat of a Snake.

That Snake flight was his area orientation. Forcing himself to change his mood, he looked at the bright side. He had never been in a Cobra prior to his orientation ride. "At least," he thought to himself, "that was something beyond flight school." The Snake ride had been interesting. Slowly smiling for the first time, he remembered his ride in the Cobra.

"Ya, that little ride was a lot of fun!"

The Snake driver had graciously allowed him to fire the gunner's minigun turret on a gun range. Kev's lack of flight time was bad enough. To Kev, the tragic fact that he had yet to fly his beloved OH-6 only compounded his ever expanding misery. Then, further multiplying his miseries, the powers to be had not even allowed him to touch, caress, and love that beautiful little bird.

Saddened, the young man was beginning to doubt the collective wisdom of Hollywood's countless cinematic productions. Grave doubts were also forming about the military wisdom of all those hundreds of paperback novels which he had so zealously read. He wondered to himself. "Did they know what they were talking about?" The media had spoken so eloquently about the great romance and thrill of combat. So far, in his tour of "combat" duty, he had experienced none of the romance and thrill. Had he been of the mind set to analyze his psychological state, he would have been forced to cry. His static situation deeply depressed him. Most of all, he hated being a "newbe." In brutal truth, being the nameless new guy meant that he did not exist.

Depressed, dejected, discouraged, and looking like a sad-eyed pup, Kev was heartbroken. For the moment, being the newbe had cruelly reduced him to a nobody standing in the settling dust. The Cav was rushing about and on its way to new adventures. Divorced from the adventure, he stood alone like an unfeeling statue. Unmoved, the dust of the helicopter rotors slowly settling on him. Watching the Cav mount up and charge off to the rescue had spent him emotionally and spiritually.

Being left behind was the worst thing that had ever happened to him. Not caring if someone was watching, he repeatedly kicked and scuffed at the dust and dirt like a frustrated little boy watching his big brothers go out to play.

"I feel like I'm . . . , I'm impotent! Look at me, will ya! I am stupidly standing here with my hands dumbly stuck in my pockets unable to do my part."

At last resigned to that which he could not control, he tried his best to graciously accept his unwished-for fate. Poor Kev was beginning to fear that he would remain a passive spectator for the rest of his life. Suddenly shocking him out of his deepening depression, his world was sharply illuminated by the bright light of hope and meaning. Unexpectedly, and coming from a surprising direction, a large man loudly called out his name. That sound suddenly lifted some of the dank dark clouds of disappointment from his head.

Startling Kev, Captain Jack Smith had come running across from his hooch with his battered flight helmet in hand. Running, while strapping on his body armor, the so-called chicken plate, he breathlessly hollered. "Johnson."

"My God. Someone does know my name!"

Quickly responding, Kev turned to the voice issuing the unanticipated summons.

Still, on a fast run, Captain Smith quickly barked some orders.

"Johnson, grab your brain-bucket and chicken plate. I need a peter-pilot, and I need him yesterday. Unfortunately for me, you are all that is available!"

Immediately jumping to the command, Kev easily slipped into his personal and private world. "A peter-pilot, on a slick, well. . . . I guess that's a start. Though, I'd rather a Snake or a Scout bird!" Interrupting Kev's private world, the Captain gave Kev another piece of information.

"We are going to fly out in 993. NOW, MOVE IT, JOHNSON!"

A more rational part of Kev was painfully aware of his true situation, status, and relative value to the Cav. That same rational part of him understood the need for things to be the way that they were. Struggling to keep himself honest, he thought about his circumstance.

"Oh well, I shouldn't complain. I'm just another new guy who doesn't have the foggiest idea about what's going on. Thankfully Captain Jack doesn't have to tell me what a helicopter is."

Suddenly sobered by the urgency of the Captains commands, he added to himself.

"Though, he'll probably have to tell me everything else." Kev's whole train of self depreciating thought took only an instant or less.

Eagerly and quickly, Kev did exactly what the Captain told him to do. Just like the inquisitive puppy that he so resembled, he had spent his every waking moment looking and listening to all that went on around him. Therefore, Kev knew that Captain Jack flew with the Blues.

"Well," he thought to himself. "This means that 993 is a Huey."

Quickly analyzing all the information that he had at hand, Kev came to the obvious conclusion that he would have to meet the Captain down at the Huey line. Without another thought, the rational and the romantic merged back into the normal Kev. Grateful for the attention, the young man moved into action like the good soldier that he craved to be.

Running full-tilt into his personalityless hooch, Kev quickly grabbed his flight helmet and chicken-plate. Trotting down to 993 on the

7

Huey line, he silently said a little prayer asking God to keep an eye on him. Anxiety ridden, the young man was painfully well aware that he didn't know much. Be that as it may, Kev didn't want to make a total fool of himself. So he prayed more pointedly.

"Dear God, I need your help. I don't want to graphically display and prove to everyone that I am a completely useless idiot. We both know that I haven't done any flying in the two months, since I got out of flight school. No doubt about it Lord, my well-trained military mind tells me that my stick work has gotten really rusty. Still, if you could please, would 'You' help me just a little bit?"

The dry, gritty dust produced by the down-wash of the many powerful rotors was beginning to settle at the Huey flight line when the breathless young man arrived. Heavily burdened with his weighty flight gear, poor Kev was gasping and panting deeply. While running from his hooch to the Huey flightline, he discovered that the heat and humidity had almost done him in. The combination of heat, humidity, and exercise had covered him with a heavy coating of sweat which was rapidly mixing with the settling white and red dust. However, Kev was happy and excited. At last, he wasn't going to be flying a Huey in flight school or in an area orientation! Panting, he wistfully thought.

"My goodness. It's true. I'm here!"

Looking at the big bird, he immediately noted that the crewchief had untied and swung the main rotor ninety degrees in preparation for engine start and take off. Very much to his surprise, he found that they had not assigned any ground troops to the aircraft. For some reason, unknown to him, only the helicopter's crew was going out on this flight. The crew consisted of Captain Jack, the crewchief and door gunner, and Kev. The young man wasn't sure what he was supposed to do next. However, Captain Jack immediately took care of that little problem!

"Johnson! Get your newbe butt into the aircraft! I hope to God that I don't have to tell you what seat you belong in."

At least, he knew that sitting to the left of the aircraft commander was where the peter-pilot sat.

Sighing deeply, he muttered to himself.

"Thank God, I know what side a peter-pilot sits on. Heck, ole Kev is so smart that he even knows what side of the helicopter to plant his newbe butt on. I bet that surprised the Captain."

Fortunately for Kev, flight instructors who had recently returned from Viet Nam did more that teach the assigned flight syllabus. Among many other things, they had told their students that "peter-pilot" was just another name for the copilot.

Cross checking his encyclopedia of aviation knowledge, Kev silently prepared himself for the unknown. He reminded himself how things were supposed to happen.

"Captain Jack is the aircraft commander. Thus, he sits in the left seat."

Firmly pulling in the reigns on his racing mind, Kev allowed the rational part of his being to regain control of his actions. Acknowledging his lack of status, Kev knew better than to say anything, to do anything, to think anything, or to touch anything. He quickly and quietly jumped into his right-sided copilot's seat. Fumbling about in excitement, he began to strap himself into his crash harness.

As he was fumbling about with his crash harness, a very surprised Kev experienced, a new, extravagant luxury. The door gunner took personal care of him as peter-pilot and helped him strap in. This strange experience of being important and cared for was totally unlike anything that he had experienced in flight school. When he finished strapping the four-point pilot's harness on Kev, the door-gunner then slid the seat armor forward. With a loud snap, the armor took up its proper residence between Kev and the door. Speaking for the first time, the door gunner slyly commented.

"There you go, sir. You're snug as a bug in a rug, all nice and safe."

Kev was not accustomed to the armor-plated seat. He noted, a little uncomfortably, that with the side armor slid forward, he could neither open nor close the door by himself.

"Whoops" he said to himself.

"In the event of a crash, the armored seat in the Huey has the big time liability of severely limiting my exit options."

He had just discovered another reality about life in Vietnam. The use of the armored seat meant that both pilots were at the mercy of the crewchief and the door gunner. Without their help, it was very difficult to get out of the helicopter. Even with that minor liability, Kev found himself very appreciative of its safety. It felt good have armor plate between him and the people who might like to do him personal harm. Pondering this newly discovered liability, he spoke to his inner self, with what he felt was an appropriate and fair amount of concern.

"If we should crash or be shot down, I'm in 'big time' trouble. Poor Ole Kev can't get out of the aircraft without someone helping him. What if the crewchief and door gunner somehow get hurt? If that happens, ole Kev is going to be in really serious trouble."

Then, grabbing himself by the shirt front and giving himself a little shake, he continued.

"OK Kev, that's enough of this stupid worrying. Remember this! You are mounting up with the Cav! Today, that will have to be more than enough for you. Trust me! Your day will come."

Captain Jack deftly jumped into his own seat. Like Kev, he too was quickly and efficiently strapped in. However, in this case, it was by the crewchief. He too had his armor plate sharply drawn forward for protection from small arms fire. Both Captain Jack and Kev had already plugged into the intercom and radios, through their helmets, when Captain Jack threw the master electrical switch on. With electricity available, the intercom was working. Gracelessly, the Captain told Kev exactly what he wanted him to do, during the flight.

The words spoken to Kev over the intercom made it painfully obvious that he was only a stupid new guy. Everyone on the intercom had no doubt about exactly what the commanding tone and eloquent simplicity of the words meant.

"Johnson, keep your mouth shut. Don't touch anything, unless I tell you to touch it. Don't do anything, unless I clearly tell you to do it. After we are airborne, when and if I have a better idea what is going on, I will brief you!"

As a postscript, the Captain added insult to Kev's battered psyche.

"Not that you will understand what I am talking about."

Bashfully and reluctantly, Kevin quietly resumed his innocent puppy-like state. His pathetic portrayal was complete with sad downcast eyes. Carefully hiding them, his feelings were more than a little hurt by the sharp status setting words which the Captain had just said to him. Yet, the thought of flying into combat exhilarated and excited him. The action, excitement, and unknownness of the moment had him bubbling over with the wonder of it all. However, understanding and accepting his lowly status, he was almost afraid to draw a breath without being ordered to do so. The little puppy felt horribly anxious, because for above all things else, he didn't want to disappoint Captain Jack. Needing to please his peers, he sat as still as a rock.

Yet, inside the private confines of his head, his ever active mind was furiously spinning. At the very least, it was spinning at trans-sonic speed. One repetitive word dominated Kevin Paul Johnson's mind with its holy mantra like cadence.

"Combat!"

One transcending thought was repeating itself repeatedly again and again and over and over in his childishly romantic mind.

"I'm in combat at last. Combat after all those months of training. Combat after all those years of wonderfully romantic dreams. Combat after all those countless numbers of novels and movies. Combat. I can't believe it. I'm finally going into combat!"

As Kev silently looked on, with a casual, yet, a very hurried practice, Captain Jack quickly cranked up 993. The big Captain had fired-up his Huey hundreds of times over the last few months. Because of his familiarity, he no longer used the check list like they taught everyone to do in flight school. Universally and religiously, the continuous use of the printed check list was religiously drilled into every student. Kev could remember his instructors pounding that imperative into his head.

"Always -- always use your check list! Never -- never trust your memory!"

Pondering for a moment, Kev spoke to his inner self.

"OK, Kev. Keep your mouth shut! This is Viet Nam and it is not flight school. This is the real thing!"

Ole Kev tried to follow the experienced Captain's deft practiced movements. In exasperation, he instantly noted to himself that he would have forgotten at least half of the check list had he tried to do it from memory.

Glancing down at the instrument panel, he noted that all the engine and flight instruments were in the green. The engine and rotor RPM had quickly climbed to flight level. Receiving clearance from the control tower on the radio, Captain Jack expertly and quickly lifted the Huey up to a three-foot hover. Kev was deeply impressed at the ease in which Captain Jack kept the big helicopter at a stable hover within the very restrictive confines of the bombproof revetment.

"I don't know," he thought to himself. "It will take me a million years to look this practiced!"

"Clear right, clear left," sounded over the intercom.

Kev marveled at the teamwork while he sat there with his mouth securely screwed tightly shut. In truth, the awe struck young man's mouth was probably hanging open and drooling. He found it all quite amazing. Captain Jack did not ask the crewmen for clearance. The crewchief and door gunner, acting as well-drilled members of a smoothly operating air team, automatically gave it to him. The pilot did not need to ask for any information. His well-trained crewmen simply gave it to him at the proper time. To Kev newbe eyes, it was like Viet Nam had psychically linked them.

Consciously noting, to himself, the smooth practiced efficiency of the crew, Kev was becoming increasingly uncomfortable with his own lack of experience. The events of the day were beginning to move far, far, far, too fast for him to follow. Captain Jack's well-practiced and deftly done actions and movements served to remind Kev just how much remained for him to learn about the art of flying a helicopter. Alas, even before he could begin to emotionally adjust to the fact that he was flying off to "injun country," they were airborne. Under the Captain's gentle touch, the Huey had smoothly taken off, cleared the perimeter wire, and was climbing to five-hundred feet. When he reached five-hundred feet, Captain Jack lowered the nose of 993 and pulled in an arm full of collective pitch. As a pilot with a mission, which Kev knew nothing about, the Captain was demanding all thirteen-hundred shaft horsepower of the Lycoming turbine.

As he sat there, it seemed to Kev, as if it were only seconds earlier when he first heard the call, "Red Bird Down." In the passing of an instant, he found himself flying through and over strange countryside and one-hundred and twenty knots of air speed. Looking down at the instruments, he saw that the air speed indicator was locked dead steady. It looked, to him, as if someone had carefully glued the indicator's needle directly to the red line. At five-hundred feet above the ground, strange and indistinguishable things and stuff quickly flashed past. The helicopter and landscape were moving so fast that Kev couldn't recognize any land marks. Speed, excitement, and the unknown before him had transformed the earth below him into a green blur. It seemed, to him, that the only thing that was lacking to turn the experience into a great movie was some deeply dramatic background music rapidly rising to a fevered pitch.

To Kev's limited and unaccustomed perceptions, the whole of God's creation was moving at an apparent supersonic speed. The rapid changes in his life were all very difficult for him to believe. So . . . he gave up trying to understand everything that had happened during the morning. Suddenly, he came to the startling realization that he still had no idea why the call "Red Bird Down" had precipitated such a rapid reaction. For that matter, as he pondered the call, he was not exactly sure what the cry "Red Bird Down" meant. He had his own disquieting suspicions, though. However, with a deep confidence that had no basis in fact, he had faith in himself. He was totally self-persuaded, that in time, he would learn his craft. What other way was there for him to look at it? As he struggled with his ignorance, Kev kept repeating to himself.

"I must learn. I have to learn. I will learn. Remember this, Kevin Paul Johnson. You have spent your whole life waiting for this moment and this mission. Don't blow it!"

With the passing of a few minutes, Kev also came to the uncomfortable realization that the countryside rushing below him was not going to offer him any useful answers to his countless questions. Therefore, he cautiously looked to his right toward the Captain. Silently speaking to himself, he said.

"My God. He is busier that the proverbial one-handed paperhanger of whom my father often referred."

Sitting in the peter-pilot's seat benignly, baffled, and bewildered, he carefully reflected upon the mind-boggling smooth operation of the air team. Uncomfortably humbled, Kev began seriously considering his place within the smoothly operating team.

Pondering upon his obvious ineptitude, another thought struck Kev.

"I am beginning to feel a little sorry for poor ole Captain Jack. Circumstance has stuck the poor guy with a peter-pilot who is the newest new guy in the whole troop."

Painfully, he reflected upon his state of lostness.

"This new guy, who happens to be me, myself, and I, is greener than the spring's greenest grass. Kevin Paul Johnson is less than useless. He is out of his element and totally lost."

Eventually, Captain Jack asked him to change a couple of radio frequencies for him. Thankfully, Kev managed to accomplish that little task, without serious mishap. The Captain then began to talk to the Command and Control aircraft. C&C's call sign was Blue Six.

Poor Kev was still feeling very much like a lonely lost little pup. More accurately, he almost felt like a beaten little pup. Having nothing to do, he listened carefully to the radio communication between the Captain and Command and Control. As he listened, Kev began to piece that situation together little bit by little bit. Struggling to understand, he translated the radio call into something simple enough for a dumb new guy to understand. Red One-Two, a Scout helicopter, a Red Bird, had been shot down by enemy fire. While Kev was listening to the radio communications, the Blues were in a firefight with the enemy. At first, this reference to the "Blues" confused him. Then, he understood that the Cav also called its own ground troops the Blues.

Distressed by the sudden reality of war, Kev also understood that Red One-Two's pilot and observer were still on the ground and unaccounted for. Were they alive or dead was the universal, yet unsaid, question. No one, in the air or on the ground, could confirm either way! Later that evening while talking with another new pilot who had arrived the same day he did, Kev told him.

"I wasn't very sure of my early guess, and would not have dared to voice an opinion. Still, it seems that I had guessed correctly. Fearfully, I had come to the conclusion the cry 'Red Bird Down' meant that a Scout helicopter had been shot down."

When Kev finished his musing, the radio conversation had ended and the briefing given to the Captain by Blue Six was completed. Captain Jack quickly filled Kev and the crew in on the details of how he would run the operation when they arrived at the crash site. Since they had time, he spoke to Kev. "Listen carefully newbe. In about ten minutes, things are going get very busy for us. We are going to take over the Command and Control function of the rescue effort. Did you follow the rest of Blue Six's briefing?"

As the Captain spoke, the speeding, thrumming, and thumping helicopter continued it's headlong rush toward the crash site.

Kev quietly said. "I think so, Sir."

The bright red needle of its air speed indicator remained

perfectly pegged to the red line as they continued racing along. Assuming that Kev was still confused, Captain Jack explained to him that the Command and Control helicopter, Blue Six, was low on fuel. He also said the Red One-Two's wingman and the White Birds would be leaving the area. The second team of Scouts and Snakes would take their place. He continued by telling Kev that their call sign for the day was Blue Three-Three. Just as Kev was about to open his mouth and ask what "Command and Control" meant, a flash of better sense told him to shut it.

This better sense came from another self-directed conversation, which went something like this.

"I may be a new guy. However, I know better than ask Captain Jack what Command and Control does. Kev, ole boy, – just watch, listen, and learn. Whatever you do, **DO NOT** ask stupid questions!"

Captain Jack continued by confirming Kev's fears about what had happened at the crash site. He told the crew that the first team of Snakes, the White Birds, had already left station because they had expended all their ordinances. In support of the people on the ground, they had shot off all their rockets, forty millimeter grenades, and minigun rounds. Wishing to make sure that everyone understood the situation, he reminded them that the Blues, meaning their own organic infantry, were also on the ground. Muttering to himself, Kev thought.

"I think that I've got it. I hope."

The Captain continued his briefing.

"When we arrive on station, we will take over as C&C for the second Red and White Teams, plus the Blues on the ground."

A good part of Jack's briefing, about ninety-five percent or better, was well beyond Kev's limited understanding. He did not know Cav tactics yet. Much to the dismay of his professional pride, Kev was not completely sure that he knew what half of the words meant! It was becoming painfully and distressingly clear to the now overwhelmed young man that he was along just for the ride. Within the private confines of his head, poor ole romantic Kev cried out in dismay.

"John Wayne, where, oh where are you when I need you? Look at me! I'm just dead weight here. I'm as useless as. . . ." Well. The language was, at best, highly colorful. The frustrated language echoing about in Kev's head well expressed his dismay.

So far, the best thing that had happened to Kev in Viet Nam was that he had a "newbe" friend with whom he could confide. Sharing a cold beer that evening, Kev continued his explanation of what happened to him. The fact that he was speaking with another newbe and was well-lubricated allowed Kev to be verbally honest.

"I have no doubt about it, my friend. The only reason that ole Kev was sitting in the Huey was because 'the book' says that a warm body, wearing pilot's wings, will be strapped into the copilot's seat. I was about as useful as a couple of sandbags strapped into the seat. Yet, on the other hand, a couple of sandbags probably wouldn't make any bonehead mistakes. So, I humbly admit and submit to you that I was, most likely, a gross liability."

The racing helicopter continued to precisely maintain its one-hundred and twenty knot maximum airspeed. With each passing moment, the geography flashing below Kev changed. They were moving from the costal plain into the rugged foothills of the Central Highlands of South Viet Nam. With the beat of its rotor thundering off the rocks, 993 rushed through the buffeting air in a deep pass within the rugged hills.

They were rapidly coming closer to the operating area of Red One-Two's Scout team. Struggling as best he could to see, Kev intently looked to his right and to his left. For him, the trees and rocks seemed to be a little more than an arm's length away. As the thundering helicopter rushed along, they became little more than a multi-shaded green blur to Kev's straining eyes. Holding his breath, he wasn't sure of anything. Deep down inside, he wanted to be scared of this seemingly reckless flying. Every carefully trained fiber of his body knew that he was supposed to be scared. When he was in flight school, all his instructors had carefully taught him that he was supposed to be terrified by this type of dangerous flying. Despite his training, he was completely enthralled by the sense of speed and power.

His transformation happened in a flash. He completely forgot everything that the flight instructors had said about low level flying. In the passing of a brief moment, he was no longer nervous. Rather, he was a normal young man awash in a churning sea of male hormones. Gloriously charging off to the rescue, he was thrilled to the very core of his being. Feelings of high adventure and romance submerged his fledgling warrior's heart. Yet, the deeply submerged rational part of his being began to question and wonder.

"Am I secretly, deep within whatever makes Kevin Paul Johnson tick, a thrill seeker or a demented adventure junkie?"

On their first mission, most pilots' minds frequently wander far afield. In this case, Ole Kev was no different. Like many of those who had preceded him, young Kevin also became hopelessly lost in his overloaded mind's vague and aimless wanderings. Unexpectedly, he was jarred back to reality by sharp words quickly barked in his direction.

"Keep your eyes' open, Johnson!"

The harsh voice, ringing and reverberating in his ears, swiftly snapped him out of his mental musings and day dreams. Then, he let his pent up breath out.

Just as Kev's breathing began to return to normal, the crewchief called to Captain Jack on the intercom.

"I see the Snakes, sir. They are circling approximately six klicks to our right."

Upon hearing this, Captain Jack immediately contacted C&C to get an up to date briefing. When the briefing was finished, the new crew, of which Kev was the junior member, took over the responsibility of Command and Control until C&C returned.

As best as the inexperienced Kev could understand by listening to the briefing, C&C told Captain Jack where the Blues were on the ground. C&C also continued his terse and tense briefing by telling Captain Jack what the situation was. He also noted that the new teams of Red and White Birds were giving the grunts gun support. As far as Kev could tell, nothing of note had changed. It seemed to him, in his fully and emotionally painful self-acknowledged inexperience, that the sick and hollow feeling in his stomach painted a very grim picture.

When Command and Control finished his briefing, Captain Jack made his initial radio contact with all the parties involved. Much to his dismay, Kev had become uncomfortably accustomed to his own level of ignorance. He had no idea what was going on. Young Kev's blind ignorance was becoming his normal and unwanted state of being. This unavoidable ignorance was causing his previously high self-esteem great anguish. He tried as hard as he could to get a comprehensive understanding of the unfolding situation. For all he was worth, he tried to deduce what was happening around and about him. Knowing that it was important, he tried to picture everybody's place on the ground and in the air as if it were part of a beautiful and priceless mosaic.

Poor bewildered Kev was doing his best to gather all the brittle scattered pieces of the colorful mosaic and create a beautiful tile of clear understanding. The struggle to understand seemed only to cause more frustration. He knew that if he was to carry his own weight, he had to quickly convert the jumble of colors and pieces into a clear picture. Still, the constant noise on the radios and the constantly moving helicopters were confusing for the overwhelmed young man. Unknown to himself, deep inside, he was rapidly maturing. This maturation was witnessed by the fact that he began to feel the first serious stirrings of a truly honest self-doubt since arriving in Viet Nam. Within the privacy of his own mind, he was deeply concerned about his worth to the Cav and to himself.

"Oh Lord, do I really know what I am getting myself into?"

Captain Jack keyed the intercom. As it had before, the click of the Captain's mike startled Kev back to the situation at hand.

"OK guys. Here's the scoop. The bad guys have the Blues tied down. They are about a klick from the crash site. The Reds and Whites are supporting them. However, nobody has seen hide nor hair of Red

One-Two or his observer. Therefore, we are going to make a couple of low slow passes to see if maybe we can get lucky and see them. If we take fire, return fire only on targets you can positively identify. Do not, I repeat, do not just randomly spray fire around! Now remember. We do not know where Red One-Two and his observer are. They have got problems enough for the moment. We, surely as the devil wears bright red underwear, don't want to shoot them up and add to their growing list of concerns."

They arrived high over the operating area just as the Captain finished his briefing. Without warning Kev, Captain Jack rapidly lowered the collective. This abrupt control movement began a sharp descending turn directly over the crash site. Frantically looking about, Kev was still unable to locate the wreckage. At the same time, the helicopter's high rate of descent put his already uneasy stomach somewhere in the upper reaches of his throat. At least, Kev sincerely hoped that was why his stomach was in his throat. The crowning blow to his deeply shaken ego would be to find out that he was ignorant, useless, and most shameful of all, also a craven coward.

When the Huey's airspeed bled down to thirty-five knots, the Captain leveled the helicopter off at fifty feet above the ground. They then began their highly exposed and very dangerous approach over the crash site. Kevin couldn't believe the experienced Captain was exposing them so boldly to enemy fire. However, at that exact moment his overtaxed mind wandered off on its own fearful journey. It returned to an uncomfortable incident from a couple of days previously.

Later that evening, sipping his sixth or seventh cold beer with his new friend, Kev continued talking. He told him about the distracting journey his wandering mind had embarked upon while descending to the crash site.

"Please believe me. I didn't want to remember it. Not at that time, at least. Yet suddenly, I remembered something very distressing from a few days ago."

He paused to think.

"It was something which I would have preferred to forget. Looking back, I suppose that a combination of fear, anxiety, stupidity, and feelings of utter uselessness had returned me to my first and only ride in a Cobra."

Kev paused to take another small sip from his beer.

"The guns needed a living sandbag for the front seat when they brought the Snake back from maintenance. Fat, dumb, and happy, I was strapped in the copilot-gunner station. Mercilessly, while I was flying with Captain Jack today, every detail of the Snake's instrument panel smashed its way back into my vivid memory. I can't believe it myself. While sitting in the Huey, I stared mesmerized at the round faces of the

Snake's front seat instruments. They were only eighteen inches in front of me. Staring into my face was a small round bullet hole. The dang thing was exactly in the dead-center of the instrument panel. While I was flying along with Captain Jack, I could clearly see the hole in the Snake's instrument panel."

The young man paused to shake his head in amazement at himself.

"For a moment, I was afraid that I could have reached out and touched it! Someone from the bad guys side had centered the deadly little hole between the airspeed indicator and the tachometer. Paralyzed, I stared at it. Arrogantly, it stared defiantly back at me. The haughty haunting hole was giving me its full and undivided attention. Someone had told me about it over a few beers the previous evening. They said that last month the copilot-gunner died from the bad guy bullet that made that neat clean little hole. Haunting and taunting me, it was boring itself deeply into my psyche. The rational part of me knew that it was just a little bullet hole and that it couldn't hurt me. However, . . . Malevolently, it continued staring at me. Menacingly, it spoke only to me. With evil glee, the little hole was telling me that I was next. Believe me. I tried to will it to go away. Nevertheless, the perfect little hole continued to stare at me from the instrument panel."

Guiltily, Kev snapped his attention back to the Huey with a very contrite start. Feeling both foolish and guilty, he looked about to see if anybody had noticed his second little lapse of concentration. Grimly determined to carry his own weight, he refocused his attention on the increasingly somber mission. Hoping and praying that he could see something of value, he did his best to help the search. Kev intently looked out the windscreen and his side window.

Yet, poor Kev couldn't believe where he had suddenly found himself. They were going so slow. It seemed to him that they were almost drifting weightlessly and aimlessly over the wreckage of the Loach. In his uninformed opinion, they were begging to be shot down. If that happened, they would crash directly on top of Red One-Two's wreckage. He strained his eyes and was looking for all that he was worth. The overwhelmed young man was looking for any signs of life while looking for Red One-Two and his observer.

He was surprised to note that the search and rescue mission was becoming increasingly personal. At last, Kev began to feel the human impact of the call, Red Bird Down. Kev remembered that he had met Red One-Two. At last, the call sign had a fragile and human face behind it. Kev had remembered that the missing pilot was the baby-faced First Lieutenant with whom he had shared a beer the previous evening. He was also looking, just as intently, for Red One-Two's enlisted observer. Yet, this part of the search felt a little different. The observer was a young man whom he had never met. Looking for, well . . . He was just looking as best he could. Frustrated, Kev continued straining vainly to see something useful till his eyes hurt. Still, he couldn't see anything. Had he been a trained observer that wouldn't have helped. Nobody else saw anything either.

When the slow flying Huey finished slowly drifting over the crash site, they turned one-hundred and eighty degrees to return the way they came over the wreckage. As young Kev and crew were turning to return to the crash site, his young, untrained, and undisciplined mind continued with its strange wanderings. Kev quickly realized, maybe for the first time in his life, what it meant to be afraid for his own life. He manfully tried to shake off the dark and dreary feelings. However, the chill of honest fear had begun to wrap its powerfully constrictive tentacles around him.

Unbidden by him, Kev's mind perversely returned to its previous musing. Greatly unwelcomed, right before his eyes, his vivid, full-color, perfect memory traveled directly back to the front seat of the Cobra. When he arrived, the neat round bullet hole between the airspeed indicator and the tachometer continued to send its tormenting message to the nervous young man. Just like a few minutes earlier, the cold and heartless little bullet hole in the Snake's instrument panel was looking directly into his now pale and sweaty face.

Without his wishing to, Kev remembered more of the ghastly story which surrounded the little round hole! A couple of drunken gun-pilots had told him the story in ghastly graphic detail. They said that copilot-gunner had been a young Warrant Officer. Kev realized that it made him much like himself. Bench flying at the club, the guys had told him that the copilot-gunner had only been in country for a couple of months. Laughing, they pointedly told Kev that the front-seater had been another useless new guy.

"That poor slob was just like you, newbe!"

The bullet, they told Kev, had struck the nameless young man full in the face.

With his untimely death, the copilot-gunner had received one small blessing. Everyone agreed that he had died instantly. Kev's foolishly romantic mind had conjured up many combat pictures over the years. Thankfully, he couldn't even begin to imagine what the wreckage of that unknown young man's face must have looked like. When he thought about the gross damage that the bullet must have done, Kev's fear of being a coward tormented him with a vengeance. He decided that he didn't want to know what the wreckage of that face looked like. The young man was afraid of how he would respond to the crass reality of a bullet smashed face. Deep in his gut, Kev was beginning to learn that romance and reality are not necessarily one in the same.

19

On the second pass over the broken wreckage of Red One-Two's Scout bird, a loud voice shook Kev from his private inner world of torment. This time, Kev's interruption from his inner struggles was quite rudely done. The excited door-gunner cried out.

"Taking fire!"

As expected, the loud voice ringing over the intercom gave a big jolt of adrenalin to the whole crew. Captain Jack immediately yelled back to the gunner.

"Hey Riley, can you see where it is coming from?"

The door-gunner frantically replied.

"No sir. I honestly can't tell where the fire is coming from."

Showing great discipline, the door-gunner chose not to return fire due to the fear of hitting Red One-Two or his observer. He never forgot that the two young men were somewhere below. But, where were they? Highly experienced, the door-gunner acted very wisely and with better discipline than Kev himself felt. He held his fire while being shot at and Kev wondered if he would have done the same. Captain Jack them pushed the cyclic stick forward, dumping the nose of the helicopter, and pulled in full power on the collective. The lumbering Huey immediately "beat feet" out of the area. Kev later told his friend at the club.

"We left post haste, I might add."

Unable to safely return fire, they quickly climbed back up to a more reasonable altitude. Kev was secretly pleased that Captain Jack decided that they could best help by staying out of the way. Staying at a higher altitude allowed the Red Birds to continue their low and slow work without worrying about running into the big ole Huey. Again, engrossed in his private thoughts, Kev sat safely wrapped in his armored seat. At a deeply personal level, the brutal reality that someone was trying to kill him, totally mystified Kev. Sorting out his jumbled feelings was hard for the young man. He had not been mentally prepared for the recent turn of events. The perplexing and scary problem, for Kev, was that he neither saw nor heard a thing when the door-gunner said that they were taking fire.

Deeply troubled, he began to think and to ponder his strangely unfolding situation. Much to his dismay, these were not a series of encouraging thoughts which were making their way across his brain's agitated synapses.

"I'm not going to live very long if I don't know when I'm being shot at. My, God, this is nothing like the movies or like the paperback books. In the world of pop fiction, the writers had made the whole thing seem so simple!"

Adding to Kev's growing list of emotional difficulties was his simplistic world view. Life had been very straightforward when he was a little guy. Like many other mothers, Kev's mother had carefully explained the different roles in TV westerns. The good guys wore white hats and the bad guys word black hats. In his current situation, from his elevated view of the ground, he saw neither white nor black hat on the ground below. Kev was troubled, perplexed, and in the strange world of Viet Nam.

"How am I to know who are the good guys and who are bad guys? How could he shoot back when I don't even know that I am being shot at? How . . . how?"

The excitement ended as the Huey slowly climbed back up to three thousand feet. Self-absorbed, Kev noted that his fear and anxiety had completely drenched him in a putrid sweat. Thinking about it, for a moment, he noted that his sweat didn't have a sweet, hard-working flavor to it. It was unlike when he had been playing ball at the YMCA. Today's soaking perspiration had a subtlety different texture and flavor to it which he couldn't quite pinpoint. After a bit, he decided he understood the difference. This sweat didn't have that invigorating wonderful feel that came as the aftermath of a hard-played ball game. At least, as they climbed, a little relief from his fear and anxiety was in the offering. After a moment, he noted that the cool breeze coming in his window offered a partially refreshing scent. Attempting to do a quick "head job" on himself, he silently wondered how much of his sweat was from the heat and how much was raw primal fear.

It didn't take the pale young man very long to decide that he didn't want to know the answer to his question. Because he was usually brutally honest with himself, he was highly fearful about the simple question's answer. Anyway, he quickly decided that he had bigger concerns than the quantity and the quality of his perspiration. What had happened to him, just a few moments earlier, was becoming all too clear. His restless mind, as it had been doing all day, wandered away from the task at hand. Like so many who had preceded him, he could only hope that Captain Jack and the rest of the crew didn't know how truly scared he had been. Later that evening, he struggled to tell his friend at the club about his feelings.

"By this time, I was so scared that I was almost afraid to look down and see if I had soiled myself."

While they were being shot at, young Kevin made a startling discovery. What he discovered was that the books and movies, which had been educating his generation, had forgotten something vital and important. This was a horrifying discovery for his romantic imagination. Feeling like the onrush of the tide at the Bay of Fundy was overwhelming him, he was afraid that he would drown in the oncoming flood tide. He had suddenly learned that sitting still and "taking it" was somewhere between hard and impossible. To let people shoot at him without being

21

able to shoot back did not seem fair.

"Good Lord, my first role in combat was not supposed to be passive!"

Rather, Kev had always imagined himself actively involved in his first combat. None of the countless paperback novels that he had read had prepared him for this uncomfortable acquiescent role.

Captain Jack looked toward his young peter-pilot and silently noted his discomfort. Though the situation on the ground was grim, a wee bit of a twinkle flashed in the Captain's eyes. The Captain slyly smiled to himself as if he were remembering something of his own history. Looking to the back, he then winked to his crewchief. He had been gruff with Kev. However, he knew a surefire cure for Kev's problem. Then, with a seemingly kind and gentle voice, he spoke to the shaken young man on the intercom.

"Ok Johnson. You've got the aircraft. Maintain airspeed and altitude and continue to orbit to the right."

Resuming his gruff persona, he changed his tone and continued.

"By the way newbe, try to stay over this specific valley."

Like the first light of dawn, a beaming radiant expression of puppy-like gratitude brightened Kev's face. It was instantly obvious to the whole crew how much he appreciated getting his hands on the controls. Finally, if only for a moment, he felt like he was more than an Army issue olive drab sandbag. Moments earlier, Kev had felt as if someone had painted the words "shoot me" in glowing flourescent colors upon his chest. Not being able to defend himself had multiplied Kev's feelings of great frustration. Wishing not to be obvious, he had tried to do his job while still making himself as small as possible in his armored seat.

As "old hands," both the Captain and the Enlisted crew instinctively knew how important it was for Kev to have something to do. They too had gone through similar anxieties as newbes. For a few minutes, Kev needed to have something to keep both his hands and mind occupied. The slightly shaken young man centered his mind on one thought as he took the controls.

"I am going to concentrate on flying the aircraft. Thank God! Now my dang hyperactive imagination won't have time to freely stroll back to the front seat of that cursed Snake. I won't be thinking about that neat round little bullet hole in the instrument panel."

Of course, the little round hole continued to trouble him.

That evening, while talking to his friend at the club, Kev described his flying with discouraging words.

"So help me, I couldn't believe how badly I was herding the aircraft through the air. Mind you. I was herding it and not flying it. I was working up a Olympic class sweat just trying to keep some semblance of altitude and airspeed. Within seconds, I was soaking through my flight suit. The darn thing was wringing wet. At least, though, I didn't smell like fear this time. I am proud to say that ole Kev just smelled of good old hard-working sweat. Man 'O' Man. I was not kidding you when I said that my stick work was a little rusty. Yet, when I mentally stepped aside and watched myself trying to fly, the word 'pathetic' immediately jumped to mind. I could only hope that Captain Jack and the crew didn't notice how hard I was working just to keep the beast in the air."

The humbled young man took a sip from his beer and continued his tale of woe.

"Good Lord, I never felt so unprepared in my whole life. Undoubtedly, it was worse than my first flight back at Ft. Wolters. Thankfully, Captain Jack was busy talking on the radios and being the C&C. He didn't see how I was busily chasing the airspeed indicator. My, so called, flying was like a cripple's wretched dance. I went from seventy knots to ninety knots, back and forth, back and forth. I didn't hear what was happening on the ground. Nor, did I care anymore. Suddenly, ole Kev was afraid that he would lose control of the bird. Well . . . So much for being a hotshot Cav pilot."

What Kev didn't know was that Captain Jack had also had "his day" when he first started flying in Viet Nam. With his own memories fresh in his mind, the now gracious Captain only pretended not to notice.

As he was fighting with the Huey, several radio frequencies were chattering away in Kev's ears. Somewhere in the midst of the radio noise, Kev heard something about the Blues still being in contact and that the second team of Snakes had expended most of their ordinances. Glancing down at the instruments, he was forced to angerly yell at himself.

"Shoot a monkey! I can't believe it. I just lost fifty feet of altitude while I was trying to listen to what was being said on the radio. How in the love of everything that is holy does Captain Jack do it? How does he talk on the radios and talk to the crew? How does he know where everyone is both in the air and on the ground? How does he do all these things and still fly the helicopter? He,s p------ me off! Darn! He does it with such grace and control all at the same time."

Poor Kev's level of frustration was rapidly climbing to an emotionally intolerable level. He felt like he was working full-time showing everyone within a hundred-mile radius what a lousy pilot he was. The young man was turning greener and greener with envy over Captain Jack's skills.

Wildly rowing the flight controls about like a first week flight student, Kev finally regained the fifty feet that he had lost while trying to listen in on the radio conversation. From a great distance, he felt a quiet and patient voice enter the tumult of his frustrated mind. For Kev, it was an undiluted sound of mercy coming through the intercom. Captain Jack benevolently took the controls of the helicopter with the utterance of three magical words.

"I've got it."

The Captain then pointed to the fuel gauge. They had used up most of their fuel. Surprised, Kev wondered where the time had gone. It seemed as if they just arrived on station. Pointing to another Huey approaching them from the distance, he told Kev that the Command and Control helicopter had returned.

"We are going to fuel up and then we will stage out of an abandoned fire base which is nearby."

He continued.

"When we arrive, we'll shut down the helicopter. Shut down, we'll wait patiently for further instructions from C&C."

Kev's response was simple.

"Thank God! At last, we are going to do something that I'm good at. I have had a lot of training over the last twelve months. I'm in the Army and I know how to wait."

Freed of responsibility, the young man gave himself guiltless permission to aimlessly stroll around inside the wide-open expanses of his head. As Captain Jack flew, Kev slowly reviewed the last couple of hours. He found it terribly difficult to believe that just two hours previously he had been standing around the base camp feeling sorry for himself. Approximately one-hundred and twenty minutes earlier, he had been another new guy with no idea of what was happening. Ignored by everybody, he was an unknown newbe with his hands stuffed dumbly in his pockets. Two hours before, he had felt like the lowest of the low. Kev had felt unbelievably useless. It was in the depths of this despair that Captain Jack had yelled to him. Then, suddenly, Kevin Paul Johnson found himself in the middle of all the action.

However, much to his dismay, he still felt left out of everything. He still felt like the lowest of the low. With minimum effort, Kev had convinced himself that he had managed to prove one thing to the Captain and crew. They were correct in their assessment of the newbe. As a pilot and officer, he was totally and completely useless. He had been shot at and he didn't hear a single shot being fired. It was possible that a man he had drunk a beer with the night before was dead. As a further blow to his ego, he had proven that he couldn't hold airspeed and altitude when he was given the controls. Poor Kev was convinced that the rawest basic flight student at Fort Wolters could have done a better job. Worst of all, in all the movies that he had ever seen, John Wayne and his type never had troubles like these.

One hopeful gleam encouraged the new guy named Kevin Paul Johnson. The last two hours taught him that nobody expects much from a newbe. Pausing his incriminating memory stroll, he placed most of his hope on that little thought. The awareness of others' expectations was all that comforted him as the Huey was quietly flying to refuel. By his silence, Captain Jack had not condemned him as a completely lost cause. When he was a new guy, Captain Jack had been in the same place. Compassionately, he left Kev alone to struggle with his thoughts. He too, was struggling with his own private musings.

During the rest of the flight, Kev, left alone to struggle with the mixed emotions of fear, excitement, and exhilaration, kept his peace. These strong, ill-defined, and uncomfortable feelings surged through him like the never-ending waves of the ocean. Newly self-aware, he struggled painfully with his newfound and self-demonstrated ineptitude. If he learned nothing else, he had painfully discovered that he had much to learn. As Kev struggled with his new reality, he decided that he had more to learn that he could possibly learn in ten long lifetimes.

The three veterans in the helicopter were kind and they left Kev alone to face his newly discovered mortality. With the perfect recollection of his mind's eye, he saw the young face of Red One-Two. Accusingly, he felt the young Lieutenant's smooth young face looking deeply into his guilty soul. Again, unbidden by free will, Kev also found himself pondering the meaning of that Snake's instrument cluster. That little round bullet hole between the airspeed indicator and the tachometer continued to mercilessly drain the contents of his romantic cup of self-confidence. Lastly, he was left alone to fearfully question his life in the Cav. He pondered.

"Will I ever truly 'cut the mustard' and 'earn my keep' with this great bunch of guys?"

More than anything else, he needed to proudly wear the crossed sabers as something that he had earned.

These probing internal questions about his competence hurt him more than any others. His self-directed accusations did not improve his self-image. Muttering under his breath, he savagely beat himself up.

"At least, if Captain Jack had placed sandbags in my seat no one would have expected the sandbags to be able to keep airspeed and altitude. This is not a good beginning, Kev. No, this is not a good beginning at all!"

Filled with dark, expectant, and grim quietness, the thumping Huey flew to the nearest refueling site. Wordlessly, the crewchief rapidly refueled that bird with two-hundred gallons of JP-4 fuel. With the tank cover secured, they took off to stage out of the abandoned firebase with the other Blue Birds. These were the other Huey's which had dropped off their troops in search of Red One-Two and his observer. While they were enroute to the firebase, the radio crackled and sent a somber message to all who were on the Cav's frequency. In hushed tones, which were depressing even through the distortion of the radio, C&C broadcast Kev's closing chapter for the day. The message, given to everyone on the radio net, did nothing to lighten the black mood it conveyed.

"Blue Three-Three, we have recovered the bodies of Red One-Two and his observer. Go ahead and take your aircraft back to the barn."

For Kev, it was too early in his combat experience to be sure what the events of the day would mean to him. For the moment, the rational part of himself was deeply suspicious that his young life had begun a profound process of radically changing. How was he changing? The humbled little puppy dog could not begin to guess. As Kev pondered, the four young men sorrowfully and quietly turned the helicopter south toward their home base. None of them spoke. Each of them was lost in his own quiet and somber thoughts. They thumped along slowly now. The four young men did not need to rush through the increasingly unfriendly skies of South East Asia.

Later that evening, Kevin Paul Johnson, who also dreamed of becoming an author, wrote in his journal:

"RED BIRD DOWN!" Without warning, a controlled frenzy of activity exploded round and about me. The little words, Red Bird Down, shook the foundations of the earth. Just a few hours ago, in my new world of Military Aviation in Viet Nam, two of the primary currents of my life have merged. Much to my surprise, this merger forms a new, more powerful, channel for my life to flow through. The first channel was formed because I have always wanted to fly combat. And, for almost as long, I have wanted to write something serious. Thus, my second channel comes into play. In the coming months, while I am in Viet Nam, I will fly combat and I will write when I am not flying.

Three little words, Red Bird Down, impact the lives which surround me like no other words that I have ever heard uttered. In the passing of a couple-three weeks, I have discovered much about the power of words. Certain words, symbols, strung-together verbal sounds, in this strange and curious life carry their own unique meanings and dark terrors. These are the interconnected verbal sounds that when spoken, cried out, and then heard shake the foundations of the world. They set the hearer's heart racing and the hearer's legs driving like frantic pistons. Furthermore, they will send the hearer's adrenalin pulsing and pounding through the veins and arteries of his suddenly tense body. Often, these heart-stopping words and sounds leave that terribly unique, fear-filled, bitter, biting taste of tin as the overpowering resident of a cotton dry mouth.

For those who have served most of their time in the Army, Marine, and Air Force base camps of Viet Nam, one of the most piercing of these words and verbal sounds is "incoming." This is the soul-piercing cry that signals the arrival of unwelcomed death and destruction. No longer is the hearer protected by the illusionary safety of the perimeter wire. Also, for those of us in the base camps, other gut-wrenching words occasionally cut through the still night air. "Charley is in the wire!" That is a terrifying cry signaling that this night could be the hearer's last.

For the many different ready reaction teams in Viet Nam the words, "friendlies in contact," raise many, if not all those same feelings and fears. These are fears which are painfully and graphically expressed with deeply personal thoughts. "Maybe this is my day to catch is, to get my ticket back to the world, to buy the farm, or to be issued an olive-drab body bag with six handles." For numberless, nameless, unknown, unappreciated, and sometimes unwillingly drafted souls humping the bush in this war, they have their words. Possibly, they have inherited these words from many previous wars. The cried out words "medic," "Oh JESUS-GOD!," Or "I'm hit" stabs into the deepest recesses of the soul with the gut-wrenching thought that I might be the next to cry out.

Those of us who are fortunate enough to roam the length and breath of Viet Nam in our frail and fragile vibrating thumping helicopters have our own code words. Just hovering and crawling along, five feet above the tree tops, looking for the bad guys creates its own specific series of verbal sounds. When spoken, these strike deep into the core of our collective soul. We are the modern day Cavalry Scouts who wear the most ancient and beautiful crossed sabers. We are the ones who are always spending our time in injun country.

For us, another string of words and sounds bring to life all the indescribable fear-filled feelings which we share with all men-at-arms. Our specific sound/noise was the mournful cry that would signal the frantic controlled confusion of a troop scramble. In the scramble, all the combat members of the troop would "mount up" on their steeds/helicopters in the middle of the fear/excitement rush of adrenalin. Three little words would always start this emotional and physical scramble. "RED BIRD DOWN." I now know these three words. Somehow, I think that they have changed the course of my life. Yet, I do not know how much they will change, mark, or even identify my life.

I do know that when the cosmic clock stops ticking, I will remember these three little words. Yet, it was only a few hours ago that the Cav introduced me to them. I can never forget these three little words, were I to try, or were I to live a million years. "Red Bird Down" cut through the stillness of that calm morning, two or three aeons ago. Or, was it just a few hours ago? I have already discovered that in our little world time quickly loses its former meaning. The heart-stopping cry, "RED BIRD DOWN," sounded at our little base camp somewhere in the middle of Viet Nam. I was as green as the spring grass. Just out of flight school, I proudly wore my spanking new pilot's wings and Warrant Officer's insignia. I was lost. The truth is, I was a replacement pilot, a nobody, a new guy, a newbe, who had no idea who or what was going on. Suddenly, I learned what that mournful cry would signal. In time, if the cry "Red Bird Down" does not sound for me, I will tell the world about it.

"Red Bird Down." Strange, they are only three little words in

27

common English. The largest of them is only four letters in length. Tonight, though, I fear that echoing call. Will "Red Bird Down" sound through our staging fields and base camps during my tour of duty? More frighteningly, will this call sound for me. That is, if I am allowed to enter the fraternity of Red Birds? Today I learned what the strung together symbols and sounds, "Red Bird Down," mean. For me, these three words mean the bitter metallic taste of fear in the back of my mouth. It means that my heart will skip a beat or two. It means that the mad scramble of friends wanting to save friends will launch itself. What is worse, sometimes, it means that somebody is dead!

As I am prone to do, tonight I muse and meditate. "Is this the great romantic adventure that I have spent my life dreaming about?" If it is, then the cry **"RED BIRD DOWN"** is not the way to begin a great adventure.

F or reasons unknown to him and unknown to anyone else for that matter, something strange happened. While at flight school, Kev abruptly fell deeply and passionately in love. While in training, he had heard exciting stories about the Aero Scouts of the 1st of the 9th Cav. Naturally, he found these Aero Scouts and their mission romantically exciting.

However nobody could convince him that he wanted to fly the old Korean war veteran OH-13 in the "new war." Yes, he knew that they were the latest turbo-charged 'S' models. Pilots who had flown them told Kev that the turbo-birds flew worlds and worlds better than the old 'E' and 'G' models. Those were the tired old birds that he flew in basic flight school. Nevertheless, 'S' model or not, it was still an old design which was powered by a piston engine. The Army had been flying them since the Korean War! Further, in Kev's lofty opinion, it was a mundane helicopter. He felt this way because it was the design which every Tom, Dick, and Harry associated with a helicopter. He thought to himself.

"Heck, when I was a kid, they even had a television show starring the old Bell type '47.' Whatever else I do, I don't want to fly television's whirly-bird!"

Surprising him one day, a small black and white picture radically changed his thoughts about flying with the Aero Scouts. That was the day he discovered that the Cav Scouts were phasing in a new gas turbine powered observation helicopter. The only thing that he saw before going to Viet Nam was a simple black and white picture of the little bird. Yet, from his first glimpse of her, he found himself deeply and passionately in love with what he discovered was a wondrous piece of flying machinery. By the power of a single black and white photograph, the lovely little Red Bird had begun craftily worming her way into his heart. It was only later, while in Viet Nam, that he came to fully appreciate her sterling performance. What had happened to many young men before Kev, happened to him. His passion for this magnificent piece of flying machinery grew and grew.

This strangely seductive little helicopter, which captured his young and fanciful heart was usually called the "Red Bird" in most Cav units. Sometimes, folks who were not Cav oriented called her a Loach. Way back when she was going through her birthing process, she had another name. The engineers who gave the little Red Bird life and personality on the drawing boards at Hughes aircraft called her an LOH. That military and manufacturers three-letter acronym stood for Light Observation Helicopter. As hard as it was for Kev to believe, some misinformed people consistently fail to appreciate her incredibly sensuous beauty. They unflatteringly describe her as an egg with a telephone pole sticking out her backside or an ugly little tadpole. Whatever someone, in their sad ignorance, might choose to call her made little difference to Kev and the many others who felt like he did. For people like Kev, she was their sensuous little Red Bird.

A young pilot's affection for his cold metallic steed may seem quaint to some folk. However, young men who developed a burning passion for her became fiercely loyal to her. For example, Kev would lovingly defend her against those with whom he argued the relative merits of different models of helicopters. More than once he strongly responded to her being denigrated by the uninformed.

"Please believe me, anything condescending you may say about my little Red Bird will never make the slightest dent into my feelings for her. She is beautiful!"

In truth, excellent reasons for his opinion and driving passion existed. The little Red Bird was very different from anything else in the Army's extensive fleet of helicopters. The pilots who had flown her either liked or disliked her strongly.

Very few, if any, who have known her, left her presence without forming an opinion. When well taken care of, she was a high-strung, and equally high-spirited little filly. She would gladly respond to the slightest gentle touch on the controls. To all who would mount this little filly, Red Bird pilots offered an emphatic word of caution. If the man flying her were not careful and if he treated her roughly, she would turn and immediately give the foolish a dreadful bite. The little bird also had little patience with those who would mistreat her. Kev instinctively understood that her bite, kick, and stomp could be fatal to the unsuspecting.

If Kev were discussing his girlfriend, most likely he would use a more human set of criteria. He would tell you about the subtle color of her hair and her eyes. Joyously, he would speak warmly about the soothing tone of her voice. Like any other man in love, he would continue by telling you of her tender gentleness and of her infectious laugh. Without a doubt, he would gleefully tell you of her superior intelligence. Not that it was anybody's business, nor would he find it appropriate to tell you, but he might speak proudly of her bust, waist, and hip measurements. That is, if he had such facts available. If he were exceptionally brave or unbelievably stupid, he might even tell you how far his girlfriend deflects the little red needle on the bathroom scale.

When young Kevin talked about his great love and passion, the Red Bird, he was forced to use an entirely different language. Kev never forgot, though he loved the little Red Bird deeply, she remained only a piece of gorgeously sculpted machinery. The United States Army, in its own unique language, spoke of Kevin's passion in cold facts. These are some of the bare-boned facts as presented in the official Army operator's manual:

"The OH-6A aircraft, manufactured by Hughes Tool Company - Aircraft Division, is basically an all metal, single engine, rotary wing aircraft. It is powered by an Allison T63-A-5A turbine engine driving a four-bladed main rotor and a tail mounted anti-torque rotor through a two stage, speed-reduction transmission. The aircraft is equipped with shock-absorbing landing skids. Primarily an observation aircraft, it is capable of carrying a pilot and three passengers (one of whom may act as a crew member - copilot or observer), cargo, or armament subsystem. The aircraft can be equipped with armor for combat operations, and can also be used for target acquisition, reconnaissance, and command and control. Dual control provisions allow the aircraft to be flown from either left- or right-hand pilot's compartment seat."

It is true that cold, hard, and unfeeling data, when it was presented in the Army operator's manual, remained nothing more than cold, hard, and unfeeling techno-speak. On the other hand, Kev's love, his Red Bird, was a highly spirited little filly unlike any other aircraft in the whole Army system. Reducing her to cold techno-speak, the Army completely failed to capture her life and spirit. Considering his mechanical passion for her, it is most interesting that this little bird was stone simple. Yet, those who flew her loved every little nut and bolt. They spoke of her as exceptionally quick and delightfully responsive. With a laughing free spirit, she was eager to respond to the lightest touch of the controls.

Red Bird pilots would caution that being a highly refined steed.

"Occasionally," they would say, "the little filly is wee bit high-strung and quirky."

To a man, they agreed that if she were miss-handled or abused, she would turn viciously upon the unwary. The silent brotherhood of Army Aviators, including Red Bird Pilots, would suggest that the ever-present UH-1 Huey was the under appreciated workhorse of the fleet. Unlike the little Red Bird, the Huey was truck-like and unglamourous. However, she was honest, forgiving, and exceptionally hard working. In contrast to the Huey, they said that the little Red Bird was the racy red Italian sports car of the fleet. Of course, she could only be the sports car of the prancing horse fame.

Little wonder that someone of Kev's deep mechanical sensitivities loved her so deeply. Star-struck, Kev found looking at her and touching her metallic flanks to be a sensuous delight. To those who understood the beauty of the little helicopter's mechanical simplicity and beauty, love was inevitable. Listening to the heartbeat of her little turbine engine whine was a first class mechanical symphony. Simply being in her presence set Kev's boyish heart a-racing. Living or not, no other had touched Kev in such a way. As unlikely as it may seem, that little bird did set many young pilots' heart a-racing. Hughes' little Red Bird delighted Kev far more than his '57 Chevy' with the Corvette engine that he had painstakingly hand built. In Kev's book, there was no comparison!

Upon his arrival in Viet Nam, Kev made a number of surprising discoveries. The urgencies of war had transported army aviation in the carefully structured world of Ft. Wolters and Ft. Rucker to a distant place and a time quickly forgotten. Somewhat surprising him, he found out that his newly assigned home had transplanted him into a strange new world. This foreign world was far more distant than just the many miles of earth and ocean that separated the sheltered world of flight school from Viet Nam. Learning to fly a new helicopter, in this case his beloved Red Bird, was done much differently in the combat world of Viet Nam.

Back in what was called the "real" world, when a pilot learned how to fly a different model aircraft, extensive classroom lectures were mandatory. Usually, most of this class room training happened prior to many instructional rides with a highly-qualified 'IP' (instructor pilot). Nevertheless, he quickly discovered that this new place, which was to become his home, wasn't the carefully ordered world to which he was accustomed. This new world was located in the Republic of Viet Nam. Furthermore, Kev's new setting in this new world was the Cav. As the ancient Biblical poet alluded, this was the place of the quick and the dead. In this strange world of never-ending death and destruction, things were done much differently. The rules of necessity dictated that everything had to be accomplished yesterday.

After begging and pleading with all the appropriate military decorum that the Army required of an officer and a gentleman, Kev eventually got his wish. The Major allowed Kev to join the Red Birds. Revealing how different things were in Viet Nam, Kev discovered that the Red Bird platoon was an all volunteer outfit. When the time eventually came to separate the wheat from the chaff, the current members of the Red Birds passéd the final judgement and gave the final approval who was in and who was out. To the best of his knowledge, this democratic process was unique to the Red Birds in Army Aviation. Kevin naturally found, that the whole democratic process appealed to his romantic nature. Greatly surprising him, he also learned that the Red Birds were quite hesitant to accept married men in their ranks. In time, he would understand the reason for the exclusion of married men. After they allowed him to join, he soon discovered that the ad hoc process of transitioning into the Red Bird had its own problems and pitfalls.

When the Scouts finally accepted him, Kev quickly began his flight training. At the time, schools with classrooms, blackboards, and cutaway plastic models were not available in all of Viet Nam for new Scout pilots. Nor was there a school with IP's who were dedicated to the single-minded task of teaching a pilot how to transition into and fly a different aircraft. That much needed luxury wasn't available to the young men learning to fly the little Loach in the combat zone. "OJT," on the job training, was the necessary paradigm of the day. Such was one of his surprising discoveries when the Scouts accepted him to fly with the Red Birds.

The in-unit transition process started with someone tossing the green pilot a dash ten and telling him to read it. Because he was going to be flying with the Red Birds, Kev was given the official Army TM 55-1520-214-10, the dash ten. That long list of letters and numbers was Army talk for the OH-6A's operator's manual. Flight training began, for Kev, with little ceremony and even less ado about the whole transitioning process. Without prior warning, CW-2 Jones stuck his head into Kev's hooch and called out to him.

"Here you go newbe."

He spoke while he flipped him a dash ten. Dropping the book that he had been reading, Kev sat on the edge of his bunk dumb struck. As of yet, he didn't understand the strange ways of his new world. However, a world of important information passed between them. Yet, the two of them exchanged no spoken words as Loach dash ten sailed gracefully through the air in his general direction.

Stunned by the casualness of Chief Jones, Kev recovered his senses and quickly lunged to catch the weathered manual which was slowly floating through the air. On the spot, he received the first and the last of his structured classroom lectures on flying the little Red Bird.

"Here you go, boy. You better get some serious studying done. If something really has you puzzled, grab me at the club some night and I'll see if I can help you."

Without another word being passed between them, Chief Jones casually pivoted about and just as casually walked out the door. Much to Kev's surprise, Chief Jones' solo flight of the bedraggled dash ten was both the beginning and the end of his formal class room instruction in flying the OH-6!

"This is a 'different' world." He said to himself.

A couple-three days later, with an equal amount of carefully stylized in-country ceremony, Lt. Simmonds introduced Kev to his upcoming flying syllabus. The Red Bird platoon conjoined two separate approaches to the hands-on OJT (on the job training) aspect of learning to fly the Red Bird for the scouts. Combat necessity forced these combined processes upon most of the Cav units in country. Totally unprepared for this OJT learning process, Kev understood that they combined these approaches to speed up the training schedule. Muttering to himself as he figured it out, Kev said. "Well, that's Ok with me." It worked like this. First, a pilot in transition got a fair, but nonspecific, number of actual combat mission hours. The "student" pilot receives these hours by flying in the place of the enlisted observer whom they would have assigned to the wing bird.

Like Chief Jones before him and with equally immortal words which serious students of the art of flight instruction had crafted, Lt. Simmonds stuck his head in Kev's hooch. With his unannounced arrival, he informed Kev of his upcoming flight.

"Hey, newbe, you're flying with me today. So, get your stuff together."

Kev was to be both his observer and student. The flight hours in which Kev was destined to enjoy the company of Lt. Simmonds was designed to kill two proverbial two birds with one stone. While he was doing this observing and flying with Lt. Simmonds, he was supposed to learn all that he could. They expected that Kev would become familiar with the tactics of aerial observation used by the Red Birds. In an effort not to waste flight hours, Kev discovered that Lt. Simmonds was more than willing to give him some stick time. The Captain expected Kev to fly the helicopter when they were not involved in the actual recon. Flying to and from the area where the recon was done would be part of Kev's training.

During their first flight together, Simmonds took time to tell Kev how he would progress into becoming a Red Bird pilot. His advancement to full flight status was predicated upon Kev's mastering the basics of flying the little helicopter. Lt. Simmonds then explained the part of Kev's training which he personally did not enjoy.

"Later, after you have made enough flights as an observer, may God have mercy upon my poor raggedy butt, you and I will swap seats. I, in turn, will become your observer as you fly in the wing position."

"Mind you," he continued after a brief pause.

"My next point is not negotiable. You must satisfy this pilot's judgement that you can fly the aircraft, sort of, and that you can fly the mission, sort of. If you can accomplish that, the Captain will then remove you from my tender loving care."

Dramatically, he paused, making Kev impatiently wait for each little bit of information which Lt. Simmonds slowly doled out to him.

"Only then, when my well-trained military mind is totally satisfied with your progress, flying skills, and ability to perform the mission, will a valuable enlisted observer's life be placed in your worthless hands. Before you say a word, I am well aware that this is not the way that it is done back in the 'real' world. However, let me assure you that you are no longer a citizen of your former world! Your worthless butt now belongs to me!"

Another part of Kev's training included a short familiarization flight in the OH-6A with the unit IP. In his case, the unit IP was CW-2 Jones. The familiarization flight consisted of flying around the traffic pattern and roundabout local area. The semiformal instructional flight would last for about an hour. During the familiarization ride, Kev would shoot about half-a-dozen autorotations to a three-foot hover. Autorotations were power off, or gliding type landings. While in flight school, Kev had found them to the most fun and one of the most demanding parts of his flight training. Lt. Simmonds had already told him that the bulk of his training flight time would come from getting stick time as an observer. In the Cav, in combat, and in Viet Nam, things didn't always work out as people had planned them. In Kev's case, he made his own familiarization ride after he had made his first flight with Lt. Simmonds.

To increase Kev's flight experience, if an aircraft was available, the Captain gave it to him for some additional flight hours flying the traffic pattern. This local training flying was usually done with another pilot who was in training. Eventually, when Kev had enough experience both in the field and in the traffic pattern, the IP would give him a fifteen minute check off flight and oral examination. Kev's check-flight would be with the unit IP, CW-2 Jones. Of course, Jones was the same talkative person who gave Kev all the minutely detailed instruction in the dash ten. It was Kev's responsibility to satisfy Jones, or at least not scare him to death during his check-ride. When and if this happened, Jones would certify Kev to fly the, aircraft. This clearance though, did not clear him to fly recon's. That important decision, to declare Kev mission ready, remained firmly clenched in Lt. Simmonds tight fist.

Flying with another transitioning pilot, Kev discovered another problem with his being a romantic type person. He was shocked to find out that not everyone shared his mystical and wondrous spirit of military romance. During his transitioning, Kev also suffered the shock to his carefully preconceived notions about flying in combat. Furthering his growing dismay with human reality, it was during this part of his training that Kev discovered a harsh reality about human existence. The men that he wanted to fly with were supposed to be Officers and Gentlemen, before they became military pilots. Yet in fact, he discovered that some are selfish and look out only for their own well-being.

Sadly, Kev's romantic view of the Cav and the war suffered its first serious damage at the hands of these frail aspects of the human condition. Rudely, he found out that some people act as if they are truly military pilots, while in fact, they are only looking for an easy way out of combat. Lastly, Kev discovered that some people are either unable or unwilling to overcome their fears. However, they will go to great lengths to cover that fact.

One day, the Captain assigned Kev to fly the local area with another newbe green pilot. This young man was also transitioning into the Red Birds. On this otherwise unremarkable day, Kevin became the unwilling recipient of a near fatal dose of aviation terror. Subject to "aviation style" fear beyond his comprehension, poor Kev experienced the most terrifying moment of his short aviation career. Possibly, he received the ultimate horrify moment which could be thrust upon a Red Bird driver.

Adding to the educational value of the flight, he learned something scary about people who did not share his romantic view of military life. Serving him well in his later flying, he also learned something vitally important about his little Red Bird's "personality." During his momentous flight Kev came to understand, at an experiential and gut level, exactly what a high-strung little filly his beloved little Red Bird was. As if this was not enough negative knowledge for one flight, he also discovered exactly how nasty her outraged bite could be.

As the strange situation developed, it seemed as if a Mephistophelean overseer chose him, as an uniquely qualified "instructor" to fly with Kev that afternoon. Later, Kev would ruefully tell those who asked that the "Evil One" must have personally chosen this very special instructor. Sent from the realm below, this, one of a kind, "instructor" was the perpetrator of a gross injustice to young Kevin's aviation sensibilities. Eventually, poor Kev's much abused adrenal system was drained of its contents at his "instructor's" brutal hands. One would think that being subjected to inhuman fear was sufficient educational activity for the poor young man. However, this was not true. The grim realities of a very human Army thrust into the middle of an unpopular war was also part of the "Evil One's" assistant's syllabus. The, so called, gentleman who was unknowingly serving as Kev's special "instructor" was named WO-1 Charley Bird.

Later that evening, while speaking with his new friend at the Officer's Club, Kev began his grim story with a confession.

"In truth, I am the last person in the world who has the right to 'cast the first stone' at another man's, so called, sins."

Nevertheless, casting huge boulders of anger, rage, and blame at Charley Bird was exactly what Kev set about to doing. Begrudgingly, Kev had suddenly come to suspect that every unit in the Army had their own Charley. To his great dismay, he found out that his unit also had theirs.

Prior to his fateful flight, Kev had learned that ole Charley was the type of guy who knew everything that there was to know about military aviation. If his superior knowledge were not sufficient, he was the kind of guy who did everything better than the average Joe. Furthermore, because of his carefully nurtured and well-inflated self-image, Charley didn't appreciate or accept unsolicited advice from anyone. Most particularly though, he refused to accept, with anything resembling esteem, advice from his peers. Like himself, Charley's peers had also just finished flight school. Kev was sure that Charley asked himself, for him, a serious question.

"What did they know that he didn't know better?"

Before Kev got totally carried away with his character assignation, he made a private confession to his friend.

"To be fair, I also recognize, within myself, a clearly marked tendency to portray an exceptionally 'strong ego.'"

It needs to be carefully noted that abundant strength of self-confidence was a common hallmark which most of the folk in Military Aviation carefully nursed and strongly projected. In short, most Army pilots had a very high opinion of themselves. The hard world of Vietnam was proving that this high self-opinion was completely justified! Flying vulnerable and fragile helicopters in a combat zone was not a job for the weak at heart. Often, this feeling of superiority got them into trouble. However, in balance, that high self-confidence was also what kept them alive when the chips were down.

In contrast, Charley had worked diligently to further alienate himself from most of his peers. He had an aloofness which most people correctly perceived as a very carefully crafted portrayal of superiority. Many of the new guys were sure that, basic to Charley's personality, there was a streak of very nasty self-serving sneakiness which frequently surfaced. His inner sneakiness made most of the pilots and enlisted folk uncomfortable in his presence. When he was present, people felt forced to always remain on guard. Simply put, ole Charley was not the sort of everyday, lunch bucket, guy with whom most of his peers wanted to share a beer or two after a hard day at the flight line. Even after a long day boring holes in the sky, most of the pilots preferred to remain alone rather than to share in his company.

Within a few days of meeting each other, Kev came to dislike and distrust Charley. In turn, Charley had made it abundantly clear that Kev was the type of commoner with whom he would rather not associate. Spending time with a new guy like Kev would serve no known useful purpose to Charley's status needs. Being the "nobody" he was, made Kev a person who was unable to further Charley's carefully planned career advancement goals.

Be that as it may, the Captain, noted that neither Kev nor Charley were flying as observers that fateful day. In a well-meant attempt to get the biggest bang for his buck, the Captain assigned the two of them to put an hour of practice flight in the local area. It was a common sense decision. Both of them needed every hour of flight time that they could get under their belts. In turn, He gave them a bird which had only an hour's flight time left on it. The plan was that when they finished flying the hour, maintenance would put it in the hanger for its one-hundred hour maintenance check. As it was, with only an hour of flight time on it, the bird was unusable for a day's recon. It appeared that the Captain was going to be able to "kill several birds with the same stone."

If for some unknown reason Charley had failed to make the reality of God's preordained social order clear, one only had to observe and listen. As for Charley himself, he regarded himself to be a superior grade of human being. In relation to a mere plebeian creature such as ole working class Kev, Charley had a crystal clear understanding of his position in life. Given the undeniable fact that he out ranked Kev by two weeks in grade, he "appropriately" assigned himself as the pilot in command. Confirming that Kev understood their status difference, he carefully assigned Kev as his copilot. Most would have split the time as pilot and copilot. But, not Charley.

Taking life in stride, ole Kev found this careful differentiation of status humorous. Such things only mattered to Charley. His out ranking Kev was by the sole virtue of the incontestable fact that he had graduated from flight school two weeks prior to Kev. Nobody in the Scout Platoon or the whole troop cared a wit about who graduated before who! That is, except Charley.

Ole Charley never forgot the, important to him, relative difference of their military status. Therefore, upon arriving at the flight line together, he immediately confirmed their little pecking order. Charley pointedly instructed, his underling.

"Kev, I want you to do the preflight on the little helicopter. Remember, be careful and double check the fluids!"

Always taking good care of himself, Charley was thus assured that Kev would be the one getting his hands dirty. Poor Kev would have to crawl around and about the dirty and greasy aircraft. This carefully preplanned division of labor allowed Charley to remain spotlessly clean while he meticulously checked out the log book. Chuckling to himself, Kev chose not to get himself all worked up into a full-blown uproar over what, in the larger picture of things, was nothing.

Throwing up a mock salute, He said.

"Yes, Sir."

Having paid the proper homage to his leader, he quietly and efficiently did exactly as Charley instructed him to do. He untied the rotor blades of the little Red Bird and safely stowed the tie down away. As with any good preflight, he walked around her carefully poking about her mechanical guts making sure everything was as it was supposed to be. Sadly shaking his head, he noted that she was an overworked and tired bird. The poor old girl was grimy, dirty, and did require extensive preventive maintenance. Even taking into consideration these distasteful surface problems, she remained militarily safe. Kev decided that she was flyable for the hour that they were going to use her.

Silently, Kev had completed all his walking around and about, prodding and poking, looking at and into, and the general meter-metering which was the heart and soul of a good preflight. He then placed himself in the left seat. This seat, of course, was the copilot's seat! Young Kev didn't want to hassle with Charley over meaningless things. Laughing, deep within himself, at the absurdity of the moment, Kev remembered who he was. Charley might have forgotten. However, Kev knew that they were both stupid newbes.

Taking a moment, he mentally made sure that he hadn't forgotten to check something during the preflight. Satisfied, he then securely strapped himself in. Charley, having already finished strapping himself in, dug out his check list. Fumbling about, he managed to get the little bird cranked up without incident. Two or three revetments down the line, a couple of the maintenance guys were working on another helicopter. They found the incongruous sight that greeted their eyes so funny that they tried not to laugh as they watched.

Charley, playing his role, cut a laughably ludicrous figure. Lest the casual observer forget, he was a big time, I'm going to win the war all by myself, combat pilot. The gentleman was in the most basic meaning, "dressed to kill" To be kind, the training mission that the two mainte-nance guys were watching just did not fit the scenario. Climbing into the helicopter, they were two "student pilots." In reality, they were just a couple of green as grass kids learning how to fly a Red bird. Their only purpose in flying was to bore holes in the sky and fly around the traffic pattern for about an hour. Excepting their personal side arms, they didn't have a single bullet or a gun to shoot one on board this helicopter. Staying in the heliport's local area, they didn't need one!

Normal practice at their heliport was that when someone was flying an unarmed bird around the traffic pattern, they flew in a relaxed setting. The pilots and crew simply unrolled the sleeves of their nomex flight suits and put on their crusty old leather flight gloves. If they were lucky, they might have the new nomex gloves. Their only other equip-ment consisted of their flight helmets carefully crammed down over their ears. The personal safety gear was a practical necessity which was always used when flying. It was understood that crashes and the resulting fires were indifferent to war or peace. As to the grievous threats of the war, they were perfectly safe in their own traffic pattern. Except for the loaded side arm strapped to their hips, they could have been driving around a traffic pattern anywhere back in the world.

Struggling manfully, Kev forced himself to stifle a laugh as he casually glanced to his right. GI Joe Charley, was apparently preparing to face the overwhelming yellow hoard all by himself. Everyone who looked could see that he was all set for the big one! He had put on his chicken plate with both front and back armor plates. The armored seat did not offer Charley enough protection. Barely able to keep his thought to himself, Kev muttered under his breath.

"Santa H Clause and all his little elves! I don't believe it. Please, tell me my eyes are pulling a trick on me. Charley has got the back plate stuffed in his chicken vest. This is unreal! Ole Charley must be the only pilot in Viet Nam to fly with the back plate!"

In comparison, some Cobra pilots did not wear a chicken plate. They reasoned that by the time a bullet got through the front of the Snake and the pilot/gunner, it would be spent. Charley, nevertheless, was taking no chances concerning his precious body. He had also put a bulky flack vest on over his chicken plate. Looking to his right, Kev correctly assumed that Charley was never one to put himself second. Nor by the looks of things, was he one to neglect his personal safety.

Only in country a couple-three weeks, Charley somehow had managed to obtain one of the new, exceptionally heavy and uncomfortable armored flight helmets. Kev didn't dare guess where the armored flight helmet might have come from. However, Charley was probably the only pilot in the troop to have one in his possession.

Struggling as best he could to keep his laugh suppressed, Kev spoke to the private recesses of his mind.

"It looks to me, like Charley is carefully protecting his self-proclaimed superior brain."

At the absurd sight of him, poor Kev struggled to maintain a semblance of composure and control. Kev continued his conversation with himself.

"It's a good thing that I am a fair bit heavier than ole Charley."

This "weighty" thought that raced through his mind was based upon aviation logic. Because, if they had been the same weight, all the personal body armor GI Joe Charley had strapped on his preciousness would have thrown the little bird completely out of weight and balance. He could just imagine how in such an extreme out of balance condition, if Charley tried to hover, the overburdened little bird would roll over on top of both of them.

Unable to contain themselves, the two maintenance men were openly laughing their heads off while watching this laughable high drama of men at war unfolding. While the two maintenance types were enjoying Charley's parody of a Scout pilot, Kev quietly sat in his copilot's seat and tried not to burst out laughing or begin crying in embarrassment. He had his sleeves rolled down and his old comfortable leather flight gloves on his hands. Unlike Charley, he only had his old battered flight school "brain bucket" carefully scrunched down over his ears to protect his head. The contrast in styles was not lost to the maintenance guys. Leaning against their revetment wall, they decided the on-going comedy as a good reason to stop working and to enjoy the silly situation.

Slowly turning toward his friend and speaking in a dramatic

stage whisper, the first mechanic turned to the second and asked.

"Which one would you like to fly with, Mr. Johnson or Mr. Bird?"

An answer came without a moment's hesitation.

"Are you kidding me? Neither of them! They're both stupid newbes. However, if I have to choose one of them, Johnson looks to be a little more comfortable. I'm not sure, but he almost appears to have a feeling, of sorts, for what is going on. Either one would probably get me killed. However, I believe that I might live a little longer with Mr. Johnson!"

For some unknown reason Kev had managed to forget, for a moment, where he was. As he looked about, the local scene reminded Kev of the profound difference between the orderly world of flight school and the world he now inhabited. The world of well-organized safety conscious flight schools with barrier-free heliports were a thing of his distant past. In Vietnam, all the Army's helicopters were usually placed in "U" shaped revetments approximately three and one half to four feet in height. The ground crews normally constructed these protective enclosures out of sand filled fifty-five gallon oil drums. If this protective wall was still not sufficiently high, the sand filled drums were then topped with several layers of standard issue olive-drab sand bags. The sole purpose of this ad hoc construction was to protect the fragile helicopters from damage in case of rocket or ground attack.

The down side was that the obvious and immediate difficulty was that the pilot was forced to hover backwards out of the protective revetment before he could line up for takeoff. Kev looked to his right, left, and forward and thought to himself in impending horror.

"Oh Lord, have mercy on me."

Standing carefully aside, the two highly amused enlisted men patiently waited to see if any more high drama or a continuation of the absurd military comedy was coming their way. They had no idea what would happen when the two green pilots attempted to take the little helicopter out of the revetment. Both of them knew that if the helicopter accidentally bumped into the revetment, a disastrous crash would follow. The maintenance people thought with the two green pilots it might happen while hovering backwards, hovering forwards or even hovering sideways. Staying within the world of combat's black humor, one turned to the other and offered a macabre wager.

"Ten bucks say that they don't make it out of the revetment."

If they bumped the solid revetment while fumbling around, it would be unforgiving to the offending helicopter. In retaliation for being struck by the hovering helicopter, the revetment would do its very best to grab the offender and cause an accident. A bump and a bang, and a great thumping, thrashing, and flailing of the rotor would signal the death of the helicopter. With the advent of this chaos, the revetment would then have finished completely ravaging the offending helicopter. This vindictive and destructive action would constitute the revetment's revenge upon the stupid newbe's incompetence. Completing the vicious act of blind revenge, a burning crash would result in a destroyed helicopter and possibly a destroyed pilot or two. It could happen while the maintenance types were watching. If so, the two green pilots would not be the first to feel the revenge of an offended revetment. Many fumbling pilots had experienced a similar fate.

Kevin Paul Johnson, the great romantic, freely admitted that he has always been uncomfortable when he is not the one in control of the situation. Like any other high-spirited pilot, it was perfectly understandable that he always wanted the aircraft's controls securely nestled in his own hands. If he could not have the controls in his hands, he wanted to have a set within his reach. Hell for him was to fly in the back of the aircraft as mere cargo. In this instance, as he had been doing ever since his arrival in Viet Nam, as a know nothing newbe, he would have to bide his time. Today's flight was Charley's flight. For the moment, Kev was primarily supposed to observe and learn. Kev had heard the scuttlebutt that Charley was not considered a smooth stick man. This widespread scuttlebutt failed to make Kev any more comfortable about not being in control of the helicopter.

However, the last thing that he needed was Charley's negative comments shared with him over the intercom. Apparently, before Charley attempted to lift the little Red Bird to a hover, he wanted to cover all his bases. With the carefully cultured and very urbane voice of a highly experienced pilot, Charley paused and politely pontificated for poor inexperienced Kev's benefit.

"You know, I have never really liked these Loachs. In my opinion, they are much too twitchy on the controls."

For a brief moment, Kev considered asking Charley an inflammatory, yet heartfelt, question.

"Why, in the love of everything that is holy, do I have to fly with a jerk, like you, who doesn't even like the helicopter?"

Pausing and pondering for a moment, he thought better of it. With the comfortless utterance of this less than confidence inspiring statement, Charley proceeded to crudely yank in a full armload of collective pitch.

Like an uncontrolled rocket, the unloaded little bird responded to Charley's abrupt control movements. It seemed to Kev that the abused little helicopter shot up to the world's most unstable high-hover. Deeply distressed, a surprised and shocked Kev found himself bouncing about in a strange neighborhood eight feet above the ground.

Speaking to himself, Kev blurted out:

"Gawd, Charley."

A normal hover somewhere between two and three feet above the ground.

"At least," Kev thought to himself, "this is a blessing, of sorts. At this absurd height, we are not going to bump into the revetment."

For a brief moment Kev just watched Charley try to hover the little Red Bird. As he looked about in abject horror at his coming death, Kev seriously considered jumping, head first, into a full-blown panic. Discarding that thought, he then looked down at his set of controls. Suddenly, he wasn't the least bit worried about being killed in the crash which he believed was a sharp intake of breath away.

Of more immediately concern, to Kev, was the frantic action of the blurred cyclic control stick between his legs. It appeared to Kev that he was about to be beaten to death with the wildly thrashing control stick. Charley was thrashing the stick about the cockpit like he was using it to whip up a cake mix rather than gently coax a helicopter into flight. Taking a quick glance down at the anti-torque pedals, Kev's already questionable confidence in Charley frantically fled from him at a continuously accelerating rate. Soon, there was no more confidence left.

Reviewing what he had seen so far, he bitterly noted that Charley's flying skills, so far, had not been confidence inspiring. His confidence and plans for the future continued to depart from his heart and mind at a constantly increasing rate. Stranded in his passive position, Kev slowly shook his head in disbelief. Ole Charley, he was something else in the Red Bird cockpit. He struggled pumping the anti-torque pedals back and forth as fast as he could. It looked like Charley was racing his bike down the steepest hill in his old neighborhood. The struggling would-be pilot was pumping so fast that he must have been riding his ancient one speed bike from his childhood days.

Sadly, Kev resigned himself, body and soul, to the inevitable cruel decision of the unfeeling fates. Left with no other option, the young man calmly closed his eyes and patiently waited to pass on to another and hopefully better place. The wild gyrations within and without the little helicopter convinced him that he was about to be transported to yet another world in a metal and flesh rendering crash.

Well . . . , that was not exactly true. Reluctantly trusting his fate to the gods of aviation, Kev began to wonder if he might die prior the inevitable crash. The gyrations of the little helicopter were throwing Poor Kev about the cockpit like he was a boneless rag doll. He was also being beaten to death by the many unyielding things his body slammed into. Protecting himself, as best he could, he was tightly gripping the grab handle by the door frame.

As he was thrown about, Kev was painfully well aware that he was not a great stick man. Nor, had he ever claimed to be the world's greatest helicopter pilot.

"But this," he said to himself "is beyond absurd!"

As he bounced about, Kev felt as if he were sitting inside a soda fountain blender running in overdrive. This absurd situation, masquerading as flying, was terrifying him! Tossing about the cockpit, the terrified young man made a holy vow. As God was his witness, he vowed to everything and everyone that he called holy. Should he miraculously survive the day, he would never become an instructor pilot. Well . . . after patiently waiting for the inevitable fiery crash and his subsequent death, much to his surprise, nothing happened.

Taking a deep breath, Kev decided to do a quick inventory concerning the condition of his own person. To his great shock, following his detailed inventory, he decided that he had not transitioned into the dreaded condition of deadness. Pleasantly surprised, he quickly noted that he didn't feel any extra physical pain. However, he carefully noted his state of profoundly deep psychological terror. Ironically though, by the way the helicopter was thrashing about, he came to the conclusion that he was going to be motion-sick.

"Good Lord!" He exclaimed to himself. "This is not even close to fair!"

"Pilots are only supposed to get motion-sick flying in a storm. They were not supposed to become motion-sick at a hover. Oh Lord! I think I am about to puke."

While he managed to hold the contents of his stomach, he felt as if he was flying through a category "really bad" storm. Continuing his deep pondering of his powerless situation, Kev came to a strange, yet highly logical, conclusion.

"To the best of my knowledge, dead people simply don't get motion sick! Therefore, I must still be alive!"

Relieved to be alive, he continued dreading the unknown and possibly short future which was awaiting him. At the same time, he sighed in deep resignation that somehow it wasn't quite yet his time to die. Fearfully, Kev slowly opened his eyes. His fate was cruelly controlled by virtue of two weeks of flight school. The "outranked" young man could do nothing except patiently await what dismal, dank, and dark new terrors might be hidden within the coming hour.

Later that day, Chief Jones asked the two maintenance men what they saw. They said.

"Chief, to begin, we have no idea by what illogical mysteries the little helicopter managed to escape unscathed from the revetment."

It had come as a great surprise to them when the wildly gyrating helicopter safely escaped the revetment. Even more surprising when it ended essentially facing down the take off lane. The younger of the two added another thought as a post script.

"Mind you Chief, it was truly the ugliest thing I have ever seen here at the heliport! And, I have seen some ugly stuff!"

The tower operator later told the Chief that he considered calling somebody because he thought that whoever was flying the little bird was unsafe. Then, with a shrug of his shoulders, he added a closing thought.

"But, Sir" I finally said to myself, "who is a PFC tower operator to make that judgement?'"

Sitting at their high hover, Kev found himself to be a properly terrified and unwilling passenger on a wildly gyrating carnival ride. The little helicopter was hovering at fifteen feet and bouncing to and fro. Dismayed, Kev noted that Ole Charley, trying to control the helicopter, was still sawing away at the pedals for all he was worth. While at the same time, he was whipping the air into a froth with the collective and control-stick. Hovering, more or less, the nose of the little helicopter was swinging both left and right about ninety degrees.

Later that night, at the club, Kev told his friend Sven about the flight.

"Call what happened next whatever you might choose. As for Kev, I positively refuse to dignify what happened next by calling it anything that vaguely resembled a normal take off. Yet, somehow or other we arrived in the air. What shocked me even more, is that apparently by accident, we eventually arrived in the general neighborhood of the traffic pattern. Fortunately for me, the big boss god assigned several gods, who had grossly misbehaved, to my worthless butt. For their punishment, they were serving their penance by being assigned to a stupid green helicopter pilot and being responsible for his safety. Believe me, those poor gods were working over time. These unknown gods whom I had previously underappreciated, made sure that no other helicopter traffic was flying about for us to blunder into. By the way, I do hope that they received overtime pay for a job well done."

Kev, still emotionally shaken, paused to take an extra deep draw from his beer. Following a healthy stretch, he continued with his story by asking.

"Sven, I am in Vietnam, aren't I? Haven't I sufficiently suffered for all the sins of my misbegotten youth? Well . . . , I guess not. Because, I was then forced to endure sitting through two or three circuits around the traffic pattern. I swear to you on a stack of Bibles, those were the most pathetic circuits ever flown in any aircraft traffic pattern. This is up to and including the first days of Primary flight training. Honest to goodness, they made my wretched flying with Captain Jack a few days ago look like the work of a highly seasoned aviation pro. Let me put it this way. To say that this sorry excuse for a human-being was ham-fisted would be a grievous insult to every member of the proud and prosperous swine family. I include, in this list, those little piggies who gave their lives to become breakfast's bacon."

About a half an hour into the flight, surpassing Kev's worst expectations, things went from bad to worse. For a reason or reasons which the tower operator said he could not remember, he asked Charley if he could modify his traffic pattern. Without thinking about the consequences of the modified traffic pattern, Charley did as he was requested. The few people at the heliport who were watching all agreed upon what they witnessed. None of them suggested that Charley and Kev were flying anything that was a recognizable traffic pattern. The tower operator was simply being very generous by calling what they were doing a traffic pattern.

Yet, things still might have turned out OK for the two of them if they had been flying the forgiving lumbering Huey. However, flying the high-spirited little Red Bird was nothing like flying a stable ole Huey. She was a head-strong little filly. When abused, she frequently chooses to turn on the abuser to inflict a severe bite. A bite, that all experienced Loach drivers would add, can be severe enough to be fatal. Made angry enough, she would kill the abuser and any others in the helicopter. As things went from bad to worse, this new traffic pattern was the last piece in the strange puzzle. Every negative thing was now set in its place to punish the two green pilots. A very angry little filly was going to bite them with a premeditated vengeance!

Well . . . the little Red Bird's time for the sweet sensation of revenge had arrived. Those clods who had so severely abused her were going to pay a price for their compassion less ways. Kev's dear Mama had occasionally described the upcoming situation thusly.

"Charley's chickens were ALL coming home to roost."

Ham-fisted Charley had now been flogging the poor bird without mercy for about forty minutes. The little put upon Red Bird decided that the meanspirited flogging by itself was sufficient to warrant severe punishment. Not satisfied, he then gave her the ultimate insult. Without considering the consequences, he was making an excessively steep approach with a light right rear tail wind.

Knowing in his heart of hearts that a flying opinion would be of no value coming from him, nevertheless, Kev spoke.

"Hey Charley. Why don't we make a go around. This approach just feels a tab bit steep for me. What the heck. Nobody is watching."

Sawing at and continuously fighting the controls, Charley persisted in forcing the little Red Bird to do something which she didn't want to do. His situation was totally unacceptable. Someone who was a full two weeks his junior who also had less flight time in a Loach was suddenly threatening his pilot's pride. In an attempt to maintain his carefully crafted image and bearing, Charley took deep personal offense at the well-meant suggestion. None of this came as a surprise to poor ole

Kev.

He angerly snapped back at Kev.

"Who is flying this machine Johnson, you or me? I've got full control of her and if we need to do a go-around it will be my decision."

What else could Kev do but keep his mouth shut and wait? This was one of the problems of military aviation. Upon occasion, rank overrides aviation common sense.

One absolute top of the list, big time "NO-NO" is boldly posted in the OH-6A flight manual. Charley's steep approach with a right quartering tail wind was it! On the back of the front cover of the dash ten, the writers have addressed a severe warning directly to the pilot. This dire warning, which was considered so critical it came before the general description of the aircraft and was printed in **BOLD** print.

In big bold letters, it warned Kev and Charley against getting into their current flight configuration. When he had studied the pilot's manual, Kev had carefully read the warning. Several different times, he had heard about this bad news situation in the hanger flying, shop talk, sessions at the club. Gripping the handhold on the door frame, a helpless Kev could easily read the proverbial handwriting on the wall. Only a fool would ignore such a bold print warning. Unfortunately, for him, Kev was flying with that fool.

They were entering the no man's land commonly called "a tail rotor stall." With a frightful gong sounding in the background of Kev's head, the hammer of doom was hanging directly over the two young heads. Sighing in resignation, Kev remembered a bit of conversation in one of the hanger flying sessions at the club.

"If your tail rotor stalls, your world will turn brown and smelly in less than a part of an instant. Furthermore, if you are not quick, if you are not thinking, and if you are not one with the little Red Bird, you are in deep trouble. She will, without hesitation or remorse, kill you deader than the proverbial doorknob!"

With a sad and pitifully resigned shake of his head, Kev came to a deathbed decision. He should not waste time worrying what color hair his, never to be, grandchildren would have.

Every pilot, military or civilian, knows that all good war stories start with three wonderful little words.

"There we were!"

Well . . . "There 'they' were."

Two green pilots were in the middle of an excessively steep landing approach. Compounding the problem, they were descending much too rapidly with a right quartering tail wind. The two green pilots were already in very deep trouble. The odds were stacked against their escaping unscathed. They did not need any more problems. Still, more trouble was relentlessly closing in on them. Charley's incredibly poor flying had totally stacked the deck against the two young men. Belatedly, just as he had done everything else in the flight, Charley suddenly realized what was happening too late to recover. They were descending far too fast and too steep. Good ole Charley was desperately trying to salvage his wounded pride. True to himself, he positively refused to acknowledge that he was too steep in this sloppy approach to landing. Making a go-around would be visual evidence that he blew the approach and that was unacceptable to a man like Charley.

His flying was so bad and his approach so excessively steep that he was still going to overshoot his intended landing spot by a substantial distance. Lost and in over his head, Charley sent his dormant brains on vacation. Analyzing their approach and looking at Charley, Kev instinctively knew that Charley's brains had traveled to a remote and inaccessible location. He stupidly, pulled back on the control-stick, flaring the aircraft, and yanked in an armload of collective. The die had now been cast, cooled, and removed from the mold. The two little white cubes, with spots on them, came up craps. The banker was calling in the loan. In other words, the little high speed tail rotor stalled! It was no longer biting the air and doing its critical job of controlling the aircraft. That tail rotor joined Charley's dormant brain. It too went on an extended vacation. The little rotor was no longer acting to counter the tremendous torque of the main rotor.

At their high power setting, trouble happened faster than one could speak about it. The little Red Bird started rapidly spinning about her rotor mast. She was acting as if the tail rotor had suddenly fallen off. When the little helicopter started its rapid spinning, Kev was convinced things couldn't get worse. Once again, he was wrong! Things did get worse!

Lost for a better idea, Charley forcefully punched the panic button right through the instrument panel! It was instantly clear as a bell to Kev that Charley had never read the flight manual. Having known Charley for about a week, Kev decided that his conclusion about Charley and the dash ten stood to reason! Ole Charley already knew everything there was to know about military aviation. Reading the dash ten would have suggested that there was something that he could learn.

With an insight, calmness, and maturity that greatly surprised him, Kev thought to himself.

"Of course, reading the dash ten apparently is only for common scum like me. Superior human beings, like Charley, don't need to study."

"There 'they' were," wildly spinning like a child's top at the ridiculously high hover. There they were suspended and spinning about the rotor mast at seventy-five feet above the unforgiving earth. The next step in the farcical flight didn't seem humanly possible to Kev.

However, good ole Charley found yet another creative way to compound his errors. Without having the slightest idea of what he was doing, Charley frantically punched the panic button harder. Yanking up on the collective, he pulled in every foot-pound of power the little bird had to give. The dash ten said that this was not a good idea. However, Charley belonged to an old, yet discredited, school. Its motto was simple.

"If a little is good, then a lot must be better."

With his latest panic driven action, Charley drove all the engine instrument needles deep in the red zones. Trapped in the out of control helicopter, the two of them spun faster and faster. The increased torque, which the screaming engine applied to the rotor system, drove their uncontrolled spin on and on. In the midst of this chaos, the abused little engine was broadcasting the heartbreaking discord of high pitched tortured screams. The heart-rendering noise assaulted Kev's mechanical sense of justice and mercy and outraged him. Continuing his mindless panic-stricken behavior, Charley sawed back and forth on the anti-torque pedals just as fast and as hard as he could. If it were aerodynamically and mechanically possible, Charley's frantic foot work served primarily to make the dangerous situation even worse.

Poor Kev hung on and sadly looked down at the communication towers and the utility poles flashing past his vision. All of those sharply rising death devices seemed to loom a hundred feet above him. It seemed as if they were leering at him as they reached out to destroy him. Finding no solace in that sight, he then looked at the rapidly spinning ground. Meanwhile, he calmly waited for his life to come to a smashing conclusion. He did know that fighting Charley for the controls would make the situation worse. If that were possible.

Up to that exciting and educational moment in their time together, Kev had only thought that Charley was just your normal run of the mill obnoxious jerk. Much to his dismay, Kev discovered a greater depth of depravity to Charley than he had ever expected possible in an Army pilot. Kev regretfully discovered that Mr. Bird was a crude ham-fisted non-pilot as well as an overbearing blowhard. Any man in the Red Birds would easily decide that these non-piloting skills would be sufficient condemnation for the man who wanted to be a Red Bird pilot. However, this condemnation was not the end of the story when it came to Charley.

In way over his head, he had become completely panic stricken. What he did next told Kev the rest of the story about what type of human being, officer, and military pilot, ole Charley was beneath all the bluster. With no advanced warning, Charley suddenly yanked his hands and feet away from the controls. He acted as if these useful flight tools had suddenly transformed themselves into flesh-eating white-hot metal. One would have thought that these controls were rapidly searing through his skin and flesh all the way to the bone. Almost weeping, he cried out,

"You've got it."

Having been painfully humbled when he had sloppily herded the Huey through the sky with Captain Jack, Kev readily admitted, that he was not a great stick-man. Furthermore, after that first combat mission, no grandiose visions remained concerning the state of his flying skills. However, he was planning and determined to become one of the best stick-men in Viet Nam, if not in all of Army aviation. Apparently though, his flying instincts, if not his skills, must have been very good. Recognizing that much remained for him to learn, he wasn't too good to carefully read the dash ten. In this case, reading and studying the operators manual was their salvation. Yet, something greater than a pilot's knowledge both drove and governed his actions. A deep instinctive urge drove Kev to ease the little Red Bird's pain and suffering. Wherever the truth may lie, Kev immediately knew what their problem was.

More importantly though, he had a pretty good idea what had to be done to save their bacon. Calming speaking, he took the controls.

"I've got it."

Then, he immediately jumped on the pilotless controls before the situation became any worse. With little else to work with, he let his instincts take command of his hands and feet. Simultaneously and in one smooth controlled motion, Kev made three distinct control movements. First, he dumped power to reduce the main rotor torque. Second, he dropped the nose to get some air speed. Lastly, he turned into the direction of the spin and into the wind. Thinking about it for a moment, Kev immediately realized that a good automobile driver would use the same reflexes if he entered a skid on an icy road.

"At last!" He thought. "I knew that growing up and learning to drive in a icy winter wonderland would pay off."

The response of the little Red Bird was as if a magic wand had deftly and sweetly passed over her protesting body. Immediately, Kev's endearing little filly lovingly and deftly answered his slightest wish and lightest touch. As always, Kev found his little bird to be a true thoroughbred with a wonderful succulent, soft, and responsive mouth. Feeling the tension leave his body, he easily swung her into a little bit of a gentle turn. Caressing her controls as if she were a precious lover, he landed her just like he had been flying with the Red Birds all his life. As he was landing the tower anxiously called and asked if they needed any assistance. A little shaken, but in control of himself, Kev told them that all was under control.

"Oh yes," he added to his call to the tower.

"Mark us down as safely landed and carefully tucked away in the barn for the night."

Hover/taxing the bird to its assigned revetment he deftly parked her. Following the two minute engine cool down period, a speechlessly enraged Kev shut her down. Emotionally wrung out, he did nothing to lessen the deafening silence which had filled the aircraft since the last radio call.

The farcical flight had so outraged and infuriated Kev that he did not trust himself to utter a single word. Wordlessly and without looking him in the eye, he handed the Log book and the main rotor tie down to Charley. Silently, he gathered his flight helmet under his arm and started grimly walking to the little Officer's Club. He was honestly afraid that if he even looked at Charley, he might physically assault him. He knew he had sufficient reason to hurt the man. Rightly, he feared an emotional and physical explosion that he might regret later. Leaving Charley, slack jawed, still shaking, and finally, blessedly silent, Kev gratefully departed the scene of the crime.

"Maybe," he thought to himself. "Charley can fill out the log book and tie the aircraft down without screwing up that simple task."

For the moment, Kevin Paul Johnson honestly didn't give a tinkers damn or a rat's rectum what the high and the mighty Mr. Bird did. As far as Kev was concerned, if Charley took a nice long walk off a short pier, it would give him great pleasure to watch the blowhard sink beneath the waves. It might have been the most merciful thing possible for all parties involved. Arriving at the club, the subdued young man ordered three quick double bourbons.

"Hold the ice and hold the water."

Grimly, he bellied up to the bar and did his "serious" drinking. Shaking like an autumn leaf in the wind, he rapidly downed them just like he was an honest-to-goodness hard-core drinker. At last, his nerves were safely swathed in a warm alcoholic haze. Wordless, he quietly wondered back to the quiet and relative safety of his hooch.

As for Charley, Kev vowed never to speak to him again. Chief Jones having heard about the incident made his own little investigation. At the conclusion of his investigation he went over to Charley's hooch. Upon his unannounced arrival, he said.

"Sorry Charley, the Captain and I just don't think that you are Red Bird material."

Charley, having quickly regained some of his imperious bearing, indignantly informed the Chief of his position on the issue!

"That stupid Loach is nothing more than a flying death trap. I was just coming over to tell you that there is no way in hell that I am ever going to fly one again."

Chuckling to himself with the wisdom of a couple thousand flight hours, Chief Jones jauntily walked away. Charley's lack of personal responsibility had quickly placed him far far beneath the Chief's contempt.

Over the next few days, Kev noted that no sense of angst,

51

mourning, or deep emotional pain existed among the Red Birds over Charley's latest imperious declaration. The last that any of the Red Birds saw of Charley, he was working as the assistant supply officer. Remaining true to himself, he was refusing to fly anything or any mission that even hinted at danger. If pressed by the Major, he would fly as the copilot in the command and control Huey flying at a safe altitude. If the great combat pilot had already flown his four hours for the month, which was sufficient to receive his flight pay, he did his best not to fly.

True to his nature, Charley always found his "good/safe" supply officer's heavy job load sufficient excuse for not flying. If the Major insisted that he fly, he usually "volunteered" to fly the mail to higher headquarters. While flying his danger laden postal missions, he carefully kept himself safe from ground fire. He assured his physical safety by always carefully aviating somewhere in the upper stratosphere. Of course, much to the delight and amusement of the enlisted folk, when he was forced to fly, he flew still safely swathed in all five-hundred pounds of his personal body armor. Nattily attired, the bold knight of the aero world continued to complete his combat togs with the only ballistic flight helmet in the troop.

THE PUPPY BECOMES A FLEDGLING

Life was good and the morning's sun began its daily climb into the clear blue skies. Refreshed by a full night's sleep, Kev climbed out of his bunk unexpectedly looking forward to a new day. He didn't understand why he was excited about a new day. However, the sour smells of the latrines and the stench of the night-soil upon the rice paddies seemed less foreboding then they previously had felt. Following his tepid shower, he casually glanced about his new world.

"Well, Kev, your new world seems pretty much as you left it last night."

Though the day was young, the morning's mist was rapidly burning off from the paddies. As usual, it promised to be another hot, humid, and generally miserable day in lovely Southeast Asia. Undaunted, he jauntily walking over to the Officer's mess. As he walked along in good spirits, the young man was whistling a meaningless tune. Celebrating his new lease on life, even the Army's breakfast of reconstituted eggs, "SOS," and bitter coffee tasted better than wonderful! Delighting his breakfast, Kev ate with a newfound gusto and purpose. Quietly chuckling to himself, he thought to himself.

"Kev, ole boy, your life is beginning to look up."

As he talked to himself, Kev allowed a big smile to fill the wide expanses of his young face. With that smile, he made a heart-felt resolution. Enjoying his breakfast, he dedicated his meal to gathering his strength so he could loudly curse the day Charley Bird's mother birthed that pile of self-centered uselessness.

Kev was delighted, relieved, and smugly satisfied when someone had told him that Chief Jones had paid an "official" visit ole Charley. His spirits soared to greater heights when he found out that Jones had given him the Scout's heave-ho. Charley, the fearless combat pilot, had been efficiently, safely, and appropriately relegated to the Scout's scrap heap The chief had effectively said that, like a crashed helicopter, he was broken and beyond economical salvage.

The only down side was that the Red Birds then found themselves increasingly short of qualified pilots. This unexpected situation forced Red Six, the Captain, to accelerate Kev's training. Unknown to Kev, Red Six asked Chief Jones if the young man was ready to drive the little Red Bird around the traffic pattern by himself. Jones told the platoon commander that he felt confident in Kev's growing abilities. Smiling, he continued.

"The kid has already shown that he was ready to fly the Loach on his own when he saved Charley and himself."

Pausing and taking a deep draw on his ever present cup off coffee.

"Captain, I think that the kid can solo."

Taking a moment to think and struggle with himself, the Captain decided to OK the flight. Agreeing with the Chief, he Oked the solo because Kev rescued Charley's and his own butt from Charley's self induced tail rotor stall. Twenty-four hours later, with the Scout's complete lack of ceremony, Kev found himself dressed in his flight gear and down on the Red Bird line. He was not sure how or why it occurred. Nevertheless, he found himself getting ready to take his first solo ride astride his beloved Red Bird. When he arrived at the flight line, being Kev, he nervously began a serious pep talk/conversation with himself.

"Well . . . , let's see now Kev. It appears that you have completed your preflight inspection. Like a good little pilot, word for word, you carefully followed the dash ten's checklist. Step by step, you peered into all the sight glasses and noted that all the oils and fluids are up to their proper level. Carefully acting as if you knew what you were doing, you walked all around and climbed over, about and through the aircraft. As far as you could tell, it appears that all the nuts and bolts are where Mr. Hughes says they are supposed to be. Furthermore, it looks as if the maintenance guys have properly attached, torqued, and safety wired, all the assorted parts that make up a helicopter. Terrified of making a complete fool of yourself, you even remembered to untie the rotor blades and have safely stowed the rotor tie down in the back. I guess that you're finished here."

Scratching his head slowly and methodically, Kev decided that he had done well so far. With the nervous itch relieved, he continued his monologue.

"Hmmm . . . This ole bird seems safe to fly. Whether or not the pilot is safe, well . . . , that could be an entirely different story. OK Kev! It is time to quit stalling. As your dad would say to you when you were a little guy 'there's no time like the present.'"

Pondering for another moment or two, he reached down and scratched himself in a more private place. He knew that he was stalling and that it was understandable. His last flight in a Red Bird had been dramatic, traumatic, and had darned near scared him to death.

"I guess that's it. Kev, it looks to me as if it is time to climb into your seat and get this show on the road. Such as it is!"

His preflight completed, and running out of excuses to delay the day's test, Kev geared himself up for action.

"All-right Kev, it's time to roll down your sleeves, put on your gloves, and cinch up your britches. While you are at it, dummy, strap yourself into your safety harness, and put your brain bucket on your pointy little head."

Ready to crank up the little bird, he dug out the rest of the start-up checklist. Fastening it to his knee board, and then fastening the knee board to his knee, the nervous young man got started. Almost shaking with anticipation and fear, Kev continued his never-ending monologue.

"OK my boy, don't get yourself all worked up about anything. Damn it, come on Kev! For crying out loud, don't get your panties all bunched up over a little trip around the traffic pattern. It is not all that difficult. Think about it for a minute. Somehow, you managed to pass your final check-ride in that ancient 'A' model Huey at Mother Rucker. Heck, even that bloody idiot Charley didn't kill you. (Though he tried hard!) You can do it kid. The United States Army gave your Silver Wings. In their great wisdom, they declared, to the world, that you are an official Army Aviator. Now go out and prove it to the rest of the troop!"

He mopped his sweaty brow and took a long and drawn out lung expanding breath.

"As far as you know, there is no reason to break a sweat today."

While taking his deep breath, Kev nervously reflected upon the importance of his upcoming flight. After a moment or two, he allowed his breath to depart with a deep sigh and shudder. As far as he could determine, he was ready to go. Before his rising anxiety gave birth to even greater levels of anxiety, he quickly reminded himself that he was just going to do was motor-motor the little bird around the traffic pattern for a time or two and burn up a few gallons of Uncle Sam's JP fuel. Maybe, if all went well, he would fly a wee little bit in the local area.

"Of course," he thought to himself.

"If he am lucky, nobody would note that a grass green pilot is driving this little bird."

With a silly grin, he knew that a complete lack of notice would be the mark of a successful solo.

Deep inside, he was aware that his upcoming little flight should be a piece of cake. Properly thought of, the morning's flight was going to be playtime. He had been with the troop long enough to know that flying when no one was going to shoot at him and no one was going to grade him was a rare luxury. Furthermore, like when he flew with Charley Bird he would also be physically comfortable because he was not going to have to wear his chicken plate.

"Well,"he thought to himself with just a touch of a hidden smile.

"Come on! It's now or never you old chicken."

Filling himself with another deep shuddering breath he plunged in.

"Here goes nothing."

Carefully going through the check list step by step and line by line, Kev wanted to fire the bird up the way it is supposed to be done. He had set a preliminary goal of being able to zip through the checklist with the speed, accuracy, and authority that Captain Jack did on his flight with him to young Lieutenant's crash site. However, first, he had to fire her up without damaging the engine, the rest of the helicopter, or his ego.

Rotor Blades - CLEAR.

Fire Guard - POSTED.

Throttle - FUEL CUTOFF position.

Starter-ignition button - PRESS AND HOLD.

N1 turbine speed 15% - twist the throttle to IDLE STOP.

TOT temperature below 927 C.

Starter-ignition button - RELEASE AT 58% N1.

Engine Oil pressure - 50 PSI AT IDLE.

N1 tach indicator - STABILIZED 62-65%.

XMSN OIL PRESSURE warning light out at 55% N2.

Generator switch - GEN.

Invertor-OFF switch - INVERTOR.

Attitude gyro - PULL TO ERECT.

Radios - ON.

Helmet - ON.

Controls - Check friction OFF, tip path plane, freedom of movement of pedals and collective, Adjust frictions as desired.

Throttle - FULL OPEN. Monitor instruments for temperature and torque limits.

Governor trim low range - CHECK N2 FOR 96 +- 2%.

Engine oil pressure - 90 TO 130 PSI.

Throttle - Reduce to idle; check both throttles for 62-65% N1 idle rpm; RETURN TO FULL OPEN.

All instruments - Normal operating range.

Anti-collision lights - ON.

Caution and warning lights - OUT, if applicable.

Instruments - Normal operating range.

N2 - 101% normal pre-takeoff setting on the ground (103% at a hover).

Fuel quantity gauge - Check indication.

Completing the cockpit check list on the little Red Bird, Kev was ready for flight. It seemed to him that the little bird idled anxiously in the revetment. Authentically excited and satisfied with his preflight, the young man was set to begin the most wonderful helicopter flight of his life. As his excitement built to a fever pitch, Kev knew that this was going to be a "historic" flight. His excitement paled that of his first solo flight in the Korean War veteran OH-13 at Fort Wolters. At last, he was in his own "front-line" combat helicopter. The young man's great adventure was at its jump-off point with the engine running and up to flight idle. Savoring the moment, Kev reached over with his right thumb and clicked the radio switch. Carefully modulating his voice and praying that it didn't crack, he tried to speak like a real, live, and honest to goodness, "Cav pilot." Praying that he sounded cool, he made his first radio call of the day.

"Tower. This is Red One-Five requesting taxi and takeoff from the Red Bird Nest."

Releasing the mike and unable to contain his excitement, Kev explosively gushed two words to the unimpressed world.

"Oh yes!"

At a dirty dusty heliport, stuck in the middle of an unpopular war, young Kev was almost overwhelmed by the greatest celebratory moment of his life. For the first time in his aviation career, he wasn't sitting in a training bird, nor was he flying a lumbering Huey slick. The young man was awestruck as he softly and sensuously caressed the control stick. In an unholy way, for Kev, this was a deeply religious moment. Strange feelings of masculine love and power cursed through his veins which throbbed with the power of his little bird.. For the first time in his pilot's life, the trigger on the control stick was a real live trigger which fired a mini-gun. It was not a radio switch! Kev, shameless romanticizing, was thrilled! Later that evening he was telling one of the new Huey drivers at the club about the flight. He ended up saying.

"Honest to God, I could feel my excited blood pounding through my veins and supercharged electrons running up and down my nerves. I sat like a star-struck fool softly caressing all the controls like they belonged to my girlfriend's body. Hypnotized, I kept lifting and releasing the trigger guard just to listen to it snap."

What else could someone like young Kev say? This was his very first flight solo in a Loach. For the first time in his aviation career, he was in command of a dedicated combat aircraft. For the first time, since getting his wings, he was in command of his own aircraft. The fact that his little helicopter was unarmed and harmless never entered his mind.

It seemed as if it had taken his whole lifetime for the young man to achieve his crowning moment. Few could understand the power and meaning of the moment. At last, he had arrived at his great goal and was flying his own Red Bird with his own call sign. He was "Red One-Five." The control tower had innocently acknowledged Kev's greatest achievement. Crashing-pounding waves of almost uncontrolled excitement were building within him. His ears were rushing with the thunderous crash of giant rollers upon the beach.

All the hard months of work at Fort Wolters and Fort Rucker become worth all the assorted military hoops that merciless Tach Officers had him mindlessly jumping through. Feeling the mechanical and spiritual life of the little Red Bird pulsing through the controls and into his very being, he was grinning from ear to ear. Kev suddenly realized that the normal screaming and yelling of the Tach Officers hadn't been so bad. The excited young man felt the truth of the moment. All the pushups, all the harassment, all the highs and all the lows of the last year which combined flight school and Officer Candidate School had at last come to full fruition. For Kev, this was the culmination of human history! Yes. Kev's long awaited Kingdom had come! He was caught up in the penultimate moment of a romantic young helicopter pilot. It was then that he knew that all the endless months of frustration and hard work at flight school had been a small price to pay to savor this moment.

Completely overwhelmed by the moment, Kev quietly boasted to himself. Despite the high-pitched scream of the little turbine engine, fearing that someone would think that he was totally loony, Kev spoke quietly to himself.

"Today, at last, I, Kevin Paul Johnson am finally my own man. For the first time in my life, I am something much more than just Mrs. Johnson's little boy. I feel wonderful and complete as a human being. How could a man want anything more?"

Steadying the control stick with his legs, he reverently reached to his collar and softly caressed his insignia.

"These are my beautiful golden crossed sabers. I can't believe it is true. In a moment, I am now going to fly my own military issue war machine. If God should strike me dead upon landing, it will have all been worth it."

Young Kev was, on top of the world. He was already emotionally "flying" at altitudes he had never dared dream about! For the moment, the glorious and wondrous feeling of being an Army Aviator was his and his alone. The sweet and creamy frosting on his delicious cake was that Mr. Hughes' delightful little bird was his treasured possession! No one, no one in all of creation was going to take this moment away from him. Kevin Paul Johnson's penultimate moment was his alone to remember and to treasure for the rest of his life.

Within himself, Kev knew that he had earned his special moment. He had paid for it with his sweat, his determination, and more hard work than he could remember. Savoring the moment, he cared little about anyone else. As far as he was concerned, the "druggies" could have their drugs and the "boozers" could have their booze. That was their business. He knew that they could never feel the soaring heights of elation that he was feeling. It did not matter to him if he died within the sweep of the clock's hand. Kevin Paul Johnson knew in his heart of hearts that there was no greater "high" in the whole world than the one which he was so fully enjoying.

The happy young man felt complete. He was in possession of his own Red Bird and his own call-sign. He was Red One-Five! After the flight he confided in one of his friends.

"I have to be honest, my head was spinning like a supercharged top that I barely heard the tower give me clearance to begin my flight. HOLY COW! I can't begin to tell how beautiful the words were than rang in my ears when the tower talked to this army pilot. 'Red One-Five, you are cleared to hover taxi and takeoff from the Red Bird Nest.'"

Generally a self-contained and private person, young Kevin returned to his inexhaustible, self-directed, pep talk.

"Ok Kev, that's enough patting yourself on the back and enjoying your self congratulation's garbage. You've got flying to do!"

Reluctantly, he accepted that the languid leisure of savoring the glories of the moment had run its course. It was time for ole Kev to carefully herd his little bird into the air. He began carefully. A pilot never started a flight so very carefully. Somehow, his ultimate moment of truth had unexpectedly slipped up upon him.

Ready to begin his great adventure, Kev gently eased up on the collective. The soft application of upward pressure on the collective increased the power in nice and slow increments. Lovingly, he was caressing his hard-earned tools of adulthood with the lightest of a touch. Cautious to a fault, he reminded himself that the little bird was empty and that the unforgiving revetment surrounded him. Perspiring heavily, Kev carried on. Desiring with all his might, he wanted to be a totally cool Scout pilot. Yet, he was very nervous. Continuing with his self-contained conversation, the very nervous young man reminded himself of the reality of the moment. Though he might not see them, some people were closely observing his upcoming flight.

"Come on now, Kev. Don't go and make a dang fool of yourself on your first official solo flight as a Scout. Dear God, PLEASE, don't let me end up looking like that blowhard Charley. It would be better if you struck me dead on the spot! Ok . . . Just think before you move any of the controls. Kev, my boy, you would look like a first class fool if you jumped straight out of the revetment into an uncontrolled hover at fifty feet."

As he lifted the collective pitch stick, he began adding a featherweight touch of right pedal to compensate for the increased engine torque. Working hard and concentrating on his fling, mighty rivers of salty flowing perspiration began to flow from every pore of his body. The little bird was lightly straining at the soft leash to soar with the winds. With the little Red Bird dancing lightly on the skids, he gently added just the thought of a tiny little touch more power. SUDDENLY he felt a great and wondrous miracle. Ole Kev was hovering, three feet above the ground. Best of all, he was in his own Loach. Kevin Paul Johnson was flying his own glorious little Red Bird! Seemingly as miraculous as the parting of the Red Sea three-thousand years ago, Kev suddenly felt like he had truly become Red One-Five.

Readying himself to back out of the revetment, Kev began applying just a little bit of back pressure on the control stick. Doing everything cautiously, he was still taking all the time he needed so he could do things right. Concerning this little solo flight, Kevin had no excuse for rushing. As the light pressure on the stick began to take hold, he began slowly backing the little helicopter out of the confining revetment. Subconsciously, he believed, as far as this flight was concerned, that image was everything. Overly concerned, almost to the point of paranoia with his performance, Kev was trying not to snag a skid on the PSP (perforated steel planking) floor of the revetment. The nervous pilot was terrified of crashing in front of God and everybody. He was almost as terrified of discovering some other, unknown to him, piloting foolishness. Then, using that foolishness to prove that he had evolved beyond being just another idiot new guy. But, had reached new depths of stupidness.

As he fretted, he began to wonder if it was an exceptionally hot day. Thinking about it for a moment, he decided that the temperature must have soared to an excess of a million degrees inside the helicopter. Stained dark by this time, his flight suit was completely soaked through. Kev felt so wet that he thought that he had just forded a stream.

Aerodynamically, the multitude of moving parts had reached an equilibrium of sorts, and the helicopter had stopped moving. He could stay suspended forever, or he could add an additional gentle touch of back pressure on the cyclic stick. He opted to continue on with the adventure. Nice and slowly, he backed the little bird out. So far, he was pleased with his performance.

"Heck," he thought to himself.

"Kev, ole boy, you looked just like an old pro backing out of this revetment."

Not wanting to leave anything to chance, he continued to repeat his silent mantra of the day.

"There you go. You've got it under control. Don't forget what kind of helicopter you are flying. She's her own little Bird and is as skittish as a half broken young filly."

Struggling and gently sawing at the pedals as he fought a stiff crosswind, he continued his continual monologue.

"In case you forgot, stupid, you better remember something important. Your little filly is even more skittish when she is hovering in a cross wind."

Working very cautiously, he safely cleared the revetment. Preparing to soar on the wondrous wings of his proud and glorious little eagle, Kev began a little pedal turn to face the helicopter into the wind. Before he began to over-control the helicopter, he quickly reminded himself not to fight the wind but to let the wind do the work for him.

In his mind, this was Red One-Five's great moment of truth. In his mind's eye, something important had changed. Suddenly, the young man was no longer Kev, the newbe. He had received his takeoff clearance from the tower as a Cav pilot! Making one last check of the gauges, he noted that all the instruments were safely nestled in the green. Nerves humming with tension, he continued his never-ending self-contained conversation.

"Well here it is Kev. It's now or never."

Beginning his takeoff with soft and cautious hands, he lowered the nose with just a slight touch of forward stick. At one with the little Red Bird, he just thought of moving the stick. A touch of the lightest pressure was more than enough. Surprising him, words from the directly lifted from the mouth of his old instructor pilot passed over his lips.

"Gentle now, gentle, do it exactly as you do it with your girlfriend and not your wife."

A little self-conscious, Kev wasn't exactly sure what that expression was all about. Having neither serious girlfriend nor wife, he had not practiced handling a woman gently or not gently. Unhampered by his lack of experience with the fairer sex and mentally shrugging his shoulders, Red One-Five began his solo takeoff.

Allowing himself a sly smile of self congratulations, which he believed that he had earned, Kev reminded himself to get back to work. There was flying left to be done. He began his takeoff doing exactly the opposite of what he did when he backed out of the revetment. With the softest thought of nudging the stick forward and applying the slightest upward pressure on the collective, he started carefully and slowly moving forward. Kev was accelerating the little bird slowly and gently so she didn't drop through his cushion of air under the main rotor. Flying without a crew or guns, he knew that he had more than a sufficient amount of power available for takeoff. If he chose to, he could easily and crudely horse the little helicopter into the air. For this flight, he was convinced that image and technique counted heavily.

More than ever before, he wanted to make a takeoff look very smooth and graceful. Needing to prove to himself and his unseen observers that he had a pilot's touch, he did his best. Kev wanted to make a smooth, graceful, and skillful takeoff like the best pilots do. While, he was emotionally flying, he never forgot that his was still both an instructional and evaluation flight. Though he couldn't see him, Kev was confident that Chief Jones was slowly sipping his ever-present cup of coffee and watching from up on the hill. If nothing else, Kev fervently wanted to be a Red Bird driver and he didn't want this solo flight to blow his opportunity to become a Cav Scout. The little Red Bird was starting moving forward ever so slowly. At last, he felt it, just a little bit of a shudder. Kev's little piece of heaven entered transitional lift. Smiling because he had done well, he and his little Red Bird were climbing into the wondrous world of flight.

The shameless romantic in Kev loved the many "B" movies he had watched as a child. Emotionally placing himself in the midst one of them, he started climbing "into the wild blue yonder." Savoring his mystical release from the clutches of his earthly bondage, the young man pondered his life and his aviation career.

"Maybe, just maybe, John Wayne did have something correct after all. This is, is, well . . . , it is exciting beyond words."

It seemed to his soaring spirits that his body would explode with joy. If he listened carefully, he could hear his heart pounding and his blood rushing excitedly in, around, and through his whole body. Suddenly, and with zero forethought or planning, the cockpit of the little helicopter resounded with soaring noise as he cried out with joy.

"Y E S ! ! !"

His gloriously isolated location gave him the freedom to make his foolish outburst of pure joy. So he continued.

"Soon, very soon now, Kev, you'll be making your contribution to the team. Then, when you start pulling your own weight, you can wear your sabers proudly."

Kevin Paul Johnson, like most of his peers in Viet Nam and back in the world, was a boy and a man struggling toward adulthood. He wanted to make his mark, dream his dreams, make his contribution. Most of all, he wanted to earn the respect of his adult peers. As for Kevin, it never occurred to him to question his country who said it needed him. Raised as he was, it was sufficient that the President said that his country needed him. It was also good to be needed. Deep within, he knew that when he returned home he would no longer be Mrs. Johnson's little boy. Somehow, when he successfully made his takeoff, he had become a man. Furthermore, he knew that real men traveled to far away lands to slay evil dragons. Smiling at his "poetry," Kev also knew that he was in a far away land populated by evil dragons. Therefore, he must be a man.

Kev was climbing smoothly "into the wild blue yonder." For him, this was like the Biblical ascension of an angel going to a place beyond human comprehension. He wanted to be singing at the very top of his lungs. However, caution stopped him. Young Kev didn't want to make a dang fool of himself, in front of God and everybody else in all of creation. Nevertheless, his unleashed exuberance was almost limitless. It was a good thing he was tightly strapped into his armored seat. If he hadn't been, he would have been leaping and dancing up and down for the sheer joy of being an honest to goodness, living breathing, U. S. Army Aviator. For as long as Kev could remember, in fact for all of his short twenty years, he had dreamed this specific dream. This special flight had been etched into his mind in a glorious panoramic living color for all the years that were his. Wonder of wonders, a simple, yet liberating, flight around the traffic pattern had become the culmination of every one of his little boy dreams. At last, Kevin Paul Johnson was an honest to goodness authentic military pilot. He was flying his own combat aircraft!

A dozen trips around the traffic pattern and a hand-full of approaches and takeoffs placed the newly ascended angel into the highest of all heavens. All too quickly, Kev found himself back in the revetment.

It was all over. His first solo flight in a Loach had gone well.

"Hmm . . ." he slowly drawled to himself as he sat contentedly in his seat.

"Red One-Five, I really like the sound of that."

Yes, yes it did sound good to Kev. Better yet, the control tower gave Red One-Five himself clearance to land. Best of all, Red One-Five managed to smoothly and professionally get into the revetment without breaking or bending his helicopter.

All too soon, the ecstatic young man had to emotionally come to earth, finish his business, and tie down the rotor blades. Taking a moment for himself, he was basking in his achievement. Sitting contentedly and quietly he listened to the soothing sound of the mechanical ticking of the cooling engine. Floating on a cloud, he completed his walk around to see if something fell off during the short flight. Relishing the glory of his solo, he even enjoyed filling out the log book and signing his name. The words that he carefully wrote in the helicopter's log looked wonderful to the young man.

"Kevin Paul Johnson, PIC, pilot in charge!"

Flying his own military bird was wonderful. To him, it was something that he could never properly explain to one who had never dared to dream such a dream. Struggling to contain his explosive exuberance and to appear cool and dignified, Kev was sitting in the cockpit filling out the log book. Yet, he could hardly believe that he was filling out the log as the PIC. Pausing for a reflective moment, he was afraid that he might wake and destroy the best dream of his life.

"Maybe," he thought to himself.

"I better pinch myself to see if it is true."

For one whole hour he flew his sensitive and spirited little bird. Those spectacular minutes of controlled flight gave him the true freedom of flight. However, it also gave him the rare, to him, freedom of adulthood. Joyfully celebrating both, he believed that he had achieved them by his own merit! His liberating experience was like that of a new-born bird being free in defiance of the mercilessly heavy clutches of gravity. With great celebration, Kev had taken the controls in his hands and climbed. The enraptured young man had soared like a bird and flown slowly and flown fast. The fledgling scout had turned left, and he turned right. Gloriously riding the gentle winds, he had turned as he climbed and had turned as he descended.

Continuing his endless private conversations, Kev excitedly

exclaimed to the world.

"Wow. Kevin Paul Johnson was the pilot in charge. I was not the copilot, nor was I the student pilot. I was the PIC."

Bouncing about in his authentic emulation of an excited pup, he was almost afraid to believe the words he had written in the log book.

"Where did the time go? A whole hour! Unbelievable!"

It seemed, to his racing mind, as if he had taken off only a brief moment previously. In boyish delight, he wanted to holler out to a couple of uninterested enlisted men, he saw working on another helicopter way down the flight line.

"What do you know? It's really true. I can fly this bird all by myself. Did you see it -- did ya -- all by myself -- I did it -- I DID IT -- I flew my own little Red Bird -- all by myself?"

Well . . . eventually his high-flying spirits reluctantly came to earth like his helicopter had done earlier. Regrettably, he knew that his flying wasn't as smooth or as pretty as the other scouts. Well . . . , to be honest, his old IP might have better described his struggling in the traffic pattern as a wee bit sloppy. Nevertheless, Kev knew that his life as a Scout pilot was slowly traveling in the proper direction. While Chief Jones sipped coffee and watched Kev from his seat near the maintenance shack, he saw something in the young man that deeply impressed him. An old hand at the business of flying a helicopter, the Chief could tell that in time Kev's stick-work would be smooth, pretty, and delightfully light. Standing alone in the revetment, Kev silently promised himself that he would be just as good as the rest of the Red Birds.

"Give me a little time and they'll see. I'll earn my keep. Before long, I'll be a real scout! No longer will I just be another dumb new guy along for the ride as an observer!"

Pleased, yet grimly determined to keep working, Kev happily headed back to his hooch with his flight gear. Watching young Kev trudge up the hill with a confident bounce in his step, the Chief smiled and silently saluted him with his battered coffee cup.

Carelessly throwing his gear on his bunk, Kev took an extra strong dose of his self-prescribed medicine of reality. Looking over the heliport, he noted that the rest of the troop was in the field. As to be expected, they were flying their assigned recon. Thinking about it, the young man forced himself to accept the cruel truth. He could believe anything that his little heart chose to believe. Solo flight or not, he knew he remained an outsider. Ole Kev knew that he was still the stupid new guy. However, he was feeling hopeful. By completing his solo flight, he was getting just a little bit closer to becoming a full member of the team. He wondered, where they were working while he was boring empty holes in the sky?

"Well," he thought to himself, "I'll find out tonight. That is, if we don't have a 'Red Bird Down!' If one goes down, I'll find out sooner."

With no other assigned duties and several hours on his hands, Kev decided to write to his old friend and mentor, Pastor Bill. He wanted to tell him what it was like to fly as an observer ans Scout in training. Before he began to write he leaned back and took a look at himself.

The first few weeks of Kev's time in-country had passed. Unexpectedly, he found himself rapidly maturing in that rarefied atmosphere which forced many changes upon the young men breathing its thin air. The, soon to be, Red Bird pilot was discovering that the world of the insular Scouts operated much differently than he had expected. As his flight hours slowly added up, he became acutely aware of his own inexperience and relative uselessness as a scout pilot. Sometimes this awareness got him down and he translated the negative feelings to his value as a person. It seemed to him that while engaged in his training process, plenty of people had gone to great pains to point out his continual condition of uselessness. Laughing about people's willingness to critique him, he rationalized their occasionally mean behavior to another new pilot.

As a wanna be author, he waxed poetically.

"They do this, just in case I might have failed to recognize my many demonstrations issued directly from my complete and comprehensive catalogue of understated utter uselessness. Furthermore, this 'condition and or state of being' of mine is graphically evident to any who might choose to look. Or, for that matter, not look."

Examining his experience, It didn't take long for Kev to lower his lofty sights. His own obvious ineptitude caused him to sadly place his dreams of combat related glory into temporary storage. Self revelation transformed his quest for this glory to a sad striving for simple competence. Eventually, it became his deepest hope that his usual condition of uselessness was boring to the people who surrounded him. He prayed that he looked like any other new guy who was walking around in a total state of confusion.

During his younger years he had painted, for himself, a highly romantic self-portrait. He usually did his "dreamy painting" while carefully studying the detailed instruction offered by cheap paperback novels and countless John Wayne movies as his structural backdrop. In these paintings, his imaginative and passionate self-image placed him at the center of a great conflict. As always, he was the great and dignified lone wolf. Without being conscious of it, he began to envision himself as the strong silent type who needed no one, yet who was the one who came to everyone's rescue. The twentieth century expression of his unrealistic self-image was born of his childlike understanding of those first glorious "knights of the air" jousting, for God and King.

Lying on his back in the grass on a warm summer's day, as a

child, he would frequently draw his Quixote like mental pictures in the billowing white cloud-filled sky. As he dreamt with his eyes wide open, he imagined himself flying with the great "knights of the air" in the First World War. He proudly would join their noble challenging each other in their fragile wood, fabric, and wire biplanes in the deadly skies over northern France. Later, his mental pictures of World War II's graceful English Spitfires and Hurricanes continued to nourish his heroic images of saving the world. Looking deep inside, he saw himself joining them slashing and eagerly straining skyward to defeat the German Junkers and Heinkles winging their way across the English Channel. Romantically, heroically, and unrealistically he often envisioned himself stopping the "Godless Hun" from bombing London and other innocent English neighborhoods. Like generations of young fools who went before him, he immediately lost sight of the short life-span of his air heros.

Whatever the particular image created in his fertile imagination might have been, deep in his heart, Kev convinced himself that he was destined, with a big D, for a glorious future. He was sure that when he escaped from the claw-fingered clutches of an unforgiving earth, things would be wonderful. Kev knew that when his eventual release happened, he would be free to rely upon his wit, his courage, his skill, and whatever other "gifts" God might choose to give him. The young man had a broad series of well-thumbed imaginative self-portraits. He was convinced that when the smoke and dust settled that he would be standing in the center of the universe. It was his self-ordained fate to battle the cunning, crafty, and cruel combined forces of evil.

Though Kev recognized that the numberless battles he would face would be without a doubt most difficult. He believed that he had emotionally prepared himself for the coming difficulties. In his imagination, the physical duress of battle did not matter. Chosen by a power beyond himself, he would come out victorious against the dastard, demonic, and dark hearted forces of some extensively evil empire. In the final chapter of his self-understanding, the unkind might say his self-delusion, he would stand abused, alone, and badly battered. Nevertheless, a victorious Kev would be standing at the very center of it all. Somehow, he knew that Kevin Paul Johnson would be the pivot point upon which the gods of war would decide the ultimate battle. Maybe, his would be more than the battle. Maybe, it would be the future of all human civilization that he would selflessly save.

With the passage of time, in his new home, Kev had become painfully discovering that his self-centered whimsy had insufficiently prepared him for Viet Nam. Thankfully, he also had been very careful to keep his dreams and thoughts to himself. Kev had observed in his, newly found and still quite limited, understanding of the Red Birds that life and death was balanced on more than his personal whimsy. To some extent, he was correct in his understanding of the Air Cav and its mission. His year of flight school and a lifetime of studying military history helped balance some of his emotional ignorance and childishness.

The Cav remained the Cav, though it had now exchanged its flesh and blood horses for iron helicopters. They still rode hard to cover the flanks, lead the thrust, and protected the rear of the army. The key of the life and the spirit of the Cav remained completely dependant upon its superior mobility on the battlefield. However, in Kevin's Cav, the twentieth century helicopter and its petrochemical fuel provided the soldier's mobility. The sensitive and compassionate part of Kev was thankful that the noble horses no longer suffer the indignity of human combat.

A serious, yet amateur, student of military history, Kev frequently reviewed his understanding of the Cav. As he well knew, the all-important mounts of the Cavalry had changed years before his birth. Gasoline and not hay fueled the mandatory mounts of the Cav units of his world. Some, like the Eleventh Armored Cav, had wheels & tracks for mobility, while three of the four troops of Kev's Cav Squadron had smoothly swinging rotor blades. What hadn't changed was the variety of missions assigned to the different types of Cav.

For example, in the Air Cav concept as recently developed and put into practice with the 1st. Cav division (air mobile)maintained the concept of the mounted infantry division. In comparison to the bulk of the army, the 1st. Cav remained highly mobile and quick in movement. The Air Mobil Cav's job continued to be a force which can reach out beyond the normal and limited reach of conventional divisions. Their mission was much different from the rest of the army which he felt remained condemned to a slow-paced ground hugging life.

Like it had been since the beginning of organized armies, conventional divisions still carried the bigger punch. The 1st. Cav (air mobile) division carried a smashingly hard punch. Much like their mounted infantry forbearers, they remained limited in as much as they were unable to punch long and hard if cut off from their line of supply. However, this Air Mobil Division was not the Cav to which Kev had aspired over the last year. The great dreamer which lived within him wanted to reach out beyond their plodding speed and mass of numbers. Emotionally, the young dreamer needed to be part of the mythical Cav of movies, romantic novels, and of the rich folklore upon which he had thrived all those years while waiting for his turn. A true romantic must remain the loner. For Kev, to be just another nameless and unknown cog in the big machine would be paramount to death.

Upon his arrival in Vietnam, with eager sincerity Kev had specifically asked for assignment to one of the several independent Cav squadrons. He had no burning desire for assignment to the mounted infantry of the 1st. Cav Division. However, he did think that the big yellow shoulder patch was pretty nifty. Remaining true to his romanticism, he positively refused assignment to a standard helicopter company. He was terrified that they would convert him to little more that a truck driver who happened to be flying a Huey helicopter. With every fiber of his being, he craved to be a part of the people who used their mobility to follow the example of the old Indian scouts. Deep within his romantic heart, he wanted to cover the flanks and to protect the rear. Heroically, he craved to be the human trip wire who would warn of the advancing enemy and by that deed save the day.

As a young man bent on living his dreams, he knew exactly what helicopter he wanted to fly, with whom he wanted to fly, and what mission he wanted to fly. Young Kev knew with all his hear and soul that he wanted to fly with the Aero Scouts of an independent Cav troop. They called them the Red Birds in his unit. When his opportunity came, he specifically and firmly asked, requested, and finally begged and pleaded to fly his beloved Red Birds.

Though he would not have publically admitted, it to anyone, Kev's foolish, adventurous, and romantic nature mercilessly drove him on to fulfill his dreams. It would not let him be satisfied to be just another run-of-the-mill, nameless, faceless GI Joe assigned to the mailed fist of the Army. Nor would his visionary turns of mind allow him to be satisfied to be either the sword or the spear. He knew that he could only be satisfied if he could be the very sharpest thrusting point of the spear, or the cutting razor edge of the slashing sword. He wanted to be in front of those in the front. Just as when he was a child, he needed to stick his nose into places where somebody did not want it. Again, like when he was little, he needed to see the things he wasn't supposed to see. Naturally, it also followed that, he wanted to listen in on the conversations that he wasn't supposed to hear.

When they called the final role, he needed to stand breathless, bruised, bloodied, battered, but not beaten, before the army's assorted commanders and generals. Being the one to give them the vital information which no one else could give them, was the internal engine which drove him. His information would, in turn, save the day.

One day, while writing to a High School friend of the female variety, he admitted some of his weakness to her.

"In my occasional lapses into, what I call, 'the Kevin's feet firmly anchored to the ground stage,' I have come to suspect that I am, in truth, a glorious fool. Maybe more accurately, I am simply a romantic fool, who is terribly out of age. Someone, a while back, told me that I should read 'Don Quixote' because I would find a kindred spirit in him. Maybe I'll do that when I am not flying my little Red Bird. Yet, even now, recognizing my own foolish nature, I hold fast to my beliefs. Say what you like, I positively refuse to give up the notions that there can be both glory and honor in my deadly profession of being a soldier. As strange as it may seem to some people, I believe that this sense of honor is possible even today, even here, and even now. Further, I know that we all pray that life would be different. I firmly believe, given the baser nature of the human animal, it will be a long time before we are ever able to live without soldiers"

Growing up, Kev had envisioned the Army as a rigidly hierarchical organization. He clearly understood that Generals told Colonels, Captains told Lieutenants, and Sergeants told Privates. Therefore, it came as a great surprise to him when things didn't exactly work that way in the Aero Scouts. The fact that someone in Washington said that he was an Officer and a pilot did not mean that his destiny was to play center stage with the Cav. He understood that when he managed to cut the mustard, the Captain would assign him to fly as a wing man. This role called for a silent supporting actor in the drama of the aerial recon. Maturing rapidly, he was coming to discover that flying on the wing position was a very difficult and unheralded mission. Furthermore, if flying the wing bird is to be done correctly, it required great skill, great dedication, great courage, and finally great concentration. The last thing the Red Birds needed in a wing man was the spirit of a loner or prima donna. He knew that it would be difficult for him, but he was committed to becoming a team player if that was what it took for him to achieve his greatest of dreams.

Kevin got the opportunity to begin to understand why he needed to change his loner attitude while flying the wing slot with Lt. Simmonds. As they covered Chief Jones, he began to come to the realization that it was Jones and crew who were the ones who held the center stage in the little drama being played out by the Red Birds. Within the two aircraft team, Chief Jones made the calls. Chief Jones, essentially, controlled the recon. Whereas, it was Lt. Simmonds in his "lesser role" who gave the mike switch double clicks acknowledging instructions or responded "this is Red One-Three, roger." Lt. Simmonds, who out ranked Jones, went and did what Chief Jones said and required of him, with or without orders so to do. Therefore, it was the lead bird who clearly held the center stage and not the rank of the pilot. Carefully observing the ebb and flow of the mission, Kev came to his new realization. When he started flying combat missions of his own, he would be playing understudy to the lead actor in the drama. Unfortunately for Kev, that was not the way that the romantic little boy had pictured things in his picturesque mind.

A day or two earlier during the two-day maintenance stand down he had written to his friend, Pastor Bill. While he was writing, he was trying to digest the mass of data, which had come his way. Kev found himself deeply pondering how things worked in the Red Birds. Sitting with his pen in hand, Kev had been trying to digest what he had seen and experienced. This included two points of view, while he was flying both that first flight with Captain Jack in C&C and the more recent missions he had been flying as the observer with Lt. Simmonds. Fortunately, Kev had always been a young man willing to learn. He had been trying to digest all the discussions and "hanger flying" that the "old hands" told when they were having a beer at the club. Lastly, he had been closely observing the very high level of respect with which all the pilots held some, if not all, the enlisted observers.

Not expecting to, Kev had discovered that something of great interest was going on within the Aero Scouts. Much to his surprise, the actual flying of the recon didn't seem to go according to his understanding of Army regulations, John Wayne movies, or even cheap paperback novels. Willing to learn, the young pilot was opening himself up to a richer view of Cav life. It appeared to him that it was, in fact, the observer in the back seat of the lead scout who was the point of the spear or the cutting edge of the sword. It was during his last mission which he flew with Lt. Simmonds that the richer view of the Cav team struck him.

He was watching the back seat observer standing on the skids of the little helicopter. As he continued to watch the lead bird, it began to appear to Kev that it was Johnny who was calling all the shots. At least that is who Lt. Simmonds said was standing on the skid. Bravely, Kev had asked him, on the way home, who the backseat observer was in Chief Jones' aircraft. To Kev, it further appeared that Chief Jones, for the most part, was following Johnny's direction. In turn, he and Lt. Simmonds were following Chief Jones' lead. Muttering to himself, Kev stumbled upon a new truth.

"The junior enlisted man telling the officers what to do, that's a most interesting idea. I guess, that's the Cav."

His training was accomplishing its mission. Ole Kev was learning during his rides as the wing's observer. Too often to be put out of mind, he was experiencing something new and unexpected. As he listened to shop talk in the club and at the staging fields he heard something that didn't initially make sense. He often heard the lead pilots making telling comments about the observers.

"Johnny told me to drift to the left. Bill told me to make another pass. Anderson told me to keep my speed up because something didn't feel right."

Walking away from a discussion at the staging field, he commented to himself.

"If I am to survive here and learn my craft I need to learn from these enlisted folk. The problem is that I don't have much contact with the enlisted guys yet. Hopefully, when I become a wing man, I'll get to know some of these guys a little bit better. One thing is for sure, all the lead pilots seem to think of Johnny as the cream of the crop. What is even nicer, is that they all seem to like him as a person. Maybe some day I'll have a chance to just sit and talk to him for a couple of hours."

Much had changed in Kev's life. The world of Viet Nam was not exactly the world that he had been expected. However, when no one was looking, he would occasionally reverently finger his golden crossed sabers as he looked at the silver wings pinned on his ball cap. Kevin Paul Johnson, having mounted up and soloed his beloved little Red Bird was now Red One-Five. He also was becoming part of the team. The twenty-year-old boy in the process of becoming a man was living his dreams, at least in part.

FIRST RECON

Earlier in the day, Kev had successfully completed his solo in the Red Bird. It was obvious to all who looked that he was as excited as a little kid with a shining new toy. However, he was far from ready to be trusted alone with this new toy. Trying to be nice to the excitable little pup, the Captain, trying to suppress a knowing grin, gave him some time off. Generally, this time to rest was a rare gift for an overworked Scout Pilot. Being the "gung ho" new guy, Kev could not appreciate this particular rare gift of time. The seeming curse of his free time put him at "loose ends." Because he harbored dreams of being a writer, he decided to put the time to good use. He wanted to capture his feelings in a letter to Bill, his longtime Pastor and good friend.

Dear Pastor Bill:

Today was one of the greatest days of my life. I have leapt another hurdle. However, I now find myself very fearful of waking up. I have this horrible feeling that I will wake and my wonderful dream will come to an abrupt end. Let me start with the good news. Ole Kev finally soloed in his own Loach! Now, in the eyes of the Cav, that makes me almost a person. To affirm my emerging personhood, I also have my own call-sign. I am Red One-Five. Though it sounds funny, around here people are frequently addressed by their call-signs even when they are not flying.

Almost as thrilling, I flew on my first recon mission with the Red Birds a few days ago. Unfortunately, I didn't get to fly as the pilot. That is, I didn't have my hands on the flight controls during the actual mission. When I left home for Viet Nam, I foolishly believed that I was mission-ready. However, I have quickly learned otherwise. More training and still more training is the standing order of my days. Therefore, on this flight, the Captain assigned me to go fly in the enlisted observer's position. My main job was to figure out what was going on.

Anyway, the boss has given me the rest of the day off. We are also having a two-day maintenance stand-down during which nobody is flying. I suppose that he cut me loose because until I "learn the ropes," at my best, I'm only excess baggage. Right now it feels like I've graduated from Jr. High School and am trying to learn my way around the new High School building. One day the Army gave me my silver wings and I was on top of the world. The next day I am a stupid nobody who is lost and constantly getting underfoot. Consequently, I thought that I would take the time to write a lengthy letter telling you what flying my first Scout-mission in Viet Nam felt like.

In this letter, I'd like to do two things. First, I'll try to tell you who we are. Second, I'll try to give you a feel for our mission. Obviously, I got my wish and I'm flying with the Red Birds. They are the Scout birds, the observation helicopters, and they serve as the eyes of a Cav unit. Properly used, the Scouts are also the eyes of the whole army. Speaking poetically, the Red Birds are just like the Indian scouts of all those old John Wayne movies that you and I enjoyed. Like it was in the movies, the Red Birds fly a distance away from the main military units looking for and/or keeping an eye on the bad guys.

With your grace, I'll continue to use the poetry and imagery of the old movies. (Hey, what do ya know? I really did learn a little bit about language from your classes.) The Red Birds are always spending their time in Injun country, snooping around and generally looking for trouble. Much to the frustration of the bad guys, our pesky little helicopters are continually putting their noses in places where they are not welcomed. While there, they are doing their best to discover what the other side is up to. Following the classical movie script, sometimes the Red Birds get a bloody nose for their efforts.

I don't remember if I told you in previous letters what my little Red Bird is like. Forgive me if I did. However, I'll just brag on her some more! Let me tell you, Bill, she's indeed a rare beauty. In my humble, and I suppose limited, opinion the OH-6A (LOACH) is the little red Italian sports car of the whole United States Army helicopter fleet. Of course, you know the nimble sports car I am talking about. It is the sports car which proudly uses a prancing horse as its emblem.

Hughes Aircraft builds the Loach. As far as military aircraft go, in truth, she is just a wee little bit of a thing. In fact, as a light weight, she weighs in at a little more than 1,800 pounds empty. Like I said, she is just a wee little bit of a thing. To give you an idea what 1,800 pounds is, your big ugly monster of Ford station wagon weighs at least twice as much as she does. My delightful little bird is perfectly egg shaped with a small tail boom and a small tail rotor tacked on the end. Although she can seat four people, she remains a very quick and agile little thing.

I would say that her heart, soul, and spirit is her little Allison gas turbine engine. It is so light that a strong man can pick it up by himself. Yet, it develops two-hundred and seventy shaft horsepower. Strangely enough, with this seemingly low horsepower for a helicopter, she will fly at an air speed of one-hundred and twenty knots. This is about one-hundred and forty plus miles per hour! Sometimes I find that hard to believe, considering that my Chevy at home has more horsepower than this little bird. On the other hand, my car doesn't fly nor does my car move as fast! I know that for a fact. I tried more than once to make my "fifty-seven" boogie down the road that fast. (Oh yes, please don't tell mom and dad about my futile attempts at flying my fifty-seven.)

Anyway, let me return to the story of my new world. I'll begin by telling you about my first flight with the Red Birds. As I mentioned earlier, I was flying as an observer. Let me point out, as I have recently learned, that not all Cav units fly the mission in the same flight, aircraft, and crew configurations. However, my unit flies what we call full teams. This means that we have two Loachs flying the "hands on" part of the recon. Orbiting above the Red Birds are two Cobras (Snakes) who are giving gun cover to the Red Birds. While flying a recon, we also have one Huey, containing the unit commander and extra radios. The Huey is flying command and control above and over the whole affair. Filling out the Cav team, and kept on standby, are four troop carrying Hueys. Twenty-five of our shock troops are assigned to these ships. These troops are to be used for insertion into the area of operation if we do find something interesting.

If there are problems, they are also available to help recover a downed aircraft and crew. Our whole unit, including these crack troops are always available as a ready reaction force for other ground troops who might have gotten into trouble. So it is much like the movies. We do recon and are also used as a "fire brigade."

The primary mission of two Red Birds is to fly as low and as slowly as reasonable and possible while they carry out their search for the bad guys. In our troop, the lead Red Bird usually carries the pilot and two enlisted observers. It seems confusing, however, the Army organizes the Cav in troops and squadrons as opposed to companies and brigades like the rest of the Army. One of the observers is in the left seat. He is armed with either a CAR-15 or an M-60 machine gun. The CAR-15 is a fully automatic, short barreled version of the M-16 rifle. The other observer, usually called the back-seater, sits directly behind the pilot in the right rear. He always carries an M-60 machine gun with about fifteen-hundred to two-thousand rounds of ammunition.

Along with his machine gun he has an assortment of white phosphorous and colored smoke grenades for marking targets for the Cobras to attack. As if this is not sufficient, the back-seater, generally carries a 40m.m. M-79 grenade launcher, with another interesting assortment of ordinances and toys. Completing his virtual arsenal, he also has fragmentation hand grenades, thermite hand grenades, and sometimes a home made bomb or two. As you can see, the back-seater in the lead scout usually has quite an impressive collection of toys and surprises if the bad guys want to come out and play.

(It seems strange to be telling you about the tools of war. Yet, if I am to tell you about my "new" life these tools are a big part of what it is all about.)

In my case however, for my first flight, the Captain assigned me to fly my training missions in the wing bird. The standard crew configuration for the wingman usually consists of a two-man crew in the helicopter. The pilot is in the right seat with an enlisted observer who is in the left seat. This enlisted observer is usually armed with a CAR-15 for which he has a large number of clips of 5.56 m.m., .223 caliber, ammunition. These ammunition clips are universally loaded with straight tracer ammunition. The resulting stream of tracers when fired at the bad guys will hopefully scare them sufficiently to make them duck and miss with their shots. In all honesty, little hope existed of my ever hitting any bad guys with the CAR-15, except by accident that is! Sometimes, an experienced observer will replace the CAR-15 with a M-60 machine gun and about a thousand rounds of ammunition. Of course, no one is going to trust a newbe like me with an M-60 machine gun!

Only one observer is assigned to the wing bird. This allows the *wingman to carry an awesome punch. His main armament is an XM-27E1 mini-gun. This powerful weapon is mounted in the back seat area and protrudes out the left side of the helicopter facing forward. This type of machine gun is a gattleing type of gun with six barrels. The mini-gun, using M-60 machine gun ammunition, has an unbelievable firing rate of either two-thousand rounds per minute or four-thousand rounds per minute. All this firepower is available to the pilot with the simple pull of the trigger which is located on the control stick. Let me give you an idea of how much firepower that is. The American ground forces' standard M-60 light machine gun fires approximately six-hundred rounds of 7.62 m.m. per minute! On the other hand, the mini-gun will fire up to four-thousand rounds per minute. This is over six times the rate of fire of a standard machine gun. Oh yes, I forgot to mention that the wing man also carries a smaller assortment of hand grenades much like the lead bird and for the same reasons.*

It is getting late. With your permission I will continue with this letter tomorrow.

Kev was very surprised to discover that he was enjoying having the day off. He started his letter the evening after his solo, but he didn't come close to telling Pastor Bill all the things he wanted to share with him. The day off gave him the time to write an "A number one" first class tome of a letter about the first mission that he flew as an observer. The evening before, he had given Pastor Bill a little background information about the aircraft and the mission of the Red Birds. The next morning, he continued with his great epistle. Most surprised, he discovered that writing gave him the opportunity to reflect upon his feelings.

For my first flight with the Scouts, the good Captain assigned me to fly as the observer with Lieutenant Simmonds in Red One-Two. If you should be interested, this would make my call-sign of the day Red One-Eight X-ray. In Army aviation, it is normal procedure for the copilot to use the pilot's call sign with x-ray added to the end. Anyway, our job was to fly the wing off Red One-Six flown by CW-2 Jones. Both Simmonds and Jones had been in country for a long time and were very experienced. Jones had been in country for ten months, and Simmonds for six months. The two of them had been flying daily missions as a team for over three months. With this level of experience, they had developed a very smooth working relationship. Oh yes, both of these scouts had configured their aircraft as I described earlier. All in all, I considered myself very fortunate to be "in training" with this experienced and smooth working team. The best description of my feelings is that I have now become their semi-accepted foster-child. The two of them have now become my mommy and daddy in my transition process of becoming a scout pilot. Mind you, I doubt that I'll call them mommy and daddy.

Since I was to be flying as Simmonds' observer he gave me a CAR-15 and about twenty-five magazines filled with tracer ammunition. Wisely, he was not going to trust me with an M-60 and all the damage it could do. Stepping outside myself and taking a good look, I am forced to admit that I was quite the sight as I began strapping into the left seat. Before climbing into the helicopter, I put on my "chicken plate." The chicken plate is a piece of ceramic body armor with a vest of sorts supporting it. In theory, the chicken plate will stop a thirty-caliber bullet from direct ninety degree shot. The manufacturer also claims that it will stop a glancing fifty caliber shot. Personally I will be quite pleased to never test the manufacturer's claim! Think about the problem this claim presents. If it doesn't live to its guarantee, I'll be unable to issue a complaint or to bring a civil suit against the manufacturer. I wonder. Do you think it is one of those strange"Catch 22" situations that the military is so good at creating?

Allthe Scout pilots also carried a Colt model Nineteen-eleven, forty-five caliber, automatic pistol. Tigers that we are, we jauntily hung this pistol on a standard Army issue web belt. In truth, most of the pilots couldn't hit the inside wall of a barn with the forty-five. Yes, I mean exactly what I just said. We couldn't hit it even if someone locked us in the barn with the doors closed. Still, we carried our issued forty-five's. Lt. Simmonds showed me that the forty-five did have one useful aspect beyond its ability to shoot. He told me to twist the holster in front of me. That way, I could use it as additional "body armor" for my more private and personal parts. Laughing, he said that it was a little heavier than a protective cup in a jock strap. In truth, I'm not sure that the pistol would be a lot of protection for that tender area of my anatomy. Nevertheless, the presence of all that metal as a shield of sorts was sure good for my morale.

Suited up, I looked far more like a fat waddling little teddy bear than a dashing John Wayne type figure. Nevertheless, I was prepared to win the war single handedly. At last, I was set to fly. With the help of Lieutenant Simmonds' normal observer, I scrunched myself into the observer's/copilot's seat. As a side note, Lieutenant Simmonds had not seen fit to speak to this newbe as of yet. Looking in front of me, I noted that a full set of flight controls was available to me. The controls were left in place just in case the pilot was to get killed or wounded. The thought was that having these controls would give the enlisted observer a fighting chance of crash landing the helicopter if he had to. I was told that some of the crewchiefs and observers could fly pretty well.

However, I quickly discovered a serious problem. When I swaddled myself in all of this equipment, there just didn't seem to be enough space to move in the cockpit. It was really cramped. Oh, by the way, did I mention the survival vest? They also required us to wear one of them. The vest had many pockets, all of which the Cav had filled goodies like fishing lines, flares, mirrors and an emergency radio. So I wondered, if one can't move about to fly the aircraft, how in the bloody blue blazes could one land it even in an emergency? I also discovered that getting into a combat loaded Red Bird, with all my personal gear strapped on and about my body took on the farcical quality of a Three Stooges building project.

To further complicate my life, I still had to manage the CAR-15, act as an observer, and not shoot us down if I needed to return fire on the bad guys. The process of "mounting up" had been a lot easier yesterday. All that I had to do was to get in and out of my little bird and fly the traffic pattern. This flight was a vastly different proposition with all this stuff hanging all over my body and getting in my way.

It did not take the proverbial rocket scientist to note that being an observer, was rapidly taking on the foreboding feeling of being an awful big job. Sitting quietly, I was getting the distinct feeling that the enlisted observer was not window dressing who was just tagging along for the ride. Thinking about it, I was beginning to uncomfortably wonder if it might be the pilot who was the one who was tagging along for the ride. I am beginning to raise this question because it appears to me that the observer needs someone to fly the aircraft and act as his driver. In turn, I think that the pilot is too busy flying to do any observing. I'll know more and better as time passes.

I have honestly struggled to play my role, Pastor Bill. However, a pro active guy like me doesn't like being the know nothing, do nothing, faceless nobody, stupid new guy! Yet, that is exactly what I was during my first scout flight. Both my mission knowledge and my flying usefulness was perfectly reflected during the mission which I flew with Captain Jack a couple of weeks ago. This state of affairs does not fill me with a brimming cup of self confidence. My first Red Bird mission quickly became another reinforcement that I was just a stupid know nothing new guy. Like Captain Jack, the first thing that Lieutenant Simmonds did was to briskly put me in my place.

"Hey newbe, strap yourself in, don't touch anything, don't do anything, and keep your mouth shut."

I don't know if all new guys get this treatment. All I can do is pray that I am not just considered any stupider than most of the new guys that come here. If I am, well . . . I'm getting painfully accustomed to the role.

After giving the question of my abilities as a new guy serious consideration, I kept my big mouth shut. I decided that I wouldn't risk asking anyone where I rate on the stupid new guy scale. I fear that someone might volunteer an answer which I would prefer not to hear. They have another name for new guys in Vietnam. Believe me, it is quite a bit less complimentary than being called a newbe. Forgive my secrets, but since you are my pastor, I won't share this obscene name with you. Sometimes it is more politely expressed when someone calls you the military acronym, FNG.

I suppose that I can only hope and pray that I am only getting the standard U.S. Army/Air Cav issue new guy treatment. The thought of being considered exceptionally stupid brings me no pleasure. With a little luck, I am getting the standard new guy treatment. I never thought that I would hope and pray that I am only average "new guy" stupid. Honestly, this treatment is enough to make you feel stupid even if you are not!

As hard as it may be for those who know and love me to believe,

77

I did exactly what Lt. Simmonds told me. Without a single comment or wise crack, ole Kev obediently put on his flight helmet and plugged in the radio cord. Then, I strapped myself into the four point crash harness. Of course, I didn't touch anything in the cockpit. Here's a news flash. I even managed to keep my mouth totally shut through the whole process. (I knew that you wouldn't believe that outrageous claim!)

Like Captain Jack, Lieutenant Simmonds' hands quickly, quietly, and efficiently flew about the cockpit of the helicopter, in their preparation for takeoff. Before I knew it, the engine was lit off, we were up at flight idle, and we had told Red One-Six that we were ready to go. I really can't tell. Maybe Lieutenant Simmonds simply might not have liked flying with a new guy. On the other hand, he may not be very talkative either. In either case, up to that time, he did not deem it necessary to address my lowly person. Well . . . he did tell me to keep quiet and mind my place.

Whatever the case may be, it was becoming clear, to me, that these guys in this Cav unit knew exactly what they were doing when it comes to this flying business. Now that this first mission is safely under my belt, my situation is becoming clearer. I am beginning to understand that there might be some very good reasons why Scout Pilots are the tightly closed society I have seen. It kinda scares me Pastor Bill, I secretly wonder if I will ever be able to act, look, or be near as competent. I mean these pilots look, sound, and act confident even before the aircraft leaves the ground. This may not make any sense, but, they swagger without swaggering.

Maybe the old hands are correct, this training time is beginning to look like a good time to keep my mouth shut and learn all that I can. Do you think that my mom was correct when she used to tell me time and time again that it was not a bad thing to keep my mouth shut? I clearly remember dear Mom's words. Heck, I should remember, I heard them often enough.

"Kevin Paul Johnson, sometimes it is a whole lot better to keep your mouth shut and let people think you are stupid. It is much better, than opening your mouth and proving to one and all that you are truly stupid."

A few minutes after we were airborne and heading out to our AO, area of operations, Lieutenant "the silent" Simmonds spoke. Somewhere in flight, he developed a new found kindness and deemed to speak to a distinctly lower life form such as myself.

"Ok Johnson. You've got the helicopter."

That meant that I was to take the controls and fly the bird. As I took the controls into my greedy little hands, the Lt continued.

"Just keep your distance from One-Six and fly this thing in a real loosy goosy wing. By the way Johnson, please try not to crash and kill me."

If I had been confused about it, my station in life was beginning to become clearer. The Lieutenant did not, in any way shape or form, feel required to build up my self confidence as a pilot or as a Scout. As far as he was concerned, confidence building and emotional support were not part of his job description. After stretching himself a bit and lighting up a cigarette, Lieutenant Simmonds saw fit to speak to me on the intercom.

"Given that you are a stupid newbe, I'll keep this really simple, Johnson. You just keep flying the wing on One-Six, and I will tell you the straightforward facts of life. For the time being you are to remember that you are positively the stupidest creature that God ever put on this good green earth. You are not to do anything without my permission, period. That means that you even need my permission to take a leak! You are to do exactly what I tell you to do, and, you are to do it at the exact moment that I tell you to do it."

If Lt. Simmonds wanted me to feel warmly welcomed, this was not the way to do it! Thinking carefully about his approach, I felt it best not to point out his nurturing omission. Seemingly without pausing for breath, he continued my briefing.

"Now, these are what our jobs are. First, my whole purpose in being here today, as a wing man, is to keep One-Six alive and well. That, my young friend, is the only reason you and I are in this helicopter. Furthermore, from this minute on, the only reason that we were born, is to keep One-Six alive and well! If One-Six calls 'taking fire,' I will turn the helicopter and fire the mini-gun directly underneath his aircraft hoping to make the bad guys stop shooting. If I get lucky, maybe I will even kill a couple of them. Perchance you should see any muzzle flashes, you are to call them out to me. Then, and only if I tell you to, you are to shoot at them with that little pea shooter they handed you on the ground. Whatever you manage to do, for God's sakes, don't hit the rotors or the mini-gun. I sure as heck don't need to be shot down in the middle of bad guy country by some stupid butt new guy! Always remember my young friend, our purpose here is to keep One-Six alive and well. The United States Army, in its great collective wisdom, created us for nothing more and nothing less. He is doing the recon. We are not doing the recon!"

Following his overwhelming torrent of words, he again became silent and withdrawn. The Lieutenant was blankly staring at the passing countryside as I was flying the little helicopter. His stare seemed to be what all the paper back novels call the one-hundred-mile stare. After a bit, Lieutenant Simmonds seemed to return. He continued.

"Now, you Johnson, have but two things to do, and hopefully even a dumb new guy like you can remember them. First, your mission is to keep me alive! However, I do not delude myself in thinking you will have any idea what is going on if things get noisy and the bad guys come out to play. Nevertheless, that is your job as the observer in the wing bird, to keep me, the pilot alive. Keep your eyes open and your mouth shut unless you see we are taking fire. If you see someone shooting at us, holler out loud and clear on the intercom. Tell me where they are and what they are shooting. Always remember that you are not a trained observer! Today, you're just along for the ride! These enlisted observers see far more than you ever will see. Even if you fly these things for a year, you will never be able to see as much as they do."

Once again he paused as if to gather his thoughts.

"The second thing that you have to learn is how the wing man flies his mission. The wing man's only mission, as you hopefully still remember, is to keep the lead bird alive. You do remember after the passing of all this time since I last told you? As far as I am concerned, you had better learn it really well. If my worst fears come to life, one of these days, it might be my wing that you are flying. You had better be planning on keeping me alive! Today, though, the monkey is firmly on my back. I have to keep One-Six alive. Then, I have to keep myself alive. Further adding to my mounting woes, I have to keep you alive. Enough said, keep your mouth shut, your eyes open, and the good Lord willing you just might even learn something."

That Pastor Bill was the most that I had heard Lieutenant Simmonds say the three or four weeks I had been with the Cav.

We flew along silently for about another ten minutes. The whole time I was sweating profusely while vainly trying to fly mostly straight and level. At last, I heard One-Six tell command and control that he was descending. I looked questioningly at Lieutenant Simmonds not knowing what was to come next. As much as it pains me to admit it, he was totally correct. I was just a stupid new guy. Furthermore, I had no idea what was going on. Simmonds then grunted over the intercom, informing me that he had the aircraft.

Spiraling down to the left, we moved a little further away from One-Six as we descended into a small valley traveling at about ninety knots. With just a small touch of his normal compassionate kindness, which he generously showers upon us new guys, Lt. Simmonds suggested that I lock and load my CAR-15. The good Lieutenant had not forgotten my stupidity. Reinforcing his earlier lecture, again, he sternly warned me not to shoot us down in my stupidity. As he was speaking to me, he turned on his master arm switch for the mini-gun, lifted the trigger guard on the cyclic stick, and put his finger on the trigger. Reaching up with his thumb, he clicked the radio on and curtly made his radio call.

"One-Eight is ready to rock and roll."

The way we flew was like nothing I had ever done before. In fact, it was nothing like my first mission with Captain Jack and I thought that was something else. The feeling of speed totally mesmerized me. The excitement of possible combat, and my own exhilarating response to it, left me breathless. What we were doing was nothing like flight school. It was . . . Well . . . it was incredible.

Racing down the valley at ninety knots, we were only about ten feet above the towering trees. My pulse was pounding like a trip-hammer as we raced one behind the other down the valley. Ninety knots is close to one-hundred miles per hour and I thought I could reach out and touch the trees! Not having any idea what else to do or what I was supposed to do, I pointed my CAR-15 out the door. Struggling to be useful, I tried to look deeply into the flashing green blur of the jungle canopy. However, I could see nothing in that sea of green which was passing just scant feet below the skids of the speeding helicopter. I also tried not to think what would happen if we hit the trees racing past us.

That's right. I didn't see and couldn't see a thing. All that presented itself to my untrained eyes was just a confusing blur of endless green stuff. This strange sea of green was flashing by faster than my untrained brain could process what the eyes really never saw. Then again, I didn't know for sure what I was suppose to look for. In truth, my "observing" didn't make any difference given that I had yet to learn how to see like a real observer. Something else was happening that was taking me by surprise. I was also trying not to acknowledge the quickly increasingly strong taste of fear that was rising like a bitter sour bile to the back of my throat. My response to this first recon was unacceptable. I believed that all Scout pilots are fearless. Chocking back the bile, I couldn't decide if I was afraid of the flying or of the unseen bad guys.

Constantly flying a highly irregular pattern through the valley, Red One-Six was slowly reducing his speed by gradual increments after making his first pass. Lieutenant Simmonds told me on the intercom that they usually made the first pass at high speed to see if we would draw any fire from the bad guys. He calmly informed me that being shot at while flying fast was better than to be shot at while flying slowly. Fast, he said, was a much more difficult target. That declarative statement made good sense to me, and who was I to question his wisdom?

As One-Six continued to reduce his airspeed we also were slowing, though not as much as he. Covering him, we would continually weave back and forth behind One-Six. Maintaining our higher speed, we were always facing him, always alert, and always ready to respond if someone started shooting at him. In time, One-Six slowed to a near walking speed as he was doing his recon. It was all new to me and I caught myself looking at his Loach. One-Six was opening up the tops of the trees with his rotor wash so that his observers could look behind and below into the trees.

You wouldn't believe it unless you were there Pastor Bill. The guy in the back seat was standing on the skid looking straight down into the rotor wash with his M-60 pointed down into the wash. Yes, he was calmly standing totally exposed on that helicopter skid. Staring into the trees, he seemed to be a naked statue before God and the world. The intent enlisted observer was a perfect target for anyone who happened to be looking. I couldn't decide if I was watching was guts and gumption, or, if it was sheer stupidity. Whatever the case, he was standing exposed on that skid. It looked like he was presenting himself as a perfect target for the bad guys.

Surprise -- Surprise. Mental musing about the back seat observer became the center of stupid Kev's attention. Forgetting my own job, I asked myself which was the predominate aspect of the observer's personality, his guts or his stupidity? Suddenly, I heard a very angry and unhappy voice resounding through the intercom. Unexpectedly it came crashing painfully into my consciousness.

81

"Hey stupid! Stop watching One-Six and get your eyes back where they belong! In case I failed to tell you, I'm planning to go home alive. That means that I am not going to allow some stupid new guy to get me killed!"

With a guilty start, I tried to jump ten feet in the air. Fortunately, my safety harness restrained me. Feeling like the damn fool which I was, I got back to business of trying to be an observer. Properly chastised, I refocused my eyes on the jungle passing beneath and to my side. Just as I had been earlier, I was looking and looking for the bad guys. Blind Kev was looking, looking for the NVA, looking for the Viet Cong, looking and looking, yet not knowing what I was looking at.

As we protected the lead ship, Lt. Simmonds gracefully turned, weaved, and wove the little helicopter from side to side. Moving at forty knots, we drifted from the right to the left, and from left to right. It might have appeared that we drifted aimlessly. However, we always kept One-Six in front of us in case he took fire. Without warning and much to my embarrassment, the would be Scout pilot began to become a little queasy. For the first time in my short aviation career I was rapidly becoming motion-sick. Desperately hanging onto my aviators pride, I said and did nothing to indicate my distress. I was not going to let anybody know just how quickly and how horribly sick I was becoming. In fear and trembling I cried to myself.

"This is just what this stupid new guy needs. If I become airsick, boy-o-boy would everybody have had fun with that."

As I came closer and closer to a miserable death by air sickness, a fleeting thought brought a snide and sick smile to my face.

"Somehow, it would be an act of justice that if despite my best efforts not to get sick, I vomited my breakfast all over Lt. Simmonds. He has earned it since he has been so kind to me."

Finally the inevitable was at hand. I knew that the end of my life as a military pilot was but scant seconds away. Dying a little bit at a time, I knew that no hope remained for me. It was but just a matter of fleeting seconds and I was going to barf everything I had ever eaten in my whole life all over myself and all over the aircraft. No doubt about it, I was going to disgrace myself. To my horror, I was going to be nothing more than another funny story told throughout the Army Aviation Community. Undoubtedly, they would call it the story of "the barfing new guy."

Seconds remained before I became another pathetic tale told at the Officer's Club till the end of all human history. After we landed, I would never be able to face the guys in the Scout platoon. They were going to laugh me right out of the troop. Worse yet, if I survived after barfing my guts out, I was going to enjoy the questionable privilege of cleaning the helicopter under the laughing supervision of its crewchief. Closing my eyes I could see a horrid picture. That pathetic picture was forcing tears of shame and horror to freely flow from my eyes. Every enlisted man on the whole base was going to be down on the flight line. Smoking and joking, they would be pulling up chairs, popping a cold one, and settling back to enjoy this pilot's final humiliation.

With no other choice left to me, I patiently suffered the coming of a gruesome slow death. Carefully listening to my vivid imagination, I could hear the laughter resounding bitterly in my ears. When I walked into the club tonight, they all would chant my story in perfect harmony.

"There he is, Red One-Five the worlds greatest -- Barfing Scout Pilot."

In desperation I prayed.

Maybe, if I had a little luck, I might just quietly discontinue my human existence and drift into quiet oblivion of death. Just maybe, I would just peacefully expire without anyone noticing my final demise. Possibly God would be gracious and the bad guys would give me a break. Hopefully, they would shoot me dead and short-circuit this coming misery. Life wasn't fair. Nothing had prepared me for this humiliation. How come John Wayne never barfed his guts up all over the patrons of the movie theater? How come none of the heros in all the paperback novels I had ever read ever barfed up their guts? Like all young men, I had occasionally drunk too much and been sick as a dog. (Please don't mention the drinking part to my folks.) However, this, was ten times worse!

My dying thoughts were neither glorious nor heroic. They were just overwhelming. Nevertheless, my misery was the canter of the world. Seeking death, I had ceased to care what was happening with or to One-Six. If he had been shot down and crashed into a towering inferno, I doubt I would have even noticed the smoke and flames. Had the world, as we knew it, ended, I would have been oblivious to the smoke and flames of the final conflagration. Unless my own situation of nauseous distress drastically changed for the better, I would have been totally oblivious to any change. My extreme distress centered my complete concentration upon me and my suffering. All my efforts were an increasingly vain attempt of trying not to make a total fool out of myself.

Suddenly, as if it had been by Divine providence, Command and Control came to my rescue. The radio rang out with some of the most beautiful words ever uttered in all of recorded human history. These were the finest life saving words ever uttered by any human being. They called us to check out a small village about twenty klicks away.

Not a moment too soon, we began to make a wonderful stable, calm, and smooth climb to altitude. As we climbed, I came to my own understanding of heaven. It wasn't quite like I learned in Sunday School. Speaking quietly, Lieutenant Simmonds then reminded me to put the safety on my CAR-15. Then, totally astonishing me, he spoke his first kind words to me since I had arrived in Viet Nam. Looking directly at me, he seemingly compassionately asked an obviously stupid question.

"How are you doing Kev?"

Apparently he had noticed the bright shade of lime green radiated from my sweaty skin. I believe that the bilious shade was mostly centered near my gill slits. Or, I suppose that it is possibly that it could have been the stark vision of the pasty white face of death that he looked at. I know that he was looking at the face of a man who with all his heart and soul was hoping to die quietly and unnoticed. Whatever it was that he saw, something had reached deeply into Simmonds vast store room of human compassion. Much to my surprise, Lieutenant Simmonds, noticed something that was sufficient to make him ask his almost tender question.

To his question of my well-being, I murmured weakly.

"I've felt better, Sir."

Looking back, I must have passed a secret scout platoon initiation by not losing my breakfast and the previous fifty meals. For at the onset of my, well . . . at least it felt that way to me, last dying gasps, he began to gently laugh. I began to get angry at his laughter. Cutting off my anger, he told me not to feel too bad about being air sick. Still chuckling, he kindly assured me that every one of the scouts on their first ride as an observer had felt the same vivid death wishes. Pausing a moment, as if to think, he then added a postscript.

"And, to be honest with you, I almost lost my cookies on my first flight as an observer."

After a bit, I gathered one or two of my wits and had gotten my long-suffering stomach back into its proper position below my throat. Life almost seemed worth living. A few moments into my reprieve we crested a hill. On the other side was the village C&C said we were supposed to check out. Lieutenant Simmonds informed me that this was a friendly village and not to take the safety off my CAR-15. He didn't want me to make any mistakes. Taking up out covering position, we followed One-Six in a quick pass over the village. All was quiet and we returned the way we came. Though I had seen nothing, One-Six said that something didn't feel right to him.

Lieutenant Simmonds must also have felt the same unease. With his voice reflecting his increasing tension, he then told me to release the safety of the CAR-15. At the same time, he slipped his finger under the trigger guard on his control stick. Unconsciously, he began lightly caressing the trigger for the mini-gun just as he did during a recon. As had become the norm for me, I was disoriented, confused, and had no conception of what was going on. The setting spread out beneath me looked so pastoral, so very peaceful, and so delightfully calm. With both Scouts keeping our speed up, we began to circle around the whole village and surrounding area. One-Six said that he was nervous about the presence of hostile forces. As far as I could see, nothing stirred and nothing caused us any threat from the surrounding area. Finally satisfied, One-Six began returning to the village.

Given everyone's, except mine, uncomfortable gut feelings, we then made another cautious pass or two. Having decided that doing it was safe, One-Six came to a standing hover over part of the village. Hovering over what I thought was a peaceful scene, he made his horrific report to C&C. While he was reporting to C&C, we continued to circle the area at slow speed protecting the lead bird. When One-Six began his report, I couldn't believe my ears. I also fear that you will not believe me. However, it is as true as it is tragic.

They were all dead Pastor Bill. Every one of them was dead. The NVA or VC had murdered all the women. They had murdered all the men. They had murdered all the children. Even the chickens, and pigs, and dogs, they had butchered them too! I don't pretend to fully understand what is going on over here. Whatever is happening here concerning the rightness of this war, I doubt that the answers are as simple as you might have me believe. Seeing such a sight makes it impossible to believe that this was the compassionate action of a group of benevolent people from North Viet Nam seeking to remove the presence of American imperialism from the South.

Eventually, C&C called up the slicks and inserted the blue platoon. To our collective horror, they cryptically confirmed the torture and execution of every living being. Let me make myself clear. Every man, woman, child, and animal in the village had been butchered. I'll spare you all the ghastly details. It is sufficient to say they did not die peacefully and gently of old age in their sleep. From what the ground troops later described to us, most of the villagers probably welcomed death as a gift from God when it finally embraced them. I am not sure what else I can tell you, except that Lieutenant Simmonds said that sometimes this happens to friendly villages. This mindless butchery is supposed to serve as a warning from the Viet Cong and the North Vietnamese about what happens to those who do not see things their way and support them.

I know that this undoubtedly is the longest letter I have ever written in my whole life. Nevertheless, I felt that sharing with you some of my feelings and observations was important. After all, if nothing else, we have always been honest with each other. I also know that I need to get this letter in the outgoing mail because it is getting late and I want to get some sleep. However, you have got to believe me when I tell you that those "valiant freedom fighters" are killing innocent civilians. These are the same people whom some of your friends are calling benevolent liberators!

Wow! I have never spent a night and a whole day writing one letter.

Until my next note, I remain your friend.

Kevin

Suddenly a voice called out to Kev. "Mr. Johnson! Hey, Mr. Johnson. Why don't you drop in at the scouts' hooch sometime later tonight? Take your time, clean up and grab some grub. Heck, we'll be home all night. It's not as if we have somewhere to go. When you get here, we'll share a cold one or two. Who knows, if we lose track of time, maybe we'll share three or four. While we're kicking back and enjoying our cold ones, we can gab a bit. If you like, I will fill you in, a little bit, on all the interesting little ins and outs of being an observer in the scouts."

Dumbstruck, Kev was not prepared to respond. However, surprised silence didn't slow the young man who had called out to him.

"After all, you'll need to know what is going on. I don't know if anyone has told you, but, for the moment, you are another peon. I hope that you don't take offense Sir. However, as of now, you're just like the rest of us little people. Really, don't worry about it Mr. Johnson. It isn't that bad. Who knows, maybe life will be interesting living as one of us peons for a little while. Ah shoot, be patient Sir. Your peon status is only temporary. Then, you'll get your own bird. What the heck, learning the way we EM types view things might be an educational experience for a future Scout. When you finally begin flying your own bird, you will have a greater appreciation for all of us, nameless little people, in the Scout platoon."

For a delightful change of pace, wonderful, exuberant, and welcoming words warmly greeted Kev that evening at the Scout line. He was feeling depressed after Lt. Simmonds and he had landed and shut down the little Red Bird. He felt so lost, out of place, and almost unwelcomed that he was near tears. Add to that what he had witnessed at the little village had deeply shaken him.

At the sound of the friendly voice, Kev had quickly snapped his head around to find the voice's source. Because he was the stupid new guy, a warm and friendly voice inviting him to share a cold one was not an everyday occurrence. Noting that the friendly voice belonged to the observer from Red One-Six deepened his sense of surprise. Coming from an enlisted man was one of the last places that expected find a friendly invitation to share a beer. The friendly young man was the same observer whom Kev had watched in amazement crewing the back seat of Chief Jones' bird. Watching this young enlisted man had filled him with a strong feeling of awe and wonder. Kev had breathlessly watched him standing fearlessly on the skids of Red One-Six, with his M-60 machine gun casually cradled in hand. That was how the young observer did his recon.

The unexpected source of the friendly voice further astonished Kev as he reflected upon the day. His world was full of surprises.

Looking up while he was tying down the rotor blades the grinning face seemed out of place. He noted that the enlisted man was a youngster himself. Silently enjoying a little humorous irony, Kev also noted that the young man was probably shaving once a week. With his inner voice chuckling, Kev thought to himself. "Well . . . , that means that the two of us are in the same shaving league."

Nodding in approval, Kev glanced at the young man's blacked out chevrons. The enlisted observer had earned, although he appeared so young, the rank of hard stripe E-5. He was the youngest looking buck sergeant that Kev had ever seen. So, Kev figured, he must know the scout business. Speaking to himself, Kev commented.

"After all, he is alive and a veteran."

Pondering a second, Kev realized that, in itself, was worth something. Calling to Kev, over his shoulder as a postscript of sorts, he shouted out.

"By the way Sir, everybody just calls me Johnny. Not to worry, my last name is unpronounceable. So, please Sir, just call me Johnny like everybody else does."

Happy-go-lucky, the young man continued toward the EM hooch.

Young Kevin had been observing and learning as much as possible with observations of the past couple/three weeks. Mirroring the Scout pilots, the EM observers in the Scout Platoon were a very clannish and close-knit bunch of guys. These observers had purposely and pointedly chosen to stand apart from the other enlisted men in the troop. Furthermore, they were like their pilots who felt themselves just a bit superior to the other pilots. They also felt themselves just a little bit better than all the other EMs' in the Cav troop. It didn't matter to them if the other enlisted men were in the grunt platoon, the ground troops. Nor did it make any difference if they were aviation types. The crewchiefs and door-gunners in the Blue Platoon, or for that matter the armorers and crew chiefs in the Gun Platoon remained outsiders. The Scouts, Red Platoon officers and enlisted alike, knew that they were the cream of the cream, the top of the crop, the very best there ever was. Kev liked that attitude. Moreover, Kev yearned and ached to be a vital part of the Scouts.

"Ah," he thought to himself, "to walk the walk and to strut the strut."

Greatly pleased by the knowledge, Kev was told that the Troop Commander did not compel enlisted men to fly in the scouts as observers. This made their commitment the same as the pilots. Membership in this platoon, which he was coming to understand as a very special platoon, was strictly voluntary. No doubt existed in his mind, Kev believed that he was on the verge of joining the most exclusive club he had ever seen. He hoped and prayed with all his heart that he was soon to be a member of the most exclusive club that he would ever have a chance of joining. Young Kev already knew that he had traveled far beyond his humble roots. Membership was almost more than he dared to place in the realm of possibility.

The growing possibility of becoming a member of this exclusive club caused his heart to soar. Listening to the conversations of the experienced pilots gave fuel to the fire burning in his heart. Scout pilots, both Warrant and Commissioned, readily admitted that they were superior human beings both braver and smarter than anyone else. Yet, he had carefully noted the deep respect in their voices when they spoke about the enlisted observers. The other pilots had already convinced Kev that these young observers were in a class of their own. Everyone in the Cav knew that the enlisted observers were highly competent and very dedicated. In many ways, the mission of the Cav pivoted upon the skills of that unique bunch of half crazy young men. Because of this, the wise and observant pilots were always bragging on them. It was only a matter of days after he arrived that Kev understood why the scout pilots held them to be considerably more than simply a cut above the best. The scout pilots whom Kev had gotten to know, always spoke of these young observers with grave and earned respect. Furthermore, they treated them with a knowing respect that surpassed all the others enlisted men in the troop or the rest of the Army.

Speaking to a friend at the club one evening Kev said as much himself.

"It is obvious, even to a dumb new guy like me, why the good Scout pilots feel so positively about their observers."

He had already seen the close teamwork in a scout bird. The Scout pilots, comfortably put their lives and their complete trust in the observers' skills on every mission. If the observer messed up or missed something he should have seen, they were in trouble. Selfishly understood, a Scout pilot stood a very good chance of becoming a dead pilot is his observer goofed. Their recon mission called for a level of absolute trust in another human being. Kev had never experienced this level of trust and commitment his short life. He had a gnawing fear that if he didn't capture and savor the experience now, he never would. Pondering what he was feeling for a moment, Kevin was sure that he never would have another opportunity. He suspected that such co-commitment could only happen in the world of combat. Furthermore, he suspected that such a situation could only happen in an all volunteer outfit. Being in both places, now was the time for him to savor the experience.

Finishing the evening meal, such as it was, Kev declined an invitation to go over to the little Officers Club and down a cold brew or two. While he would have greatly enjoyed a beer or two with the other new pilots, he had an important appointment. Having foregone the opportunity to be with "his own type," he began warily walking away from his personal safe haven known as Officer's Country. Tentatively, and not at all sure of himself, he slowly started down the steep hill. He started chuckling to himself as he noted a delicious irony. The enlisted barracks were physically situated at a lower level than the officer's barracks. Like 99% of his peers, Kev had never spent any off duty time in his short military career with enlisted people. Not at all sure what to expect, he made his way into what was for him a no man's land.

Pondering the meaning of his military life and his place in it, he truly didn't know what to expect at the EM barracks. Though he had been an enlisted man before going to flight-school, he had already been set apart at basic training. All of the young men who were going to Warrant Officer Flight training served in the same platoon at basic training. Directly following basic training, with the members of his platoon, he left for flight school. From his first day of flight school, Kevin Paul Johnson had always been a part of the world of officers and officer candidates. Although, while in flight school, he had held an enlisted rank (E-5) as an officer candidate. This in no way prepared him for the mind set and life style of an enlisted man.

Unaware of his own feelings, he was walking into a great irony. While the Army said he was an Officer, he was not truly one of them. His background was much different. In truth, he had far more in common with the enlisted folk than he did with his brother officers. Yet, Kev also found himself far removed from his element. As was becoming the norm, John Wayne and cheap paperback war novels had not prepared him in the slightest way for his newest encounter with real life.

The sad fact of Army life was that he didn't have the slightest idea of how to act as a very junior Warrant Officer in enlisted country. Despite the painful knowledge of his unpreparedness, he was willing to try. Kev hoped and prayed that he might walk away from that EM hooch a little bit wiser than when he entered their private world. The possibility of self-improvement was a powerful incentive to him as he walked down the hill. As much as it pained his battered ego to admit it, he knew he was a babe in the woods when it came to being an Aero Scout. Kev was sure that the time spent with the enlisted observers guaranteed an improvement of his Red Bird skills. No one had, as of yet in his very short combat career, accused him of not needing to learn more. He told no one how inadequate he actually felt. However, he knew that his pool of aviation knowledge was very shallow.

While he was walking down the hill to the enlisted hooch, Kev quietly reminded himself that he was going to the enlisted folk's house and home. For all intensive purposes, it was very important to him to always remember that he was their guest. Kevin was a very well raised young man. He knew that Mrs. Johnson would insist that her son show these young men, at the very least, this level of respect! Walking down the hill, Kevin Paul Johnson began to firmly beat one fact into his head.

"I am not their commanding officer, nor do I have any command function over these guys. They have invited me to be their guest for the evening."

He continued talking to himself.

"Don't forget. Kevin Paul Johnson is still the stupid new guy."

The soon to be visitor reminded himself that these young men were his own age, and in some cases they were even younger than he. However, they were still the combat veterans! He continued to remind himself of the "facts of his life."

"Kevin, you are still a radiant shade of green behind the ears. These guys probably all know that quite recently a wanna be Scout was more than a little green around the gills."

Fearing that he might have forgotten something, he continued to remind himself of the things which were important to him.

"Remember! Ole Kev is the student. Tonight, the enlisted men are going to be my teachers. Therefore, I will show them the proper respect which any good student shows his teachers."

Just before reaching the EM's hooch, the strangest and foreboding thought passed through Kev's mind. He remembered reading a short story or piece of mythology in High School. It was about a man who had to choose between two doors. Behind one of the doors was a dragon. However, behind the other was a lovely princess. He had a rough idea what the dragon might be. Officers did not belong in enlisted quarters, except for official business. If the Major found out about this visit and decided that it was improper, Kev knew that he was in for an butt chewing at the least. The princess though, that image had him confused. He had not seen anyone who vaguely looked like a lovely princess among the enlisted folk. Females did not belong behind the door at this hour. If they had any prostitutes present, he decided that he would leave before he saw them. Shrugging off his strange thought, he decided that he would not find a princess behind the wooden door.

Tentatively, he knocked on the rough wooden door to EMS' simple hooch. Preparing himself, he kept clear thoughts and self reminders of politeness and respect safely lodged in the forefront of his mind. Not knowing what to expect, he anxiously waited for the door to open. The door of their hooch quickly swung open and Johnny warmly invited him into the loud boisterous smoke-filled room. Someone had a stereo blasting away in the deep dark recesses of the room. Cranked all the way up, the stereo was playing what Kev was beginning to recognize as the unofficial anthem of the U.S. soldier in Viet Nam. When the refrain came, all the young men sung with great gusto, if not proper pitch and tone. Celebrating their communal life, the exuberant enlisted men in the room joined in with the refrain. "We got to get out of this place, if it's the last thing we ever do."

Kev guessed that roughly fifteen of these young enlisted men occupied the long room. Most of the young soldiers were dressed only in their, United States Army standard issued, olive drab skivvies. Looking about, it appeared to Kev that all these young men were of rank E-5 or below. Thinking about the young men that he saw round and about himself, Kev also doubted that any of them had yet to see his twenty-first birthday. Finding himself in the midst of a noisy group like this was wonderful. Immediately relaxing, he felt completely at home.

Thinking about it, Kev knew that these were his kind of people. To a man they seemed to be exciting and exceptionally vital young men. Mostly draftees, they had no time for pretensions and career advancements. The rich flavor and texture of the room overflowed with their youthful laughing, joking, and carrying on. These guys were acting just like carefree young men do all over the world. While Johnny was introducing a cautious Kev to all the enlisted guys, some kind soul thrust a cold frosty beer in his hand. No one stood on rank or ceremony. Kicking back, with their gracious help, for the first time since he arrived in Vietnam, he immediately began to feel just like one of the guys.

Finishing his introductions, Johnny grabbed a cold frosty beer for himself out of the little fridge. After he popped the top and took a long draw, he invited Kev to step out into their patio. Arriving outside, Johnny laughingly offered him Kev his choice of one of the many beach chairs that they had scattered about outside their hooch. The colorful scene outside the hooch was just like many other strange things that Kev had already seen in his short time in Vietnam. The small electric fridge filled with beer and cokes in almost every hooch being another case in point. These brightly colored webbed beach chairs seemed so totally out of place.

Never-the-less, this place called Viet Nam remained locked in the olive-drab world of three military forces. Sadly, Kev knew that Viet Nam, itself, was deeply immersed in the throbbing throes of self destruction. Kev had just discovered the tragic consequences of this land's suffering. It was a place at war with itself. Knowing this, to his minds eye, bright holiday colors seemed to be so discordant. New in country, Kev still thought of these brightly colored chairs as strictly belonging scattered upon the white beaches of his beloved Cape Cod.

When they had become comfortable, Johnny opened the conversation with and important question.

"Before we continue talking Mr. Johnson, what would you like us to call you?"

They knew that normally enlisted and officers alike address an Army Warrant Officer as Mr. -------. Whereas, a soldier's given rank and name is used to address all other ranks in the Army. Pausing for a moment, Kev found himself thinking of a High School Shop teacher the students had been so fond of back in the world. With little or no hesitation, he gave Johnny a suggestion.

"Just to call me "Mr. J."

Kev figured that this would be low keyed enough that the EM's wouldn't think of him as uppity. He was also somewhat confident that this "address/title" would not get him into trouble with the Major for being excessively familiar with the enlisted folk. The young man, who was so much like those who surround him, would have much preferred operating on a first name basis.

Kev had been a member of Uncle Sam's Army long enough to know that what he would have liked would eventually cause problems. Much like his High School Shop teacher "Mr. C.," he knew that such a first name arrangement would not work well in the long run. Though he felt, and most likely, was more like these enlisted folk than he was like his brother officers, he also knew that he was not one of them. He would face the real possibility that sometime in the near future of asking these young men to risk their lives. They would have to take that risk based upon his word and command alone. Pausing and thinking about possible command problems, it seemed that working on a first name basis might make that most unpleasant task difficult at best. More likely, working on a first name basis would make it impossible. Once again, Kev had discovered that his vast and highly vicarious experience by many of the paperback war novels' about men at war offered him little help. He was beginning to understand what worked in pulp fiction did not always work in real life.

Johnny and Kev passed the largest part of the next hour sharing stories of their growing up in their own home towns. The childhood tales and stories they shared were normal for boys their who were turning into men. The spoke of playing ball, building fast cars, chasing girls, and all the other things that average American boys do. Sitting together sharing a cool one, the two of them were like all the countless young men in all the militaries the whole world over. With pride and joy, they shared pictures of the special ladies which they had left at home. When Johnny showed Kev the picture of his high school sweetheart, a catch and a warm tenderness richly colored his voice. Radiantly smiling and glowing with love, he then told Kev about his plans.

"When I get back home, Sally and I are going to get married and forget this place. The Army drafted me and sent me to this overgrown cesspool. That's OK. I'm not the only one. We made a deal and I'll extend my tour for six months. When I finish the six-month extension, the Army and I will forever part our ways. Then, Sally and I are going to make a bunch of kids and get back to living like real human beings."

When Kev's turn came, he admitted that he had no clear plans residing in his future. Greatly surprising himself with his blunt honesty, Kev quietly spoke.

"I envy you Johnny. When my time here is finished, I'll go back to the world. However, I've never done that well with women. I fear that most of my dates in High School were sympathy dates. Maybe, just maybe, if I get back to Ft. Wolters, that gorgeous little girl with the raven black hair will continue to go out with me. The Good Lord knows, she's too smart and too beautiful for the likes of me. I can't imagine that she would be foolish enough to become my wife."

He paused dreamily.

"Yet, it would be wonderful if she would."

Later that evening, Kev realized that he had discovered something about this young man which drew forth a refreshing honesty from his soul. He did not understand what the intangibles that made up Johnny were. Possibly, it was only the beer and the warm air. Whatever it was that moved Kev, the young man did not need to impress the young Sergeant. However, Kev found himself truly envying him for his clear view and well-thought out plans for the future. When the two of them were well into their fourth or fifth beer, Kev began to completely relax.

"Maybe," he thought, "I've found a 'soul mate.'"

Continuing to open himself up, he told Johnny that at this point in his life he was simply going to take his year in Viet Nam one day at a time. Understandably, Kev wasn't quite ready to tell him, or anyone else for that matter, that he had dreams of being a writer some day. It just didn't seem an appropriate moment for Kev to talk about wanting to be a serious writer in a confusing world filled with death, desolation, destruction, war, and warriors.

The two young men began to run out of things to say and their conversation slowly sputtered to a halt. The conversation was getting uncomfortably personal for the young men who were normally taciturn about such private things. As if by design, six additional enlisted folk came out of the hooch. Preparing for a long evening, they carried another half a case of ice cold beer. Pulling up something to sit upon, they gathered around to join in the conversation. Kev felt like he was relaxing in someone's back yard as he glanced about. Completely at ease, they sat themselves about on an assortment of homemade chairs. Most of these were created out of the soft pine boxes that the rockets for the Snakes come in. The young men cracked open additional beers and they filled the air with laughing confusion, insults, taunts. Immediately they started sharing the foolish mistakes that they all had made during recons. Sitting in the midst of this wonderful liveliness, they offered Kev a totally overwhelming assortment of advice that might serve to keep him alive during the coming year. At the very least, he hoped and prayed that this advice might serve to keep him out of fatal trouble.

Several young enlisted men had a beer or three too many under their belts. One of them, feeling the effects of his beer, shouted over the din of the seven young men who were all laughing, talking, and shouting in young male harmony.

"For goodness sake Mr. J., whatever you do, don't go and shoot yourself down tomorrow!"

A cacophony of hearty laughter and drunk young men in the fullness of life, served as a backdrop to the comment. Immediately, several observers tried to reinforce his point. They reminded Kev that the M-60 machine guns that they used in the Loach's were free guns. By this, they meant that the guns were hand held. Bell Helicopter, in the Hueys securely mounted their M-60's. Wisely, Hughes did not install mounts or mechanical stops to limit the travel of the Scout's machine-guns. Whereas, there were factory installed mechanical stops in the Hueys to keep the gunners from hitting the helicopter. Such was not so in the Loachs. Surprisingly, the foolish could shoot themselves down! Laughing and yelling back and forth, they told Kev about some poor soul who recently had managed to shoot three holes in his rotor blades.

When the wounded bird came home to land, everybody at home base could hear the shrill whistling of the wind through the bullet holes. The distraught observer vigorously tried to convince everybody and anybody that the bird's wound was the result of enemy ground fire. Unfortunately for him, upon inspection, the bitter truth of the matter was quite clear. By examining the angle of the bullet strikes on the rotor blades everyone could see that the observer had hit his own aircraft. In unison, all the observers told the rest of the story. They said that the pilot of that helicopter had some very choice and colorful words to share with the young observer. Very colorful words, they added, as they were words that the young man's mother would not have approved of lately. They further described the incident in great and dramatic detail. Anybody within a ten-mile radius of the heliport could clearly hear that graphic one-sided conversation. The seriously offended pilot screamed and hollered while the unfortunate observer took his medicine. Kev wanted to know who the pilot and observer were. However, he decided that he hadn't earned the right to know.

Another of the drunk observers, laughing almost hysterically, pointed an accusing finger at Johnny. With a great show of solemnness, he told Kev to watch very carefully where the hot ejected shells go from the M-60 if and when he is firing it. Again, as apparently they had done many other times before, the observers joyfully told the story. The incident took place several months previously. Johnny was in the middle of a hot firefight with an NVA unit. While shooting, Johnny had somehow managed to put three of the red-hot ejected shells down the back of Lieutenant Simmonds' flight suit. They said that the spent shells burned the skin on the back of his neck convincing poor Lieutenant Simmonds that he had just been shot. Believing that he was near death, the scared pilot almost crashed the helicopter in his near panic. The lieutenant, they continued, had remained quite angry for several days. Only when the burns on the back of his neck stopped hurting and began to heal over did he cool down. Embarrassed by his near panic, he had promised to get his revenge on Johnny. The story had a good ending. When he had finally healed, even Lieutenant Simmonds had to laugh at his piloting antics as the hot shell casings seared his neck and back.

As the gales of laughter slowly subsided, the conversation turned to a more serious note. This change began a movement toward the flavor and texture which Kev had been seeking as he traveled down the hill to their quarters. One of the observers said that with time and practice, an observer learns to use all the senses God had given him. Of course, they all assured Kev that the eyes were still the most important part of the observer's bodily equipment. Nevertheless, the young men collectively agreed that a successful and living observer used everything that God had given him.

Another of the guys interjected a strange thought, to Kev, with these words.

"Don't forget Mr. J., you can also smell gooks!"

Speaking as a well-tuned chorus, all the observers agreed on one thing. If they told the pilot that they had a "heavy gook smell," it was the wise pilot who believed them. In time, they guaranteed me that even the dumbest pilots eventually learned to smell the camp, cooking, and personal smells of the Viet Cong and the NVA. Thinking about what he had just heard for a moment, Kev laughed. He then told them that for the time being he would have to trust their highly trained smellers. One young man with six too many beers under his belt blurted out an ill thought comment.

"Not to worry Mr. J., your smeller is big enough to make a good scout!"

Absolute silence followed the young man's verbal oversteps. Kev did not want to spoil his time of learning. In response to the accidental overstep, he immediately fingered his nose, laughed, and added his own observation.

"By golly, if size has anything to do with it, I've got an excellent start."

Seeking to quickly change the subject and relieve any possible discomfort, another young observer jumped into the conversation. He emphatically told Kev not to wear one of those new sound proof helmets.

"Sir, maybe these new helmets might help save your hearing."

His tone took a graver note as he continued.

"However, remember that dead men do not need good ears."

Another voice piped up.

"It's really nice to know when somebody is shooting in your direction. So listen with both your ears Mr. J. New guys may not realize it, but, even over the sound of the engine, you can hear the bad guys shooting."

Kev decided that it was a good time to keep his mouth shut. He could find no useful reason for volunteering that on his first mission with Captain Jack that he had not heard the bad guys shooting.

As evening wore on, the riot of youthful noise began to settle down. Seeking to continuing his very valuable "classroom time," Kev asked Johnny about the responsibilities of the two observers in the lead helicopter. He wanted to understand exactly why the two Red Birds flew in different crew configurations. Johnny reminded Kev that the lead bird, with two observers, can't mount a mini-gun.

"Sir, I understand that giving up the capability of firing four-thousand rounds a minute is difficult for the pilot. It has to be tough not to be able to shoot back yourself. However, the payoff is well worth it."

"Removing the mini-gun," he explained, "gives the lead bird a three-hundred and sixty degree circle of observation when flying with two observers."

Johnny added that using two observers greatly improved mission performance and safety.

"When we use two observers and they have two M-60 machine guns the lead bird has three-hundred and sixty degrees of effective M-60 coverage and protective fire."

Giving greater detail, he added, that if the helicopter flew with the mini-gun, the entire right side of the helicopter was unable to fire at the bad guys. What Johnny said to Kev made good sense to him. He decided that if he ever flew lead that was the configuration that he would choose.

Kev had been so engrossed in Johnny's teaching that he hadn't noticed the other enlisted guys wandering away. Nevertheless, Johnny willingly continued acting as Kev's private tutor when he asked his next question.

"Why do you fly the backseat and not the front? I would think you would enjoy getting an occasional chance at the controls."

Johnny gently laughed, and then continued. He explained that the rear-seater had the prime observation responsibilities and he would normally be the most experienced observer on the team. Pausing to take a draw from his beer he continued.

"Of course, Sir, the lead scout pilot is also the most experienced pilot on the team. I admit that getting a little stick time in might be fun. However, when I am in the back seat, I can see much more. You've been in the front. Heck, A guy can hardly move about when he is in the front. However, when you are in the back you can really move about. Some of the guys, myself included, like to stand on the skid. When you are on the skid, you can see the whole world."

A look of concentration came over the young Sergeant's face. It appeared as if he were weighing a question. Having come to a decision, he spoke quietly.

"I hope that I am not speaking out of turn, Sir. Our job is to find the bad guys. Then we back off and let someone else fix them. The lead scout doesn't need a mini-gun."

Johnny, remaining true to his understanding of the mission, strongly emphasized that a wise pilot would follow the rear-seater's direction as much as possible.

"So you see, Sir, while it is fun to try and fix the bad guys, we're a whole big bunch smarter when we let the big boys take over."

Laughing, he added a postscript.

"There are a few times I wished that I had taken my own advice."

In the short period of time that had passed, Kev had learned more about the nuts and bolts of the mission then he had during the rest of his time in country. The young man was like a dry sponge in the presence of water. Young Kev couldn't absorb enough and he still wanted more.

"Tell me Johnny, how does a back-seater see anything? When I was 'out there' today, I couldn't see a thing."

Chuckling for a moment, Johnny continued.

"Well Sir, if you get a good back-seater, he will try to undo everything you learned in flight school. The first thing that he will want you to do is to fly the helicopter so that the rear-seater can look down into the rotor wash as the trees part. To do this, he is going to ask you to fly out of trim. That is, you will have to fly kinda sideways with the front-seater leading the way. I'm sure that you got yelled at for that in flight school."

Kev laughed and shook his head remembering his instructors beating on his helmet and making him look at the needle and ball. Johnny continued.

"Sometimes, Sir, we'll let the pilot fly in trim. However, we'll ask him to fly low enough that the rear seater can look into the tree-lines, or caves, or whatever other lateral view he might wish to have while looking for the bad guys."

The night wore on and Johnny continued his teaching duties. He then explained that the front-seater usually was a less experienced observer. Continuing to define how a three-man crew operated, Johnny restated that the wise pilot always followed the directions of the rear-seater. The exceptions were if it made flight conditions unsafe. Fearing that he might have over-spoken, Johnny quickly added.

"Of course Sir, the pilot is always the boss."

A good part of the time, the pilot usually flew the helicopter in a slight crab. This was to give the rear-seater the best possible view of the ground.

"I might ask you to fly crabbed to the left so that I can look forward. Or, I might ask you to crab to the right so I can look behind us."

While flying in a crab, the front-seater had the responsibility of covering the "rear." The "rear," Johnny defined as the area at which he wasn't looking. He emphatically stated that both observers had the responsibility that if the bad guys fired, they were to immediately cry out "taking fire."

Following the "cry," the observer would throw the white phosphorous marking grenade they carried. He explained to Kev that the safety pin was already straightened out to make it easier to pull. Lastly, he added, they would then and only then return fire at the bad guys. While the observers were following their script, the pilot would break away, make his report to command and control. As the lead bird was making its hasty retreat, Johnny told Kev that the wing bird would then engage the target with its mini-gun. This gave the Cobras time to begin their roll-in on the white, willie peter, smoke.

Surprised, Kev noted how the hours had rapidly passed by. At the same time, the volume of beer that they had consumed was finally beginning to make its presence known. Well, at least, it was beginning to make itself known to Kev. His head was spinning and his bladder was painfully full. Johnny and the other observers had thrown more information at him than he could possibly consume in a single sitting. As a closing thought, Johnny added a bit more to Kev the sponge.

"Mr. J., you'll learn lots of tricks from your observers, but most important is to keep your eyes open. By the way, Mr. J., look carefully for the things that just don't seem to fit the picture properly. If something is out of place, it will jump out at you if you allow it to. Whatever you do, don't spend your time looking for something specific. The reason for this is that while you are looking for that specific thing, something else will jump up and kill you dead. Nevertheless, don't worry Mr. J, you won't see much at first, but in time it will all come. Honestly sir, if you don't try too hard and just sorta go with the flow, everything will work out just fine and dandy."

With that hopeful closing note for Kev to chew upon, they decided it was time to call it a night.

Wishing Johnny, a good night, Kev, staggered and struggled up the hill to his hooch and fell into bed. The night was like every night for the past couple of weeks. Piles and random jumbles of various and assorted thoughts filled Kev's overworked mind. As he had every previous night, he sorted out the confusion spinning about in his mind. His undeniable conclusion remained the same as it had been for the last few days. He didn't have the slightest idea what he had gotten himself into by volunteering to fly Red Birds. As sleep began to take hold, his closing thought was to wonder what he was doing smack dab in the middle of "his" far away and poorly defined war. Exhausted, he began drifting off to sleep. Or, he was passing out. Humbled, he offered a little prayer to God. Understandably, Kev asked that he would not make a complete fool of himself on his next mission. Feeling both foolish and selfish, he added a short postscript to his prayer.

"Dear God please let me stay alive long enough to learn my trade and do something useful."

IT IS ALL DIFFERENT

It seemed to Kev that the thump of his head falling on the pillow had just finished echoing when morning painfully arrived. Dragging himself out of his bed and checking the flight roster, Kev found himself again flying with Lieutenant Simmonds in Red One-Eight. This pleased him. Flying with the same crews as they did the day before offered the young man a touch of the familiar. Groaning at costly effects of the previous evening's excess beer, he offered a bit of a laugh to his thoughts.

"Another day and another dollar. Hopefully, my suffering has no effect upon the war effort."

Looking toward the coming mission positively, Kev believed or hoped that he should have a better grasp of what was going on during a recon mission. Smiling, he ambled over to the mess. It was time for a cup of coffee and a sampling of the Army's horrible excuse for breakfast.

Though he had eaten the Army's worst, Kev was still smiling happily as he carefully pre-flighted the Red Bird. Thinking for a moment, he had no regrets about spending all evening and the wee hours of the morning with Johnny and the other EMs'. During the evening, he had learned about the observer's job and a bit about the observers themselves. Buoyed with a new confidence, he felt that he had a little better understanding about what Lt. Simmonds expected of him for today's mission. His self-reflections had a positive note to them.

"I might be as useful as a sandbag. However, I am now an intelligent sandbag."

The enlisted folk had told Kev that the crewchiefs, who were normally the front-seat observers, came with the aircraft. However, the back-seaters usually flew with the same lead pilot. Also, pilots usually flew the same aircraft. Knowing this, when Kev arrived at the flightline, he wasn't surprised to see that Lieutenant Simmonds normal observer, and crew chief was there to launch the aircraft. As he had the day before, the crewchief helped Kev strap-in. A few small things had changed and this delighted Kev. Though he was still very green, the little change made Kev feel as if he belonged. The young enlisted man immediately began kidding Kev.

"Mr. J., words fail me. I can't tell you how much I appreciate having a newbe Warrant Officer assigned to me."

With a big smile on his face, the crewchief continued!

"With you flying in my place, I can probably get the day off."

"That is," he carefully added, "if I can manage to avoid the all-encompassing clutches of the maintenance sergeant."

Lt. Simmonds, overhearing the conversation, added a comment. Supporting another scout in his battle against the Army in general, he felt that it was worth added his two cents' worth.

"I won't tell the sergeant, if you won't."

Life offers many wonderful teachers, and experience is the best of all. The day before, Kev had gone through gyrations and convolutions of climbing into the helicopter. When he arrived, the Cav had issued him a huge pile of equipment. Assuming that he was supposed to use it all, he had strapped everything all over his body. This time, getting into the little bird was much easier. While his entry was easier, he was not graceful about the process. Not knowing any better, he had tried to fly his first mission with a flack vest on. He found it so restrictive that it made movement almost impossible. It was then that he noticed that neither Lt. Simmonds nor Chief Jones had worn one.

Laughing, they later told him that a flack vest was much too cumbersome when worn with the chicken plate, survival vest, and pistol in the front seat of a Loach. Willing to learn from their example, he had immediately gotten rid of that hindrance! When Lt. Simmonds twisted his forty-five into his groin, Kev felt absolutely no shame in moving his forty-five to a position in front of his groin. He believed that protecting the family jewels was honorable. After all, no one knew what the future might bring. Though he admitted not doing well with the ladies, he still had the faint hope of eventually getting to use the family jewels productively. Well protected, he was ready to go.

This time, when Kev had arrived at the flight line, he felt as if something unseen had changed. The crewchief's kidding and the other pilot's advice was a welcomed change. At first, the sense of change puzzled him. He knew that he was still the stupid new guy and far from a full or useful member of the team. Eventually, in all his encyclopedic wisdom, he decided that the change had something to do with being "blooded." The young romantic was not exactly sure that he knew what the word meant. However, "blooded" was a graphic word he had seen used frequently in those numberless cheap war/adventure novels that he had read. Smiling to himself, he realized that he liked that word. Being "blooded" had a good feel to it.

Other thoughts crossed his mind.

"Maybe it has something to do with the fact that, with the grace of God, I managed not to barf my guts out yesterday."

Kev, being Kev, was quietly slipping into his inner world.

"Oh no, my stupid mind has gone and wandered off again. Here I am psychoanalyzing myself wondering if it were just self confidence from my night with the EMs'?"

Quickly returning to reality, he decided to quietly enjoy the change. Lieutenant Simmonds was quite clearly in a better mood than the previous day and that was good enough for Kev. Kev was progressing and The Lieutenant was changing the way things were done. Like the previous mission, he cranked up the aircraft. However, when the Red Bird was up to full operating RPM, he told Kev that the controls were his.

"Ok Johnson, tell you what we're going to do. Unless I say something different, I'll control the radios and you will fly the bird out to our area of operations. This morning, while we're flying out to the AO, I want you to maintain a nice loose formation on One-Six."

. A small smile crossed his face as the Lieutenant continued.

"What the heck, I'm willing to bet that even a dumb new guy like you should be able to handle that little task."

"Wonder of wonders," Kev thought to himself.

"This is nice. Lt. Simmonds' tone is delightfully different!"

Thankfully, for Kev, the biting sarcasm of yesterday's flight was absent. A more confident Kev found Simmonds' light-hearted banter refreshing. The payoff was that it took part of the edge of young Kev's performance anxieties. Now that his first mission had "blooded" him or whatever the proper term might have been, the tone was comradely. It felt, to Kev, that the joking and teasing was like that of an older brother to a younger brother. At last, Lt. Simmonds light bantering tone gave him a wonderful sense of belonging.

"Well . . . ," Kev thought.

"Things are beginning to feel a whole lot better today."

Though he felt more accepted, this is not to say that he felt that he had earned his membership in the team. Still, at least for the moment, young Kev felt that he was just little bit closer to being a member of the Cav team.

"You've got it."

With the Lieutenant's words of encouragement, Kev took over the flight controls of Red One-Two. Drawing a deep breath, he carefully tried to lift the little bird to a hover in her sandbag revetment. "Wow!" Kev continued to discover that each new day was offering its own surprises. Intellectually he understood what happened. However it surprised him that the combat prepared Red Bird was nothing like a lightly loaded instructional aircraft.

"Ok," he said to himself. "So be it."

Lifting up on the collective, he pulled in more power and nothing happened.

"Well . . ."

Kev pulled in more power. Grimacing, He continued lifting up on the collective stick trying to get his little Red Bird unstuck from the earth's hungry grasp. When the helicopter's struggling and straining had convinced him that the bird could never fly, something began to happen. Frustrated, Kev was convinced that he had lifted the collective to the mechanical stop.

At last, the combat overloaded bird struggled awkwardly and

tentatively to a low hover. For a moment, Kev feared that he had put on some excess weight. A decided downward tilt to his side of the aircraft served as evidence to his new found fatness.

"Ah, I know what it is. It must be the weight of the mini-gun bolted just outside my door. Oh yes, the two-thousand rounds of ammunition stored just behind me for the mini-gun just amplify this out of balance feeling."

While he might have understood the why, the downward tilt to his side remained disconcerting as he had never hovered a helicopter that wasn't level from side to side.

Having stabilized the low hover, Kev risked a quick look at the engine instruments.

"Jimney H. Christmas, the N1 gauge shows 101%."

Kev knew that 101% on the N1 gauge was just about every ounce of power that the little turbine engine could pull. Further adding to his surprise and distress, he noted the position of the TOT needle. Turbine outlet temperature was nudging the bottom of red line. Suddenly, Kev felt boxed in. He knew that if he demanded even a tiny bit more power for flight it would seriously damage the little engine. Very carefully he began applying gentle back pressure on the cyclic stick. He couldn't sit there all day. It was time to begin backing the heavily laden bird out of the revetment. Working to lift the little bird to a hover and back it out of the revetment began another step in his learning process. This time, Kev was learning how incredibly difficult it was to fly a combat-overloaded helicopter. Way back when, the instructors at flight school had only talked about the difficulty of flying an overloaded helicopter. Kev's lack of experience, with an overloaded helicopter, was understandable. The safety of the students had precluded the possibility of practice flying an overloaded bird.

Displaying what he felt was a gross lack of flying skill or grace, Kev finally managed to bump and scrape his way backwards out of the revetment. He was filled with bitter self recriminations.

"This is not an impressive beginning to this flight. Damn it, this amateur display makes me feel like I am a beginning student back at Fort Wolters."

Kevin's world was quickly turning, as all pilots say, "brown and smelly." He was feeling like a miserable student who had yet to win his solo wings. In fact, the struggling young Kev was feeling like a student who was beginning to seriously worry about washing out of flight school. Unknown to Lt. Simmonds, embracing those feelings of failure was easy for Kev. The hopeful Scout pilot had learned, painfully and intimately, what the fear of failure and washing out of flight school felt like.

Kev hadn't quite been the last in his class to solo. Yet, he had been well entrenched in the bottom third of his class. Within the dreadfully deep and dark recesses of his mind, Kev moaned and cried out.

"Oh when, oh when would I have the confidence and learn the skills of a Captain Jack or a Lieutenant Simmonds?"

With his vivid imagination racing at full speed, he fearfully thought the worst. The darkest and most dreadful of all his demons assailed him.

"Maybe I just wasn't cut out to be the swashbuckling hero pilot of my dreams? God knows. I have yet to prove that I can fly worth a tinker's darn."

Following One-Six, at a slow and low hover to the takeoff lane, Kev did a very careful left pedal turn. A right turn would have taken more power than the little turbine was going to safely give them. To his credit, Kev remembered that a right turn would have caused an increase of pitch in the tail rotor, thus requiring more power. So he wisely chose to do a left turn which reduces the amount of pitch in the tail rotor.

"That's something, I guess."

Being a stupid newbe had reduced him to taking, and celebrating, what little aviation victories he could find. Beginning his takeoff, Kev lowered the nose a touch and the little bird began to slowly inch forward. He had completely forgotten how heavy the bird was and she started forward quickly. Just as quickly, she fell off the cushion of air the main rotor had built up under her. As a result, the skids immediately struck the tarmac with a firm thump.

Months before, Lieutenant Simmonds had suffered the same struggles himself. To Kev, he did not seem the least bit perturbed by the young pilot's seemingly pathetic struggle. Appearing unconcerned, Simmonds continued to puff contentedly away on his cigarette. His relaxed stance was as if he were at the club enjoying a cold beer. Cross-checking his brain functions, Kev reminded himself that it was not a good time to be ham fisted on the flight controls. Struggling he maintained a semblance of control after the skids banged the tarmac. He used just a slight touch of back pressure on the stick. It was the right move. Reluctantly, the poor overloaded bird shook and shuddered herself into the air. With the skids kissing, well . . . , banging hard into the tarmac once or twice more before they were freed from the unforgiving clutches of the ground, they were off.

As had become the norm, his new experiences surprised Kev. He discovered that the takeoff with an overloaded Red Bird was almost dangerously hypnotic. During the drawn out takeoff run Kev found his eyes fixated upon the ground directly in front of him. It seemed as if he were in a trance. Dangerously distracted, he discovered that each and every little pebble and blemish in the tarmac mesmerized him. As these pebbles and blemishes slowly and painfully passed beneath the skids, Kev almost forgot to fly the helicopter. Remaining absolutely motionless, he carefully set the controls perfectly still. He wanted them to be as if they were firmly set in stone. Flying as smooth as he could, he maintained the N1 at 101% with the TOT just nudging the bottom of the red line. Not one extra foot pound of power available for his use if he made a mistake. The struggling fledgling was using all the engine power which was available to his unskilled hands.

In his short time in country, Kev had watched many dramatic takeoffs by overloaded Charley model Huey gun birds. He had found himself captivated by these Charley model gun birds from other units. Many new pilots experienced a visual excitement as they watched those struggling three-bump-and-off into the wild blue yonder overloaded takeoffs. As green as he was, he could appreciate the extraordinary level of skill which was involved. Those exciting take offs never failed to fascinate him. He found it quite a sight to see the door gunner and crewchief running beside the heavy birds until the last moment. Then, when it seemed almost too late, they jumped on board as the bird began lifting into the air. A logical part of him found it hard to believe their reasoning for doing this. Just so that they might carry a few more rounds of ammunition, or just a couple more grenades seemed both silly and stupid. While he watched them, he had thought to himself, how thrilling it must be. What a charge it must be in those Charley model gun birds as they struggle over the wire overloaded with many finely honed killing tools of modern man.

Things and views can change quicker than a person might like. Quite unexpectedly, Kev found that he was now looking at a combat overloaded takeoff through the other end of the telescope. His whole point of view had suddenly twisted one-hundred and eighty degrees! When his hands were on the flight controls, a struggling takeoff wasn't nearly the exotic experience he had thought it would be. With the deft movement of the perception telescope, Kev had suddenly become another one of those scared and nervous crew members. Ole Kev had become almost paralyzed with fear while he was staring at the rolls of barbed wire which were rushing upon him. With painful clarity, his overwrought imagination suddenly came to the conclusion that those rolls of barbed wire were malignantly alive and vicious. Their purpose in life was to reach up and snag his skids. Their whole reason for existence was to flip his little Red Bird on her back killing her and her crew.

Like many before him, Kev quickly discovered that the real-life "thrill" of an overloaded takeoff was a vastly "different" experience. It was nothing like day dreaming about piloting such a skilled takeoff. Much to his romantically idyllic dismay, Kev found that the menacing wire was rapidly rushing upon him. He had become psychotically possessed with a horribly distressing thought. In seconds he was going to crash and then be smashed into thousands of bloody little pieces. If the coming horrific crash did not kill him, he would then be burned to death in the following fire. The hardest thought of all for him was that he would never have heard a single shot fired in anger. Or for that matter, he would never have accomplished one little heroic deed for the good of humankind.

Much to his dismay, this possibility of a less than heroic and glorious concluding chapter on his life's story was rushing upon him and reaching up for him was horribly bitter. The experience of an over-loaded takeoff was beginning to leave a very bitter metallic taste in his now dry cotton waste-filled mouth.

Eventually, Kev began to relax. The little bird reluctantly entered a laboring climb to altitude. After a couple of moments, he felt able to slightly reduce the power demands. It hurt his mechanical sensibilities to work the frantically spinning little turbine so hard. Settling into a climb he was not surprised by his physical reaction to combat flight. Like his first flight, he found that he had soaked through and through his nomex flight suit. Having never done well in High School biology, this puzzled him. Kev wondered where the seeming endless gallons of nervous smelly sweat came from. Whatever the case might have been, soaking through a flight suit in anxiety and fear was becoming an everyday occurrence. Though it did not surprise him, it was an occurrence which he wasn't enjoying. As before, self-doubt, his constant companion, reared its ugly head. Kev questioned himself and the gods of military helicopter pilots. The nervous young man was questioning if he would ever again fly in a dry comfortable flight suit. Fearing that he wouldn't like the answer, he didn't ask any of the other pilots what the condition of their flight suits were when they flew.

Kev looked over at Lieutenant Simmonds in wonderment. As he did when Kev had the controls, he was calmly smoking a cigarette. Apparently, he was totally unperturbed by Kev's rough takeoff. Quietly flying along, poor Kev quietly wondered to himself about his presumable lack of piloting skills. He found his situation and condition discouraging.

A routine morning's take off with a heavy helicopter had caused him to break into such a fearful sweat. He feared what would happen to him when he had to fly the same overloaded beast at the tree top crawling speeds of Red Bird combat? Wound up as tightly as a human being could be, he knew that he could not fly smoothly.

Anxiety ridden, he was becoming horrifyingly convinced that he didn't have what it took to be a Scout. If someone had even said as much as a little "boo" to him, he believed that his body would have exploded into a million or more pieces. The tension overload was enough to cause him to sit and tremble almost uncontrollably while he was trying to fly. Believing that he was so tense was impossible for the romantic hero that was hidden deep within. He struggled with many questions. How could a morning's takeoff wind him up so tightly? He was simply attempting a normal early morning's take off in lovely Southeast Asia.

Kev fearfully wondered to himself.

"What would I have done if I had heard enemy fire while my hands were full trying to keep the helicopter from crashing during takeoff?"

Whatever it was that he was doing this morning in lovely South East Asia was subject to debate. He decided that he was not going to try to convince anyone that Kevin Paul Johnson had been in control of the helicopter. As Kev struggled to fly and with himself, Lt. Simmonds enjoyed a silent chuckle. It was clear, at least to him, that the aircraft was flying Kev and not the other way around. As a pilot, Ole Kev was still just along for the ride. Well, so much for the young man's many wonderful dreams of gracefully climbing into the wild blue yonder to save the world from the forces of evil.

Unfortunately, Kev decided that he wasn't quite yet ready to join his brothers in arms/wings of the embattled RAF. They would still be taking off in their Spitfires and Hurricanes to take part in the heroic Battle of Britain in Kev's mind. Much to Kev's regret, his heroes would continue flying against the invading hoard of Germans and making the world safe for Democracy without him.

The day was not lost nor was all of life negative. Despite his inner tension, Kev found himself enjoying the still quiet of an early morning's flight. The fact that it came following his emotional trauma of the takeoff made the experience sweeter. In time, the serenity of the morning returned his pulse to a near normal rate. It was so calm that the early morning air was glass smooth. Such conditions made for a delightful flight as they passed over the momentarily peaceful rich bright green rice paddies of central Viet Nam. Kev had read that before this little conflict had gotten out of hand that this country had been the bread basket of all of South East Asia. He began to see another Viet Nam with his current overview of the world which was truly beautiful. Heck, even a boy from a mill town could sense the productive possibilities in that horizon of rich bright green rice paddies. It was so calm and beautiful that it was almost like one was taking a restful relaxing drug. The sweep of the horizon felt like the calming effects of his morning "coffee" drug. This view made it difficult to believe that a vicious war of brother against brother was taking place just below.

Spread itself out below Kev was a delightful and restful Currier & Ives pastoral scene. Flying along, he watched the local men and women who were out cultivating and planting. Surprising him, he found that watching them doing the things that make the rice grow was very calming and pleasant. He noted that the people below looked so peaceful, pastoral, and harmless in their ever-present cone shaped straw sun hats. In each of the little villages and hamlets that they flew over, smoke was gently rising from the morning cook fires. Looking carefully, Kev saw that the children were running around playing their games just as children throughout the world do. It was so domestic that just outside one of the villages, Kev saw old mommasan squatting on a paddy dike taking care of her morning constitutional. Sadly though, the presence of the noisy war machines was her normal background noise. As the gaggle of helicopters roared over her head, old mommasan didn't even raise her head in acknowledgment of their presence.

Kev was surprised that he could smell the smoke of the morning's cook fires at their altitude of about a thousand feet. Though the cooking smoke didn't smell of his city home, nevertheless the smoke still smelled of home. Little wonder, he thought to himself, that the French loved this place. He could understand why they didn't want to leave it following the Second World War. On his first orientation flight, Kev had seen some of the haunting ruins they had abandoned. Those estates in the secluded valleys of the highlands seemed shrouded in a mystical fog. He was sure that it must have been an almost idyllic life for them. For the moment, it seemed to Kev that if it weren't for this war, this would be a wonderful part of the world in which to live. In fact, he thought that it would be a good place to raise a family. More so, he suspected it would have been wonderful to be a wealthy white land owner. With lots of peasants to work your land, life would have been very good, very good indeed. Surprised by his thoughts, he noted, with embarassement, that his thoughts were neither democratic nor egalitarian. Nevertheless, he believed that the colonial French period must have been wonderful for the French.

Pausing for a moment, he did a quick reality check. In the midst of his quiet revery about pastoral peace, another side of the world below remained carefully hidden. Kev reminded himself that by night an unknown percentage of these people would pick up their AK-47's and SKS rifles. When they did that, some of these simple farmers would spend the night doing their very best to kill Kev and all of his friends. As the young man's days in Viet Nam were passing by, he was growing up. He was beginning to suspect that the total human experience becomes full of uncomfortable little paradoxes when childhood remains only a memory. Such were the conflicting thoughts that Kev found bouncing back and forth in his head. The world passing beneath his feet was so confusing to him as their small flock of war birds droned peaceably along their way to the chaos of combat.

"What a crazy paradox this place is." He said to himself.

What an absolutely crazy paradox this strange place was turning out to be for him. Just in Viet Nam for a short time, and he found himself falling in love with its apparently serene beauty. Ironically though, in the midst of this serenity, Kev found himself flying a machine specifically designed to kill and destroy.

"Possibly," he thought to himself, "the artificial tranquility of this morning's moment is, in fact, artificial."

Caught up in the immediacy of the moment, he was content. Kev decided that he would be happy to spend an eternity at the controls of the Red Bird. What could be better than drinking up the beauty of this moment in flight? During the delightful season of the morning's flight, he had forgotten all about the glory of his cheap war novels.

Somewhere, somebody has written that all reflective moments of peace and quiet must end. So it was for the young man enjoying an idyllic moment. The troop arrived at their assigned area of operations. The little bird's intercom crackled. Sadly, Viet Nam reminded Kev that all pleasant trips down his friendly "what if lane" must end. Like most of his other trips, down the creative "what if lane" of his imagination, this trip ended abruptly. As they were crossing a heavily wooded ridge, Lieutenant Simmonds' voice interrupted his day dreaming with Simmonds taking the controls.

"OK, I've got it Kev. It's time for us to go to work. This is the valley where we will do our recon this morning."

As was his frustrating habit, Kev's private little world had totally engrossed the resources of his mind. Embarrassed, he did not remember the morning's quick briefing. Adding to his embarrassment, he had not been paying any attention to where they were or where they were going. Lost in his thoughts, Kev has just been an obedient little puppy following Red One-Six and enjoying flying. He had been acting as if he had no war or navigation responsibilities to be concerned about.

Angry and frustrated, he chastised himself!

"What a big dummy I am turning out to be! No doubt about it, it was a good thing that nothing happened to the Lieutenant. Heck, I wouldn't have been able to find my way home. Well . . . I suppose, in an emergency, I could have turned east and found the ocean. Shoot. I probably couldn't find my butt in the outhouse."

Frustrated to the point of tears, he began mentally beating himself up.

"As stupid as I am, turning east toward the South China Sea and then turning south is the full extent of my navigational skill. The Good Lord only knows if when I reached the ocean I would have had sufficient brain power to turn south and not north!"

Not for the first time, he found that he was lost smack dab in the middle of Vietnam. Talking to a friend later that night at the club, he continued to beat himself up.

"There it was, slapping me in the face. Ole Kev was making another one of the typical new guy mistakes which he seemed to have become so fond of making. Yep, Ole Kev, he's right on the ball one more time! He's not paying the slightest attention to what is going on! No wonder, I thought to myself, that the other Red Birds didn't trust a new guy."

Just as they did yesterday, the team of Red Birds crested the ridge at speed and began to go to work. Lt. Simmonds keyed the mike and said to Kev.

"Ok newbe, time to earn all that good combat and flight pay that Uncle Sam is giving you."

Responding to the Lieutenant's word, Kev grabbed the CAR-15. Drawing the bolt back, he locked and loaded a clip of twenty tracer rounds into the receiver. As a new guy and not a trained observer, the Scouts were not going to trust him with an M-60 yet. Good old-fashioned common sense said that he would do less damage to himself or to someone else with the CAR-15. Senior scouts were always concerned about someone getting excited and making a mistake.

That was OK with Kev. The enlisted guys had told him enough horror stories to make the point valid. He had never fired the M-60 machine gun. Were he to have a jam, he would have been hard pressed to clear it in the middle of a firefight. The young man's newfound humility made him acknowledge that he really didn't want to be any more of a liability to the team or to himself than was necessary. Using the much smaller CAR-15 in the confines of the little cockpit was also much easier. The M-60 was much bulkier and heavier when complete with the long and heavy belts of ammunition etc. Kev doubted that he could have safely handled it within the confines of the little Loach.

Fumbling about, Kev got himself adjusted and ready for the recon. Lieutenant Simmonds slid the aircraft out to Red One-Six's right side. Taking up his covering position, he positioned the little bird about one hundred meters to the right rear. From this position he could fire the mini-gun directly under One-Six if the lead bird received fire during the recon. After making the initial high speed pass, just like yesterday, they drew no ground fire. For Kev, it was still open to question if he would have noticed any ground fire unless the bullets happened to hit him. Red One-Six slowed to a near walking pace and began the serious work of the recon.

As One-Six slowed, Kev could easily see Johnny standing seemingly naked on the skids. All that held him in place was a single webbed cargo strap. He had attached it to his safety harness and to a cargo ring in the helicopter. The young observer was peering deeply into the double canopy jungle looking back and forth. Johnny was a strange, other worldly sight. With the M-60 following the movement of his head as if mechanically slaved to his eyes, he merged the human and the mechanical. In his left hand, with the pull ring of the safety pin looped through the handle of his M-60, was a willie peter marking grenade. Johnny was ready to throw the white grenade as a target for us and the Snakes if One-Six were to receive ground fire.

The two Red Birds had made about three passes back and forth in the valley when One-Six made his first report on the radio. He said that he had discovered some well-worn trails. Acting as Kev's instructor, Lt. Simmonds told Kev that One-Six would begin working his way up one to see where it led. As One-Six continued slowing, Lt. Simmonds picked up their speed to about thirty or forty knots. Flying as the wing bird, they were weaving back and forth behind him. The whole time Lt. Simmonds was always keeping the mini-gun essentially pointed toward One-Six. Kev noted that the Lieutenant's face reflected his continual readiness. With the cryptic announcement of well-traveled trails being visible, the tension in all the aircraft increased markedly. No one said anything directly about it. However, everyone on the radio net could feel the tension. Cautious anxiety and tension were like an actual living presence in Kev's cockpit and each cockpit. The hunt was on!

As the recon was taking shape, Kev pushed his head, arms, and the little CAR-15 out of the aircraft. With all his heart and soul, poor Kev was frantically trying to see something. He craved to see anything. Nevertheless, all that he saw was a confusing blur of dense growth flashing beneath him. The only differentiation he could discern was that it came in many and varied shades of green. With the increasing level of tension, Kev also found himself getting a little bit scared. His inability to see anything but green was convincing him that a complete army or maybe two armies could be just below him. What bothered him more was that he feared that he would never be able to see them. Muttering to himself, he sadly commented.

"God, I couldn't see them even if they had a thousand tanks and trucks."

By this point, Kev knew that they could have killed him, or something even worse, before he became aware of their presence.

The unfolding drama happening somewhere below him was forcing the young man to acknowledge his own uselessness. As Kev reluctantly recognized his total bewilderment, One-Six called on the radio to announce that they had discovered a small base camp. The discovery caused Kev's heart to skip a beat. Pausing for a moment, One-Six continued.

"Six, there are fifteen — maybe --- twenty hooches and a handful of bunkers scattered about on the ground."

He continued.

"It looks to me as if the bad guys are still living here and are in the neighborhood."

With a click, the radio message ended. Kev wanted to know more. What happens now? As if answering Kev's question, One-Six came back on the radio.

"Six, if the bad guys are at home, they are ignoring me."

Command and control advised him to proceed with caution. Therefore, he move away and carefully reconed the whole area. He wanted One-Six to make sure that he wasn't walking into a trap of one sort or another. The two Red Birds spent another fifteen minutes looking all around the base camp area. Red One-Six reported that all he could see were the hooches and bunkers but that there was no ground activity nor was there anyone moving.

"Apparently," he said, "the bad guys have all gone to ground or they have taken the day off and are all out trout fishing."

Of course, in the case of ole Kev, the newbe, he saw nothing. His untrained eyes saw more of the ever present dense green jungle flashing directly beneath the helicopter. The Scouts saw nothing else of the bad guys either.

With One-Six's report of no enemy activity command and control issued some orders.

"One-Six, why don't you and your wing start burning some of the hooches and see if we can get the bad guys to come out and play."

When C&C told One-Six to put the hooches to the torch, Lt. Simmonds quietly told Kev that he should keep his eyes open.

"Things might get really hot quick in a hurry."

"Keep my eyes open!"

Frustrated, Kev saw that statement to be ironic understatement.

"If I open them any wider, both my eyeballs will fall out of my head! Why? Because. Nothing will remain to hold those poor blind useless things properly in place."

Over the next couple of minutes Johnny dropped five or six willie peter grenades. They burst with billowing white clouds of chemical smoke and immediately set four or five of the hooches to burning brightly. At last, as the hooches went up in flames, Kev could see something of the bad guys. Well . . . , the sad truth was that all he could see were the already burning hooches. Surprising Kev, no outraged response came from the people on the ground. Accordingly, command and control decided that the bad guys were not going to come out and play. With the lack of response from the ground, C&C called up Lt. Simmonds.

"Red One-Eight, I want you and the newbe to help burn those

hooches. Fuel is getting a little short and I don't want to have to finish the job later."

Acting as if he knew what he was doing and that he could really see something, Kev had kept his mouth shut. Following C&C's orders, Lt. Simmonds set Kev loose.

"OK Kev, it's our turn now. Put me directly over one of the other hooches. When we are set, then drop one of your willie petes on it."

Kev wanted to cry like a frustrated baby when he keyed the mike.

"Sorry sir, I can't see a thing."

Try as he might, the only hooches which he saw were the ones that were already brightly lit by towering flames. His "scouting" blindness was totally humiliating poor ole Kev. He had been looking in vain for what seemed like a lifetime. However, it was but a couple of minutes. During that time though, One-Six had managed to set two more hooches on fire. The burning of the hooches was just like the rest of the recon. Kev looked and he looked hard. He struggled mightily to see through the endless blanket of different shades of green which was spread directly below him. In the end, a disheartened Kev felt as blind as a new born kitten.

A soft laugh and quiet chuckle, which was both understanding and slightly frustrated, unexpectedly filled Kev's ears. This quiet and sympathetic laugh was the last thing that Kev expected while they were at war with the group of hooches that he couldn't see. Lt. Simmonds then kindly offered to help poor bewildered Kev. He told him not to feel bad about being blind and that he would place him directly over one of the hooches. Unwittingly adding to Kev's feelings of complete humiliation, he said that he would even tell him when to drop the willie pete. Later that night, Kev explained what happened to one of his new friends who flew Huey's.

"I peered intently into the ever present dense greenness below me which the rotor wash had opened in the jungle canopy. At the same instant Lt. Simmonds asked me if I saw it yet. Suddenly, I saw it. Just below me, there it was! Shoot! I couldn't believe my eyes. Lord, there it was, no more than forty feet directly below our hovering Red Bird. It was bigger than all of life. It seemed bigger than my High School and city hall combined. When I finally saw it, the thatched hooch was maybe twelve feet by twelve feet. Contrasting all the shades green. It had a bright yellow straw roof suggesting new construction. At Simmonds' command, I dropped the willie pete grenade. Mission accomplished! I smugly enjoyed the wonderfully satisfying explosion of white smoke. In its own way, the bursting grenade looked beautiful with bits of flaming white phosphorous streamers spraying outward in all the directions of the compass. At last, I had done it. I had struck my first blow for God,

113

country, and self as a fledgling scout. The hooch caught fire and was blazing merrily away. The score for the mission, an even dozen hooches for One-Six, and one hooch for ole Kev!"

Well . . . , maybe Kev had not totally won the war in Southeast Asia all by himself that afternoon. The radio had not announced that the bad guys were begging to unconditionally surrender. As they climbed to altitude, they were leaving the flames and smoke behind them and Kev had contributed. Finally, Kev felt as if he were of a little bit more value than an old sandbag. With almost no pride, he pulled off an unashamed act of self deception. He did this by assuring himself that a sand bag would have been unable to pull the pin on a willie pete and toss it out of the helicopter. Kev was aware that this wasn't a big contribution to the war effort. Still, by this stage of the game he was grasping at straws in his feverish desire to make some sort of contribution. As was his well-earned reward for putting up with a useless new guy, Lt. Simmonds gave Kev control of the Red Bird. Leaning back and enjoying his free ride as a passenger, he lit up his ever present cigarette and instructed Kev to follow One-Six to the refueling site.

Much to his surprise, the little bit of self confidence or self worth Kev had earned with the dropping of that willie pete on the hooch aided his flying skills. As a graphic demonstration of his growing skills, he managed to both land and take off from the fueling site. This small accomplishment thrilled Kev. For Kev had done it with an acceptable amount of control if not actual skill. The young man didn't crash or look like a fool. He knew it was a fair effort, because it did not earn even a grin or a quiet snicker from Lt. Simmonds. Of course, while they were fueling, Lt. Simmonds allowed Kev the honor of doing the actual refueling of the Red Bird while he held the controls. Such again, was his reward for putting up with the newbe. Ole Kev got to do the dirty work.

Being as new at things as he was, Kev found that task to be fun. He had never gotten to handle the hose and refuel a helicopter while she sat at flight idle before he came to Viet Nam. This hot refueling, which was normal in Viet Nam, was something which he had never done at flight school. Grinning foolishly, young Kevin Paul Johnson was enjoying every new aviation related experience that was part and parcel of his new life.

Twice more, Kev and Lt. Simmonds flew recons. However, these were uneventful. At the end of the day as they were returning to home base, Lt. Simmonds had Kev do the flying. Not only did this give him a break, but it also served to give Kev additional stick-time. Just as they had on the way to the AO, Kev was delighted to be flying along with the whole troop. As he looked about, he saw a gaggle of helicopters. It consisted of four Red Birds, four White Birds, four Blue Birds, and C&C. Smiling to himself, he felt a small measure of pride in becoming a part of the Cav team. With the sun setting and the sky darkening most everyone in the troop sensed a calmness. Quietly and contentedly, their aircraft continued flying along in the still evening air. A serene beauty, with position lights on and red rotating beacons flashing, added to the poetry of the moment. Looking about, Kev could visualize this scene as the backdrop while the closing credits of a film about the Cav in Viet Nam. Hollywood would scroll it down the dusky colored big screen. This calming atmosphere must have also affected Lt. Simmonds. He surprised Kev by asking him a little about himself.

Trying not to make himself appear foolish, Kev gave some of his biographic basics.

"Well Sir, home is a medium sized, declining mill town in New England. It's nothing special, but it's home."

Continuing, Kev said that he had been a so-so athlete and managed to do just enough studying to graduate from High School. Speaking honestly, he shared with Lt. Simmonds that he had been working at one of the many mills at a meaningless job.

"I hate to admit it Sir, but, I was going nowhere. My future consisted of forty years in the mills and then Social Security. It may seem strange to you, but, the Army Aviation Warrant Officer program was my ticket out of the treadmill. God knows. I always wanted to fly military aircraft. Without a college degree, this was the only way."

Flying for the Army was his great avenue of escape from the trap into which Kev had felt himself falling. Though he tried to hide his romantic nature, as the two of them continued their conversation, ever more of it was slipping out. As Kev opened up, he told the Lieutenant now that he was away from home, he had come to realize that his folks were among his greatest heros. Speaking with loving pride, he continued.

"My Dad has spent his whole life working in the mills for criminal wages. I am very proud of him. He has never complained and always done his very best for his family."

Kev continued.

"My Mom can make a home out of next to nothing and she can even make a can of spam seem to be a special meal for her family."

At that point Kev shut up for the conversation was getting uncomfortably personal.

Having said more than he meant to, Kev was naturally curious about Lt. Simmonds. His curiosity seemed fair to Kev. They had been spending a fair amount of time together. Though Kev didn't know much about him, he quickly discovered that the Lieutenant came from a world much different from his own. So he asked him about himself.

"Sir, If I might. Would you tell me something about yourself?"

Simmonds laughed and said that he didn't have much to tell. His dad was a small town lawyer in Iowa. Apparently, the Lieutenant's dad made a very good living. The detailed description of the house in which Simmonds grew up and his description of his childhood was far different from Kev's experience. Simmonds continued that he had attended Iowa State University for four years and had majored in pre-law. He continued by telling Kev that he was ROTC and had applied for flight school. He decided to attend flight school because for the nine months he attended flight school he would receive twenty-five dollars a day TDY. This money was in addition to his full flight pay and his normal pay as a lieutenant. He continued that flight school was a deal which he simply couldn't pass up. When he finished his ROTC commitment, he planned to go to law school and eventually set up a law practice much like his dad's.

The Lieutenant then laughed and pinpointed the differences between the two of them.

"Kevin my friend, we're really quite different and we have lived in different worlds. I'm here because this is what I have to do to get where I want to go in my life. Whereas, you are here because, in truth, you're a hopeless romantic. As an idealist, you honestly believe that you are going to make a difference by your being here. In fact, I bet you're probably a lifer at heart."

Kev truly didn't know what he was the most shocked about when the Lieutenant shared his last comment with him. First, was it because Lt. Simmonds had read him like a book? For it was absolutely true that he had no plans for the future other than to enjoy flying Uncle Sam's helicopters. The frosting on the cake was that he was getting paid for it. For him, that was as close to heaven as Kev ever expected to get. Kev had started to come to the realization that sometimes he lived in what was almost a romantic dream world. The young man was also finding out that his life was not a carefully reasoned life. That the Lieutenant had seen through him, was a shock. No one in Kevin's world had his future so carefully planned out. The greatest shock went right to Kev's heart and soul. All his life he had dreamed of flying, whereas the Lieutenant was flying simply because the money was better than leading the troops on the ground. Kev was really learning to like and respect Simmonds, but they obviously came from much different worlds.

HE'S A RED BIRD – HOWEVER HE'S STILL KEV

Pastor Bill had often spoken to Kev about life. The poet has fluently suggested the same thing. Concerning human existence, some things never change. Flying with the Red Birds, Kev was discovering that time always continues its ever forward and ever tireless march. He also discovered that time continues marching along its own assigned path and usually ignores the individual's desires. Tirelessly, it marches even when most folk are no longer aware of the resolute presence of time's inflexible marching orders. This is and was time's never-ending march. Such was Kev's philosophic and poetic excuse for not writing to his friend, Pastor Bill. Time and its countless demands had taken over his life.

The grind of daily missions was slowly wearing the young man down. Six flight hours a day was a long time. Six flight hours flying low and slow protecting his lead took its physical and emotional toll. Kev's six flight hours were far more taxing than the same six hours in a Huey. Kev felt that all of his six flight hours were like being in a Huey on short final to a potentially hot LZ. Six flight hours a day was also starting to apply a little tarnish to his golden veneer of idealism. It had been at least a month since the last time that he attempted to sit and try to capture his feelings.

Many changes, personal and group, had taken place since he came to Viet Nam. Flying with the Red Birds was only the first of them. Sitting in the peaceful quiet of his hooch while thinking about the changes of his life, he was puzzled. Kev was not at all that sure when his change to something/someone different from what he was before had happened. Nevertheless, one day, without his really knowing, or really being aware of any change of his state of being, the world had changed. Kevin Paul Johnson was no longer the Red Bird's stupid new guy. Somewhere along the way, he had become a full-fledged member of the Red Bird team.

However, he was enjoying his time in a "romantic's heaven."

"I thought it would never happen," he told his friend Sven.

"At last, I think and I pray that I am earning my silver wings. Of which, everyone knows, I am so overbearingly proud. Now I am Red One-Five!"

This change of status, did not mean that he was, by any stretch of the imagination, a highly skilled scout pilot. The young man's knowledge and services were not yet in great demand. His lead pilots accepted him, but they knew that he had much to learn. Yet, deep within himself, he came to believe that he had now become more of a help than a hindrance to the Red Bird's mission.

Several meaningful changes had taken place in Kev's two months in country. CW-2 Jones finished his tour of duty in lovely South East Asia. The Chief was very happy to get orders to go to Ft. Rucker in Alabama. He was hoping to set up housekeeping with his new wife and raise a bushel basket of rug rats. "Rug rats" was a new term for Kev. However, he thought that it was something to look forward to someday. Ole Chief Jones was also looking forward to leading a quiet life of a flight instructor. He expressed a strong preference for having American helicopter flight students trying their very best to kill or maim him for life. This seemed much better to him than having the bad guys trying to do much the same thing to him.

He said that he would find the change of "enemy" very refreshing. For him, it was important to have the people that were trying their best to kill him speak a language which both understand. It was his heart felt contention that the people who are trying to kill him should clearly comprehend his urgent communications. Ole Chief Jones wanted those folk to fully understand each and every one of his flowery words while he loudly cursed them out. With his incredibly eloquent fluency of graphic language, they would miss something if they didn't understand him. As Kev thought about it, being able to clearly and forcefully express his feelings of distress to those who sought to harm him had a positive merit to it. He agreed with the Chief.

"The people who are trying to kill you should know the emotional distress they are causing by their actions."

Most likely, poor old Jones would end up teaching Vietnamese Students who could not speak much English. Kev knew that the Army was beginning to train more and more Vietnamese to fly helicopters with the hope of turning more of the war over to them. However, it was most likely that the wisdom of the United States Army would assign Chief Jones to teach them. That meant that it would be as it had been for the last year. The people who were trying to kill him, this time students, would miss the full depth, width, and impact of his wonderfully colorful eloquence.

When Chief Jones returned to the States, his observer Johnny, decided to join the Blue Platoon. Kev had been flying Jones' wing a couple of weeks before he left. One day, when the other team was out on recon and he was sitting alone, Johnny plopped himself down for a gab. Without a preamble, he began to speak.

"You know, Sir, I've been watching you on our wing. In my humble opinion, I think you're getting the hang of things."

A big smile spread itself upon Kev's face. Compliments were still few and far between. He was enjoying this one. Curious, he asked Johnny what his plans were now that the Chief was leaving. Just before Johnny was about to speak, the local girls showed up with their cokes and bread. Kev bought both of them a cold coke and a nice warm French bread to go with their conversation.

Johnny spoke while munching on his bread.

"Well, Sir, I have decided that I would enjoy spending my remaining time in lovely South East Asia sitting around waiting. When the Chief leaves, I'm going to join the Blue platoon."

Kev nodded and Johnny continued.

"The way I see things, it will be a refreshing change spending only an hour or two on the ground a couple/three times a week. I believe that I have spent my fair share of hours standing on a skid looking for the bad guys."

Kev said that he could understand. Johnny continued.

"Thinking about it, I have come to the conclusion that I would like to have some big fat trees to hide behind when people are shooting at me."

Cutting the conversation short, Johnny thanked Kev for the coke and bread and went back to his bird and the Chief.

What Johnny didn't say was that he found it difficult to trust any other pilot after working with Chief Jones for so long. Kev could understand that. He had been with the Red Birds long enough that he was beginning to understand the importance of the crew members having complete confidence in each other. When he had been training with Lt. Simmonds, he observed the guys that had been flying together for several months. At first he was impressed with their team work. Later, as he continued to watch carefully, he understood that the observers and pilots share the same aircraft and risk. As a result of this shared danger, a very unusual and strong bond develops between them. His extensive readings of his cheap war novels had called this experience of combat friendships, the "bond of brothers."

Writing to Pastor Bill one night, he shared some intimate thoughts about what he had seen.

I never really understood what they were talking about in the many war novels I have read. The authors frequently referred to a "Bond of Brothers." I wasn't even sure if such a bond or such a band of "true" brothers was humanly possible. However, these days, I am beginning to gather a limited insight to the bond. This "mystical" bond is far deeper and much more intense than the ones we had in high school. It is even deeper than the ones we had on the basketball or the football team. My current concern is that I might never earn my entry into this mystical bond. Yet, I also fear that if I do enter this bond, someday I will be forced to leave it. Thinking about what I just said, military tradition has some weak points. To me, it seems a crime that once a crew lands, the "real (read rank and structure conscious) Army" does not allow the pilot and observer to continue their friendship and close working relationship. In the so called real Army

119

this is verboten. Sometime, I will have to share my feelings about the real Army and the combat Army.

A couple of weeks later, when they had returned from flying, Johnny and Kev had a very long talk. They were both down at the Red Bird line setting upon a revetment. Their intense conversation was one of those quite rare and very serious talks that doesn't need a six-pack of beer to lubricate it. In fact, it didn't even need a single can of beer to make the words flow or to get the conversation jump started. It just happened. During the previous couple of months, Kev had decided that Johnny was quite a guy and would gladly seek his counsel whenever possible.

What surprised him most about the young observer was that Johnny was just as gung-ho as the day he arrived in country.

"No," Kev thought to himself.

"That's not quite correct. Johnny is a true professional soldier in all the positive aspects of the word."

If only one guy in the unit believed in doing a proper job in this crazy place, it was Johnny. As Kev was thinking, Johnny shocked him.

"You know, Sir, good ole Uncle Sam drafted me. I'm just putting in my time, waiting to go home, get married, and make lots a babies."

For Kev, Johnny was a good example of the ironic paradox that so well defined his experience of Vietnam. The best observer in the platoon was a draftee. He didn't want to be in Viet Nam. He didn't ask to be a part of the war. However, since he was, given who he was, Johnny was going to be the best of the best in the little Cav unit. Although the two of them had become friends of a sort, Kev was not sure that he fully understood what drove him. Kev believed that he would have been angry if someone had sent him to war against his better wishes. Yet, Kev had to greatly admire his spirit and dedication to the mission.

Johnny and Kev covered many subjects in their conversations. Looking forward to a new "career," Johnny talked about the grunts.

"I don't know. After spending all this time looking at the dirt, I think it will be fun to go down there and play in it."

It was obvious that Johnny was going to tackle being a Blue with the same enthusiasm he had brought to being a Scout.

"Sometime," Kev thought to himself, "if I can discipline myself to continue writing, I am going to have to write about the grunts. Those dudes are about as crazy as the scouts. Well . . . , sometimes, they are just a little bit crazier."

Kev already knew that a finer bunch of shock troops could not be found in all of Viet Nam. While the Army didn't call them "Shock Troops" those guys were. Johnny told Kev, and initially it surprised him, that several of the observers transferred from the grunts because of the flight pay. Wishing to receive flight pay made sense to Kev. Being red-blooded Americans, they too believed in the profit motive. All the flying members of the Cav were quite fond of their flight pay. Johnny continued.

"After a few months of sitting around waiting for action, some of the grunts get itchy. Having the chance to play with the bad guys every day appeals to them."

Pondering for a moment, he continued.

"I suppose you could say that they are the reverse side of my coin."

From his first flight, Kev recognized, that the grunts were a great bunch of guys. The Scout crews probably appreciated them more than anyone else in the Cav. If they needed them, they would be there as quick as the Blue Birds could deliver them. One heart-stopping call said it all. That call was "Red Bird Down." If that call resonated through the Cav, the grunts were the very first guys on the ground. Their only purpose, from the moment the cry goes out till the mission is finished, is to get some poor unfortunate Scout crew safely back home. Their single-minded sense of purpose was sufficient reason to make them all epic heroes in all the Scouts' books.

It was getting late that evening and only the insects were flying down on the Red Bird line. Peaceful, it was one of those quiet moments that occasionally get shared by people, Johnny made a powerful statement to Kev.

"Mr. J., I don't know why, but I really like you. I've also got a gut feeling that, some day, you are going to be a great scout pilot. I want you to know, something though. While I won't be flying with you, I'll still be keeping a close eye on you."

With a wry smile Johnny continued.

"Furthermore, if you ever go down, I'll take good care of you. When you're on the ground, don't worry about a thing! Just look to the sky and I promise you that I will be riding on the skid of the first slick heading your way."

Kev nodded his head silently. The warmth and honesty of Johnny's concern left him uncharacteristically without words.

In the, so called, rough and ready setting of men at war, Johnny's faith in him deeply touched young Kev. He was greatly impressed by Johnny's quick willingness to take him under his wing. Painfully well aware of his limitations as a Scout pilot, Johnny's pledge was reassuring. Kev hadn't gotten so cocky, as to think that he didn't need someone occasionally taking good care of him. The young man knew that he had not grown out of his puppy stage.

While he was no longer a pest and underfoot, he had yet to become the mean old junk yard dog. Pondering and then thinking that it would be a dramatic sight, Kev silently prayed that he would never have to look up at the lead slick. His sense of romance had its limits. He didn't want to be on the ground watching the lead slick coming to his rescue with Johnny standing on the skid. With that, they went off to bed and they didn't speak again except in casual passing for quite a while.

When Chief Jones made his trip across the big pond and went back to Ft. Rucker, some team changes were necessary. In the Chief's absence, Lt. Simmonds inherited his lead spot. No question about it, at least in Kev's mind, Lt. Simmonds deserved to fly lead. Even Kev, with his lack of experience, could see that he was turning out to be one really fine scout pilot. The Lieutenant had developed an unbelievable nose for the bad guys. It seemed to Kev that Lt. Simmonds had his own personal guardian angel. He had an uncanny ability to escape unscathed from all his encounters with the bad guys. In fact, as far as anyone could remember, his little bird had never been hit by ground fire.

When all these changes happened, Lt. Simmonds became convinced that he had unknowingly and unwittingly angered the gods in charge of Aero Scouts! While everyone else thought he had a guardian angel, he disagreed. He suspected that he had somehow greatly angered the vengeful gods of Aero Scouts. How else would he have inherited Kev as his wingman? When told of the change, Kev felt sorry for Simmonds. The first thoughts that passed his mind were about their first flight together. Quietly chuckling to himself, Kev remembered Simmonds' less than encouraging comments about his being a newbe and his ability as a pilot. As scary as it sounded, for ole Lt. Simmonds, flying his wing was now Kev's whole reason for existence.

A new mantra began repeating itself in Kev's mind.

"I now live solely to keep him alive, just as it had previously been his whole purpose in life to keep Jones alive."

With the usual foolish and misplaced confidence of youth, he made a profound yet also solemn promise to himself.

"I swear by everything I call Holy, as long as I am flying the wing position, the call 'Red Bird Down' will not sound for my team!"

He further said to himself.

"The Good Lord willing, I will be able to live up to this vow while maintaining silence about it. Only God and myself need ever know it."

He had seen and experienced enough to realize that he had made a horribly arrogant vow. Maybe he was growing up just a little bit. At least, he had enough wisdom not to say his vow aloud.

Because he was an inexperienced Scout, with only a coupe of months under his belt, the Captain assigned Kev a very experienced Specialist four observer named Chuck Frank. It surprised him to note that Chuck was a little older than most of the other observers and pilots. In some ways, it was not a good match. Kev maintained much of his eager friendly puppy-like demeanor. Chuck, in contrast, was not quick to talk, or to get friendly with anybody in the unit. Everyone agreed that Chuck was very much the classical loner. He had a wiry lean build and almost a dark brooding air floating about him. When they were together, Kev could feel the dark brooding permeating the air. This young man was unlike any of the other observers that Kev had come to know with the Red Birds. Most of the guys were quite young, full of life, youthful foolishness, and unbridled enthusiasm about everything. Several times, as the two of them flew in and out of the area of operations, Kev tried to start a general conversation. Kev was always disappointed. The best and longest response that he ever got from Chuck was a begrudging grunt or three.   One day, in exasperation Chuck said that he was not interested in talking with Kev.

"I don't mean to offend you, Sir. However, I don't like officers and lifers. I'm tired of this place and I don't want to talk. So, please, let's do our job and go our own ways."

Following his rejection of Kev's offers of friendship, with emphatic clarity, he made his position in life clear.

"I have ninety days and a wake up and that is all that I am interested in."

If Kev had failed to understand him, he repeated himself.

"Ninety days and a wake up!"

It was not that Chuck wasn't civil or militarily correct, for he was. An unhappy man, he chose to spend his emotional time somewhere else. He was not at all invested in having any more to do with Kev as a person than the mission required of him.

Carefully watching Chuck, when he was not with him or in his aircraft, Kev noted that he didn't speak much with the other observers either. Chuck quite simply went quietly along his own way doing his own thing and not bothering anybody. This made Kev feel a little better.

"At least this proves that his treatment of me is not unique," he told himself.

Kev was still disappointed, because he knew nothing about him as a human being other than as he proclaimed, ninety days and a wake up. Of course, each day that passed made it one less day and a wake up declared in Chuck's mantra. As Kev watched him, it seemed to him that a dark brooding cloud concealed deep feelings which were pent up inside him. It appeared to Kev, that the dark brooding cloud foretold of an explosion waiting for a time and a place to happen.

Kev, correctly suspected that Chuck was not pleased about having to fly with a new guy. Flying with this new guy, Chuck believed, probably correctly, that it put him at unnecessary and unacceptable risk. It greatly increased his chances of not walking up the boarding ramp to the shinny big freedom bird. Walking up the homeward bound boarding ramp was the culmination of his ninety days and a wake up.

Sadly, Kev understood that it is not his place to bother him. So, they developed a distant, yet functional, working relationship. Ole Kev drove the helicopter and Chuck traveled along as the observer. Chuck spoke with, and to, Kev only as necessary for the mission.

After a few futile attempts, Kev gave up offering him the chance to fly to and from the mission area. Kev knew that most of the observers enjoyed the chance to get some stick time. The observers usually had fun doing a little straight and level flying. But, not Chuck. When the two of them were flying back and forth, Chuck lit up a cigarette and stared silently into a private unseen distance. Cast aside, Kev had no idea what Chuck saw in the unfocused distance. Very competent, in his own non-involved fashion, Chuck was teaching Kev about being a Scout. When they had shared a few flights, Kev became convinced of one thing. Chuck was in many ways quite the opposite of Johnny.

Whatever may have been going on with Chuck, he was not meanspirited or anything like that. In fact, Chuck continued to be a great help to Kev as he was learning to fly the wing slot. He showed Kev that flying a combat wing was unlike formation flying in flight school. In flight school great emphasis was placed on flying a precise distance and position in relation to the lead aircraft. Flying the Red Bird's, Kev was discovering, sometimes, maybe even frequently, was quite the opposite of what he had been taught in flight school. Philosophically, he was beginning wonder if most of human life turned out much the same. That is, school and life had little in common.

In the Red Birds, the wing bird was always on the move in relation to the lead. Sometimes it is sliding to the left and other times sliding to the right of the lead bird. Sometimes the wing fell quite a distance behind. Other times they allowed themselves to get close. Kev had learned much of this under Lt. Simmonds' tutelage. However, critical to Chuck's teachings, Kev began to understand that there was no shame in protecting himself also. Flying the covering wing for the lead scout did not mean that they had to make a big fat juicy target out of themselves in the process. In reality, the job was quite the opposite. Chuck said it bluntly one day.

"Sir, with all due respect, the wing can't cover the lead bird if it has stupidly become a smoking hole in the ground."

When Kev had absorbed Chuck's crude reality, he continued.

"The absurd state of being a target, and trying to get somebody to shoot at you is strictly the lead bird's job."

Following a moment's thought, Kev decided that he was happy with that situation. Telling his friend Sven at the club about his feelings, he said.

"Being a target is not a job for which I currently would choose to submit a detailed application Nor would I beg for the job."

After he had a couple of weeks of missions under his belt, Kev decided that he would be happy to spend all his days flying the wing. The first part of the job was not to get himself shot down. While at the same time, he was to make every effort to assure that the lead bird is not shot down.

In a quick note to his friend Pastor Bill, he explained his job this way.

In the wing bird, we go to a great effort to fly a highly varied flight path and an unpredictable one at that. While at the same time I always have the minigun, my new found toy, available. I try to keep myself positioned so that we can deliver a devastating barrage of fire under the lead bird if he receives fire. It is difficult flying, yet it is also a fun type challenge.

Kev spent many hours thinking deeply about his new observer. Eventually, he decided that Chuck was quite typical of many of the young men whom good ole Uncle Sam drafted and sent to Viet Nam. Kev didn't have to be a rocket scientist to know that Chuck did not want to be in the Army. If the observer had chosen to spend his days in lovely South East Asia, Kev didn't think that he would be hearing Chuck's mantra so frequently. The constantly repeated and endless mantra was wearing on him. He was getting sick and tired of listening to "ninety days and a wake up" delivered with its overtones of pent up anger.

Listening to Chuck's mantra, he realized that he did not know what it was that made a man like Johnny tick. Kev pondered. Logic led him to believe that, in the same position, he would have been very angry and would have done as little as possible. Following that logic, he would have expected to find Johnny feeling and acting more like Chuck. Yet, in Kev's observations of him, Johnny was much different in his attitude. As the weeks passed, he found it increasingly hard to understand Johnny's enthusiasm. Young Kev continued to ponder and came to a conclusion.

"If one were to say I am enthusiastic that would be understandable. I have spoken of and shown some of my romantic willingness to be here and do my bit."

In many ways, he understood the differences between Chuck and himself better. After all, Chuck never asked to come to Viet Nam!

Looking back to one of their first missions together, the picture began to come into focus. Kev began to get a better feeling for Chuck and his natural distrust for him. Flying that mission Kev had proven that he was a serious threat imposed upon Chuck's dream of resuming his normal life back in the world. Having read far too many of his paperback war novels, Kev got overly excited during one of the first missions that he flew with Chuck. It had been a quiet day when suddenly the lead bird had taken a little bit of rifle fire from a small island on the river. In retaliation, C&C instructed the Red Birds to work it over a little bit. After

125

they shot it up, they were to go back for another look-see. For some reason, C&C didn't want the Snakes to expend their munitions.

Most likely, C&C wanted to let the Red Birds have some fun shooting up the small islet.

When C&C gave the two Red Birds permission to play, Kev immediately and excitedly checked his brains at the door. For Kev, this was not necessarily a new phenomenon. Frequently, both his father and Pastor Bill had suggested that he kept his brains safely stored in cold storage. Whatever the case might have been, Kev got carried away. Excited at the prospect of playing little gun-bird, he stopped thinking about ground fire. Carefully lining himself up at seven-hundred feet and began a straight gunnery run in on the little island. Trying to do a good job, he was flying a schoolbook gunnery approach. Straight as an arrow, he aimed his little Red Bird and its mini-gun at the island. Careful not to burn out his mini, he was using about two second burst with the mini-gun. Pleased with himself, Kev was covering the whole island with little dust explosions where the bullets struck. Suddenly, Chuck came completely unglued. He started screaming at Kev.

"What in the love of God are you doing? I'm not about to have a Gook rice farmer kill me because of some stupid newbe! Damn it, I'm not going let some rice farmer kill me because of a stupid newbe who is insanely bent on making a great big fat juicy target out of himself. Stop flying like a target or I swear to God I'll shoot you myself."

Shaken y the outburst, Kev later told Sven what happened on the flight.

"I broke away from my firing run, with what I believed to be a perfect textbook curve. Oh yes, I can confidently tell you that it was just as smooth as a new born baby's bottom. Of course, just like they taught us at flight school, I did not overfly my target. For what it is worth, this was my first chance to play gun-ship and I wanted to make a classical firing pass. At least, I think that I did that part correctly. I would like to say that Ole Chuck, speaking in a calm and rational way, explained to me the problems with my textbook gun run. Such was not the case!"

"Chuck spent his time screaming and yelling. He was saying something about his not wanting rice farmers killing him in a meaningless war. A war, he added, that he didn't want any part of. If nothing else, I'll give Chuck his due. He did finally get his point through my thick skull. When I think about it, he was correct. It made absolutely no sense to make a straight in approach giving the gunners on the ground all the time in the world to adjust their fire. He loudly explained to me that a gun run was just like all the other parts of a recon. It is always wisest to present as difficult a target as possible to the bad guys. When he finished screaming, his logic had made its point. I promise you that the firing pass upon that little sand island was the last textbook gun run that I have made."

Kev was struggling to come to terms with the rapid changes that were happening to him. Flying the Red Birds in Viet Nam was like nothing that he had ever done before. The rules and values of the world that he came from frequently did not seem to apply. Also, his Hollywood and cheap novel education wasn't helping understand what was going on. He needed someone to talk to. Yet, he wasn't comfortable revealing too much of himself to his peers. With no where else to turn, young Kev found himself frequently writing to his friend Pastor Bill. Kev felt so comfortable with Bill that he wrote candidly of his experience of combat and of his feelings.

Dear Pastor Bill,

Sometimes, when I think deeply about it, my being here is very strange. In many ways, and I can't believe I am saying this to my Pastor. As you probably suspect, the hopeless romantic in me honestly believes this whole combat thing is what I was born for. This is my great adventure and the greatest contest of life. I know that I shouldn't be, but, I am glad to be part of it. Explaining that to you is hard because you are my pastor and because of your personal opposition to this war. As much as I loved playing both basketball and football, what I am doing here doesn't compare. As much as I loved the contact, the sweat, the struggle, the pain, and the playing to win, it doesn't compare.

This experience is qualitatively different. For me, this experience is much, much better. It has a sharper flavor, a richer texture, and is painted in brighter deeper colors. I suppose one could call it the big leagues of gamesmenship. At times, flying combat feels almost like an addictive drug. When I am not flying a mission, all that I can think about it getting back into my aircraft and playing the game again.

You know how it is. When you love the game, you play at school, church, or at the YMCA and you play your heart out. If you are as crazy as I have discovered I am, you will more than willingly spend your body to win the game. Yet as I think about it today, when they post the final score and when the playing field has emptied, what does the game really mean? Winners or losers, for the most part, the opponents remain friends. Following the game, everyone goes out for a coke or a beer. In the end, the game doesn't really mean a thing. That is, when you look at the big picture of human existence. Should you win something like a state championship, it is a transitory fame. Fifteen minutes after that game is over, everyone has, properly so, forgotten what the final score was or even who the players were. I would suspect that if you play pro ball, at least you could hope for a bigger pay check the next year. Further, as a pro, if you are really lucky, some kid might want a baseball card with your smiling face on it. Limited, though it be, that becomes your limited contribution to the course of human history.

I know that we radically differ on this point, but, at least to me, this little war of ours somehow means something. Feeling that somehow

127

this war means something, in turn, I believe my being here means something. I honestly believe that we are trying to help some folk make their own choice about whom they want to run their government and in turn their lives. We are trying to stop, as they say, the dominoes from falling in increasing numbers to the Communist. That much, the falling of the dominoes, seems clear enough to me. I am continually amazed how much in the way of communist military supplies, we capture. You know, guns and bullets the things that kill us, come into this little country over the borders of neighboring countries. Please remember that "the us" I speak of here are the kids who used to be in your confirmation class. Even if you are correct, if everything we do in this place is wrong, the stakes are high. If we lose this game, our history will forever change some people's lives.

In some ways, combat has surprised me. God help me. I find this flying in Vietnam this, excuse the term, "whole adventure" exceptionally exciting. I have come to the conclusion that what makes this so different from anything else I have ever done is how the head score keeper tallies the score. The unchangeable part of the scoring is that if I lose this game, I die. I really lose the game and truly lose big time. Then Kev loses once and for all. This type of winning or not winning will make a real difference in the intensity of the game. Well . . . , at least it makes a big difference to me and maybe a few others. What can I say? Kevin Paul Johnson is fully convinced that THIS LITTLE GAME COUNTS FOR SOMETHING!

In an ironic way the way that we play this game is sad. I say this because we will share no cokes or beers with the other team when this little game is over. At least no cokes and beers will be available for us, the players on the field. The stakes that we play for, on this playing field, are for keeps. The winner takes all is the first, last, and only rule of the game. I have discovered that this is the game that I have always wanted to play. Yet, I am also beginning to better understand all the Chucks over here. Guys like him have never wanted to play this winner take all game. Worse yet, they can't understand why someone is forcing them to play. Maybe you did affect me far more than you will ever know. Part of my feelings has changed since I have been here. I don't think that I can really condemn them like I did before. I am beginning to understand their wanting to stay alive and saying the heck with this kind of stupid game.

Let me try to explain my new found feelings this way. You remember how you took me out quail hunting with you a couple of times. Of course, you recognized that I never seemed to enjoy it quite as much as you did. Yet, maybe what I am doing here compares in some shadowy form with that enjoyment you found in your hunt. I can remember how you enjoyed the hunt. When you carefully and skillfully crept up on a covey of quail and then flushed them into a panicked flight, you were carefully controlled and excited. Then, maybe if you bagged one or two, it would bring delighted laughter to your eyes. You tried to explain to me how it was a contest of skill. Your hunting expertise and shotgun skills were pitted against all the survival instincts the birds had developed over the countless centuries. I even remember you admitting once that when you

128

had gotten a really good bag that there you felt something primal, savage, and brutal about the hunt and the kill. The basic and raw emotion sent your blood racing. Maybe, for you, getting a good bag was like winning the state championship.

I have spent time reflecting upon what I am feeling and our hunting together. Have you ever thought about what happens if you lose your little hunting game with the quail? Honestly, have you ever thought about it? Think about quail hunting for a moment my friend. What is the worse thing that is going to happen to you if you lose? You will be out a few bucks for some shotgun shells, a hunting permit, gas, etc. As far as I can see, at the very worse you might be cold and tired, and maybe even a little bit cranky when you get home. Who knows, maybe you would even catch a little head cold or something? Still, win or lose, nothing really changes for you when you play that game. When it is all finished, you will still have that fine shotgun your dad gave you. You will still have a warm bed in the parsonage. Fatigued, you will more than likely have a good night's sleep. Of course, you will still have to write Sunday's sermon on Saturday night and will do your usual good delivery of said sermon. (Just a little dig about your writing habits, to show you I still love ya.)

I have learned one thing over the last couple of months. I have found that when I get back home, I will not feel as excited about going quail hunting with you as I did in the past. True, I will still enjoy the walking through the woods and fields with you while you hunt. I might even enjoy the challenge of the stalk. However, I won't bother any more with carrying a shotgun or doing any shooting. For me, there just is no challenge or joy left for me in that game. For you see, I find no real cost to going down in defeat when you play that particular game.

Pastor Bill, I don't know if I should even try to tell you how I am feeling about my part in the war. However, you are my friend and you have always listened to me. Or for that matter, I don't know if you will ever be able to understand me. Maybe all of my writing is just an exercise for me. It is letting me think out loud on paper. After all, I was once one of your confirmation students. Thinking about it, I am not all that sure that you really want to know my feelings about the ultimate hunt that I go out on each day.

Yesterday I did it. Today I did it again, and, tomorrow I am going to do it again. Although it is not even close to many things that you taught me, I fear that I love it. I love my hunt.

Tomorrow morning, I am going to go walk down to the flight line. When I arrive there, I am going to give my tired old bird a very careful pre-flight. I don't want any unexpected problems that using a little caution and common sense can help avoid. When I am sure that everything is where it belongs, properly bolted, and safety-wired it together, I'm ready to get in the bird. I am going to roll down my nomex sleeves and carefully fasten them to protect my arms from flash burns if I should blow up. Completing that, I will strap on my chicken plate, survival vest and all my other assorted odds and ends which I strap to my body. Completing all these tasks, I will check my forty-five automatic and make sure that it is loaded, just in case I might need it. Lastly, I will move the holster in front of my groin as a little added armor. Of course, I do hope that I won't need it. Mind you, I am not foolish enough to leave a bullet in the chamber. Lastly, I will carefully place my little M-2 carbine beside my seat where I can also get it quickly. Should I find myself as the Red Bird which has gone down, I'll need it.

Then carefully climbing into the crowded cockpit, I will put on my helmet and then my nomex gloves. These will help to protect me in the event of an unsuccessful hunt leading to my being shot down and having the air craft catch fire. Following all of this, I will turn some knobs, throw some switches, then pull the starter trigger, and light the fire. By this time, I am going to be wide awake and fully alert and looking forward expectantly to the day's hunt. Once we are airborne, my observer and I will then test-fire our weapons. He'll test his machine gun, and I'll test my mini-gun. Satisfied that they are working properly, we will fly out to the fields and woods seeking our game. I might add, we'll seek our most wily, cunning, and dangerous game.

Like your quail, the place where we go to hunt is home to my game. We are the intruders in his neighborhood. We are the hunters and he is the hunted. It is our job to flush out the biggest covey we can and try to bag as many as possible. If the covey is large enough, we will call in some other hunters to aid us. However, a big difference exists in our hunt. Our game is far smarter than the little quail that seem to have excited you so. He is a top notch expert at the ancient art of camouflage and he will not readily panic. Most of the time, in fact, he doesn't panic at all. In our case, he is ready and exceptionally skillful at fighting back from his carefully constructed concealment. He can often see us before we see him and frequently we are forced to find him as he is shooting at us. He is shooting at the hunters, who have now become the big fat targets. Quite often, his guns are far bigger than ours are! Remember this my friend, our dangerous game is not a harmless little quail of the fields and valleys.

More than once, while I was out hunting, our quarry has turned the tables on us. In a flash of time's sweeping second hand the world changes. Far quicker and more dramatically than I can ever say it with words, the hunter has instantly become the hunted. When this happens, when you are the hunted, everything changes. Ever nerve of your body and being screams with life's tension, fear, and hope. Suddenly, you become vibrantly awash in a surging sea of adrenalin. As the druggies say, a rush surges through your whole personhood that can't even be spoken of unless you share the same experience. The best I can say is that you are intensely alive in that individual moment. When that happens, I am more intensely alive than I will ever be if I should live for a million plus a million more years. Each second is closer to a complete lifetime. These are unique seconds which some of us savor. Each sound, sight, and smell is more powerful than the previous one. The sensual and emotional intensity is higher than you have ever experienced in the entirety of your existence. You think. You react. You're quick. Or, you are the loser in this game. Bang, you're dead! "Red Bird Down!"

Just like at home during the deer season, while we are on the hunt, we carefully scout his trails. We read the signs of his passage through the fields and woods. We try to get as deeply into his head as humanly possible. Then we try to stay one step ahead of him. Sometimes, not as often as we would like, we are better than he is. Sometimes, when we are sneaky enough, we can flush him because he wasn't ready for us or he was looking in the wrong direction. Occasionally, we can even catch him when he is between his little holes. Upon occasion, we can even bag him. However, even then, we very rarely catch him in panicked flight. Our quarry is not like the quail back home fluttering away from us in panic. He fights back viciously. Cornered, he does his best to make us bleed and pay heavily before we can win that particular inning of the ball game. To be honest, panic totally ruins the higher quality of the hunt. If we do force a panicked flight, like one sees with the covey of quail, then the odds are no longer fair and the hunt is soured for me.

When we go hunting, we assemble the team. Everyone on our team knows the stakes. The five of us on our team are keenly aware that a mistake by me can mean the death of the lead ship and its three young passengers. Or, a mistake by my observer could mean our own death. We share a wonderful sense of purpose and trust. All of the little stupid things which so many people back in the world seem to think are so important just disappear. The things that people are willing to hurt each other over, just melt away into their proper place of nothingness. For the moment, at least, it is just you and your brothers in the midst of the definitive hunt. You need each other. You are perfectly willing to lay down your life for each other. Teamwork is life. Mistakes, laziness, and selfishness are invitations to death and defeat. Sometimes, I think that I could stay here forever. As strange as it sounds to you, it might be worth it if I could spend eternity playing ball on this well tuned team.

Maybe I will try to write an essay on what I'll call the "Band of Brothers" experience. If I ever complete it, I'll be sure to send you a copy.

Whatever the feelings are that I am experiencing during the fantastic hunt, they are intense. These are far more vital, far more alive than the so-called joy one receives from a pay check earned pumping gas for countless grouchy, middle aged, fat ladies. I am talking about the people who quickly complain about a speck on their windshield, and then whine to your boss trying to get you fired! In fact, when I think about things this way, I find myself admiring your patience as a pastor leading a volunteer group. I often wonder how you can possibly put up with a life and death blood fights that have happened in our church. For example, do you remember the fighting, tears and resignations over the color of the carpet in the east parlor of the church? Over here, I have learned not to care in the slightest bit if a carpet is installed in the east parlor. Who cares about the color of carpet when the stakes of the hunt are so high? Life is far too precious and vital for that petty foolishness!

Like I said earlier in this little tome, grabbing the shotgun and hunting quail does not hold a candle to this new hunt which I have discovered. In fact, I suspect, that when I return home, I will never pick up a rifle or shotgun to go hunting. Forgive me for saying this and I mean no disrespect. However, I have discovered, at least for me, that quail hunting, or deer hunting, or any other sport hunting is really a loser's game. I say this because, in fact, you can't lose no matter how long you play that game.

Although the poet suggests that some things never change, I think that my time here with the Red Birds is changing me quite profoundly. Some of the changes I suspect are good and some of the change is not all that good. Whatever the case may be, I know that I am changing. I know that it is changing my values and deepening my appreciation of life. I don't know what the outcome of this whole year will be. Maybe you won't like me by the time that I get home. All that I am sure of is that something deep inside me is undergoing a constant molding and changing!

Well, I suspect that this epistle is getting a wee bit oversized. If it gets much larger, I will have to ship it out parcel post. If it ever gets mailed, remember I suggested that this might just be an exercise in thinking. Please don't show it to my folks. If they weigh the number of words used here against the little notes that I scratch off to them, I suspect that I will be in a whole heap of trouble. Further, I doubt that I want to share my feelings about the hunt and its thrills and dangers with them. I doubt that either mom or dad would understand. Maybe, I don't give them enough credit. A perennial problem of youth, the wise old heads tell me. Nevertheless, I am grateful that someone listens to me. That is one thing that you have always done well in addition to being a good friend. Pastor Bill you are a good friend, I might add, who has stood by me when we have differed so radically about my being here.

just Ole Kev

LIFE AS A SLICK DRIVER

Thoughtfully quiet, Kev spent the evening working at his custom-made writing desk. In a reflective mood, he was feeling guilty about the superior attitude he had been developing. As the months had passed, he had begun to become more than a little arrogant in his accomplishments. Or maybe better said, he had become understandably overbearing in his new status as a Red Bird. The changes in his attitude were to be expected. In the military, looking down one's nose at those who do not belong to your elite unit is the norm. Such a superior attitude may put some people off. However, that feeling of superiority was part of the spirit of things within the Red Bird community.

The Army accepted that self confidence was critical to making their unit elite. When the Scouts go out on their hunt/recon, they do not know what surprises the bad guys have in store for them. Unconsciously, Kev discovered that if they are to survive and be successful it was necessary that they know that they are the best of the best. Conversing within his own head, he thought to himself.

"I think flying with the Red Birds is similar to playing baseball. If we go up to bat against a great fast ball pitcher what is happening in our heads makes the difference."

Pondering, with his pen in hand, he began thinking about baseball. Chewing on his pen, he began carefully searching his memory. He struggled to remember the poem about the Great Casey coming up to bat. Though he could remember the story line, he could not remember the poem. Suddenly, he had an inspiration drawn from his own Little League days. Rather than write about Viet Nam, he would scribble an essay about baseball in his journal. The Great Casey, his Little League days, and Viet Nam seemed to all tie together. Protecting the innocent he changed the setting and the name of the Little Leaguer.

His turn comes and the little boy comes up to bat. The setting is a small town and everyone in town is attending the local Little League baseball game. Little Tommy is only 10 years old. He is not very big for his age. Possibly, he weighs 100 pounds when he fills his pockets with pretty rocks and the other priceless treasures which little boys carry. Dragging his baseball bat behind him, Tommy slowly wanders up to home plate. Planting his feet firmly in the batters box, he screws his batting helmet tightly on his head. Looking straight ahead, he sees the **massive 12-year-old** *who is towering over him on the pitching mound. He gulps in anxiety.*

As little Tommy looks up, the massive 160-pound 12-year-old begins his windup. With a heave and a grunt, he throws his fast ball. As the ball races toward him, Tommy notes that the pitch will be a little inside. Deep within Tommy's brain critical facts are rapidly flashing from synapse to synapse.

"The baseball is hard. This big kid throws fast. If the baseball hits me, it will hurt really bad!"

When the speeding baseball reaches home plate, a crisis of faith confounds the little boy. He closes his eyes and steps deeply into the proverbial bucket. *(That is, he steps away from home plate.)* Suffering from multiplying anxieties, Tommy takes a mighty swing. Of course, our little friend misses the ball by a country mile. And, the umpire hollers out -- **"STRIKE!"** His coach yells encouragement to him. He tells him to stop stepping in "the bucket" or he'll never hit the ball.

Unexpectedly, the 160 pound, 12-year-old monster, smiles. He has Tommy right where he wants him. When he stepped into the "bucket," Tommy told him that he was afraid of the ball. Totally confident, the smiling monster rears back and throws his second pitch. This one is a little closer to the fearful little boy who is up to bat. Once again, deep within Tommy's brain, critical facts are rapidly flashing from synapse to synapse.

"The baseball is hard. This big kid throws fast. If the baseball hits me, it will hurt really bad!"

Anxiety wins and fear rules. Our little boy just jumps back away from the speeding baseball. And, the umpire hollers out — **"STRIKE!"**

A third time, the 160-pound 12-year Godzilla like creature smiles. As he did the first two times, he rears back and throws his fast ball. This third pitch is on the outside part of the plate. In fact, it is further away from Tommy than the previous ones. A third time deep within Tommy's brain, critical facts are rapidly flashing from synapse to synapse.

"The baseball is hard. This big kid throws fast. If the baseball hits me, it will hurt really bad!"

Anxiety wins the battle and fear rules the day.

As he did the two previous times, Tommy squeezed his eyes tightly shut. Mirroring the previous two pitches, he stepped away from the plate. Stepping deeply in the proverbial "bucket," ole Tommy swung in vain. Like before, he missed the pitch by the proverbial country mile. Every human ear within the confines of the ball field heard the results of Tommy's fear and anxiety. **"STRIKE THREE -- <u>YOU'RE OUT!</u>"**

Would little Tommy have struck out anyway? It is possible. We'll never know. However, when Tommy looked up and saw the big twelve-year-old he was doomed. He doomed himself with his own thoughts. "The baseball is hard. This big kid throws fast. If the baseball hits me, it will hurt really bad!" If the batter doesn't believe that he can hit the ball, he is doomed to strike out!

Satisfied with his little essay, Kev put his pen down. He remembered how he had feared the big twelve-year-old. Little and afraid, he had been doomed to strike out.

"I suppose," he thought to himself, "I shouldn't be surprised at that."

The connection to Viet Nam was clear to him. If he were as afraid of Victor Charles and his cousins from the north as he had been of the big kid, he would be in trouble. Speaking to his empty room, he emotionally grabbed his baseball bat and charged up to the batter's box.

"I can hit this son of a gun any time I want to. He may be good. However, he isn't good enough to strike out ole Kev."

With that affirmation, Kev had become part of the breed of Red Birds.

The Red Birds pilots, more so than most, had an overbearing belief that they are the best, the boldest, and the bravest in all of Army Aviation. More times than not, their superior attitude goes straight to their pointed little heads. At least it did in Kev's case. If they were at the little Officers Club and the beer, bourbon, and war stories began to flow, they started shooting off their mouths. Frequently, the less experienced the Scout, the louder the mouth worked. Within moments, it became the Scouts against the world. They were better that the gun pilots. They were better than the heavy helicopter pilots. Unarguably, they would affirm that and they are definitely far superior to any slick pilot in the whole wide world. Scouts hold one exception.

This exception is the Medivac pilots. Universally, the Scouts knew that the "Dust Off" boys have the baddest biggest, boldest brass gonads in the whole wide universe. Just ask them what the score is. They'll set you straight on that issue in a flash. Kev ego was no exception. That is, he was no exception until he was unexpectedly humbled.

His most recent education in the art of humility started during a normal run of the mill day. The Red Birds saddled up early in the morning and were spending their time doing a quiet recon of a long valley. It was a familiar valley which they had snooped around many times before. In some ways, working a familiar area made it an easy day for them. Being well acquainted with the area, they could detect changes in the bad guy's activity that much easier. Small changes in the topography jumped out as they did their recon. As had become Kev's normal custom, he was flying Lt. Simmonds' wing. It had been a very uneventful day with little activity from the bad guys. For a change, the bad guys had decided to remain hidden and tolerate the Scouts poking around in their back yard.

The two of them were on their third recon of the day. With about an hour's worth of fuel left, C&C received an urgent call from Division. The folks at Division had a recon patrol out which had gotten into some trouble. The recon grunts on the ground needed an immediate extraction. Countless bad guys were quickly closing in on them and the tired grunts were badly outnumbered. Division asked the Cav to provide additional support and gun cover as needed. Slicks from the local lift company were enroute to extract the grunts. The Major accepted the mission and they immediately set out at their best possible speed. As they were clipping along, just above the tree tops, Kev thought to himself that this would be exciting change of pace. The day had been too boring for his taste. The thought of charging to the rescue set his pulse pounding. He felt like a Cav-man at his best. Full of himself, he muttered.

"This is why I am here."

Division had given them good coordinates. Following the Snakes, the Red Birds quickly found the Grunts. It was easy to find. The area was a bee hive of activity. Four slicks were in a high orbit along with a C&C ship. In addition, four Charley model gun ships were making firing runs in support of the people on the ground. To this group of friendly helicopters, the Cav added their own. They brought C&C, two Snakes, Lt. Simmonds, and Kev. The sight of all these helicopters gave Kev a good feeling. Seeing this much effort being expended to help/rescue six unknown grunts who were in trouble was encouraging. Unfortunately the grave situation quickly changed that warm feeling of Kev's to a feeling of deep unrest and unease.

As he listened to the radio net, Kev didn't like what he heard. A very dangerous and unstable situation was unfolding on the ground. Nobody could find a suitable landing zone for the slicks to pick up the grunts. Everybody knew where the good guys were. They also knew where the bad guys were. Sufficient gun support was available, with the four Charley model gun birds and the Cav's two Snakes. The fly in this smooth ointment of helicopter support was that they had no way to extract the good guys. Six grunts against a possible company of NVA. The taste and textures of this operation were getting very rough and sour, exceptionally fast.

Division C&C called Kev's C&C, Blue Six. He informed Blue Six of an additional problem. He did not have any slicks equipped with jungle penetrators available. Hopefully, he asked if any of the Cav's slicks waiting back at the staging field were so equipped.

"Long Leg Six negative to jungle penetrators. Please stand by five while I talk to my Red Birds. I want them to take a look-see. Break-break, Red One-Eight, this is Blue Six. Did you monitor?"

To which Lt. Simmonds responded that he had.

"Red One-Eight, have you got any suggestions now that you have had a quick look at the area?"

The two Red Birds had immediately started their own look-see upon arriving at the area. There were no low flying birds and they were able to get a good look. Lt. Simmonds coordinated with the Charley model guns on another frequency. They began their quick recon while the two C&C birds were talking. Simmonds responded.

"Six give me a minute or two. I think I saw an area we can possibly get a Red Bird into."

Dutifully, like a good little puppy dog, Kev followed Simmonds as he gave a tiny shale-covered clearing on the side of the hill/mountain a much closer look. Beginning to sweat, poor Kev believed that he read Simmonds' thoughts in increasing horror. Trees, seventy-five feet tall, surrounded the little clearing. It was much too small for a Huey. Complicating matters, it appeared that the ground had a thirty-degree slope.

"No way," he thought to himself. "There is no way in all of God's creation that I can get a Red Bird into that little confined area."

Comforting himself, he reminded himself that Lt. Simmonds was not known for his foolishness. Kev was sure that they would soon begin looking a little further afield. Shaking his head in disbelief, Kev dared not contemplate the impossible.

With a little burst of static Lt. Simmonds keyed his radio.

"Blue Six, this is Red One-Eight, can you get the grunts to move about two hundred meters up the side of this hill?"

Inwardly, Kev groaned.

"I know that he's not even going to try. Dear God, tell me that he is not going to try."

Kev's panicked thoughts and prayers went unheard by the capricious gods of Scout pilots. Lt. Simmonds continued.

"With a little luck, I think that One-Five and I can get them out."

With an exploding feeling of impending dread and doom, Kev forced himself to look at the postage stamp size opening on the side of the hill. Speaking with a voice that sounded like an executioner's, Blue Six responded.

"It's your call One-Eight. What do you need?"

Kev felt like crying. He wasn't sure if is was from fear of not being a good enough pilot or just plain naked fear!

"Break, break, One-Five, follow me and monitor the radio."

He was his wingman, what else was he going to do.

"Blue Six, this is One-Eight. With your permission, One-Five and I will land on the sandbar about five klicks on this blue line. If you can get a couple of the Charley model gun birds to orbit them, we'll leave the observers. I believe that they will be OK with their three M-60s and three thousand rounds of ammo. One-Five and I will strip our birds and go in and pick up the grunts. Both of these birds are pretty strong. I'll go in first and pick up three of the grunts. As soon as I clear the LZ, One-Five will go in and get the other three."

A pause followed as Blue Six came to a conclusion. He then keyed the mike and gave Lt. Simmonds idea his blessings.

"One-Eight, if you guys are game, we'll give you all the gun cover you need."

The two little Red Birds quickly landed on the sandbar. Immediately the observers began to strip their aircraft while the pilots held the controls at flight idle. When the two birds took off, they left their crew members, machine guns, grenades, and all their assorted toys which go bang. They even left Kev's cherished mini-gun on the little island. By the act of pulling three quick disconnect pins, the observers robbed Kev of his beloved security blanket. Sadly looking at his mini-gun assembly resting upon the sand almost broke his heart. The observers immediately began setting up a circular defensive position. C&C saw to it that they were well covered by a pair of Charley model gun birds. For the observers this wasn't a bad situation. They had three-hundred and Sixty degrees of open ground extending all the way out to about three hundred meters. Further, insuring their safety, anyone who wanted to get to them had to cross a minimum of fifty meters of slowly flowing river. With their three M-60 machine guns and thousands of bullets, and the two Charley model gun-birds over head, they were as safe as they could be in Vietnam. They were possibly safer than if their mothers had wrapped their loving arms about them.

Deprived of his security blanket, Kev immediately felt as naked as the day he was born. Not that he remembered anything about the day he was born. For the moment, he had a good imagination though. While the observers were stripping the little helicopters, Kev recalled how he had gotten into their interesting situation. Lt. Simmonds had proven to Kev that he is a great team player. Before the two of them got to the sand island, he called Kev on the radio.

"Well One-Five, are you prepared to try something new and exciting? Would you like to become a slick driver for a day? You'll be one of only two OH-6 slick drivers."

By now, he knew Simmonds well enough to know that this was his way of saying that playing unarmed slick driver was strictly a volunteer effort. If he wanted, Kev could choose not to take part. Simmonds would then make two separate trips into the little LZ to get the grunts and think no less of him.

Listening to the Lieutenant's conversation with Blue Six, Kev had already framed a number of cryptic responses prior to receiving his call. They ran the full course of his mounting anxieties.

"You have got to be kidding me. I'm not nearly that stupid! Give me a break, even slick drivers have door gunners."

Another response that came to his mind was fearfully honest.

"I'm sorry One-Eight. I don't believe that I'm a good enough pilot to get in and out of that LZ."

Both responses were an honest reflection of his fears and self doubts. Given the heroic image of himself, which he had so carefully crafted, he had a problem. In the end, only one response was possible for Kev to give to Simmonds' request. Putting on his best "cool Cav guy voice and sounding far more sure of himself than he was, Kev responded.

"One-Five is right behind you One-Eight."

Continuing on an overly confident note, Kev spoke. He had his image to maintain.

"Where thou goest, there goest I."

Not wanting anyone to see the "condition" of his "condition," Kev kept the shaded visor down on his flight helmet. Two highly divergent, yet closely related, memories surprised and struck him. The first memory was of boating with his grandfather when he was a very small boy. The second thought came as words long forgotten from the old King James Bible.

"Fear thou not; for I am with thee: be not dismayed; for I am thy God: I will strengthen thee; yea, I will help thee; yea, I will uphold thee with the right hand of my righteousness."

He wasn't ready for either thought to flirt through his overloaded mind and wasn't sure that he had time to get "religious.".

Then, with a small private grin, he warmly remembered boating many years before with his grandpa. The two strange memories gave him the answer to his fearful problem. Relieved, he stuck his head back into the upcoming rescue and silently hollered to himself.

"Kev, have someone wake up that useless Warrant Officer Pilot who shares my quivering body. When he becomes coherent, if he can, tell him that he just accepted a tough mission."

Kev's Grandpa, many years previously, had passed through the doorway we call death. However, he continued teaching his little grandson how to deal with legitimate fears.

Studying the foreboding clouds of his fear, Kev remembered. Not long before his death, he and his grandfather had gone boating. It was a lovely summer day and they motored across the bay to the sandbar. Grounding the boat upon the sandbar, the two of them walked about the sandbar looking for pretty shells. (At the time, Kev was still a very little guy and looking for pretty sea shells with gramps was just fine with him.) When they grounded the boat, both thought that it was full low tide. Surprising them, while they were walking, the tide went out farther. Suddenly, the grounded boat was hard ashore. The hour was getting late. Not withstanding the time, together they couldn't push the boat off the sandbar.

The problem was that Kev's grandpa had already had three serious heart attacks, and Kev was just a little pip squeak. The little boy didn't have enough beef. His grandpa couldn't exert himself because of his heart condition. Concerned, if for no other reason than Grandma would skin both of them alive for being late, Kev asked his gramps what they were going to do. Like a wise grandfather, he spoke calmly and quietly.

"The most important thing Kev is that we are not going to panic. We have got a little problem, but, everything will be fine. The two of us just need to think about the situation. If we put our heads together, I'm sure that we'll come up with an answer."

With that, Kev's gramps sat on the boat's gunnel and got his cigarettes. It was a pack of Old Gold's. Kev quietly chuckled to himself and wondered why he remembered that his gramps always smoked Old Gold's. The gentle churchman he was, he sat quietly, carefully lit up a cigarette, and spoke to the little boy.

"Kev/boy, God gave us the tides. The tide went out a little. Now, do you remember what happens after the tide goes out? In time, the tide will come back in. When the tide comes back in, it will float the boat off the sandbar. After the boat floats, we can go back and let Grandma chew us out for being late."

In a couple of hours the tide came in and the floating boat vindicated Kev's Grandpa's faith. The rising waters displaced my fears and floated their boat free.

It only took a moment for the whole parade of events to pass down Kev's memory lane. Not all of it made sense to him. He was at war and wasn't sure about God's place and position on the war. Yet, he was going to be saving lives and not taking them. He was confident that God was the author of life. Therefore, if God were the author of life then God should bless the coming effort. Thinking about the tide, he wondered what it might have meant. That was another question. Maybe gun birds were like the tides. Sometime they had to go and refuel and rearm. However, in his experience, they always came back. Suddenly confidence filled him. He was going to be saving lives and it was the high tide of gun birds. He was going to have his two Snakes and the two remaining Charley model gun birds that weren't protecting the observers on the sandbar.

The young man was the prisoner of an emotional roller-coaster. He was rapidly vacillating between soaring exhilaration and demeaning fear. His emotional tide turned and went out as he bitterly spoke to the privacy of his heart.

"I could be waving my hat over my head and yelling charge or some other stupid thing. Even if I were that stupid, I still would have felt as defenseless and naked as the day I was born! Ole Kev is armed to the teeth and ready to take on the yellow hoard. HA!"

140

Well . . . Kev did have his trusty, dusty, rusty forty-five tucked into his groin. As a backup, he also had his little M-2 carbine tucked beside his seat. Sighing in deep resignation, Kev pulled in the power and lifted off. For a moment, his imaginative thoughts seemed a bit far-fetched. Nevertheless, he thought he heard some nasty and sarcastic laughter ringing in his ears.

Sadly shaking his head, Kev came to a disconcerting self mocking conclusion. Somewhere, a legion of slick drivers was laughing uproariously at scared little Kev. He knew who these slick drivers were. Thy were the same Huey pilots whom he had insulted over the past couple of months by calling them glorified truck drivers.

The young man's colorful imagination went into overdrive. Sitting back, he was watching his little drama unfold. He was sure that each and every one of those slick drivers was leaning back in his chair, sipping a cool one, and enjoying a great big laugh at Kev's rapidly mounting terror. Yep! They were all leaning back in their chairs watching the fearsome Red One-Five. Laughing and joking, they were pointing out his trembling at the prospect of doing a simple troop extraction. The truth was as plain as day! They were probably even having a cold one as they enjoyed the show.

"Well, let them laugh," he thought to himself.

"They do it all the time and they go into these LZ's armed with two door gunners."

Kev hadn't gone into a confined area, let alone a postage stamp sized LZ like this since he was at Ft. Rucker. Continuing his theme of self-confidence boosting, ole Kev rambled on.

"I'm better and braver than all of them because I'm totally naked. Furthermore, I'm going to land and pick up troops who might be under fire without a single gun to defend me."

While the observers had been stripping out the little helicopters, C&C had gotten the tired and scared grunts headed toward the little LZ. In turn, C&C assured the two Scout drivers that the troops would be in position by the time the they arrived. Lt. Simmonds keyed his mike.

"Blue Six, make sure that the grunts approach from the down slope side. I don't want them walking into the rotors."

Six had been on the ball and was quick with his response.

"It's already done, One-Eight."

On the positive side, for both the Red Birds and the grunts, the two remaining Charley Model gun birds and the Snakes had forced the pursuing NVA to go to ground. This meant that the grunts had managed to disengage from them. With a little luck the LZ would be cold. Kev would not be disappointed if no one were shooting at either Simmonds or him when they were on the ground.

As the gun birds made their firing runs on the down slope side of the hill, Lt. Simmonds began his approach. He was making it look so effortless that it could have been a practice approach at Ft. Rucker. Scooting in quickly, Lt. Simmonds sharply flared the little helicopter on short final. Orbiting about three-hundred meters away Kev was bathed in sweat. When Lt. Simmonds was on the ground, C&C called Kev.

"OK One-Five, he's picking up the grunts. You can begin your approach."

Just quickly and effortlessly, One-Eight lifted off the ground, and was out of there with the three grunts safely aboard.

As the Lieutenant was lifting off, he called Kev.

"Red One-Five the LZ is cold. Be aware though, I did receive some scattered fire on approach. It is a little tough in there. When you land, you're going to have to hold position in on one skid. There is about a thirty-degree slope in the LZ."

In some ways, this was not the kind of information that Kev needed to hear. Already shaken, he knew that a more positive report on the condition of the LZ would have greatly cheered him up. He had painfully noted that he was going to have sufficient problems landing in the LZ, that is, without trimming some branches off the trees. Given this added information only added to his growing anxiety. Grimacing, he muttered to himself.

"Gramps, at the moment, I could use some of your patience, calmness, confidence, and faith."

Lt. Simmonds had confirmed his anxieties. He now realized that he wasn't even going to be able to have both skids on the ground while the grunts threw themselves into the helicopter. This was a maneuver that he had never done. For safety reasons it was only spoken about in flight school. They never practiced it. The only reason he continued his approach was that he had seen Simmonds safely get in and out of the LZ.

"Maybe," he thought to himself, "I am too chicken to chicken out."

Ole Kev received a few scattered rounds of small arms fire on his short final. The sound of the enemy gunfire barely penetrated his consciousness. He was so afraid of crashing in the postage stamp of an LZ, he forgot to be afraid when he took fire. Grimly, he flew on.

Struggling and gritting his teeth, Kev got the little bird into the LZ. Though large trees surrounded it, he survived without making any fresh tossed salad out of the foliage. Remembering what they had taught him in flight school, he placed the up slope skid on the ground. Keeping the helicopter level with the controls, he slightly lowered the collective. This placed one skid firmly on the ground. Maintaining some lift with the rotor, the other skid hung in the air. Looking to the up slope side, the rotor disk was about eighteen inches above the ground. Kev prayed that the grunts would remember to come from the down slope side. He would have trouble maintaining stability as they got in the helicopter. However they would not get hit by the twirling blades nor would they pull the helicopter's rotor disk into the ground up slope.

Ducking under the twirling rotor blades, the three tired, dirty, and scared grunts rushed out of the tree line. Kev breathed a deep sigh of relief. They were on the down slope side. The first two dove into the back of the little Red Bird setting her shifting about and dangerously rocking. Fighting the controls, Kev managed to keep her from crashing. He then hollered at the third one to toss his pack in the back and get into the observer's seat beside him.

"For God's sakes, stay close to the helicopter and keep your head down!"

Struggling not to bang the controls about, the third man got in beside Kev. They were great! He wondered if it were possible. Ruefully shaking his head, he was sure that it couldn't have been possible. Yet, it appeared that the three grunts wanted to get out of that little LZ even more than he did. In far less time than it takes to tell, the three of them were in. Over the noise of the little turbine Kev hollered to the grunt on his left.

"Anybody left?"

He assured Kev that this was the lot.

So far, so good, he was still alive and had three happy grunts onboard. Kev keyed the mike.

"Red One-Five is safely outbound."

He made the call to assure that none of the gun birds would shoot him up as he exited the small LZ. As far as he could tell, if someone had been shooting at him on the way out, he didn't hear it. Poor Kev was wired so tightly that he couldn't possibly have heard anything over the blood pounding in his ears. He was just as afraid as he had been on landing. Only this time he had two new problems. Three young men were depending upon him. He also had to make a near vertical takeoff. As they struggled over the towering trees at full power, he hollered at the grunts to lay down some covering fire. This close to safety, Kev wasn't the least little bit bashful about being afraid. Desperately, he wanted the bad guys to keep their heads down. With all the engine instruments touching their red lines, the little Red Bird staggered over the trees with the three grunts. Each of them was rapidly emptying his M-16 into the tree lines. Luck was with Kev. Nobody shot them down nor did he create any freshly tossed salad on the way out either. For both, young Kevin Paul Johnson was very thankful.

143

The five minute flight back to the little sand island was wonderfully anticlimactic. Somewhere in route, Kev started breathing again. Unnoticed by him, his pulse dropped back to a more normal human level. As he approached the island, he noted two empty slicks which were waiting to relieve the little Red Birds of their happy passengers. The two of them landed and throttled back to flight-idle. Emotionally exhausted, they decided to shut down. Red One-Eight made the call to C&C.

"Roger that, One-Eight, we'll keep the Snakes orbiting till you rearm and get out of there."

Their six passengers shook hands all around. The scene made Kev smile and he felt some pride in a job well done. They were very appreciative of their first ride in a Red Bird. Left unsaid was the fact that they had gotten a new lease on life. Then, one of them made a comment that horrified Kev to the very marrow of his bones.

"If we're ever in another tough spot, we'll call on you guys. The slicks could never have gotten us out of there. Now we know that you guys can. Who knows, maybe you'll see us again. We usually work six man teams. Six men, two Loachs, the math works out perfectly."

It took the five of them a little longer to reload their Red Birds than it took to strip them. This stood to reason. No lives were at stake. Kev and his observer also discovered that it was easier to remove his mini-gun and dump everything out of the bird than to remount the mini-gun and reload both birds. They worked up a sweat supporting the weight of the mini-gun while another observer tried to line up the pins. However, this time they weren't in any hurry. Low on fuel, they could not return to the area of operations without first refueling.

C&C called Lt. Simmonds and said that he was calling it a day. "Bring the boys home."

He told the two of them to refuel and join up with everybody back at home base. That little bit of information didn't break Kev's heart. The mission totally washed him out and didn't think that he had anything left. With none of them complaining, they refueled and headed back home. It was a delightful talkative trip home. Kev's observer, not Chuck on this flight, talked a mile a minute. He just kept on rattling on endlessly about his adventure as a hard core grunt on the little island.

"You should have seen us, Sir. We set up the 60's to cover one-hundred and twenty arcs with the ammo carefully laid out. Then we dug ourselves nice little depressions and waited."

Kev responded. "It sounds to me like you guys had the situation well in hand."

Happily complaining, his observer continued.

"Well, Sir, we were a little disappointed. We kinda thought that if the bad guys dropped in for a cold one and a smoke things might have been interesting. The way we saw it, Sir. With the Charley birds overhead and our 60's we could have really rocked and rolled. Who knows, we might have become heros."

The excited observer finally asked Kev how he had enjoyed his own "little" adventure. Pausing for a moment, Kev carefully considered his answer. He decided that his momma was right when she had told him the honesty was the best policy.

"To be honest, I was scared spitless. I was lost without my mini. In fact, George, I even missed you and your M-60. I swear to God I don't ever want to sit on the ground naked like that again. Don't you dare quote me, but I would hate to be a slick driver sitting in a hot LZ. That takes guts --- a lot more guts than I've got."

Lost in thought, he didn't have much else to say on the trip home.

Well . . . Ole Kev added another vow to his ever growing list of vows.

"I will never again give slick drivers a bad time calling them just glorified truck drivers. They might spend most of their time being truck drivers. Still, they more than make up for the easy life each and every time that they go into a hot LZ. Setting their helicopter on the ground and waiting for someone to shoot them is a tough way to make a living."

As if the issue were ever in doubt, Kev decided that he would stay in his beloved Red Bird.

"At least," he said to his observer, "I have my trusty, dusty mini-gun to shoot back at the bad guys when they are angry with me. Better yet, I don't have to land and become a big still target. Fortunately, when people are shooting at me and it gets too hot, I can also run away if that suits my needs. Ole Kev does not mind running away and coming back later with his big brothers."

Flying as a Scout, Kev was rapidly discovering that the fickle gods of military aviation are capricious and difficult taskmasters. Their demanding world includes difficult, harsh, and shocking truths. Following his turn flying as a slick pilot, Kev discovered another truth about his life as a member of the Aero Scouts. He discovered that when flying with the Red Birds, "it" is bound to happen. Sooner or later the odds will eventually catch up with most of the bold young pilots. Every morning, the young men of the Aero Scouts crawl out of the sack and meander down to the flight line. Upon arriving, they kick a tire, and light the fire. Day in and day out, they willingly launch their little helicopters into the North Vietnamese Army's unknown and unfriendly greetings. Once in the air, they then go out looking for trouble. When they fly as Red Birds, they will always be worlds apart from the missions of the guys who fly the ash and trash missions. A slick occasionally stumbles into trouble. The Red Bird is **ALWAYS** looking for it.

After Lt. Simmonds and Kev had their opportunity to play slick drivers, Kev promised himself that he would be nicer to Huey drivers. Unfortunately, from the way he viewed the world, promises to be nice to perceived lesser beings were much easier to make than to keep. The precocious child within felt that he would be highly irresponsible if he missed an opportunity to jab and twist the knife in a little bit. He believed that in all reality, what Huey drivers flew were glorified duce-and-a-halfs mounted on skids. In the eyes of most of the Scouts, the Huey pilots were truck drivers. As truck drivers, they spent all their time moving their assorted supplies and troops from one safe location to another safe location. Kev wished one sad fact were not so, but, he'd seen it all too often. To Kev it seemed that too many of them, should they hear a shot fired in anger, turned tail and ran just as fast as they possibly could. Of course, Dust-Off also flew Hueys. However, the Scouts knew them to be a breed apart.

Again, Kev sincerely wished his feeling about most slick drivers were more positive. His feelings were frequently reinforced when he was wandering down a line of slicks waiting at a staging field for a mission. Often, he saw sights which made his blood stop flowing and freeze solidly in abject horror. When he examined their door guns, more times than not, he saw rust on them! From the point of view of a Red Bird, this was an unforgivable sin. Someone who is ready for and willing to deal with trouble would never have a rusty door gun. Maybe he only saw it a couple of times. However, his mind multiplied it beyond its reality.

Having recently played a slick driver, the rusty weapons he saw greatly bothered him.

146

"Maybe," he thought to himself, "I should take a closer look at my negative evaluation of my friends? However, I listen to the tales told in the club. If they should get shot at, they make it sound like the world ended. After the rivers of beer start flowing through our little club, their war stories are even more outrageous than ours. I wonder how they win the war with rusty door guns?"

He reflected sadly.

"I would be a rich man if I had a nickel for every time I have heard one of these guys refuse a resupply mission just because the LZ was hot."

It seemed to Kev, from his limited experience, that if the bad guys are shooting, the LZ was too hot for the slick drivers to handle.

On the other hand, the young men flying with the Red Birds got shot at almost every day. That's what the Aero Scouts did. As regular as clockwork they got shot at. That's how they earned their flight pay and their combat pay. They flew around fat dumb and happy playing target for every kid drafted into the North Vietnamese army. As strange as it may have seemed to the outsider, many gun-birds went for days on end without hearing a shot fired in anger. Again pondering his world, Kev reflected.

"I suppose that I am being unfair. The pilots can't hear anything when enclosed in the cockpit of a Snake with their air conditioner running full speed."

However, the kids in the Red Birds heard almost every shot which was directed at them. They saw almost every muzzle flash. Inconceivably, a couple of them have had the horror of feeling the muzzle blast of a hidden antiaircraft gun drumming upon their pants' leg. Kev had learned that the world of the Red Birds was a far different place and experience than the world of most of the helicopter drivers in Vietnam.

When flying the Red Birds, "it" was bound to happen. The truth is that getting shot at, was what these young men and boys seem to do best. The proof of this statement could be found down at the Red Bird Nest. When a person took a moment and looked carefully at the flock of little birds, the evidence jumped out at them. All of them had multiple patches made out of scientifically flattened beer cans. The overworked folks in Maintenance had this drill down to a science. Stomp the ole Budweiser can flat, she was ready to go. Pop-rivet the can, or cans, properly into place and the hole is patched. Then, finish painting them with bright green zinc chromate paint. There you are. Presto, it was good as new. Now to be fair to the maintenance guys, they did the best they could. When they were really living high off the hog, and if it was available to maintenance, their repairs got fancy. Then the little birds would get a little olive drab paint dabbed over the bright zinc chromate.

Adding a little more depth and color to this picture was the condition of the plexiglass bubbles. A casual observer didn't have to look very hard while walking about the little birds to see something quite thought provoking. Most of the, Budweiser can-patched, little birds also had nice little round holes in the plexiglass. What was most amazing, to those who flew these little birds, was the vast number of places a bullet could "safely" strike a Red Bird. That is, the number of strikes the little bird could take without destroying the aircraft and/or wounding a crew member. Sometimes, when taking a good look into the cockpit, one could see an entrance hole in the lower plexiglass and an exit hole in the upper plexiglass.

Upon close examination, it looked as if the bullet, which made the holes, should have gone through the pilot's head. However, most of the pilots were looking out the door as the bullet made its journey through the cockpit. Yet, when some pilot played "connect the dots," so to speak, it occasionally did some serious damage to his psyche. Writing to Pastor Bill, Kev once commented about playing "connect the dots."

"I promise you, having experienced this exciting little game of connecting the dots between little holes in plexiglass rattles me. Thinking about it definitely has me mumbling to myself for days on end."

As Kev discovered, the law of averages would eventually catch most Aero Scouts. It was simply bound to happen. If someone choose to play in the big leagues, someday one of the guys on the other team was going to throw a fast ball straight at his thick skull. Kev would ask people to think about the world of the Red Bird for a moment. How often could a pilot come home unscathed with the wind whistling merrily through newly created holes and assorted fluids leaking out of his little bird? Eventually, it happened to him. How often could he blindly go charging in to protect his lead bird as the lead tried to evade ground fire? How often could he willingly take on heavy antiaircraft weapons to protect the lead bird while he ran for his life?

At first blush, the questions may seem foolish and even rhetorical to the seasoned Scout pilot. However, they were not. How often could he deliberately go slowly trolling around as a big fat slow target trying to draw fire from the bad guys without incident? Yet, these troubling questions didn't change Kev's romantic commitment. Ole Kev never complained about being a Red Bird. He couldn't conceive of doing anything else while he served his tour in Viet Nam. Eventually though, even the dumbest Scout pilot found himself in a cold sweat while he made his morning walk down to the flight line. With a start and a catch in his throat he eventually comes to the painful realization that it was bound to happen. If it doesn't happen today, then maybe, it will happen tomorrow. Nevertheless, it would happen. It happened.

A few days later, Kev wrote about it to Pastor Bill.

A wondrous unexplainable thing is taking place here. I am not sure that I can adequately explain this strange mystery. Whatever it is, it is not the stuff of cheap paperback novels or a novelist vivid imagination. I also know that it isn't the stuff of ivory tower thinking or a PH.D. in Political Science. Nor, for that matter, is the mystery the stuff of a preacher's pulpit, as important and meaningful as your sermonic stuff has been for me over the years. For sure, it is not the stuff of a careful accountant's clean and clear column of numbers or some lawyers guardedly reasoned thinking. Nevertheless, whatever this unexplainable mystery is, it is! It exists and it is real!

Maybe some can never understand this mystery if they have never heard the call "Red Bird Down." Possibly, even if a person has heard the call Red Bird Down or a call similar to it, unless he is the Red Bird down, it remains a mystery. I suspect that it is only when someone is the Red Bird which is downed can he learn something and experience something uncommon. What this person learns is something that very few men or women ever have the opportunity to discover. I believe that this person then experiences the new truth of the Bond of Brothers. Within the trauma of those moments the experience forever carves something new, and yes even wonderful, upon the heart and soul. The downed Red Bird discovers what has been, as if by some form of divine magic, created within this extraordinary volunteer group.

Trapped in the unnatural world of being on the ground, the pilot's world is illogically stood upon its head. Unwilling trapped in a strange world, the downed pilot begins to learn. He learns that most incredibly and most unreasonably, that in this day, age, and place, people are willing to die for their brother. Or, at the very least, they are willing to put their lives at great risk for the downed Red Bird. It is true, and as a Red Bird, you've done it yourself several times for someone else. Like any other good Scout, you've hung it all out for your buddy. It did not matter if he were a nameless grunt on the ground. You didn't even think much about it at the time. As I have stated before, that is what a Red Bird does. He is no longer a self-centered child. Suddenly, in a fearsome upside down world, you find that you are the Red Bird who is downed. However, when you have become the "Red Bird Down," it is a new ball game. As the downed pilot, you begin to walk the seemingly endless miles back to the dugout. While trudging along, you are hoping to catch a ride home after striking out on a high hard one.

Well . . . , so much for my supposed heroics. I would prefer to weave and color a spellbinding story about how I was shot down in smoke and flames during my heroic last stand. A last stand, I might add, where I had fought, the countless godless hoards, to my last bullet. Ole Kev would love to weave a tale of a chivalrous last stand where he made the world safe for democracy and the American way of life. Or at the very least, I would like to tell a tale of a spirited last stand where I saved a fair damsel in distress. Obviously, such a dramatic romantic explanation would be completely acceptable to me. I fear to report that my recent walk

149

back to the dugout, after striking out, wasn't particularly glorious. As a point of fact, one might say that I suckered on a slow curve ball that I couldn't have hit with a cricket bat the length of broom stick. Well . . . , strike three and suddenly I was walking back to the dugout. Walking back, I might add, with my head hung in shame and my tail neatly tucked between my legs.

Kev's sad story of suckering on the slow curve ball had a quiet and humble beginning. During the course of the morning, the two little birds had been snooping around a familiar little valley. The two of them had visited that neighborhood often. After about a half an hour, the evidence convinced both of them that good number of bad guys were hanging out in the valley. Try as they might, they could neither find them nor convince them to come out and play. Using all the tricks that they knew, the two of them still could not entice the bad guys to come out and play. As the day wore on and they were deep into their second mission, Kev found himself rapidly losing his edge. The day was calm, warm, humid, and it had developed a quiet soothing rhythm. One might have called it a sleepy tropical day which someone had lifted directly from a dime novel. Ole Kev, safely swaddled in his chicken plate, was almost asleep in his slowly moving helicopter. It was not surprising that he was getting a little bit drowsy.

Unexpectedly, Kev's radio drove something shocking and painful through his emotional synapses. It felt like the smashing and flesh searing impact of a hundred thousand volt jolt of electricity driving itself into every nerve fiber of his body. Without the benefit of a gentle pre-amble, he was shocked into burning wakefulness. His whole body quickly overflowed with a brimming charge of urgently injected adrenalin. Abruptly, Kev's heart pounded and every nerve stood on vibrating edge. Lead's controlled, yet also semi-panicked cry, accomplished Kev's physical and emotional transformation.

"Taking fire,"

Two words shattered the sultry stillness of both the setting and of his drowsing soul. Trained instinct and repetitive practice took over. Kev frantically stomped on his left pedal to bring the mini-gun to bear under lead's bird.

Kev's only thought was to offer his lead bird protective fire. At the outer edge of his vision, he also saw a rippling series of bright red-orange muzzle flashes. Before the unnerving sight could even make its shocking electronic impression upon his now frantically awakening brain, his own quiet little world exploded. One of the bad guys had fired a full thirty rounds from an AK-47.

"This isn't fair," Kev thought to himself.

"This bad guy is breaking the rules."

He was shooting directly at Kev, his observer Joe, and his little Red Bird! Deep in the recesses of Kev's brain he was stunned, shocked, and surprised.

"This is not how it is supposed to be done. He is supposed to be shooting at lead!"

The result of the bad guy's marksmanship was two new holes artfully making their appearance in the plexiglass between Kev's observer and himself. The bullets entered and the bullets exited. For the moment, it appeared that the bullets entered and exited without doing any damage to either Kev or his observer. Well at least, they did not appear to do any physical damage.

Two startled Red Birds immediately dropped their noses and pulled in power. They quickly exited the suddenly unfriendly neighborhood. It was time to regroup and to rethink their strategy. Lead checked himself out first. Finding that neither he nor his two observers were any worse for the wear, he informed Kev of his positive status on the radio. Kev and his observer Joe also did a quick inventory in the cockpit and then of their bodies. All the engine instruments remained in the green, exactly where they had been all day. There seemed to be no new or strange noises coming from the power-train. So they decided that the transmission and rotor systems were O.K. Finished with the aircraft, both the excited young men quickly completed comprehensive, personal inventory of their bodies. They couldn't find any places that hurt which hadn't been hurting when they first took off. Further encouraging them, they didn't appear to be leaking any vital body fluids. Therefore, they decided that they were OK.

Neither Joe nor Kev had a degree in higher math so they didn't consider taking their pulses. Silently, the two of them concluded that they couldn't possibly comprehend such large numbers. Speaking to Joe Kev made his own observation about his pulse rate.

"I don't know about you Joe, but I cannot count that high with my boots still on my feet. I need all my toes if I want to count that high."

Kev then keyed the mike.

"Joe and I are doing fine. We've got a couple of new holes in the plexiglass. However, we've escaped any serious physical damage. If you're ready to to go back in, we'll follow."

Because the two of them were young, foolish and manly Cav people, they could not allow themselves to give lead a report on their physic condition.

Given their emotional condition had either of them the brains which God should have blessed them with at birth, their radio call would have been different. They would have requested to return to the staging base. Once at the staging base, they could have completely check out the little bird for further damage. Nobody would have thought the worse of them for that act of common sense. That was what they were supposed to do. It was SOP to land as quickly as practical after receiving battle damage. Upon landing, they could then make sure that they had not missed any vital damage to the helicopter. Everyone in the troop understood that having the helicopter fail in the middle of a firefight due to some unseen and unknown battle damage was stupid. Of course, the two young men were young and foolish. More important, they did not want anyone to think that they had just been scared spitless. Given their current mindset, they were asking for trouble. Wanting people to say that the two of them had more guts than brains, they decided to continue with the mission.

Not that the issue was in doubt, however, the two young men confirmed their absence of brains with that decision. By continuing their mission, they proved that neither of them was fully competent to continue the mission. Lead then decided to enter the valley by the back door to surprise the bad guys. Nerves strung just as tautly as a high "C" piano wire, Kev dutifully followed him into the little valley. His primary job remained the same. The mission of the wing bird continued to be providing cover and protection for the lead bird. By this time, Kev had been flying the wing bird for a couple of months and he had proved his growing competence. If he were assigned a good observer, he was confident enough to let his observer do a little snooping. Without needing the observers help, Kev could maintain the watch over the lead bird by himself. For this mission, Kev had Joe flying with him as his observer. They didn't fly together often, but Kev knew him to be an excellent observer. Therefore, he had great trust in him and his judgement. This was where things really began to get brown and smelly for the two of them!

Kev continued in his letter to Pastor Bill.

Given his experience and my relative inexperience, I was confident in his abilities. When Joe asked me to slide a fifteen or twenty feet to the left, his side of the aircraft, I followed his directions. Stupidly, without even looking, and clearing myself, I did exactly what he asked me to do. What happened next is strictly Kevin Paul Johnson's fault. I was the pilot. I was the so-called boss of the bird and responsible for our safety. Well . . . The Cav held that I was the responsible party. Looking back, I wasn't necessarily intelligent enough to be responsible. To be honest, I was not at all responsible. My brain had up and gone on an extended vacation. Half in shock, I was still stuck deeply pondering the meaning, and the cosmic significance, of the four little holes that had suddenly appeared moments earlier in my plexiglass.

It would seem that Kev had sufficient adrenalin pumped into his loudly singing nervous system. Unfortunately for him, he was about to go into a total emotional and physiological overload. Without warning, he heard horrible loud grinding, crunching, shredding noises. A pronounced pitching up of the tail of his lovely Red Bird accompanied these wretched noises. The gruesome sound of wholesale destruction instantly broke his heart. Furthermore, it didn't do his pilot's ego any good either!

Instantly, he became sick to his stomach. It wasn't horror which turned his stomach. No, it was the realization that he had committed a bone-head mistake. Well . . . , Kev needed to have only one synapse slowly snapping in his seldom used brain to know exactly what a bonehead mistake he had just committed. When moving those few feet to the left, Kev had created his latest disaster. He had gloriously and successfully managed to put the tail rotor of his little bird into the middle of a big ole hardwood tree.

With a brokenhearted groan of emotional, psychic, and egocentric pain, he knew the natural result of such seldom seen stupidity. His little helicopter had magically become Uncle Sam's newest one-hundred-thousand dollar vegamatic! What was taking place behind him was exactly as he had seen demonstrated on national television advertisements. Unwillingly, he looked to the rear of the helicopter. Much to his horror, but not to his surprise, he saw a fountain of shredded green stuff spitting in all the directions of the compass. This shredded, chopped, and carefully mixed green stuff was rapidly spewing forth from the Red Bird's little high speed tail rotor. However, there was one startling difference from the television ads. In this case, Kev was not smiling as he flew the self-destructing latest kitchen wonder of the modern mechanical age. He had not planned on making hardwood salad.

Continuing with his confession of stupidity to Pastor Bill, Kev explained what was happening.

Obviously, I don't know what you may have read in the past. Nor do I know what glorious aviation wonders you have witnessed on your television set. Or for that matter, I do not know what your perceptions of helicopters are. However, one place exists where my little Red Bird is vulnerable, fragile, tender, weak, or all the above. The Loach's weakest point is the furiously spinning tail rotor. That is, the little tail rotor on my self-destructing helicopter. It was gloriously involved in a self-destructive orgy and serving as the focal point of my little Red Bird's spectacular imitation of a vegamatic.

With ever increasing horror I was aware that in a few seconds one of three things was going to happen. With more luck than I was enjoying, the tail rotor would run out of trees upon which to destroy itself. The second possibility, which was more likely, given the way my day was going, was that the tail rotor would not run out of trees. Therefore, it would succeed in its kamikaze mission against the tree. A more drastic possibility was that I would take out my handy, dandy government issue forty-five. With the pistol safely in hand, I would blow out what remained of my seldom used brains on the general principle of gross stupidity. At least, that would save the government the cost of a court's martial.

153

Fortunately, God apparently has a deep and abiding concern for drunks, fools, and scout pilots. At that moment, his recent display of flying skills convinced Kev that he was very over qualified for at least one of these three categories. Lest the reader be confused, Kev was not thinking that he was, in any shape or form, very over qualified as a scout pilot. Adding definition to his problem, he was stone cold sober. Reduced to near tears, he was repeatedly screaming a single word in his mind.

"STUPID — STUPID — STUPID . . ."

Thankfully, training, instinct, and the grace of God chose to intervene for him. Reflexively, he quickly lowered power and turned to the right hoping to get the little Red Bird safely on the ground in essentially one piece. Kev was aiming for a little clearing which he had just passed. Thinking to himself, (actually praying to himself) he believed that with a little luck he could make it to the ground before he experienced a total tail rotor failure.

All Scout pilots KNEW that if the tail rotor fails in the little Loach, the pilot is in very deep trouble. Tail rotor stall in his flight with ole Charley Bird had given Kev on the job training.. Further compounding his black comedy of errors, Kev had virtually no airspeed and was over some big ole trees. This situation put him in a great big heap of deep dark trouble. Thankfully, he was traveling down the hill and could ease the strain of the damaged tail rotor by lowering his power demands. Despite a reduction in his demands upon it, the little rotor was all but destroyed.

Loud mechanical mayhem was taking place at the end of his helicopter's tail. The death rattle of the tail rotor was causing Kev to grimace in horrific pain. The little high speed tail rotor was rattling, thrashing, thumping, screaming and generally threatening to tear itself free from the helicopter. Kev found that the shock of the moment reduced him to following pure instinct. He was not relying on his totally overloaded and completely shut down brain. The terrified young man hit the radio button on the cyclic stick with his thumb. Crying out in a panic-stricken voice, at least six octaves higher than his normal radio voice, Kev announced his plight to the world.

"Red One-Five is going in with a tail rotor failure."

The all-powerful need to preserve a little of his dignity as an Army Aviator had taken hold of Kev's brain. In a distant deep dark corner of his prehistoric brain, snugly submerged in the reptilian brain stem, a latent synapse slowly came to life. This slowly snapping synapse told him to be careful.

"Don't advertise, to all of creation, that you are an incompetent fool who is pretending to be a United States Army Aviator."

Nourishing this latent tendency of self preservation, Kev carefully limited the self incriminating information which he shared with the world. He had quickly come to the realization that there was no need to tell the whole world what had happened. It was sufficient that he knew that he had just shoved his tail rotor in the biggest tree in all of Vietnam. Kev also knew that the tree into which he had shoved his tail rotor was the biggest and meanest helicopter destroying tree in both the North and the South! As he descended toward the little clearing, Kev had another dismal thought.

"Through the power of one man's gross stupidity, I have just created the world's most expensive vegamatic!"

And so, he made his fateful radio call.

"Red One-Five is going in with a tail rotor failure."

That was Kev's last radio call for the day. Things were suddenly getting busier and busier in his little cockpit. Looking forward, he noted, with dismay, that there were several small trees in the little clearing. At best, he had marginal, tail rotor control. Adding to his woes, the ground had a steep slope upon which to land. He had not forgotten another imposing and important fact. How could he forget? He was playing an away game at ole Victor Charles' home field. Kev and his observer were no more than two klicks, about a mile and a quarter distance from ole Chuck. Acting unfriendly, he had put four little holes in the plexiglass. As Kev prepared to crash-land, he clearly remembered the appearance of the four little thirty caliber holes. Their magical and unnecessarily abrupt appearance was what began the nearly fatal shut down of his brain.

Totally ashamed because of his lapse of concentration, Kev later told Sven about the landing.

"I am not sure how we arrived safe and sound on ole mother earth. Thinking about it, I doubt that it was anything that I did that caused it to happen. Nevertheless, with a bump, a slide, and a scrape, I managed to get the battered little bird on the ground. The way my day had gone, I was surprised to manage it without any additional damage. For an instant, I almost smiled to myself. At least one thing had finally gone kinda of right."

"Now," he thought to himself, comes the interesting part."

Pausing to consider the situation, He continued.

"If my buddies in the gun-birds can keep the bad guys at bay, maybe we can manage to sling this bird out with one of our Hueys. The least I can do is bring her back home."

Anyone who cared to look would have seen how bad poor Kev was feeling. He would have hated to have destroyed what is left of his little Red Bird.

155

"After all," he continued to himself. "She is/was a very good bird."

To be forced to destroy her on the site would only have added additional hemlock to Kev's overfilled cup of misery. Kev wished that he could have said that the pilot who made the successful landing was exceptionally good. It would have been a soothing balance to his emotional tumult. Aware of the possibility of fire, he quickly shut off the fuel supply and shut down the master electrical switch. Shutting down the bird began the process of stopping the self-destructive dance from continuing its frenzied jitterbugging on at the end of his little bird's tail.

Pausing for a moment and taking a deep breath, Kev looked about and tried desperately to gather his few remaining wits. In shock, he realized that he didn't have the faintest idea if anybody knew where they were. Kev knew that his intimate encounter with the big tree had deeply rattled him. He thought to himself.

"God, I wish that I had part of my brain functional and on line. If I had just a little bit of a brain, I would have taken ten seconds and called command before I shut the bird down. Then C&C would know that for the moment, we are safe and bodily sound on the ground."

The young man knew that he was in deep trouble. He was not a grunt! Filled with foreboding, Kev's mind was filled with black thoughts.

"The Army hasn't trained me to play ball down in this league. Good Lord, my well-qualified and aggressive opponent, ole Chuck, is only about two clicks away. Then again, maybe he is behind the tree just to my right. I don't know where the heck he is. After all, this is his home field and he has already graphically shown me that he doesn't like me playing in his back yard."

However, Kev was sure that ole Chuck was ready, willing, and quite able to show him how they played hard-ball in the Vietnam division of the major leagues. Rearing back, Chuck had already put one fast ball just under Kev's chin getting his full, complete, and undivided attention! After the fast ball had throughly rattled him, ole Kev swung and badly missed the slow curve. With the next pitch, the completely rattled young man could easily strike out.

It would be a grave mistake to believe that Kev's brain mysteriously decided to begin normal function after he safely set the little bird on the ground. In his case, normal function was no longer possible! Kev's burned-out brain remained overloaded! Joe and Kev were both scared and totally out of their element. In fact, both of them were very very very scared. Accepting his command responsibility, Kev yelled to Joe to grab his M-60 and several belts of ammo.

"Meet me in the little depression directly in front of the helicopter."

Pausing for a moment, he added a post thought.

"Leave your helmet on until you arrive safely."

Kev didn't want him getting brained by the main rotor which was still turning at a good clip.

The wounded Red Bird may only have been a little helicopter with a light rotor system. Nevertheless, at speed, those spinning rotors will kill a man dead if they hit him on an unprotected brain bucket stuffer. Reaching beside his armored seat, Kev grabbed his little M-2 carbine and pointed it out the door opening. He had traded some of his treasures for the little carbine because he could stuff it beside his armored seat. For the moment, he was glad he had it. Like a good wing man, he was planning to give Joe cover during his run to the depression. Though, by this time, Kev admitted to himself, he was quite fearful about the possible results of his effort. The way his day had been going, nothing good would come of his effort. If he had to shoot, he feared he would miss the bad guys and probably shoot poor ole Joe in the back. Fortunately, Joe made it safely to the depression and set up his M-60. It was Kev's turn to leave the broken bird. Remembering to leave his helmet on, holding his carbine in his right hand, he leapt out of his broken helicopter. Ole Kev was unwittingly emulating his greatest John Wayne "over the top" mode!

Wham! Slam! Crushing blinding pain! Suddenly, Kev's whole right arm went instantly, totally, and completely numb. The smashing impact of something truly awful threw him to the ground. Bewildered, befuddled, baffled, and afraid he lay upon the ground. Mostly stunned, he struggled to understand what had happened.

Groaning he wondered, "what else can go wrong?"

As he gathered his bearings, he continued.

"After all this, I've been shot. I think?"

His head slowly cleared and the fog of his confusion began to slowly dissipate. Amazed, he discovered that he was in one piece. Still somewhat bewildered, Kev slowly looked up while his eyes came into focus. Thankfully, at least Joe seemed OK. As of yet, the bad guys hadn't shot him. Unaware of Kev's problem, good ole Joe was still carefully watching the tree line. Dutifully, Joe remained intently covering Kev till he could join him. Still unable to move his right arm, Kev noticed his little carbine lying a couple of feet away. As he slowly reached for it with his left arm, he discovered a deeper sense of horror. Slowly and painfully, it dawned upon him what a complete idiot Mrs. Johnson's little boy had turned out to be!

He quietly muttered to himself, noting that he was a total fool and a complete idiot.

"Good Lord! I can't believe it!"

With indescribable horror, he was disgusted to note that the barrel of his carbine was bent about forty-five degrees! This whole situation had become absurdly unbelievable. For the moment, Kev refused to believe what he knew to be true. While Kev was doing his John Wayne impression and leaping out of the broken little bird, he topped his vegamatic routine. Reaching new heights of gross human stupidity, he managed to add an insult to injury. As horrifying as it was to him, when he was leaping from the helicopter, he had stuck the carbine into the still turning rotor system.

The grim horror and black irony of his day was threatening to destroy what remained of his brutalized psyche.

"Now," he thought bitterly to himself, "would truly be an exceptionally good time to quit. This is the last straw. If I had any dignity, I ought to blow my brains out with my handy, dandy government issue forty five and do the world a favor."

Yet, a great fear arose concerning that plan to regain his sense of honor.

"I'll probably screw that up too. Somehow, someway, and undoubtedly very creatively, I'll only manage to grievously wound myself. Therefore, I'll succeed in becoming a greater burden on the war effort."

The humbled, ashamed, and totally mortified young man groaned with an emotional and psychic pain beyond measure! Red One-Five wanted to crawl into a hole and die unseen. Nothing in all his years came close to this on his humiliation scale. On a scale of one to ten, Kev was sure that he had reached a hundred in humiliation and mortification!

"God bless Joe," thought Kev.

The young observer brought the first ray of sunshine into Kev's dismal black night. He pretended not to notice the latest of Kev's bonehead stunts. Kev was deeply thankful for the "nonobservance" in that seemingly endless string of total brain failures. Scuttling along in a crab-like crawl, Kev made his way over to him. Settled into the little depression, they were back to back.

"How utterly ironic," Kev bitterly thought to himself.

"I've finally made one of my great dreams happen. I've created my own glorious last stand. It's two against the world! If this is what I wanted, how come today feels like a nightmare?"

Settling in a little deeper, Kev took his watch over his 180 degrees. Bless his soul, Joe didn't say anything about the carbine which Kev so abruptly modified for shooting around corners. Laying out his two fragmentation grenades and loading a bullet into the chamber of his forty-five, Kev Whispered the next logical question.

"Joe, is there any evidence of the bad guys?"

A blessed one word answer was directed to the heart of all Kev's current anxieties.

"Nope."

The feeling began to return to Kev's right arm. Looking down to the right side of his battered body, he could detect no substantial damage, at least to his arm. Kev then did a quick inventory of his ego. Finishing the inventory, he muttered in self-directed rage and frustration to himself.

"I can honestly say that no one has bruised my carefully nurtured ego. My stupidity has not bruised it at all! At this critical juncture in my personal history, my stupidity has destroyed me. I am little more than a scared lost little boy with a totally shattered ego. Kevin Paul Johnson is a useless piece of dog turd."

Poor Kev was feeling so bad, so stupidly useless that, for a fleeting instant, he even thought of welcoming death or capture. It seemed to him, at least for that passing moment, that capture would be preferable to facing his peers. Death, that would solve all his problems. Without even closing his eyes, Kev could clearly hear the bitter laughter from the Officer's club ringing in his ears. Though he had been in country about three months, he was still considered a "new guy" by the older hands. With that in mnd, he was sure what tonight's conversation at the club was going to be like.

"Hey, did you hear what ole Kev did this time? No, tell me, what did ole Kev manage to do this time? Well . . . , he stuck his tail rotor into the biggest helicopter eating tree in all of Vietnam. What a newbe jerk!"

He could only pray that Joe would keep his mouth shut about the carbine.

Two or three minutes quietly passed. Much to their surprise, Joe and Kev found that they were still breathing, alive, and most surprising of all physically unharmed. The expected yellow hoard from the north had yet to arrive and bury the two of them under their onslaught of gross numerical superiority. It was blessedly quiet. As the racing beat of their hearts slowed, they found that their new world was uncomfortably quiet. Listening carefully, they could hear the lead bird searching for them a little to the north. Looking up, they could also see the snakes slowly circling high overhead.

Thinking about their plight, it was deathly quiet. It almost felt like the quiet before the storm. Were they to be honest with themselves, their plight had left them feeling like two lonely and very scared little boys. Maybe it would have been a little bit better for them to have known exactly where the bad guys were and what they were up to. Maybe the waiting for the unknown end was worse than the end itself when it finally comes. The two of them found that they had too much time to think and ponder after all the excitement of the last few minutes.

No words passed between the two of them. Without the sharing of a single sound, Joe and Kev made a silent vow. Young and male they still had their ego's with which to contend. They were in Asia, and should they survive, they needed to save face. While listening to the drone of lead looking for them, Joe asked a question and made a confession. He had been too scared to notice at the time if Kev had made a radio call while they were crash landing. Kev quietly responded to Joe's question.

"Yep, I told them that we were 'going in with a tail rotor failure.'"

Joe simply grunted in response. He did not need Kev to remind him that he was the one who coached them into the tree. A sympathetic Kev could only hope that Joe's memory did not make him feel as bad as Kev did. As God was his witness, Kev was not blaming him one little bit. Nope, ole Kev was going to accept full responsibility for this one.

"However," he thought to himself, "if no one asks, I'll be very happy. I for one, am not going to volunteer any extra information about the recent events."

Following an inner sigh, Kev continued his inward conversation.

"After all, both Joe and I can agree that the tail rotor did fail. As far as I can see, no need exists for us to go into the trivia and minutia which were the cause of the failure! I didn't lie when I said 'tail rotor failure.'"

Little doubt existed in Kev's mind about Joe's intentions. Joe was not about to volunteer any extra information either. Kev was glad that the two of them had respect for each other. That meant that they were not going to waste any time or effort laying blame on each other's doorstep. Furthermore, neither of them was totally stupid. They weren't about to volunteer, to God, and everybody else their method of inventing the U. S. Army issue one-hundred-thousand dollar vegamatic.

Lying back to back, the two young men could hear their lead Red Bird getting closer and closer. They had no way of knowing if a Snake had seen their poor little bent and broken bird as she fluttered to the ground. Hopefully, the circling Snakes had already seen their little bird lying broken upon the ground. The Cav painted the tops of the dog houses and the 45 degree tail stablizer day-glow orange for just that reason. This made it easier for the Snakes keep track of the Red Birds. Also, because everyone knows that it eventually will happen. Kev decided, listening to the pattern of his search, that lead had a good idea where they were. For the moment, lead was carefully scouting out the area between Kev and Joe and the place where they last saw the bad guys.

Kev's mounting anxieties and fears wished that lead would come running directly to them. If only to make sure that the two of them were all in one piece. Just as Kev's anxieties and fears mounted to the point of an impending explosion, lead suddenly popped up over the trees and flew directly over them. He made no indication that he had seen the two young men. The lack of acknowledgment didn't surprise Kev and Joe. Lead wasn't supposed to help the bad guys find them by hovering directly over them. At last, Kev and Joe knew the score. That made them feel a little bit better. They knew that their lead bird had seen them. Help was on the way.

Suddenly, life seemed terribly ironic to Kev. The electrifying call "Red Bird Down" had already resounded and reverberated throughout the staging field. The two young men knew that the back up teams of Red and White Birds were in the air. Having been there, they knew that the back-up teams had pulled the engine power gauges all the way to the red line. They also knew that the four or five troop carrying slicks were waddling to take off. Kev and Joe were comforted that the Slicks were fully loaded with their twenty-five grunts armed and ready. However, the tension felt by the two young men was becoming almost unbearable. Quivering with anticipation, they knew that it was only a matter of time before their salvation arrived. Best of all, they knew that nothing in all creation would be allowed to stop their saviors. They felt this assurance because, for the Cav, the rest of the war had been placed on standby status. That status would not change until they had recovered the downed Red Bird.

While they huddled fearfully in their little depression, the two young men remained hopeful because they were the Cav. They had done the same recovery drill several times. While comforted, another thought troubled them. Both Kev and Joe knew that they were very scared. They briefly talked about going back to the bent bird and getting some more ammunition for the M-60 and a few more grenades. Deciding that it was quiet and that there was no need to take any unnecessary chances by exposing themselves to the unknown, they sat tight and kept their mouths shut. All that remained was for them to do was to wait patiently and say their quiet prayers. Each of them was hoping that the other didn't know that he was praying.

Well trained, the lead was doing his job properly. He had returned to where the two Scouts had last encountered the bad guys. If he had stayed above them to give them cover and support that would cause a problem. He would have served as a magnet drawing every bad guy who had eyes to see and ears to hear to them. Lead purposely chose to move away. Doing so, made it less likely that the bad guys would know exactly where the two young men were. If they are exceptionally fortunate, the bad guys will not even know that they went down. Lead was following good tactics and theory. However, the presence of lead and his M-60 machine guns would have comforted Kev and Joe.

For the two young men on the ground, the sun was warm and a balmy breeze was blowing gently over the two of them. In another setting, it would have been a perfect time and location for a quiet summer's snooze. Their pulses eventually descended a little below the two hundred mark. Understandably, their normative safety felt exceptionally good for the moment. Eventually, the slight hint of the quiet drowsiness they enjoyed prior to the four little holes appearing in their plexiglass reappeared. They were not really drowsy, per say. However, after their swimming in adrenalin for the last forty-five minutes, they were close to being relaxed. Such post excitement feelings were understandable. Kev and Joe were assured that the call "Red Bird Down" had gone out and the whole troop was responding. Considering that they were still on the ground, all was almost well with their part of the world. Looking toward the little bird, Kev decided that maintenance could probably fix it. Luck had been with them. They suffered no injuries other than to their brutally savaged pride and ego. Best of all, they knew that help was only fifteen to twenty minutes distant.

Some things never change in the world of aviation and aviators. For any and all airplane drivers, being stranded on the ground is always a very different and a very scary situation! Aviators are not grunts. Suddenly, not much more than a klick away, their balmy tropical solitude was abruptly broken. The two of them clearly heard the sharp staccato bark of an AK-47 fired on full automatic. Then in response, they heard the slower return fire of an M-60. To their heightened senses, both weapons sounded as if they were only feet away. Day dream time was quickly and violently ended. With another large shot of adrenalin being directly injected into their blood streams, they came completely alert. Obviously, lead had found some bad guys on the move. It also seemed reasonable that they were heading in Joe and Kev's direction.

Looking to the friendly skies, they saw the two Snakes begin their firing run. Their strange viewpoint surprised them. Snakes at work and play looked very different from the ground. From their new perspective, the dance of the Snakes remained a deadly and beautiful aerial ballet. Yet, a more private fearful feeling was quietly injected into the dance when they saw it from the dance floor. The feeling took on a personal quality. No longer was it a lovely aerial ballet watched from a safe professional distance. As the Snakes fire their rockets, they could hear each individual 2.75 inch rocket ignite in its pod with a loud crack. Following the crack of ignition, they listened, and watched. The deadly rockets streaked purposely, followed by their trailing smoke, toward the ground. After the last few minutes of silence, the violent explosion of their ten pound warheads was incredibly loud making the earth shudder. The two of them could also hear the mini-guns firing. Unable to hear the firing of the individual rounds, it sounded to them like the ripping of heavy cloth. All the destructive commotion was too close and personal for comfort. With the Snakes firing into the trees just before them, suddenly, a thousand meters was not very far away.

Fearfully fascinated, the two young men carefully shifted their positions without sharing a word. Silently, they acknowledged the changing situation. Facing the direction in which the other aircraft were engaging the bad guys, they waited and hoped. They were no more than a foot apart in the little depression which they currently called home. In preparation for the worse, Kev carefully examined the belted brass bullets. He may not have been a grunt. However, he knew that these little bullets must feed freely into the M-60 should they need to defend themselves. Without a spoken word, their status positions were reversed.

Though they were still a team, Joe now took on the role of leader and Kev became the supporter. Joe had the machine gun. Joe had months of experience using it. All Kev had to contribute were two grenades, his trusty, dusty, rusty forty-five and a day's worth of bonehead mistakes. Alone and afraid, some things did not need to be expressed with words. The two of them knew that Kev would follow Joe's direction on the ground as quickly as Joe had followed Kev's in the air. Theirs was neither the time nor the place to stand upon rank and position. The two young men were Cav men and Aero Scouts. They were wise enough to allow skill and experience to chart their course. Now was the time to concentrate upon survival, not status.

For a fleeting moment, Kev pondered the value of his skill and experience. Evaluating himself, he could only hope that Joe didn't know how truly scared he was. Now that the proverbial fat was in the fire, he cursed each and every cheap paperback novel that he had ever read. He swore, that if he survived the day that he would never watch another John Wayne movie.

"Yes," he said to himself. "Like a fool, I dreamed of a dramatic last stand. Why didn't anyone tell me what it is like to be this scared and in way over my head?"

At this point, Kev felt so irrational with fear that his greatest fear was no longer death. A final blow threatened the young man's tattered and shredded dignity. He became gravely concerned that he was going to soil himself to top off his whole sad comedy of errors! Speaking to Sven later that evening, he said.

"Make no mistake about it, I fully believed that I had earned the right to soil myself today."

The noise generated by the Snakes protecting them was climbing to a crashing culmination. It sounded to Kev like the closing of a Wagnerian opera. Looking to the source of the protective noise, they watched in awe as the two White Birds were expending all their remaining munitions. In one loud smoky final pass, the rockets, forty

163

millimeter grenades, and mini-gun tore up the trees and ground. Less than a thousand yards in front of them, the earth trembled with the force of the multiple explosions of grenades and rockets. Providing a background to the thundering explosions was the high-pitched song of the ripping rippling fire of the mini-guns.

Both Joe and Kev hoped with all their combined heart and soul that nothing could possibly survive such an attack. However, the two of them had been around long enough to know better than that! At first, Kev was almost frozen in place with panic. He started thinking that hundreds of bad guys must be advancing through that hail of fire just to capture him, Mrs. Johnson's little boy.

Not wanting Joe to know how scared he was, Kev gathered his remaining wits about him and looked up. The sight of the second team of Snakes orbiting overhead surprised him. Reassured, he slowly let his breath out and stopped fidgeting with the M-60 ammo. An unstoppable yellow hoard wasn't charging them, yet. The first team of Snakes was only making sure that the bad guys went to ground and dug in for a little while. No point in the Snakes taking all those munitions home when they could put them to good use. Just as Kev was about to point out the new Snake team to Joe, the second team of Red Birds came roaring right over the top of them.

Quickly returning to the two downed scouts, the Red Birds began carefully searching out the area near and about them. They were making sure that the landing zone would be as quiet as possible for the Blue Birds. No one wanted any nasty surprises when they arrived with their valuable load of grunts. The fickle gods of good fortune had finally smiled upon Joe and Kev. No more than fifty feet away from the two scared little boys was an LZ which was large enough for two Hueys at a time. As Kev and Joe watched, the lead Red Bird carefully hovered down into the LZ. Very cautiously, he turned his little Red Bird 360 degrees about its axis. He did this so that his observers could look directly and deeply into the tree lines. Eventually, he satisfied himself that this was the best possible place to put the grunts.

The lead Scout, having chosen his LZ, marked it for the approaching troop laden slicks. When he did that, Kev heard the unique pop fizz of a smoke grenade being dropped into the clearing. Bright clouds of purple smoke began to billow out of the small olive drab canister. Gently driven by the prevailing breeze, they rolled along the ground like a gaily colored fog. It was so pretty that in another circumstance, Kev might have said that the circus was coming to town. Kev thought to himself.

"This can only mean one thing. The slicks are finally inbound with our rescue team."

As he took in the dramatic picture unrolling before him, he could almost hear the lead Red Bird's call on the radio.

"LZ marked with goofy grape."

Sitting in his stupidly chosen ringside seat, Kev found himself to be two people simultaneously. He was both submerged in and, in the same breath, totally out of his element. The situation was fulfilling part of his romantic nature. Red One-Five was the center of all the Cav's helicopter action. He painfully reminded himself that he was not flying. His mission has drastically changed.

"D----- Kev, watch the tree line in front of us. Pay attention! Start looking for bad guys sneaking in for a crack at the Blue Birds. After all, the two of us might very well be the perfect human bait for an elaborate helicopter trap. For God's sake, you do not want the Hueys to be ambushed just as they touch down!"

A little farther away, the second team of Red Birds and Kev's lead were still busily engaged with the bad guys. Without straining, the two young men could clearly hear the slow hammer of the M-60's mixed in with the sharp bark of AK-47's. The noise filled their ears while the second team of Snakes was preparing to roll in. Their purpose was the same as the first team. Put the heads of the bad guys deep into the ground. Putting the bad guys under fire was greatly slowing their advance upon Kev and Joe. In the deep recesses of his brain, the young man from the wrong side of the tracks in an old mill town was impressed. A whole Cav troop and more than a million dollars of equipment had been committed to his rescue.

In his candid letter to Pastor Bill, Kev commented.

I should have been thinking only of helping Joe keep us alive as we awaited our rescue. My whole being should have been highly tuned to a fever pitch, ready for the worse. Since we were on the ground, bad guys, who had escaped observation by the Red Birds, could still capture us. As the old saying goes, "we were, hardly, out of the woods." Escaping and evading the bad guys was the only place where my mind should have been. However, as had been my custom all day, my mind wondered as I tried to take in the whole air show unfolding for my benefit. This undisciplined wandering of the mind had been going on all day. It started when those four little bullet holes in my plexiglass derailed my thinking process. I had yet to get my mind back on track.

Eventually, I got my mind focused on the business at hand. In the distance, I could hear the deep thrumming of the main rotors of the Hueys carrying the grunts. I couldn't see them. Nevertheless, I could clearly hear them and follow their progress. From the sound, I decided that they must have been making a low fast approach. Such an approach made sense. The rest of the troop didn't know for sure why I was on the ground. Our Blue Birds didn't know if the bad guys on the ground were waiting in the LZ. However, they knew that much shooting was going on. They were showing great wisdom by being cautious. Like a great shimmering ghost, popping up over the ridge less than half a klick away, the lead slick suddenly appeared. He already had his nose pulled steeply back in his deceleration flare. Outlined against the sky, I could see that our troops were standing on the skids. The sight boggled even my vivid and colorful imagination. The picture only lacked bugles, pennants, and sabers to be completed. They were coming to save Joe and me.

"My God," Kev thought to himself.

Suddenly he had found himself submerged in yet another feeling of horror. He had never realized what a huge target a Huey made with his fat belly silhouetted against the sky. Seemingly, it was taking up the whole horizon. Once again, Kev took back every degrading thing he had ever said about slick drivers. He thought the worst and the best.

"Santa H. Claus, that slick is such a big fat target. Good Lord, even I could shoot him down with a bow and arrow. This slick driver, whom I have laughingly harassed and called a garbage truck driver has guts. He is exposing his vulnerably fuel-laden-belly into what is most likely a very hot LZ to save my raggedety butt. That, my friends, takes big brass gonads."

After the day's black comedy of stupid errors, Kev knew that Mrs. Johnson's little boy did not rate someone taking that much of a risk for him!

What happened next doesn't get written about in paperback war novels. For that matter, they don't depict it in "B" grade war movies. What was happening to Kev was not sufficiently macho for pulp novels and "B" grade movies. However, it was real and it was happening. He was having trouble seeing clearly. If Joe had noted his difficulty, Kev would have said that it was sweat falling into his eyes that were blurring his vision. Nevertheless, Kev knew better than that. The young warrior's eyes were filling and overflowing with huge tears. His throat was constricting. It definitely felt like he was about to cry. He was having trouble breathing. The reason for all this was as clear as a cold crystalline mountain stream to ole Kev.

Looking at the right skid, of the leading slick Kev was suddenly overwhelmed. Brightly colored Christmas lights and birthday cake candles were shining. Overarching the gay, holiday lights were countless rainbows. Christmas presents, birthday cakes, and Easter celebrations were wrapped up in a single package. Standing, completely exposed directly before his eyes, was the living symbol of his salvation. Suspended twenty-five feet in the air was the living miracle of the band of brothers. Standing on the Huey skid, twenty-five feet in the air, one hand holding his M-16 and the other holding onto the helicopter was Johnny. Disbelieving what his eyes were telling him, Kev knew what was going to happen next. Johnny had told him. Nothing could hold back the tears of joy, shame, and salvation when Kev saw Johnny.

The rapidly decelerating and descending helicopter was not going to touch the ground before the symbol of his salvation leapt into action. The grunts weren't going to wait that long. They knew the risk to the Huey. Before the big bird stopped and before it could touch the ground those wonderful fools were going to leap into the waist-high elephant grass. Kev wouldn't have leapt that distance on a bet. Nevertheless, they were going to blindly jump off into elephant grass, risking life and limb to save Kev and Joe. That was the type of people the highly focused young men were. Jumping off, risking life and limb was what they did. They were the Cav and they were going to reduce the exposure to enemy ground fire that the big fat Huey had on the ground. These twenty five young men were going to risk everything for their brothers.

Kev continued in his letter to Pastor Bill.

As I watched, slack-jawed and in awe, the first one to jump from the lead slick was good ole Johnny. Like a freeze frame film, I watched him fearlessly and purposefully push off from the relative safety of the helicopter. Frame by slow frame, I watched him slowly descending fifteen/twenty feet through thin air. As he drifted down, I watched him carefully gather himself for the shuddering impact with the hard earth. He hit the ground. He tucked and rolled once. Without pausing, even for the briefest of an instant, Johnny gathered himself with his M-16 at the ready. Like a very carefully staged play, he and his fellows raced in our direction. Without giving us more than a quick glance, all but Johnny raced right past us in the direction of the bad guys. First things first, they set up a defensive perimeter to protect Joe and stupid Kevin.

No one noticed anything special about me or about my condition. I doubt that anyone had the slightest idea of what was going on inside me. I don't think that I am ever going to tell anybody. My problem is that I don't know how to tell the story. How can anybody, who hasn't needed it, understand salvation? (That thought gives me a little better appreciation for the problem of preaching the Gospel!) Yet, I am also convinced that I was crying like a baby during this whole landing. Honestly, Pastor Bill, I can't remember much else after I saw the slow running freeze frames of Johnny's jump into nothingness. It's the truth. I can't remember seeing anything else after Johnny's squad ran past me. The rest of the troop insertion must have taken place. Other helicopters must have landed. Yet, I simply can't remember seeing the other three Hueys unload their troops. In fact, I don't even remember getting on the last bird for evacuation. Before you think that I totally blanked out with an emotional overload, I do clearly remember one life changing thing.

I remember Johnny sending his platoon to form a perimeter between us and the bad guys. He paused for a moment and made a life changing statement. **"I told you Mr. J., if you ever went down, I'd be the first one there . . . "**

A couple of days after Kev wrote the bulk of his letter to Pastor Bill, he added a postscript.

I've been thinking and I want to share a thought or two with you. Please feel free to respond. In truth, I would greatly appreciate your thoughts on this. I don't know if you would approve of my using the Bible this way but it has helped me. As Johnny spoke to me, I thought of the verse that you have often used. It goes something like this.

"Greater love has no man than this; that he lay down his life for his brother."

If it were not for the other day, I doubt that I would have ever understood. When Johnny leapt from that skid, it became clear!

My friend, I believe something powerful and possibly even Divine is at the center of this "Band of Brothers" experience. Whatever this wondrous thing I've experienced might be, I know that it defies human reason and simple explanations. This inexplicable thing, whatever one might wish to call it, happens. It even happens when a stupid fool like me tries to cut down the biggest, meanest tree in all of the Viet Nams with his tail rotor. Even in the midst of such unbelievable stupidity, his brothers will be there.

Pastor Bill, please allow me to add a postscript to my postscript. Under no circumstances let anyone read this little epistle! I have just proven that I am an incompetent jerk, buffoon, and all around general stupid idiot! Furthermore, I have proven that I do not belong anywhere near a machine anymore complicated that a dull spoon. Maybe another day, when I am older and no longer am concerned with other people's opinions, you can share this with someone.

A week later, the little Red Bird came out of maintenance with a new tail rotor and a new main rotor blade to replace the one Kev had bent! The guys in maintenance gave him a bad time but everyone accepted that such things happen in the Scouting line of work. That is everyone but Kev accepted it with good grace. He remained horrified at his own bone-headed stupidity!

Flying scouts in Viet Nam frequently reminded Kev of sailing upon the deep blue waters of his beloved Cape Cod Bay. His delight in such flying came from the addition of movement in a third dimension. When he first became an Aero Scout, someone had told him about the joy of playing with and in the winds. That more experienced Scout was right when he spoke about playing in the wind with the little Red Birds. Consequently, at times, Kev found it very difficult to accept that he was having fun in the world of Viet Nam. Looking about, he recognized, that the land was a paradox of self mutilation. He also acknowledged that his personal world was becoming a great paradox. He would kill, lest someone kill him first. Yet, he was having the time of his life! It was almost painful for him to admit that he sailed the winds with a broad smile upon his face. For young Kev, this totally innocent, childlike, enjoyment of sailing the winds was almost sinful. How could he smile so warmly in the face of all the death and destruction?

Coming from his working-class poor background, Kev had not had much opportunity to do much sailing. In fact he had not sailed nearly as often as he would have liked. Nevertheless, occasionally he did have the chance to enjoy sailing with a friend who had a small catamaran. He found it a soothing and delightful feeling to use and play with the wind. Prior to his first day's sailing, he had never thought of the wind as a childlike friend. However, in the wind, he discovered a playful friend with whom he could romp and childishly delight. When he could, he spent sunny afternoons running joyfully with the wind at his back. For Kev, sailing was a glorious experience. The sails, taut with a powerful unseen energy behind him, offered him a previously unknown freedom. That unseen power that set boiling froth at the foot of the bow, and left a white frothy churning wake behind the boat, was glorious. It filled him with a feeling of marvel and mystery.

Not surprised, Kev delighted in flying the wing bird and scouting around in the highlands. Flying and sailing with his lead bird was a wonderful way to make a living. That is, if he had to be in the midst of a war. Poking his nose into the many nooks and crannies in the rocks and little blind valleys became a captivating game of hide and seek. As a Red Bird pilot, he could enjoy playing the wind as he did his job. Ask any pilot. An honest pilot will say that flying is like deep restful sleep punctuated by startling nightmares. Flying Red Bird recon, like all other flying, consisted predominately of hours of soul stifling boredom.

Like other flying, being an Aero Scout, the pilot occasionally finds his idyllic time painfully disrupted by brief instances of stark raving terror! During the long hours of near boredom, Kev gratefully rediscovered that creative, yet invisible force, which readily brought a smile to his face. This was the force which flowed over the hills and gave him the updrafts, eddies, and swirling currents. He then became an experienced wing pilot spending countless hours playing his little games.

Enjoying the company of his invisible playmate, the wind, Kev was satisfied to allow the lead pilot to do his recon. When lead was poking around in a little depression, Kev caught the updrafts on the lea side of the surrounding hills. Playing in the winds, he seemingly floated around weightlessly using little or no engine power. The game had become a delightful contest. The object of this game was to see how much fuel he could take home at the mission's end. He did this by "gliding" and floating lightly around on and with the wind. It, the wind, became his friend and not his enemy. The game was harmless. It offered the young man a challenge while he kept an eye on the lead bird. In fact, the game offered Kev some useful training. More experienced pilots had told him that conserving power and fuel was a sound practice. They were looking toward the time when Kev's turn would come to fly the much heavier lead bird. It was heavier because it flew with two observers, two M-60 machine guns, more ammo for the M-60 than was carried for the mini-gun, and as many grenades and other explosive devices as could be crammed into the bird!

As to Kev's playing with the wind, he had seen what happened when Charley Bird had fought the wind rather than use it as a friend. Using the wind as a friend came as natural as breathing the same life giving wind.

With the passage of time, Kev became a competent wing man. As his competence increased, he also discovered that he loved flying the wing bird. This surprised him greatly, given his inner desire to play center stage in a great military drama. The romantic young man discovered a rare kind of military freedom which came with his mission. Possibly, it was the freedom which was born out of a lack of structure from a military text book. Flying the wing, Kev had but one responsibility and care.

If he took care of his responsibility, circumstance allowed him to play his little games with the flighty and fickle wind currents of the Highlands. His mission had been diligently and forcefully drilled into his young head by his combination friend and nemesis Lt. Simmons. Well trained, Kev quickly discovered that even in the midst of playing in the winds, his responsibility was very easy for him to remember. Expressed in its simplest form, it was Kev's never ending mantra as he flew his little bird.

"I live to keep the lead bird alive and well."

The division of labor pleased and suited Kev's desires. It was lead's responsibility to find the bad guys and then to fix them. If he were unable to fix them, then he asked someone else to fix them. The young man was thankful that it was also lead's responsibility to coordinate all the multifaceted happenings of their mission together. As the months passed by, Kev quickly saw that it took a long time to understand the many things which are involved in an aerial recon. Aware of his limitations, he was deeply grateful that it was his single-minded responsibility to keep lead alive. Given what he had learned about himself and his neophyte skills, Kev felt that he was in the right place. Sometimes, when he thought deeply about it, the lead's responsibilities overwhelmed him. When he did his deep thinking, he was thankful that all that was required of him was a trained reflex. Kev felt that he was not ready for the responsibility of flying the lead Scout. For the first time in his life, he had found a comfortable notch and ole Kev really liked things the way they were.

As with all good things, time continues its restless flow. Because of time's flow, things change. The months of flying, without his really noting their passing, had drifted into hoary history and he was no longer a newbe. Many older pilots had rotated back to the world. Their usual tour of duty was for twelve months; that is, unless someone volunteered to extend their tour in lovely Southeast Asia. With the natural evolution of things in lovely Vietnam, the Cav promoted experienced wing pilots up to flying lead slots. In turn, the Army replaced these wing pilots with much less experienced pilots. These less experienced pilots were the new batches of lost and confused newbes. Much to his personal dismay, it was now Kev's time to fly the lead bird.

Captain Grant, the Scouts' platoon leader changed Kev's world. The Captain was a wizened and ancient old trooper of twenty-two or twenty-three years of age. One day he pulled Kev aside and gave his the news of his unsought promotion to lead. Complain as he did, Captain Grant did not allow Kev to turn his promotion down. Unfortunately for him, young Kev's days of wine and roses had come to an abrupt end. Like it or not, as of that conversation with the Captain, he was going to have to earn his keep as a scout! From newbe, to wing man, to lead, Kev's changes felt like they were coming rapid fire.

Finding himself abruptly thrust into "Scout" adulthood took Kev by surprise. Adulthood was not as easy as he had thought it would be when he was a young teen. Assigned to fly lead Scout, Kev was painfully discovering that adult responsibility was not all that it had been cracked up to be. One of the strangest surprises of moving begrudgingly into adulthood was his changing relationship with Pastor Bill. He had found, in his former confirmation teacher, a man with whom he could share the strange and frightening experiences that were bombarding him on a daily basis. A few years earlier, Kev would not have dared to be so candid, honest, and forthcoming with his mentor and pastor. Pastor Bill remained his "Spiritual Mentor." However, he was fast becoming a dear friend and Kev's closest confidant. So, he wrote often, carefully sharing the confused thoughts and feeling that he did not dare share with his parents or anyone else he knew.

"Countless miles and many months separate us. My friend, let me affirm an important thing. My respect for you as Pastor, person, and friend has never changed. Rather, it only grows richer and deeper. I say this because we do deeply disagree about some things which are basic to my life. Yet, in the midst of disagreement, we still seem to draw closer."

It comes as no surprise that we stand on opposite sides of the dramatic issue right now. I have discovered that the moral issue of the U.S. involvement in our delightful little war is fraught with the potential of conflict between us. Pausing and thinking about our substantial differences, your letters sometimes surprise, but always, please me very much. I am deeply grateful that you are still interested in continuing our conversations. Thank you very much for that wonderful expression of trust and friendship. Even in this distant place, you are teaching me that friendship is an expansive and wonderful thing. It is much larger than I ever imagined it could be when I was a protected child at home.

It remains my heart felt prayer that these life and death issues, with which we struggle, have become the true cement to a deep and lasting friendship. Stepping back and looking from a neutral distance, I fear that we occasionally appall each other. The activities and beliefs, which we share in our letters, frequently separate us by distances far greater than the many miles between us. Yet, on the other hand, I do hope that we stimulate each other to seek deeper levels thought and understanding. I keep copies of what I write in my personal diary. Much to my surprise, I find that this new found discipline of writing has become very stimulating and forces me to think at a new and deeper level. Therefore, I still hope to put something in writing together on the other side of this year of combat. Dare I speak of the tomorrow that I look forward too?

"I pray that my writing will eventually become a book?"

Regrettably, my free and easy time of silently enjoying my flying and floating upon the unseen pillows of the air currents as a wing pilot, are ending. Red Six, Captain David Grant, my Scout Platoon boss, has informed me that he wants me to begin to fly as a lead scout. Acting just like a spoiled child, I dug my heels in and balked. (No responses are necessary or required , about my being a spoiled brat!) I argued, whined, and pleaded. Feeling desperate, I seriously considered throwing myself on the ground for a good bout of screaming and pouting. Strenuously, but in vain, I attempted to convince Captain Grant that the Red Birds would be wasting a great talent. By wasting a great talent, I mean, my self proclaimed and very extensive skills as the best wing pilot in all of Red Bird history. Try as I might, I could not convince him that it would be a criminal waste of a great talent if he converted me to lead.

Of course, my extensive carrying ons and highly creative pleadings turned out to be a completely wasted effort. The good Captain even told me, attempting to stroke my ever active ego, that I was too good a stick man to remain just a wing pilot forever. After that, The good Captain firmly declared that he needed me to fly lead. What a change that was from Lt. Simmons many negative comments not a few short months ago! Of course, the Captain's argument about needing me didn't change any of my childish ways.

Not withstanding his arguments, I continued my balking, pleading, and arguing. In the end, he drew his last ace from the bottom of the deck. He leaned back in his chair with a big smile dangerously spread upon his face. I should have been ready to be trumped. Having carefully set me up, he then told me that Johnny had agreed to rejoin the scouts and fly as my back-seater. Pausing, I thought for a moment. Then, I decided.

"If Johnny is willing to take a chance with me, I guess that I will also have to be willing to take a chance with me.

Working closer with him than he had before, Kev quickly discovered that his young platoon leader was a nice guy. He promised Kev an easy first couple of days as he learned the dos and don'ts of his new job. Knowing that he had lost the battle, Kev gave in,

"Ok Sir. You win. Just tell me what you want me to do and Johnny and I'll give her a shot!

Having been in-country nine months, Captain Dave was a highly experienced lead himself. Being a good leader, he then scheduled himself to fly Kev's wing for his first few missions. He did this to personally keep him from getting in too deeply over his head. As much as he dreaded it, Kev's day of reckoning eventually came. It was time for young Kevin Paul Johnson to lead the hunt. The Captain had assigned ole Red One-Five to run at the head of the hunting pack. However, Kev was grateful that Captain Dave was going to be right at his heels and protecting his back door.

He was totally confident that John Wayne would never have said such cowardly and disgraceful things about not being ready to fly lead Scout.. Not even within the private confines of his head would "the Duke" have thought such negative thoughts. The fact remained that a nervous Kev had secretly hoped that his wily and dangerous game would be on vacation for a few days. The newly hatched lead pilot knew that he would have his hands full just trying to fly the over loaded lead bird. It seemed to Kev to be both ironic and illogical, but, the more important of the two Aero Scouts had the least margin for error. The lead scout bird was the helicopter which had to fly the slowest. Frequently it was forced to hover out of ground effect. Ground effect, being a special kind of lifting force near the ground that requires less power to sustain flight. Because it carried a bigger crew and more munitions, Kev's lead bird would also be the heavier of the two birds. So, of course, it has the least excess power margin for this demanding kind of flight.

As much as he wanted to avoid the responsibility for the whole team, Kev's time had quietly crept up upon him. He shared his thoughts and self-doubts with his friend at the club the night before his first flight as a lead!

"Don't tell anybody, Sven. However, I am not at all convinced that I am ready for this job as lead. It seems as I was the stupid newbe yesterday and now I am a lead. Something is out of wack with this whole Vietnam war thing. It just don't make no sense. I tell you, things are going much too fast for Mrs. Johnson's little boy!"

Unable and unwilling to find a place where he could hide from his upcoming mission, ole Kev forced himself to waddle down to the Red Bird Line. Assuming that his perceptions was different from the other pilots, the picture he had of himself climbing into the little Red Bird for takeoff always amused him. He had told Pastor Bill about all the assorted equipment that they strapped on their bodies. Months had passed, yet, it still caused him to chuckle quietly when he looked at himself. A scout pilot going down to the flight line was quite a sight. He waddled down with a chicken plate, a flight helmet, 45 cal. pistol, a survival vest, emergency radio, personal camera, etc. (It seemed as if every pilot in Vietnam carried his camera with him when he flew.)

Kev was thankful that he didn't also have to wear a parachute like his heros strapping into their Spitfires and Hurricanes of the Battle of Britain. Loaded down as he was, he had enough trouble getting into the little helicopter.

Waddling down to the Red Bird nest, Kev discovered that Johnny was already at the helicopter along with the crewchief, Pete, who would be flying as the front seat observer. The experienced observer greeted ole Kev with a positive affirmation.

"Don't worry Mr. J. This is going to be a piece of cake. Pete and I have carefully checked her out. This ole bird is loaded, ready, and in tip top shape. Not to worry about a thing, Mr. J. AND! I haven't forgotten my promise to keep you out of trouble."

A bright red flush slowly crept up Kev's face as he savored the meaning of the promise. Johnny's words were filled with warmth and with the knowledge that he hadn't forgotten that he had assigned himself as Kev's personal guardian angel. The previous evening, Kev had told Sven that he was thrilled that the god's of aviation had assigned to him a guardian angel named Johnny. As he was talking, he then remembered that during Confirmation, Pastor Bill frequently spoke of God coming to people and being with people through other people. Still feeling the warm flush on his cheeks, Kev finally believed his old Pastor and friend. Somehow deep inside himself, he knew that God had taken enough interest in him to send him Johnny.

Musing to himself, Kev thought.

"God. I don't know what I ever did to deserve this kind of love and protection. However, I want to say two words about it. Thank you!"

174

As much as he wanted to, Kev could put it off no longer. It was truth time. Walking around the little bird he checked the fluid levels and kicked the tires in preparation to light the fire. Well . . . , he actually kicked the skids. Finishing his walk around inspection he climbed in, threw a couple of switches, and lit the fire. After the usual whomp of the little turbine lighting up, everything concerning the little bird checked out satisfactorily. All the gauges were in the green and ole Kev's big flying test could no longer be delayed.

An unknown and sharply pointed question had been haunting his professional well-being. His haunting question was simple to the extreme.

"Could Kevin Paul Johnson handle a heavy bird?"

Mr. Hughes of Hughes aircraft rated the OH-6A for a gross weight take off at two-thousand and fifty pounds. Usually, the Scouts flew the wing birds at the max military gross weight of two-thousand-four-hundred pounds. Someone had told Kev that they figured that the combat weight of a lead bird was roughly three-thousand-four-hundred pounds. Well . . . , while preparing for this flight Kev began thinking very grave thoughts.

"The book says that this bird won't fly carrying such a heavy load."

Kev quickly concluded that he was in very deep trouble. This disquiet had him muttering darkly to himself.

"So much for The Rev. Norman Vincent Peal's Power of Positive Thinking!"

Filled with less than positive thoughts, Kev began his first flight as a lead pilot. He started by pulling ever so gently upon the collective pitch lever. He was cautiously adding power and seeking the point of balance. Kev didn't need the helicopter lunging into the side of the sandbag revetment. With his mental fingers tightly crossed, Kev began his historic flight. The power gauges, torque and N1, swung up nearer and nearer to their red lines. At last, they stabilized. The gauges' message was clear. "That was all that there was and there was no more!" Wish as he might, no more power was available to him from the overworked little turbine.

If he even thought of pulling in more pitch with the collective, the main Rotor N2 R.P.M. would start bleeding off. Then, the low R.P.M. warning beeper would begin blasting into his ears. Everything stabilized and they just sat there in the revetment not quite ready to fly. The little helicopter was sort of dancing and tip toeing. Old 662 was not about to come to a six-inch high hover. Obviously, the struggling little bird refused to come to the three-foot high hover. The book instructed the pilot to maintain that hover before takeoff. Kev was beginning to think that he would have to lighten his bird. He muttered to himself.

"Throwing something out is the only way that this ham-fisted pilot can get it off the ground."

Suddenly his guardian angel spoke quietly and unobtrusively into his ear.

"Not to worry Mr. J. You've got her dancing lightly on her skids. Just hold your power steady and without really moving the stick, just think a touch of back stick. Believe it or not, this will slide her ever so slowly and gently backwards on the PSP toward the takeoff lane."

The Cav made generous use of PSP, Pierced Steel Planking, to create their parking spots, runways, and taxiways over the dirt and mud.

"Relax Mr. J. Trust me. This old trick works just as slick as whale poop. If she starts to hang a little bit on the PSP, just wiggle your tail rotor a touch or two, that will usually break her free."

Low and behold, to Kev's surprise, delight, and pleasure, Johnny's softly spoken recommendations worked perfectly.

"A most interesting situation," Kev thought to himself.

"In this highly structured military world, an enlisted backseat observer is telling an officer-pilot how to fly."

Again, Kev discovered that in the Red Birds, they often stood things upon their heads. Kev was beginning to believe that such cooperation and respect could only happen in the Red Birds. Whatever the case was, Johnny obviously knew what he was talking about. After a little bit of time, not to mention a couple/three gallons of perspiration liberally donated by Kev, he got her backed out. Somehow, he got her aligned, more or less, for a takeoff.

Despite his internal and vocal insecurities, Kev's assignment to fly lead thrilled him. To most people, it would be a little thing, maybe even meaningless. However, for Kev, it was an important part of overflowing world of romantic dreams. It might have even been vital. With the passage of the months, he had been slowly climbing the ladder of his dreams. Acceptance to flight school, flight school itself, assignment to the Cav, becoming a Red Bird, and then flying a combat aircraft had been steep steps.

Now, the Cav had assigned him his personal aircraft. Ole 662 now belonged to Kev. In fact, they had even stenciled his name on her side. WO-1 Kevin Johnson! He just had to get a picture, showing his name, with himself standing beside her. He was planning to get lots of copies for Pastor Bill, his folks, and everyone else he knew.

As usual, with his mind stuck in imagination overdrive, he was putting the cart before the horse. First, he had to return to the problem at hand. In great apprehension, he looked down the takeoff lane. It was one hundred and fifty yards, or four hundred and fifty feet in length. He noted sadly that it was not quite the ten thousand feet of concrete as used by the Strategic Air Command. Thinking about the short take off lane, increased his anxiety. Then, he looked carefully, dubiously, and fearfully at the four foot high rolls of barbed wire situated at the end of the takeoff lane. To add to his mushrooming sense of discomfort, he glanced past the barbed wire. In the close distance, he saw the utility line strung fifteen feet up in the air.

With an uncomfortable gulp from the cup of humility, Kev knew that the take off was going to be a major league struggle for him. In all his wide readings of war novels and in all the John Wayne movies he had seen, Kev could not remember the hero was struggling with his current options. As far as he could tell, ole Kev's primary options were limited to either throwing up all over his flight suit or emptying his bladder into his flight suit. Neither of these options thrilled him or came close of his carefully nurtured self image.

Carefully noting that his little helicopter was one half ton over max military gross weight, Kev was very unsure of himself. He was becoming very deeply troubled by the possibility of exercising both of the above mentioned options. Exercising either option was not the way that he would choose to begin saving the free world and American mother-hood! The magnitude of the problem was abundantly clear to him. He wasn't sure that the tired, old, and overloaded war bird, which wouldn't/couldn't hover, could clear the barbed wire. If he accomplished that impossible task, no way existed for her to safely clear the utility lines.

As his mind frequently did, it overloaded at the prospect and traveled south for the winter. Kev found himself hoping that when they told his parents that he died in a fiery crash on takeoff, they would end the tragic story there. He also prayed that the messengers of his ultimate demise would be brief. Most of all, Ole Kev prayed that they wouldn't tell his folks that he also killed two enlisted men due to his gross ineptitude as a pilot.

It seemed as if someone, who stood close by, knew Kev's needs before he did. As before, his guardian angel calmly whispered into his eager ear.

"Here you go now, Mr. J. Do exactly the same thing you did as coming out of the revetment. Only this time, we do it in reverse. Or, should I say do it front ward. Hold your power steady and just think forward pressure on the stick. Now, just let her slowly slide forward on her tippy toes."

Out of ideas, Kev thought to himself.

"Who am I to argue with my guardian angel? I need to have confidence in him. He has done pretty well by me thus far."

He pondered for a rare theological moment.

"Maybe this is what Pastor Bill meant by faith?"

With Kev just thinking forward pressure on the stick, they slowly started sliding forward. The little helicopter's movement was almost impossible to detect. However, ever so slowly, they began picking up speed.

With the barbed wire gleefully preparing to grab her skids, old 662 gave herself a little shake and shudder. At the last moment they gained transitional lift. Much to Kev's delight, she finally lifted a couple of inches into the air. The little bird was denying the gravity bonds of her terribly overweight condition. The young man was grateful for the mystery of transitional lift which happens at twelve to fifteen knots of forward airspeed. Not an aeronautical engineer, Kev wasn't prepared to explain the aerodynamics that gave them a touch more lift! However, he was perfectly willing to accept its gift of flight. Suddenly, with a light hop, skip, and bounce or two, the three of them were essentially airborne. With just the slightest touch/thought of back pressure on the stick, Kev traded a little airspeed for a touch of altitude.

"Wonder of wonders," Kev thought as he ever soooooooooooo slowly let his breath out.

They had cleared not only the barbed wire, but also the utility lines which were greedily reaching up for them and threatening to kill the three of them. When he heard Kev's expulsion of breath, Pete who was the crewchief and flying in the front seat, opened his eyes.

Kev told his friend Sven later that evening.

"We staggered into something that kinda/sorta, more or less, resembled level flight."

The soothing voice of Kev's guardian angel gently broke the silence on 662's intercom.

"See. I told you Mr. J. No sweat. After all, flying this heavy bird is just like the seduction of a very pretty girl. Soft, easy, and gentle does it. Then, in due time, this ole gal will gladly give everything you want and then some more as a bonus."

"Well . . . ," Kev thought to himself. "Apparently, all my previous youthful attempts at seduction had most likely been crude and ham fisted."

His lonely fate, the young man eventually and most sadly determined, was that he, unlike all his paperback book heros, was to die a very frustrated virgin.

"Whoops!" Kev thought to himself.

"I should be careful about telling this part to Pastor Bill the next time I write to him. Oh, what the heck. I have worse sins than my teenage attempts at seduction."

Pastor Bill had quietly frowned upon his attempts at seduction. However, they were all frustrating, dismal and disheartening failures. In response to Johnny though, Kev just sorta grunted into his mike. He was hoping that this meaningful grunt assured Johnny that he fully understood the subtle points of this conversation. Admittedly, he didn't understand much or anything about the gentle seduction of pretty girls. Therefore, he had difficulty understanding the clear relationship that it had to flying overloaded, war weary helicopters?

Upon arriving at their area of operations, Kev quickly glanced down at his fuel gauge.

"Wow!"

The little round gauge surprised him how much fuel 662 had burnt just getting to the AO. Kev remembered that basis physics, a course in which he had not done that well in High School said something about his fuel situation. The fuel gauge made that physics lesson painfully clear. Laughing at himself, he looked back at High School.

"Be truthful, Kev. Other than 'recess' was there ever a course that you did well at while you were in school?"

With a chuckle and a shrug, he went back to the problem at hand.

The heavier the bird, the more fuel it took to keep the helicopter in the air. Now that he was flying the lead bird, he knew that he was going to have to pay much closer attention to fuel consumption while he was doing his recon. The last thing he needed to do was to commit another boneheaded stunt. Running out of fuel in the middle of injun country would qualify as a truly remarkable one. Poor Kev was still receiving plenty of well-deserved comments about the day he turned his little helicopter into the world's most expensive vegamatic.

In the end, he had been unable to defend the damage to his main rotor. Much to his shame, he was forced to admit to shoving his carbine into the still turning rotor. In his heart of hearts, he knew that he didn't need to go to further extremes to prove what type of urine deficient pilot he was. He knew that, to the rest of the Cav Troop, he happened to be an idiot equipped with Army Aviator wings. He felt fortunate that they needed him. He also knew that the Captain was forced to assign Kev to fly lead. However, he believed that he had not earned it.

White Six, the Troop Commander was flying Command and Control for Kev's first mission as lead. A few minutes after they arrived at the AO, he told Kev which valley to recon. White Six wisely suggested that Kev not rush into things. Patiently, he told Kev to take his time getting his feet wet.

"Remember, Son, You can't always tell how deep the water is at first glance."

Kev's radio crackled, this time it was Red Six.

"O.K. here's the scoop One-Five. I don't want you to go getting over anxious on me today. Take a couple of minutes and keep your airspeed up for your first few passes. We've got plenty of time. Get the feel of things, One-Five. Whatever you do, please, don't be in a rush to get low and slow. You have got months to learn your trade as lead scout. Also, always remember that these lead birds fly one whole heck of a lot different from flying a wing bird. Give up too much airspeed while you are heavy and you can really, quick in a hurry, find yourself deep in the brown smelly stuff. In fact you can get yourself into big time serious trouble."

"That's true enough," Kev thought to himself.

"I might not be your basic rocket scientist. For that matter, I'm not ready to be a brain surgeon either. Nevertheless given a little patience, I know that these guys can teach me a thing or three."

With each passing day, the young man had already discovered that he had much more to learn. He was reminded of it at take off time as he was struggling to get the heavy bird out of the revetment and then take off. He now knew that flying the lead bird had been an entirely different proposition from flying the wing bird. A single struggling take off in the morning had already taught him a great deal about flying the heavy lead birds!

The young man was very unsure of himself. However, he was becoming ever more grateful for the unique set up of the Red Birds. In the real Army, or at least the peacetime Army, Kev would never have had his "ace in the hole." The near feudal system of military life made it difficult for information to travel up the ladder from the Enlisted people to the Officer types. Therefore, the uniqueness of the Red Bird way was evident when they began to let down from their higher altitude.

Johnny, currently serving as Kev's guardian angel, was unobtrusively filling Kev's earphones with life saving information. These were the little things that would allow him to do his recon and return home at the end of the day to enjoy a cold beer or three. Though he had been flying the wing for several months, he had never shown the wisdom to study and learn the many tricks of flying lead. For this oversight, he was becoming very regretful.

While they were descending to begin the recon, Kev decided that it was time for him to get his act together. It saddened him to know that he frequently pledged to get his act together. However, he was responsible for too many people to be sloppy in doing his homework. Thankfully, Johnny was quick, yet tactful, in speaking up.

"Mr. J., I recommend that we first take time to check out the tops of these hills. It wouldn't do for us to be slowly chugging along in the valley and have somebody shooting down at us from the hill tops."

Johnnie's recommendation made good sense to Kev. Deciding that it was time for him to use his brain, he commented to himself.

"Who am I to argue with his greater experience?"

If someone were shooting down at them, they could not safely return fire if they had to shoot upwards through their rotor system.

"On the other hand," Kev thought to himself.

"With a small helping more of my bad luck and stupid decisions, I could top my great vegamatic incident. As far as I know, I'll have to shoot myself down to do that."

An old hand had told Kev that this had happened before.

"Yes," Kev thought.

"What a fitting ending that would make for my less than illustrious military aviation career."

The flight wore on and Kev became more comfortable with his ability to handle the heavy bird. Even so, he had almost no confidence in his abilities to lead the recon. Leadership required more than a well-trained reflex! After ten or fifteen minutes, following Johnny's tactful guidance, they drifted down to the floor of the valley. Looking about, Kev remembered the valley. The memory was not very helpful to the young man. His previous trips had been in the much different guise of a wing man. Also, they had almost no contact with the bad guys on those previous trips. Either, the bad guys weren't at home at the time or, they couldn't find them to invite them out to play.

Flying along, young Kev found that he was of two minds. Tearing at his ego and his common sense, part of him would like to have discovered an NVA base camp or something equally grand. It would be rewarding to prove his worth as a lead scout on his very first mission. The other part of him, the more logical part, remained very happy with no contact with the enemy. If he had less contact with the enemy, he felt that this would offer him less opportunity to make a four star fool of himself. Because of his glorious vegamatic incident, he now feared continual harassment from his fellow pilots more than he feared enemy guns and bullets.

Kev was surprised to discover that though they had burned off a substantial amount of fuel, ole 662 remained sluggish at the controls. Sighing to himself, he commented.

"A heavy bird is a heavy bird."

He was thankful that he finally had a sufficient power reserve to allow some very slow flight. At least, this was quite a bit better than the problems of the take off. Lighter, he had sufficient power to begin the serious part of the recon. To properly fly the recon, he knew that it required that he fly no faster than at fifteen to twenty knots of forward airspeed. As Kev was finally able to slow down, Johnny continued with his instructional duties.

"If you're ready to move on to new and challenging things, I have something that I would like to try, Mr. J."

Kev grunted his affirmation for new and wondrous stuff.

"If you're ready, I would like you to add some left pedal and fly this ole bird a little bit out of trim. Good, now as you can see, we are flying in a slight crab. I guess you could say it is kinda of sideways. This gives both of us a really good view as we mosey quietly along our way. At the same time, this also allows Pete to look behind us and see everything that the rotor wash has opened up underneath us. Sometimes, I'll ask you to change the crab. When you do this, Pete and I will change views."

Kev was surprised how the different configuration of the lead bird affected everything that he did. Partially protected by the two-foot square piece of armor plate, Johnny was sitting directly behind him. Kev had never had an observer anywhere but to his side in the co-pilot's seat. Sitting, with his feet hanging out the door, Johnny had a bird's eye view of the world. He also was strapped into the aircraft with a monkey harness securely attached to the floor. Since he was strapped in, he couldn't fall out should he get shot or slip. Johnny would sit, or stand on the skids, during the recon with his M-60 machine gun cradled in his lap. Should they be shot at, he had a white phosphorus grenade ready to throw to mark the spot where they received fire. Pete, who was also the aircraft's crewchief, sat at the familiar place to Kev's left. He too had his M-60 pointed out the door ready to return fire as well as a Willie Pete at the ready.

Flying the unarmed lead bird, (read no minigun made Kev feel unarmed), Kev discovered that he had become little more than the taxi driver. He was discomforted because he didn't have his wonderful minigun to play with should the bad guys come out. His responsibility was to fly the bird and "run things." Obviously, the three of them hoped and planned on seeing the bad guys first and getting the first shot in. First sight was important to Kev as he was now "unarmed." This was the new way that Kev would, most likely, spend the rest of his days in Vietnam. Going as low and as slow as possible they continued looking for the bad guys. All in all, playing the passive role was difficult for Kev. At least, that is how he initially saw his role.

Several days later, . . .

Dear Pastor Bill, I will never forget when I was in your confirmation class. You sometimes poked a gentle loving fun at my black and white view of the world. For the sake of avoiding a fight, I won't mention that I am currently noting the same black and whiteness in your own view of the world. We'll save that discussion for a later time. As much as it pains me to consider the possibility, maybe your words contain a touch of truth. At times, I'm just not sure what to do with them. Yesterday we had a mission that profoundly troubled me. With your grace, I'd like to share part of it. Daily, I am discovering that a great number of gray areas are involved in this war. Unfortunately for me, in his detailed instruction 'Manual of Combat Understandings & Ethics to American Youth,' John Wayne managed to overlook these countless gray areas.

As the three of them were quietly chugging along doing their normal recon, their pace picked up. Johnny discovered what appeared to be fresh earth work taking place at an old abandoned bunker/tunnel complex. Being hard-working Scouts, the discovery pleased the three of them. This sort of activity was exactly what they were looking for. With freshly turned earth scattered about, Johnny saw a positive indication of VC or NVA activity. Slowing to take a much closer look-see, the bad guys rudely greeted them with a smattering of ground fire. Nothing came really close to them. With nothing coming close to them, the scattered and poorly directed ground fire was nothing that should have scared them. Nevertheless, it was more than enough to raise Kev's pulse rate.

Laughing to cover his tension, Kev keyed the mike.

"Between you and me Johnny, one shot aimed in my general direction still gets my full and undivided attention."

Agreeing, Johnny responded.

"No doubt in my military mind boss, they got my attention. Shooting at me is a clear indication that the bad guys are at home and in a foul mood."

For some reason, totally unknown to the three of them, the bad guys didn't seem to want them to drop in for a visit and conversation. But, they were normal red-blooded American boys. Therefore, they decided that the negative reception called for a lively response from them. The three of them felt it was a sufficient excuse for them to spend some more time visiting their new found friends and neighbors. Pete piped up.

"Maybe we can all share a cold beer or something when we got to know each other."

When Kev had finished reporting to him, White Six decided to insert the ground recon unit. These were the good folks Johnny used to work with. In fact, they were the same good folk who picked Kev up. That was when he did his, much talked about and world famous, vegamatic routine. The radio crackled. "Red One-Five, I've called in the ground platoon and told them to prepare for a hot insertion. While they are in route, I want you to pick out an LZ, recon it and establish an approach pattern." While studying the situation, Kev thought that about 300 meters to the north there was an acceptable LZ for two ships. Poking around a bit, he could find no evidence of the bad guys having prepared any nasty surprises.

Thinking for a moment, he decided to bring the Hueys in from the east. As they took off to the west, he wanted them to make a hard right break. That way, they didn't fly over the bad guy's neighborhood. Even the newest of the new guys knew better than to offer big fat slow targets. Kev was quickly learning that the varied responsibilities of flying the lead scout kept him busy. Musing to himself, he pondered the multiple balls that he had to juggle.

"Well . . . it looks like my lazy days of quietly riding about on the floating air currents are finished. Maybe I don't need my mini-gun. I have enough to think about as it is!"

For Kev, watching the unfolding drama of a troop insertion was much like watching a well-drilled football team on the field. Just like the coach diagramed it, the troop-laden Slicks approached the LZ. He called the lead Snake sending them into motion.

"White Two-Niner, this is Red One-Five. I'd like you and your wing to make a rocket pass over the LZ just before the Slicks arrive."

The Snake driver double clicked his mike, by that acknowledging Kev's request. The next words he heard over the radio were simple in their directness.

"Two-Niner is inbound and hot."

While the Slicks were on short final, Kev asked the Snakes to finish preparing the LZ.

"Two-Niner, would you and your wing place a mini-gun curtain on the north and south side of the LZ."

From what Johnny and Kev saw, he wasn't expecting any opposition to the insertion of the ground troops. On the other hand, given Kev's recent history of poor decisions, he decided that a little added caution was appropriate. Ole Kev wasn't going to see a slick shot down because he hadn't covered all the bases.

Continuing his writing to Pastor Bill, Kev commented.

In a strange military way, the combat insertion of the Blue Platoon was a thing of exceptionally rare beauty. I know you will have trouble with that notion of something being beautiful in combat. For the moment, if you would, please accept me at my word. As the first two Slicks were on short final, the Snakes made their final gun run of the insertion. They were very protective of their charges. In fact, they almost appeared to be mother hens caring for their little chicks. Maybe they were more like junkyard dogs. The two Snakes swooped down, one on the right and one on the left. Their deadly curtain of mini-gun fire was protecting the Hueys when they were at their most vulnerable. One thing I have observed over the last few months, when it comes to taking care of their own, none do better than the Cav!

Kept very busy watching, screening, and directing the insertion of the Blues, Kev watched a sight unique to the Viet Nam combat veteran. That, sight which may never be repeated, was the airmobile helicopter insertion of crack combat troops. By this time, Kev knew that their Blue Platoon was as crack as they got. He found that the experience of watching this insertion was like watching the deft movements of an option quarterback. Before the first two Slicks had even touched ground, they were emptied of troops and dipping their noses in their quick escape from the kill zone. Immediately upon hitting the ground the inserted troops had fanned out and established a tight security zone about the LZ. Because of their zealous protection of the LZ, one could possibly have imagined that the second two helicopters contained their mothers with the picnic baskets.

Maybe it was just the beauty that Kev saw in fine team work that touched him. He loved to watch good team work, be it the football team, the factory, or the field of arms. On the other hand, maybe it was simply his wide streak of romanticism that moved him to near tears.

The insertion of the Blues did not finish the young man's day's work. Flying the lead bird, it was his responsibility to direct the Blues to their objective. In this case, he was carefully directing them to the location where Johnny had seen the raw earth evidence of some fresh activity at the bunker/tunnel complex. Once they arrived, then the Blues would begin a thorough recon. They could see more than the Aero Scouts ever did from their helicopters.

"Hopefully" Kev thought, "they will rudely bump into the folks who had been shooting at Johnny and me."

Kev decided that the gods of the Aero Scouts were smiling upon him. He was thankful that Johnny had three of four months of experience with the Blues. With this experience, he was able, to offer safe advice to them during their cautious advance toward the bad guys. As he had been all day, ole Johnny was making the inexperienced Kev look pretty darned good.

Flying protectively over and around them, the three young men in the Red Bird could occasionally catch glimpses of the infantry types. The ground troops were moving cautiously and quickly from cover to cover. For Kev, it was an education watching them advancing and carefully protecting each other along the way. In a matter of minutes, they safely achieved their goal of the complex. Then, without pausing to rest, the grunts set up their security ring. Like all the members of the Cav, neither they nor their officers believed that anyone should die stupidly. The grunts accomplished their objective without having had any enemy contact. However, from his vantage point Kev found the time from insertion to the setting up of the security zone an unnerving experience. As the grunts advanced, he feared that they might get an unpleasant surprise due to his own inadequacy as a new lead scout.

A cold and clammy thought/feeling had struck Kev as the Blues advanced on the ground. It was something like waiting for the second shoe to fall in the apartment upstairs. Time seemed to lose all its meaning and impact. As anyone who has ever lived in an apartment well knows, from the moment that the first shoe falls, everything seems to stop and wait upon the second bang! Kev impatiently waited for the shoe to fall. He knew that the bad guys were down there somewhere from the early part of the recon. The three young men had distinctly heard them banging away with their rifles and their AK's. The thought of the grunts getting caught in an ambush he missed horrified him!

When they had established a perimeter, the Lieutenant in charge of the Blues called Kev on the FM radio.

"Red One-Five, we have discovered a new tunnel entrance and are preparing to send the 'rat' into the tunnel."

That little call reminded Kev how varied life in the Cav really was. In a matter of moments the prime recon of the Cav had gone from flying above the ground. With the approval of the Major, it had changed to walking along the ground. A few moments later, the discovery of the tunnels again changed the nature of the recon. This time, it became crawling in damp dark tunnels below the ground! Kev told Pastor Bill what his impression of the "tunnel rats" was in his latest letter.

I will readily grant you that my view of our troops in Viet Nam is biased. Nevertheless, I believe that the Cav people are a curious, strange, and even terrifying admixtures of both the brave and the foolish. In fact, I usually put us in the Red Birds at the very zenith of that list of strange folk. After all, we are the flying targets. Given what I have seen so far, I am forced to admit that the "tunnel rats" are in a league all of their own. I personally think they are just plain, CRAZY, nothing more, nothing less. They are just plain, CRAZY. Furthermore, everyone in the Red Birds agrees with my assessment. Let me tell you what I saw this "rat" doing.

Painting a word picture for you, I'll try to capture these strange and wonderful people. I was safe on the top layer of our little trinitarian world, floating in the air. The grunts providing security on the middle layer, were standing firmly on the earth. At the base, the tunnel rat serving as the bottom layer, was removing his combat gear. He was stripping down to his fatigue pants, boots, and green T-shirt. He did this in preparation to enter the tunnel below the surface of the earth. The man was, I might add, a skinny little fellow. That made it easier for him to crawl on his hands and knees while exploring the tunnels. Picture this in your mind, if you can. His friends in the Blues were slowly lowering him, by his feet, head first into the tunnel entrance. In one hand he carried a flashlight and in the other a 45cal. pistol. That was all he was taking with him as he entered that dank, dark, and foreboding enemy territory. Lest I forget to tell you, they had securely tied a rope to his feet. If something went wrong, they could haul him out quickly.

Slowly flying over the site, Kev visibly shuddered in his seat while thinking about the tunnel rat. As he was looking at the events below him, his imagination wandered. He was thinking of someone lowering him into the two-foot square opening armed only with that flashlight and the 45. As vivid as ole Kev's supercharged imagination could be, even he could not imagine entering that tunnel under any circumstances. The guys in the Blues had told him what the tunnels were like. They were too narrow to turn around in. Furthermore, the tunnels are unlit, clammy and damp.

These earthen tunnels were not union built! Therefore, as a good blue collar kid, Kev questioned their construction standards. He also knew that the tunnel rat must also contend with possible booby traps. If he survived the booby traps, an unknown enemy in an unknown location was waiting for him. The guys in the grunts had also told him that if the rat had to fire his forty-five in that restricted space that he would be stone deaf for several days.

Kev had already decided that he would positively hate to be put to the task. In an inner conversation about the tunnel rats, Kev had said to himself.

"If they told me to go down one of those tunnels, I do believe that I would gladly accept a Court's Marshall rather than go. A long vacation at Ft. Leavenworth would be an acceptable alternative to being a tunnel rat. No doubt in my military mind, I would prefer to make little stones out of big rocks for the rest of my life. That would be much better than allowing anyone to lower me head first into one of those dark holes."

Morbid curiosity took over Kev's mind. He came to a hover at fifteen feet over the tunnel entrance. Then without warning, what sounded like two or three muffled gunshots came from within the tunnel complex. With that, the silence below was abruptly shattered. As if on cue, the Blues frantically began reeling in their friend. They were praying that he remained tied to the end of his rope. Taunt arms flashing hand over hand, they were pulling him back as fast as humanly possible. As the young soldier's boots appeared at the tunnel opening, a couple muffled explosions came from deep within the earth. Following the soft explosions, a section of the tunnel complex collapsed.

Happening faster than Kev's mind could process all the movement, roughly a dozen men in NVA uniforms jumped out of previously undiscovered tunnel entrances. As they appeared, they immediately started shooting their AK-47's at full automatic. As they fired their long burst of fire, they ran from the Blues. Apparently, the tunnel rat's intrusion into their sanctuary had just flushed the game. Just like the hunted game they had just become, the bad guys were scattering to the winds like a covey of quail while shooting at everyone.

Within the confines of the little Red Bird, teamwork and training immediately kicked in. Without a word being exchanged, Johnny and Pete got some shots in at the fleeing NVA. They excitedly yelled that they saw a couple of the bad guys go down. The good news was that the bad guys had not hit any of the grunts. While they were engaging the NVA,

Kev called in the Snakes to roll in. In all the excitement, the radios were filled with much excited yelling. The Blues were yelling for support on the FM. The Snakes were yelling for directions on the UHF. Lastly, C&C wanted an immediate update on the situation on the ground. With everyone demanding Kev's attention, he struggled to untangle the situation. It scared him that he was the guy who was responsible. Kev was the quarterback and C&C was the coach.

Adding to his confusion, the relief team had arrived on station when the explosions and shooting began. His little bird was becoming dangerously low on fuel and this was forcing him to leave station. Quickly briefing Red One-Four, they left the supervision of the rest of the mission to him. He had no choice. It was time to pull up stakes and get some fuel. He really didn't want to go. His self-proclaimed heroic image demanded that he should stay for the action. He had a nagging fear that he had missed something when he briefed One-Four.

"It is enough," he rationalized to himself, "that we found the complex and we got things started."

Yet, he felt incomplete, like he hadn't completed his job.

As they flew back for fuel, Kev asked Johnny his opinion about the mission. Specifically, he was concerned about his part in it. The young men had come to recognize that Johnny's wealth of knowledge could not be over appreciated. Good and bad experience had taught him some of his limitations. Therefore, he knew that Johnny could save his life as long as he wasn't too proud to tap into his wisdom. Thankfully, at least for the sake of his ego, Johnny gave him quite good grades for the last flight. Then, said he, further stroking the raging fires of Kev's fast redeveloping ego.

"You know Mr. J., we might just become the greatest Red team ever."

Later developments prompted the final part of Kev's latest letter to Pastor Bill.

At a more personal level Pastor Bill, let me share with you my concerns, struggles and confusion concerning the outcome of my first mission flying lead. If I read the news and your letters correctly, what happened today reflects the concerns, struggles and confusion we are all facing these days. I'm speaking of our military commitment in Viet Nam. After we had returned to the Bird's Nest, I went to the club to grab a hamburger and a cold beer. While I was sitting at the table with Red One-Four, he told me an upsetting story.

"When the dust had finally settled, we had gathered six or seven bodies from the tunnel complex and the surrounding area."

At this point, having found and fixed the bad guys, we would call it a successful day. In proper Cav fashion, we had found the enemy and we had accordingly fixed him.

Reflecting back upon what happened today it makes me wonder about this whole thing. As best we can understand, fearing capture, the NVA had blown up their underground facility. Totally unknown to me, I am afraid, what Johnny and I had discovered turned out to be a crude underground field hospital. Before I go any further, please let me make a strong point for reference and clarification. The NVA and the VC never put red crosses on their field hospitals.

According to their rules they themselves routinely shoot at our hospitals. I have also seen how they use the red crosses on our Medivac helicopters as their aiming point. All our hospitals and Medivac helicopters, I might add, are unarmed and clearly marked with bright red crosses. I have a friend from flight school who flies Medivac. He has told me that most of the hits he receives are usually within the bright red cross. He correctly surmises that the bad guys use the red crosses as their aiming point. As far as the VC and the NVA are concerned, there doesn't seem to be a Geneva Convention. Hopefully, as you read this letter, you remember that they have both refused to sign the Convention.

However, as if finding a field hospital and having it blown up in my face wasn't enough of a problem for me to deal with! Things got more complicated. The Blues compounded my personal ethical problems by identifying one of the NVA whom we killed as a doctor. PLEASE NOTE THIS POINT VERY CAREFULLY! He was armed with an AK-47. The doctor was loudly proclaiming his status as a dangerous combatant. He was shooting at the Blues when they killed him!

What bothers me so deeply is that he still was a doctor. The man was supposed to be saving lives, not taking them. Pastor Bill, believe me when I say that none of us are here to kill doctors, nurses, or alike. However . . . , we are here to kill the soldiers of an invader. How are we supposed to tell the difference if the Doctors are armed and they are shooting at us? Furthermore, how are we supposed to know the difference if their medical facilities are undifferentiated from their combat facilities?

Let me assure you of one thing. The very complex ethical issues of this place are not discussed only by clergy, educators, and high-minded students. Those of us in leadership positions, no matter how trivial, struggle with these same ethics and issues. Though you wouldn't know it by following the popular media, the Army trains us to ask these questions! Sitting at the club sharing our burgers and beer, both Red One-Four and I felt that this had been a successful day. We had done our job to the best of our ability. The Red Birds in as much as we had found some bad guys and had fixed them had completed their mission. On the other hand, One-Four and I both found ourselves troubled by the day's events.

Perhaps One-Four said it as well as anyone can say it.

"What are you going to do Kev? You fly into the area and the bad guys start shooting at you. You shoot back and ask questions later. They build an aid station/field hospital and then do not identify it as such. For reasons unknown to us, they then blow it up and break out. While escaping, they are shooting and trying to kill as many of us as possible.

189

Unfortunately, in the midst of it all . . . we kill a doctor. It don't make no sense. We would have taken the surrender of noncombatant doctors and nurses and treated them very well. It just isn't right. Still, . . . what are you going to do?"

After taking a long thoughtful draw on his beer he continued.

"I have some really mixed feelings about the whole thing. If they are willing to fire rockets at our aid stations and hospitals, how are we to respond. And, if they are dedicated and enthusiastic about shooting up our Medivac helicopters, isn't the turn about fair play?"

No glib answer came to ole Kev's mind concerning Sven's question. Neither did the two of us like what happened during the mission, but . . .

I don't know if this makes the confusion of things clearer or not for you Bill. I do know that I fear the "media" getting its teeth into a story like this. They would have a field day. Cringing inside, I can see the whole thing in print and on the six o'clock news. We will all quickly become mad butchers of men and women dedicated to peace. They will pontificate that we should be put away for the safety of all humanity. Proudly, those with all the answers will say that we should be locked up forever and ever.

Yet, the brutal fact is that the situation just isn't that clean. It isn't black and white like so many would want to believe. Like it or not, here a different set of rules defines the game of life. In fact, the VC and NVA have established a savage set of rules. I have played under them too often to ignore them. Nor can I pretend that this obscenity doesn't happen.

I believe I told you about the village we saw when I first got in country. That is a good example of the difficulties we face here. In my opinion, the crime is that it is the unfortunate nineteen-year-old draftee who is struggling to survive and do a job who gets slapped with a broadly drawn black brush. When in reality, it is a very grey world both here and back in the "world!" I wouldn't lie to you, Pastor Bill. I fly with these good men, kids, if you will. They are just trying to do the job that old, fat, bald professional politicians in Washington sent them to do. We are here because, like politicians, the North want to take over the South. I might add, this is a job we have to do after our own politicians have very carefully tied our hands behind our backs.

Till the next time, pray for us. For, in fact, we remain the same kids who were in your confirmation class a couple of years ago.

Johnny and Kev had been flying together for a few weeks. With the passage of time, they began to get the feel of each other. It felt good to Kev working with someone who understood the mission as competently as Johnny did. When they flew together, Kev felt confident. His knowledge and experience of Johnny convinced him that they were going to make a very fine team. Speaking to his new wing pilot at the club one evening he described his feelings this way.

"I'll tell you one thing about ole Johnny. It already feels as if he were to cut for the basket on a breakaway, we would score. Somehow, I would immediately know that he was cutting without even looking in his direction. Again, without looking up, I am confident that I could hit him with the floor length pass which he is expecting. Lay up! Two points! We score and, of course, the good guys go on to victory."

However, Kev's emotional roller coaster also contained some deep dark valleys. He had begun to get the feeling that, for the most part, there was a lack of clear purpose in the American presence in Viet Nam. He still believed that he was part of the good guys' team. Time hadn't changed one important thing in his outlook. Young, but rapidly growing up, Kev continued to believe that he was fighting for some greater possibility. Yet, he had gotten the uncomfortable feeling that they were not accomplishing anything of consequence.

"Possibly," he thought to himself, "we have more troops over here than we can use effectively."

As it has been since the first armies, the military bureaucratic tail was much larger than its fighting head and teeth. Whatever the case might have been, Kev was beginning to feel that they were getting nowhere fast with their little war.

One day seems to blend into the next day with no substantial change in the war. Day in and day out, Johnny and Kev flew over the same pieces of real estate. It seemed that they did their little recons without a final goal in mind. Frustrating them, they continued with even less accomplishment. The Army could put troops on the ground any time they chose. If they put enough of these troops in place, they could hold the ground far if they remain in place. Nevertheless, it was like water slowly and constantly seeping through a sand dike. The minute they turn their backs and relaxed for but the briefest of an instant, the bad guys were back in place. Within a day or two it was just like they had never been there in the first place. At times, the whole effort felt like a great study in futility.

Don't misunderstand Kev's feelings. His experience in the Cav was not negative. It was the overview, the bigger picture, which was distressing him. The bright moments seem to make their individual efforts worth something of lasting merit. However, these moments did not necessarily move toward a glorious conclusion of the war effort in South East Asia. The brute fact of futility remained for those who were in the rank and file. Their greater goals in Viet Nam were unclear. Kev saw the bright and shiny moments in the individual efforts of very honest people like Johnny. Yet, not just in Johnny, but Kev also saw brightness in all the rest of the everyday guys. These everyday guys included junior grade officers, enlisted, and drafted folk, like Johnny.

The "Striped Pants Crowd" in Washington and the "Brass Hats" in the "Five-Sided-Funny-Farm on the Potomac" didn't offer any well defined goals for the average soldier. Given the situation, the best thing that Junior Officers, like Kev, could do was redefine their mission. Many felt that they should do their utmost to bring "the boys" home alive. With the passage of the months, Kev joined them in striving to bring them home in one piece. They fought and died to bring home as many American boys as they possibly could while still trying to accomplish an ill defined mission

Johnny and Kev had one of those days that made them feel good about themselves and the mission they were struggling to accomplish. They were in another valley about ten miles east of the site where the bad guys had killed his young Lieutenant friend. That was where Kev had flown his first combat mission with Captain Jack. For some mysterious reason Division's intelligence wennies had decided that they wanted to put some people on the ground. It would be a difficult task. Good Ole Mother nature had exceptionally heavily forested the upper part of that valley with triple canopy jungle. That meant that almost impossible to put a sizable body of troops on the ground from helicopters. A painful lesson or two had previously been learned in that valley. If Division didn't put troops on the ground in a sizeable number, they would not come home.

Because Division needed to insert a large body of troops by air, they had sent Johnny and Kev out to that valley a few days earlier. Their mission was to look for a location which they could make into a landing zone (LZ) for Slicks. An almost insurmountable problem was immediately apparent. The length and breath of the valley was all triple canopy jungle without a single suitable landing site. To counter this "little problem," the Army and Air Force people had worked out a nifty little plan. They decided to create, what most folk called, "The Instant LZ." To accomplish this, they planned to use a huge bomb which had been nicknamed a daisy cutter.

Giving this uniquely military solution of the LZ problem some thought, Kev decided that the plan was about par for the course. He had learned that only the United States Military Mind in Viet Nam had this level of so-called wisdom. Who else, but the military, would crack open a walnut with a twelve-pound splitting maul? Creativity and elegant solutions to perplexing problems created and drafted by the Military Mind was not something that he had often experienced. In his neck of the woods, thundering crudeness had become the norm. When all else failed, they always decided all that the Army required was a much bigger hammer. Therefore, in another move designed to save the taxpayers a few dollars, the Air Force offered to help. They discovered some twenty-thousand pound bombs left over from the Second World War.

A ten-ton bomb was a really BIG bomb! For example, a heavy full-sized American sedan might weight up to two tons. That means that this bomb weighed as much as five sedans. In Kev's part of the world, the bombs the Air Force was dropping on North and South Vietnam were much smaller. They were either five hundred or seven hundred and fifty pound bombs. When war broke out in Viet Nam, the Air Force no longer had a combat aircraft which could deliver such a large bomb. The Air Force had decommissioned all the aircraft with huge bomb bays when atomic bombs were developed and became reliable. When the Air Force wanted to make a really big BANG, the A-bomb had become their main noisemaker.

Of course, the Air Force, like the Army and the Navy, loved bigger hammers. However, this situation of a surplus of big bombs caused a wee bit of a problem. The Air Force could not safely deliver these huge conventional bombs to their Communist friends in the north. However, it would be such a shame to let these bombs just sit around or scrap them. It was un-American. The bombs were already bought and paid for.

Not to worry though, a group of the whiz kids from the Five-Sided-Funny-Farm on the Potomac came up with another new whiz-bang system. Those crafty whiz kids had developed a way that a C-130 transport plane could then be the deliverer of the massive bomb. Using radar control and knowledge of the weather and the winds, at the proper time, they could solve the delivery problem. They could deploy a parachute out the back cargo door of the transport plane. When the parachute caught the slipstream, it would then drag out the bomb which they attached to a cargo pallet. After clearing the cargo aircraft, the 20,000 pound bomb would then disengage from the pallet and float gently to earth at the end of its parachute.

The next part was a little tricky. It was important that the bomb went bang before it contacted the earth. Otherwise, it only made a big hole in the ground, but not the helicopter size LZ needed. To insure that the bomb would explode at the proper height, they attached a long probe to the nose of the bomb. Upon striking the ground, the probe would set off the bomb just above ground level. Exploding at this altitude, theoretically it knocked down a radius of trees, creating and area large

193

enough to land a Huey in. With this genesis the name became obvious, instant LZ. At least that is the way the whiz kids said that it was supposed to work.

To be fair to the whiz kids, the instant LZ concept wasn't necessarily that bad a system. Usually, the towering explosion blasted a fair radius of trees down. Hopefully, the thunderous blast effect created the instant LZ as advertized. Like so many other wondrous ideas created by the whiz kids behind their desks, this high/low tech notion did not always work exactly as advertised. Far too often, several large tree trunks, denuded of their leaves and branches, would remain standing in the newly created LZ. The blast effect would fully denude these remaining trunks of all their branches and leaves. For some unknown reason, the offending trees always seemed to stand directly in the middle of the LZ. (In self-defense, Kev blamed the remaining tree on the capricious gods of war who put his tail rotor in another tree during his infamous Vegamatic incident.)

It didn't take a PH.D. whiz kid from MIT to figure out what striking one of these large trunks would do to a helicopter rotor system. Ideally, the first helicopter would land its troops just as the dust settled from the explosion of the massive bomb. It was felt that the explosion of a twenty-thousand pound bomb would assure that anyone left alive on the ground would be suffering from shock and concussion injuries. Given this, the wiz kids assumed that those on the ground who survived would not be in any condition to contest the landing. The difficulty was that this whole system would only work if the big bomb knocked down all the trees. As always, the gods of war worked hard to bring the ideas and dreams of mere mortals to tears.

Far too often, several substantial, helicopter eating, tree trunks were left standing despite the appreciable explosive effect of a twenty-thousand pound bomb. That situation, with a couple or three stripped tree trunks left standing in the middle of the LZ, should not have come as a great surprise to anyone. At least, it shouldn't surprise anyone familiar with the nature of the tropical hardwood jungle. The size and strength of the massive hard woods to be found in the Vietnamese jungle defied the bigger hammer principle. Given this problem, which rendered the LZ unusable, the unique and wondrous military mind came up with plan number two.

If some hardwoods were left standing following the bomb's explosion, a lone Huey would then hover as close to the ground as possible. When the bird was in position, a special pioneer team would then repel down long ropes from the hovering helicopter. The whiz kids would equip this pioneer team with woodsmen's tools, chain saws, axes, etc. Their job was to quickly clear out the remaining stumps. To the whiz kids, this situation didn't present a very substantial problem. The

Washington whiz kids had convinced themselves that if any bad guys were on the ground, they would remain stunned and shocked by the force of the bomb's explosion for a fair amount of time. Thereby, they would be unable to interfere with the pioneer team.

As usual the whiz kids omitted at least one crucial item in their ivy tower minute planning. Tropical hardwoods do not cut down nearly as easily as soft southern pine. In fact, cutting them down takes a long time and can eat up several chains on a chain saw. Precious time, is the brutalist of enemies to people on the ground surrounded by hostile forces. Furthermore, big bombs and chain saws make lots of noise. The whiz kids did not know that the bad guys were nosey neighbors. All these noises would naturally arouse their curiosity. This was where Kev & Johnny came into the saga of the wiz kids wondrous idea.

For this operation, someone at the division level had been doing some constructive thinking. They decided to have the instant LZ created on the spot which Kev and Johnny had picked out for them. Continuing with their smart thinking, Division used the Cav to cover their flanks while they were making the insertion. It looked good on paper because covering the was a mission which the Army had in mind when they formed the Cav. Therefore, when it came time for the troop insertion, the Cav was flying in the area. Kev and his friends had a "ring-side seat" when the Air Force dropped the "Big Bomb," the daisy cutter. All who were there agreed that the bang of this big boy was quite impressive. However, Kev and Johnny knew that this big time bang would gather more than the passing interest of every bad guy in about a ten-mile radius. Johnny keyed the mike and commented.

"If this doesn't bring the bad guys running, I'll eat my dirtiest and smelliest pair of olive drab skives with salt and pepper."

As the dust was settling, the pioneers rapidly repelled down the ropes dangling from their hovering Hueys. First, six pioneers repelled from one Huey, and then six more repelled from the second Slick. Division equipped them with their axes and little chain saws. As an afterthought, for their own protection, they were allowed to carry their M-16's and a few clips of ammunition. Their "little" job was to quickly clear away the half dozen remaining trees so their buddies could join them. Just as the people in the field feared, these hardwood trees were not to be felled nearly as quickly as the whiz kids had planned.

Unfortunately, the situation began to develop just as Johnny and Kev suspected it would. Quickly complicating the lives of these military woodsmen, a dangerous and potentially deadly curiosity by their nosey neighbors, the bad guys, took place. Within less than fifteen minutes the twelve pioneers on the ground were forced to quickly trade in their chain saws and axes for their M-16's. However, this little exercise, of playing grunt, wasn't in the whiz kids game plan. Unexpected by the wiz kids from the safety of their desk, these pioneers were fighting the now dangerously curious NVA for their lives. This was not part of the game plan!

Most of the young pilots in the Cav believed that the people fighting the war from behind their desks did not have a passing thought about the war. Nor did they believe that these Remington Raiders gave a passing concern for the unfortunate people they sent to fight it. The young pilots also believed that those who opposed the war from behind their desks probably also gave little thought to the men who were caught up in it.

The lost truth, in both sad cases, was that the bad guys were not anything close to stupid. What was unfortunate for the American kids, was that the bad guys never took the time to carefully read the script which the whiz kids wrote for them. Adding to the risk of the situation, the pioneers were neither regular nor heavily armed ground troops. Given their mission to cut down trees, they were not properly equipped to defend themselves against a determined enemy.

Both Kev and Johnny were distressed that many people did not realize the bad guys had learned much during their years of war with U.S. Forces and the French before that. After all, they didn't rotate home after a year's tour of combat duty. They knew that the Army's and Air Force's overwhelming and total control of the air could devastate them if they caught them in the open. Their best survival tactic, given the overwhelming American firepower, remained getting in as close and personal as they could to the people on the ground. By always attempting to maintain a tight engagement, the bad guys would make it impossible for the troops to effectively use either air power or artillery. When they did that, they stripped the people on the ground of their strongest arm of support. The Red Birds struggled with that problem constantly. Using their overwhelming firepower occasional created too great a risk of killing their own people and tied their "helping" hands.

When the pioneers got into trouble, the Scout's real mission of the day began. For once, Kev and crew found themselves wonderfully rich in fire support which made Kev happy. Division had a pair of Air Force F-4 Phantoms standing by in high orbit. They also assigned two pairs of Charley model gun ships to support the rest of the insertion. The Cav's four Snakes were also available. As always, they kept two of them in the air covering the Red Birds. All in all, this was an impressive amount of air power. Yet, as rich as they were in air power, it might not make any difference. Unfortunately, all this might in the air couldn't help anyone, if the bad guys were close enough to engage in hand to hand combat with the small number of pioneers.

Inevitably, Vietnam had developed into a static war. What made it much different was that it was being fought with multiple layers of command only a helicopter flight away. That being so, more than enough experts and others were orbiting overhead. Being typical Senior Officers, they made themselves readily available to give advice and issue orders. It seemed to Kev that command and control helicopters were stacked to the heavens. Not counting Kev's own command and control aircraft, the Division commander was in his own helicopter. Above him, another general from somewhere or another was cluttering up the sky in his helicopter. Kev wasn't sure, but he thought that a couple of Colonels were wandering about also and generally getting "underfoot."

Enough aluminum was moving around and about in the air over this partially finished LZ Kev was wondering if there was an airport nearby. Thinking about all the aluminum floating about, Kev thought that they should have had a control tower in the middle of the LZ. Just for flight safety, he felt that they needed it to reduce the danger of midair collisions. When the bad guys attacked, the pioneers began crying for help on the FM radio.

Adding to the confusion that cry for help kicked off, that naturally started the generals acting like generals. Unasked, they were giving the pioneers endless stupid, useless, and meaningless instructions. The generals were also issuing their string of meaningless instructions on the UHF radio to all the aircraft in the area. Not to miss the opportunity, they were issuing orders to each other, and anyone else who might be foolish enough to listen to them. Everybody was talking, hollering, yelling, and issuing orders all at the same time. Unfortunately, nothing worth noting was happening. That is, unless someone considered that the pioneers were in immediate danger of being overrun and killed as something worth noting. In the colorfully descriptive military parlance of the day, it was turning into a first class rat's nest.

Thankfully, that day, the gods of war had made at least one good soldier available. He was a man who knew his business. That soldier's soldier was Kev's big boss. He was their unit commander, the Major, Yellow Scarf Six. Cutting through the noise and confusion on the radio net, the Boss called Kev. He asked him to come up another frequency on the VHF radio. For a change, ole Kev had one of those stupid things which worked.

Writing to Pastor Bill, he once said of the Major.

I have to say it straight out. The Major is a good man and a darn good soldier. When I am feeling cynical, I suspect that, and that alone, was why the Brass Hats had passed him over for Lieutenant Colonel. Over the years he had probably told one or more Remington Raiders a thing or three they clearly didn't want to hear. My dear friend, I have discovered that the act of "calling it like it is," can really hurt your promotion prospects in this man's army. I suppose the same can be said for most of life. I'll find that out later.

197

Kev's boss, the Major, tended to be quite abrupt, and as usual, he was right to the point.

"Red One-Five, do you think that you can help those people on the ground?"

Without taking a moment for thought, Kev keyed his mike. Of course, Kev, a young man who had never been previously known for careful deliberation before he acted, responded positively.

"Six, if you can get all those noisy brass hats out of my way and get everybody off the radio net we'll do what we can to fix this sorry situation."

God bless the Major, he was just the man that the pioneer team needed. When it came time for him to take charge, taking charge was exactly what he did best. Trusting the Major's leadership, Kev rolled ole 662's nose over and pulled in an arm-full of collective pitch. From his lowly point of view, it was time for him to come up with a brilliant plan if the Major didn't have one for him. Listening to the radio as he moved into position, smiling, he clearly heard Yellow Scarf Six take charge. It was his plan to take care of those kids on the ground. At this early stage of his own military career, ole Kev didn't care whose feelings he hurt or whose toes he might stomp upon in the process. Speaking up, he took full advantage of his rank. A Jr. Warrant Officer was not considered a political animal. Most considered themselves civilians in uniform. Therefore, Kev had no problem asking the Major to get all the brass out of the way so he could go to work.

"Attention all aircraft this is Yellow Scarf Six. Clear the LZ area immediately! I am sending my Red Birds in."

It seemed as if the boss had yet to lift his finger from the mike when something or other Six, started to protest. Undoubtedly he was one of the growing mob of self-important generals which they had underfoot. Kev's boss responded in his finest I'm in command and I'm taking charge voice to the unneeded interruption.

"Something or other Six, I will cheerfully discuss this with you later. Go to a higher altitude. Right now! My Red Birds are going in!"

Surprisingly enough, the generals were at least intelligent enough to recognize a soldier's voice when they heard one. Immediately all those helicopters which had previously been in Kev's way, and each other's way, quickly clawed their way to a higher altitude. Unexpectedly, the great-grandfather of all military miracles occurred. The radio net went totally silent. Every pilot in the Cav found the blessed silence unbelievably wonderful. Who would have thought, Generals being quiet and letting the soldiers fight the war? That was unheard of in Viet Nam. Kev smiled a little self-satisfied and malicious smile. If something went wrong and he didn't survive the day, that was OK with Kev. He'd now experienced military heaven in Viet Nam.

Kev's friend Sven was normally a lead pilot. This mission found Kev thankful that Sven was flying as his wing man. Sven was just the kind of wing for which the day called. He was a good man and friend, an excellent stick man, and most importantly, a very cool head in a fight. Though normally a lead, Sven always flew an excellent wing. Furthermore, Kev found that trusting him with his life and the lives of his crew came natural. Wisely, Kev elected to stay on the UHF so that everybody could monitor his conversations. Everybody included the brass hats, his own people, and even the F-4s overhead. He keyed the mike.

"Sven, I'm going down into the hole. Please, keep your speed up and get ready to give me some serious mini-gun when I call for it."

Without pausing, Kev continued with his instructions.

"White Two-Five, as soon as I get a good eyeball on the situation, I'm going to call you guys down to deliver some serious pee. Don't expend everything on your first pass. I can't say for sure, however I fear that I might need you for quite a while."

Since he was on a roll, Kev continued issuing orders.

"Six, you better call up the other team and get them here muy pronto. I suspect that I am going to run out of bullets and ideas real fast."

It was clear to the rest of the Cav that under Johnny's tutelage, Kev had come a long way, since his first mission as a lead pilot.

Everyone's response was exactly as Kev expected. He was the quarterback and they were an excellently drilled and a well-practiced team. They were almost immediate with their return calls. Sven was first to respond as Kev's wing.

"Roger One-Five. In case you are curious, I now know that you are certifiably insane. However, Red One-Four is with you all the way as always."

The Snakes responded with their usual great support.

"Roger, roger Red One-Five. We humble White birds are always at your beck and call."

Biding his time, the boss was last to respond.

"Red One-Five this is Yellow Scarf Six. I'm way ahead of you son. The second team is cranking as I speak. Now don't you go doing anything stupid. We have enough to deal with right now. I don't want to have to pull you out of that hole too."

With that call, Kev knew the boss was just telling him to be as careful as the situation allowed him to be. With a wonderful feeling of confidence, Kev knew that the Major was a great commander. He wouldn't interfere with the man in charge of the operation. He had given Red One-Five the mission and now it was his call. His job, though he was Kev's boss, was to support him so that he could get his job done.

Unknown to him as things began to heat up, it was turning out to be the day in which Kev finally understood why he had given up the mini-gun. If a day ever was going to allow the three man flight team to prove itself, it looked like this one was the day. Giving up having the electronic trigger of his mini-gun at his beck and call had been very difficult. Ole Kev loved the wonderful little trigger which would pour out two-thousand or four-thousand rounds a minute. However, he quickly came to the conclusion that such an impressive amount of firepower wouldn't help the people on the ground. What was going to be of greater help to them was having three-hundred and sixty degrees of free M-60 coverage at six-hundred rounds per minute. Kev already knew that trying to fly the bird while trying to be as small a target as possible inside his armored seat, and run the show would keep him fully occupied.

It was clear to him that he wasn't going to have time to play with a gun. Before Kev had even called Red One-Four and told him that he was going down the hole, he had the beginning formation of an idea. Now it was time to see if it would work.

"If this works," he said to himself. "I'm going to call it my 'Hail Mary' play."

Slowing, he approached the semi-finished LZ. Speaking to Johnny and his front-seater he issued his instructions.

"OK guys you know the drill. No shooting unless you have an absolute positive "id" on a bad guy. If there is any doubt at all in your mind, just don't shoot. I don't want to take any chances on hitting any friendlies. OK? Now this is what we are going to do. I am going to hover right down as low as I can over the friendlies on the ground. When we get there, we are going to cover them. We'll keep covering them until I come up with a brilliant, or even a semi-brilliant idea about how we are going to get them out of this mess."

Pausing a moment, Kev continued.

"Any questions? I'm open to any astute suggestions before we go down the hole."

He happened to glance over at the front-seater. Sighing deeply, Pete shook his head no. Johnny keyed the mike and responded. "Let's do it boss. It's time for us to rock and roll."

Flaring the aircraft, Kev bled off all his forward airspeed. Preparing to descend into the semi finished LZ, he radioed the pioneers on the ground. They didn't need the radio to hear a lot of small arms fire coming from both M-16s' and AK-47s'. For the moment, none of the ground fire was directed at them. The three young men in the Red Bird knew that their moment of idyllic quiet was about to undergo a radical change. The truth was that drawing the enemies' fire away from the folk on the ground was a big part of Kev's so-called plan.

Switching to his FM radio which was what the ground troops always used, Kev called the people on the ground.

"Crocket One-niner, this is Red One-Five, are all your people inside the LZ."

He responded to the affirmative. Kev then continued.

"Crocket One-niner, I understand I can now kill anything outside the blast area."

Later that evening at the club, and a casual discussion over a cold one everyone thought Crocket's response was classical. It reassured Kev to know that this guy was a cool customer. He was keeping his head and Kev honestly didn't know that he would have done the same in his place.

"Roger that Red One-Five. You and your friends are more than welcomed to kill anything outside the blast area. In fact it would make us very happy campers if you killed everyone and everything outside the blast area."

For the first time, Kev had the positive feeling that they would get the pioneers out the LZ in one piece. Though, he admitted one uncomfortable fact only to himself. Kevin Paul Johnson remained painfully short one grand and concluding idea. Feeling slightly frustrated although he was awash in a sea of adrenal secretions, Kev grunted to himself.

"How in the heck are we going to get these guys out of here?"

As the little Red Bird crossed the line of demarcation between the virgin jungle and the blast area, Kev called the people on the ground again.

"OK, Crocket One-niner, this in Red One-Five. I'm the little helicopter hovering directly above you. I want you and your people to 'go to ground' because we are going to start killing anything that moves! Get under a log. Visit your friends, the moles. Or, crawl in a hole and make like a snake's belly because we're getting set to rock and roll up here. When we turn up the music, you are going to have a whole big bunch of hot brass raining down upon your heads."

Fulfilling some of the expectations of Kev's "plan," the bad guys had seen them. Without taking a vote, they quickly decided that the Red Bird was a much juicier target than the folks on the ground. Exactly as Kev had hoped planned, the three of them were beginning to receive the bad guys' undivided attention.

"So far, so good." Kev thought to himself.

Shooting at Kev and crew meant that they were not shooting at the folk on the ground. Better yet, they themselves had not received any hits. Receiving no hits was most excellent! Kev asked Johnny and Pete the crew-chief if they could see the friendlies. They responded that they could. It was time. Kev hit the intercom button.

"OK guys, this elevator is now going down. I am going to do some fancy 360 degree pedal turns. While we are spinning about like demented fools, your job is to put down some serious fire and kill anything that moves!"

The little bird quickly descended into the hole. Just as quickly, they were surrounded by green and the thick wall of impenetrable towering trees. Maneuvering at random, the little Red Bird sought to avoid the increasing volume of ground fire. They spun to the right. Changing direction, they spun to the left and rapidly ascended fifteen feet. Just as quickly, they descended ten feet.

At one point, Kev saw a green trace go between the rotor system and his head. While at the same instant, he saw another green trace go between the skids and his lily white butt. Later at the club, he admitted that he didn't know where the four ball rounds went. He knew that they were supposed to be sandwich meat between the tracer rounds which went above and below him. Noting no superfluous holes in his body as the tracers burned their deadly image into his retinas, he decided that all was well. The little bird took a hit or two. So far it wasn't anything serious. She kept flying and both the observers vigorously hammered away at the bad guys with their M-60's.

Over the FM radio, everyone with a radio could hear the pioneers shouting encouragement and cheering the little Red Bird on. Understandably, they were enjoying the slugfest directly above their heads. A casual listener might have thought someone just scored the winning basket in the State Basketball tournament. Obviously, their no longer being shot at greatly added to their exuberant pleasure. Somewhere in the midst of this dramatic one helicopter war, Kev asked Red One-Four if he found anything that he needed to know about. Giving Kev something else to worry about, Sven said that more bad guys were about two-hundred yards away to the west. He added that they were heading directly toward the LZ.

Sven told Kev that he would keep them off his back.

"Don't you worry about us One-Five. At the moment, Hank and I are keeping them really busy. You just keep playing your silly little games in that there hole in the jungle!"

Kev called the Snakes down on this new group of bad guys and asked Sven to direct their fire. Sven had them make repeated passes. He also told them to conserve their ammo and only use a couple of rockets on each pass. He was afraid that Kev might need them real soon. Everyone hoped that this would keep these bad guys from moving in on the pioneers and Kev's little bird. White Two-Five, with his usual dry humor, added to the surreal atmosphere.

"Red One-Five and One-Four, my number two and I take great personal pleasure offering our personal delivery services to the guys flying in the toy helicopters."

So far so good! Kev's little Red Bird had already accomplished possibly more than he had hoped to achieve. They were drawing the enemy fire away from the folks on the ground. Entering the slugfest, they were giving the rest of the Cav time to get the pioneers out. Kev was pleased, but he also knew that this approach would only buy a limited amount of time. They only had about four, maybe five-thousand rounds of M-60 ammunition on board. At first blush, that might have seemed like a lot of bullets to spray around. While in fact, their ammunition was fast running out. The way that they were spraying bullets around the area, it wouldn't last much longer. Furthermore, the law of averages said that it was only a matter of time before the little Red Bird found itself in deep trouble. Given the growing volume of fire directed at then, before long, they would receive a fatal hit. If that happened, they would crash in a towering ball of flames directly on top of the very people whom they were trying to save. Kev knew that it was time to get some other people involved in the game before the time clock ran out on everybody.

Kev then hit the mike for the UHF radio.

"Red One-Four, this is One-Five, I'm getting some really heavy fire from the edge of the standing trees to the north west of the LZ. Can you make a couple of close-in passes with your mini? I need it really tight on me. I say again. I need it really tight. Place it so tight that I get exceptionally nervous. But, for God's sakes don't shoot me down. I've got sufficient problems to keep me fully occupied at the moment."

When Kev finished speaking with One-Four, he decided that it was time to conserve ammo. Drawing a deep breath, he then told the observers to stop putting down suppressing fire and to only shoot when they had a target.

Sven then responded to Kev's request for close in support. With grim determination, he spoke.

"Red One-Five, this is One-Four, I am inbound east to west DO NOT STICK YOUR HEAD OUT! I'm going to put my fire right in on top of you."

Then the little boy, which was part of all of them, spoke up.

"Oh, by the way One-Five, I'm curious, do you have the twenty bucks you owe me? Firing now, at two-thousand."

With that, the characteristic sound of a slow ripping heavy cloth announced the firing run of One-Four. Exposing himself as much as Kev was, Sven was making a very slow gun run. At the same time, he was scientifically walking the fire up and down the tree line. That death dealing minigun really got the bad guy's attention because Kev and crew stopped receiving any fire. For the moment, the two Red Birds had turned the tables. Fearing for their lives under the terrible onslaught of Sven's minigun, all the bad guys went to ground.

If anyone can call such a display of purposeful death beautiful, then Sven's gun run was beautiful. From the loud screaming, shouting, and cheering on the FM radio, the pioneers clearly also thought that it was beautiful. Kev saw that a slow mini-gun pass with a Red Bird at 30 knots is truly an awesome sight. This was the first time that he had clearly seen the receiving end of things. Red One-Four was shredding the trees and underbrush with his mini-gun. Looking at it, it seemed doubtful, to him, that anything could live under the weight of such concentrated firepower. It looked so good that he called One-Four and asked him if he could make a couple more runs just like that. He assured Kev that he could. Sven keyed his mike.

"Roger that, One-Five. By the way, Hank said that he is pretty sure it was forty dollars that you owed me."

Moving back to Red One-Five down in the little hole in the trees, the situation remained the same. The little Red Bird continued to do its left and right, descending and ascending pedal turns. It had never left the LZ which had been under construction. Johnny and the front-seater continued carefully firing an occasional burst, either to keep the bad guys honest or shooting at something they saw. Both told Kev that they were down to less than five-hundred rounds each. That was not good news to Kev. Five-hundred rounds of ammo doesn't last long in an M-60. It was time to check with the troops upstairs and see if anyone had come up with a brilliant idea for stage two. As for Kev, he knew that he had overdrawn his account at the idea bank.

Stage two raised the problem of how in bloody blue blazes to get these people out of the hole.

"White Two-Five, this is One-Five, say ammo status, please."

Kev knew the Snakes had to be getting low on ammo just like he was.

"One-Five, we've got about a dozen rockets each and a few bursts of mini. We're conserving ammo and only firing one pair of rockets on each pass. We're just trying to keep these other guys from giving you a bad time. By the way, Sven needs that forty dollars to pay my beer tab."

Kev keyed his mike.

"Roger the beer tab White Two-Five, good work and thanks. Yellow Scarf Six, have we got the second team in sight? I'm getting dangerously short on bullets. I don't want to sound overly concerned about the situation. However, at the moment boss, I'm unstrapping my forty-five and getting ready to throw it at someone."

As always, Kev's boss was right on the ball. He always tried to stay two or three plays ahead of the opposition and usually succeeded.

While Kev was busy spinning around in circles and using up all his bullets, thankfully he was using his head. Yellow Scarf Six was coming up with part two of their unfolding plan. This plan was, your basic create things as you go along plan. The eventual goal was to get the pioneers out of their big deep hole. They were the Cav. The Cav improvises. Complex plans, they believed, were for the dull-witted.

"Red One-Five, this is Six, two questions for you. The second team is about zero five from our location. Can you guys hang on that long? Secondly, I got two Slicks equipped with jungle extractor winches. Do you think when we get the second team on site we can winch these guys out?"

Kev answered affirmatively to his second comment/question. He then told the Major that One-Four's close-in fire and his own M-60's had apparently taken some starch out of the bad guys. The boss was staying right on the ball because his next call went to the four Charley model gun ships which had been orbiting.

"Backstop Six, this is Yellow Scarf Six, my boy Red One-Five is getting a little low on bullets. I think that he could use some playmates down there. Can you put down some rockets and mini if he tells you where?"

Backstop Six responded immediately.

"That's a roger-roger Yellow Scarf Six. We were getting a little afraid that you Cav guys weren't going to invite us to your little rock and roll party."

Backstop Six then called Kev and told him that he had four Charley model gun birds at his beck and call. He added that one of them was a heavy hog with nineteen pairs of rockets and a 40mm grenade launcher mounted on the nose of the helicopter. Kev knew that meant that the others had seven pairs of rockets and two mini guns each. What was also nice was that Kev also knew that all of them also have two door gunners with M-60's. Equipped as they were, the Charley gun birds offered Kev quite a welcomed addition of close-in firepower. Furthermore, if he used it well, Kev was beginning to believe that the Cav could pull the rescue off with a little help from their friends.

The plan had now come into a clear focus in Kev's mind. The three of them, in the little red Bird, were still doing slow climbing and descending pedal turns. At the same time, the observers were letting out short three and four round burst to keep the bad guys honest. Kev keyed the mike to lay his rapidly forming plan on the table.

"All aircraft on the net this is Red One-Five, here's the scoop. I'm going to stay in the hole till I either run out of ammo or the Slicks with the jungle penetrators push me out of the way!"

Kev cut the conversation off as Johnny pointed out movement to the west. "Wait one, please."

205

Kev rekeyed his mike.

"I want the second White team to take over from the first team. We need you to keep those bad guys to the west face down in the mud. I also want the second Red Team to marry those Slicks. I mean make passionate love to them while they're inbound! When I land, I want you to tell me about all the little helicopters you made. That way, the only way for the bad guys to shoot down a Slick is to kill a Red Bird first. Lastly, on my command, I want Backstop and friends to dump everything they own in one pass covering all three hundred and Sixty degrees around me."

Kev paused for a second to gather his breath.

"Backstop, I would like your heavy hog to plaster the west side. That's where the fire has been the heaviest. Correct me if I'm wrong. It is my understanding that all you Charley model drivers are getting a little old. Therefore, I understand that you guys like to do it low and you like to do it slow. So I'm really trusting you with my Lillie white butt!"

Backstop Six quickly cut in.

"Doing it low and doing it slow is the best way to do it sonny!"

With a little chuckle, Kev continued.

"And Six, please tell the good folk on the ground to really go to ground this time. It is going to get seriously noisy around here before their taxi arrives. Any questions?"

No questions were forthcoming and Kev hadn't planned on there being any. These guys were all pros, Cav and non-Cav.

Having made all the transportation arrangements which he could think of, Kev gave the boss a quick call.

"Six, this is Red One-Five, I can't see a darn thing down here in the hole. Would you get all of the dance partners lined up and headed my way? I'll monitor on the radio. Oh, and by the way boss, I'm getting really short on bullets. So . . . , please make this happen very quickly."

When Kev finished, the three of them in their little helicopter continued to do their own private little dance number in the LZ. Anxiously, Kev monitored the change of Snakes with White Five taking over with his team. Then the boss called.

"One-Five, this is Six. The Slicks are two minutes out and the Red Birds are snuggled right up to them. Are you ready for Backstop?"

Kev rogered him and continued.

"OK Sven, it's time for you to get the hell out of here. I'm getting a new dance partner for this fast one. I'll meet you south in a little bit. By the way, you're a low life liar! I only owe you ten bucks and I'm going to buy everyone at the club drinks with it tonight!"

"Backstop, you're in. It's time for your guys to rock and roll. Please remember this little guy down here is your dance partner now.

Whatever you do, don't step on my toes cause I'm betting it'll hurt like hell if you do."

The next words on the radio began the thundering beat of Army Aviation style Rock and Roll.

"Backstop in hot."

With that, all the points of the compass in the whole world began to explode in smoke and flames. Two point seven-five inch rockets, mini guns, and forty millimeter grenades were going off everywhere. As far as Kev was concerned, nothing could have lived through the inferno. In the midst of Dante's Hell, Johnny keyed the mike.

"Jiminey H. Cricket Boss, when you pick dance partners, you definitely do know how to pick the noisiest ones on the floor."

A couple of minutes later the radio crackled again.

"All Backstop aircraft clear and cold."

That was Kev's cue.

"Red One-Five is out of bullets, and is outa here. I'm going south for vacation in a place where the people are friendlier."

With that, the young man pulled in an armload of collective and vacated the neighborhood post haste. The leaving, though, was much nicer than the arriving. As they flew away, the bad guys were no longer shooting at the pioneers. In fact they were no longer shooting at the little Red Bird, or at anyone else. All things considered, everybody and everything was in quite good shape. They still had about an hour of fuel left and the bad guys hadn't hit anything vital on the little Red Bird or any of the three young men. Checking with Red One-Four, Kev found that he had about an hour fifteen worth of fuel. However, he was bingo ammo on his minigun. Bingo, meant that he had exhausted his ammunition. Kev then called Yellow Scarf Six for instructions.

"Six, this is Red One-Five and One-Four, we are clear of the area with a little more than an hour's worth of fuel. We have expended virtually all our M-60 ammo. What are your instructions?"

As always, the boss was right on the ball. If Kev went back to refuel and rearm at the firebase, it could be as much as forty-five minutes before they could be back on station. The brute fact was that they were not out of the woods yet. The hoist equipped Slicks had just begun their extraction. This was a combat zone. Things over and in the LZ could go to hell in a hand basket in seconds. It was logical that the boss wanted Kev's team available as soon as possible. The snakes had no choice but to return to refuel and rearm. However, the boss had another plan for the Red team.

"Red One-Five, I want you and One-Four to head south to LZ Jones where the lift Slicks are staging. When you arrive at Jones, I want you to beg, borrow, or steal every bullet you can from the Slicks. After you rearm, return here post haste. I have already arranged for the Slicks to share their door gunner's ammo with you. They will be ready for you when you arrive."

LZ Jones was an abandoned patch of red earth situated at the mouth of the valley. It was about ten to fifteen klicks to the south of their present location. That meant that it was less than five minutes flying time away and that Kev and Sven could quickly reenter the battle. The Cav often used it as a staging field. However, when they staged out of it, they had to provide their own ground security. This LZ/staging field was one of the numberless ironies of the Viet Nam war. Unbelievably, though the bad guys owned the open ground surrounding it, they never bothered most people staging out of there. It was only six to ten miles away from the bad guy's country. That was real estate into which Americans could not travel in less than company size strength. Go figure!

The two Red Birds made their approach to the abandoned one-thousand foot tar runway which went down the center of the LZ. As they made their approach, they saw that the lift company tied down an even dozen Slicks there. Each was complete with their ground pounder types. These were the first group of the troops which they had scheduled for insertion into the LZ which the pioneers had been preparing. The crewchiefs and gunners from each slick were scurrying about and removing some of their ammunition from their door guns preparing to hand it over to the Red team.

Without shutting down, just rolling the engines back to flight idle, the observers relieved the eager helpers of the much needed ammunition. When the task was completed and the ammo properly stored, they took inventory. The generous slicks had rearmed them with about one-thousand rounds for One-Four's mini and about seven-hundred and fifty rounds for each of Kev's observers. It was not as much ammunition as they would have liked, but at least it did put some sting back into their stingers if they needed to use them again. If things went sour during the extraction of the pioneers, their little bit might come in helpful and buy a little time till the Snakes returned fully refueled and rearmed.

Partially rearmed, the two pilots immediately brought their rotor systems back up to operational RPM. Quickly taking off cross field, the two Red Birds headed back to the scene of all their previous excitement. By this time, the adrenalin overload of the previous few minutes was beginning to wear thin. Nevertheless, all five young men were ringing wet and totally exhausted. Kev asked Johnny and Pete if they were ready to go back into the hole if necessary. Trusting Kev as their "team leader," the two men responded honestly.

"Don't really want to boss. Still, if we gotta, we gotta."

The two of them mirrored Kev feelings exactly!

As they approached the area of operations, Kev called Six and told him of their status. Thankfully, he said that the Cav's slicks equipped with the jungle penetrators had extracted all the pioneers! Six then instructed them to rearm, refuel, and return to their staging base. He then added a complimentary comment.

"Division Six was very impressed with your performance One-Five. He was also very surprised when I told him that you were a Junior Warrant Officer. The good general said that Santa might put a Silver Star or a Distinguished Flying Cross in your Christmas stocking. Good work son."

That night Kev decided to forgo his usual beer ration for something with a little more celebratory kick. He and Sven closed the club after singlehandedly, well, dual-handedly, destroying almost two quarts of good bourbon in the process. Sadly, they agreed that they had not won the war either single or dual-handedly. On the other hand, both felt justifiably good about themselves because ten or twelve pioneers got another chance for life. Red One-Five and Red One-Four had played a significant part in the drama that saved their lives.

For a change, that night the young pilot slept the sleep of the innocent. Or, maybe well-lubricated ole Kev slept the sleep of the blind drunk. Whatever the case might have been, Kevin Paul Johnson felt useful and worthy of his golden sabers. For the moment, he felt that his time in Viet Nam had not been totally in vain.

GONE FISHING

Kev's time moved on in the lovely vacation spots of Southeast Asia. Gathering experience and expertise, he was enjoying some very good days. Other days, well . . . , he decided that they're just his share of the bad day allotment. Then occasionally, he suffered one of those forgettable days. Or, at least days that he wished, from the very bottom of his heart, that he could forget. Those were the days that made him feel a little more foolish than he usually did. When one is a twenty-year-old Junior Warrant Officer, those foolish days can be very painful. As with most folk, with the passing of the months, Kev discovered that his very foolish type of days started off like any other day. Writing to Pastor Bill, he explained how those days began.

Dragging an exhausted body out of the rack, the average bold Scout pilot takes care of his morning constitutional in the Officer's five holer. Following the communal celebration of humanity, he grabs a cup of the so-called coffee served at the mess. Gagging the wretched mess hall coffee down, the suffering and badly hung-over pilot gathers his gear, and shuffles on down to the flight line. (Of course, little Kevie has never been that badly hung-over pilot.)

Up to this point, a Scout's day remains essentially normal. Resigned to another day's missions, a tire is kicked and a fire is lit in the old bird. Lifting off into the wild blue yonder, as usual, the Scout has no idea what surreal and strange surprises await on the other side of the horizon. However, when one is flying in lovely Southeast Asia, strange and unusual things frequently do happen. These are the horrible and unbelievable things none of the instructors could ever prepare you for back in flight-school days.

One of those unreal days began like all the rest. The boss, flying C&C, began by leading his mixed gaggle of helicopters off to war. Kev's team did not object that the day was starting slowly. While the boss took the first team into the field, his team topped off their fuel. Following an uneventful refueling of their Red and White birds, they went directly to the staging field. Familiarity offered comfort as this was a field which they had often used in the past. Upon their arrival they parked and carefully shut down their birds. Almost immediately and as usual, the usual flock of young Vietnamese sales girls surrounded them The girls briskly set about their business of selling cokes, bananas, and lovely warm French breads.

Feeling in a generous mood, Kev happily purchased cold cokes and warm French breads for Johnny and Pete who was the crewchief flying the front seat. While they were sipping their cokes, they casually looked about. Suddenly, a sight which none of them could remember ever having seen before shocked and greeted their unbelieving eyes. Kev should have known that when his eyes focused on the absurd, it was going to be a unique day. Lo and behold, ole Sven had reached deeply into his pockets and had bought his new observer a coke. It was common knowledge that Sven's pockets were so deep that they reached to his boot tops. Neither Kev nor Johnny thought that Sven's arms were long enough to extract money from his deep pockets. This new found generosity, by Sven for his newbe observer, was sufficient reason for Kev and Johnny to stroll over and begin to harass him with great gusto. After a bit, the two of them tired of the game and they made their way back to ole 662.

So far, the two young men felt that it was going to be a wonderfully lazy day. Without sharing a word or a detailed plan of action, Johnny and Kev grabbed their chicken plates in preparation to use them as pillows. When they had properly propped up their chicken plates against one of the little bird's skids, they were prepared to enjoy the war. The two young men did what was proper and natural to good soldiers. They stretched out to doze in the warm sun. They agreed that grabbing a few z's on company time was a sweet something to savor. Dedicated soldiers, they were intent upon following an old saw about military life. It goes something like this.

"A good soldier never stands when he can sit. He never sits when he can lie down. And, he never stays awake when he can sleep." For the moment, the two men were striving with zeal and dedication to be excellent soldiers!

When the temperature was hovering comfortably in the low eighties and a refreshing breeze blowing, the experience of an early morning nap on company time became exceptionally sweet. When life was slow paced and enjoyable, even the strange smells emanating from the nearby village seemed warmly pleasant. More asleep than awake, the two fierce warriors stretched out comfortably. Someone passing by would have thought that they were two bathers basking in an expensive resort's sun. Passing the time with an occasional word, they found themselves delightfully alone and at peace with the world. With the war temporally forgotten, they dreamed their boyish dreams.

Pete, their front seater, had wandered off and was talking with two of the crewchiefs from the Blue platoon. His absence allowed them to enjoy the uniqueness of their silent and unspoken closeness. Unplanned by either, their silent communion had become part and parcel of their life together. Kev didn't understand what it was about Johnny's presence that comforted him. However, he knew that when he was with him, somehow he felt much safer. That comfort was sufficient. Sometimes, not asking questions is best.

Only the good Lord knew why Kev felt any safer when he was with Johnny. Neither of them were case studies in wisdom and caution. As often as Kev had gotten them in trouble, ole Johnny matched Kev's foolishness step for step. If Kev came up with a dumb idea, Johnny instantly agreed with it. Then, off the two glorious fools would go getting into more trouble. And, if Johnny came up with a dumb idea, Kev was just as quick to agree to a new way and even more creative way of getting them into trouble. Everyone knew that they were a team. The only question among their friends in the Cav was their level of sanity or insanity.

Casually glancing down at his watch, Kev was surprised at the passage of time. C&C had yet to call them out to relieve the first team. Groaning inwardly at the prospect of returning to work, he began to slowly gather his flight gear in preparation. If things followed their normal pattern, they would soon receive C&C's call to mount up and head out. Where they would go was unknown and that was OK with them. Resigning himself to the cruelness of life, Kev threw his chicken plate into the pilot's seat.

Stretching and getting the kinks out, he began to superficially inspect the aircraft. Just making work for himself, he was leisurely walking toward the engine compartment. He began opening the engine compartment when the runner from the Blues' radio relay came over to him. The young runner told Kev that C&C wanted his team to wait for his return from the area of operations. Continuing, the runner said that the Major mentioned something about division giving them a change of area. Well, waiting a little longer was OK with the two young men. They were in the mood for a listless lazy day. A Norman Rockwell painting with two fishing poles, a can of worms, and a creek would have completed the picture of their desires.

Within ten minutes of being told to mark time, they heard the heavy thrumming of Huey rotor blades. Unbidden by conscious thought, Kev smiled to himself. He suddenly realized that the heavy slap of a Huey rotor system would always mean Viet Nam to him. The biting blast of a rotor wash induced sand storm announced the arrival C&C and the first team. Trying not to make everyone miserable, they quickly landed and shut down their helicopters. Suddenly, the pace of life at the staging field quickened. Before C&C's rotors stopped turning, everyone expectantly gathered about the Major for a quick briefing.

The long and short of his briefing was that the intelligence weanies at division had a new bug up their butts. Kev and his team were supposed to immediately check out a valley outside their normal area of operations. None of them had been in there before. Therefore, Johnny and Kev began looking forward to a new adventure. The Remington Raiders at Division had come across some questionable intelligence. Someone told them that there was supposed to be a battalion or better of NVA types hiding in the valley.

Quickly finishing his briefing, the Major knew his boys. He asked them if they were ready to go to work. Yet, he already knew what their answer was going to be. Without looking behind himself, he walked away and climbed back into his helicopter. Sven and Kev looked at each other and silently shrugged their shoulders. As they were trotting back to their Red Birds, Sven commented.

"I am afraid that the Major wants us to earn our flight pay today."

Chuckling to himself, Kev's thoughts drifted back to his Dad. Almost every day when he grabbed his lunch bucket and went off to work, he would make the same comment. Looking back, his dad's observation of the human situation seemed most appropriate. Slapping his front seater on the back Kev sounded just like his dad. With a playfulness which surprised him, Kev mimicked his dad.

"Another day. Another dollar. If the intelligence weanies want us to look into things, that's what we'll do."

With his great and profound philosophical insight into their military life together, they strapped in and lit the fire. Keying the intercom as they took off, Kev was feeling musically minded. Seeking to cheer them up, Kev loudly serenaded his hapless crew.

"Hi ho, Hi ho, its off to work we go."

For some reason, a chorus of enthusiastic boos immediately assaulted him.

Fifteen minutes later the two little Red Birds crested the ridge leading into their new hunting ground. Johnny keyed the mike and offered his first suggestion of the day.

"Let's keep to the high ground and keep our speed up boss."

That seemed like a darned good idea to Kev. He was still half asleep and not feeling very bold. Cautiously, they spent the next fifteen minutes checking out the high ground by cruising around at forty knots. After what the intelligence weanies had said, they were surprised. Cruising along, they found nothing along the hills and ridges to suggest any recent use by the bad guys. By now, both of them were completely awake and beginning to feel frustrated by the lack of action. If they were forced to give up their lazy morning, they believed that the bad guys should offer a good reason for doing so.

"Enough of this." Kev thought to himself.

Keying the mike, he suggested to Johnny that they begin to poke around in the valley floor.

He had been looking at Viet Nam for months. Surprising him, over the months, he had fallen deeply in love with its strange and beautiful magic. The apparently empty valley below him was a heart-breakingly beautiful sight. The length of it was a patchwork of light green abandoned rice patties. In turn, the light green of the paddies was set apart by blocks of deep dark green double canopy growth. Forming a distinctive line of rich green growth down the middle of the valley was a fair-sized stream. Matching their earlier mood, it was meandering slowly. This stream, or blue line as they were apt to call it, ran generally north south following the valley. While they were drifting down the side of the hill toward the valley floor, Kev asked Johnny how he thought they should continue. Thinking for a moment, he laid out a plan.

"Let's just poke around here for a bit boss. If we don't find anything, then let's check out the blue line."

Kev called up to C&C and told him what their general approach to the recon was going to be. The Major's quick response was typical of his trusting leadership style.

"Roger that, One-Five. Keep me posted and let me know if you need anything."

With the Major's blessings, they began to carefully poke around the valley floor.

Following their well-read script, the three of them began sticking their collective nose into the many nooks and crannies of the valley floor. It didn't take Johnny long to see that the bad guys hadn't been in that valley for a long time. The lack of evidence painted a clear picture. The undisturbed nature of things also convinced Pete and Kev that the bad guys were not in the area. Nevertheless, the recon fully engrossed them. Their's was a different war. It was not a war of large units. Therefore, they knew that it only took one draftee bad guy to upset the delicate balance of the moment. Give him a single rusty bullet and the time it takes the heart to beat once and he'll ruin their day. For that reason, if no other, they continued to carefully search about the valley floor with all due caution.

After a few more minutes, the situation remained the same. They were finding very old evidence of the bad guys and nothing recent. The three of them agreed that it was time for them to take a good look at the blue line. Kev called up C&C and informed him of their negative findings. Then, he told the Major that they were going to check out the blue line.

Upon closer inspection of the river, they found the setting of the river to be a bit different than they had expected. The close up view was much different from when they first looked at the valley. Kev hadn't seen a river quite like this before in all his recons of the highlands. Without human notice, through the countless centuries, a geographical oddity had formed. The ancient, slow moving, and very muddy river had cut a ten-foot-deep channel. Strangely enough, the banks of the sluggish river were almost straight up and down walls of hard clay and mud. In fact, the walls were perfectly straight and sheer.

To Kev's amazed eyes, it was as if the river were slowly flowing down the streets of Manhattan. They were slowly passing over the river for their first pass when Johnny suddenly called out. When the tachometer monitoring Kev's heart returned from the red line, Johnny asked him to return over the river from a different direction. Naturally, Kev asked him what he had seen to get his attention. His response was that he thought that he had seen some old bunkers dug into the sheer banks of the river.

Banking to the right, Kev was keeping the river in Johnny's view. Maintaining caution, he planned on returning to the river on a different heading. Opting not to cross directly over the possible bunkers, he aimed for a point approximately fifty meters further down the river. While they were moving into position for their second look, Kev called C&C. He wanted to inform him of the possibility of bunkers. Everyone else on the net could also monitor the conversation. If the bad guys were at home, the three of them wanted everybody to be on their toes. Johnny then keyed the mike. Shocking Kev, he was feeling a little bold or playful.

"Tell you what I'd like you to do boss. Drop down until the skids are almost touching the water and head toward the bunker at a walking speed. That way, I can look directly into their front door when we get there!"

To Kev, it was beginning to feel uncomfortably like one of Johnny's bright ideas which would get them into deep trouble. Still, like a good little Scout Pilot, he did exactly what his back-seater told him to do. He gently lowered the collective and applied a slight back pressure on the control stick. This slowed the little Red Bird. She then slowly settled until she stabilized on her downdraft a couple of inches above the water. Reluctantly, a nervous Kev started a slow speed troll up the river. Silently, laughing to himself, he had a picture of an idyllic country scene.

"This looks like something from Courier and Ives or Normal Rockwell," he thought.

"The only thing missing is a couple of fishing poles sticking out of our little Red Bird."

Later, at the club, Kev was trying to tell Sven what the mission was like. Though, the mission had created its share of excitement. The picture of the slowly approaching bunker entrance had struck him deeply.

"I swear to Almighty God, if I had reached out with my hand, I could have stuck it deeply into the bunker's opening. With my breath held, I was waiting to count muzzle flashes. Sven, why in the blazes do I let Johnny talk me into such things?"

Ole Sven only smiled and he drew deeply on his beer. Not answering the question, referring to Kev & Johnny, he knew that one was as bad as the other.

Looking at the banks to his left and right, Kev felt the first faint stirrings of an attack of claustrophobia. If muddy water hadn't been slowly flowing below them, the depression would have made a perfect helicopter revetment. Scaring him, he uncomfortably noted that the rotor disk was below the top of the river bank. However, it did offer a strange comfort. If a bad guy had been standing out in one of the abandoned rice patties, he would not have seen them.

"At least" he thought to himself, "he could not shoot at us."

However, Kev knew that this was not a very comfortable place to be flying a little helicopter. It wasn't its natural element. True, the little Red Bird might have two M-60 machine guns for defensive fire. That wasn't enough here because she wasn't flying in the open freedom of three dimensions.

The three of them knew that their first line of defense was always their high maneuverability and quick speed. Kev found only discomfort in the knowledge that both of his first line defenders had been negated while they flew between the imposing river banks. Nervously looking to his left and to his right, he could only see sheer mud and clay walls! If someone started shooting at them from the river, they would have to climb first. Then, and only then, could they turn away from the ground fire. Increasing Kev's anxiety, was the fact that climbing would expose their vulnerable underbelly to enemy fire.

Filled with fear, foreboding, and dread, Kev was holding his breath. He was waiting for his final vision as a living human being. As he grew increasingly nervous, Kev had become convinced that his final sight, would be of muzzle flashes as the opening to the bunker came into his full view. Stepping outside himself, Kev took a good look at the pilot of the helicopter. He noticed that this scared pilot had, suddenly, somehow gotten considerably smaller. Defying all the known laws of physics, he had managed to hide 99% of his body within the small, yet comforting, confines of his armored seat. Even with this defensive cowering, if someone decided to stick a rifle out of the bunker, well . . . he knew that the pilot was a dead man.

Johnny unexpectedly keyed the mike. Startled, poor Kev thought he must have jumped straight through the rotor system. When the painfully loud click in his ears startled his musing spirit back into his body, every muscle twitched and jumped! Only the Good Lord knew why they didn't crash and burn when Johnny startled him so badly!

"It doesn't look like anybody has been here in the last couple of months, boss."

The mike clicked off. Kev tried to regain his composure. Just as suddenly, Johnny came up with yet another brilliant idea. Keying the mike again, ole Johnny suggested that they get permission for recon by fire.

Thinking about Johnny's suggestion for a moment, though he would liked to have, Kev couldn't find any serious fault with it. A rational part of him wanted to find a fault, any fault. However, another part of him, which he sometimes called his spirit of adventure, thought that it would be great fun. He decided, if they were shooting into the bunker entrances as they approached them, it might be safer for all of them. Their own fire entering the bunkers would make it very difficult and dangerous for the bad guys to shoot at them. His carefully trained military mind came to a decision.

"Any action that discourages the bad guys from shooting at us was a pretty good idea."

Thinking a little longer, he amended his thought.

"Any action that discourages the bad guys from shooting at us is a great idea."

The whole time those thoughts bounced about in his head, they remained at a stationary hover looking into the first empty bunker. Kicking himself in the butt, Kev decided that it was time to get moving. Keying up the radio, he called upstairs to the boss. They didn't want to start "shooting the place up" without getting permission and letting everyone know what was going on.

"Blue Six, Johnny and I would like to continue up the blue line doing a recon by fire of the bunkers dug into the bank."

Six gave his permission. Also, pausing for a moment, he suggested that Johnny use his M-79 to lob a grenade into each bunker as we went past.

Before the echo of his conversation with Blue Six faded away, Johnny's voice took the Major's place in Kev's ear.

"I got a good copy on the Major, sir. Carefully following the boss' orders, I have locked and loaded my trusty, dusty, and rusty thumper. I suggest you just maintain an easy walking pace up the blue line. You know what, Boss. I think that this is going to be as slick as whale poop. You just drive the taxi, boss. Pete and I will do the rest."

Keying up his radio again, Kev called his wing man Sven.

"One-Four, we're going to begin 'shooting up' these bunkers with M-60 and thumper so don't let the noise disturb your daydreams. We'll holler if we get any response from the natives."

Kev smiled to himself.

"Good ole Johnny, he likes to play with his Army toys."

Kev doubted that the radio waves had reached Sven before he heard the first hollow bump-like thump of the M-79 being fired.

Many people thought that M-79 was one of the most interesting weapons in Viet Nam. The M-79 fired low-velocity, forty millimeter grenades, and had been used widely the ground troops. Most of the time, the Scouts didn't use one. However, the task current called for a thumper. Most of the guys found that shooting one was fun, both in the air and on the ground. The grenade moves so slowly that the person firing it, and anyone standing close by, can follow it's flight. When the shooter is not in fear of his life, he frequently finds himself shooting and correcting his shots like he was tossing a baseball. Kev had fired one several times from the ground. He loved to watch the slow flight of the round as it arched through the sky. The little boy in him also enjoyed the satisfaction of the loud boom at flight's end. He, too, liked his Army toys.

Boom! A small cloud of dust and smoke slowly exited the entrance of the bunker. At first, Kev had feared that they were too close for the grenade to arm itself. Wrong again. Johnny had carefully placed his first round right through the front door. He exclaimed excitedly.

"I put it directly into their living room, boss."

If anyone had been at home, Johnny undoubtedly left him with a throbbing headache and then some!

Unrecognized by all, at the moment, Johnny had created a monster that was preparing to swallow them whole.

Using the boom of Johnny's first shot as the crack of a starter's pistol, Kev nudged the little Red Bird forward. It was like they were taking a slow stroll up the blue line and skipping rocks across the river. Like the young boys, which they were, their recon by fire quickly became a contest of sorts. When the bunker appeared on Pete's side, he would put twenty-five or more rounds from his machine gun into the entrance. While his M-60 was pounding away, he was keeping a score of sorts. When the bunker appeared on Johnny's side, he would carefully lob a grenade into the entrance making sure that he informed the crew what a great shot he was.

Surprising Kev, the three of them didn't completely deteriorate to the point of cheering and keeping a scorecard. At the very least, they were too professional for that level of foolishness. The sobering fact was that some bad guys could be waiting for them as they slowly made their way up the river, prevented that kind of foolishness. Yet, they did get caught up in their little game.

The poet, in the practice of his art, sometimes speaks of time seemingly slowly grinding too a halt. That was a close, but not an exact description of what happened to Kev and crew. But, it was close. They had become totally engrossed in their little recon by fire and had not paid any attention to the passage of time. As the pilot, Kev concentrated carefully on maintaining a walking pace up the blue line. At the same time, he was very careful about keeping the twirling rotors out of the unforgiving river bank. He had learned what trees can do to tail rotors. Much to his dismay, his friends frequently reminded him of his minor misjudgement and his creation of the $100,000 vegamatic. Therefore, he did not want to learn what mud and clay could do to main rotors.

Pete and Johnny kept their concentration zeroed in on the bunkers with a second eye scanning a little further afield. They were being careful that the three of them did not receive an unpleasant surprise. They were confident that they could trust Sven and the White birds to keep them in visual contact and protect their butts. Suddenly, Sven's unexpected call startling them. Red One-Four's call deeply troubled Kev.

"Red One-Five, I've lost you. Where in the bloody blue blazes are you?"

Kev couldn't believe what the radio had told him! Such a thing was not supposed to happen. A wingman never lost sight of the lead bird! True, he might occasionally put his tail rotor in a tree. HOWEVER, a wing man never – never – never lost sight of his lead. Not trying to control his frustration, Kev snapped an angry reply right back to him.

"You great-big-dummy, we're right on top of the blue line. Shoot! We're exactly where we have been for the last half hour!"

Kev was confident that One-Four would quickly regain eyeball contact with them. Therefore, he returned his concentration to the job of staying in the center of the river. The task of flying the little Red Bird was taking a little more concentration than before. Without his consciously noting it, the banks of the river had started to, ever so slowly, close down on them. Angry, Kev decided that this little incident, of leaving him uncovered, was going to cost Sven. He was trying to decide exactly how much beer Sven was going to buy him for pulling such a bone-head stunt. However, he knew that ole Sven would immediately get an eyeball on them. The miscue would only damage One-Four's pride and put a dent in his pocketbook.

As with much of the rest of his young life, things, including his flying, never seemed to work out according to Kev's carefully thought out plans. While Kev was returning his concentration to his flying, Sven made another distressing call which caused Kev to cringe. This second call to the Snakes had a deeper note of concern in it.

"White Two-Five, do you have One-Five in sight? I still can't find him."

Kev immediately decided that this bonehead stunt was going to cost Sven at least a full week's ration of beer at the club!

"Negative One-Four. I lost him just before you made your first call. Break, break, Red One-Five we have all lost sight of you. I recommend that you come to altitude so that we can all get a good eyeball on you."

Enough was enough. Kev was as angry as he ever got. At that moment, if you asked him what frustrates a Scout pilot more than anything else in the whole world, he could have answered in a flash. The answer to that question was straight forward and simple. It was having his covering aircraft lose sight of him. That was even worse than his losing sight of the bad guys. Kev's next radio call made his frustration exceptionally clear.

"What in the blazes do you mean you can't see me? For crying out loud, will you guys get your heads out of your butts! I'm sitting right on top of the blue line!"

Left unsaid in Kev's radio transmission, but understood by all, was the postscript.

"You guys are all blind idiots."

Unperturbed by Kev's call, White Two-Five carefully and patiently repeated his request that the little Red Bird climb to altitude. Resigning himself to the fact that deaf, dumb, and blind idiots surrounded him, he relented. With great aggravation, anger, and sarcasm, he told everyone within the sound of his voice exactly how he felt.

"Roger, roger, Red One-Five is climbing to altitude. **NOW!**"

Madder than the proverbial wet hen, Kev prepared to grab a handful of collective. As a demonstration of his anger, he decided to dramatically pop up to altitude like a rocket shooting out of a launcher. That way, he figured that the blind and brainless dolts above could find him. Pete, who had often flown with Kev, well knew his flair for the dramatic. He also knew that Kev was highly p----- off. For reasons unknown, he happened to look directly up Panic stricken, he immediately mashed down on his mike button. With his voice rapidly climbing countless octaves above his normal, he screamed in uncontrolled panic.

"Jimminy H. Christmas boss. **Don't climb!**"

His voice continued to rise in pitch and volume as he repeated himself.

"Dear God, sir, whatever you do, don't climb!"

Snapping his head up to the vertical position, Kev graphically and explosively added his two cents worth.

"Holy, s---!"

Deeply engrossed in their recon by fire, the three of them had not paid attention to anything else. They had not noticed that the trees had decided among themselves to artfully entrap them in a deep green canopy. Kev muttered to himself.

"Shoot . . . , we're the deaf, dumb, and blind idiots who have no conception of what was happening. If we get out of here, once again, this one is going to cost me big time."

While Kev had been concentrating their recon by fire, the banks of the river had slowly tightened down upon them. Simultaneously, the branches of the trees had silently and carefully interlaced themselves directly above them. At that sight of the interlaced branches just above him, a Scout's natural paranoia immediately set in. With his paranoia in full swing, Kev began to seriously wonder if these were secretly Viet Cong trees.

"OK. OK." He said to himself.

"Possibly, I slightly exaggerate my paranoia. Maybe the interlaced tree branches are only Viet Cong sympathizers."

Whatever the case might have been, their situation had suddenly become uncomfortably tense. The overhead branches and the tight river banks had effectively trapped the little Red Bird. She had become a trapped flying machine who found herself in a place where she could not and was not supposed to be or fly.

When the trees embraced them, the problem became visible, or better yet invisible, to their escorts. They could no longer be seen trolling down the blue line and nobody knew where they were. The only way their situation could have gotten worse, except for the bad guys deciding to fire at them, was if they had tried to climb through the trees.

"Thank God," Kev thought.

"At least Pete didn't let me creatively ruin our day by playing the vegamatic game again. This time, I would be doing the vegamatic thing with the main rotor!"

His sphincter painfully tightened with the knowledge of what he almost did in his flamboyant anger. Kevin Paul Johnson had almost smashed the little helicopter into the shaded green canopy above him. If he got out of this, Kev knew that he would suffer from crippling constipation for at least a month or more.

With the passing of the months, Kev found one ancient Viet Cong trick which he hated above all others. In the Cav, they called it "the old instant tree trick." Many young men flying with the Cav, mostly Scouts and Gun Bird drivers had almost fallen victim to that old VC trick. When the pilot is looking in another direction, the VC pop a specially genetically crafted seed into the ground. Then, when the pilot returns his eyes to the direction of his flight, presto, a big surprise greeted him. An instant, one-hundred and fifty foot tall, helicopter eating tree suddenly would spring up directly in the middle of his flight path.

The old "instant tree" trick had been the source of many laughs at the club. However, for the pilot who looked up and saw wall to wall tree, it wasn't funny. Most of the Cav pilots believe that the best minds in both Russia and China collaborated to produce this seed. Well-lubricated one evening, Sven told Kev that he thought that the CIA should make a priority of investigating this hellish secret weapon and how to neutralize it.

This time, the fiendish devils had almost gotten him. Ole Kev had almost fallen for a new and unusual twist on the old instant tree trick. Painfully gagging on a large portion of a tough old crow, he sheepishly keyed the mike to report his position.

"Ah . . . guys, I do believe that I know exactly where I am now. Believe it or not, I'm still on the blue line. Yes, it's true. Little ole Red

One-Five is still on the blue line. We just happen to be trolling along, fat, dumb, and happy under the trees at the moment. Sorry about that. Give us a minute and we'll come back out where you can keep an eye on us."

Oh how he hated feeling like an idiot. Here he had been bad mouthing the other guys when it wasn't their fault that they couldn't see his little Red Bird. As was his habit, ole Kev had shot his mouth off without thinking. Kev had screwed up and not the other guys.

Having successfully chewed, eaten, and swallowed, several bitter mouths full of that tough old crow, Kev needed to do something about the situation. Choosing the obvious solution, he keyed the mike.

"Johnny, clear me for a one-hundred and eighty degree pedal turn."

All that the red-faced pilot was concerned about for the moment was getting out of that mess as quickly as possible. Hovering six inches over the water with tree branches overhead was no place for his little helicopter! Johnny didn't make poor Kev feel any better.

"No way boss. If you try it, you'll put our tail rotor into the river bank."

That was not exactly the response that he wanted to hear! However, it was the truth. According to Kev's "game plan," Johnny was supposed to clear him for a quick pedal turn and an embarrassing exit stage right. As to their next move, the three of them did not need to cast secret ballots. They shared the same conclusion about the wisdom of putting their tail rotor into the river bank. One horrid thought centered Kev's thinking! He had no desire to play a new, different, and highly creative variation of his infamous one-hundred-thousand-dollar vegamatic routine.

He did not want to hear the answer to his next question. With a heavy heart, Kev forced himself to key the intercom again.

"Johnny how far do we have to back hover before I can turn this beast around?"

Totally fearless or just blessedly stupid, Johnny didn't bat an eyelash at their precarious situation. He happily informed Kev that he'd only have to back hover for a distance of about one-hundred meters. Maybe a little more.

"Hey, not to worry boss, Pete and I will guide you."

"This is just great," Kev thought to himself.

"I'm the guy who suffers crippling multiple panic attacks when backing fifteen feet out of a revetment. What in the blazes am I going to do now?"

With the gear shift lever safely placed in reverse, and carefully listening to Johnny's coaching, they began their unseen journey back to where they had started.

Eventually, the backed out far enough to be seen. Laughing, the Major then suggested that they pull up shop and go home. As for Kev, he was not in the mood to argue.

Ole Kev bought the beers for Sven, for the Snake pilots and gunners, and he even bought the Major a couple of cold ones at the club that night! Were they small minded, they might have asked for a public apology for Kev's abuse on the radio. However, being renowned Cav pilots and full of mercy, they found it more enjoyable to deplete Kev's wallet. The Major, speaking for everyone, through his laughter said.

"Mr. Johnson, I must tell you that this is absolutely the best tasting beer a Warrant Officer has ever bought me! I thank you for it and the next time you are buying for everyone, please remember your poor old boss."

However, this time Kev was deeply enjoying the laughter which he had created. He hadn't broken a bird and no one got hurt. As for his ego, he was a Scout and he had ego to spare.

Somewhat to his dismay, Kev discovered that the Major wasn't finished. Somehow, he knew that he had a few more digs and comments coming his way. As he was leaving the club, straight-faced, the major had a question for him.

"Hey Kev, don't forget to tell all your buddies the next time you see a windmill?"

Another day and another time and it was ole Kev's turn to offer the interesting suggestion. Kev's latest suggestion got their blood flowing. It was the first mission of the morning and, as always, the three of them were looking for new and creative ways to get themselves into trouble. Sometimes, Kev and Johnny were like two little children. What one didn't think of, the other one did and they both got into trouble because of it.

During his months in country, Kev had discovered many interesting and exciting places in Viet Nam. Happy Valley was one of the more interesting ones. It was a nondescript, twenty mile long, valley known to almost every combat soldier in the Central Highlands. Infamous, it was also known to those in the Central Coastal region of Viet Nam. Year after year, no matter who the personnel or which American unit was present, Happy Valley essentially remained the same scary place. The little valley was Charlie's home field! Years previously, Charley had set up housekeeping there fighting the French, then the Japanese, and then the French again. Having paid for it in gallons of blood, he was not going to move out because the Americans requested that he do so.

Writing to Pastor Bill, Kev commented.

I hope that the name Happy Valley causes no confusion. Let me be clear about this place. We did not call it Happy Valley because it had the best bars, steam houses, and brothels in all of Viet Nam. Of course, it is possible that some of these accommodations did exist for the pleasure of the permanent residents. I doubt that I'll ever know the answer to that for sure. Still, if they existed, I didn't know of a single GI who had frequented these establishments. Happy Valley had a noxious and notorious reputation as the place that the average, run of the mill, American soldier did not relish visiting.

Of course, Johnny and I held a somewhat different view of things. Many who knew us had said we were moderately crazy. People said, that upon careful examination of our mental state, one might correctly suspect that neither of us was firing on all cylinders. Others, colorfully suggested that our elevators did not go all the way to the top floor. The beer drinking crowd suggested that we were a couple cans short of a six pack. Uninformed people thought that our apparently perverse desire to go where we were not welcomed would eventually get us killed. Maintaining our reputation, we always yearned to visit Happy Valley for a cold one.

Good Ole Mother nature had nestled this quaint little valley in the deepest part of the Central Highlands. It was an undisputed fact that this little piece of real estate clearly belonged to the North Vietnamese Army and their Viet Cong cousins. They had a long term lease written in the blood of many young men from many places. It had been several years since Americans had been in this one-hundred-mile square area in force. The tragic facts of the war remained unchanged. When reconnaissance ground troops went in, more often than anyone at a command level wanted to admit, they never came back! In the mildly poetic language of the Red Birds, this was injun country.

Though Kev never saw it himself, he was completely convinced that the bad guys posted a large NO TRESPASSING sign at every entrance to the valley. Every pilot in the Cav agreed as well as those pilots of different outfits, whether someone saw the sign or not, the bad guys enforced this no trespassing sign with near religious zeal.

The brass, as is an occupation hazard to the grunts, continued to ignore the bright neon no trespassing signs. Safely manning their typewriters, the Remington Raiders claimed that the signs were invalid. Following orders, the Major assigned Red One-Five the dangerous task of taking a look-see. They were supposed to make sure that the bad guys had not left! The lowliest private knew that the bad guys had been in residence so long that the signs were in Vietnamese, French, Japanese, and English. This same lowly private knew that the bad guys were not leaving

When the Major told Kev, over the radio, where they were going, he had mixed feelings. As always, his finely honed Scout's ego relished the challenge. However, his brain, which was functioning for a change, was less enthusiastic. Kev keyed the mike to share his feelings with Johnny and Pete about the wisdom of the mission.

"Most likely, some staff weenie safely hidden in his air-conditioned office dreamed up this little trip. I bet you that he accomplished this difficult task just before he went to the club for his steak and mixed drinks."

He continued briefing the two of them.

" Heck, it seems like an easy enough job. All we are required to do is to find the 'bad guys' base camp in preparation for a combined air and ground assault sometime in the future. That looks easy enough, on paper!"

Just before Kev and his team began their reconnaissance, the radio crackled. It was the Major who was flying C&C. He told them, in his concerned fatherly manner, to be careful.

"One-Five, keep your airspeed up and 'go in hot'."

He wanted them to go in with guns firing. That was just fine with Kev. The boss continued his stern fatherly advice.

"For God's sake, don't go and get yourself shot down! You and Johnny be careful. If you go down, I am not sure we can get you out! In fact, I doubt we can get anyone out with anything less than a full division and a wing of Fox 4's!"

Johnny and Kev both knew, though they said otherwise, that they were not considered important enough to the war effort to rate a full division for their rescue. Personally, though, they felt that they were more than well worth the effort! A Cav troop, committed to them, was attractive. However, a full division would have been more attractive.

Without further ado, the trumpeting of bright brass bugles, or the roar of a standing ovation, they began their recon. Red One-Seven was flying the wing dutifully following Kev. As a team, they spread out and let down from their higher altitude. Immediately the two little birds started snooping around the high ground beginning with a high speed recon. After a few minutes of snooping around, all was quiet. Between them, they had not heard a single bullet being shot at them. Ole One Shot Charley didn't seem to be home. The three young men took this as a good sign.

Speaking the intercom, minutes later, Kev and Johnny came to agreement. The way which they were reading the signs along the ridges, pointed to the valley floor. If they went into the valley, they felt confident that would find the enemy base camp. Acting a little bolder than cautious maturity would dictate, they decided to go down and do a close look-see at the valley floor. If they wanted to find the bad guys that was where they had to go. So far, everything had been going well. They had not yet received any ground fire.

Kev commented to Johnny, "maybe the bad guys have already heard of us. So, they decided to dig in for the duration."

It was time to continue their infamous, tradition of having more guts than brains. Less informed souls had made other unkindly suggestions concerning their tradition. Most of the Slick drivers said Red One-Five's tradition contained more stupidity than brains. Furthermore, they said that it had nothing to do with guts. Whatever the case might have been, they descended, down into the deep dark valley. Their first pass down the central part of the valley was high speed. Deeply disappointed, they received no response from anybody who might have been in residence.

Not responding, to them and to their knocking on the door seemed rude. Their disappointment served as a further indication of their tireless dedication to their infamous tradition. However, the staff weanie who assigned them the mission wanted intelligence. He didn't understand that they couldn't see anything during a high speed pass. All that they saw was the green blur of trees rapidly passing beneath them. Eventually, they felt forced to slow down if they wanted to see anything. Though it was very dangerous, and the Major told them not to, they did it.

Foolishly, Kev and Johnny were disappointed at the lack of a greeting. Pete remained quiet. He was the saner one. The two young men felt that their only option was to slow and get serious with their snoop.

As they slowed, C&C received a radio call. They all remained on the same frequencies so they were all kept up to date.

Kev wrote in his journal of his feelings about the news he received.

It was wonderful news. A pair of F-4 fighter bombers came on station and offered us some additional air-support. While it is true that Johnny and I, for some unknown reason, are considered infamous. It pains us to admit that some people have the nerve to debate the nature of our infamy. Nevertheless, big friends like a pair of F-4s are always welcomed when we go out to play with the bad guys. Sometimes, I think that we two fools are like a couple of little guys at a bar. We like to start fights that the big guys have to finish.

Johnny was taking his turn as the idea man. Sounding both gleeful and frustrated, he commented over the intercom.

"Hey boss, maybe we just need to knock on the door a little bit louder? Who knows, maybe they just didn't hear us?"

Pausing to think for a moment, Kev responded.

"Well . . . ? Tell you what Johnny, we saw some hooches a little way back. Why don't we go back, shoot the place up a bit with a good old-fashioned recon by fire? If they don't respond, we'll burn down a couple of hooches. While they burn, we'll sit back a bit and see what happens. Maybe after we get their attention, they will be willing to come out and play with us."

Pausing a moment and foolishly getting caught up in things Kev continued.

"You know, you're right, it seems like a real shame to come all this way and not get to play with our friends."

Kev had taken over and Johnny was in full agreement.

"Well . . . what are we waiting for boss? Let's Rock and Roll?"

Kev took a moment to tell C&C what they had planned to do. C&C wasn't exactly thrilled with the idea. Nevertheless, he reluctantly gave it his blessings. They quickly returned to where they had seen the hooches, and Rock and Roll they did! Johnny was firing his M-60 from directly behind Kev, while Pete was firing away on his M-60 beside Kev. Ole Kev then decided that it was time to knock at the front door a little bit louder. The two crewmen tossed out three or four Willie Pete grenades. This got two or three of the hooches merrily ablaze.

Continuing in his journal Kev said.

"That's when things got really busy, quick in a hurry. Quicker than I can possibly tell it, everything went to heck in a handbasket. Just like my good friend the Apostle Peter from the Bible, I got the three of us in stormy water well over our heads!"

Like always, ole Kev had spoken and acted without carefully counting the consequences! Apparently, the disturbed residents of Happy Valley were card-carrying members of the NVA. Not unexpectedly, they had taken violent exception to their homes being set on fire. Their angry responses seemed to come from out of nowhere. Heavy machine gun fire came from more than a dozen different directions. The NVA spit restitution and revenge from hidden positions which the three of them had missed in their anxiousness to play games. What erupted was the most intense antiaircraft fire that Kev had ever received. No doubt about it, Red One-Five and crew were suddenly playing hard-ball with the first team. Shocked, Kev screamed in the radio in unashamed, stark, sheer raving terror.

"**TAKING FIRE . . . TAKING FIRE!!!**"

He was as terrified as he could be and continued to cry out.

"They are throwing everything but the kitchen sink at me."

Kev and Johnny had been around a while and they were known commodities. They got excited, became dramatic, and frequently acted with unnecessary "flair." However, they didn't rattle quickly. Their terrified screaming got the full and undivided attention of everybody on the radio net. Chronologically they might still be a couple of kids. However, they were also combat veterans and knew the score. Kev had already been shot down a couple of times. Johnny had also gone down a couple of times. That was in his first tour with the Red Birds. As Kev viewed the developing situation, this time there was no question. This was going to be Kev's last mission. It didn't take a first class rocket scientist to note that they were in the deepest trouble that the two of them had ever managed to stir up! Again, Kev cried out in pure terror.

"They are throwing everything but the kitchen sink at me!"

Maybe Kev was always a wingman at heart. He always tried to protect his wing and gun birds. Instantly analyzing his plight, the rational part of Kev knew that he was already dead. Reflexively, he keyed the radio and screamed at his wing man.

"One-Seven get the h--- out of here!"

He was the target of all the fire. If he acted fast, maybe his wingman could escape the trap by making a run for it. Without lifting his thumb from the mike button, Kev then yelled at the Cobra helicopter gun-ships.

"Break -- break, White Birds get the h--- out of here! Heavy caliber antiaircraft fire, do not, I repeat, **DO NOT ROLL IN!**"

A grim determination took over the emotional flavor of the little Red Bird. Committed to making their deaths expensive, they responded to the situation. Stoically accepting the unacceptable, the three young men knew that they had arrived at their appointed destination. They were alone and stranded somewhere, smack dab in the middle of the Biblical Valley of The Shadow of Death! Johnny was standing on the skids returning fire for all he was worth. Pete was grimly matching Johnny bullet for bullet. Their return fire really didn't make much difference.

228

They were low, slow, heavily overloaded, with heavy antiaircraft shooting at them from below and down on them from the sides of the hill. It was problematic enough that Kev stirred up a nasty little hornet's nest. Not satisfied, Kev had to go one step further.

Overconfident to the point of stupidity, he had stumbled into an artfully created anti-helicopter trap. Kev knew, that he and Johnny didn't own enough finesse between the two of them to be planning on telling war stories at the club. They were clearly doomed. Kev's concern was the safety of his wing and the Snakes. Remaining remarkably clear-headed, Kev considered the torrent of ground fire making him their point of focus.

He thought to himself.

"I see no need for anybody to join me in this foolishness."

Powerless, all that he could do was pray that everybody had followed his commands and beat feet. Regarding radio conversations, he and Johnny knew that their friends were listening to Red One-Five's final recon.

Red One-Five was like a wounded animal beset by a pack of hungry wolves. Surrounded and unable to move, the wolves were viciously tearing away at her flanks. She had begun, what Kev felt, was her final struggle for life. Johnny was still returning fire from the skids and Pete was matching bullet to bullet in this final confrontation for their survival. In desperation and acceptance of what was, Kev lowered the nose and pulled in every ounce of power the little turbine would give him. She was like an overloaded semi-trailer pulling away from a stop light. Struggling to move, the little Red Bird, oh so terribly slowly, began to accelerate. Airspeed and altitude meant life for them, neither of which, they had in excess. Understandably, he had completely forgotten about the orbiting F-4's.

Having banished every thought from his mind but their upcoming death struggle, a new voice in his earphones startled Kev. Quite literally, it felt like the voice of the great and the holy coming from the heavens. This new voice on the radio net turned out to be the secular voice of salvation caressing their ears. Presenting itself in a slow pleasant Southern drawl, Kev heard an unexpected sound of hope in his headphones.

"Red One-Five, you'all just follow that/there blue line. You'all just keep moving on down the delightful little river at best possible speed. Phantom Two-Two and Phantom Two-Three are inbound. And, we're hot!"

They did not politely ask everyone to clear a path for them. The F-4 drivers knew that they had a meaningful mission that measured its value in human lives. By God, they were going to do their best to save Red One-Five. It was the Cav's responsibility to get the h--- out of their

229

way! Kev was not in a position to be proud. However, the young man was glad that the F-4's had not forgotten him. He told Sven later that night.

"Who was I to argue when the big boys wanted to join our game? Unfortunately, my best possible speed had yet to move beyond a slow walk. I knew that it was going to take me a long time to get out of the kill zone."

Dodging trees and staying over the blue line, he couldn't see the whole drama unfolding from his position in the cockpit. Ole Kev had his hands full trying to survive blundering into Happy Valley's hidden anti-helicopter trap. Johnny keyed the mike and admitted that he had to watch the air show. He explained his logic and fatalism.

"What the h--- boss. You know that we're s------! I just gotta see this."

Looking back over his shoulder while he continued to fire his M-60, he gave Kev and Pete a vivid and colorful running commentary. Between Johnny's colorful commentary, Kev's own imagination, and what he did see, this is what happened.

The two pilots of the two F-4's snugged up their safety harnesses and pushed their control sticks and throttles forward. Pushing their throttles o afterburner and their control sticks forward, they sent the two lethal war birds plunging directly into Happy Valley's antiaircraft firestorm. Charging to the rescue, they came hurtling down and inbound.

Men with a mission, they did not pull-up at the prescribed two-thousand feet for a ground attack. Nor did they pull-up at the danger-ously low one-thousand feet. Still, they did not pull up when they arrived at five-hundred feet. At this altitude, they were far below the hills surrounding the valley and much of the antiaircraft shooting down at the little Red Bird. All the way down to the deck screamed the two avenging F-4's. Phantom Two-Two and Phantom Two-Three were inbound. They were plunging to Red One-Five's rescue at better than five-hundred knots. That translates to almost six-hundred miles an hour!

In writing to Pastor Bill, Kev did his best to relay some of his powerful feelings about the two Phantom drivers.

I can never know exactly what happened in those two cockpits. Nevertheless, I am inclined to think that something affected these two F-4 drivers with the foolhardy and romantic malady that frequently got Johnny and me in trouble. Not to insult them, however, I think that they were Scouts at heart. Whatever the case, those two guys are now prime characters in my book of life. Forgive me. Two guys are in each aircraft. In a terrible and strange way, it was a beautiful example of the military art of combined services supporting each other. I might add though, how they did it was clearly foolhardy! Yet, I know one thing. Had they been shot down, Johnny and I would have figured a way to get them out. On my word of honor, we would have gotten them out. We would have done it even if we had to commit the whole of the United States Army, Air Force, Marines and Navy in Vietnam and then walk out with the four guys on our backs.

If Kev had not seen the attack with his own eyes, he would never have believed what happened. For sure, he would not, for even an instant, have believed anybody telling the story. However, they did what they did. When the two F-4s dropped their napalm, the front shackles let loose first. The front shackles were supposed to release first. What Kev would not have believed was that before the rear shackles let loose the napalm canisters struck the trees splashing their hellfire. This meant that the napalm burst into killing flames before the canisters were completely free of the F-4's. Kev saw the smoky burn marks all the way down the sides of their avenging aircraft. He knew that the two big jets must have suffered damage from their own high explosives which they had also dropped. Aware of the risk those Jet Jockeys were taking, Kev couldn't speak for the huge lump in his throat. Adding to his discomfort, the young man had trouble seeing for the tears streaming down his cheeks. He knew that those lovely Air Force fighter jocks were risking shooting themselves down.

At the frozen moment in time, illuminated by bursting napalm, Kev felt a miracle taking place. Phantom Two-Two and Phantom Two-Three, "truly were one" with Red One-Five as they shot past them at the Red Bird's tree top altitude. He could not believe the message of salvation his eyes were sending him. Thundering past him on full afterburners were two big Phantoms right on the top of the trees. The big, bad, and beautiful F-4's were within fifty feet of the little Red Bird. The bright red blue cones of flames shooting out of their exhaust were punctuating the urgency of their quest. Passing on both sides of the hounded and harried Red Bird, their twenty millimeter Vulcan cannons were firing with the sound of ripping canvas.

In Kev's opinion, they were the best friends for whom a man could ask. To his delight, Kev's new found friends were carving a high explosive path for their escape. Too emotionally moved to speak, the three young men watched with mouths agape. Hopeful for the first time, they continued their grim struggle for survival. However, they were very thankful to be in the company of some bigger and tougher friends!

With afterburners belching flame and the characteristic black smoke of the F-4, Phantom Two-Two and Phantom Two-Three came to the end of the valley. They did beautiful crossing and climbing turns. Again the radio crackled with words of salvation.

"Phantom Two-Two and Phantom Two-Three are inbound hot."

Having swapped sides of the valley, and they pointed their deadly aircraft toward the valley floor. This time, they returned in the other direction. Looking directly at the onrush of avenging angels, Kev could see the unfolding thrilling drama first hand. He told Sven.

"It was unbelievable! They were right down on the deck! Releasing their napalm just like they did on the first pass, they made the bad guys notice that my big brothers had joined the game. Charley knew that my two big brothers were p-----! The jelly-like napalm was bursting into flames before it had cleared the big, bad-a---- birds. Passing us with their Vulcan cannon firing six-thousand twenty millimeter rounds a minute, they were like something out of a big screen movie."

"Sven, it was like this. Heading directly for me, at near sonic speed, were two of the squattest, ugliest, and meanest looking aircraft I have ever seen. Those Fox 4's were brutal to behold. As they came screaming down the valley, I could see the shock waves flowing across them in the humid air. When they dropped the napalm and opened up with their 'pistol,' they were all business. Flames and fire were everywhere.

The bursting napalm formed Dante's rolling billowing smoke and flames of hell. Additional white flames of hell were shooting out, at least twenty feet, from their pistols. As they passed, I could see twin cones of blue red welders torch flames coming from their afterburners. Those big twenty mike-mike shells were creating a tornado of shredded trees twenty feet to our left and right. Our mean and nasty big brothers were creating a wonderfully safe path for little Red One-Five and crew to follow. The safe path they created for us was a virtual dead zone! If our friends in the F-4's had anything to do about it, this time, the howling wolves would not bring down the wounded prey!"

For the next couple of minutes, while the little Red Bird was clearing the valley, it was strangely silent. The red-hot M-60's had finished speaking their staccato piece. No idle chatter filled the radio net. Best of all, no NVA guns were spewing forth their hatred. The gross brutality and killing efficiency of the Phantoms left everyone, on both sides of the conflict, stunned and silent. Finally gaining some airspeed, Kev cleared the valley. When they were finally safe, a collective sigh reverberated through the battered little Red Bird.

Kev's pulse rate eventually returned somewhere below the five-hundred mark. As he gathered his wits about him, the pleasant slow Southern drawl of Phantom Two-Two caressed his ears.

"Red One-Five are you'all O.K.?"

Keying the mike, Kev cryptically responded. "Thank You!"

After a pregnant pause, he continued.

"Phantom Two-Two, we owe you big time. You and your friends can come play in our ball park any time you want. If you and Two-Three are ever in our neighborhood, drop in our club. We'll keep you drunk for a month."

Kev didn't know what else he could say. He remained stunned

and shocked from nearly being killed. Furthermore, the gift of the efficient and brutal salvation he had just received had placed him in an emotional overload. Kev's savior spoke again.

"Red One-Five, Two-Three and I had a good time playing in your ball park. You'all ever get in trouble again, just give me a call."

With one last click of his mike the gentle Southern drawl gave Kev his parting instructions.

"You'all stay out of that valley now, you hear!"

With that, both did aileron rolls and left the area.

When he was telling Sven all about the incident that night, the hopeless romantic in Kev, gushed excitedly.

"One might be tempted to say things ended in the finest Hollywood tradition. Phantom Two-Two and his silent side kick Phantom Two-Three flew off into the deep red sunset."

When he finished talking with Phantom Two-Two, the Major radioed Kev.

"Red One-Five, this is White Six. What's your status son?"

Happy to answer, he immediately responded to the boss.

"Six, this is One-Five, we're still flying and breathing sir. Give me about zero-two and I will give you a more thorough status report."

The three young men in the little Red Bird did their superficial inventory.

"White six, this is One-Five with my status report."

The Major didn't respond so Kev began his report.

"We're a little shaken up sir. Thank God. Nobody is hurt. We expended most of our ammo and we're getting a little low on fuel. The bird has taken several hits, but, nothing serious. All the gauges are in the green. However, it sounds like we took at least one rotor hit, maybe two. Request permission to refuel and check her out more throughly."

The Major's next decision was an easy one. Two problems pointed to the same conclusion. First, he had a badly shaken crew that he did not want to put back into the meat grinder. His second problem made it easy for him to spare the ego's of the young crew.

"One-Five, after you refuel and rearm, if you consider your bird airworthy for a one-time flight, I want you to put a circle red X in the log book and head for the barn. Just to be on the safe side, I am going to send One-Seven along with you to keep you from getting lonely."

Chuckling softly, the Major keyed the intercom and spoke to his pilot in the C&C bird.

"Dwayne, you know that if he makes it safely to refuel, he'll fly that wreck back himself. No way in all of creation will Kev admit that his bird is unsafe for him to fly. I can read his mind. If maintenance can fly it back, then by God Kev can fly it back!"

An older, second tour pilot, Dwayne responded with a soft

chuckle.

"I know sir. No one has ever said that Red One-Five was either smart or cautious. Still, as God is my witness, you and I will never see a better Scout!"

Bursting out with a tension-relieving laugh, the Major cautioned his pilot.

"Dwayne, for goodness sake, whatever you do, don't tell him that. In his heart he already knows he's the best that there is. If we tell him, he will be more impossible to live with. That is, if being more impossible is possible for that crazy fool."

On the way to the refueling site, the three of them decided that they would check out the battle damage before refueling. If maintenance had to sling-load it back under a Huey, they wouldn't want the extra weight of ammo and fuel. When the fueling site came into sight all heaved a sigh of relief and Kev made his call.

"LZ Fishbed, this is Red One-Five inbound with battle damage. We request hover-taxi clearance to park and inspect our aircraft before refueling."

The tower gave them their clearance and they set down to carefully meter-meter things. While the rotors were spinning down, both Pete and Johnny quickly jumped out. Childlike curiosity was killing them. Johnny had seen a couple of holes in the clamshell engine doors. Sure enough, they had taken a couple of hits, but they had passed through without hitting any engine components. Pete also discovered a couple of hits in the dog house. The bullets had torn up the air-cleaner while passing through. Pete was worried that the engine must have ingested some foreign matter. Kev assured him that the TOT gauge did not suggest any engine damage.

"After all," Kev assured him. "It got us this far, didn't it?"

With a doubtful grunt, Pete accepted that the bird would probably get them home.

By then, the blades had stopped turning and Kev was studying the hole in a rotor blade. His wingman, being as curious as the crew, had found something interesting. He called the whole crew over and showed them the hole in the tail boom. Three sets of eyes got very wide as they exposed the tail rotor shaft. A matching hole went through the shaft with only a little bit of it tearing. Kev decided that this tearing was due to the high speed of the shaft when it hit it. After much discussion, Pete very reluctantly agreed that it would hold.

"After all," said Kev with his best optimist voice. "It got us this far!"

While they were closing the tail boom, Johnny suddenly started shouting.

"My God! Pete, Pete, come here quickly. Will you look at that,

Mr. J's seat is missing."

Without missing a beat, Kev continued to calmly close the tail boom. Making them wait so that they didn't think him easy, he finally responded to their needling.

"Why shucks Johnny, you know exactly how that ole seat disappeared. About ten seconds after the shooting started, I sucked that little charmer right up to a place where the light doesn't shine. Only me and my proctologist know for sure."

That started uproarious laughter by the five young men who were looking over the battered bird. It was exactly the medicine that they needed.

A couple of days later, Kev wrote extensively in his journal.

I believe that this whole incident is part and parcel of the irony of combat. Most likely, I will never know who Phantom Two-Two was as a person. I never saw his face. He was, in many ways, just an invisible savior's voice on a radio. He was the one who was coming to my aid. I don't even know his rank, not that rank is very important once combat begins. However, I do know one thing. I know what Phantom Two-Two and his wingman Phantom Two-Three did for us that afternoon. No doubt about it, he is the man who saved our lives. Lastly, I do know that I carefully followed his advice. Considering what he did for me, I felt that Phantom Two-Two's advice was good enough for me. Command and control didn't ask us to go back for another look see. Johnny and I did not go into that valley again!

Already I have difficulty believing the whole Happy Valley thing happened. I find it difficult because so much detail is missing in this story. Even as I sit here writing, in reality, I can only guess that Phantom Two-Two was a Southerner. The only evidence is his drawl and his "you'alls" on the radio. Still, I have no idea exactly where in the south he was born, who his parents were, or where he went to school. Nor do I know who his friends are, what his age is, or many other countless details that make up the knowing of another human being. In fact the only name I know him by, and the only name he knows me by, are our military call signs. Then again, as people maybe we would not like each other. Not that liking each other really matters in combat. All I really know is what he, Phantom Two-Two did. He saved my life!

Later, that same evening Red One-Four and Kev were sharing a couple of beers and rehashing the day's exciting events. Over the months, this hanger/club flying had become their frequent custom. One-Four had been flying team lead for the other Red Bird team and had missed out on all the fun in ole Happy Valley. Sometimes Kev thought that he was the smarter of the two. Ole Sven, showing his wisdom, was not the slightest bit disappointed in missing out in all the fun. Maybe if he didn't have Johnny, he too would feel different. Kev was telling One-Four that if Phantom Two-Two had said something else to him, he would have done it. Had he said "hey you'all, let's make another run through there. With a little luck, we can pinpoint those antiaircraft batteries and take them out. After we do that, it will be safe for you to finish the reconnaissance. After all, there's no sense in quitting now." Kev told Sven that he and his crew would have gone back into Happy Valley, guns a'blazing!

"Strangely enough, he had earned that kind of authority/power over my life. I believe it was because of his actions."

He emphatically added a postscript.

"However, I am also very – very – very thankful that he said to me, 'you'all stay out of that valley now you hear!'"

Quietly thinking for a moment or two, Ole One-Four popped the top on another beer as they sat upon the old rocket crates arranged in front of the pilots hooches. Kicking up his feet, Kev saw a deep philosophical look set in his face. That thoughtful look took over just before he became profound. Kev hadn't thought that they had enough beers for profound statements, yet. Apparently, they had enough. Ole Sven began.

"AUTHORITY! That is an interesting word you have chosen Kev. Let me bounce a couple of thoughts off you tonight. It is clear to me that Phantom Two-Two's authority was not in the badges of rank that he wore on his shoulders. All we know of his military rank is that he was a commissioned officer in the Air Force. Furthermore, his authority could not have come from the family's connections. We both know that his authority was not in how much money that he had in the bank back in the world! Money doesn't mean much of anything over here. At least money doesn't mean a thing to us Red Birds." Pausing for a moment, Sven's face lit up. "Well . . . , it does pay for the beer."

Presumably it was profound philosophy time. Philosophy, they had discovered over the preceding months was thirsty work. So, Kev also leaned back and popped the top of another cold one. Picking up on the flow of things, he pondered.

"Maybe, we based Phantom Two-Two's authority upon the way he acted. The proof's in the pudding. He had saved my life at risk of his own! That, my good friend Sven, was good enough for me to do as he wished!"

Relieving some of his heavy philosophical thirst, Kev drew heavily on his beer.

"Think about it this way Sven. I remember exactly how today felt. When my pucker factor had gone off the scale, I heard the soft southern drawl in my ear phones. 'This is Phantom Two-Two and Phantom Two-Three we're inbound hot.' Something important was left unsaid."

"What he didn't say was, 'This is all you need to know. I will save you!'"

Kev looked deeply within for a moment and decided to take a

chance on exposing himself.

"Let me use some of my Sunday School thinking for a moment. Using the Psalmist words, I think I know what happened. 'He, Phantom Two-Two, entered the Valley of The Shadow of Death.' This he did for my sake! Accepting the risk involved, he was willing to enter that valley with me. Because he joined in my danger, I listened to him when he told me to stay over the blue line. I continued to listen to him when he told me to stay out of that valley. As for me, today Happy Valley was the Valley of The Shadow of Death."

They sat upon their top quality custom-made ammunition box furniture. Together, the two young men sat and slowly sipped on their beers. Though they were together, they were both also alone. Musing upon the day, the two of them became totally preoccupied with private thoughts. That was some very deep thinking for a couple of young Warrant Officer Pilots just out of High School. After an indeterminate amount of time Sven spoke up again.

"I think you've got something Kev."

"Oh, how?"

"Think about how we get so many of our leaders over here. When we first meet them, we have no way to tell the good ones from the bad ones. We simply are stuck, good or bad, with whoever gets sent to us from the Five-Sided-Puzzle-Palace on the Potomac!"

Having made that point, he leaned forward with a new intensity.

"It seems to me that leadership/authority has nothing to do with titles, earned or honorific. Leadership/authority, it has nothing to do with stars, eagles, oak leaves, or even bars on someone's shoulders. Rather, it seems clear enough to me, that the quality of leadership/authority has everything to do with what a person is and does. The true leader of men rises when the 'fat is in the fire' and the troops need good leadership to save their bacon. If you want my opinion, these are the only ones we should have to listen to. The ones who prove themselves by taking care of the troops."

Kev felt the conversation was getting dangerous to military discipline and all that sort of thing. Nevertheless, he could see that Sven had made a telling point. Knowing who should earn their respect and whom they should risk their lives for was becoming their most pressing problem. Using previously undiscovered wisdom, Kev decided that it was time to end the conversation. He was afraid that they would say or do something stupid with all their drunken wisdom.

"Tell you what Sven, I am going to my hootch, grab my note book and write for a couple of hours while today still remains fresh in my mind."

Sven laughed with a touch of bitterness and responded.

"Sounds like a good idea. As for myself, I am going to get as stinking drunk as I can. Then, I guess I will continue waiting for some fool in Washington or the Puzzle Palace to do me in. I am sure that someone will find a new way to tie my hands, take my guns away from me, and then send me somewhere to get killed!"

Later, the journal continued.

Though the day kinda ended on a bitter note, I went to bed feeling good about ole Kev's contribution. True enough, Johnny and I had jumped into the deep end of the pool. As always, we did it without checking the depth of the water. That takes more brains than we seem to have. Then again, we had also experienced the best part of the American effort here in Viet Nam. Phantom Two-Two and Two-Three had reminded me of that. Despite what Jane Fonda and alike say, Uncle Sam has filled this place to overflowing with good people trying to do their jobs. In fact, unlike back in the world, risking their lives for other strangers was routine. Ya, lots of problems happen because of the numberless idiots micro managing our actions. They don't help any by telling us that we can't cross invisible lines. These are the same lines that the other guys cross with impunity. However, today, I had seen what was best about the people at the forefront of life. We had even managed to put a bit of a hurt on the bad guys.

"Overall, it was not a bad day!"

Beset by a sleepless night, Kev's mind would not rest or give him any peace. It was as if he had forgotten to do something. Maybe it was more like a critical piece of a hidden of an important puzzle was missing. The restless young man had tossed and he had turned, all night long, in his incompleteness. However, the answer lay just beyond his grasp. Flying and the romance of combat was involved, but he could not see how. Reviewing "his path," he had accepted that he wasn't going to fly the awesome Fox-4. Slightly disappointed, he felt that his children and grandchildren would not be enamored by his flying a helicopter. When he thought about it, he found that his little Red Bird lacked the glamor he sought.

"That's it! That's the missing word. That's the answer!"

John Glenn had named his WW II Mustang "Glamorous Glenna" after his wife. He had named all his later aircraft, including the Bell X-1 in which he had broken the sound barrier the same. Ole 662 needed to be named. She needed her wondrous personality expressed. People needed to know that she was far more than just a little flying machine. His little bird was his faithful and magnificent steed. She was his friend and companion. Jumping out of bed at dawn's light, he knew what he was going to name her. "I shall call her, 'Rocinante,' the faithful steed."

With that out of the way, he could proceed with work.

After carefully naming 662, Kev then tried to understand why the rugged hills and valleys of central Viet Nam constantly got him into trouble. It made no sense to him. He never got into trouble when he occasionally flew in the flat lands. However, when he was flying over the primitive hilly country, he felt a call and challenge from their stone age ruggedness and beauty. Disconcerted, he wondered why he couldn't savor flying above the primitive grandeur in peace and quiet. Yet, he continued to sing the same sad song with the same tear-filled refrain while he was poking around the beckoning green hills and valleys of Viet Nam.

Whenever he got himself into trouble, inevitably, his new dilemma occurred directly on the top of a hill or deep down in a hidden valley. Eventually, Kev decided to accept the obvious. The changelessness that had become Kev's Vietnam continued as he marveled at a world which he had never previously experienced. Whatever this place was, clearly it was not his picturesque, peaceful, and pastoral New England.

Surprising no one, least of all himself, Red One-Five again managed to get himself well over his head while he explored the pristine primitiveness of the primordial land. Suddenly, he was, feeling the boiling fervor of brewing trouble heading his way. Increasingly anxious, he didn't know the where or how of his coming. However, he felt it coming. In the blink of an eye, he found himself in a huge cast iron pot of water. Adding to his misery, the bad guys had heated to a vigorous, violently rolling boil. Not only was the water hot, he knew that he was to be dinner's main course. In his imagination, the only thing lacking was the dancing of half-naked savages' banishing spears.

As new and exciting things always did for ole Red One-Five, they began innocently enough. The Major had him quietly poking around a new valley. Try as he might, he had not turned up anything of substantial interest. Humid warmth and the constantness of the triple canopy jungle was a gently lulling influence. Fighting sleepiness, he was fearful that he would lose his edge in the boredom of his recon. Earlier in the day, Big Boss Six, something or other, had been pressing Kev's boss to find something interesting for division to become involved in. During their pre-mission briefing, the Major had thoughtfully informed the Red Birds about division's dire need to stir up some trouble. Upon hearing the news, Kev poked Sven in the ribs and irreverently commented.

"Looks to me as if someone needs to add a star to his shoulder boards."

Laughing quietly, the two young men shrugged their shoulders at the seeming normalness of the situation. For them, a recon was a recon. They had long since given up trying to understand what the Army was doing in Vietnam.

Neither Kev not Sven had made any grandiose public statements about how much they liked being Scouts. However, this request to start a fight was right up their alley. Unrecognized by them, they loved to start a fight that someone else would have to finish. In a very candid moment, Kev repeated to Pastor Bill.

"Most of the good lead pilots remind me of the mouthy little guy who is always causing trouble at the corner bar. Once we get things really cooking on high, we are like the mouthy little guy. We run away as fast as we can. When the rough stuff begins, we prefer to leave the big boys alone to duke it out."

Try as they might, neither Red team could find anything that might be of interest to Division. Big Boss Six wanted a legitimate excuse to make the poor ole crunchies from division come out to their neighborhood and play. However, neither Kev nor Sven had helped him. Both young men knew that Division's grunts felt little to no disappointment in their negative findings. God had yet to create the grunt who liked walking a million miles through the bush while carrying sixty pounds of ruck, rifle, and rations. Nevertheless, they diligently continued to look for trouble because that was what Big Boss Six wanted.

Interrupting his concentration, the UHF radio unexpectedly crackled in Kev's ear. The Major said that Big Boss Six had flown into the local area and he had made a suggestion. He wanted the Scouts to move farther west about two miles. Just as it had happened a hundred times before, Big Boss Six had made his suggestion from his safe vantage point of ten-thousand feet above any possible bad guys. Kev was flying 662, renamed Rocinante, and Pete was in the front seat. At the Major's radio call, ole Pete quickly quipped.

"Shoot boss, I bet that the friendly gentlemen from the North couldn't reach Big Boss Six with the biggest SAM missile they have set up in downtown Hanoi!"

Kev felt that it was a loser's bet. So, he didn't take Pete up on it. Laughing, he retorted.

"Pete, it is not fair to suggest such a terrible thing. Everyone knows that the Big Boss Six has a very special Command and Control Huey."

At that point, Johnny couldn't pass up the opportunity to join in with the straight man's line.

"Excuse me sir, but what's so special about that C&C bird?"

"Why goodness me. Guys, it is the only Huey in Viet Nam equipped with an oxygen system for pilot and crew."

Over-stepping himself a little bit, Pete added his last comment.

"What's the scoop, boss? Do you think Mr. Bird might like it up there?"

While he was laughing inside, Kev knew it was time to cut things off.

"OK guys, cool it! In case you've forgotten, we've got to go to work."

Well . . . when Big Boss Six made a suggestion, the little peons considered it a definitive order. The three young men in the little helicopter knew who the little peons were. Recognizing their lowly standing, they obediently followed command's suggestions, read orders. Red One-Five and crew pulled up stakes and moved camp to the west.

While they were doing that, Kev thought of a friend's brother who was a Second Lieutenant in the Marine Corps. He had attended the Naval Academy and upon graduating received his commission. When he heard that Kev was about to receive his Warrant, he sent him a small section from a handbook he had at the Academy. Kev knew that this was meant for Midshipmen at the Academy. However, he kept a copy of it in his wallet as a reminder that it also held true in the "real Army."

"Juniors are required to obey lawful orders of seniors smartly and without question. An expressed wish of a senior to a junior is tantamount to an order if the request or wish is lawful."

"Well," thought Kev. "Moving two miles isn't that difficult."

Apparently, everything looked just calm and peaceful from higher altitudes. Neither the Major nor Big Boss Six said that they saw anything of note. Kev knew that meant that neither Command and Control ship saw anything that raised concerns about the safety of the little Red Birds and their orbiting Snakes. The Major was good and Kev was confident that if they had seen something, he would have told him. Figuratively hitching up his belt, Kev set himself to work. Johnny had taught Kev to always check out the high ground at the beginning of a recon. That is exactly what they did under Johnny's careful direction! When they were satisfied that the hill tops were clear, then, and only then, would they start to check out the lower levels of a valley. One hill top, and then a second hill top, checked out with nothing more that some well-worn foot paths. Kev was quickly rediscovering his edge as the tension mounted. All the evidence that they had seen strongly suggested that the bad guys were or had recently been in the local area.

Dutifully, Kev reported their findings to Blue Six, the Major. Apprehensively, they began a cautious approach to the next of the high hills surrounding the valley. However, something, which eluded their grasp, didn't feel right. The three of them shared their growing discomfort on the intercom. They hadn't had the opportunity to see the recon area from higher altitude and felt like they may have missed something important. However, Big Boss Six wanted them there yesterday and he hadn't reported anything suspicious. Speaking rapidly and nervously, Kev kept up a constant chatter with Blue Six and the White birds. Usually, during a recon, Kev was very quiet on the radio unless they had contact with the bad guys. The Major had flown enough with Kev and Johnny to know that something in the air was making them very tense. Concerned, he called.

"One-Five, do you smell something bad?"

Kev responded immediately.

"Yes sir. However, as of the moment, I can't say what's bothering me. For what it is worth sir, Pete and Johnny feel it too!"

Lowering the nose of his little Red Bird and pulling in an arm load of power, Kev made for the next hill top. This rapidly accelerated the little Red Bird up to thirty or forty knots making them a more difficult target. Then, rolling to the right, his side of the helicopter, he pulled in maximum power and began a zoom climb to the top of the hill. **Bam! Bam! Bam!** Five, ten, maybe fifteen rounds of fifty-one caliber anti-aircraft started shooting at them no more than a dozen feet from them. Horrified, Kev and Johnny felt the hot muzzle blast banging on their legs. The two of them didn't exchange a word. No words were necessary. They knew it. The future had become fact and no F-4's were close by to save them. Abruptly and rudely, the bad guys had transformed them into three dead men flying in a little helicopter! It was only a matter of seconds before the heavy anti-aircraft rounds tore the three of them into hundreds of bloody little pieces.

"Break - Break. All Cav aircraft, heavy caliber anti-aircraft fire! Break contact immediately! Break down the valley to the south! Hit the deck! White Birds do not engage! Number two, follow the White Birds out the valley at best possible speed. I repeat. White Birds do not engage. Everyone on the Yellow Scarf net, Get the h--- out of here! I'll join you guys later."

The way Kev saw things, his wing man or the two White birds would get themselves blown out of the sky if they tried to help him. Terrified, Kev wasn't trying to be a hero. However, he accepted that the grim situation was his problem. He had stumbled into the anti-aircraft trap like a rank and raw rookie. Anger replaced fear. This was the second time in a couple of weeks he had stumbled into a trap. Kev was supposed to be the hunter and not the hunted.

"Well . . . ," he thought to himself. "It will only be my problem for another second or two."

"Join them later. Ha! Now, that's a laugh."

Just as suddenly as it had started, it stopped. Unexpectedly, the fifty-one had stopped firing! Finding that they were still very much alive and well, the three young men in the little helicopter were surprised and shocked. A heartbeat later, the reason for their reprieve began to become clear to them. It appeared, that if they stayed below the crest of the hill, they were safe. At least, they were safe for the moment. The bad guys couldn't depress the muzzle of the heavy, anti-aircraft, machine gun low enough to shoot at them. If nothing else, the Mexican stand off, of sorts, gave them a moment's breather. However, they were well aware that their good fortune wasn't going to last all day. If nothing else happened to ruin their day, they would run out of fuel soon enough. Drawing upon his deep pool of leadership skills, Kev came up with a big fat blank. He didn't have a ready answer for the potentially fatal, problem they were facing.

Later that night, Kev wrote in his journal about how he initially felt when the fifty-one opened fire on him.

Never let anyone say that when he was totally terrified, Kevin Paul Johnson was too proud to ask for help. Most likely, I had involuntarily deposited a smelly dark brown coating inside my skivvies. However, I decided not to address the odorific problem of brown and smelly skivvies. Putting first things first, I didn't figure that I would be the first man to die in combat with a big brown load in his britches. Keying the intercom, I mentally crossed my fingers that someone on this helicopter was a whole big-bunch smarter than I was or that I had been.

"Anyone have a brilliant idea or two that you would like to share with me? If you happen to have one, now is a really good time to do so! Because, I am afraid that the minute that we make a break for it and head down the valley, that gun is going to have a clear shot at us. I promise, when they're done with us, it ain't going to be a very pretty picture. By the

way, let's keep this little piece of information just among the three of us guys. Between you, me, and the lamppost, I think that we're in some very deep s---. Whatever happens, though, I don't want the other guys coming back to try and get us out of this mess."

People have an incredible variety of responses to danger and fear. Some like Charley Bird, as Kev had discovered months ago, freeze up. Others, and Kev had occasionally done so himself, got twitchy and highly excitable. Some, and Kev truly envied those people, become cool as a cucumber fresh out of the ice box. The largest number of folk, grimly grit their teeth, bear down, and do the best that they can. These people are usually hesitant to acknowledge their fear. Generally, Kev acknowledges his fear. At times, he seemed to embrace it as something evil with which he must compete. While he was competing with his fear for ultimate control, he usually got a little mouthy and sarcastic. Finally, when he had come up with a plan of action, he then boldly challenged his fear and the source of his fear. This was when ole Kev was at his best and at his worst. The problem was that he could become brave to the point of being foolhardy.

Two quick circuits around the crest of the hill and Kev won the battle for ultimate control over his fear. With that critical battle won, his fangs came slashing out of both sides of his mouth. Uncontrolled, they smashed their way straight through the worn metal floor of the cockpit. He was mad as h---. However, what was worse in his eyes, he was professionally embarrassed by stumbling into another trap.

"By God!" He said to himself.

"If, I'm going to die, then by C-----, I'm going to die on my terms, and on my terms alone!"

Pride and ego are a two-edged sword. It got Kev into trouble. Now that he was in trouble, he decided that it was time to cut with the back edge of the sword.

Kev's fight with the anti-aircraft gun suddenly became very personal. The heavy gun had surprised him and scared him almost to death. Its profound threat to unarmored helicopters had deprived him of his Cobra gun cover. He knew that the Snakes would probably be "dead meat" if they took on the gun trying to protect him while he was busy escaping. Ole Kev had never lost a Snake. He was proud that no Snake had taken as much as a single hit protecting him. Foolish to others, possibly, it was an important part of his protective instincts. Kevin Paul Johnson wasn't going to allow anyone to change that score card.

The bad guys had broken up their smooth team work and this made Kev mad. Using but a handful of bullets, a crew of three to five bad guys had forced the Cav to run from the valley. Embarrassing to Kev, it was like the Cav was running with its collective tail tightly tucked between their legs. Suddenly, the hot blood, began throbbing and pounding through his veins. This surge of pride and emotion gave Kevin Paul Johnson no choice. It was time to even the score!

Savagely, he stabbed at the intercom button and spoke in a coldly calm voice.

"Here's the hot skinny, guys. I'm really p----- off! We're going to take that SOB out! Now, guys, give me a couple of good ideas."

Johnny immediately responded.

"I'm with ya boss. That SOB just scared me out of ten years of life. He's got exactly what's coming to him."

Fearing that they were going to turn and attack the anti-aircraft gun, a third voice, belonging to Pete, issued a low groan of dismay over the intercom.

"Dear God, help me. I am going to die with two homicidal maniacs!"

A second or two passed without a brilliant idea being tossed into the arena. The mike clicked. A quiet and hesitant voice spoke.

"Somehow, I just know that I'm going to regret suggesting this. What do you guys think about a mini arc light?"

Just as Pete had instinctively feared, two enthusiastic voices greeted his hesitant suggestion by sounding their total approval. Muttering something to himself about two homicidal maniacs who were determined to get him killed, Pete grimly went about tightened up his crash harness.

One of the most awesome, if not always the most effective, weapons employed in Viet Nam was the B-52 "arc light" attack. The big old eight-engine B-52, first entered the Air Force inventory in the early fifties. Boeing specifically designed her to deliver nuclear weapons over a vast distance. The Air Force had not designed the majestic old bird for the type of war that the political types had dictated for Viet Nam. Nevertheless, she could haul an impressive tonnage of conventional bombs. Trying to develop a devastating, yet conventional, area weapon, someone thought of modifying some older B-52's. By adding some wing pylons and modifying the bomb bays, the grand old girl could drop something in the neighborhood of thirty, seven-hundred-and-fifty pound bombs. Unseen and unheard at thirty-thousand feet, she could drop all these bombs in a single continuous string. When these conventional bombs struck the dark jungle at night, the flash of them exploding, rolled across the ground below. It looked like a giant welder's electric arc was being struck upon the face of the earth.

The unfortunate troops who found themselves at the receiving end of an arc light, usually never knew what hit them. Once, in a beer soaked discussion, the Scout pilots agreed that an arc light was almost unfair. Without sound, sight, or other warning, suddenly the earth would heave up and explode. The theory held that they would so stun anyone who survived that they would be unable to offer any meaningful organized resistance for a long time. Most of the people in the Cav believed that, generally, an arc light only made kindling wood and tore up the earth. Having seen one from the air, the concentration of fire power nevertheless deeply impressed Kev. In full daylight, he could clearly see the bright welders arc being struck by the exploding bombs.

Sometime, long before Kev joined the Cav, an enterprising Scout got the interesting idea that the little Red Birds could copy the big boys. Most likely, after a case or two of beer, the idea of the mini arc light was born. In practice, the lead scout would fly, at twenty to thirty knots, over a bunker complex, small base camp, or other suspected enemy concentration. As they passed over it, they would drop as many fragmentation grenades as possible. Over time, the Cav style mini arc light became well refined. The most important innovation was the placing of a couple of open hooks in the door frames. After their pins were straightened out, the frag grenades would then be suspended upon the hooks by their rings.

When the time came to drop them, the hooks allowed the crew members to rake the grenades out like bunches of grapes. Just as a static line opened a parachute, the hook pulled the pins and released the spoons on the grenades. In fact, they came to a point where a good lead bird could put twenty-five to thirty grenades into the area roughly the size of a football field. It wasn't a B-52 strike. No one pretended that it was. However, for anyone on the ground, who wasn't well protected, it was just as devastating. Furthermore, it did serve to save the Snakes' rockets which cost one-hundred and twenty-five dollars each.

The bad part of the situation was obvious. The well-hidden fifty-one had trapped Kev. He had no Snakes, no rockets, no wingman with a mini-gun, and he was quickly running out of fuel and time. Other bad guys would soon be moving into position to shoot at him as he circled the hill.

On the positive side, Kev had now unsheathed his fangs. He had not done, nor was he going to do a rational cost analysis of their next move. By this point, Kev was well beyond doing a rational analysis of anything. This does not mean that he was caught-up in a berserker's blood lust. Yet, Kev and Johnny's blood was pounding fiercely in their veins. They were determined to kill that fifty-one cal. anti-aircraft gun or die trying! The whole meaning of life was that straightforward to them. Pete, on the other hand, did not share their lust for the kill. However, he trusted them. Best of all, he knew that when Kev's fangs were drawn, they would win. Not only would they win and tell tall tales about it later. When they counted their day as finished, they would have put a serious hurt on the bad guys.

One and a half turn around the hill and the three of them were set to go. Safety pins had been straightened out on every fragmentation grenade in the little helicopter. When he was ready, Johnny keyed the intercom first.

"All set boss. I've got fifteen hanging on hooks with straight pins and four with pins pulled in my hands."

Pete quickly chimed in.

"I've got eight on hooks and four in hand, with pins pulled." Kev acknowledged both and added his contribution.

"Pete set me up with eight on hooks. If nothing else, I do believe that we are going to be going for the record on this one, guys."

During the couple of minutes which had passed since the fifty-one opened up on them, Kev had eventually gotten their airspeed up to ninety knots. He felt confident that this would give him enough airspeed to make their attack and begin their escape. Making a quick mental check, he decided that everything was set for them to even the score.

"OK, guys. Here's the straight scoop. With just a little luck, they have had great difficulty tracking us by sound only. I'm going to red line the power and then zoom-climb the hill to the crest. I want you guys to be ready for the hairiest helicopter ride of your life. When I start the climb, I am going to pull back hard on the stick. I promise that it will feel like she is going all the way over on her back. As we crest the hill, I am planning on facing the opposite direction from which we have been going. Hopefully, that'll cross them up. If they are where I think they are, when I crest the hill and level my wings, we'll be right on top of them. We're going to dump our little basket of eggs right on their heads before they even figure out where we came from. I'll call the drop. Remember, don't drop till you get my command! Everybody set?"

Pete clicked his mike button twice in acknowledgment.

Johnny responded. "Let's do it. Let's fix this b------."

"Ready . . . ? Now!"

Without consciously thinking about it, somewhere deep within, Kev knew that it was time to find out if he were as good as he thought. Trusting his flying instincts and spacial awareness, he went for broke. Holding his breath, Kev yanked the collective stick to the upper stop, pulled the control stick all the way to the back stop, and about half way to the left. Groaning and shuddering, the airspeed quickly began to bleed off and ole Rocinate began climbing like an express elevator. Kev had no idea what the instruments were indicating. Looking over his left shoulder, and through the rotor disk, Kev was watching the side of the hill which appeared to be beneath him. He was trying to keep his orientation in relation to the hill.

Hearing the low RPM warning in his earphones, Kev eased the

upward pressure slightly on the collective stick till the beeper stopped. The forward airspeed bled off to almost nothing. Then, Kev pushed the control stick most of the way forward. Rocketing up the hill, it seemed to those inside her, that the little helicopter was upside down and standing on her tail. The clock stopped and Kev wished that he could have been on the outside watching. Hughes Helicopter never designed their little Loach to do the things that Kev had coached her into doing! He was making her fly like she was an F-4 cooking on both afterburners!

At the apex of his zoom climb, about twenty-five feet above the top of the hill, the laws of physics finally equaled out. The vengeful little bird stood still and became weightless for an instant. Kev then stomped in full left pedal, reduced the collective a bit, gave her hard right stick, and pushed the stick to the forward stop. He felt vindicated. His instincts had payed off in spades. An angry young man had turned the tables on the bad guys. The little Red Bird was once again the hunter to be feared. She had become the hawk who scented blood and was about to smash the mouse! For the brief instant, which once or twice in a lifetime seems to last for an eternity, the vengeful hawk was weightlessly suspended above her vulnerable prey.

Nose down, Kev had pointed ole 662/Rocinate directly at the menacing AA site. A separate part of Kev, who was observing the whole thing, marveled at what was revealed to his eyes. The little bird gave him a panoramic view of the bad guys. Pointing its muzzle about thirty degrees to his right was the fifty-one caliber AA gun. At last, the target was easy to see, no longer was it covered by camouflage. Fifteen foot long tongues of flame were jetting from its muzzle as it vainly spat forth death. Tasting the joy of a clean kill of pure vengeance, Kev was unconcerned. The little Red Bird was not where the bad guys had expected it to be.

Suddenly, the clock began rapidly sweeping forward. The little Red Bird started to slowly swoop down upon the abstract figures in NVA uniforms. Somehow disinterested, Kev watched them as they were scurrying here and there seeking cover. Other distant men were cranking furiously at the traverse wheel of the AA gun. In desperation they were trying to bring it to bear upon the swooping hawk. Holding his eagerness carefully in check, and coldly looking at the scene before him, Kev knew they had only one chance to kill that big gun. The game clock had stopped ticking and only this play remained. One play would bring the game to its deadly conclusion. In Kev's mind, it was gamesmanship at its best. Winners take all and no consolation prize for the loser! It was the only way to play the game!

From the edge of his vision, he saw muzzle flashes. They sprouted from several AK-47's and were dotting the area. Shutting them out of his mind, he totally ignored them. Emotionally zeroed in on the kill, Kev bore down on the slow dive. Thumbing the mike button, he loudly hollered.

"Now! Now! Now!"

Jamming his left leg under the collective stick, he controlled both pedals with his right foot. Simultaneously, he transferred the stick to his left hand. With his right hand freed, he frantically raked off his eight fragmentation grenades. Everyone was doing his part. Vindicated, Kev had finished the hard part of the flight. Almost as an afterthought, he was adding his little bit to the rain of death showering down upon the AA site.

With speed, building rapidly, Kev continued his dive down the other side of the hill to the valley floor. Turning and twisting, he began running for his life. Just as the rim of the hill flashed past him, the sweetest symphony his ears had ever heard rewarded his audacious flying. A rolling thunder of many small explosions silenced the booming base beat of the AA gun. It was a special thunder thumped out by more than thirty frag grenades of a Cav style mini arc light.

For the first time in the last five, or less, minutes, Kev allowed himself to breathe. They were part way down the valley doing one-hundred and eighteen knots and all remained quiet. If that AA gun and it's crew was still operable, it had a clear shot at the fleeing Red Bird. Thankfully, it hadn't shot at them yet. They must have killed it. Relieved and exuberant, Kev keyed the intercom.

"I think we pulled it off guys."

Just as Kev finished on the intercom, a concerned voice finally got past the blood lust pounding in his ears.

"Red One-Five, where in the bloody blue blazes, are you?"

"Oops! Sorry about that Blue Six. I got a little preoccupied and forgot to keep you informed. We're about half way out of the valley and will be at your location in no more than zero two. The three of us are just fine and we are awaiting the pleasure of serving your needs."

With a well-earned, and justified, touch of pride in his voice, Kev added.

"Oh by the way sir. We just killed the fifty-one! If you want to go back in and get it so we can take it home, we're ready to go."

"Negative on that, One-Five. Big Boss Six decided that the valley was a little hotter than he was looking for. He told us to pack up our bags and call it an early day. We'll meet you back at the barn."

Later that evening, at the club, the beer was flowing by the gallon. The Cav pilots were getting a little rowdy as the Major sipped a beer at the little bar. Full of life and the spirit of adventure, Kev and Sven invited him to join them for a moment. Joining them at their table, the Major asked.

"OK Johnson, shoot straight with me. Did you guys really take out that fifty-one?"

Sobering slightly, Kev put on his straightest serious face and assured the Major that Pete and Johnny had taken it out.

"I'm just the truck driver, Sir."

Sven could take it no longer.

"Sir. That's not the story that I heard. Pete and Johnny told me, and I quote. 'That was positively the best (many descriptive and colorful words) piece of flying that they had ever seen.' They should know sir. They've flown with all of us. Who would know better? They were right there when it happened. Those two guys agreed that Kev had delivered them perfectly for the mini arc light. Pete even added. 'That crazy SOB even added eight grenades of his own to the pattern while flying one-handed!'"

Full of cold beer, excitement, and young life, Sven was completely fired up. Nothing was holding his exuberance back.

"Sir, I was thinking."

Kev and the Major groaned in unison. They found the thought of Sven thinking amusing. Ignoring their unfounded disrespect of his intellect, he continued.

"It's not fair that the Air Force pukes get all the great missions. I think that we should become the Army's first 'Wild Weasel' outfit. What the heck, Sir. All the necessary parts are in place. We mere mortal pilots can spend our time unmasking AA batteries. When we find them, we'll have ole Kev along to kill them for us."

Laughing and shaking his head, the Major responded.

"I don't know, Sven. The Air Force guys might just get a little upset if we use inexpensive little Red Birds to do a job that they need Fox 4's to accomplish."

Going along with the joke, but also, with a generous helping of beer, a little enamored with the idea of being a Wild Weasel, Kev quickly spoke up.

"Sounds like fun to me, Sir. I'll give it a shot, but only on one condition. That is, that we get to use ole Sven here for AA bait."

The whole conversation was getting to be too much for the Major. Laughing, he excused himself with his own semi-serious comment.

"I'm going to go now. If I stay here any longer, you two brainless idiots will talk me into something that we'll all regret when we sober up."

One night, several weeks later, when he was pouring over his notes, Kev was carefully ordering his letters, journal notes, and other writings. Noting his own changes, as a person and a pilot, he put all the events of his tour in a reasonable chronological order. According to the dating of this letter he wrote it after he went on R&R. However, he seemed to have his own reasons for placing it just after he had his successful encounter with the anti-aircraft site. Maybe, he recognized the need for an occasional dose of humility.

Dear Pastor Bill,

It's been a little while since I have written to you and I am sorry. If I work hard enough at it, I am sure that I could come up with an impressive list of compelling reasons for my not writing. For the sake of brevity, and honesty, I save the paper. Anyway, I have been keeping up with my personal writing. In fact, lately I have been having a lot of fun with it. With your permission, I'd like to share a little short story. I know that it is still a little rough. However, I know that you can read through that. It is about a Scout pilot whom I know intimately well. The story line is about how he had gotten a little full of himself. After reading it, let me know what you think. In an effort to protect the "innocent," please remember that it is purely a piece of fiction. Any resemblance to a living person is purely accidental.

Ole Red Niner-Nine slowly woke and stretched with a great feeling of self confidence.

Life was good." He thought to himself.

Over the past couple of years, he had earned his wings and his sabers. Having dutifully served his apprenticeship, he was now the lead Scout. Best of all, everybody agreed, even those who didn't like him, agreed that he knew his business. When it came time to teach a new wing man the tricks, or prepare an experienced wing man to fly lead, the boss always called on Niner-Nine. In his opinion, the Army had not invented a mission which was too tough or too dangerous for him to refuse its challenge. His only requirement, when he was flying the challenging mission, was that he be the man in charge. A self-satisfied smile slowly appeared upon his face, for he knew that he was good enough to get away with that little demand of control. The closest he came to a personal problem was that he had few friends. However, the absence of intimate friends didn't bother him. He was too busy being the best of the best to notice his loneliness.

Niner-Nine had just begun his second mission of the day when someone from higher-higher gave his boss, who was flying command and control, an emergency radio call. Some desk jockey from Division told the boss that troops were in contact and that they were requesting air cover. Higher-higher continued by telling the boss that all the other air assets in the area were committed. Always willing to help troops in contact, the Major, Niner-Nine's boss, agreed to come running with his Scouts and Snakes. When the Major told the Red and White birds of the situation, Niner-Nine calmly took it all in stride. As far as he was concerned, it was a typical, quick response, mission for the Cav. If he had flown this rescue/support mission once in the last few months, he'd done it fifty times. As far as he could tell, the folks in charge had said nothing that should cause him to get too excited. Pushing the nose of his little Red Bird, Rocinante, over and pulling in power, he followed the Snakes at his best possible speed.

Approaching the area where the ground troops were in contact. With great pained drama, Niner-Nine groaned over the intercom.

"S---, this is just what we need! It looks to me like, at least, ten command and control Huey's are going to be clogging up our airspace and radio net. I'll bet that more than a thousand pounds of collar brass is circling aimlessly around in the sky wearing out helicopters and wasting the Army's JP-4. With my luck, this whole thing is going to turn into a first class three-ring circus."

When Niner-Nine began his negative observations, he was about two minutes away from the ground troops. The whole time, he was carrying on about how much he disliked having the "brass" interfering with his work.

In self-defense, his two young observers were sadly shaking their heads in unison. They had frequently heard this lament. Ultimately, as a form of self protection, they had learned to tune him out when he climbed upon his soap box. The two young men had little sympathy for his, so-called, suffering at the hands of the brass. Just as Niner-Nine was either winding up or winding down his cynical comments, the Major began his briefing.

With the click of a mike keying a radio, the Major's briefing began.

"Red Niner-Nine, this is Blue Six. Apparently, we've got a couple of platoons of friendlies pinned down by some ground fire. They say that they are unable to disengage or move forward without receiving heavy fire. This is what I'd like you to do. Take your team and move up the hill to the north of them and see if you can find the source of their trouble."

Niner-Nine rogered the Major. Pausing for a moment, he realized that he had missed a piece of important information. He called back.

"Blue Six, this is Niner-Nine. Could give me the radio frequency for the folk on the ground? I must have missed it. Before I get started, I'd like to get a good handle on things?"

Without pausing the Major responded.

"Just stay on the UHF push, Niner-Nine. Talk to Sod Buster Three-Two. He can take good care of you."

Something about the Major's instructions didn't ring true in Niner-Nine's head. Whatever it was that was bothering him, he just couldn't quite get a handle on it. It felt like an itch that he couldn't quite reach. In fact, it felt more like an itch whose source he couldn't find. Shrugging his shoulders, he keyed the mike.

"Sod Buster Three-Two, this is Red Niner-Nine. I'm in the little Loach overhead. Please give me the exact location of your people and where the bad guys are."

That nagging itch was still bothering him. It was there, somewhere. That persistent itch was making him irritable because he could neither identify it nor could he reach it. He had learned that when he had a nagging itch to pay close attention to it until he could identify what was irritating him. The chance always existed that, this time, it would be the little itch that would get him killed. While he waited, for what felt like an excessively long time, for a return call from Sod Buster, he keyed the intercom.

"Stay on your toes guys. Something here just doesn't feel right."

Finally . . . Sod Buster came on line.

"Niner-Nine, my people are all in the draw directly below you. The enemy fire seems to be coming from the north. My people think that it comes from about fifty to one hundred and fifty meters up the hill."

"Thanks Buster. I have a clear copy of your position and the position of the suspected bad guys. Could you tell me what kind of weapon's fire you have been receiving?"

Sod Buster responded. "Wait one."

D---, there it was again, that itch. It was driving poor Niner-Nine crazy. Something was terribly wrong. Something just didn't fit the picture. Whatever it was, it was giving him a throbbing headache like a TV out of focus. In fact, . . . it almost felt like someone was lying to him. Or, at the very least, someone was not telling him the whole truth and nothing but the truth, so help them God.

Finally . . . Sod Buster came back on line.

"Red Niner-Nine, my people tell me that they have only received small arms fire. They say that it has been mostly SKS and a little bit of AK-47 fire."

Somewhere deep within the recesses of Niner-Nine's skeptical brain an ugly thought began to creep to the surface.

"Someone was lying to him!"

The vague, out of focus, thought gradually became clearer to him. It was as if someone was slowly turning up the rheostat on a ten thousand watt light bulb. By tiny increments, it went from hardly perceivable to brilliant searing white. Barely trusting himself to speak, he slowly keyed the mike. Pausing for a moment to maintain control of his growing anger, he slowly spoke.

"Sod Buster Three-Two, please state your exact position."

He waited for the answer he knew, but didn't know yet. Sod Buster responded.

"Red Niner-Nine, I don't understand your question."

He recognized a stall when he heard one! Red Niner-Nine was rapidly becoming furious. Ole Niner-Nine angerly thought to himself.

"How in the h--- am I going to help the people on the ground with people playing these stupid games?"

The reason for talking to Sod Buster on the UHF radio was becoming uncomfortably clear. Struggling, but, nevertheless keeping his temper in check, he slowly repeated himself.

"I say again. Sod Buster Three-Two, please state your exact position." With the tone of his voice showing that the question clearly puzzled him, Sod Buster responded. "I'm circling above you in the Command and Control helicopter."

Inside his little helicopter, Niner-Nine exploded. From his mouth came forth a string of highly colorful and carefully crafted creative oaths. He didn't key his mike while making his picturesque comments about Army brass in general. However, his observers clearly heard every wrathful word through their helmets and over the roar of the helicopter.

"That's why we were using UHF radio," he said to himself. "He is flying in a Command and Control aircraft using the UHF."

"The people on the ground always use FM radios."

Sometimes, from his limited perspective, Niner-Nine just couldn't understand what was going on in the Army. As he saw it, people on the ground were in trouble and some Yo-yo was busy playing middle man. Didn't the people in command and control know that the best thing to do was to let him talk directly to the folk on the ground? That way he could have a first hand feel for the situation and how he could help them. If only the "brass hats" would let him do his job!

Gathering himself, and control of his, now frayed, temper, Niner-Nine keyed the mike.

"Sod Buster Three-Two, please give me the radio push for the people on the ground."

Sod Buster's answer was quick in coming.

You don't need it, Niner-Nine. I can take care of all the communications."

That was not the answer that he wanted. He wondered to himself how people, who were supposed to be in command, could be so dense.

"Was the jerk, up there, afraid that he would get cut out of the loop and by that lose his medal of the day?"

Again, he managed to gather himself and his, now soaring, temper. Speaking a little firmer, he made his radio call.

"Sod Buster Three-Two, please give me the radio push for the people on the ground!"

The answer surprised him. Yet, it didn't make the slightest bit of sense. Sod Buster had phrased his answer as a question.

"Red Niner-Nine, do you mean to tell me that you can talk to the people on the ground?"

That question was, to Niner-Nine, the proverbial straw that broke the camel's back. For a moment, he found himself sputtering and unable to form coherent words in response. He knew that he was losing control of his temper. Losing his temper no longer bothered him. He didn't care. He shouldn't have to control his temper when dealing with people who were terminally stupid.

"Didn't that idiot know that lives might be at stake?"

Niner-Nine let go of his temper and savagely keyed the mike. Almost yelling, he let loose a week's worth of frustration.

"Sod Buster, give me that G-- D---- radio frequency! I can talk to anyone I like. I can talk to anyone in all of Vietnam and the rest of Southeast Asia to boot! H---, I've got as many radios as anyone in this stinking little two-bit country. My radios have radios! Stop worrying about being cut out of the loop and give me the G-- D---- radio frequency before you get some of these people killed with your little ego games!"

An oppressive silence filled the radio net. A funeral would have been noisier. No one spoke for at least a minute. Realizing what he had just done, Niner-Nine had the most terrifying thought of his whole military career. He was listening to his own funeral.

"I've just hollered at, swore to, and grievously insulted a Field Grade or General Grade Officer. I'll be lucky if I only get twenty years at Ft. Levanworth doing hard labor."

In the little Red Bird neither observer dared to breathe and the cloying silence still filled the net. A small click broke the intense quiet burdening the radio net, and a calm voice spoke.

"Red Niner-Nine, I understand that you speak fluent Vietnamese."

Silence, again filled the radio net.

Kev placed Pastor Bill's next letter directly after his little fictional story.

Dear Kev,

I loved your little short story. Before I say another word, let me encourage you. Keep up the good work. You kept me interested right from the first word. Yes, I remembered that it was not about a living person. However, I suspect that I do know who the "hero" of the story is. Don't worry my friend. Your little secret is safe with Pastor Bill. I'll treat it as if you told it to me in confession. Believe it or not, we've all been there. Everyone of us, at different times, gets an over blown self-image. Heck, I've shot my mouth off more than once without knowing all the facts of, or about, the situation. Why should "Red Niner-Nine" be any different from the rest of humanity? I think that such discomforting happenings are all part of growing up.

Anyway, I liked the story line and I had no idea what the "little itch" was. Keep working on your writing. Ending in "silence" was masterful. At least it seemed so to me. I've ended in "silence" a couple of times myself. You may have a talent. If nothing else, your willingness to use real life and then help us poke fun at ourselves is something that we all need to hear. . . .

"Pastor Bill"

Many months of flying and combat had passed. Unrecognized by young Kev, he was being reluctantly driven into adulthood. When he arrived in Vietnam, he was mentally prepared for adventure but not for responsibility. Despite his best efforts not to allow such a terrible thing to happen to him, Kev was maturing and embracing his responsibilities. Pastor Bill also noted the subtle changes in one of Kev's letters.

Good heaven's Bill, the passing months in Vietnam are starting to scare me! The many dark, dank, and dismal feelings which are lurking inside me are beginning to terrify me. I don't know why, but, I find that I am beginning to feel like and talk like my grandparents. Surprised that the months have passed so quickly, I suddenly find myself temporarily in the transient barracks at Da Nang. As far as I know, only one thing is worse than being stuck in a transient barracks.

Unfortunately, that one thing which is worse has assaulted me. I am surrounded by wall to wall brain-dead jar heads! Jar heads are Marines, for you nonmilitary types. At least, some things never change. Army guys don't like Marines and, in turn, Marines don't like Army guys. Drowning in a sea of newbe jar heads, I am painfully waiting to go on R&R in Australia. Like my grandparents, all I can think about is time.

"Where has the time gone?"

Pastor Bill, I honestly don't understand it. When I look at the clock, I'm not much more than twenty years old. Scratching my head, I wonder. How did I get to feel like a worn out old man? Leaning back and thinking about my life, it seems like it was yesterday that I arrived in-country. Closing my eyes, I can picture little Kevin Paul Johnson, a few months ago, standing dejectedly with his hands in his pockets. Like many others, I arrived at the Cav as another fresh faced, yet faceless, newbe. The latest newbe was easily picked out of the military crowd. His new, crispy, bright green jungle fatigues stood out like a strobe lite neon sign in the middle of the night's desert. He was bouncing around exactly like the silly and eager little black pup that took up residence in your house three years ago.

Kev's mind slowly drifted in the still quietness of the transient barracks. Pondering deeply upon the many changes which created him, he slowly let his breath out. Stretched out on the bunk, he looked down at the lanky stranger's body attached to his ancient mind. Harsh soaps and bright sun had bleached the jungle fatigues which he was wearing. They were a pale reminders of the bright olive drab green that they had been when issued. The picture he saw seemed frightfully poetic.

His faded fatigues were just as bleached out, torn, and tattered as he was feeling. With an almost bitter chuckle, he glanced about at the fifteen or twenty young enlisted men who shared the transient barracks with him. Each individual man/boy looked so fresh and different from his own self image. Uncle Sam's United States Marine Corps had outfitted each boy in his own spanking new, bright crisp green, set of jungle fatigues. Looking a little closer, Kev could easily see their fold marks from their storage in stock. Somehow, it made him sad to see the eagerness in some of their faces. It reminded him of himself not that far in the past.

Strangely enough, Kev found that he could be thankful for the situation as it stood. Chuckling quietly, he looked about him at all the new replacements. To a man, they were all newly minted, straight from boot camp, Marines. Glancing about, he was glad that they were also all young enlisted men. That made it possible for Kev to maintain his illusion of privacy and solitude in the open barracks. As young enlisted marines, just released from the rigors of boot camp, they did not know much about the ways of the military.

Even so, they knew a few important things. Just as Kev also knew a few things, way back when. First, they knew that his bleached out fatigues marked him as someone who had been in country a long time. Being normal new guys, excitement and anxiety filled every bright green clad one of them. Some, like Kev of a few months ago, also had feelings of romance and glory, and endless questions. They all faced an unknown tomorrow that might place them at risk. However, none would break the unwritten etiquette and risk of bothering Kev with their anxieties and endless questions. Being exhausted by it all, that was just fine with Kev.

Further assuring Kev's privacy, the young enlisted men knew that he was an Army Officer. Kev was sure that most of them had never seen, met, or even heard of an Army Aviation Warrant Officer. Nevertheless, they knew that he was some kind of an Army Officer. Furthermore, they were totally and efficiently, Marine style, brutalized against bothering an officer. For the moment, Kev gratefully accepted some unknown Marine Drill Sergeant's gift of peace and quite.

Alone in this strange place, he found it to be an interesting situation sharing in the same barracks with these young men. Some Marine clerk probably did not know what an Army Warrant Officer was. Kev assumed that was why he found himself placed in these barracks with young enlisted Marines. Such a mistake would not normally happen in the Army. Nevertheless, he discovered that the moment was sufficient with its own pleasure. Not a social animal, he was silently enjoying the peace and quiet of his own company and private thoughts.

Like his grandparents frequently did, Kev looked wonderingly at the strange world in which he was forced to live. Not having a better response to what he experienced, sometimes he slowly shook his head in dismay at all that he did not understand.. More often than not, the incongruity of the whole human situation baffled him. His situation, which some people laughingly called life, apparently was slipping beyond his comprehension. Earlier in the evening, Kev was following his carefully developed and trained military instincts. With little better to do, he carefully scouted about the large and extensive Marine base. Boredom, curiosity, and a desire drove his scouting mission to enjoy his transient freedom of movement.

Delighted, he discovered that a USO, "Bob Hope" type, show had been scheduled for later in the evening. This show was going to be on the other side of the compound. The Marines had scheduled it for later in the evening, when their, heavy duty base camp work day had ended. Much to his delight, he had discovered that there was supposed to be a Playboy Miss Some Month or another at the show. With the instincts of a trained Aero Scout, he suspected that she would be prancing around on the stage sometime during the show. Kev was sure that she would drape a very minimal amount of clothing upon her perfect little body. The visual pleasure would have to be a morale builder.

"Or," he thought to himself, "maybe a morale destroyer."

Thinking about what he had just discovered, Kev suspected that ole Pastor Bill would not approve of his interest in the nocturnal activities of the Marine base. Always one to make a game of things, he playfully said to himself.

"Kev, ole boy, even in your dottering old age, this could be interesting. The sight of Miss Some Month or another prancing about on the stage may be an enjoyable sight."

Male biology being what it is, Kev decided that the show deserved the careful personal attention of ole Red One-Five. Carefully rationalizing, he thought to himself.

"I am the lead scout pilot. Due to my position of great responsibility, I need to meticulously scout this situation out for the good of our Cav unit."

Strategically, Kev doubted that the fearless Cav types would, any time in the foreseeable future, be launching an Air Mobile assault against the Marine bastion of Da Nang. However, his training demanded that he know the exact disposition of the enemy so that he would be prepared for the unknown. He reasoned to himself, that knowing where the compound's recreational facilities were, was an important part of their military disposition. Anyway, every Army Officer knew that the Marines were always the enemy and he needed to be prepared.

Much of the first blush and dime novel romance of being a real live soldier and officer in Uncle Sam's Army was fading. In turn, Kev's military complexion was losing most of its freshness and bright bridal blush. Nevertheless, he still cared deeply about the troops. Without any conscious thought, he instinctively tried to do his very best by them. Pausing for a moment, he assumed a mission and formed a plan of action.

"I am responsible for the health and welfare of the troops. It is time to act like it!"

While he was at the transient mess tent, he rounded up about a dozen US Army enlisted folk who were also waiting to go on R&R. Dedicated to "his" men, he would lead them on an important mission of mercy.

The jar heads had not seen fit to tell Kev or the enlisted folk about the evening's show. It pleased Kev to see that most of these enlisted men were combat types. These were his kind of people! They spent most of their time out in the bush chasing and fighting ole Victor Charles and his many cousins migrating down from the North. Standing tall, rising to his full command authority and responsibility, and wearing a big grin, he formally addressed them.

"Gentlemen, it is my great and good pleasure to volunteer my leadership and extensive experience for a great mission of mercy. In volunteering to join me, your mission will be solely for the benefit of the fighting men of the United States Army."

Noting the high quality of his voluntary leadership, all the enlisted folk eagerly volunteered for their secret mission. The men were ready, willing, and very anxious to do an in-depth recon of the possibly delightful and charming assets of Miss Some Month or another.

Having done his usual excellent job as the lead scout, Kev and his new command prepared for their moral building mission. Carefully snooping about and scouting things out, Kev had discovered where the Marines were going to hold the show. As he continued his recon, he had also discovered that they had scheduled the show to begin exactly at 19:30 hours. With military percussion and precise timing which would have done General Patton's Third Army proud, Kev led. His fearless little band arrived at the fenced off entrance of the amphitheater. This was where the show was about to begin. Arriving on location at exactly at 19:15 hours, Kev's volunteers prepared to enter.

Leading from the head of the column, where else was he to lead from, Kev proudly presented his newfound command at the gate. Immediately, he encountered the omnipresent Marine M.P. The M.P. was most beautifully presented. Representing the long arm of the law he was complete with his mandatory stiffly starched uniform, side arm, night stick, chrome helmet, and spit-shined boots. Kev, grungy and worn out, snickered to himself.

"My oh my, this poster boy Marine is so pretty. I think that I want to take him home with after the war and put him in the front yard! Then I'll enjoy watching the cute little birds poop on him and the dogs lift their leg to mark him."

The beautifully attired Marine MP looked down with obvious disdain at the motley group of ill kempt Army combat types. Kev's new command consisted of typical grunts from the bush. He presented his battle-hardened troops for admission. They were complete with gaunt faces, thousand mile stares, faded torn fatigues, floppy boonie hats, and broken down worn out jungle boots. At the sight of them, the gorgeously outfitted M.P. stepped forward.

He informed the field weary soldiers that this show was only for "recruiting poster" Marines stationed at Da Nang. He added, in case the stupid Army types did not understand, they did not allow transient Army types to attend. Before Kev had the opportunity to challenge his authority, the M.P. noted the faded blacked out insignia of rank on Kev's beat-up old fatigues. Snapping his best parade ground salute, he then told Kev that he was authorized to admit Army officers. However, he was not allowed to admit Kev's enlisted folk.

Incensed, Kev tightly clenched his jaw. The pressure hurt so badly that he feared that his teeth would break from rage. Attempting to control his greatly shortened temper, he spoke slowly and clearly. He had been told that one had to speak slowly to jar head, if one expected to be understood. A couple of weeks later he told Sven of the incident.

"I was so mad that I had a stark raving stupid attack. Amazingly enough, I began to try to reason with a pretty Marine M.P. Trust me, that was a completely wasted effort! Trying to reason with a parade ground Marine M.P. ranks exceptionally high in the top ten of my stupid ideas since I have been over here in lovely Southeast Asia. I quickly discovered that an unpainted rock has more native intelligence than a Marine M.P."

He was beginning to get exceptionally incensed, angry, and blindly enraged. Lo and behold, another beautifully attired rear echelon Marine made his entrance. It was his turn to add to their little drama in the midst of the endless Viet Nam war. This, also very beautifully attired Marine, was a Major. According to the mystical ways of the military, he outranked Kev. He firmly informed Kev that the M.P. was correct in his enforcing his orders. The Major did however, patronizingly allow that as an Army Officer, the Corps cheerfully invited Kev to attend the show. However, his gracious offer did not change the unfairness of the situation. The compound full of Remington Raiders was not going to allow Kev's new, all volunteer, command entrance. The opportunity to view the fabulous female charms of the lovely Miss Some Month or another was not for such lowlifes.

"At this point" he told Sven, "I lost any semblance of control which I might have had over my temper. Without thinking about it, I snapped this pompous, fat a--ed, Remington Raider my prettiest parade-ground salute. Then in a carefully controlled voice, I responded to his patronization.'Thank you sir, but I'm a combat soldier. Therefore, I positively refuse to treat my troops as second class citizens!' Finished with my pronouncement and condemnation, I pivoted about on my heel and quickly marched away. If I didn't leave immediately, I was afraid that I would say something which I meant from the very core of my being. I knew in my heart that my next comment would be something which I would regret later. That later date, most likely, would be at my General Courts Martial which would send me to good ole Ft. Leavenworth for insubornation."

Disappointed, disillusioned, and angry the enlisted folk left with him. As an Officer and Gentleman, young Kevin was the most embarrassed he had ever been in the Army. It was worse because the Marines' behavior caused it. All that Kev could say to the enlisted folk was an apology.

"I'm sorry guys. I guess I just don't know who the enemy is in this war."

With that sad observation, Kev disbanded his new command for the lack of a mission. A young private turned to Kev and spoke kindly.

"Sir, we think that you should go back and see the show. Heck, we're used to this kind of treatment, we're just stupid grunts. After all Sir, war is hell when you fight it from behind a Remington typewriter!"

The young man's, cryptic comment surprised Kev. Without thinking he blurted out.

"Thanks guys. However, I've got my pride too. If you guys aren't good enough, then neither am I! Anyway, they need the R&R. It is a tough war when you have to spend all your time writing each other up for commendations. You guys take care now."

Returning to the transient barracks and feeling sadly disappointed by the omnipresent military B.S., Kev slowly stretched out on his bunk. Though he was angry, he found it to be quiet and peaceful lying, alone with his thoughts. Taking advantage of the moment, he allowed himself to slip into the foggy never-never land of half sleep. Glancing down, a moment later, at his oversized fancy Seiko aviator watch, he noted that he must have fallen asleep.

Suddenly, it was about one in the morning. Quietly smiling to himself, he allowed his imagination to carry the moment. He assumed that Playboy's Miss Some Month or another had put on a few more clothes than she had been wearing previously in the evening. For a moment, he kinda felt sorry for her. Without a doubt, the poor girl was trapped at the Officer's Club, besieged, and surrounded by a battalion or more of Ruthless Remington Raiders.

To a man, they were feverishly seeking to find a way to remove, not only her clothes, but also her pretty petite pink panties. Chuckling, Kev could easily imagine their highly creative war stories. Yet, he knew that all the stories had a single-minded purpose. The Raiders were tossing their tall tales about in sadly lamentable attempts of seduction. True to their kind, they were trying to convince her that she should comfort their troubled souls with her sexual favors. If the poor girl was that gullible, then she was in deep trouble!

The Ruthless Remington Raiders would have her believe that all of them suffered greatly in their heroic combat feats. After all, everyone in Viet Nam knew that war is hell. True to form, a few of the less sensitive and more enterprising individuals were trying to find ways to offer her a little cash gift. All that they would expect in return was a couple of hours of her private company. To Kev's mind, if most of these long suffering and epochally heroic Remington Raiders were not so pitiful, they would be unbelievably hilarious.

With a deep war weary sigh, Kev clasped his hands comfortably behind his head. He decided that it was time to begin a deeply serious, fully in depth, and militarily necessary, study of the backside of his eyelids. **CRUMP -- CRUMP -- CRUMP!** Alert sirens started to wail all over the compound. Then, with a total disregard of Kev's peace and quiet, some mindless idiot ran through the barracks screaming in apparent panic.

"Everyone to the bunkers! Go to the bunkers now! Incoming! Incoming!"

Mumbling to himself, Kev negatively responded to the confusion which was upsetting his rest.

"Incoming, no s--- Sherlock!"

Sighing deeply and wearily, he took careful stock of his military situation. Quickly completing the task, he discovered several things that made his decision for him. First, Kev was bone tired. Secondly, he was beginning to get very frustrated. Finally, he was flat worn out. Furthermore, he had no idea where the closest bunkers might have been. Carefully reviewing his options, he did a quick cost analysis in his head. Finishing his difficult and complex calculation, he decided that the safest place for him was to remain comfortably stretched out on his bunk.

His inventory of military hardware was nonexistent. He didn't have any personal weapons. If he were to reach out, no pistol, no M-16, and no survival knife would be within arms' reach. It was not a situation that he liked. However, he could do nothing about it. The military bureaucracy required him to check all these items into supply when he left for R&R. He might have been in a combat zone, but he was unarmed! The basic problem, that he faced, was clear enough to Kev. If he were to run about in the dark, not knowing where the bunkers were, he'd be a fool. At best, he'd be scurrying here and there like some stupid chicken with his head cut off. In turn, he thought.

"I'll probably break my dang fool neck falling into a hole or something."

The evening's torment did not end with the sirens and jerk running through the barracks. With incoming 122's still occasionally falling on greater Da Nang, the gods of war would give him no rest. Another stupid fool, this one also wearing a Marine uniform, started running through the barracks yelling and screaming.

"Gooks in the wire! Gooks in the wire!"

"Great," Kev thought to himself. "Well . . . I know that I am not dumb enough to go out into that dark confusion. We are in the middle of a rocket attack with some idiot yelling that the bad guys are in the wire. With all this going on, some other idiot will think that the bad guys are about to over run this massive Marine base. If I am stupid enough to step out into that situation, most likely, some trigger-happy jar-head will fill my body with an even dozen M-16 bullet holes."

With a sense of finality, seasoned with the self-ordained personal wisdom of his advanced years and great combat experience, Kev rationalized his decision.

"I'll just stay comfortable in my rack. It is as safe as any other place that is available to me."

"What the heck," he continued to rationalize to himself.

"While the jar heads are running about in panic, I'll roll over and catch an assorted 'Z' or two."

With the soothing crump of 122's, the wailing of the alert siren, and the occasional undisciplined burst of M-16 fire in the background, Kev began to drift off. Experience had taught him that he needed to catch a few 'z's' whenever he could. He was still in Vietnam, and one sleeps when one can. As he began to enter that wonderful never-never land of sleep, the gods laughed. The mental retard of a yelling jar head, completely outfitted in his never used combat gear, reappeared. Again, he ran through the barracks. Noting that Kev was not running around in a complete state of panic, the Marine rudely shook him to a state of wakefulness. Kev groggily listened to his incessant and loud demands that he join him in his growing, Marine style, group panic.

Several weeks later, laughing over a cold beer, Kev painted the picture for Sven.

"Well . . . my sense of humor, by then, had departed. I patiently tried to explain to this idiot that the Chicom 122 rocket is an area weapon. This meant that I stood an even chance of getting killed in a bunker, or, of getting killed while stretched out sleeping in my rack. Furthermore, I continued to patiently explain to him my current combat situation. 'Listen to me very carefully, stupid. I am not going out there where some thoughtless idiot has foolishly given rear echelon Marines live ammunition. If I do that, I will probably get myself killed very dead by friendly fire.' Finally, I offered him a deeply personal suggestion. I did this just in case he hadn't yet gotten the general drift of my displeasure. Frustrated, I added comments concerning my personal disdain for his running around and upsetting the beginning of my R&R. Lastly and with great gusto, I kindly suggested to him that he leave me alone and go do something that happens to be anatomically impossible with himself. With that closing suggestion, I rolled over and pointedly ignored him."

The gods of war eventually saw fit to smile upon Kev. In time, the rocket attack sputtered to a halt. It quieted down, and the base camp jar heads eventually settled down. With the rocket attack slowly sputtering to a stop, the rear echelon Marines quieted down. They were no longer running about and indiscriminately shooting off their M-16's.

The months had changed Kev. Something dark and depressing, which was fermenting and churning deep within him, troubled him. Innocence and the free sleep of youth had become something that only existed somewhere in his vague memory. This, disquieted rumbling within, told him to get out his pen and paper. Sighing like an ancient man, he went over to the day room where he found a light and a table. Sitting down, he began to write in his ever-present journal. He kept hoping that his extensive writing would eventually come to some useful purpose. If nothing else, he had discovered that writing did help him to order his jumbled thoughts.

"Tonight" he muttered to himself, "if I keep busy writing, it will keep me from killing an even dozen stupid Marines."

When in doubt or troubled, Kev always unburdened himself to Pastor Bill. Therefore, he continued with his letter.

Nothing new for me tonight. I woke up just before the rocket attack. I hate it, yet, I wake up almost every night from the same thing. Most of the time, my dreadful memories cause me to break out into an almost icy sweat. Painfully, I remember the haunting face of the night's disquieting dreams. This is the face that only I can see through my mourning veil of strictly private tears. This is the face of my dreary, depressing, and dark nights. Oh Lord, the face is so silky smooth and soft that it is almost like a girl's face. It is full of the hopes and dreams of youth. In the world of my darker memories, not one weather-beaten line of maturity is etched upon this haunting face of my dreadful, deep, and dark torment.

In fact, the young owner of this face does not shave the whiskers of male maturity from its baby smooth skin. For the tragic truth of the human folly called war is that this is a face of a young soldier who does not need to shave. The terrifying, yes even criminal, truth of the matter is that one cannot shave what one cannot grow. It does not matter how much one might want to shave like a grown man. One can't shave what one can't grow. The obvious reason the boy of my haunting memories cannot shave this face is that this baby-smooth face has not physically passed from boyhood to manhood.

Oh yes, I almost forgot. God, I wish that I could forget. However, I can't forget a single detail. My dank and dismal nights will never give me peace nor will they let me forget. A "wana be," silly little mustache, almost appears upon the upper lip of the face which exists only in my haunting night time memories. If the picture of it didn't haunt me so, it would be ironically funny. Were one to look very hard at his upper lip, one might almost see that silly little mustache of wispy colorless hair. My nightly vision is so clear and true. It makes my skin crawl in continually relived horror. Violating my peace, it is like the past has violently taken over the present. I can plainly see his hair. It is light brown and boyishly unkept. When the sun shines upon it, just the slightest shading of a red highlight glistens in the lively reflection. Forgetting no detail, the vivid vision reminds me with almost every night's torment. An exuberant, youthful, and joyful bounce define the step of the boy struggling to be a man of my memories.

A couple of weeks, maybe a month before the beginning of the haunted dreams, Kev met the owner of the boyish face. That face, and Kev's nightly torment, became as linked as clouds and rain. Kev never expected to have expected the "little-boy" face to burn itself into his being. The owner was just another in the, now, long line of faceless newbes. Initially, nothing existed that was remarkable about the fresh-faced newbe who was just out of flight school.

His boyish face belonged to another faceless new Warrant Officer assigned to the Cav. TK was the name that everyone immediately called him. TK was military shorthand for "The Kid." Like the rest of them, TK had finished High School and gotten accepted into the Aviation Warrant Officer Program. In due time, he completed flight training and arrived in Viet Nam. The marked difference was that he completed the task a couple of months before his nineteenth birthday. There was a second remarkable feature to TK. When Kev first looked at his baby face, he honestly thought that the owner was sixteen and not one day older.

If Kev had been a policeman back in the world, and he saw TK driving a car down the road, he would immediately have pulled him over. Any cop worth his wage would have asked to see his license, not believing that he was old enough to drive. When the Scout pilots learned that he was still eighteen they immediately started calling him "the kid." This was shortened very quickly to TK. Like the rest of the Cav's pilots he had been assigned a call sign. Red some number or another was his call sign. Strangely enough, no one remembered it or ever used it. To the rest of the pilots, his youthful looks were so overwhelming that even on the radio he remained, to all the unit pilots, just TK. That "handle" became his call sign!

Although calling him TK may have seemed a little cruel, TK took it all in stride. Resolutely and cheerfully, he made it his badge of honor. Calling TK their mascot was also unfair to this, one each, olive-drab, government issue Warrant Officer Pilot. Regardless, to most of the Cav pilots, within a few short hours of their meeting him, that is exactly what TK functionally became. For some unknown reason, all of those "old guys" took him under their collective wings trying to take care of "The Kid!" In his presence, the Scouts had suddenly become wizened old men of twenty, twenty-one, twenty-two, even up to an ancient twenty-five or more.

Kev continued his letter to Pastor Bill.

This evening, I sit here with my pen in hand and think about the dark torment of my nighttime hours. This sadly human story seems so blackly ironic. For you see, as often happens, by this time in my Vietnam journey, I was the well-seasoned old pro among the Scout pilots. I had already been shot down three times, you know. With the turnover of pilots the Captain made me a lead pilot. Not only was I a lead, but I was the most senior lead Scout Pilot in our armed reconnaissance unit. Popular wisdom proclaimed that Red One-Five was supposed to be the best. Because this was the popular wisdom, everybody turned to One-Five for advice about the art of being a Red Bird.

The emotional cost of this fame, I was soon to learn, was higher than anyone should have asked me to pay. At least, the cost was higher that I felt I was able to pay. No longer was my time all my own. Life without a care no longer was mine. The days had long since passed when my only job was to play with those wonderful expensive mechanical toys which Uncle Sam had given me. My days of playing in the fickle winds of the highlands had long since drifted into horary history. Unknown to myself, I had become saddled with more responsibility than any man or boy of my age should have to carry.

Lonely nights have shown me something terrible about the high emotional cost of good leadership. In my gut, I know that everything happened because I was Red One-Five. Being Red One-Five, TK had became my special responsibility. TK's arrival has inexorably changed my life. I may not like it or have liked it. However, my life will be forever different. In fact, I fear that my life will continue changing unto the time that the rivers of time cease to flow for Red One-Five. As long as my mind and memory continues to function, I will never forget this blackest of incidents. Kevin Paul Johnson will forever wonder about his own responsibility for it, and in it, and during it. It all began so innocently. My friend and boss, Captain Dave Grant, Red Six, approached me one day and set this story in motion.

"One-Five I am going to make TK your wingman since you are my most experienced scout. Obviously, he is a little green. However, I think he will be OK in time. Please, try not to let him get into any trouble."

Though I wish it with all my heart and soul, I cannot change what has happened. Not even God can do that. Since the moment that I met TK, the master clock of all creation has kept on ticking without missing a beat. Because of this, I have discovered that time has mindlessly continued its march. Heartless, it gives us absolutely no personal regard. These truths change nothing. What was is what is. Searing painful memories continue to viciously smash their way into my sleep. The bitter tasting irony of my time with TK only gets worse. Touchie feelie people can say what they will. However, time has not healed any of my wounds. Furthermore, I am far from convinced that it would be right or just if time healed these wounds.

I was the seasoned pro! More than likely, I was little more than an overblown legend in my own fertile imagination. TK, on the other hand, was just the green kid. I have to admit, that to the objective outsider, I looked like ole TK's High School buddy. Looking back, I can find only one minor exception. Our only true difference was that no hint of a red highlight was to be found in my unkempt brown hair. At that nefarious moment in time's merciless march, I too even had one of those silly little "wanna be" mustaches! Oh, how strange and how terrible time can be. It changes and, yet, nothing changes. Advancing years requires Kevin Paul Johnson to commit one morning a week for his face shaving duties. I am not anything at all like those grizzled old combat soldiers portrayed in all those glorious Hollywood pictorials.

Frequently, during the quiet of the night, when no one was looking, Kev prayed. Sometimes, as he prayed, his whole body would tremble and tears would streak his childlike cheeks. He continually prayed that part of his memory might fail. The young man feared that only death would erase his memory. If God would not grant his simple request, he prayed that his memory might at least soften and fade. It seemed to him that, for reasons that only the Holy One knew, God would not grant his prayers. Poor Kev could not forget a single dishearteningly painful moment from the "incident." Night in and night out, he was forced to relive the story repeatedly in his head. He told no one of his mythic hill climbing and then his sliding back to the bottom. Praying, he was hoping that time would ease the burden of his heavy rock. It didn't seem to. The emotional torment became a merry-go-round without joy, without end, and without a brass ring.

Prior to the merry-go-round of morose memories, he and TK had flown together for maybe three or four days. At first glance, this may not appear to be very much time spent together. However, three or four days can be a lot of flight hours in a Red Bird. It is about six or seven a flight hours a day. Red Bird pilots are embroiled in the pressure cooker commonly called combat. Even when no one is shooting at the Red Birds, the pressure cooker is red hot. As Kev looked back on those couple-three days, he honestly felt that TK had the makings of a very good wingman. Just as Kev had when he was a wee bit green, TK was making his share of flight school-induced mistakes. To TK's credit, Kev instantly noted that he had a uniquely native understanding for the very difficult and thankless job of being a wingman. All the Scouts agreed that despite his limited amount of flight hours, TK was quite a good stick man. Within those two or three days Kev was beginning to believe that the two of them were going to make a good team. Talking to Sven after the second day of flight, he said. "We're a matched pair, he and I, both of us sporting our silly little mustaches."

Best of all, speaking from ole Kev's understandably selfish point of view, TK worked very hard at mastering the skills of being a wing pilot. Young and as green as he was, TK was completely dedicated to keeping young Kev alive, whole, and well. Having remembered his early days and early lessons saw that TK was a quick study. Keeping the lead pilot alive, whole, and well remained the thankless job of a wingman. Ole Red One-Five felt that TK already did it well. As the lead pilot, Kev got the glory, the official and unofficial pats on the back. Sometimes, he even got the shinny little medals pinned on his chest. In turn, the unseen wingman just kinda tagged along, always lurking somewhere in the shadows. At least, Kev was convinced that this is how it must have looked to someone who was on the outside looking in.

For the most part, in their limited time flying together, the two of them had not had very much serious contact with the enemy.

"Well . . ." Kev said to Sven. "Come to think about it, the day before, I had gotten myself in a wee little bit of trouble in a box canyon."

Before the day's flying was finished, Kev's little bird had taken several small arms hits and he had all the excitement that he wanted or needed for the day. Between missions, Kev continued to tell Sven of TK's potential.

"I would be criminally remiss if I didn't tell you, ole TK sure did a good job saving my bacon. Without his quick thinking and guts, I might still be trying to get out of that darn box canyon with my skin unpunctured by AK-47 fire."

Almost every night when Kev closed his eyes, he reluctantly and vividly harkened back to that day. That day is the same day he tearfully prayed that God would allow him to forget. As it was, things promised to be boring for the two of them. Young fools that they were, they wanted some "real" action. His "day of haunting horrors" began as a quiet day of boring holes in the air and not finding any bad guys willing to come out and play. Two flights under their belts, four hours of recon, and they had no contact with the enemy. After refueling, Kev and TK landed at the staging field to which they were assigned. They fueled their two little Red Birds, which were completely armed and ready for action. It was their responsibility to always be ready to instantly respond to a call for help.

With the Red Birds parked and ready, if needed, TK sat beside Kev. Relaxing in the shade of a Snake, TK offered an eager new guy observation.

"You know Kev, this is not the kind of day that I went to flight school for."

Reflecting back upon the days when he too was an eager bouncie young pup full of p--- and vinegar, Kev smiled. Unknown to him, he offered horribly fateful words which seemed to ordain the horror to come.

"Cheer up TK, who knows, maybe you will get lucky and things will get hot and heavy for you on the next mission."

For the moment, as it was so many other times in Viet Nam, it was a hot humid listless time. They quietly waited to be called out to relieve the other Red team. With nothing better to do, several of them were killing time. They were whiling the minutes away in that time honored way of all pilots since the Wright Brothers first struggled into the air at Kitty Hawk. The group of young Warrant Officer pilots was taking turns telling outrageous war stories. When the colorfully inflated war stories petered out, they began telling outrageous female conquest stories. Some wiser ones among them were catching a few z's.

Like an unexpected bolt of lightening, striking out of the clear blue, sunlit sky, they got a scramble call!

"TROOPS IN CONTACT!"

Exactly as they would have responded for the call, Red Bird Down, the Red and White birds scrambled into the air. All of them did their best imitation of the scrambles of Spitfires and Hurricanes lifting from their dispersal fields in the Battle of Britain. Like the young pilots of that generation, they were grim, fatigued, and determined to do their best for their brothers who were calling for help. By this time, Kev saw nothing romantic about such a scramble! He understood that when they scrambled, usually people were dead or dying.

At the call "Troops in Contact," they tossed their cigarettes about the compass rose. Jumping up, they kicked cups of water, coffee, and soda to the side, as they scrambled to their feet. Energized by a burst of adrenalin, they ran full tilt to their Red Birds and Snakes. The slashing sabers of the Cav cranked the combat-worn turbine engines of their birds into reluctant life. As their rotor systems came up to operating speed, they were off. Urgently, they dragged the poor abused helicopters, protesting, shuddering, struggling, and groaning into the air. All this was done without the benefit of a checklist or careful check of instruments and controls. Troops were in contact and in danger!

Their Loachs and Snakes were, for the most part, tattered, tired, and war-weary aircraft. The four birds awaiting the next recon were very heavily overloaded. They carried every bit of death dealing munitions the crews could shove into or bolt onto them. Quicker than one would think possible, the poor old birds, more or less and very reluctantly staggered, sometimes stumbling almost drunkenly, into the air. Like the checklist, flight school safety and decorum had been forcefully cast aside for the good of the troops in contact.

Once airborne, Kev called his wingman on the UHF radio.

"TK, follow me, and let me know if you can't keep up. We'll go low level all the way. Let's not waste any time climbing to altitude."

Kev pushed the nose of Rocinante over and pulled up the collective control. He was dragging the engine power all the way to the edge of the red zone. Troops in contact justifiably demanded all that his war weary bird could give him. Dodging and twisting around the taller trees, he was closely following the contours of the uneven terrain. With ole 662 protesting the abuse, Kev continued pushing his little bird to go as fast as she could. He could ask no more from her. Called to the rescue, she was mechanically maxed out. According to the safety standards of flight school, this was very reckless behavior. However, they believed that the situation compelled them to demand everything from their helicopters. The Cav was responding to ground troops, who to the very best of their knowledge, might be battling for their lives. All the pilots and crewmen knew that their timely arrival might be the difference between life and death.

Wishing to be prepared for whatever he might encounter in the next few minutes, Kev called up their controlling agency on the VHF radio. The more information that he had at his disposal, the quicker he could help the people on the ground when he got there. For the moment, he had to assume that the ground troops were fighting for their lives. For all he knew, the folks on the ground might be in hand to hand combat and about to be overrun by the bad guys. As was their SOP, he had not received a radio call from his wingman. None was necessary. Therefore, Kev assumed all was well with TK and his observer.

After about ten maybe fifteen minutes of frantically racing to the rescue of the ground troops, the controller suddenly called off the mission. As always, no one saw fit to give the Cav any details. Kev assumed that the crisis, whatever it might have been, had passed. It could have even been a false alarm. Theirs was not to question why. Accordingly, the Red and White birds could stand down, refuel as necessary, and return to the staging field. Keying his UHF radio, Kev called to his green wingman. He was planning to go to the refueling site and top off.

"Did you hear that TK? False alarm. We can return and refuel."

TK made did not response to Kev's radio call. Unconcerned for the moment, Kev repeated his radio call.

"Did you hear that TK? False alarm. We can return and refuel."

TK probably just didn't hear him. The response to the second call was a very empty haunting silence filling his ears.

"Radio failure!"

Kev half prayed and muttered both half aloud and half to himself. Hopefully, he questioned his two enlisted observers.

"Can either of you guys see TK?"

270

As lead scout, he was flying with two young observers rather than mounting a mini-gun. Yet, Kev had felt half equipped and uneasy all day. Johnny was on R&R. For this mission, he wasn't in his usual place in the back of Kev's Red Bird. Therefore, both the observers were younger and less experienced than Kev would have liked. They were so young that they couldn't even grow a silly little mustache like the older more mature pilot types. After leaning out of the helicopter as far as possible and searching diligently, they keyed their intercoms.

"No boss we can't see him anywhere" was the stereo response from both of them.

"Oh, God." Kev groaned uncontrollably.

A large knot was forming in the pit of his stomach causing him to feel like vomiting. Wingmen don't disappear! Wingmen are forever!

He feverishly hoped that his fertile imagination would remain, just that, an overworked fertile imagination. Without a word, Kev earnestly prayed that the pictures forming in his mind had no connection to reality. His imagination had already envisioned the worst for TK and his young observer. Unable to see TK, they did an immediate 180 degree turn and began retracing their flight path. Red One-Five and crew began fearfully searching for TK and his observer.

While searching, they were continuously calling on all their radios and frequencies. A somber silence filled the little helicopter matching the dreadful silence on the radio. Disquiet and discomfort filled the little bird. None of the usual conversation and silly banter on the intercom, which was a hallmark of flying with Red One-Five, was taking place. The three of them remained deeply immersed in their own private worlds. Each of them were saying their own private and personal little prayers to whatever it was that they themselves called holy.

They returned twenty kilometers. As they were flying the twenty long kilometers, they looked, called, hoped and prayed. For twenty long kilometers the three of them feared the worst. At last, they found TK and his observer. Unfortunately, they saw tragic evidence of the unkind fate suffered by these two young men/boys from about five klicks distance. Just as Kev's normally overactive and vivid imagination had visioned, and then had harshly recoiled from, they found TK and his observer. The two young men were resting under many a pilot's final black marker. Their simple and somber death marker was a towering rolling cloud of oily black smoke. Kev didn't need to have five stars pinned upon his uniform and thirty years of military experience to see that they had crashed and burned. A somber sorrow filled voice quietly sobbed in his head.

"Oh God no. TELL ME IT IS NOT TRUE! Not TK. He's just a kid!"

As he sobbed and screamed within his head, the White birds called him. They too had seen the smoke and were joining up to offer him gun cover.

With the passing of the months, Kev's combat reflexes were sharply honed. He never forgot that he was in the middle of an ill-defined combat zone. His first thought, and appropriate concern, was that enemy ground fire had somehow brought TK down. Accordingly, when he confirmed that a downed aircraft caused the towering black smoke, Kev called in the Blues.

"Red Bird Down! We've got a Red Bird Down!"

He needed them to secure the crash site. The god's of war were being exceptionally cruel that bright and sunny afternoon. By the time the Blues had arrived on their own scramble, what happened was obvious. Enemy activity was not to blame for the untimely deaths of the two boys.

Enemy activity wouldn't have changed the fact of their horrible deaths. However, Kev wanted and sorely needed to blame the enemy and not something or someone else for the horror that he saw on the ground. Slowly flying about the area, it had become unavoidably obvious to Kev what had happened to TK and his observer. The three of them carefully reconstructed TK's flight path. When they did that, they saw the top of a tree on TK's last flight path, which was freshly broken down. The tired, old, and very war weary Red Bird which TK had been flying, had struck the tree. For reasons which will always remain unknown, somehow they clipped the top of a tree. That was why two young men and a little helicopter lay crumpled, broken, and burning on the ground!

Looking down at his fuel gauge, it felt like a gross betrayal to him. However, he had no choice. Kev was forced to refuel and return to the staging field. It would be a while before the ground troops could do anything at the crash site. The fuel soaked wreckage that contained TK and his observer was still burning hotly. An exceptionally somber and quiet Red Bird left the cemetery pyre of TK and his observer behind. As they flew away, the smoky pyre continued to billow a dreadfully dark message into the clear blue skies.

More than anything else that he could think of, Kev hated not to be in complete control of any situation. Putting the towering markers of somber black smoke behind, he was forced to admit to himself, that nothing remained for the three of them to do. It was time for them to go. They had done their job. Unfortunately, they had found the crash site of TK and his observer. They would have preferred to have found them flying along lost or something. Nothing remained for Red One-Five and crew to do. TK's future was out of their hands. Kev was as sick at heart as he had ever been. What was worse, he was sick to his stomach and felt like throwing up. He could see in his fertile imagination, all too

272

clearly, what had happened to TK and his observer. Their final agonizing moments/seconds filled his sorrowing heart.

Sitting upon the rough red earth at the stage field Kev was trying, with all his remaining strength, not to break down and cry like a little boy. Fighting an intense inner battle, he was forcing himself to remember that he was Red One-Five.

"D--- it, Kevin Paul Johnson, you are a seasoned combat pilot in the United States Army and not a little boy."

Sitting on the hard earth with a silly little mustache, he would not allow himself to cry. Kev wanted to and needed to, but he didn't. He had been faithfully and carefully taught by John Wayne, and his likes, that real soldiers did not cry. Sitting alone with his head dejectedly cradled in his hands, in his mind, Kev replayed TK's and his observer's final moments. Maybe it was serving as a perverse form of self punishment.

Within the recesses of him mind, he saw the whole crash sequence in painfully crisp and clear detail. The images that filled his head were complete with sight, sound, and smell. The horror of the crash radiated from somewhere deep within the creative core of his mind's eye. Kev thought to himself, maybe it was pilot error? After all, TK still wasn't throughly accustomed to their war-weary combat overloaded aircraft. Still, Kev reminded himself that TK was a very good stick man. Part of Kevin needed some type of logical answer to understand the mystery of this unnecessary and untimely death. Dissatisfied with his answer, he eventually surmised that TK's tired, old, war weary Red Bird had failed. Possibly, it just couldn't make enough power to get over that last fateful tree. After a bit, Kev bitterly and accusingly thought to himself.

"In the final analysis, it doesn't really make any difference how it happened. TK is dead. And I, Red One-Five, was the one who was suppose to keep an eye on him."

To even think as Kev was thinking may strike some people as a little arrogant. Whatever might have happened, TK was flying the little helicopter and not Kev. However, Kev took his responsibility to take care of TK with a deadly and earnest seriousness. Nevertheless, something called mature responsibility condemned Kev to the deepest depths of his being. He believed that he could feel what happened in total painful detail, when no one else possibly could. He could see, hear, and feel it crisp and clear like no one else. Sitting alone on the rough red earth of the Central Highlands of remote Viet Nam, staring off into the horizon, he shuddered with fear and revulsion. Gagging, as if to vomit, his imagination took to soaring flight.

Thud! The skids and bubble of his helicopter hit the top of that last tree. The gravely injured helicopter uncontrollably and inevitably begins to nose over. Fatally wounded, it is pointing itself directly downwards toward the hard and unforgiving earth. **SHEAR, STARK-RAVING, UNFATHOMABLE TERROR** fills every synapse of two young minds. The raw emotion mercifully tries to shut down TK's and his observer's all too fragile human brain's ability to function and feel!

The solid ground is rushing up at unspeakable speed. Frantic now, driven by inhuman panic-stricken desperation, TK pulls all the way back on the control stick. Yanking the collective stick to the stop, he pulls in all the power available. He is pulling the power all the way into every red zone on the instrument panel. The terror-stricken pilot is unconcerned about damaging the screaming little turbine engine or little transmission. Most likely, heart rendering and horrible cries of fear and desperation are forming on both their lips. Finally, just maybe, if TK and his young observer are lucky, their story ends. During the last few seconds of their cruelly shortened existence, the gross brutality of a life ending crash quickly ends the tragic drama.

Involuntarily, a cold nausea filled Kev, and he deeply shuddered with revulsion. As always, his imagination offered him no peace or quiet.

If their luck continues to be as bad as has led them to these final seconds, human words and thought will be inadequate to express what happens next. These final seconds will take eons and ages more than the fullness of time. The closing seconds will take forever and forever and once again, they will take forever. These final seconds will take a long drawn out lifetime. The worst horror possible is that maybe it will take a couple of minutes or more before their final day reaches its fiery conclusion. **PAIN --- PAIN --- PAIN!** All that time and creation has left for these two young mens is the merciless, all consuming fire.

For the moment, Kev had been mercifully left to his own thoughts and feelings. Friends, formed in the world of the Cav, know when to give someone room to grieve. At last, it is time to allow himself to weep. Within the confines of his sorrowing soul and confused consciousness Kev cried out.

"The heck with all the books, movies, and other 'B.S.' that tells me how I must feel. The heck with those who tell me how to respond to another seemingly meaningless death in this great and wonderful human glory which we call war."

For Kev, one thing existed for sure concerning TK and this war of his. The steps he once watched, will no longer bounce. No more silly little "wanna be" mustaches will cause him to chuckle as he talks to his wingman. The greatest cruelty was not something that Kev would personally know. Sometime in the future, no one will ever see any grey hair replacing the brown hair with the reddish tint on TK's head.

About two hours later, Kev got a subdued call from Command and Control.

"Kev, I need you to strip your little helicopter."

His somber mission required no guns, no armor, no bullets, and no observers. All that remained for him to do as the lead scout was to fly his empty Red Bird to the crash site. The reason the Major called him to fly the mission was simple. The landing zone, next to the crash site, was too small for a Huey.

"Maybe," he thought to himself, "there is something right and proper about my flying this mission."

To Kev's mind, a grim poetic justice of sorts seemed to be at work. Then again, maybe his friend the Major was trying to start a healing process for the young man. That thought never came to Kevin's tormented mind. Traveling with his guilt and thoughts as grim and haunting company, he would have to take his little OH-6A into the landing zone.

With unwelcomed suddenness, everything that was important in Kev's world had done a quick turnabout. Red One-Five was doing exactly the opposite of what he was supposed to be doing. Earlier in the morning they took great care to load two machine guns, thousands of rounds of ammunition, grenades, and many other tools of death, fire, and destruction. Regrettably, sad circumstance had forced them to remove it all. Guns, bullets, grenades, and even the armor plate were removed from their accustomed locations in the little observation helicopter. The three young men made quick and quiet work of stripping 662. The two young enlisted men also had their private thoughts. TK's observer had been a bunkmate and friend of theirs. When the task had been finished, Kev's two observers loaded all the paraphernalia of war and themselves into a slick. That was how they were going home.

Kev sadly loaded 662 for her coming mission. The crewchief from C&C silently handed him an olive-drab body bag. It was a six-foot long reinforced plastic bag. It was equipped with a full length zipper and six handles. Another crewchief silently handed Kev a couple of standard cargo tie downs. Wordlessly, Kev secured these three sad items of cargo in the back of 662. Securing himself in the pilots seat, Kev fought back the mounting tears of rage, frustration, and pain. With a heavy heart, Kev then fired up 662 for his final mission of the day.

In all his dreams of military flying, Kev had never envisioned, for himself, such a terrible and painful mission. His final mission for the day was to pick up TK's charred, smashed, and broken body. The Blues had yet to find the observer's body. Apparently, the impact threw him quite a distance from the crash site. Some optimistic souls still maintained a slim hope they would find him alive. Kev's wretchedness of heart told him otherwise. He landed his little helicopter at the crash site and immediately smelled the sickening sweet, pork like, smells of burnt human flesh well known to experienced combat pilots. Somehow, he already understood that the sickening smell would live with him every night when he is forced to close his eyes and face his memories.

The ground troops were all understandably ill from the smell of TK's charred remains. Kev felt that simple human decency couldn't ask them to do any more with the body. To ask them to do such an inhuman task was not fair. Kev reminded himself of his responsibility.

"It was not their lapse in leadership which caused this situation."

Driven by something deep inside himself, he knew that he would have to shut down the helicopter and do his duty as he understood it.

"He was my wingman after all. Even if it were but for a few short days."

Before shutting down, Kev keyed the radio to talk to the squad leader of the Blue's.

"Blue Three-Niner. This is Red One-Five. After I shut down, I will do what needs to be done."

The young lieutenant who was the squad leader was a laughing joyful young man with whom Kev had shared a beer or two. His response was subdued and relieved.

"Thank you, One-Five."

From Kev's journal.

The walk from the helicopter feels like a million-mile death march. I reluctantly and wearily drag myself over to the still smoking remnants of TK. Driven by remorse, I want to say and need to say a prayer. Why oh why can't I remember any of the prayers Pastor Bill taught me? Unashamed and with tears running down my cheeks, I kneel before this unrecognizable hunk of charred meat and reverently bow my head. Inadequate human words form on my lips.

"Dear God, please take good care of TK. I didn't."

As gently and reverently as this totally obscene thing can be done, I care for TK. A sensitive young grunt feels my torment and he offers to help me. I thank him, but gently decline his offer. Hopefully, his feelings are not hurt and he understood that this is my responsibility and duty. Borrowing his entrenching tool, I carefully place what little remains of TK into an olive drab military issue body-bag.

The stench of his charred burnt, once young and vibrant flesh, makes me gag and wretch constantly. With the young grunt holding the bag open, eventually, I roll the charred obscenity into the plastic bag. Gathering the bag into my arms, I begin TK's last and longest journey. A few more steps and I place the bag in the back of 662 as if it contained my own sleeping child. Then, I gently tied TK into the back of my Red Bird. He won't fly my wing on this mission, dedicated as he was, to keeping me alive. Everything in the whole world has now been forever changed. For the finishing action of this grim day, I will fly as his personal escort. God willing, maybe he will allow me to fly with him as a friend. Kevin Paul Johnson will start TK on his long lonely journey home by bringing him to the folks at graves registration. Grave's registration in turn, will send him

276

back to his mom, dad, and pretty little girlfriend. Hardened by endless repetition, they will ship him home in a box marked do not open. Escorting him on this first leg is not much. However, it is the last act of kindness I can offer ole TK.

Tormented, Kev had written of his nightly troubles to his friend and confidant.

Oh Pastor Bill, I'll always wonder. I suspect that I'll always wonder because mine is a question without an answer. TK was not yet nineteen. How could he possibly be dead because of a false alarm? Was TK's death another obscenely inflated price paid to the gods of pathetic leadership and unclear goals? In this meaningless instance, why did he have to die? Was it because of some self seeking politician? Was it because some brass hat in the Pentagon was seeking another promotion? Was it just a mistake? Or, was it because of Kev's own pathetic leadership and unclear goals?

"Wake up Sir. Your plane leaves for Australia in an hour."

OF SLOBS AND SOLDIERS

With a deeply satisfying roar of man's aviation triumph and power, the four big jet engines blasted out their farewell message of fire and smoke. Comfortably resting his head against the headrest, Kev enjoyed the reassuring push of explosive fire as the big jet liner accelerated down the long concrete runway. Looking out the window, he silently bid friendly Sidney Australia a sad goodby. As the big bird started to climb into the distant heavens on its way back to Vietnam, he began settling in for a long flight.

Relaxed and enjoying himself as he looked to the ground below, he had a wonderful view of Sidney's nice new opera house. Shaking his head ruefully, he wondered why he had never gotten around to see it. He had wanted to see the magnificent white structure. It was high on his list of things to do. Yet, he never did get there. For the better part of his R&R he had slept, rested, and done nothing. It seemed as if he had a million or more things which he had wanted to do while he was enjoying his R&R. However, he had spent most of his time sleeping.

"Well," he wryly said to himself. "This has not been an R&R about which all the guys are going to want to hear."

He made his inner observation because it was a standing joke that they should rename R&R. Rather than "Rest and Recuperation," many felt that they should call it "Intoxication and Intercourse." Given the opportunity, a young and healthy man's thoughts turn to young women. For their five days of R&R, most of the married guys went to Hawaii to see their wives for the first time in months.

None of these married guys that he had spoken with had seen much of Hawaii. For the most part, they had enjoyed an active second honeymoon. They were well acquainted with the decor of their room and a restaurant or two. One or two had said that they got as far as the bar of their hotel. Slowly shaking his head, Kev envied them and said to himself.

"Having a woman who will travel halfway across the world to spend five days in bed with you must be wonderful."

In their own turn, many of the single guys spent their R&R in one of the large Asian cities. They would return with tall tales of drunken debauchery. Though he wasn't completely naive, Kev found it difficult to believe their stories. They said that a young and beautiful woman could be "rented" for the five-day period at a couple hundred dollars, or less. Young, male, and healthy the thought of renting the services of a young professional woman had intrigued him.

However, he did not want to be in an Asian city. He was fast becoming sick of Asia and all things Asian. Furthermore, he wasn't all that sure that he wanted to spend five days with a "rented" woman. Most

278

of his single buddies thought him a little strange to be uninterested in lovely talented professional companions. Inexpensive, beautiful, and talented though they might be, it didn't seem right to Kev the romantic. Always and forever the hopeless romantic, he wanted the woman who was with him to care for him as a person. How could he celebrate a relationship if she were only concerned with the size of his bankroll?

"Nope! I'm going to keep my mouth shut. No one will believe me if I tell them. Worse yet, if they believe me I get laughed out of the club."

Looking out at the clouds below, he slowly shook his head in private wonderment. His seat was hardly warm and he wasn't sure where the time went or what he had done with it. When he arrived, he went to the hotel which the R&R people had recommended. It was nice, clean, and quiet. Someone who was highly perceptive must have looked at him and seen right through him. His small room was exactly what the doctor had ordered. When he walked through the door, he knew that he had everything that he needed. He had a soft bed with clean soft bright white sheets, quiet and blessed air conditioning, and what little noise that filtered into the room was quiet and muted. The ever-present artillery didn't pound, the jet turbines didn't scream, and countless rifles didn't crack in the background. For the weary young man, the hotel was a little piece of heaven on earth.

As the big bird leveled off, he smiled at the strangeness which surrounded his fuzzy memory. It wasn't as if he had done any substantial drinking.

"Heck, I've drunk more in a single night at the club than I did the five days I was here. I'll be darned if I know what's happening to me. Maybe, I'm getting 'Old Timer's' disease. That's it, my poor old arteries are hardening and before I know it, they are going to put me in the 'Home!' That's why the last five days are all a confused blur."

Laughing within the private confines of his mind, he knew what had happened to him. He had emotionally checked out. Shutting down his overwrought mind, his concerns, and worries, he had quietly wandered here and there as a stranger in a strange land. As a blessed change, the strange land upon which he wandered did not threaten the young stranger to itself.

That was the most amazing thing of all. When he got off the big airplane, he was halfway around the world. Alone in another hemisphere, it felt like he had climbed into a wondrous time machine for a strange and wonderful trip. True, they drove on the wrong side of the street. It was also true that their dollar bill looked strange without a picture of ole George on it. They also had some funny names for things and places. Not meaning to insult, he had laughed when he discovered that a drug store was a chemist shop. Thankfully, no one heard him.

Yet, Australia didn't feel all that different from his world. To Kev, this new land was like looking in a slightly distorted mirror. Everything seemed a tiny bit out of phase with the world of his youth. It was like he was flying ever so slightly out of trim. Things didn't feel quite right. However, he did not feel as if he were in any danger. Somehow and in many ways, this world he had just visited seemed to be living fifteen to twenty years in the past. As he slowly strolled about, he almost expected to see Wally, Beaver, and the "50's" gang suddenly walk around the corner. He immediately felt safe and comfortable. Everyone he met spoke his language. Though, they did speak it with a strange, British-like, accent.

Secure in the familiar strangeness of the new place. He spent most of his waking daylight hours slowly strolling about, just going here and there. This surprised him, for he had never been a person to stroll aimlessly. Yet, being freckless and free with nor responsibilities or calender was wonderful. Kev poked his head into countless little shops and meandered down the paths of little parks. Like countless tourist who had preceded him, he stopped in the touristy gift shops. While browsing, he found a couple of little gifts for his family. Suddenly, he saw a little Kuala Bear. Inside, it had a little music box which played Waltzing Matilda. It made him think of a little raven-haired beauty, from Texas Woman's University, who had so warmly touched his heart. In his most foolish dreams, he dared to imagine that she would spend her life with him. He bought it for her because it was soft, beautiful, and filled with a special music like she was.

Listening to the deep drone of the jet engines, he thought of the cuddly little Kuala Bear. He smiled warmly with an unaccustomed good feeling. Never one to blindly follow the crowd, Kev did things his own way. The quiet strolls and buying that little bear had been the high point of his R&R. Ole Kev knew that his time in Sydney lacked the excitement of others' R&R's. Chuckling to himself, he knew that he wasn't going to try and explain his actions to his buddies. For the most part, they wouldn't understand. Ole Kev had not had a "wild" R&R. However, flying with the Red Birds had given him sufficient excitement to last several lifetimes. While the big bird was droning across the endless expanse of ocean, Kev also felt a deep pang of self-disappointment.

The bold young Scout pilot wished that he had been equally bold with the raven-haired beauty. He knew that he should have shared all his deep feelings for her, with her. Yet, he didn't know how to accomplish the task. His folks were not demonstrative nor were they passionate people. The young man honestly did not now how to speak of his passion and keep himself under control all in the same breath. It was possible that his passion scared him more than the bad guys did. He just didn't know. Yet, he knew he was disappointed in himself.

With another frown, he spoke to himself.

"Oh why, oh why didn't I ask her to marry me."

Slowly shaking his head, he continued.

"At least you could have asked her to wait and marry you when you return to the world. But, no, not you Kev, you kept your mouth shut. No, no, you're too stupid to open up and tell her how you felt. You have to be noble. After all, you could get killed and leave her a widow. Or, if you did ask her to marry you before you left, you could have died and left her with only a ring and sad memories. However, you never asked her if that was a risk that she was willing to take. BIG DUMMY!"

For a moment, disappointed silence filled his head.

"Admit it, stupid. You're afraid. Ole Kev may be 'Hell on Wheels' in a Red Bird. However, he's afraid to open himself up to the most wonderful person who has ever entered his miserable life. John Wayne has taught you well. Bullets are one problem. However, a good woman's love is an all together different situation."

After severely chastising himself, Kev lapsed into a brooding internal silence. He had gone to a couple of the recommended clubs to sample the nightlife. It wasn't all bad. The young Scout had enjoyed a couple of cold "Foster's" and had his usual ration of bourbon and water. Gathering his courage, he had talked with a few of the local gals. Yet, his heart wasn't in it and it seemed that they could easily sense it. To them, he was probably lonely and boring.

Bored, and worse yet, he found that he was terribly boring to himself. Therefore, he went back to his room early. Lost in a different strange land, he decided to enjoy a soft bed and clean sheets. Reviewing his performance at the night club, it made him wonder why the raven-haired beauty ever gave him the time of day.

"The Good Lord knows that, even at my best, I'm not a party animal nor am I a brilliant conversationalist!"

As he was shaking his head wistfully, a small smile, filled with self-directed laughter, crossed his lips. On his second night at the club, he met a nice girl who's company he enjoyed. Strangely enough, she was the perfect note of irony for his R&R. He had specifically waited and gone to Australia because he was tired of Asia and all things Asian. So, who does he spend the night talking to? He spends it talking to an Asian girl from Thailand. She was a college student. They talked and danced a few times in all innocence.

If any of his randy friends could have seen them together, doing nothing, they would have immediately driven him out of the Scouts.

One of the days, when she didn't have any classes, she gave him a guided tour of Sydney. She was bright and bubbly about her studies and being in Sydney. He felt that the Chamber of Commerce should have hired her as a tour guide. They also met two other nights at the club. They repeated their first night of mostly talking about everything and nothing. Occasionally, they danced. As he remembered his little tour guide, a light chuckle slowly escaped from his lips. Speaking to himself, he reminded himself that he had the "honor" of the Scouts to uphold.

"I'll never tell anyone about her. And, if I ever do, I'll not mention that I only danced with her and never kissed her."

True, his buddies might think him pathetic. Yet, he had made his choice of what he wanted and needed. He was comfortable with that choice.

Slowly drifting off to sleep with the hypnotic hum of the engines lulling him, he was satisfied with his R&R. Thinking of the soft double bed and the clean crisp sheets, he continued smiling. For the first time in months, the young man felt both rested and clean. Seemingly, he had spent hours standing in a steaming hot shower washing Vietnam out of his hair and skin. He had willingly checked out of his dangerous and deadly world and joyfully traveled to a private place of unique peace and quiet. Enjoying the solitude and the soft cleanliness of civilized life, he had with quiet gusto celebrated becoming a non-being. No choices, no decisions, and nobodies life was in his hands. All in all, it had made for a perfect five days.

All too soon, the tires of the big bird had thumped down heavily upon Da Nang's long concrete runway. As Kev had expected, the war continued in his absence. And, he was again a part of it. Catching a military shuttle flight, he returned to his beloved Red Birds. Stunning him with its suddenness, it was like he had never been gone. Immediately, decisions, choices, and combat thrust him back into the pressure cooker of flying the little Red Bird.

Five days of R&R, in Australia, served only to wake in Kev the sad knowledge of his emotional condition. He had become war weary over the passage of the many months since he was a newbe. He had been told that R&R was supposed to refresh him. It was supposed to work that way. However, it did not seem to be working out. For some reason that he did not understand, when he returned to the Cav, he seemed to be more worn out than when he had left.

Maybe a brief visit to a normal world, even if it were not the good ole US of A, was not a good idea. The presence of happy unarmed people along with the everyday commerce of life had made things worse. Unfortunately, it served to brightly highlight how much of his youth he was missing. Kev was very surprised to discover the presence of flush toilets, clean sheets, and hot showers had affected him so deeply.

Returning to Vietnam, everything was as it was before. People came and people went. Yet, the menacing shadow of the ever-present war cast its cold darkness upon all that he did. Try as he might, he could not shake the nagging and growing feeling of futility. At best, the war felt like it was stalemating. Young men from both worlds died in droves. With the setting of the sun, everything in lovely South East Asia returned to "normal." With the approach of darkness, the only ground that the Americans were sure that they controlled was the ground upon which they stood. Yet, as darkness set on their world of war, even the ground beneath their boots could be contested. Vietnam was like that when Kev arrived in country and it appeared that it would never change.

To those who flew with the Cav, Kev's depression and frustration was completely understandable. It was the way things were and the way things seemed to have always had been. He had been back with his unit for three or four weeks and had not had a day off. On average, he flew four or six hours of recons every day. As it was before he left on R&R, each flight ended with the same questionable results. He never asked the bothersome questions aloud and very seldom asked them in the privacy of his head. Yet, the questions were constantly hanging on the tip of his tongue like a drop of water hanging on the faucet's lip.

"With all our effort and blood, are we accomplishing anything worth the cost? Have all these, seemingly countless, deaths made the world a better place."

Shaking his head, he would sometimes wonder if big city cops felt the same frustration and lack of accomplishment in their endless job of controlling crime.

Strangely enough, when Kev wasn't bothered by dark and dreadful dreams of what he had experienced, he slept like a baby. Yet, maybe it wasn't strange. The young usually work hard, play hard, and sleep hard. He was young and heathy. When he had the opportunity to sleep, he slept soundly. Continuing his life of ironies piled upon more ironies, sleeping like a baby was exactly what got him into the most trouble he had ever gotten into while in the Army. Only Kev could find such a creative way to begin his relationship with the new Major.

Kev's Vietnam Army was a strange place of highly divergent worlds. In Kev's case, the only military world that he knew was the Army involved in war. When at war, the Army usually becomes highly focused on its mission. This is one of its great strengths. However, when at peace, the Army leans heavily on its traditions and rituals to maintain its identity. In his case, Kev joined the Army, went to flight school, and then was sent to Vietnam. Every part of his experience was focused upon the war in South East Asia.

The young man's total emotional and physical focus was upon the job of flying the Army's helicopters. Most of the young Warrant Officer pilots in Vietnam were very much like him in their focus. Frequently, they would joke about their unique military status as neither real/Commissioned officers nor as enlisted men. Generally, they called and considered themselves civilians in uniform. For most of them, it was sufficient to master their field and fly their machines. As for the many colorful traditions and rituals of the military life, they cared little. Typically, they were woefully ignorant about that part of the Army.

Back at the beginning of time, when Kev arrived in Vietnam, he had been the eager puppy who was always underfoot. In time, he found his place. However, little or nothing had marked his arrival. Like thousands before him, he had been another new guy learning his place as a cog in the big green machine. Therefore, when he heard that they were getting a new Major, he thought little about it. In his ignorance, he assumed that the old Major would clean out his office and that the new Major would move in. Then, in time, as the new Major learned the ropes, his presence would be felt. Kev knew that the new Major was arriving and that they were having a maintenance stand-down. Tired, war-weary, and becoming increasingly disillusioned, he never put two and two together concerning the mysterious ways of the Army.

He and Sven had spent the previous evening on an important mission of discovery. Always curious, they wanted to know exactly how much bourbon they could drink in one sitting. Having made a valiant effort to drink the club dry, they then staggered back to their bunks when the club closed for the evening. By mutual agreement they had set out on their important fact-finding mission. It seemed proper as the next day was a maintenance stand-down and they could sleep in. As Kev fell into his bunk, he passed into a dreamless oblivion where time, responsibility, and proper Army protocol meant nothing. Passing a few hours in drunken oblivion might not have been noble. However, oblivion was exactly what he deeply desired.

It was close to two in the afternoon when Kev eventually rejoined the world of the living. When he awoke, his mouth tasted like an open sewer had run through it and then dried out. Adding gross insult to the night's injuries, somewhere in the deep dark recesses of his skull, a malicious alcohol powered demon had set off a thousand-pound bomb. Paying the price for the previous evening's excesses, he contemplated shooting himself as a cure. As he suffered, his first thoughts centered upon his painfully throbbing head. However, only the thought of suffering additional pain kept his quivering hand from reaching for his forty-five. Whatever his condition may have been, he was confident that he could never feel worse that he was feeling at the moment. Not for the first time in his life, the young man was terribly wrong!

Had Kev been asked to consider whom he would least like to see at the moment, and had his befuddled mind been working, he would have said Charley Bird. Given the choice between a fully armed NVA regular and Charley bursting through his door, he would have chosen the NVA regular. As was typical to Army life, no one gave him a choice in the matter. Suffering from a terminal hangover, his fate was not of his own choosing. Expressing his feelings of utter contempt, Kev groaned in deep emotional pain when Charley burst into his hooch.

"D--- it Johnson! What the h--- is the matter with you? I simply can't believe that you are as stupid as you act. You better get your ragged a-- in gear. You've got thirty minutes before reporting to the new Major. If I were you, I'd try to get cleaned up and try to look like a soldier for a change. In case you are interested, the new CO is quite p----- at you for missing his Change of Command ceremony this morning."

Kev's forty-five was within easy reach. An evil thought caused him to smile. Giving in to the evil thought, he gave a fleeting thought to shooting Charley. That, he thought, might put him out of his misery. From Kev's point of view, the little jerk was enjoying himself excessively. Given Kev's self-induced suffering, Charley's level of loudness was physically painful.

Before he could come to a carefully reasoned decision about shooting Charley, the unwelcomed tirade continued. Savoring his supposed position as a close confidant to the new Major, Charley leveled his parting shot.

"You don't have any idea how much I am going to enjoy this. Your days of 'Wine and Roses' are over, Johnson. Trust me, my friend, the new Major is a <u>real soldier</u> and he isn't going to put up with any more of your silly B--- S---!"

Scrambling about in a frantic attempt to clean himself up and make himself presentable for the new Major was a painful task. Kev carefully searched his highly defective memory. He could find nothing stored in his befuddled mind concerning a Change of Command ceremony. Try as he might, he couldn't remember being told about the Major's ceremony. Pondering the abrupt end of his military career, he thought of his drinking buddy Sven.

"Well, . . . I wonder if I'll meet ole Sven at the Major's office?"

Getting angrier by the moment, another negative thought about Mr. Charley Bird slowly passing through his bewildered brain.

"Ah, . . . This whole thing makes me very suspicious that ole Charley was supposed to tell us about the Change of Command. Sandbagging us by keeping his mouth shut would be just like that little weasel. H---, we all know that he'd sell his mother, grandmother, wife, and sisters into prostitution if it would make him look better in the Brass' eyes."

Having vented his spleen, Kev ran down to the Major's office expecting the worst.

Preparing to receive the most eloquent butt chewing of his life, he nervously straightened himself up, as best he could. Drawing a deep breath, he cautiously knocked on the Major's door.

"Come in."

The Major's voice from the other side of the door immediately dashed Kev's dim hopes for a reprieve. The Major was sitting in his office and patiently waiting for Kev to make his appearance. Unfortunately, that meant that Charley was not pulling an elaborate practical joke on ole Kev. Yet, Kev knew that he had only been fooling himself with that vain hope. Pulling practical jokes and playing strange pranks on the other pilots was not Charley's style. Such childish foolishness did not fit his self-serving agenda. With the sound of the Major's voice passing through the muffling door, Kev knew that he was a doomed man!

Removing his hat and stepping promptly through the door, Kev assumed a proper military brace. With his feet set at a perfect forty-five degree angle, his back ramrod straight, and his eyes resolutely fixed at the wall directly above the Major, Kev whipped out his best salute.

"Warrant Officer Johnson reporting as ordered, sir!"

Except for his rank, he could have been back at flight school. He felt like a nobody Warrant Officer Candidate quaking in fear of his life, and yet to be career, before his Tac Officer. However, arriving for this interview, he wasn't afraid of busting out of flight school. Sadly, he felt that the stakes were much higher.

While Kev was painfully sweating out his fate, the Major leisurely sorted through some papers on his desk. While steadfastly maintaining his eyes fixed directly on the wall, Kev got his first look at the new CO. This guy was a different kettle of fish than Kev was accustomed to! His flight suit was immaculately clean, perfectly tailored, and carefully pressed. He already had all the appropriate tags and patches perfectly sewn on. In contrast, Kev's flight suit was torn, faded, oil stained, and rumpled. The battered old thing was exactly as he found it at the bottom of his laundry bag where the cleaning girl had put it. Like the rest of the Scouts, he usually wore no rank or unit insignia. At best, he looked like a refugee from a bombed out village.

The last time that Kev saw a pressed flight suit was on a gorgeously attired VIP pilot in Saigon. At the time, the pretty pilot was driving around some older guys with a mess of stars upon their hats. He had heard rumor that this new Major had last commanded a VIP outfit. Looking at him, Kev decided that the rumors were probably true. If so, Kev and the other flying slobs in crumpled uniform could be in for a really bad time!

Hoping that it didn't show, Kev began trembling. If he had been afraid that he was in trouble before, he was now convinced that he was in big-time trouble considering the Major's mode of dress! The Major's face was so clean shaven that he must have shaved a second time during the lunch hour. Glancing at his hair, Kev sadly noted that it was one-half inch shorter than regulation. Even the top of Major's desk was spotless! Its surface was clean and polished, and the only items sitting upon it were those being used. Carefully placed upon it were the Major's nameplate, one pencil, one pen, and the specific papers at which he was looking.

In dark and dismal despair, Kev realized that Charley was right in his triumphant proclamation of Kev's dark and dismal demise. This new guy clearly appeared to be a <u>real soldier</u> in Charley's world view. Only the future would tell if this guy was a combat soldier. As he continued trembling inside, Kev began to have serious doubts about his future in the military. He had planned to fly Uncle Sam's helicopters for thirty years — however . . .

Eventually, the Major decided that Kev had suffered sufficient anxiety. Slightly leaning back in his chair, he casually looked up and spoke softly.

"So, . . . You're Mr. Johnson. At last, I have met the infamous Red One-Five. Before we go any further, please correct me if any of my assumptions are wrong, Mr. Johnson, somehow, I get the distinct impression that you don't like me. If my feelings are correct, then, why don't you like me? Tell me, did I do something to offend you? Is that why you decided not to come to my change of command? I sure hope that I didn't offend you."

Poor Kev's heart and spirit sunk to the soles of his feet. Had he doubted it before, he now knew it. He was a dead man. The new Major was going to very slowly crucify him. Then, he was going to make the remainder of his short life miserable. Powerless, the young man could do nothing but stoically die with as much dignity as humanly possible.

"Well, Mr. Johnson. I pride myself as a fair man. Now is your chance to speak up. There's just the two of us in the room and you have my permission to speak freely and honestly with me. As the new Commanding Officer of this ragtag outfit, I want all my Officers to like me. Please, Mr. Johnson, if I've offended you, I need to know how I did so. But, if you don't tell me the nature of my offense, I can't apologize and I can't change if I don't know what I did wrong."

If the Major could have listened to the confines of Kev's head, he would have heard a drawn out groan of intense emotional pain. Having carefully set the table for his "Junior Warrant Officer" feast, the Major leaned a little further back in anticipation. Slowly tapping his pencil on the palm of his hand, he patiently waited for Kev's response to his questions. It a split second, the scared young pilot formulated approximately ten-thousand excuses. Just as quickly, he rejected all of them. Despairing, Kev opened his mouth and began to speak.

"Sir, I didn't . . . I . . ."

He snapped his mouth shut. The Major continued to patiently wait.

At last, the condemned man opened his mouth and spoke with

a soft controlled voice which admitted to his status as a "dead man."

"I have no excuse, Sir. You, Sir, are the offended party. I can do nothing except apologize."

Having said all and the only thing that he could say, Kev shut his mouth and awaited the coming pronouncement of his fate. Graphic visions of living at Ft. Leavenworth flashed before his eyes. A horrid vision of making little rocks out of big rocks for the rest of his earthly days occupied the forefront of his tortured mind. Slowly and sagely nodding his head, the Major leaned forward and coldly looked Kev directly in the eyes. Cringing inside, Kev tensed and waited for the expected explosion. Completely in the wrong, he knew that he had to take whatever was coming his way. However, the knowledge of his guilt didn't make it any easier as he waited for the Major to speak.

"Mr Johnson, you are positively correct about two things. First, you have no excuse for what did not happen this morning. Second, you are sorry. In fact, you are about the sorriest looking pilot and officer that I have ever seen in my almost twenty-years of military service."

Kev's heart sank further as he listened to his military sins being carefully multiplied by the Major. It was not a good day, and it wasn't getting any better. Nor, did he see any improvement on the near, or for that matter, the far horizon. Had he not been an officer and gentleman in the midst of a war zone, he would have been reduced to tears.

The young man was terminally hung-over. He was also on the top of the Major's personal "S" list for missing the Change of Command. Adding to his woes, he knew that he looked like a wretched POW who had been living in the same flight suit for the better part of a month. He was so dispirited that he kept his imagination in check. Doomed, he knew that his most vivid and colorful imagination of his coming fate would pale beside the Major's self-righteous wrath. It seemed to Kev that the Major was very carefully weighing his words which served to add to his rapidly expanding feelings of dread and doom. Finally, it appeared that the Major had chosen the words that he liked best. Internally cringing, Kev waited for the second shoe to drop.

"Well, Mr. Johnson, I've heard some very interesting stories about you. It seems that my predecessor thought very highly of you. You might not know it, but he has written you up for a couple-three DFC's and other assorted pretty ribbons. I've also spoken to your platoon leader, and he also speaks very highly of your work as a Scout pilot. It seems that I'm stuck with you because you are the best that there is."

He paused for a moment. Poor ole Kev was dumbstruck. He knew that his ordeal was not over. However . . . He began to have a very faint hope that he wouldn't be taken outside to face a firing squad at dawn.

"Before you start patting yourself on the back, they both noted that your 'military skills and polish' need a good bit of work. Your platoon leader says that you're a great Scout. However, he added that you have a long way to travel before you can call yourself a soldier. Mr. Johnson, let me offer you a small bit of free advice."

Kev was beginning to consider breathing. He had been holding his breath since the Major began speaking.

"Son, there is more to soldering than driving a helicopter!"

The Major paused and slowly played with his pencil for a moment. It was as if he were weighing a great decision.

Nodding to himself, he continued.

"Having said that, here's what we're going to do. We're going to forget that you 'forgot' my Change of Command ceremony. When you walk out of this office, you and I will start with a fresh piece of paper. However, I'm putting you and the rest of this motley mob of malcontents, misfits, and malingers on notice. From now on, being the best Air Cav Troop in Vietnam is not sufficient. This outfit will look like and act like soldiers of the United States Army. Do I make myself clear, Mr. Johnson?"

Before Kev could respond, the Major continued.

"You're dismissed, Mr. Johnson."

Wanting to jump for joy, Kev saluted and wheeled about on his heel to leave. However, before he got to the door the Major spoke with what Kev later decided was a vaguely playful voice.

"Oh Kev."

Shocked by being addressed by his first name, he almost fell over as he turned back.

"Yes, Sir."

A slow knowing smile spread across the Major's face.

"As you know, Kev, we are continuing with the maintenance stand-down tomorrow. From what I can see, most of the pilots are rather worn out and could use the additional rest. The Good Lord knows that the birds need a lot more work before I'll consider them safe fly. Nevertheless, while the Army may be in camp, the paperwork war continues. You will learn more about that if you manage to stay in the army. Be that as it may, I was wondering if you might do me a small favor."

Before Kev could answer to the affirmative, the Major continued.

"Would you be willing to report to Mr. Bird's office at O-Seven-Hundred hours and pick up some paperwork that needs to be flown to Squadron?"

Happy to be let off the hook so easily, Kev smiled and readily lied to the Major.

"Yes, Sir. I'll be very happy to go over to Charley's office and take care of delivering the paperwork to Squadron. If you like, I'll check with everyone else in Administration and see if anything else needs to be flown up to Squadron."

Smiling, the Major waved him out the door. He had been around for a good number of years and easily recognized Kev's face-saving lie. Greatly enjoying himself and his gentle form of punishment, he added more to Kev's mission list.

"Oh Johnson, before you go tomorrow, take a moment and check with 'Top.' He'll know what else you need to take care of."

Morning came early. The previous night Kev had tried to find a flight suit that didn't look like it had been through the war. It was a vain attempt. He had only two flight suits to choose from and both of them had been through the war. Therefore, he didn't have a meaningful choice. Almost twelve months of combat alternating between the two suits had taken their toll. A hands on type pilot, he was a natural magnet for every speck of dirt, grease, and homeless crud to be found on, in, or near a helicopter. When the crewchief was poking around things, Kev was always underfoot and somehow getting dirtier than the crewchief.

Adding to his general disheveled look was his physical and psychological nature. Kev was the kind of guy who could put on a freshly cleaned and pressed class "A" uniform and look as if he had spent the previous two nights sleeping in it. He always needed a haircut. However, with his flying schedule and natural rebelliousness, his hair was a very low priority. His leather boots were old, beaten-up, worn-out, but very comfortable.

When he got up, heedful of the Major's priorities, he vowed to turn clean up his act and look like a soldier. After a busy ten-minute attempt, he gave up his hopeless quest. For Kev, as always, it was a losing battle. He could spend his whole life trying. In the end, he would never look like a parade-ground or recruiting-poster soldier. As a result, his own self-image was very clear. Ole Kev flew his little Red Bird and found the bad guys. Working at that military task, he was a very good soldier. As for "spit and polish," he was a very poor soldier. The young man made his choice of what kind of soldier he would be when he arrived in Vietnam. The mission came first, and looking pretty came in a very distant second.

Looking about the rubbish and rubble that liberally littered the floor of his hooch, he eventually found his battered old fatigue cap. Of course, It was exactly where he left it. Well, . . . not quite exactly. Sometime the previous evening, he had kicked it from its allotted parking place on the floor into the dirty dusty corner. Jamming the misshapen faded rag upon his head, he reluctantly headed toward the Administration Building. Enroute, he passed by the mess hall and grabbed himself a cup of old duce and a half drain oil which was pretending to be a cup of coffee. While it wasn't exactly delicious, it did have enough kick to wake the dead, and that was exactly how he felt and what he needed. It was his day off and a chance to sleep in. However, much to his dismay, ole Kev was going to Charley's office to play airborne mailman.

When he stepped into Charley's office, he was immediately assaulted with an overpowering urge to vomit all over his clean desk and floor. Kev couldn't believe the sight that greeted his eyes. That Olympic class kiss a-- had, at last, out done himself. Kev was dumbstruck. The assistant Supply and Admin. Officer was wearing a spanking new, freshly pressed flight suit complete with all the proper insignia. The absurd sight served to increase Kev's growing anger, pushing it in the general direction of uncontrolled rage.

As far as Kev was concerned, the little jerk shouldn't have a flight suit. He never flew unless he needed his monthly hours to get his flight pay! Furthermore, for the past three months, Kev had been begging and pleading for a couple of new flight suits and a new pair of boots. Charley had repeatedly told him that they were not available. However, as Kev looked down, he noted that ole Charley's feet were also freshly shod with highly polished new boots. Apparently, the place where he had gotten his ballistic flight helmet was still open for business.

When Kev came through the door, Charley greeted him like they were long-lost friends. Winning the battle of wills, though it was touch and go for a wee bit, Kev refrained from drawing his forty-five and shooting the little weasel.

"Kev, I'm glad to see you. The Major told me that you volunteered to the admin. flight up to Squadron for me today. I can't tell you how much I appreciate your doing that. I'm just so backed up that I can't make the flight."

Simmering, Kev translated Charley's self-serving prattle.

"What I'm saying is that I have my four hours of flying in this month. That's enough for me to get my flight pay. Therefore, I'm not flying."

Not sure how much of the Major's ear Charley had, Kev slowly ground his teeth to the nubs while maintaining his stony silence.

Looking at Charley's desk with its name plats, one pen, one pencil, and two pieces of paper neatly placed upon it, Kev searched his stomach for some exceptionally vile bile. He found the growing urge to vomit overpowering. Strange, as overworked as he claimed to be, Charley had found time to have his hair cut one-half inch shorter than regulation. But, then again, that was good ole Charley. He had his priorities.

Unable to drag up any nasty vomit and rapidly losing his

patience, Kev spoke softly.

"Charley, don't play games with me. I'm too tired and too p-----
off. Just give me the junk that has to go up to Squadron. Later, if you
have the time to do your job, maybe you can get me some new boots and
flight suits."

His voice dripping with sarcasm, Kev continued.

"I've only got about one-hundred and fifty hours this month. So,
I've got to build up my time so that I can keep my control touch."

As Kev was walking out, Charley was about to tell Kev that boots
and flight suits were not available. Suddenly, he had an attack of sanity,
and he realized that he would do much better by keeping his mouth
shut.

Though he was not pleased with his "mission" for the day, Kev
had decided to make the best of the situation he had created. Yet, his
little encounter with Charley served to sour his attempt to view the flight
"positively." Fortunately, his other encounters with people at the Admin.
Shack went much better. The old "Top" Sergeant went so far as to tease
him about becoming one of the Major's favorites the day he took
command.

"Mr. Johnson, you never cease to impress me. It only took you
a day and now the Major knows your face and name."

Smiling Kev responded. "It's a gift, Top."

A grand human being, the gentle old "Top" Sergeant had a warm
spot for his Junior Warrants. (He was old enough to be a father to most
of them.) Though they technically outranked him, he tended to adopt
them as wayward children. In turn, most of them were pleased with their
adoption. That is, with the illustrious exception of people like Charley
Bird.

"Mr. Johnson, I've never seen a young Warrant Officer get a
Major's attention as quickly as you did. Your friend, Mr. Bird, has been
falling all over himself trying to get the Major's attention. Yet, just by
being yourself, you have already had a nice chat with him in his office."

Kev laughed and repeated himself by telling Top that it was a
special skill of his.

Top continued.

"However Sir, just between the two of us, I wouldn't worry about
it. I put in a good word for you, and he seems to have taken everything
in stride. In fact, he was quite impressed that you 'volunteered' to fly this
morning."

Kev laughed and added a postscript to the conversation.

"Well Top, it was not one of my finest hours."

Making quotation marks with his fingers, Kev continued.

"Anyway, the boss did ask me to 'volunteer for this hazardous

292

mission.'"

With his dark mood delightfully lightened by the wise old "First Shirt," Kev strolled down to the flightline. Maintenance was working on his bird and they asked him to fly Sven's. Flying someone else's bird didn't bother Kev as they were all war-weary. In was an hour's flight to Squadron and he knew the flying Sven's bird would be nicer than taking his own. The Audio Direction Finder worked in that bird, whereas it did not work in Kev's. However, he wasn't worried about using it to navigate. He's planned on flying IFR. In Red Bird talk that meant "I follow the roads." He would rather dial the ADF to Armed Forces Radio and listen to some nice tunes as he flew along than worry about using it for navigation. When the crewchief asked if Kev wanted him to go along, he said that he was free to do as he pleased.

Thinking for a moment, the young man responded.

"Well Sir, if it is OK with you, I'll ride along. It's a maintenance stand-down and if I hang around, the maintenance Sergeant will put me to work on the hanger queen."

Thinking about how much he liked being sent out to work on someone else's project, Kev laughed and gave him instruction.

"Well, George? Don't you think that you should mount up before the Sergeant finds out you're goofing off with a deadbeat Warrant."

The flight quickly became a relaxing and enjoyable break in Kev's normal routine. Fortunately the morning air was both still and cool making it a delightful morning for flying. With the ADF tuned to Armed Forces Radio the two young men flew along listening to an assortment of popular rock and roll. As the leisurely flew along, they enjoyed an hour's conversation about everything and nothing. In another setting, they could have been two young men out cruising and heading to the beach to check out the babes. Surprising them, the hour passed very quickly, and suddenly they were tying down the aircraft at Squadron. With nothing for him to do, Kev excused the crewchief and told him to go over to the EM club for a cold coke and a burger.

"George, why don't you cool it for about an hour and a half. Then, meet me back here."

Despite his earlier futile efforts, Kev still looked like he was a refugee from a terrible disaster. Like many other parts of his life, he called it a "gift." Shrugging his shoulders, he mashed his battered cap on his head and started trudging toward the admin. building. He had several stops and suspected that he would have to bring some stuff back to the troop. Armed with a silly grin and almost enjoyed his "punishment," he casually went about his business as the Cav's messenger boy.

After sticking his head into several offices, all his tasks were completed and he started back to his little bird. Burdened with the mail bag and another package for the Major, the return trip was not as pleasant as it had been earlier. The sun was high in the sky and the humidity was Vietnam oppressive. Sweating heavily, Kev was no longer enjoying his "punishment."

If he had looked bedraggled earlier, Kev only looked worse as he trudged back to the helicopter. Large sweat stains were forming in his armpits and down his back. He had the front of his flight suit unzipped about five or six inches in a vain attempt to feel a little cooler. Adding to his unmilitary appearance, his hat was pushed way back on his head showing a mop of sweaty brown hair which did not meet military standards. Kev was hot and stinking miserable. If there was any doubt, he looked the part. Grimly moving to his helicopter, he had two thoughts. The first was the wonderful cooling breeze that he would enjoy when they became airborne. He second was that his friends were back at the club enjoying the feeble air conditioning and sipping ice laden cokes. Frustrated, he muttered to himself.

"D--- it, that's where I belong."

As he reached his helicopter, he tossed his assorted cargo in the back of the little bird. Deciding that he would tie it down in a moment, he wearily sat on the edge of the cargo deck with his feet dangling to the ground. Pushing his battered hat a little further back upon his head, he took a deep breath. Cursing the capricious gods who hated him, he then sighed deeply in frustration. As he was letting out his breath, he noted a pair of legs approaching. The approaching legs were beautifully encased in freshly starched jungle fatigues. Adding to the military correctness, the jungle boots on those same legs were carefully spit-shined. Yet, he questioned what kind of an idiot would wear starch and go through that trouble for his boots. If the wearer didn't know, Vietnam was a land of heat, humidity, mud, and people bent on killing Americans. Being hot, unhappy and generally miserable, he thought no more of it.

Suddenly, his peace was broken when he heard a voice bellow.

"Hey trooper, don't you salute an Officer?"

Kev's internal voice questioned the motives of the noise makes.

"What kind of a Jack A-- is that, bellowing at some poor EM working on the flightline?"

Looking down at his own mud-caked and worn out boots, he noticed that the pretty jump boots were directly in front of him. Initially amused, he found it to be an interesting study in contrast. If he hadn't been feeling so frustrated, he might have perused the thought for its own humorous value. However, the interrupting voice bellowed out again.

"Hey, YOU, trooper! I'm talking to you. You there, sitting in the helicopter. Stand up when I talk to you!"

It slowly dawned on Kev that he was the one being bellowed at.

If he hadn't been so hot and frustrated, he might have laughed at the foolish situation. However, bad mood or not, he didn't find being yelled at by a stranger amusing. Rather, it made him very angry.

In his evil imagination and frustration, Kev formed a malicious plan of action. With an exaggerated slowness born of frustration and a low grade tolerance of idiots, he would slowly push the brim of his hat to the vertical position. This would obscure the only rank that he wore. He had pinned his blacked-out wings and Warrant bar to his battered cap. Continuing with his exaggerated slowness, Kev would slowly look up. Allowing his eyes to slowly travel up the immaculately starched uniform, he would settle his gaze upon the freshly scrubbed face of the very young Captain. Kev also noted that he did not wear aviator wings and that he was not a member of the combat arms. Then, with a voice dripping with insolence and a barely contained rage, Kev would quietly speak.

"Captain, is there anything that I can do to help you?"

However, his little used common sense kicked into gear, he had more than enough trouble with the Major. He did not need any more problems. Therefore, he slowly jumped up and spoke respectfully, though reluctantly.

"Are you speaking to me, Sir?"

In his imagination, he gazed into the young Captain's face with a broad monovalent smile spreading across his face. He was watching the freshly scrubbed and closely shaven face go from bright red to a lovely mottled purple color. Burned out, worn out, and generally frustrated, he would have some fun at the expense of the pompous a-- standing in from of him. Kev could imagine the young Captain becoming so enraged that he would be having trouble controlling himself. With specks of spittle flying from his lips, he would demand to know where Kev's pilot was. Getting into the swing of things, Kev would smile sweetly and respond.

"Captain, I fail to see where that is any of your business. If I'm not mistaken, you don't belong on the flightline."

Continuing to live in his imaginary world, Kev was hoping that the little jerk would over-pressure his hydraulic system, blow a gasket, and drop deader than a doornail at his feet. From the expression that would form on the Captain's face and the color of his skin, Kev would be sure that his wishes were about to be granted. Waiting, he would sit quietly. Maintaining his sweet smile, he would stare into the Captain's eyes. Because he wasn't responding, the Captain would have to break eye contact and roar.

"Trooper, you stand up when you speak to an Officer. You address him as sir. You also salute an Officer in your presence!"

When he finished with his eruption, Kev would slowly nod his head as if he were carefully weighing the Captain's words.

However, as much as he wanted to, Kev was not going to allow his angry wishes and dreams to overrule his limited common sense. He felt that something was going on in the Squadron that he did not fully understand. If the new Major and now this Captain were any indication, somebody higher up was cracking the whip.

"Maybe," he thought to himself. "If we are not going to be allowed to win this war, at least we are going to look pretty not winning it."

Continuing to live in his imagination, he would remain sitting and would casually look about all three-hundred-and-sixty degrees of the compass. Sitting and kinda rocking, he would continue to smile sweetly. Then, without a preamble, he would speak as if to a child.

"By the way Captain, do you have any idea where you are? Before you try to answer that difficult question, I'll give you a small hint. All the helicopters parked here tell me that we are on a flightline. When we are on a flightline, we don't salute. It is considered a serious safety hazard. Please believe me, Captain, it would ruin your whole day if you walked into a spinning tail rotor while saluting. I for one, would hate to see you ruin a good tail rotor. They are very expensive."

While he continued imagining that he was standing insolently before the obnoxious Captain, old Kev thought that he would sit on the cargo deck. Then, seemingly unconcerned, he would slowly rock back and forth. While rocking slowly back and forth, he could continue to stare at the Captain. Suddenly, he would be in no hurry to return to his Cav troop. While he was mad enough to chew nails and spit rust, he would decide to enjoy himself.

However, he wasn't enjoying himself or living in his imaginary world. The reality of the situation was straining his patience. While not standing at ridged attention, he was standing straight when he spoke to the Captain. Though they were on the flightline where people had to be aware of taxiing aircraft and spinning rotors, this was not enough for the Captain.

The little Captain continued with his tirade.

"God d--- it trooper! You'll stand at attention, address me as sir, and salute me!"

With that, he made a move as to grab Kev's flight suit and shake him. Angry and shocked that the Captain was going to lay hands on him, Kev stared deeply into his eyes and slowly shook his head no. Wisely, the Captain backed off.

"OK, if that's the way that you want it. We'll wait until your pilot returns."

Again, in his imagination, Kev slowly began to chuckle. Speaking softly, he would finally end the silly charade.

"You could have a long wait, Captain. You see, I'm the pilot of the little bird. Furthermore, my name is not trooper. I'll thank you to respectfully address me as Mr. Johnson. Maybe they forgot to explain that to you in charm school. However, that is the proper way to address a Warrant Officer. Despite what lofty opinions you may hold, I am not one of your little troopers that you enjoy lording your power over."

When he finished, Kev would stretch, stand up, and look down upon the pretty little Captain.

Biting his lip till it almost bled and fighting to control himself, Kev spoke softly.

"With all due respect, Sir, we have a very good reason for not saluting on the flightline. It is a safety hazard and a very dangerous practice. People have been killed by propellers and rotors when saluting. I meant no disrespect by not saluting. Also, I apologize for not standing when you approached the aircraft. Life is kinda casual on the flightline. With all the pilots being Warrants and Commissioned Officers, standing on ceremony tends to become confusing. Sir, though I may not look like it to you, I am the pilot."

With a sense of growing dread, Kev realized that the obnoxious Captain was not finished with him. Shifting about and straightening his hat, Kev attempted to remain calm and in control of his rapidly growing anger. He was afraid that the clock on his patience would run out and that he might just punch the little jerk in the nose.

After a moment, the Captain regained a fraction of his composure. Trying to maintain his superiority, the overbearing little Captain began with a contemptuous tone.

"Well, Mr. Johnson. You may be the pilot and a Warrant. However, I still outrank you."

Kev muttered, under his breath. "No s--- Sherlock!"

Gathering steam, the Captain continued.

"I expect, as military tradition demands, a salute and to be addressed as Sir!"

Kev overriding impulse and compulsion was to punch the little jerk in the face. While he held that impulse in check, he didn't discard it. If all else failed or if he was pushed much harder, he would reconsider the option.

"Captain, as I explained but a moment ago, there is no saluting on the flightline."

In his imagination, Kev added a postscript.

"Also, I will not call you Sir. You are intruding on my flightline and do not belong here. I'll address you as Captain which is militarily correct. Someday, if you earn it, I might call you Sir."

However, the Captain was not finished. "Not by a long shot," as Kev's dad frequently said. He began demanding to know Kev's unit and his CO's name so that he could report Kev's disrespect. This harping only served to multiply Kev's shock and anger. Countering his passion and excitable nature, Kev had maintained his emotional control and had been verbally respectful. Though he had not saluted and would not salute on the flightline. It was a matter of principle inasmuch as most good Aviators believed safety rules overrode all other rules.

A man of apparently great energy, the Captain then began chewing Kev out because of his sloven appearance and because he was not wearing any insignia of rank on his flight suit. Living in the real world, poor Kev tried to get a word in for his defense.

"Sir, . . ."

The Captain cut him off and continued his tirade about his not looking like an Officer and pilot. Frustrated, almost to tears, Kev tried again.

"Sir, if you'll only listen for a moment. I'm not in a VIP outfit. I fly combat every day."

His pleas fell on deaf ears. Angry, frustrated, and with confused tears filling his eyes, Kev tried one more time.

"Sir, I only have two flight suits and this is my best one."

It wasn't working.

"That's no excuse, Mister! You look like a slob! The next time that you come to Squadron, I expect you to look like an Officer and gentleman."

Just as the Captain was beginning to wind-down, George, the crewchief, returned.

George, completely unaware of the contest of wills, jauntily walked directly up to Kev and the Captain. Of course, he didn't salute. Not saluting and, if possible, looking worse than Kev, he earned a malevolent stare from the Captain. Ignoring the Captain, he spoke to Kev.

"Mr. J., is there anything that I can do for you?"

Looking up, Kev was relieved to see the crewchief.

"Ya, George. Would you please secure the packages in the back and untie the rotor? While you do that, I'll escort my friend the Captain out of the way so that he doesn't get hurt."

When he finished speaking, Kev firmly took the infuriated little Captain by the elbow and led him away from the helicopter. Angered at the seemingly abrupt treatment, the Captain started to protest. However, before he finished his first word, Kev held his hand up for silence.

When they were safely out of earshot, Kev turned to the obnoxious little Captain.

"Captain, what I am going to say to you is for your benefit. Please believe me that I am speaking respectfully. Yet, I'll be honest enough to admit that I am also speaking with great anger. Looking at your clean starched uniform, spit-shined boots, and bright insignia of rank it is obvious that you have never been out in the field. I am also pretty sure that you have never heard a shot fired in anger. So, I'm going to tell you something that you might not want to hear. We don't wear rank in the field! Nobody who wants to go home is stupid enough to make an obvious and easy target out of themselves. Speaking of targets, saluting in the field is strictly forbidden. If ole George, over there, were to salute me, I would pull out my forty-five and shoot him on the spot. In the same light, if I were to salute my Major, if he didn't shoot me first, someone else would. And, we never salute on the flightline, it is a serious safety hazard!"

The Captain was about to retort and Kev held up his hand.

"Sir, I'm going now. If you believe that you must, then report me to my Major."

As before, Kev didn't add his postscript.

"After all, what's he going to do to me? Send me to Vietnam? You see, Captain, at heart, I'm a civilian in uniform. The truth is that I could give a rat's rectum less about all your silly little Army games. However, if you ever get the guts to come out into the field, please be sure to wear your shiny railroad tracks. That way everybody will know that you have rank. Tell you what, if I should happen to see you in the field, I'll whip my biggest baddest parade-ground salute on you. After that, if a sniper hasn't shot you full of bullets, I'll have all my boys whip a big one on you. However, I'll never salute you on the flightline. Will that make you happy?"

With the little Captain standing slack-jawed, Kev turned and walked away. He was terrified that he would tell the little jerk the rest of what he had just been thinking.

With the tension and anger washed out of him, Kev jumped into his seat and fired-up his little bird. When they were safely airborne and following the road home, George came up on the intercom.

"Mr. J., what the heck was that all about? I've never seen a Captain look quite so mad."

Laughing softly as a cover for the flood of tears which were marking his rage and humiliation, Kev keyed his mike.

"Oh, it's nothing to fret about, George. It was just another Remington Raider learning the sad facts of life about Vietnam. Hopefully, he's a newbe and eventually will learn. Tell you what, let's go home to some people that we know we can trust."

JOHNNY

Frustrated by an apparent lack of progress or purpose in the war, Kev wrote to Pastor Bill.

I just don't know any more. What seemed straight forward and black and white a year ago, has somehow changed. The band seems to just keep marching on and continuously playing the same old tune. The "sweet sounding music" of my life is beginning to sound like a needle stuck on a phonograph record. Again, a few words of the song and then click. Again, a few words of the song and then click. Repeatedly, again and again, we hear the same old words and the same old song. The merry-go-round continues its endless circles with an occasional rider thrown off. According to what I read, some people, back in the world, students apparently, are clamoring for our hides. Why are we the targets? As best I can tell, they cry for our scalps because we are trying to do the job which the President sent us to do. At least that's what is happening according to your letters and the newspapers.

Struggling to justify his experience, Kev pondered upon the world of Vietnam.

"What difference does all the blood make? Nothing seems to change. A couple of kids killed here. A few days later, a couple more kids killed somewhere else."

For dramatic background music, the artillery thundered its heavy base beat. Fleets of helicopters took off. Later in the day, most of the helicopters landed.

"What's new?" He asked himself.

The sun rose and hours later, the sun set. The bad guys killed the Lieutenant and his crew during Kev's first mission in country. Months later he got shot-up, not for the first time, at the same hill where they killed him. TK died in a meaningless crash, and now this. Deep inside, Kev understood that his was "but to do and die." Nevertheless, he couldn't control the number of troubling questions rising from deep within.

"Are we getting anywhere with our little war? Or, are we just playing some stupid geopolitical game which goes on and on without meaning and without end?"

Kev just wished that he knew.

His good friend Red One-Four had his own negative answer to their problem. In his charming, yet highly cynical philosophy, he would repeat.

"My friends, the problem is that you think that there is an answer when there is no answer. We can only try to cope with the absurdity of the moment."

His suggestion was to stay as drunk as humanly possible when not flying.

"Then," he said, "when not drunk, wisdom suggest that one should try to ignore the slowly spreading stupidity."

Stupidity, Sven firmly believed, filtered down from Washington and the Five-Sided-Puzzle-Palace on the Potomac. When Sven was drunk enough, he would proclaim his angry truth to anyone who would listen. He firmly believed that a Captain, Lieutenant, or Major somewhere out "there," was getting his "combat ticket" punched. That was the man who was zealously dedicated to getting him killed. He explained to Kev that their only dedication was to assure their own promotion up the military ladder of success. A little radical, one might think, but some things the young pilots had experienced caused them to question everything.

Continuing his letter to Pastor Bill, Kev said.

Well . . . I tried the beer. I tried much harder with the hard liquor. Neither of them changed anything for me. I only get sick, sicker, and finally sickest of all. Yet, occasionally I envy Sven. Somehow, he seems to cope with the stupidity that gets men and boys killed for questionable results. Furthermore, maybe because he is such a charming cynic and my good friend, he also does a highly credible job with his mission.

As he told Pastor Bill, Kev tried Sven's approach of staying as drunk as humanly possible. Physically suffering every hung-over morning, it did not work for him. He knew that he would have to find his own approach to the problem if he wanted to remain sane. However, he had no idea what sane was in a world filled with boys killing boys. As he struggled to make sense out of the senseless, he was reminded that his mamma always told him to "dance with the girl you brung."

Giving himself a little pep talk when he was frustrated, he spoke to his inner self.

"Consequently, I suppose that I have little or no recourse but to pick up my pen and my note books and keep writing."

Upon occasion, his writing had helped him to try and sort out his thoughts on paper. Yet, he was discovering that his attempts, at writing and remembering, were exponentially harder than he expected. Writing his first five-hundred word essay in Jr. High School had been easier. Nevertheless, Kev hoped that through his pen and paper, he could keep the spirit of his special brotherhood alive for a little longer than fate had decreed.

Taken from Kev's notebook:

Today was my worst day in Vietnam! No, I take that back. Today was the absolute worst day of my life!

If any historical poetry or justice is to be found in this place, something remarkable should have stood out that morning five days ago. Something profoundly cruel in the stars and planets should have marked such a fateful day. However, inhuman reality set another stage. That morning was all so unremarkable. It promised, for lack of a better expression, to be just another boring day in Southeast Asia. That's the truth.

Yep, it was just another day in Vietnam. Nothing of merit or note was changing in this melancholy sea of changelessness. At least it wasn't raining. So, maybe it was a better day that some for yet another nameless handful of GI's to die. However, the unasked question remains unanswered. When is it a good day to die? Maybe the politicians and diplomats were talking around the table in Paris today. Then again, maybe not talking but spending their time posturing and pouting. Talking or not talking, nothing seems to make a difference in this strange slice of hell. It was another boring day in Southeast Asia. It was a day that saw another handful of GI's heading home, in U. S. government issue aluminum caskets.

Like countless other days, pilots and crew slowly ambled down to the flight line to pre-flight their helicopters. It was just another of the Cav's changeless routines done before going off into the wild blue yonder. It was a rite to battle. Maybe? Who knows? Check all the fluid levels, oil, hydraulics, and fuel in the Hueys, Snakes and Loachs. Make sure all the assorted nuts and bolts were in their proper places, correctly fastened, and safety wired as required by Army regulation. Do a quick check of all the guns and armorments to make sure they were ready. When those daily tasks are completed, then "kick the tire and light the fire."

When firing up their birds, some of them would use the checklist they had long since memorized. Others, would not. Some like Red One-Four, who was fatally hung-over as usual, could easily do this mindless task without even thinking about it. Nothing new, nothing different, it was just like the various morning task of countless GI's all over the world.

Someone down the flight line asks anyone who will listen.

"Hey, what day of the week is this?"

Everyone working the line will have to stop and think a while. Who knew? Who cared? What difference did it make? It was just one day closer to going home. That was how most of them dealt with things after a few months in country.

From a thousand feet in the air, the deceptively peaceful ground quietly slipped beneath them. It had spread its panoramic carpet before the helicopters countless other times during the past few months. That morning C&C assigned Kev's team to fly the first recon. With Kev's team flying the first mission, Red One-Four and his team set up at their usual staging field. During the passing months, Kev decided that their order of things was a kindness of sorts. Back at the staging field, Red One-Four was trying to figure out how to shoot himself. His only fear was that he would get court marshaled for destruction of government property.

Undoubtedly, Sven believed that a bullet in the head was the quickest way to end the misery of his daily hangover. However, when the time came for him to go to work, he was always OK. He always was able to do his job. Furthermore, he was always darned good.

As they headed to their area of operations, Johnny and Kev couldn't decide to be happy or disappointed at the day's prospects. Division had assigned them to look into an area which they had frequently visited. Usually, very little, if any, enemy activity took place in that locale. The mission looked to be just a routine check just to make sure that no significant changes had taken place about which "higher/-higher" should know. Kev sighed quietly to himself. He decided that it was going to be one of those days. It was going to be another meaningless day where they put in their time on the job and then went home for supper.

"I suppose," he thought to himself, "we are not much different from the people back in the world. We'll keep repeating the same task till we die. Only, I fear that we won't die of old age. We'll die of a mistake or a bad guy who was better at his job than we were at our own job."

As they had, countless times during their months together, Johnny and Kev descended from their higher altitude and began to sniff around. As far as they knew, no one lived permanently in the valley. Neither had anyone worked the abandoned rice patties for years and years. Though, little existed to interest them militarily, a delightful pastoral gentleness colored and flavored the whole length of the valley. Nothing human or of human construction moved or stirred.

The grass gently fluttered in the wind and the clear water bubbled down the shallow river or stream that slowly meandered through and about the center of the little valley. Experience had given them a very good idea where the bad guys would hide out. If any were home, they expected to find them on the west side of the valley. Flying, seven or eight klicks to the east on the gently rising slopes, everything was very quiet. It was only because they had frequently flown their mission that they could keep a healthy tension in their work. Frequently surprised by an apparently peaceful scene, they would not knowingly let their guard down.

The three young men in Red One-Five carefully combed the countryside for about an hour fifteen, maybe an hour and a half. Slowly and carefully, they made their search. Cautiously, but in random patterns, they traversed up and down the gentle slopes. They were looking for a sign that there was enemy activity in the immediate area. They saw nothing of note and drew a blank on any ground activity, friendly or an enemy. Then, as they bumped up against their fuel limit, Red One-Four and team came on station to take over the recon. It took no more than a minute to bring them up to speed. Informing Red One-

Four where they had looked and what they hadn't found, Kev turned the little bird about and departed to refuel. Following a quick refueling, they landed at the staging field. Settling down to relax and maybe catch a few z's, they patiently and peacefully awaited their next turn on station.

After they had parked and were awaiting recall, the three of them bought cold cokes and some bananas. The ever-present Vietnamese girls were carrying on with their coke, banana, and bread business. This was not at all unusual as they used this staging field often. These local sales girls were not strangers to them. Over the months, some might suggest that very foolishly, the men from the Cav had come to trust them. This staging field was just an old abandoned one-thousand-five-hundred foot long asphalt landing strip built who knew when. For all they knew, twenty years previously, the French might have built the little landing strip, or even the Japanese before them. No permanent detachment of American or Vietnamese troops was currently present. Therefore, whoever used the staging field provided their own security. Presently, the little field, being in the so-called, backwaters of the war, was wonderfully peaceful and quiet. Kev and Johnny agreed that it was a good place to take a nap in the shadow of the helicopter while they waited. As always, they were hoping that the next call that they heard on the radio was not Red Bird Down!

Rudely interrupting his much desired morning nap, C&C called for Kev's team to return to station. Pete, the crewchief, Johnny, and Kev strapped themselves into their Red Bird. In the timeless way of all soldiers, they began muttering, complaining, and carrying on. Kev believed that the pre-mission cussing and cursing started that forever to be damned day of ancient history. That was the day when the politicians drafted Og and Ug into the first cavemen's army.

Given that they attached no urgency to their return, Kev very carefully babied his helicopter into the air and traveled slowly to their area of operations. He had learned that conserving both fuel and helicopter whenever possible was a wise idea. Most of the pilots chose not to push the tired, worn, and, war weary helicopters any more than was strictly necessary. Far too many accidents had happened when they pushed helicopters and pilots unnecessarily hard. Aviation lore said that the number one killer of pilots was "Get home itis." Experience had shown Kev that the little saying held true. He believed that a cousin of "get home itis" had killed TK. Someone had pushed the panic button and TK's bird had been pushed beyond its limits.

About five klicks away from Red One-Four and team, Kev gave ole Sven a call on the radio.

"Red One-Four, what have you got for me today?"

He responded with his situation report.

"All seems quiet One-Five, except in the draw just east of my current position. Though we couldn't see anything, my back seat tells me that he heard good ole 'one-shot Charley' popping off a round at us now and then."

Thinking for a moment, One-Four commented.

"If C&C doesn't have a better idea, I suppose you could spend some time and see if you and Johnny can flush him out."

Sven's casualness about tracking ole one-shot down was because the Scouts generally considered the ole boy more of a nuisance than anything else. He would pop out of his little hole in the ground and fire a single shot at them from his antique, and probably rusty, SKS rifle. Just as quickly, he would disappear. Ole one-shot almost never hit anybody.

Most likely, he was some rice farmer. Everyone agreed that he was only a part time Viet Cong guy who was shooting off his month's allowance of fifteen or thirty bullets. From his lack of accuracy, everyone assumed that he was anxious to return home. Most of the guys were sure that he would rather work his fields and make a living for his brood of kids and loving wife.

It appeared to Kev that it would continue to be a slow and quiet day. As they let down from altitude, he punched the intercom and made a suggestion to Johnny.

"Well . . . what da ya think Johnny, shall we try to flush out ole one-shot? That ole boy is getting to be one great big pain in the butt."

Kev waited for Johnny to finish carefully arranging himself. Sometimes Kev thought that he was worse than an old woman. Everything had to be just so. First, he had to settle himself carefully on the floor with his legs hanging out of the helicopter. Eventually, when he was comfortable, he placed his M-60 machine gun across his lap and loaded a belt of bullets in it. Satisfied, he prepared his willie pete marking grenade. When he finally was satisfied with the arrangement of all his stuff in his little world, he answered.

"It seems like as good of an idea as we've got for the moment, boss."

After he spoke, Pete concurred. In the routine which had reinforced itself through numberless repetitions, they began with a semi-high speed check out the ridges that surrounded the draw. When they saw nothing and nothing had happened, Johnny and Kev agreed on their next course of action. It was time to descend into the little draw.

A couple of minutes after they had descended into the draw, Johnny cried out on the intercom.

"There he is. Ole One-shot. I heard him!"

Kev asked. "Johnny, have you got him pinpointed enough for us to call the Snakes in?"

"Not really, boss. Let's work our way to the north and then come back down a little east of our last path."

The idea seemed rather good to ole Kev. Unhurried, they carefully worked their way around to come down in the same general area. However, they were not flying the same path they flew the first time. To make that mistake would have been breaking a cardinal rule of the Red Bird recon. <u>Never fly the same route twice!</u>

About five minutes later they were slowly sliding down a hill, just south of the original position. Johnny triumphantly cried out.

"I heard him again, boss. This time though, I've got a very good idea where he is."

With that announcement, boredom had passed into history. Alert, the three of them, in the little Red Bird, were keyed up with the primal excitement of the hunt. Again, Kev asked Johnny if he thought they should call in the Snakes.

"Tell you what boss, I've got an idea."

Kev patiently waited.

"Mr. J., here is what I would like us to do. Swing out over the valley and then come in toward that big clump of trees that we just passed."

Looking back, with perfect 20/20 hindsight, Kev knew that it was not a good idea. After the fact, Kev realized that it was a deadly stupid idea. However, though it was not an excuse that he would accept from anyone, he and Johnny were caught up in the hunt. Dropping the nose of the little helicopter, pulling in power, he tried to pick up speed. He swung the little helicopter out over the valley floor at maybe one hundred fifty feet. They weren't going fast enough to be safe. At best, they were doing thirty-five/forty knots. As they started the turn back toward where Johnny thought ole one shot was hiding, Johnny began laying down short burst suppressing fire with his M-60.

With an abrupt, unexpected, and unwanted silence, Johnnie's M-60 ceased firing. At the same time, Kev heard what he thought was, a surprised grunt over the intercom. Not knowing why he stopped firing, he called to Johnny over the intercom.

"What's happening, Johnny?"

In response, he heard only silence from the back-seater. Kev risked a quick glance over his shoulder. Johnny had pulled himself all the way back into the helicopter. At first, that puzzled Kev. Then, the shocked expression on Johnny's face scared him. Something unwanted and unpleasant had etched deep lines, which was a cross between surprise and pain, deeply into his boyish face. What he saw, scared Kev like he had never been scared before.

Scared by his vision, Kev wasn't sure what had happened to Johnny and he viciously blocked his worst fears. However, he knew that whatever had happened was far more important than looking for ole-one shot. He immediately broke away from the draw and began clawing, at max power, for a safer altitude. Simultaneously, he mashed the key down on his radio.

"Number two lay some heavy mini-gun fire in the draw. NOW!"

As his wing man broke into his firing run, he continued talking on the radio. The shaken pilot asked the Snakes to roll in hot. Without pausing for breath, switched keys on the mike and Kev hollered at Pete on the intercom.

"Jesus Pete, find out what is wrong with Johnny. Oh God, tell me that I am wrong! I'm not sure, but I think one-shot hit him!"

Pete rapidly unstrapped his crash harness and stuck his head and one shoulder past the bulkhead to check on Johnny's condition.

Pete couldn't reach Johnny, but immediately he began sobbing and crying into the intercom.

"Jesus-God Mr. J! Johnny has been hit, and he is bleeding all over the place. My God Sir, I think he is dying on us."

Kev thought and prayed to himself.

"It simply isn't possible. No way could ole one-shot have hit him. Johnny and I are an unbeatable team."

Unbelievably, somehow ole one-shot had hit Johnny from a distance of maybe three hundred meters straight out from the draw. Despite Pete's near hysterics, Kev refused to believe that it was possible. One-shot had managed to hit a moving target using his, Chinese copy, rusty antique Russian, single shot SKS rifle.

Kev quickly told Pete to strap back in and take the controls of the helicopter. He had decided to try and reach Johnny from his closer position. It made good sense to him because Pete could fly straight and level and Kev was closer to where Johnny lay. He took the time that it took to for Pete to strap back in to inform C&C of their situation and asked them to please stand by. When Pete took the controls, Kev finished unstrapping himself. Like Pete, he could only get his head and one arm past the bulkhead. Again, like Pete, he could not reach Johnny. Looking back at Johnny, Kev was shocked, momentarily speechless, by the large, blood-soaked mess that greeted his eyes. He honestly didn't believe one human being could lose such a massive volume blood so quickly.

Desperately hoping that things weren't as bad as they looked, he hollered at Johnny. Continuously praying, within himself, he asked Johnny if he could hear him. Johnny looked up and weakly shook his head yes. Some of his blood then pulsed through the hand with which he was applying pressure on the gaping bullet wound. Johnny's hot blood was sprayed Kev directly in Kev's face! He couldn't believe, with the shock of being so grievously wounded, that Johnny would have any presence of mind. Yet, he had applied direct pressure to the wound. That sight reinforced what Kev already knew. Johnny was good people and wise beyond his years. It was obvious, from the spurting of blood, that they had hit him in an artery. Sometime later, a doctor told Kev that it must have been the femoral artery that was spraying so forcefully.

Using his head, far beyond his knowledge, or his years, Kev took command of the situation. He told Pete to turn the intercom on. That way he wouldn't have to use the switch he couldn't reach. It was time to help Johnny and for some reason, Kev knew exactly what had to be done.

"Now listen very carefully to me, Johnny. I want you to take off your other glove. When it is off, I will tell you what I want next."

Using his teeth, Johnny somehow got the glove off the hand that was not clutching the raw wound in his upper leg.

"God," Kev thought to himself. "This would be so much easier if I could just reach him."

However, Kev didn't feel as if he had the time. He was deathly afraid Johnny would bleed to death before they could get him safely to the ground.

"Now, when I say so, **AND NOT A MOMENT BEFORE I SAY SO**, remove your hand holding pressure on the wound. Then, quickly find the big vein that is doing all that bleeding and squeeze that vein tightly shut with your fingers from your bare hand."

Kev then gave him a couple of seconds to gather his wits. Taking a deep breath, Kev then asked him, "ready?" Johnny shook his head to the affirmative. With a silent prayer to the God of the helpless, Kev then told him --

"DO IT!"

Johnny might have been in shock, so Kev wasn't going to trust his memory. Coaching each move, he began his instructions.

"Let go with your glove hand. See the big vein?"

He shook his head yes.

"Now grab that pulsing vein with your fingers and squeeze it as tightly as you can. Squeeze as if your whole life depends upon it!"

Within the briefest part of an instant, the God of the helpless had answered Kev's prayers of desperation. When he squeezed the pulsing artery, Johnny's bleeding had stopped! It was but a trickle of what it had been a moment earlier. The volume of blood which Johnny was losing still appalled Kev. At least it wasn't near as bad!

"OK now Johnny, just sit tight, we're going to get some help. I promise!"

Wiggling back into his seat, Kev took back the controls. When he was set, he called C&C and told them one-shot had critically wounded Johnny. The Major may have been a new guy. However, he was at his best form.

"One-Five, we have got Dust-Off warming up. Do you want him to come out here and get your observer?"

Kev paused and thought about it for a brief instant. If they had their Blues immediately available with their corpsman present, Kev would have gone for it. However, there would not be a corpsman to care for Johnny while they waited for dust-off. It didn't make any sense to Kev. He feared that Johnny would bleed to death before he received the skill level of help he needed. With that being the situation, Kev responded.

"With your permission Blue Six, I believe that I can get my observer to the aid station and a doctor long before Dust Off can get out here. He is bleeding so badly I'd like to leave now and red line it all the way to the aid station."

Apparently C&C must have used the same logic Kev did. Without pausing to think about it, Blue Six responded positively to Kev's request.

"Permission granted Red One-Five. Also. I am going to send a Snake to escort and clear the way for you. God speed, son!"

Lowering the nose of Rocinante, Kev made a wide sweeping turn to gain airspeed and maneuver room. It was time for his faithful steed to become a thoroughbred racehorse. They needed both airspeed and room to climb the mountains/hills between them and the aid station. While Kev began maneuvering, he immediately pulled in every ounce of power available in ole 662. Pointedly, he ignored the engine instruments which were rapidly swinging their needles into the red danger zones. Thinking only of Johnny, he pulled in power till the main rotor speed gave a hint of bleeding off. He hated to abuse the equipment like that. Today, though, he knew it was necessary. Somehow, he also knew that ole Rocinante also knew it as she leapt forward eagerly.

"Pete, unstrap and keep and eye on Johnny. Talk to him. Encourage him. I don't care what you do. Sing to him if you have to. Just don't let him go to sleep or pass out. If it gets difficult enough to keep him awake, remind him he will die if he lets go of that big vein!"

From the back, Johnny must have been listening. He keyed the intercom with his, blood soaked, gloved hand. Seeming to gather a hidden reserve of strength, he spoke weakly.

"I hear you lima charley boss. You just pay attention to driving this darn thing and ole Johnny will do his job just like he always does."

A ghost of a smile creased Kev's face. At last, he felt a little better because his friend Johnny hadn't lost any of his fight. Continuing to try and encourage him, Kev quickly shot back.

"Johnny, it's my turn today, this time I'm the one riding in on the skids to save your worthless butt. So, you just hang tight buddy. You hear me. Hang tight!"

Rocinante wasn't high enough to clear the hills that separated them from the aid station. For safety sake, Kev decided to lower the nose further. He wanted to gain all the speed that they could before they climbed the side of the hill. Kev kept busy joining Pete in encouraging Johnny and talking to White Two-Three, his Cobra escort. White Two-Three was being helpful by taking care of all their radio communications. From somewhere in the dark recesses of his head a strange mantra kept repeating itself again and again, and over and over.

"Speed is life. Altitude is meaningless. Speed is life."

The mantra was telling him something which he had tragically forgotten a few moments earlier when he was hunting ole one shot. Speed was life and too little speed or too much altitude was, in the Red Bird business, death.

Unbidden tears flooded Kev's eyes and a massive lump of pain and guilt was firmly lodged deep in his throat. He had made one bad mistake so far today. By all that he held Holy, Kev was not going to make another mistake, period! What he had done wrong was painfully clear to him. It started when Johnny had asked him to swing out over the valley for our last run in at the draw. Without clearly thinking things out, Kev had unthinkingly placed them right in the middle of, what they called, the kill zone. They were slow, maybe one hundred and fifty feet over the ground, a perfect, unobstructed target. Even ole one-shot Charley had a good chance of hitting that kind of fat target. Angry at himself, Kev muttered.

"Johnny is paying, possibly the ultimate price, for my unforgivable stupidity. It is not his fault. I knew better. I was the aircraft commander, the pilot. It was my decision how to fly, not his. Now, Johnny is bleeding to death because I was more interested in the stupid hunt for a minor nuisance than I was in keeping my crew alive. How could he ever have trusted me?"

The grim reality of the situation broke into Kev's muttering. He received a timely mental slap in the face from some unknown source. Mentally pausing, he accepted that there was plenty of time, the rest of his life, in fact, to beat himself up for his oversights. For this moment, all that mattered was getting Johnny to the aid station alive.

This mission was now far too important for Kev to worry about his oversights. They were descending at the one hundred and twenty-knot redline of the Red Bird. Kev gradually leveled out the speeding little helicopter directly on the tops of the trees. The skids were all but brushing the tops of the taller trees. If someone was down there who didn't like them, they would not have time to fire at the Red Bird before it was far past them. The base of the hills was rapidly approaching. Kev began shedding a little of his airspeed to climb the hills. He continued climbing right on top of the trees. Though it appeared reckless, Kev was flying in a way designed to limit their exposure to additional ground fire. While, moderately concerned about limiting their exposure to ground fire, he was primarily concerned with rushing his precious cargo to the doctors.

Pulling back slightly on the stick, Kev began a gentle zoom climb up the side of the steep ravine. Turning left and then right he dodged the taller of the trees. Ole Rocinante shuddered slightly at the demands they were placing upon her. Nevertheless, she did a magnificent job and offered no complaint. Although they were climbing a moderately steep face of trees and rock, she maintained almost seventy knots. Kev couldn't ask any more from his faithful old friend. Wallowing in his own guilt, Kev began to believe that his helicopter was far more reliable than its pilot. As they climbed, he noted a little, notch-like, pass to his right. If he went through there, that would save them about a hundred feet of climbing. Turning toward it, the little helicopter shot through with about ten feet to spare on each side of the rotor system.

At last heading out toward the costal plains, the ground rapidly dropped away below them. Kev risked a quick look over his shoulder to Johnny. He was pasty white, breathing raggedly, and sweating profusely. Despite his condition, Johnny rewarded him with a grim smile.

"Hang in there buddy. I'll get you to the medico's even if I have to over speed and over stress every single little nut and bolt of this old bird!"

White Two-Three called on the radio and said that he had cleared them straight into the landing strip. He said that they were then cleared directly to the aid station's helicopter pad. To Kev, their destination was so close, only about ten or twenty miles away. With Johnny slowly bleeding to death, he also knew that it seemingly was millions upon millions of miles away.

"The hell with it." He said to himself.

"I'm going to push her harder than anyone has ever pushed an overloaded little Loach."

Holding the power steady, just into the leading edges of the red lines, Kev started pushing their airspeed. Almost frantic, he lowered the nose and started the down hill part of the flight. He had already over torqued the main transmission, over sped the N1 compressor turbine, and brought the exhaust temperature well into the red. By this time, the whole power train was already officially scrap metal! It only waited for the flight to end before maintenance condemned it.

311

Whatever Kev did to her mechanically, no longer mattered. All that mattered was that the little bird somehow held together for the next twenty miles! Kev decided that it was time to trade their altitude for more airspeed as they screamed down to the costal plain from the hills. One hundred and twenty knots was the red line.

Disregarding the red line, the needle swung past and settled, for a moment, at one hundred and thirty knots. He lowered the nose of the helicopter a little more and it swung to one hundred and thirty-five knots. He then pushed her even harder and she reached one hundred and forty knots. Arriving at one hundred and forty-three knots and she was getting very squirrely. One knot faster and, Kev feared that she would flip onto her back with a retreating blade stall. He had read about retreating blade-stall. In flight school, they had taught him about blade-stall. Now, for the first time, he could feel its deadly hand greedily reaching out for the three of them. Retreating blade-stall or not, Johnny continued to bleed to death.

The trade off, altitude for air speed, was paying off in spades. Judging things in his head, Kev noted that they would have altitude to spare when they arrived at the landing strip. He gently eased the power off, just enough, to bring the engine instruments solidly back into the green. This slightly reduced the pitch in the rotor blades. As a byproduct, it took them a little further from the greedy clutches of blade-stall. Safely removed from the clutches of blade-stall, Kev lowering the nose just a touch more. Carefully, he eased the airspeed up to one hundred and forty-five knots. That was faster than he had ever heard someone flying, a combat loaded Red Bird. Though it appeared reckless, he was planning things carefully.

If . . . ole Rocinante didn't come apart, on them, in midair, all was looking good. It appeared that they were going to cross the approach end of the runway at one hundred and ten knots and about fifty feet of altitude. Kev had been given a straight-in approach. No other helicopter was near them or interfering with their direct approach to the runway. Every American pilot in the area was pulling for Johnny's survival. True, they might not have known his name. Names didn't matter. They were all doing their bit for him by staying out of the way!

"Thank God," Kev thought. "That this is not like back in the world. People here got out of the way of an emergency vehicle."

That was the way it was supposed to be!

Crossing the threshold of the runway, Kev dropped his power down to zero. Then he flared the little Red Bird radically, trying to kill off their high air speed.

"Oh S---! Great, now a 'big time' main rotor over-speed to top things off!"

312

He had asked too much of his faithful little bird. With the over-speed, Kev had definitely reduced the whole power train to scrap metal. Not that it was an issue to him. Nevertheless, Kev's faithful little helicopter was still giving her all. Kev pulled in a little pitch to stop the rotor from over speeding any further. He kept her nose high and floated rapidly down the runway to kill their forward momentum. With a single fluid motion, they swooped onto the large red cross marked helipad and landed with a heavy thud. It was not a time of finesse. Ducking under the still turning rotor, four corpsmen rapidly unloaded Johnny onto a waiting stretcher. Although he was unconscious, he was still tightly grasping that pulsing artery in his fingers. The corpsmen brought him directly into the triage area.

Rapidly unstrapping himself from his seat, Kev was shutting the little engine down as fast as he could. Breathlessly, he asked Pete to finish the shut down and tie her rotor down. Throwing his helmet onto his seat, Kev ran breathlessly into the triage area. He arrived as the doctors began to work on his wounded friend. Upon his arrival, the NCOIC (non commissioned officer in charge) immediately turned to Kev. Looking at blotches of Johnny's bright red blood on Kev's face and neck, he asked if Kev were injured.

"I'm fine Sarge. Please take care of Johnny."

As if he didn't hear Kev, the sergeant spoke by rote.

"I'm sorry sir. You are going to have to leave."

Very quietly, but with deadly intent, Kevin responded. Unconsciously dropping his hand to his pistol, he spoke softly.

"NO! I am not going anywhere! I'm sorry sergeant, but I'm not leaving till I know my boy is going to be OK!"

With his announcement of intent, which bore no argument, Kev began to gather Johnny's equipment. He picked up his side arm, chicken plate, and bloody flight-suit remnants. Scrambling to save his life, the medics had cut all of his equipment from Johnny's blood soaked body. Understandably, the NCOIC began to get a little indignant with Kev for defying him. Before he had a chance to get started, a Doctor spoke to Kev.

"Are you his pilot?"

Barely able to keep from crying, like the scared little boy he had just become, Kev softly whispered his response.

"Yes Sir."

"Let him stay sergeant, from what the tower told us he has earned it."

Kev stood fearfully and quietly. He felt like an expectant father in the maternity waiting room. Feeling useless and powerless, he stood with his hands jammed in his pockets. With his chemical rush exhausted, he began to tremble in fatigue and emotional release. Nevertheless, he was still unwilling to be anywhere else in the whole world.

Well-regulated chaos surrounded him. It was a chaos which he could not possibly follow. This was not his world and he could not understand what was going on. As Kev stood by, the medicos hooked up bottles of blood and plasma. They worked like tightly controlled, yet still frantic, demons over Johnny's wounded leg. After, what felt like, an unbelievably long time the Doctors stepped away. Silently, the orderlies then began to wheel Johnny away to Kev knew not where.

Not knowing what this action might have meant, but being gifted with a very active imagination, time stopped for Kev. He didn't dare draw a breath. The Doctor, who moments before had said Kev could stay, turned to him and comforted him. Smiling softly through his fatigue, he spoke.

"I think he is going to live son. I don't know how you got him here alive. Nor, do I know how he managed to hold onto that artery. Still, what is important is that you guys did it. At this point though, I want to be honest, I honestly don't know about saving the leg. However, whoever thought of grabbing that artery saved his life."

With that he walked away before Kev could open his mouth to thank him. Watching the doctor recede into the aid station, Kev began to breathe again.

Later that evening he made a few notations in his notebook.

. . . While I might have made a stupid mistake, a cardinal Red Bird error, flying into the kill zone, I also might have totally destroyed a helicopter getting Johnny here. Johnny possibly could even lose his leg. Yet it looks as if he will live. At this point, I could and would ask no more! I will gladly take whatever may come to me If Johnny lives.

Suddenly, feeling like he was a character in a strange and mysterious movie, Kev was standing in the now strangely quiet and empty room. He was alone with the NCOIC. For some reason, he noticed that he had yet to even remove his flight gloves. Wearily, Kev slowly stripped off his flight gloves and released the Velcro holding his chicken plate closed. Suddenly, he felt like he would collapse from exhaustion.

Noting that Kev seemed to be weaving on his feet, the NCOIC took a closer look at him. Seeing the streaks of tears running down Kev's young cheeks, he apologized.

"I'm sorry Sir, but I was just doing my job. I never know what someone will do if something happens to their buddy on the table."

Thinking a moment about the weight of the loaded side arm he was packing gave Kev good reason to pause guiltily. Then, noticing Johnny's loaded pistol loosely gripped in his hand, Kev looked at him and said.

"That's OK Sarge. All of a sudden, I think I understand."

Turning to leave, young Kev paused momentarily as if he had forgotten something. He turned back to the old sergeant.

"Hey Sarge, thanks for taking care of Johnny."

With that, it was time to go out and tell Pete that they got Johnny to the aid station in time. With more luck than they deserved, the rest was in the hands of God.

When Pete saw Kev coming out of the aid station, he came running toward him at full speed. All in the same breathless breath, he told Kev that they wouldn't let him into triage. Gasping for air, he then asked if Johnny made it. The bottom of Kev's face should have fallen off from the width of his grin as he gave Pete the good news.

"I don't know how he, or they, did it, Pete. The Doctor said that Johnny was doing better than they could dare hope for."

Following the good news, they returned to poor old Rocinante. The sight and amount of Johnny's blood, which was slowly dripping out of the little bird, again, appalled Kev. Looking in at the large pool of blood spread over the rear decking made him sick. Wordlessly, he and Pete secured Johnny's equipment in the back. They were careful to keep it well away from the coagulating blood which was turning dark and dreadful.

As best he could remember it, Kev told Pete the whole story. Impressed by all that he had seen, Kev slowly shook his head in wonder. He told him of the organized chaos in the triage room that saved Johnny's life. Then, almost as an afterthought, he told him about his little confrontation with the old sergeant.

"You know Pete, as the old Sarge and I spoke, I suddenly understood why he wanted me to leave. He was smart. If I thought they would let Johnny die by doing some stupid thing or just not caring enough, I probably would have shot all the doctors!"

Suddenly, he shivered at the brutal thought that had came unbidden to his conscious mind. Shocked by what he had suddenly realized, Kev knew the terrifying truth in what he had admitted. He could coldly kill a man who was not in combat. He knew that such horrid knowledge would haunt him the rest of his life!

When he finished, silence filled the air between the two of them. Pete must have wondered what he would have done if he had been the one in the triage with Johnny. Turning toward Kev, he then asked the $64,000 question.

"What do we do now, Sir?"

Kev didn't know what he wanted to do. He was overcome by the events of the last hour. Still, he was sure that he would have liked to have gone to sleep. Then, if he were lucky, he could have woken up back in his bed at his parent's house.

"I tell you what Pete, I think we need to go over this poor old beast with a fine tooth comb. By all rights she shouldn't be flown again. Whatever we decide, we've got to move her off this dust-off pad. I don't want to be blocking it if someone else needs it."

Pete was no fool. He knew exactly what Kev had done to their helicopter. He was the crewchief and would be responsible for a good part of the repairs. Working as a team, the two of them spent about a half an hour going carefully through her. Rocinante had given them no warning lights during the flight or the landing. Yet, they had abused her very-very badly. They were trying to decide if she would be airworthy enough for a one-time flight back to maintenance. Finishing their inspection, Kev asked Pete's opinion.

"Well Pete, what's your honest opinion? Can we go to the stage field, clean her up, and then take her home?"

Scratching his chin for a moment, Pete's mind went to work and he confidently responded.

"She's a darned good bird, Sir. She got Johnny here. I believe that she has earned our trust by now. I'm sure that she'll take us home."

Defeated, yet on the other hand they were not truly defeated. Thoughtfully, the two young men strapped into ole Rocinante. It was deathly quiet. A critical part of the team was missing. The two young men knew that the usual horseplay and banter that set the three of them apart from the rest of the Scouts was not going to be enjoyed again. Kev and Pete regretfully accepted they wouldn't see Johnny flying with the team again. All that they could do for him now was to pray for the Doctors' skill and that he would keep his leg.

Keeping his mental fingers crossed, Kev carefully cranked up the old girl, with Pete keeping an eagle eye on the instruments. She fired up, kept everything in the green, and started sweetly humming like they had never terribly abused her. With everything in the green, Kev cautiously tested the flight controls. They were both pleased to note that, each in turn, responded properly. So, Kev gently lifted her to an easy hover. Ole 662 had sufficient fuel to get to the staging field and then to home base. So, they didn't need to refuel.

When Kev asked for takeoff clearance from the control tower, their caring response surprised and warmly touched him. This was a very busy airfield/heliport. If it were a normal day, there had been a couple hundred, or more, landings and takeoffs since they came zooming in. The control tower operator, before giving them clearance, commented/questioned.

"Red One-Five, we hope you got your observer to the aid station in time."

Kev found it difficult, no, he found it all but impossible to talk. His large emotional lump had found its way back into his throat. He gratefully responded as the tears freely flowed down his dirty – blood splattered face.

"Thanks tower. We did it, with your help. The medical types think he will make it."

That evening, he told Sven how much that controller touched him.

"Whoever that controller is, because he thought humanely of and asked about Johnny, he is special. I will always pray that there is a warm place for him in heaven when his time comes."

With that, the tower operator bid them goodby.

"Red One-Five, cleared for takeoff and we're glad he's doing OK."

After a short and uneventful flight, they approached the staging field and landed. Kev knew that he probably didn't have the right. However, he asked Pete to intercept and divert any people coming their way.

"Pete, I just want to be alone. Please, will you do all our talking for us?"

Kev had radioed ahead and they all knew that Johnny was alive at the aid station. Graciously, Pete said that he understood and didn't mind running interference for Kev.

"Boss, I'll just send everybody away and ask them to give us some peace. Don't worry about offending anyone, everybody will understand."

They landed and shut down the helicopter, just as they normally would. As people approached with their questions, Pete ran interference.

Gathering some rags, Kev grimly began to clean Johnny's congealing blood out of the back of the helicopter. Pete, upon returning, started to help Kev with the unpleasant task. The reality of Johnny's wound suddenly struck the young man. He quickly began to sweat, sway, and turn pale. Noting Pete's difficulties, Kev spoke up.

"Don't worry about it Pete, I'll finish cleaning. Tell you what, you go get me a couple of buckets of water from the stream and I'll finish the job."

A few days later, he told Sven.

"Looking back, I suppose it was a penance of sorts for me. Scrubbing Johnny's blood allowed me to be alone and quietly cry. It also allowed me to do something constructive. I still didn't want to talk to anybody."

With his hands and arms running red with Johnny's spilt blood, Kev was working out his own fears, anger, and guilt. In his journal, Kev described his losing it.

As I was scrubbing all that blood and softly crying, the Vietnamese girls with their cokes, bananas, and bread made their poorly-timed appearance. When they saw the mess which I was cleaning up, they became all excited at the bloody evidence before their eyes. All of them speaking at once began to question me about who had been hurt, etc. Maybe, these teen-aged girls were honestly concerned. Maybe, they were doing some sort of intelligence work for the Viet Cong. I honestly didn't know, and I truly didn't care.

Unable to control myself, I exploded! I was screaming, yelling, and sobbing while driving them away in a threateningly insane explosion of my own pain and loss. Pete and a couple of the other enlisted men came running over and quickly led the girls away. Wisely and kindly, they left me to do what I needed to do. I believe that there must have been a quiet understanding among all the people at the staging field of what I needed to do. Mercifully, I was left alone to finish the gruesome cleaning of poor old Rocinante.

As Kev was cleaning up the last of Johnny's blood, C&C landed. Before the main rotor had coasted down, his crewchief came running up to Kev and said that the "old man" wanted to see him as soon as possible. Kev was walking toward the command and control Huey, while the Major was climbing out and stretching the kinks out of his body. Without any preamble, he quickly addressed his thoughts to Kev.

"Kev, you did a d--- fine job getting Johnny to the aid station. I gave them a call on the way back here and they told me that your observer is stable. In fact, they say the Doctors are convinced that you saved his life."

Thanking him for the news, Kev looked dumbly at him. He no longer knew what to do, or what to expect. However, his estimation of the new Major as a man and as a leader soared like a screaming rocket.

The Major continued. "Is your bird flyable?"

Kev quickly and briefly told him all about how much abuse which they had heaped upon ole 662. He added though, that he felt that she was safe to fly back to maintenance, on a circle red X. Continuing his description of Rocinante's condition, he added, that he had pretty much destroyed the power train.

"Well, if you think that she's safe, I want you and Pete to take her back to the barn. And, by the way son, I would have done the same thing you did. By God, I'll trade a helicopter for a man's life any day of the week!"

With that, he gave Kev a pat on the shoulder and walked away to take care of one of his many other concerns.

Kindly dismissed, it was time for Kev to gather up Pete and go home. Just like when they sat upon that big red cross, they carefully cranked up the poor old bird. Pete religiously watched all the gauges for the first hint of trouble. Everything checked out just fine and dandy with the gauges and with the flight controls. One would have almost thought that she was a spanking new bird straight from the factory with the quiet

318

uneventful flight she gave them home. Maybe, the ole girl somehow knew how badly the two young men needed the reflective time in the clean and still air above that forever bleeding and suffering countryside.

Upon landing, they didn't say much to each other. They were emotionally worn out and had long since run out of words. Understandably, both preferred to remain deep within their private thoughts about what happened. Pete tied down his helicopter. While he was doing that, Kev wrote a detailed report into the log book, of the many abuses to which they had subjected her. Regrettably, Kev was quite sure that the itemized listing would force maintenance to install, at the very least, a new engine and power train. Thinking about all the over temps, over torques, and over speeds they had forced onto her uncomplaining back and shoulders, he grimaced.

He suddenly realized that it was a major miracle that she got them home. Pete then took the log book over to the maintenance shack and Kev wearily trudged back to his hootch. During his, seemingly forever climb up the hill to the officers' hooches, he heard the rest of the Cav returning to roost. A bitter thought filled his mind.

"GOD! Nothing changes. It is just another day in Vietnam. This time, all the helicopters came back if not all the men."

Three or four hours later, in the still of the night, Kev had taken his usual seat upon his custom-made rocket box chair. He was quietly sipping a coke and staring aimlessly into the depthless blackness of the night sky and his own soul. Sven wandered over and plopped down upon his own rocket box chair. Sipping his usual beer, he didn't say anything and was apparently content to keep Kev company. Thinking about it for a minute, Kev decided that the Major had asked Sven to keep an eye on him. The Major knew that Kev had been in combat a long time and had suffered other losses. Most likely, he had been told that this loss was more personal and painful than any other Kev had experienced.

Kev thought about the Major's gift for a minute, and it deeply touched him. Musing to himself, he thought.

"You know Sven, it's true, I wept for poor ole TK, though I barely knew him. Somehow, this is much different. Johnny was my friend. It was a strange friendship. In fact, I don't know if he considered me a friend. However, I did him. We didn't drink beer together and we didn't chase girls together. Nor, for that matter, did we even socialize together. That was not what our friendship was all about. It was about something different. Yes, our friendship was something bigger than a couple of boys growing up."

He reflected upon this in his journal.

Maybe the best way of thinking about our friendship was to say it this way. Through countless combats great and small, somehow though, there was a constant. As the poet would say, "through thick and thin, Johnny and I had always been there for each other." I suppose, we *eventually became like a couple of old married people. When flying our recon, we could end each other's sentences. I don't believe it yet. **My dearest friend in the whole world has been taken away from me.** Furthermore, deep in my gut, I know that I was the one who had screwed up. I am no longer a child. Yes, I know that nothing in all of creation is ever going to change that fact! Still, I already miss the assurance of his presence behind me and I have yet to fly without him.*

The sound of approaching footsteps broke the soothing silence which the two young men were sharing. As they looked up, Sven greeted the approaching figure who must have been drawn from a cheap novel.

"How's it going, Chief?"

It was CW-3 Sterns, their Maintenance Officer. He was a classically gruff, crude, and unapproachable character. Chief Sterns was so distant from the rest of the pilots that none of them knew if he had a first name. They always called Sterns Chief or just Sterns. On his own time, he hung around with the Senior NCO's on base who were more his age. Someone had told Kev that once, in the distant past, he had been an NCO. Most of the young pilots guessed that he was about ninety years old. Furthermore, he was just about as crotchety as a frustrated arthritic ninety-year-old. However, everyone-Red Birds, White Birds, and Blue Birds-voted unanimously that he was an excellent maintenance officer. As they watched him, he was continually doing both major and minor miracles in supplying the pilots essentially flyable helicopters.

Given that the Chief was not exactly a social animal, Kev held little hope that he was here to ask us about Johnny's well being. More likely, he was deeply upset at the damage done to 662. He would get upset enough at the normal and expected battle damage to our aircraft. Once, several young pilots had even heard him giving their former CO a royal chewing out over expected battle damage. Furthermore, like any good maintenance officer he was more than a little possessive about "his" helicopters. He took every bullet hole as a personal insult. Without as much as a preamble he started in on Kev.

"Johnson, what's this s--- about hitting one hundred and forty-five knots in 662?"

With escalating volume he continued.

"You made a mistake with that number --- RIGHT JOHNSON!"

Wanting to walk away from the confrontation, but also knowing that the Chief needed the straight skinny if he were to do his job properly, Kev responded.

"Sorry Chief, but that's what I did to her."

Thinking about it later, Kev could not understand how he kept his cool as long as he did. Maybe, it was because Sterns was Kev's elder and his superior in rank. Possibly, Kev just needed to justify himself and his actions.

"Chief, I'm really sorry, but I honestly had to do everything that I wrote in that log book to save Johnny's life. . . . I would do it again if I had to!"

Afraid to say anything more to him, Kev turned his back to the Chief Sterns. He was hoping and praying to end this confrontation before it went a single step further. The military pilot in Kev was in no mood to argue with Sterns. This was a man who was afraid to fly out and recover a downed aircraft for fear he might get shot at. Kev's very low opinion of Sterns' personal courage was shared by most of the pilots.

Sputtering silence occurred when Kev turned his back. A string of venom quickly followed this sputtering laced obscenities shouted at the top of Sterns' leathery lungs. Intermixed was a comment that went something like this.

"Why you, insolent young pup! What the hell, do you think you are, some kind of doctor or something? How dare you give me all this work because in your stupid opinion someone might be dying? Do you have any idea what I am going to have to do to get that helicopter back into the air? Don't you know that I work like a dog so stupid little boys like you can play games with your little helicopters . . . ?"

Another string of screaming followed this pointless tirade. Then, venom laced obscenities were pointed directly at Kev's person!

Again, Kev's journal describes his feelings best.

. . . I don't know how else to describe it. It felt as if something fragile and brittle snapped within me. Maybe it was the proverbial last straw on the camel's back. I clenched both my fists so hard they hurt and my fingernails drew blood. Rising slowly to my feet, I stood about five feet from Sterns. Glaring at him, I could see every detail on his livid red, spittle flecked, face. At that instant, much to my later horror, I realized how enraged and evil I felt. Although I had killed a few men in combat, I had never wanted to kill a man before that very second. Another word from his foul mouth, and I would have beaten him to death with my bare fist! Taking a small step toward him, I hissed through clenched teeth.

"Shut up Sterns."

The d--- fool didn't know when to shut up and quit. Purple-faced, he began to gather up a lung full of hot air so he might continue his obscene diatribe against my person. That, I could almost accept. What I could not handle were his inhumane statements about Johnny's life not being worth a helicopter. I began my second slow stride in Stern's direction. Before my right foot reached the ground, Sven, reading my mind, tackled me. As Sven tackled me, three of the many pilots who had come running from the hooches to see what the commotion was about, also held me down. I didn't resist or fight them. Lying there, I looked up to see the rest of the Red Bird pilots removing Sterns from the area. They were removing him in, what would best be described as, a less than gentle fashion. I was finished. Physically and emotionally exhausted by the day and my pain, nothing was left in me. A wet dish rag would have had much more internal substance than I felt as they restrained me.

Sven, bless his, huge alcohol-preserved, yet warm loving heart, best captured the utter pathos of the moment.

"This whole thing is inhumanly and insanely stupid! The idiot politicians in Washington and the stupid brass hats in the Five-Sided-Puzzle-Palace on the Potomac don't know what they are doing. And, we are dying. The NVA and the Viet Cong know exactly what they are doing. And, we are dying. Now, this stupid war has even reduced to us fighting with each other over a stupid machine. What did I tell you Kev, this whole exercise is insanely stupid!"

With the evening's excitement seemingly over, everybody drifted back to their hooches. Kev got up to call it a night and Sven asked if he were going to write.

"Nope, not tonight. I wouldn't know what words to use."

Nevertheless, Kev wrote.

I woke up in the morning with my boots still on and only partially covered by my mosquito netting. It didn't matter. I didn't care. Johnny was not going to be flying with me.

Five days later, the sun has set again, and yet another GI goes home in his government issue aluminum casket. This is Vietnam and I continue to write.

Really, I can hardly believe that the last time I saw Johnny, the orderlies were wheeling him away on a Gurney. The doctor told me that he was pretty sure Johnny would live. The next day, they moved my friend quickly, by helicopter, from the aid station to the closest evacuation hospital. That is where the medical types continued to stabilize him. A day later, they moved him, by Air Force C-9 medical evacuation jet, down to Na Trang on the southern coast. In one way that saddened me, for it was too far away from me to grab an aircraft and run down to visit. At that point, my helplessness reduced to me keeping him in my nightly prayers. It was so painfully passive. That is, when I remembered to pray. However, the Major, bless him, somehow could keep me updated with increasingly good reports on Johnny's progress. The medical people even felt that Johnny could probably keep his leg. Though, I suspected, that in all honesty, I would never see him again. That was something positive and helpful to hold onto. It did make me feel much better that he would walk properly.

Kev would not have gone as far as to say that he was in a celebrating mood. Yet, he felt good enough to go to the club and have a couple of beers with Sven and the guys. As they were sitting at the table enjoying a beer and a burger, they saw Captain Dick Henn coming over toward their table. Neither Sven nor Kev really liked to fly with the Captain as their wingman because of his overly excitable nature. However, this did not mean that they disliked him.

"Hey Cap, how is it going? Join us for a beer or two, if you would like."

Taking a seat, Captain Henn said.

"No beer for me tonight. But, thanks for the invite. However, I'll take a seat because I need to talk to you, Kev."

Sven made to get up and leave them alone. Raising his hands to stop him, the Captain told him he could stay for it concerned all of them.

"I don't know how to say this Kev. So . . . I guess that I'll just say it straight out. Johnny died last night on an Air Force C-9."

Pausing a moment, he filled in a blank or two.

"The medical people were evacuating him to Japan."

A million negative emotions flashed through Kev when he heard that Johnny died. White as a sheet, he was blankly staring straight ahead. Kev was afraid to believe what he heard. His hands trembling like autumn leaves in the wind, and a river of tears was streaming down his face. He really didn't want to know, but he asked.

"How did he die, Dick?"

The Captain began to speak with an understandable discomfort. This was because everyone in the Cav, possible except Chief Sterns, knew how close the two young men had been. Captain Henn told Kev what the Major had told him not fifteen minutes earlier.

"The medical people had Johnny packed up in a body cast to protect his leg while they were moving him. Apparently, sometime during the flight, while he was asleep, the artery in his leg began bleeding again. He bled to death in his cast. If it is any help, he never woke up and he never felt any pain. No one knew that anything was wrong because all his blood stayed in the body cast. Only when they went to move him from the C-9 to the hospital in Japan did they discover he was dead."

An excerpt from Kev's Journal which should have been published in the New York Times. Of course, it could never be printed by the Times. It didn't fit their editorial understanding.

. . . Oh God, I needed to throw something, or to strike out, or to hurt somebody. One half of me was blindly and insanely enraged and the other half was crying. Hurt, confused, angry, and almost out of control, I blurted out.

"I don't understand Dick. Didn't they have nurses and doctors on the plane? What were they doing playing cards or flirting with each other while Johnny died?"

I couldn't control myself any longer. Self control was stupid. It didn't matter that I was in our little Officers Club. It didn't matter that I was in front of all my peers. I started to quietly sob and mumbled something about it all being my fault that Johnny was dead. Our excitable little Captain did something which I thought was extraordinary for him. He reached across the table and firmly grasped my forearm gently and kindly. When I looked up, he said to me.

"Damn-it, listen to me Kev, we all know you accomplished a miracle getting Johnny to the aid station alive. Nobody is blaming you for this, least of all Johnny. It is just a tragic accident now."

Motioning Sven to follow him, the two of them left me alone in my grief.

I wish Pastor Bill could have been there. I did not want or need him to comfort me. No, I wanted him to witness what happened next. Our little Officers Club, which was filled with maybe fifty pilots from different units became quiet. They gave me peace to be in my own sorrow. As I put my head on the table and sobbed for an enlisted man most of them didn't know, they were all moved with compassion. Don't ask me how I knew. Yet, I could feel their deep compassion encompassing and even caressing me with a gentle love for a brother. These gentle souls were carefully caressing my grief. Ignorant and mindless fools claim that they are the so-called savage baby killers and blood-thirsty monsters. Unknowing fools claim that these lovers of my soul are preying upon a gentle and helpless people. Oh God how I wish that Pastor Bill could have been there. He needs to see and know these good people.

After a couple of minutes, maybe a little longer, I got up and began to walk. At the door of the club, I bumped into the Major. He looked at me kindly, like a father who was unable to heal a child's bruised knee and take away the hurt. This heartless leader of baby killers and savages spoke very softly.

"I'm really sorry, Kev. You did well. God knows that you did all you could do. I want you to take tomorrow off, no flying for you. . . . I wish there was something more that I could do for you. I know how close you and Johnny were . . . "

Eventually, Kev found himself sitting on Rocinante's revetment. She was still in maintenance, so the revetment was empty. The darkened revetment was as empty as Kev felt. He was just looking at the ground trying not to think or to feel. Somehow, his old friend Sven must have known where to look for him. Lighting a cigarette and taking a deep drag upon it, he spoke.

"Look, my friend, I know that most of the time I am nothing but a cynical, yet, in my humble opinion, clearly charming, drunk. Despite rumor to the contrary, I do note a few things. You and Johnny loved each other more than brothers. Everyone in the Red Birds knows that. More times than I can count, either one of you would have gladly died to save the other. This time, Kev can't save him and Johnny can't save Kev. Kevin, let's not let him really die. Please, do what I can't do. Write! Tell the story. Tell people about this chaos. Tell them that no matter what others may think, even if no one allows us to win this war, Johnny and the thousands of other Johnnys here are good people."

Getting up and flipping his cigarette aside, he stopped and looked intently at his friend. A Sven whom Kev had never met before turned and whispered.

"Please, write our story. The world needs to hear it."

. . . *Despite, or because I only learned a few hours ago that Johnny died, I write.*

In the wonderful silence of the evening, Kev sat quietly remembering and pondering. He was morosely thinking about TK's charred remains and Johnny's, lifeless body. Trembling, he knew both lay still and silent in graves somewhere back in the world. Kev found himself deeply saddened. Writing to Pastor Bill, he said of his troubling thoughts.

"One minute, we are a gang of little boys laughing like all other little children. Yet, just a quick moment later, any one of us can be another faceless statistic."

The sobering truth of their tenuous lives continually hung over the young heads of pilots and enlisted men alike. It reminded them that they had many things to learn quickly. They struggled to learn while they were enjoying their government-sponsored vacation in lovely South East Asia. Yet, within a month or two, most of them quickly learned to seize the moment.

"Carpe Diem," the seizing of the moment, does not come naturally to a nineteen or a twenty-year-old boy becoming a man. Like most of their peers in normal society, these young men firmly believed that they would live forever. As with everything else concerning the human condition, occasional exceptions do occur. However, these exceptions would always be someone else. A few, were like Sven. They quickly became fatalistic. Looking about, they would decide that a seized moment might be all that fate would allow them. It was quite common for Sven to bitterly comment, after he was well into his nightly beer ration.

"Eat, drink, and be merry for tomorrow we die. I only wish that I understood why we are dying!"

The ever hopeless romantic, Kev looked at his life in Vietnam differently. He deeply enjoyed flying his recon missions as the only pilot in the helicopter. It appealed to his individualism. Initially, he questioned nothing and enjoyed almost everything. He soon discovered that a single pilot, flying a combat helicopter, however created a problem. If the pilot were to be shot during the recon and was unable to control the aircraft, it would be pilotless. Therefore, the helicopter would crash.

Turning the clock back for a bit, I reintroduce a character who has been an important part of this little book.

During one of his first missions as a wing pilot, Kev had the human reality of the problem of only having one pilot in the helicopter pointed out to him by a young enlisted man who later went on to be his regular crewchief.

His education began innocently enough. When they were taking off on a mission, Kev's (then) new crewchief, PFC Pete Hammonds, asked him if he would teach him to fly. Flying as Kev's observer, Hammonds sat in what was normally the copilot's position to his left. Thinking about his crewchief's request, it seemed reasonable. Kev saw no reason that he couldn't try to teach the young man some basic flight skills. If nothing else, Kev thought that it would be fun to play instructor pilot. It would be nice to give the guy some enjoyment. He was well aware that life for the enlisted folk was usually quite hard and if he could give him a little fun, all the better.

Good ole Uncle Sam had equipped their little Loach with flight controls for both a pilot and a copilot. At the time, Kev was quite green at the Red Bird business. Complimented by the thought that he could teach, he found the young observer's faith in him refreshing. Due to his general inexperience, Kev did not think very deeply about the possible meaning of his young crewchief's question. Not understanding what was going on, ole Kev innocently asked him why. Hammonds answer, as was customary between officers and enlisted people in the Red Birds, was a simple and honestly straightforward one.

"Sir, I might need to land this helicopter some day."

Pete's pointed comment took Kev aback for a moment. He paused and thought for a bit about the crewchief's request. At first glance, it made little sense. Young and invincible, he automatically thought to himself.

"I'm always going to be here."

Then, with a sharp twinge of guilt, Kev finally understood what he meant. Emotionally taken aback, Kev saw the wisdom of Pete's need to have some control over his situation. After all, they were flying in a combat environment. Though he preferred not to think about it, it was completely reasonable to think that something could happen to Kev as the pilot. After another moment's thought, Kev realized that he too might benefit from the educational effort. With the selfish thought of basic self-preservation in mind, Kev began to seriously teach ole Pete some basic flight skills. The two of them had ample time to practice as they were flying back and forth to their operations area. Much to his surprise, Kev was enjoying playing instructor pilot.

"Maybe," he thought to himself, "when I go back to the world, I can become an IP at Ft. Wolters. I think that would be a lot of fun."

Within a few short practice sessions, Pete became acceptably good at straight and level flight. In fact, the young enlisted man could do a fair takeoff. Surprised by Pete's seemingly natural skill, Kev's ego was a little dismayed that Pete could do a proficient take off with a combat loaded wing bird. However, he consoled himself with a basic aviation truism. Each takeoff demands a subsequent landing. Unfortunately, landings were a skill that ole Pete simply couldn't master. The two of them tried and tried. Every day that they flew together, they worked on both Pete's flying and his landing skills. Kev was so determined that Pete would eventually safely land the little helicopter that he no longer did any landings when Pete was flying with him. However, their working and struggling together, as far as landings went, bore no fruit.

The final result of Kev's instructional effort's was always the same. Working and grappling with it every day, Pete manfully struggled to safely land the little helicopter. However, the result was always the same. Just before they crashed, Kev would be forced to seize control of their laboring, staggering Red Bird. He told Sven of his frustration.

"It never fails. Every time he tries to land the bird I have to grab the controls to keep ole 'stone-hands Pete' from killing us both."

As their weeks flying together passed, Pete showed no improvement. Kev began to doubt that Pete would ever be able to safely crash land the aircraft if he needed. Selfishly, Kev hoped and prayed that Pete would never have to save his life.

In the end, fate and circumstance made for a very dramatic story about human flexibility. It all began one of those wonderful five days that Kev spent in the "Land Down Under" on R&R. In Kev's absence, Pete was flying with another wing pilot. The two of them were trolling low and slow as they covered the lead. Nothing unusual had marked the day. They were just doing their recon on a remarkably unremarkable day. The weather was good, the breeze was light and steady, and they were quietly snooping around. As always, they were looking for the bad guys.

Suddenly, and without any warning, a burst of automatic weapons fire came streaming up from the trees. Before poor Pete could even think about what was happening, his whole world turned brown and smelly. As often happens, in combat and in aviation, things moved faster than the human mind could comprehend. Before the shock of seeing all those green tracers flying up at him was impressed on his overloaded mind, Pete was in more trouble that he ever imagined possible. The situation was putting Kev's educational effort to the ultimate test.

Pete's first and trained reaction was to return fire with his M-60. However, before he could return his own shots of anger and fear, Pete found himself terribly alone in a very hostile world. He heard and felt the multiple thuds of the helicopter taking many small arms hits. Something deep inside Pete told him that they were in deep trouble. Yet, before he could even mutter a well-earned "aw s---" to himself, he heard a pained grunt and a sharp cry from his pilot.

The pilot, seeing his knee explode from the impact of an AK-47 bullet, reflexively cried out on the intercom. As Pete looked over to him, the wounded pilot was passing out from the combination of pain and shock. When the wounded pilot began to loose control of himself and his helicopter, the little Red Bird started to flutter about dangerously out of control.

To the casual observer, it might have appeared that Pete was in way over his head. It was true. He was only eighteen years old and still a child in the eyes of most adults. Furthermore, he had only been in the Army six to ten months. However, he was well trained. More importantly, he was highly motivated by his situation. Without consciously thinking about it, he immediately knew what he had to do. He frantically grabbed the flight controls. If nothing else, Pete discovered that the instinct of pure self preservation was a powerful motivator. Looking to his right, ole Pete saw the gory sight of the pilot's shattered left knee. He didn't have time to do more than note it. Ignoring the enemy fire, Pete grimly set about gaining control of the little helicopter.

Keeping his head, and doing his best to control the little helicopter, Pete looked a little closer at his wounded pilot. It was obvious, as his head lolled about and his breathing became ragged, that the pilot was passing out. The shock, pain, and the loss of blood which was pouring out of his shattered knee was more than the pilot's body and mind could handle. This time, the landing was, in a fully concrete sense of the phrase, a do or die situation for the young crewchief. He was alone. Ole Kev was in the "Land Down Under" and could not save him! This time, Red One-Five was not going to be available to grab the controls and recover from another bad landing attempt! Taking a deep breath, Pete muttered to himself.

"Oh God, I'm in deep s--- now!"

Sharing a beer or three with Red One-Four, who was flying the lead bird that day, Sven told Kev that ole Pete turned in an impressive performance. Sven said that his observer saw the aircraft suddenly stop and stagger. He said that it was as if a massive gust of wind had struck it. Straightening itself, the little bird then seemed to flutter in place. Frantically yanking at the flight controls, and pouring on the power, Sven reversed roles with his wingman. He positioned himself to offer both cover and support to his apparently wounded wingman. After he had taken another draw from his beer, Sven told Kev that he could see that the helicopter was being over controlled by whoever was flying it. Poorly though it may have been, Sven sensed that someone was controlling it.

Pete then came on the radio.

"Sir, my pilot has been shot."

Gathering his breath and controlling himself, he added .

"I'm afraid that he is passing out!"

This announcement sent anxious tremors up every listeners' spine. It wasn't that Pete was an observer that added to the rising tension. It was simply that it was Pete.

Everyone knew about Pete's seemingly countless attempts at landing a Red Bird. His attempts were the source of many humorous stories told by the Red Birds. In fact, Kev kept hoping that these funny stories would eventually drown out the great Vegamatic incident. The Scouts had made many friendly wagers while watching Pete try to land. Unfortunately for Pete, they never bet on his success. Cynically, they only bet on how long it would be before Kev grabbed the controls. Disregarding the negative legends of Pete's flying skills, C&C calmly asked the young observer what he wanted to do. Rising to his full eighteen years of manhood, Pete confidently responded.

"Sir, I am scared, no I'm sure, that my pilot is going to die if he doesn't get help real soon. I am going to land in the river in the valley we just passed. That way, someone can pick him up and take him to the hospital."

Sven said that the new Executive Officer was flying C&C for the mission. It was one of his first as C&C. However, he impressed Sven with his levelheaded response.

"We've got a good copy on your intentions, son. You've just become the lead bird. Today ole Pete leads, and the rest of us will follow."

Double clicking the mike, C&C immediately got to work on the rest of the rescue.

"Break, break, Red One-Four, you take it from here while I call up Dust-off for the pilot."

Sliding about one hundred meters to the left side of Pete's bird, Sven keyed his mike when the XO finished.

"Hey Pete, this is your old buddy One-Four on the phone. I'm about one hundred meters to your left. If you don't mind, I thought that I would keep you company for the time being. It is probably a little lonely in there. Here's what I would like you to do. You just fly that ole bird straight and level. While you're doing that, I'll aim you in the right direction. We'll get you and the pilot safely down on that sand bar, lickety-split."

Struggling with his controls, Pete had Red One-Four gently coaching and encouraging him. Sven quickly had Pete herding the little helicopter in the general direction of the valley where he wanted to land the wounded bird. That was the valley where the young observer remembered the attractively soft sandbar. Sven carefully and gently coached him like he had been an instructor pilot for a hundred years or more.

"OK . . . , here we go. Pete, today, it's just the two of us. You can do me a great big favor by just pretending that you've got ole Kev sitting right beside you talking you through this. Don't bother messing with the radio while we do this. You fly the helicopter and I'll do all the talking."

Laughter filled the airways for a moment. It was Sven's attempt to lighten up the extremely tense situation.

" You know Pete, they tell me that I'm pretty good at talking and that you're pretty good at landing. With all that going for us, it sounds to me like we are going to make a first class team. Did you know that Ole Kev told me, the other day, why you haven't completed a landing? He said that always having him right there beside you makes you nervous. Well, my friend, today is your big chance. You haven't got a single reason in the whole wide world to get tense about things!"

Sven tirelessly kept up the encouraging chatter during the next three minutes of straight and level flight. Arriving at the river, Pete was surprised and relieved to see that Sven had gotten him lined up with the long axis of the sandbar. Luck was with them. A light wind was running straight up and down the axis of the sandbar. This breeze would make Pete's landing simpler because he wouldn't have to worry about a cross wind. It looked like everything was working out pretty well for Pete and his unconscious pilot.

C&C had contacted a Dust-Off bird that was in the neighborhood. In turn, he was rushing to the scene. When they had checked earlier, no bad guys were active in the valley. Lastly, C&C had also scrambled the Blues to secure the landing site. The grunts and their four Hueys were less than five minutes away. Sven drew a deep breath and began Pete's landing approach.

"OK Pete. We've got everything lined up properly. It's time to lower the collective stick a little bit and begin your approach."

While all the pilots and crews collectively held their breath, Pete began his wobbly approach to the sandbar. Listening in, they all mentally crossed their fingers and muttered little prayers for Pete and his pilot.

"You are doing just fine, Pete. Airspeed is bleeding off beautifully. There you go, buddy. Now give her just a touch more back stick. You are looking really good, guy. OK Pete, . . . you're at fifty feet now and doing about twenty knots. Bring the nose up . . . just a little bit more. Now, add just a touch more power to slow her."

Pete was doing very well. Ole Pete's approach might not have been a demonstration approach done by a top notch Instructor Pilot. However, it was better than most of the sloppy, every day, approaches that most of the pilots made.

"You're looking good Pete. You're looking really good, ole buddy. Ok . . . , just think a little forward stick and slowly reduce your power."

Pete must have realized that he was hovering at eight feet and was almost home free. Suddenly, what had been a good approach began to fall apart. For no apparent reason, the little helicopter began to wobble about all three axises. Instantly, Sven knew that Pete was over controlling the little bird. Disaster was but seconds away. Speaking as calmly as he could, he frantically mashed down on the mike.

"Hey Pete relax. Just take it easy kid. You are doing great. Now, lower the collective a little bit and you're going to gently kiss ole Mother Earth. Heck, I'm going give you an 'A+' for the ride up to this point."

Try as he would, Sven's encouragement and attempts to calm the young crewchief down was all in vain. In understandable desperation and fear, Pete was wiping out the cockpit of the little bird with his wild gyrations on the controls. Before Sven could get in another word, a skid struck the ground. He was helpless to do anything except watch the unfolding disaster. Losing control, Pete was rolling the little Loach into an expensive ball of scrap metal.

Somehow, in all the dust, noise, and destruction, Pete kept his head about himself. While the little bird was on her side flopping, thrashing, pounding and banging herself into scrap, he cut the fuel flow and electrics. Continuing to keep his head about himself, Pete immediately dragged himself and the unconscious pilot out of the wreckage. Thankfully, Dust-Off was already on short final and would land before the last of the dust settled. Again, keeping his cool, Pete, grabbed a rag, and immediately applied it as a pressure bandage to the pilot's shattered knee. This staunched the flow of blood. The landing might have been ugly to the extreme. However, he probably saved the life of his pilot.

Well . . . as they told everyone in flight school.

"Any landing you can walk away from is a good one."

Based upon his ultimate result, every pilot in the Red Birds agreed that this was undoubtedly the best landing Pete had ever completed. Of course, it was the only landing that Pete had ever completed. But, he had saved his pilot's life as well as his own life! Overall, that was a very good day's work for a scared eighteen-year-old crewchief!

When Dust-Off lifted off with Pete and his pilot, all that remained was for the grunts to land and strip the radios and guns out of the wreckage. Pete had been exceptionally effective in his destruction of the little helicopter. The only things worth stripping were the mini-gun, ammunition, M-60, and assorted munitions. Unbelievably, even the radios were destroyed. When they had finished stripping Pete's newly minted ball of expensive scrap metal, the grunts put the remains to the torch.

Later, with a flair for the dramatic, Sven told Kev that "a pillar of smoke marked the historic site of Pete's first completed landing."

As they had many times before, the Cav called it a day with a pillar of smoke rising as a backdrop.

A couple of weeks later, following his stay at the hospital, ole "stone-hands Pete" returned to a hero's welcome. The medical types had kept him there for observation of his emotional state and to allow his battered body to heal. Everyone agreed that it had been quite a traumatic and heroic time for him. With the Major's blessings, the Doctors had wisely used his many cuts and scrapes as their excuse to keep him for observation.

Acting as if nothing of merit or note had happened, Pete immediately returned to flying with Kev. With youthful insensitivity, Kev unmercifully began kidding ole Pete about his landing skills. Laughing, he reminded Pete that he had completely, totally, and irreparably destroyed the helicopter he crashed. Yet, on a semi-serious vein, Kev continued the conversation.

"Pete, what the heck am I going to do with you? I leave you alone for five short days and suddenly you think that you can land a little Red Bird without my help."

Eventually, when they had finished laughing, Kev shifted his conversation from a semi-serious to a serious vein. Curiosity was getting the best of him! He asked him how he ever did it.

"Pete, ole buddy, how did you pull it off? I really want to know. How did you ever successfully crash-land that old bird?"

At the age of eighteen, Pete's simple and faithful response became a powerful inspiration to Kev. Not realizing how profound his words were, Pete quietly spoke.

"Well sir, it seemed to me to be the opportune moment to learn how to land the aircraft!"

Pete saw the moment! He then quickly and bravely seized the moment. All this from a scared eighteen-year-old kid in a far away place! Pete's quiet words had not finished echoing in his head when Kev decided that was how he wanted to live the rest of his life. Kev had matured enough during the last few months to fully appreciate what Pete had accomplished when he overcame his fear and acted decisively.

While they were flying home, Pete continued with his story.

"To be honest, Sir, I chose the sandbar because I knew it would be soft. I figured when I finished rolling her into a little ball, the two of us might still be alive."

Laughing, Kev responded.

"I see that I taught you well, Pete. I always look for the softest tree when I'm going down."

With that, the two little boys continued to chuckle the rest of the flight home.

Later that night, Kev thought long and hard about Pete's profoundly simple answer. After a bit, he decided that it was a straightforward expression of how most of the young pilots tried to operate. Kev would argue, with anyone who wished, about the quality of the folk in the Cav. Most of the pilots and crew were proud to say that they were flying with an Air Cavalry Troop in Vietnam. Only a limited sense of modesty kept them from saying so.

They did not mind always being on call to help when someone needed it. To a man, they felt that it was a great honor when someone called upon the Cav. It did not matter that it could happen at a moment's notice. One and all, they wanted to help ground troops when they needed a little more help or were in serious life threatening trouble. To these young men, being on call might be to provide aerial gun support, or aerial reconnaissance, and even using their own ground troops as needed for friendly forces. No matter who issued the call, or where they were to be found, Kev and his friends happily answered the call of the moment.

Sometimes, it was difficult for these young troopers to keep up their spirits. However, in time, Kev and his friends learned not to listen to the many puffed-up pundants and their profound pronouncements. Nor did they listen to the so-called experts who were shooting their undisciplined mouths off back in the world. While they might not speak directly of it, these young men felt that what they did was very good. Furthermore, for the most part they felt that their's was a very honorable calling. Higher headquarters assigned their little Cav troop to what the Army commonly called a ready reaction mission. This made them responsible for almost a full quarter of their little, unknown, and far away country called Vietnam. They felt an unspoken pride because they were the first on call in the heart of lovely South East Asia.

Deep in their hearts, they gladly accepted the task of aiding any of their brothers who might be in trouble. In many ways, it was a wonderfully glorious mission for a romantic young fool such as Kev. Sometimes he liked to look through the eyes of a romantic fool such as himself. Once he spoke of his vision in his journal.

When people call for us, we drop what we are doing and come charging. Symbolically, we charge off into the dark dangerous unknown with flags and pennants a-flying and lances lowered. Just watch for us when the call goes out. If you keep your eyes open, you will see us rushing over the hill and across the dale. Like in the movies, it frequently seems as if we are always arriving just in time. When we arrive, of course, we always save the day. What we do is, essentially, just like they did it in all the John Wayne movies. Best of all, and most surprisingly of all, often this is in fact the truth. We do exactly that. We came a'riding o'er hill and dale to the dramatic rescue. God help me, I love it and I live every breathing moment for it.

Yet, another side of their collective life was not as dramatic or exciting. It was dark, dreary, and dismal. Kev, with his self-image overflowing with romantic pictures, occasionally was struck speechless by the shocking, brutal, and inhumane experiences of war. These were the difficult times when he continued his maturing into a leader and into an adult. One day, while Kev was flying, they got an urgent call for help from ground troops in trouble. It seemed to be the usual call for help that the Cav received. Little did Kev suspect, at the time, that this call for help would be different from any other cry of pain that he had answered.

Writing to Pastor Bill about it, he said.

Looking back through the corrective lenses of my personal history, it was a call for help that is going to leave me troubled for a very long time. Maybe, it will trouble me for the rest of my life. Still, maybe it is also a call that has shown me something I desperately needed to learn about being a leader. If it did nothing else, it made me pause and take a deeply piercing look at Kevin Paul Johnson.

The dawning of Kev's new insight began a few klicks away from where he was doing his recon. Initially, it sounded like another repeat of the normal. An unidentified ground unit had gotten itself into some kind of trouble. Needing assistance, they radioed for help to anyone who would answer their call. In this case, the Cav was in the neighborhood and the Major was in command. Keying his mike, he told Kev and his wing man to pull up stakes. It was time to go to work. People were in trouble and they needed the Cav's help.

Therefore, Red One-Five and his wingman immediately lowered the noses of their helicopters and poured on the coal. While they were enroute, C&C informed Kev that the infantry people had gotten into a very nasty firefight. Adding to the urgency of the mission, he said that the grunts had taken some serious casualties. C&C continued to say that they still had at least one person on the ground who was badly hurt.

When Kev arrived where the grunts were in trouble, he immediately discovered that the infantry folk were very willing to call it a day. However, before they could return to their base, they needed help in disengaging from the people who were trying to kill them. To do that, the folk on the ground also needed assistance in getting their wounded out and sent to the field hospital. For the moment, that was all the information that Kev needed to know. It appeared to him that the mission was exactly the reason he came to Vietnam.

Without a word spoken, the White Birds quickly assumed their ever-present protective orbit over the area. At the same time, Kev also set to work at the tree top level. C&C had given him a good fix on the ground troops and Kev contacted their platoon leader. Quarter-backing his team, the Major had given Kev the proper frequency on the radio and the call sign of the platoon leader. To Kev's way of thinking, everything was as it should be. Kev keyed the mike. "Red Dog Five-Three, this is Red One-Five." The response from the ground was immediate.

"Red One-Five, you have Red Dog Five-Three. I read you, lima charley."

Having made contact, Kev immediately started getting a feel for things.

"Red Dog, I am in the little Loach overhead. We just arrived at your location and I have clear visual contact with some of your people. Are you under fire now?"

Red Dog had the first good news of the day for Kev.

"Negative enemy fire, at this time, One-Five."

Kev paused for a second or two to decide what he was going to do. Keying up the mike again, he continued.

"That being the case Red Dog Five-Three, I am going to take five and meter-meter the local area. When I finish, I'll get back to you and we'll find a way get you guys out of this mess."

As Kev and his observers began looking about, they got a good read on the problem. Fortunately, things weren't as bad as they had first feared. Red Dog Five-Three had already managed to extract all of his hurt people, except one. Yet, C&C had previously told Kev that it had been an expensive morning for the folk on the ground. During the battle, the bad guys had seriously wounded four of the young men/boys of this infantry unit. The first order of business had been to evacuate the wounded to the hospital. Red Dog and Dust Off had accomplished the first task prior to the arrival of the Cav. However, Kev knew that Red Dog had to be one angry and frustrated Lieutenant. He knew that he too would be if he were in Red Dog's place.

What was going on didn't seem fair. All of the ground pounder types who had been wounded had received their wounds while they were trying to get the remaining wounded guy evacuated. The folk on the ground simply could not reach him without getting themselves all shot up.

Red Dog Five-Three was not the only one who found himself becoming very angry. Taking the whole situation in, Kev was becoming both angry and sick to his stomach. Unfortunately, the bad guys had confronted his friends on the ground with a vexing problem. Kev was sick and angered because Red Dog's problem was not at all unusual in his tormented little part of the world. With a sense of sadness and futility, Kev gave his report to C&C. The report was one that had been given often in the history of warfare. As was their practice, the North Vietnamese were using a wounded man for bait. At a purely logical level, it made good sense to them. They were well aware that the Americans would not leave one of their own behind while seeking their own safety.

Without having all the minute details available to him, Kev had a painfully clear picture of the situation below. Every time the men on the ground got close to their stranded comrade, the North Vietnamese would manage to wound another of their number. The situation was, without a doubt, a painful, frustrating, and miserable time for all the people on the ground. After Kev looked around and carefully evaluated their distressing situation, Red Dog Five-Three asked Kev for whatever assistance the Cav could offer them.

From Kev's point of view, Red Dog's request was legitimate and understandable. Being asked to hang around and help distressed no one in the Cav. None of them liked the sad and sobering situation that Kev was describing. As far as the people in Cav were concerned, it was their business to take the necessary risk involved. Furthermore, they were now angry and emotionally involved. It had become more than another mission. Everyone, who was mounted up, wanted to help the people on the ground recover their wounded friend.

Within three or four minutes of his arrival, Kev began receiving some light and scattered ground fire. Nevertheless, he could clearly see the still form of the man, actually boy, on the ground. Flying carefully, he maneuvered his little helicopter to the position where he wanted it. He was seeking to place himself, directly over the spot where the young trooper lay. When he arrived, he stopped and hovered directly over the unmoving form of the young G.I.

Settled into position, the little Red Bird was hovering not more than fifteen feet above the still form. Surprisingly, with all the engine noise and the down-wash of the rotor beating down upon him, the young man wasn't stirring. The boy's lack of response bothered Kev. Pursing his lips, Kev hoped that he was only unconscious. As Kev looked down upon him, he noted that he was sprawled out, spread eagled, and face down. He seemed so young. To Kev's eyes, he appeared to be a broken rag doll discarded and draped carelessly over some small boulders. Writing to Pastor Bill a few weeks later, Kev spoke of the incident.

Sitting here today writing and reflecting, I do not need to close my eyes to clearly see his bright yellow hair. Waving about, it looked almost like fresh shiny corn silk which the rotor-wash of our hovering helicopter was ruffling. Somehow, he appeared peacefully unaware of the tumult surrounding him.

Mechanically suspended just a few scant feet above that still body was turning out to be one of the strangest moments Kev had ever experienced. At the time, he didn't realize how powerful his surreal moment of comprehension would be. Somehow, the whole bizarre little drama was becoming stranger and stranger. Unknown to Kev, in a few moments the whole situation was to become emotionally threatening to him. As Kev's grotesque, emotionally charged, drama was unfolding the little bird continued hovering directly over the still body. With the seconds slowly ticking by, Kev began to suspect the worst.

Remaining suspended above the still form, the little helicopter was occasionally receiving increased scattered ground fire. However, the crew did not sit still. Nor did they remain objective and passive observers. In their turn, the two observers were continually firing back at the North Vietnamese with their M-60's. The purpose of their return fire was twofold. First and foremost, they wanted to protect the boy with the wind ruffled blond hair while he was lying still and exposed upon the ground. Secondly, Kev and crew sought to protect their own lives. Like it so frequently does, the clock of combat sped up and their little war began to escalate. Within moments, it appeared to Kev that all the North Vietnamese in South Vietnam were shooting at the larger and more valuable target.

What he was forced to do next deeply disturbed Kev. It was not something that he wanted to do. Yet, he was forced to break away because the increasing volume of ground fire. The ever increasing amount of ground fire was just too intense for the fragile helicopter. In defense of Kev's act of fleeing, his bird had taken several enemy hits. Thinking of his crew's safety, Kev decided that he could no longer safely maintain his position. For the moment, he had to abandon the young man with the wind ruffled blond hair. Quickly breaking away from the increasingly intense ground fire, Kev called the troops on the ground. With a deep sadness coloring his voice, he told them that the man on the ground wasn't moving.

Keying the microphone again, he reluctantly shared his painful observation with the Lieutenant.

"Red Dog Five-Three, I am afraid that your man is dead. He never moved or gave any indication of life while we hovered directly above him."

After a thoughtful pause, the man on the ground responded.

"That's affirmative Red One-Five, he is a 'KIA'."

Something deep and primal within Kev suddenly snapped. Everything that had gone on to this point was horribly wrong. He had been shot at and Rocinante had taken a couple three hits from the heavy small arms fire. He and his observers had willingly risked their lives for the young man with the wind-ruffled blond hair. However, it still took a moment for what the young lieutenant on the ground said to make its full impact on Kev.

Instantly, explosively, and selfishly, he was deeply angered, totally outraged, and struck almost speechless. He believed that the situation had become unreal, unbelievable, and unfair to him and his crew! Kev was shocked, enraged, and almost speechless. Without thought of personal safety, he had put his crew and self at great risk. Unbelievably, they had taken several hits from ground fire for someone who was KIA! Before he understood what had happened, Kevin Paul Johnson lost control of both himself and of the situation.

Much later, after he had cooled down, and when he put his words and thoughts to paper, he was very deeply ashamed of himself. Yet, at that strange moment in his private history, he did not feel that way. When the Lieutenant told him that the boy on the ground was already dead, all rational thought departed from his head. Uncontrolled, he exploded on the radio with an almost blind animalistic rage. Without thought for anyone except himself and his crew, Kev vented his feelings which were, by then, devoid of reason or compassion.

"I can't ------- believe this! You almost got me and my crew ------- killed! What in the ---- is the matter with you people?"

In the instant he said it, his thoughtless outburst emotionally shook him in its intensity and selfishness. Later, when he had thought and pondered deeply about it, Kev wrote about his confusion and feelings in his journal.

Immediately following my grossly immature outburst, a very pregnant, yet deathly quiet, pause was loudly broadcast across the width and the breath of the radio net. The obviously young Lieutenant, Kev had already noted his youth from the tone of his voice, quietly and maturely responded.

"I'm sorry Red One-Five. That was my mistake. I should have told you that he was KIA. However, that doesn't change a single thing! Let me make myself clear. I am not, I repeat, I am not going to leave one of my boys sprawled out on the rocks to rot! He came here as one of mine! Furthermore, he is going home as one of mine! If you don't want to risk your crew any further for a KIA, I understand. Please believe me. I deeply appreciate what you and your crew risked. BUT, that doesn't change a single thing as far as I am concerned. All of my boys are going home. Do you understand? All of my boys are going home with me!"

After drinking a couple of shots of straight bourbon to calm himself, Kev continued in the privacy of his journal.

Powerful feelings of shame and remorse washed over me and pulled at me like an overwhelming rip tide. These gruesome feelings felt like they were threatening to remove me from all human companionship. At that moment, I believed that Kevin Paul Johnson no longer deserved the bars upon his shoulders. In fact, I believed that he no longer deserved to be called human! I suppose that a therapist would have to call it shame. Awash in this sea of deep shame, I was foundering. Sick to the center of my heart, I found myself wishing that I could immediately find a close cosmic black hole. With the Grace of God, I could then fall deeply into it never to be heard from again. I just wanted to disappear forever. It was a million times worse than being caught with my hands in the cookie jar.

Just as the one way train of my black thoughts was rushing me toward emotional oblivion, the radio broke into my dark and dreary thoughts. It was the Major. Clearly not meaning to, he added more red hot coals to the personal fiery hell which was promising to be my eternal torment. The major made a simple, yet profoundly wise, statement.

"It's your call One-Five."

That was all he had to say about the situation.

"It's your call One-Five."

Yet, he was wrong. It was not my call alone. My observers had a right to comment about risking their lives on this one! I owed them the same respect that the Major gave me. Pausing long enough to ask their opinion, I then responded.

"With your permission Six, the three of us would like to stay on for as long as it takes to help these folks out."

The young Lieutenant quickly spoke up after listening to the exchange between the two of us.

"Thanks One-Five, I appreciate what a tough call that was for you."

Deeply humbled and emotionally troubled, Kev stayed on all that morning. The job of recovering the boy's body was very difficult and time consuming. During the morning, the Cav switched teams twice. As God was his witness, a subdued Kev and his crew helped as best they could. To no one's surprise, the bad guys were determined to extract their full values from the baited trap. Before the day had been completed, a couple of the aircraft were shot up a little bit.

Fortunately, they received no significant damage and could remain on station. Both teams of Snakes and Red Birds had to rearm and refuel a couple of times. At the conclusion of the arduous situation, Kev was exceptionally proud to say that they all helped that young lieutenant. Kev's dark adventure and journey into the recesses of his soul had an honorable ending. Red Dog Five-Three took all of his boys home with him.

That evening, Kev made a lengthy entry in his journal.

Sitting here at my makeshift desk, pen in hand, I pray that I am beginning to grow up. The pieces of this complex puzzle called life are slowly beginning to come together. In fact, I am seeing my place in the Cav in a new and deeply meaningful way. Reviewing the day, it is just possible that I have begun to learn an important lesson about the meaning and possibilities of belonging. The Major was, as always, very wise in offering me the opportunity to stay and help the young Lieutenant. By his grace, I had made a surprising discovery about the positive possibilities of my own military life.

My most important discovery was that the boy with wind-ruffled yellow hair honestly and truly belonged to that young lieutenant. I also realized what the life enhancing power of this belonging meant. The young lieutenant wasn't going home without the young boy who was sprawled out upon the rocks below me.

Ironically, I never knew the boy's name. However, in my world that lack of knowledge is normal. No one else in the Cav knew him by name. Interestingly enough, I now know that being aware of the boy's name wasn't important for those of us in the Cav. To us, he was simply, one of us. He was just another GI. We needed to know nothing else to do our job.

That fact of his being one of us, in and of itself, was sufficient knowledge for us to act. However, what Kevin Paul Johnson needs to burn into the deepest pathways of his mind is that the dead boy's young lieutenant knew his name. His lieutenant knew who he was. He was a precious human being. Furthermore, even in death, the boy with wind ruffled yellow hair was not going to be abandoned by his Lieutenant. The boy's Lieutenant cared for, and about, him even if others were willing to abandon him!

Kev spent a considerable amount of time pondering and looking back upon his new found wisdom. It was his heartfelt prayer that he had become just a little bit wiser than he was that morning which took him by such surprise. Uncomfortably, he had come to recognize his own selfish childishness. Kev's understandable lack of maturity, compassion, and unacceptable self-centered ignorance, had been well proven when unloaded in rage on that poor young lieutenant. As he meditated upon the day, he came to believe that it was the beginning of something new for ole Kev.

In a unique, to him, theologically profound moment, he wrote to his old friend Pastor Bill.

I have recently been to a strange and terrifying place. I'll call it the deep dark recesses of my soul. Thankfully, while in that terror-filled place, I saw the words of Jesus come to life in human action. Today, I have a much greater appreciation for the power and hope of the words of Jesus of Nazareth. If I remember correctly, Jesus said something like this.

"No man has greater love than this, than to lay down one's life for one's friends."

Traveling in that strange and terrifying land, I recognized that selfless love is one of the most beautiful sights a man can experience.

THE RING

Sitting back and enjoying a cool-one one evening, Kev propped up his feet and slowly surveyed his kingdom. Thinking to himself, he decided to climb upon his self-ordained pulpit and pontificate for the benefit of his friend Sven.

"You know what -- The poet is correct, 'time waits for no man.'"

Without his noting its waters flowing along, the rivers of time had slowly traveled passed him, while remaining intent upon their own journey. Deeply drawing down on his beer, Kev was in his pulpit and on a roll.

"You know, unbidden and very much undesired on my behalf, suddenly, Kevin Paul Johnson has become an old guy in the Cav."

Casually looking around, he had suddenly become aware of the change. The majority of the people who were present when he became a member of the Cav, had somehow disappeared into thin air. For the most part, they either were dead or had returned to the world. Finishing his profound observations, he continued.

"You know, Sven, I don't know if I like being an old guy."

Pausing for a moment, he thought and then continued with his pontificating.

"Gawd, I hated being a newbe. Yet, it did have its advantages. No one expected anything from me and I fulfilled their expectations. Now . . . Though . . . I don't know.

With the arrival of more leadership, both official and unofficial, he found himself thinking more deeply than he had ever been accustomed to doing. Sometimes, he would enter deep conversations with his friend. Mostly, he found himself taking large blocks of time to reflect on his thoughts with pen and paper. Trying to make sense of his "authorhood," he began to wonder why he was writing. Pen in hand and brooding and yeasting, he constantly questioned what he was trying to accomplish with his pen and paper.

"Am I to teach? Am I supposed to entertain? Or, am I to exhort? I wish that I knew. Sometimes I think that I am writing because I am fighting in Vietnam Vet and I no longer believe that we are accomplishing anything?"

Eventually, he came to the conclusion that his questions were not ones which he could answer with a simple yes or no. If a clear yes or no answer existed, then such a simple answer completely eluded ole Kev. He decided that he could only write out of his own experience, his own feelings, and his own struggles. All of that somehow had become mixed up into a single complex package. A package, he had found, that persistently defied any logical explanation.

Unable to answer his own questions clearly, he continued to write as often as he could. Mostly, he wrote about his life in the Red Birds. He wrote because he felt compelled by something that he did not understand. However, Kev found much to write about concerning the people and events which were shaping his life.

The young writer found himself continually challenged as he continued his journeys down the proverbial memory lane. With his pen poised over his writing tablet, he remembered another very powerful incident which was coloring his life.

It had been a rare and beautiful day for flying. The air was moist and warm. As best he could tell, an almost small southern town, with a sleepy feeling, which softly colored and flavored the rich atmosphere. Though it was moist and warm, the day was not oppressively hot and humid like so many others. Kev found that the air was so wonderfully smooth that it was as if he were gliding the aircraft on a glistening sheet of slippery plate glass.

Letting down from higher altitude and beginning the day's recon was an uneventful pleasure. Delighted to be flying, he would never have thought that he was beginning on another strange and frightening adventure. This adventure was one which would stir up and refocus recent troubling memories. By the day's end, he would be personally, painfully, and emotionally reminded of the boy with the wind-ruffled yellow hair.

Deeply enjoying the delightful flying conditions, he found himself slowly drifting the little helicopter down the side of a hill as they looked for the bad guys. True, he was very selfishly enjoying every moment of his flying. However, he remained true to his daily task and toil. Flying his normal aerial reconnaissance, Kev was, as always, on the lookout for any sign of the bad guys. Looking about for almost an hour, he had found none. Months earlier, he would have been frustrated and chomping the bit with anxiety.

By this time, he had seen too much and done too much to get easily frustrated that easily. Enjoying the rare moment of aviation delight, he deeply sighed with genuine contentment. It was a good day and the flight was turning out to be a strangely serene moment which only rarely happened to Kev. He found himself so completely wrapped up in flying, and in his recon, that the larger world was quietly put on hold.

For the moment, he managed to forget that they were in the middle of a life and death war. The strange sereneness of the moment altered the color and complexion of the flight. It made it difficult for him to accept that he was ardently looking to kill other people before they managed to kill him. Engrossed up in the placid moment, the three young men, mounted on faithful Rocinante, gently drifted down the hill. Smiling to himself, he commented to his active imagination.

"Lord, Now this is what I call flying. I love these mountains, their beauty, their challenge to flying, and playing in the strange and unexpected winds they throw at me. I can't think of anything else that I would rather be doing."

Contented or not, their heads were sticking out the doors and they were diligently looking for the bad guys. The strange experience, of the moment, was very inexplicable. The land below them was so quiet and peaceful that they might have imagined themselves sitting in a boat on a still millpond. Sitting in their little boat, their fishing lines in the water the young men were untroubled by pesky fish. For the moment, the war seemed very distant and completely unreal to the young men.

As it was want to happen in the constantly unpredictable life flying with the Red Birds, the situation was too good to be true. Another mind-numbing surprise was about to be sprung on the three young men. Without warning, their world took a nasty turn for the worse as they slowly drifted down the hill. It happened when they were gliding past the mouth of a cave. Lost in their own private worlds, they were floating peacefully through the still air.

Suspended in an unworldly world, the little helicopter was slowly descending the side of the hill. She was traveling at little more than a leisurely walking pace when their artificial world of peace and quiet exploded. It was while they were looking deeply into a cave that the pleasant calm and unreality of the day came to a disquieting end. Not seeking his permission, the entirety of Kev's life changed. Something that looked like the slow, steady flashing of a strobe light signaled this abrupt change. That strobe-like flashing was signaling the instantaneous end of Kev's peaceful world, both artificial and real. Furthermore, it was no more than fifteen feet before his eyes.

Though he was powerless to do anything about the flashes, his mind exploded in consternation and confusion.

"Holy S–t"

Stunning and shocking, Kev was unable to fully comprehend what he saw. Less than fifteen feet from his blank face, appeared the deadly repetitive muzzle flashes of an AK-47 firing on full automatic. Subjectively, time stopped. He felt, that if he had chosen to, he could have easily counted the distinct flashes of the slowly pulsating strobe. It was like no other experience he had ever had. Much later, he recounted his feelings to Sven.

"I know that my mind counted every flash of death and doom."

For Kevin Paul Johnson, the experience was internally true. The repetitive, strobe-like, flashing horrified and mesmerized him. This bewildering experience of looking at his own death was not John Wayne, Hollywood fake, slow motion. Though it was unbelievable, it was also deadly real and it made his blood run cold with horror. Yet, it was in stopped time.

Kev later wrote in his journal.

FLASH! FLASH! FLASH! Thirty times, the repetitive FLASH, FLASH, FLASH was burning itself indelibly into my numbed brain. I felt that all I had to do was reach my hand out. If I did so, I could have easily touched each of the mesmerizing flashes of deadly strobbing light. The repetitive flashing was like a slow motion Morse code of doom. Part of my boggled mind understood its message and reacted with unspeakable, yet screaming, horror. Yet, my poor addled brain could not come close to comprehending the apparently hidden meaning of the code! I felt like this strobbing/flashing code was trying to tell me something important.

Somewhere, exceptionally deep in the dark unconscious recesses of his numbed mind, Kev heard a horrifying screeching noise. It was the terrified screaming of his back seat observer. Pausing for a moment and listening closely to the noisy cacophony, Kev also heard something which he thought he should recognize. All of a sudden, he realized that it was his own voice screaming in pure stereo with his observer. As if acting on the director's cue, they were both screaming identical terror-stricken words.

"TAKING FIRE! TAKING FIRE!"

Unfortunately, their cries of terror made no difference. Unknown to them, both were screaming in raw panic into what was an already dead and destroyed radio. In a perfectly timed cadence with the slow pulsations of the deadly cold flashing coming from the cave, Kev slowly began to understand the deadly meaning pulsating message. He was aware of everything that was happening about him. While at the same time he could not understand how it was happening to him on such a quiet, idyllic, and peaceful day.

The strident shrill sound of death surrounded him. He clearly heard the metallic ripping and smashing noise of each AK-47 round. Each steel jacketed round was tearing its way through his poor doomed Red Bird. With his brain almost seized up in an overload condition, Kev never considered voicing his worst thoughts. It wasn't necessary. He knew that his Red Bird was going down. His faithful friend, companion, and steed Rocinante was doomed.

Momentarily resigned, he assigned his fate to be the same as her fate. Despite the sound-deadening quality of his flight helmet, he clearly heard the wretched grinding death scream of the engine. Strangely enough, the mechanical death of the little engine was a horrific experience for the stunned young man. It tore at him more than the dim knowledge of his own coming fate. As the consummate lover of fine machinery, the little engine's tormented voice tore deeply at the fabric of his heart. Confirming Rocinante's death scream, he heard the main rotor's low RPM warning horn crying out its strident message of doom over his headset.

Through the sound-deadening of his flight helmet, Kev was forced to listen to mechanical agony. His heart felt the crunching rendering of finely sculptured metal lovingly crafted by Hughes Aircraft. Working the controls made little difference. Following the mystical Morse message of thirty flashes of the strobe, nothing connected to his flight controls, or in his control, worked. Gravity had become the complete master of the moment, of the little Red Bird, and of Kev and crew. Helpless to do anything, he watched mechanical destruction fill his horizon. The rapidly spinning rotor blades exploded when they impacted with the splintering hardwood of Southeast Asia's trees. The unfolding drama was a surreal experience.

Incomprehensively shocked, by what he witnessed before the little helicopter hit the trees, Kev had seen one of the four rotor blades detach itself from the rotor head. Continuing the surreal picture of unbelievable happenings, Kev later described it.

"The sight of rotor blade sailing through the trees seemed to be like something from a grade "B" movie."

Helpless to affect his world, he calmly watched the detached rotor blade slowly sail away from him. Useless to him, the lonely rotor blade silently disappeared into the deep gloom of the trees. As the slow motion picture continued, Kev felt that he could count the individual leaves on the tree branches which were all so slowly passing before him. As the crew and dead helicopter were apparently gently drifting and wobbling down through the massive trunks and branches, for the first time in his life, Kev found himself powerless to control his fate.

With a rude abruptness, Kev's internal clock suddenly resumed normal speed. In the passing of another instant, the cruel reality of the moment uninvited and discourteously, smashed itself deeply into Kev's stunned consciousness! All that he had seen and experienced in the passing of a couple of seconds had not prepared him for what was to happen next. It should have. However, it did not. The dying Red Bird suddenly and unexpectedly impacted upon the unforgiving ground. The strange drama he was witnessing became painfully real when it struck the earth with a bone-jarring, back-breaking, body-smashing crash.

Yet, the shock of the resounding impact further befuddled and bewildered him for a moment. Maybe, it was for more than a moment that he found himself befuddled. In the midst of it all, Kev discovered that judging time when the clock seems to have stopped was very difficult. Overwhelmed, the young man didn't know for sure how long he sat dazed in the shattered helicopter. Eventually, his head began to clear.

Much to his horror, Kev's carefully constructed world had also come crashing down with his little helicopter. One instant, he was peacefully enjoying his flying. The next instant, he was looking about the shattered cockpit groggily trying to gather his wits about himself. Looking to the rear of the helicopter, his heart froze. He saw the most horrifying nightmare of every pilot since the Wright Brothers started it all at Kitty Hawk. All so slowly, his greatest fear came into a hot fiery focus., Remaining befuddled and bewildered, at last he became afraid. Kev looked over his left shoulder to where the back-seater worked.

Leaping red, white, and blue flames filled the back of the aircraft. The rippling roaring red of JP-4 fed, flames overwhelmed his powers of reason. Nearing panic, he frantically looked about for his crew. Neither of his observers was in sight. Confused and distraught, by their absence, he had no idea what had happened to them. However, the fact that they weren't in the fire offered him his first hit of limited comfort.

Nevertheless, his mounting fear was threatening his survival. He saw raw fuel was pouring all over the place from the ruptured fuel cell. Though he knew that it was a trick of his mind, he thought that the flowing sounded like the thunder of a huge waterfall. Yet, it couldn't be. He shouldn't have been able to hear it through the roar of flames and the insulation of his flight helmet. Looking down at his feet, much to the young pilot's horror, he saw that the raw fuel was even splashing around his boots. The primitive part of his brain was screaming at him and flashing pictures of TK's remains through his battered brain.

"**Run Kev! Run!** Your going to be burned alive!"

Simultaneously, a more rational and functional part of Kev silently prayed.

"Dear God. PLEASE tell me that this is a nightmare. Please tell me that all the fire and fuel which surrounded me is part of a terrible fictional dream!"

He prayed that he was sound asleep wandering around submerged and lost in the foreboding dark and dreadful recesses of his mind. With painful slowness, the haze of his muddled mind continued to clear. Fighting to stay alive, he willed his mind to begin working faster that the events which were overtaking him. Yet, overwhelmed and overloaded, his brain was taking its own sweet time. Surrounded by his coming suffering and death, try as he might, he couldn't get his mind to function properly. At a great distance, he heard the muffled boom of exploding ordinances. Struggling to find its source, he realized that it was in the back of the aircraft.

Without thinking about the consequences, Kev snapped his head about to see the source of the noise. At that moment, his internal clock returned to the freeze frame mode. His eyes were greeted by a wall of exploding white-hot flame created by exploding willie pete and high

347

explosives mixed with JP fuel. The sight of this wall of flamed added to his overload of horror. Flaming death was slowly and resolutely advancing upon him. Dante's horror, was threatening to engulf him. What he was witnessing was the leading edge of the explosion. The rational part of him couldn't understand how he could see what he saw.

Having seen many and caused not a few explosions himself, he was mystified. Kev knew that explosions move too fast for the human eye to track their movement. Yet, the experience was just like when the little helicopter was crashing. His whole world was moving in Hollywood style, high tension, slow motion. The crash had created a movie maker's dream-scape only inches away from him. Resigning himself, Kev assumed that this white hot moment was to be the final chapter in the short book of his life! Scrunching up into a tiny ball in his armored seat, he quietly awaited his oblivion. Clearly remembering what happened to TK, Kev prayed that his searing experience of death's fire would end quickly. Thinking about burning to death paralyzed him. Much to his surprise, his personal oblivion did not come.

Astonished to find that he was unhurt except for some minor burns, Kev's brain began to send him continued urgent messages. At last, the rational part of his brain caught up with the primitive and they began to work together.

"Kev, ole boy, now would be a really good time for you to take an exceptionally active part in saving your sorry butt."

Taking quick stock of his uncomfortable situation, Kev gave his big-time Army boss credit.

"Thank God that Uncle Sam provides good fire resistant flight suits!"

Finishing his quick thank you, he began crawling through the flames and the wreckage of what had once been his dear friend. In route, he said a silent "good-by." It hurt to give up his long sought goal, and the grand meaning of his young life. He was saying good by to his friend, his companion, and his personal Red Bird, good ole Rocinante.

Physically falling out of the wreckage, Kev caught his balance and quickly assumed a deep crouch. He quickly swivelled his head about while trying to get his bearings. Then, looking back at the floor of the flaming Red Bird, Kev caught a quick glimpse of his expensive camera. Surprisingly, the flames had yet to get to it. Still dazed by the series of shocks to his mind and body, he wasn't thinking quickly or clearly. For a brief second, he thought about going back to retrieve his precious camera from the burning wreckage.

Sanity immediately took the upper hand in his inner struggle. Kev wisely decided, he wouldn't need a camera where he was most likely going. That is, if he were lucky enough to live that long! The selfish little boy in him added its two-cents worth. He would be darned if he was going to give his new thirty-five millimeter camera to the bad guys if they killed or captured him. With a finality of purpose, Kev spoke his first words since Rocinante assumed her final resting place.

"Let the stupid camera burn!"

Young Kevin had a very good idea of what his physical condition was. Completing a quick inventory, he decided that physically everything was working. However, he knew that he was a little more than addled and had grave doubts about his mental condition. Furthermore, he knew that he was completely out of his element. He was a scout pilot and not a ground pounder. What Kevin Paul Johnson needed most was a drastic change of luck! While he was capable of limited thought process, he knew that he wasn't at his sharpest. Being brutally honest, Kev knew that he remained bothered, befuddled, and bewildered. It was to be expected. He realized that the swift change from a quiet, almost lazy, feeling to the distressing condition of being a fugitive had completely overcome his thought process.

Fortunately, he quickly found, or was quickly found by, his two crew men. During the crash, they stumbled and fell into a deep depression in the rocks and brush a few feet below the wreckage. The force of the crash had battered, bruised, broken, bloodied, and badly shaken the three young men. Furthermore, they were more terrified than any of them had ever been in their young lives.

"Well . . . ," Kev thought to himself, "at least **I am very terrified!**"

Nevertheless, they did not forget their military training. While they huddled together in the deep depression, no one spoke a word lest they be heard by the bad guys. Carefully emptying their pockets, they did a through inventory of their military assets. Among the three of them, they had two pistols, eighteen bullets, and one fragmentation grenade.

Most likely, it was shock. Whatever it was, a grim gallows' humor suddenly gripped Kev. As the ranking man, he analyzed their massive arsenal. Then, he tried to formulate a useful plan of action. Shaking his head ruefully, he thought to himself.

"Granted, we might not be the high-powered brass hats staffing the Pentagon. For that matter, I am not trained in formulating sweeping military operations. Nevertheless, it is up to me to come up with a plan which will get us out of here. Unfortunately, I don't need to do an exceptionally careful analysis of the situation to recognize that we're not in any condition to act offensively. I guess this means that we will not march directly north, quickly seize Hanoi, and then demand unconditional surrender from the NVA!"

The young Warrant Officer and his two young enlisted men immediately recognized that their first course of action was to do their best to stay alive. That was a straight-forward mission that they willingly embraced. To accomplish their first objective, they needed to escape, and evade the bad guys. However, they faced one unescapable fact. All three knew that the bad guys would be diligently looking for them.

Like three scared little children, they were fearfully crouching deep in their little hole in the rocks and brush. Passively listening, they heard the NVA soldiers cautiously walking in the underbrush. Their noise only served to heighten their growing terror. It surprised Kev to clearly hear the NVA whistling signals and directions to each other. L-istening to their movement, they could faintly hear them talking in whispers to one another. He had never been this close to the bad guys.

"Strange," he thought to himself. 'I have almost daily heard them shooting at me. However, I have never heard them speaking."

Several weeks later, with his gallows' humor remaining in its ususal strange condition, Kev commented to Sven.

"It didn't take a whiz kid from the Five-Sided-Funny-Farm on the Potomac to figure out that we were the special objects of their attention. It was a form of attention, I might add, that I did not wish to receive"

Continuing in his sports imagery, Kev sized up their situation. He knew that the rule book said that their death or capture would make the bad guys the winners in the sad game which they were playing. In the end, no one needed to tell the three young men what they needed to do. With their limited firepower, they were unable to offer any meaningful resistance. Though they said nothing, Kev noted that both of the observers had sprained and/or dislocated knees. Running or extended movement was out of the question. Ever the serious romantic, he never gave a passing thought to leaving them. Such a thought was beyond his consideration.

Yet, their injuries severely restricted their mobility. With no other options available to them, they pulled themselves as deeply as possible into their little hole. The three of them were doing their best imitation of a frightened flock of ostriches. Yet, the powerful fear which gripped them convinced them that the bad guys would hear them for the fearful shaking and rattling that their bones were making.

Giving him no respite, Kev's vivid imagination suddenly decided to turn itself on. Watching its Technicolor production, he almost laughed out loud at himself. His memory of Hollywood's great heros had given him a picture of himself that did not jive with any of his romantic notions of combat. After all, Vic Morrow as the tough infantry sergeant in "Combat" would never be caught dead hiding in this hole shaking with fear and terror.

"For sure," Kev thought to himself, "the glorious, gutsy, and grizzled sergeant would not have been wondering if he would soil himself. Hollywood's hero would have a dashingly devious plan to save everybody. Best of all, it would be completed within an hour!"

"Most likely," Kev reminded himself, "it would take less than an hour. Commercials would take their share of the allotted hour."

Rationally, Kev knew that their situation was so pitiful that it bordered on the absurd. He felt neither romantic nor glorious. Rather, he felt like he was caught up in a tragic black comedy written by a sadistic and emotionally tormented mind.

Eventually shutting down his technicolor imagination, Kev's mind decided to drift to his writing. He realized that his words would never be sufficient tools to describe his painfully dragged out moments of impotent terror.

"How," he thought to himself, "can I ever described these feelings of dark and dreadful doom and personal destruction?"

Huddling fearfully in their little hiding place, the three of them heard the rustling of the underbrush coming ever closer and closer. For what seemed to be the fiftieth time, Kev nervously, and quietly, opened the cylinder of his thirty-eight caliber pistol while wishing he still had his forty-five. He needed to make sure that he had his six bullets. Frustrated, he couldn't believe that the pilots had to turn in their forty-fives so that the observers could trade in their thirty-eights. The observers had been playing quick draw with their thirty-eights and someone thought this was a good fix. On the spot, he vowed that if he survived that he would get his forty-five back. He wanted its knock-down power!

Seeing what Kev was doing, the back-seater made sure that the pins were straight on their two fragmentation grenades. Also noting the preparations of the other two, the front-seater checked his forty-five to make sure he had chambered a round. They quietly waited for the short sharp finish to their final hunt. It was inconceivable, to them, that the NVA had not yet discovered them. Closer and closer came the telltale noise in the underbrush! Kev became convinced that the bad guys were playing a perverted game of cat and mouse with his fears and imagination.

Sweating profusely, Kev refused to believe that the bad guys had not seen them. The voice of a cornered rat screamed inside his brain. It shrilly cried out for him to jump up and finish the whole thing. It told him that waiting and being patient was wrong.

"Maybe, just maybe" he thought to himself. "Maybe I'll get lucky and surprise them. Possibly, I'll take two or three of them out before they get me."

With the greatest act of will of his whole short life, he just barely managed to restrain himself. Yet, he felt as if he would explode into a million pieces in his mounting anxiety and the demands to bring the drama to its conclusion.

Noting one of his observers tensing up and licking the sweat from his upper lip, Kev gently laid a soft restraining hand on him. It was obvious to him that his young enlisted man was thinking exactly the same thing he was. They were Aero Scouts. These young men were neither chosen nor trained because they were passive people by nature. The waiting and feeling like a scared rabbit in a hole was emotionally killing them.

"Better," all three thought, "just to get it over with! Then it will be done. One way or the other the game will be finished!"

It seemed impossible. Yet, their position became ever more precarious. The bad guys were virtually on top of them. Honestly believing that the bad guys had not seen them, was impossible. Kev became increasingly convinced that the NVA soldiers were playing mind games with them. Yet, they knew better than to waste time. They had to know that a rescue force was on the way. The bad guys had gotten so close that the noise of their movements seemed deafening to Kev's ears. He was so tense that he was afraid that he would scream!

Knowing that any second mow, he would explode from the tension, Kev peered through a crack in the rocks. He saw a bush move. Then, he saw an NVA boot cautiously move forward. Terrified, Kev stopped breathing. Reaching back, with hand signals he pointed out the boot to his observers. Like him, they too stopped breathing. A strange, stupid, and self-destructive urge came upon Kev. Not believing his own feelings, he wanted to reach out the short twelve inches and touch the boot. Part of him needed to confirm that his eyes were not playing cruel tricks on him. Thankfully, the little boy could no longer move and give in to the insane urge. Fear driven, total paralysis had attacked his central nervous system. His body would not obey the commands of his brain. Unable to act, he did not tell the searcher where he was.

Later, when he tried to write of the experience, Kev didn't know how to describe the endless lifetimes of sweat stinking of fear. Huddled in a little knot, the three of them were completely powerless. Violent, vindictive death was but twelve scant inches away.

"Carefully hidden in a deep crevice in the rocks and brush, clear as day we saw the bad guys. Trembling, we saw their legs and boots clad in NVA issue equipment! Those well-armed men were so close to us that they must have smelled the stink of our fear. Had we chosen to, we could have reached out a hand and touched them."

Like the dawning of a new thought, captured in the dialogue balloon above a cartoon character, Kev clearly understood his terrifying situation.

"WE WERE ALONE! AND, TO THEM, the men in a foreign uniform looking for us, **WE WERE NOTHING!"**

He had never felt such an overwhelming emptiness like that before in his life. With a dismal haunting destituteness, Kev suddenly knew that he had become less than nothing. He had read about the feeling. Now he understood it. With the tables turned, he had become a meaningless game animal. However, like the quail he and Pastor Bill used to hunt, he could not bolt in frantic flight. He had two hurt crewmen to think of. Their presence saved his life. Had he bolted as he wanted to, the terrified young pilot wouldn't have gotten five steps. The tables had fully turned. After all his "hunts" as a Scout, he suddenly and truly understood what it was to be the defenseless hunted prey.

He later wrote in his journal.

It is with a deep sense of gratitude that I can report the end of this story. It doesn't end with the three hunted little boys waiting for the inevitability of their death or capture. However, to tell the story properly, I need to move the calendar forward and introduce another wonderful person. As I write this, I believe that he represents the heart and the soul of the Cav. For me, he is the symbol of the better part of all of us.

Unlike back home, one day is just like any another day in Vietnam. Looking back, I am not surprised how our strange relationship evolved. Like an unexpected lightening bolt out of a cloudless blue sky, he arrives quietly and almost unseen onto my life's stage. Looking back, I can't remember exactly what day of the week it happened. Nevertheless, I do remember no big to-do happened at the troop level to announce his arrival. In another setting, the man's rank and position deserved official and ceremonial notice. To most of us, he was another fresh-faced green newbe. However, this green newbe was the Captain, the Executive Officer of our unit. That made him the number two man in the whole troop. Yet the truth of the matter was that to the very best my memory has to offer, one day he was simply present, one of us, and quietly doing his job.

Strangely enough, at first, I didn't see that he didn't fit any of my many preconceptions and prejudices. I had never in my short military life seen such an unpretentious young Captain! Please understand that he held his rank with dignity and that he was completely professional in all his conduct. He didn't try to be everyone's drinking buddy and best pal. Yet, he didn't "lord" his position. Somehow, as if it were a gift, he managed to balance being warm and friendly with being a commander. Almost at once, I came to love and respect him as I have never loved a man before or since in my short life.

Let me take a step back from that statement. I didn't love him like I did Johnny. I couldn't. That would have been impossible. However, he comes in a quarter step behind Johnny and all the others are several laps behind.

To the outside observer, who knows me, my warm feelings for him are very interesting. I say this because I am not exactly a spit and polish type of guy. Whereas, he was the only West Pointer in our unit. Further adding to the irony, I was an immature Warrant Officer Pilot who had no great love for commissioned pilots. To add, greater depth, to the irony of my affection for this man, he was the Executive Officer. That is the most thankless job in any military unit. The unfortunate XO gets to do all the dirty work that the commander wishes to avoid. This unavoidable dirty work includes general discipline.

Kev and the Captain made their acquaintance outside of their carefully structured military world. One afternoon on their small basketball court the two of them began their strange and quiet friendship. Sometime in the distant past, someone had built the basketball court at the heliport. This is where the relationship began innocently enough. It was a rare day off and Kev was alone and out on the court. Lost in his own world, he was absently shooting buckets. For the moment, he was enjoying being an innocent child at the playground. Shrugging off the pressure of his job, as only a young man can, Kev was just trying to forget where he was. Wrapped up in his passion of shooting baskets, it seemed to Kev that his, soon-to-be, friend appeared out of nowhere. One minute Kev was enjoying his solitude. The next, he had a playmate.

Slim and quite erect, Kev's new playmate stood maybe six foot two. Standing quietly in his gym shorts he softly asked if he could join in shooting a few buckets. Though Kev was quietly enjoying his solitude, who was he to tell the quiet new guy he couldn't shoot a few buckets. Basketball had always been Kev's passion and most active social outlet. The young man's response was predictable. Pausing for a bit, Kev responded and threw him the big round ball.

"Here you go guy. A little company will be enjoyable. After you warm up a bit, if you like, we can play a little one on one."

After the new guy threw a couple of shots through the hoop, they got down to some serious body banging one on one basketball. He won the first three games before Kev managed to pull one out. They played all afternoon in the hot sun sweating out their frustrations with life in general. As a junior Warrant Officer, admitting the Captain's markedly superior competence was a great blow to Kev's athletic esprit. Nevertheless, later that evening at the club, while he and Sven were sharing a cold one, he told Sven.

"Darn it, Sven. You know, for a Captain, the new XO has a real sweet touch with the leather. I won't say that he suckered or hustled me because we didn't play for money. However, it didn't take me very long to note that he had played the game a lot. Furthermore, he clearly loved playing round-ball."

Prior to that afternoon's playground play, Kev had not met the new guy officially. That didn't bother him. For the most part, he didn't care much about anything beyond what was going on in the Red Bird Platoon. The competitive situation was potentially humorous. Kev loved to win, bang bodies, and play hard. However, ole Kev did not know that this was the new Executive Officer. Had Kev known that this new guy was the XO, he might have cut him some slack. That is if he had been

Charley Bird. But, that was Charley's way and not Kev's way. In his mind's eye, when the new guy put his hands to the leather, they were equals.

In a short time, this first afternoon, the two of them were playing serious playground round-ball. They were giving each other a hard time and banging their bodies together as equals. The joy of physical competition made it a truly delightful little emotional oasis of their own creation. The two of them played round-ball for several sweaty hard-working hours. Their celebration of life, on the round-ball court, caused them to quickly forget that they were involved in the serious business of killing and dying. For those blissful hours, which passed more like moments, they were a couple of young kids playing their pick-up games at the playground.

Playing round-ball or not, Red One-Five was a well-trained observer. They had only played a couple of minutes when he clearly saw "THE RING." Noting the ring, Kev knew that his opponent was what the "common folk" in the rest of the Army called a Ring Knocker. Much to his delight as they banged bodies, Kev's playground partner was a real live West Pointer. That difference in rank and status only made the competition sweeter for Kev. The two young men never mentioned the minor issues of the "Point" or of rank. They were engaged in the serious business of playing a little one-on-one and that was more important. A West Point Ring had no place in, nor any meaning to, the oasis like setting of childlike play which they were celebrating.

Looking back, after a couple of months of reflection, Kev commented in his journal.

My Captain was a uniquely gifted officer and a true leader of men. The lean and serious West Point graduate clearly understood the difference between work and play. Intuitively, he honored and celebrated our need to balance both. I am willing to say, as Pastor Bill had often preached about, that in our secular setting, the quiet man was gloriously "POOR IN SPIRIT."

Writing about the "day of the strobe-like flashes," Kev tried to capture his feelings.

If I should live to one-hundred, and if I am to lie drooling and senile in my bed at the "home," I will never forget. I will never need to close my eyes to recall the sight. With almost no control over the falling junk, which previously had been good ole Rocinante, I was along for the ride. Seemingly from a distracted distance, I watched the trees greedily part and swallow us and our helicopter. It was like watching the maw of a great beast feasting on a little tidbit of a helicopter. When the beast was satisfied, we smashed into the ground.

Much later, everyone who was flying that day told me that the aircraft exploded upon impact. All the assorted explosives on board created a large black and white mushroom cloud. Exploding, it marked the spot where the greedy beast ate us. The men in the other helicopters, including the Captain, who saw the crash had to know that no one survived the explosion. They had seen much death and destruction and knew that nobody could walk away from such a crash and explosion! They were sure that their only remaining task was to collect the bodies and return them to our families. That is, if it were possible!

When the towering black and white mushroom cloud began rising from the trees marking Kev's crash site, all the radios in the Cav instantly came to life. After a bit, military order returned and the initial flurry of demands for information, instructions, and orders ended. It was then that the front seat gunner of an orbiting Snake made the most poignant and telling statement said by anyone that day. Tom, believing that he was only speaking on the intercom, mashed down upon the floor mike button. What came out was a graphically expressed feeling of shock which he shared with his pilot. Unknown to himself or his pilot, he had the radio on and not the intercom. To history and to everybody else who was also on the radio frequency, he loudly proclaimed what most of the pilots felt.

"I'll be damned! I don't believe it. They finally got the son of a bitch."

Ole Tom did not exaggerate his feelings. Everyone who had seen the crash and the subsequent explosion believed that Tom's cryptic analysis of Kev's plight was brutally true. Having witnessed the same death marker, the Captain ordered the Blues to land. He was sure that theirs would be the gruesome task of gathering up the three shattered bodies. The least they could do was see that the Army returned the bodies to their families. In the tradition of the young Lieutenant who had previously humbled Kev, the Captain was going to bring all his boys home. Later, Kev wanted to ask the Captain what he had thought when he saw the mushroom cloud. He hoped that the Captain had a gut feeling about the toughness of his round-ball opponent. However, Kev never did ask the question.

When the time came for the troop ships to discharge their cargo, no one was surprised at the greeting that they received. As each of the troop carrying Hueys landed with their load of Blues, the same folk who had shot down Kev met them with intense ground fire. By this stage of the war, the bad guys knew the Americans very well. Maybe they knew the Americans better than they knew themselves. They waited because they knew that Kev's friends would come for his body. The reception committee was ready when the Hueys arrived.

As expected, when they transported the grunts into the landing zone about four hundred meters away from Kev, they were greeted "warmly." When they took off, two of the big Hueys had been pretty well shot up by automatic weapons fire. Of course, the three young men could not see what was happening from their hiding place. They did not

356

need to. From the noise, they could mentally construct an accurate picture of what was happening during the insertion. Their imaginations caused them to cringe in fear for themselves and for the blues.

Huddled in their hole, the three young men were close enough to the LZ to hear the Cobra's suppressing fire of rockets and mini-guns. Both sides were loudly playing their assorted instruments of death. They could also clearly hear the M-60's of the Hueys, the AK-47's of the NVA exchanging fire as the Slicks landed. Eventually, after the troops had landed, the three scared boys were relieved to hear the return fire of the friendly M-16's. Very surprised to still be alive, Kev was sure that Command and Control was in for a very long day. Despite his own difficult situation, Kev didn't envy his friends and the fight that they faced.

The sudden and unexpected downing of a Red Bird and then developing ground combat with the Blues was going to keep Kev's friend, the Captain, fully occupied. Being the ranking man, the scared young Scout pilot didn't share his rapidly developing fears with his two hurt two observers. He though them only to himself.

"If they don't see the bigger picture of what is happening, so much the better. We have got enough to worry about as it is."

However, Kev was growing very concerned that the Cav's ground troops would never reach the crash site without unacceptable losses. In fact, the scared little boy in him was afraid that eventually they would have to withdraw. Kev knew that it was not the Cav way. However . . .

Kev's overloaded mind was far more addled than he would have been comfortable admitting. Comprehending the big picture and keeping track of the players was much different from his new "ground's eye" point of view. Dealing with the changes from an initially warm lazy day which was filled with sleepy boredom that was quickly converted to brain numbing terror was difficult. Understanding it or not, he found himself bruised, burned, sweaty, scared, and trembling in a hole in the ground. He knew that trapped on the ground was not the place that he wanted to be. In his heart, he was a bold Scout pilot and should be quarter-backing the rescue effort. The Captain should be acting as his wise coach as they preformed a Cav-style miracle. More than anything else, he hated not being in the game. This time, however, he was the sought-after "game."

In sharp contrast to Kev, his friend the Captain was flying the Command and Control Helicopter. The Captain was clean, safe, and sound flying over the Area of Operations. Thankfully, he was the West Pointer who had a natural understanding of his men and of his job. Better yet, as far as Kev had been concerned, he played a decent brand of round-ball. However, Uncle Sam's Army had very strictly defined the Captain's job within the drama of the current Cav recon and rescue. The good Captain was destined to remain in his C&C helicopter all day long. All his combat action would consist of flying lazy circles at two-thousand-five-hundred feet of altitude. From his lofty viewpoint, he would control the unfolding operation. The lanky Captain's only butt breaks would be to land to refuel. Even then, the helicopter was kept running while he refueled.

Huddled in his little depression, scared, dirty, and powerless Kev remained Kev. Unable to control himself, he let his mind slowly drift for a moment. He found himself quietly wondering to himself what the Captain might be thinking. Most likely, the XO, his ole round-ball partner, had seen it all. Maybe, he saw the crash of the little Red Bird! Undoubtedly, he saw the large explosion and mushroom cloud rising. It must have looked to be a dramatic marker over Kev's freshly created aviator's grave. Unknown to Kev at the time, the XO had heard all the radio comments. This also included Tom's cryptic and colorful commentary on Red One-Five's plight. Something that Kev would never have expected happened twenty-five-hundred feet in the air.

From the safety of twenty-five-hundred feet in the air, he directed the big Huey's to unload their rescue force. Working with Kev's wingman, he directed the slim Snakes to let loose their protective firepower. From twenty-five-hundred feet in the air, and talking with their command Sergeant, he heard the yelling, cries, and hollering of the ground troops as they engaged the bad guys.

Unable to personally intervene, he had uncomfortably listened to the Huey pilots' fearful calls that they were taking heavy fire and taking hits. Talking with the grunts, he listened to the constant background staccato of M-16's and AK-47's exchanging fire. Wisdom dictated a different response. However, his people were in trouble and he was a West Point trained Infantry Officer and a pilot. Maybe, he never said one way or the other, the knowledge that his round-ball partner and two crewmen were trapped on the ground also affected him.

After the new XO had taken in all the information from twenty-five-hundred feet in the air, the most astonishing thing in young Kev's whole military life took place. What happened in the cockpit of the Command and Control Huey was beyond his comprehension. Cynically, ole Kev thought that he understood how selfishly career officers acted in the war the government would not allow them to win. However, he discovered that he did not understand the slim young Captain at all. Kev's new friend, the Captain who could dribble a basketball equally well with his left or right hand, was made of much sterner stuff than that!

From his vantage point twenty-five-hundred feet in the air, a very special Ring Knocker shook his head and came to a surprising decision. Shocking his co-pilot speechless, he chose to disobey standing orders. An honorable man and natural leader, he chose to risk a courts martial and to risk the end of his own budding military career. Less surprising to Kev, he chose to risk his own life and limb for one of his own.

Rather than travel a safe career path, Kev's round-ball partner did both the extraordinary and the unexpected. Having come to a decision, the Captain promptly landed his own Command and Control Helicopter. Unconcerned about his personal safety, he placed his precious body in the center of the bullet infested LZ which was recently vacated by the troop-carrying Hueys. Upon landing and dismounting in true Cavalry-man's fashion. Without looking back, he grabbed his steel pot and his M-16. Leaving C&C to his copilot, the XO took decisive command of the ground troops in their rescue or recovery attempt.

"John, I'm going in with the Blues! You have flown lotsa C&C so you just became C&C. Get the crew Chief up here and work with White

Two-One. I'm sure that the two of you can run the show till I get One-five and his boys back."

With that, he dismounted.

While the Captain was making his decision to take charge on the ground, the situation at the crash site was improving. For the first time since they were dreamily enjoying their flight, life and their possibilities for tomorrow was beginning to look a little better for Kev and his crew. When the Blues landed, they had immediately drawn the attention of the bad guys who had previously been looking for the three young men. For the moment, none of the bad guys seemed to be close to Kev and crew. The bad guys had a good idea where Kev and crew were. However, the presence of the Blues on the ground, presenting a much greater threat, took over their attention. The three young men heaved a silent sigh of relieve.

With this break in the action and change of attention by the bad guys, Kev's emotional roller coaster continued its thrill ride. Feeling that his information could not wait, one of Kev's observers whispered additional bad news into his ear.

"Mr. J. when we were shot down, I fell into a hole and a gook was there. He had an AK and he was going to shoot me. Thank God . . . I beat him to the punch." Gathering his breath, he continued. "I shot him flush in the face with my forty-five."

Pausing for a moment, he then continued whispering his story into Kev's ear.

"Dear God, I hope that they don't find him till we're gone, boss. Not only did I kill him, he's a big time mess! I blew most of his face and head away!"

Gravely nodding his head, Kev now had another troubling thought which he did not need. Mumbling to himself, he played out another scenario.

"Now, if they capture us, we are in really deep trouble! The bad guys are not going to be very pleased with us! I'm sure that the dead guy's buddies are going to be looking for revenge. If I were one of them, I think, no I'm sure, that I'd feel that way."

With the observer's grim announcement, the three of them settled back to await their fate.

When he was a little guy, Kev discovered time does not always move at a uniform speed. He rediscovered that abstract change in the law or non-law of physics as Rocinante, in her death throes, slowly settled into the trees. Back when he was a little guy sitting in the dentist's chair, he noted that the sweep second-hand of the clock moved with agonizing slowness.

Huddled in a hole, the bad guys had reduced Kev to a scared little boy who had no control over what people might do to him. The situation was worse than sitting in the dentist's chair. Waiting for death or worse, he found that the sweep second hand of the clock was pausing for an eternity between each click. The slowed clock stood in sharp contrast with his rapidly pounding pulse.

During an infinite pause of the slowly sweeping marker of time, Kev looked carefully into the face of one of his observers. He was fascinated to note a bead of sweat begin to form on the young man's forehead. Like the three of them, the glistening bead of sweat seemed trapped in a static bubble of time. Somehow, the stopped clock suspended it between action and inaction. Finally, with infinite slowness, it began a slow trek down the observer's forehead. A clean mark showed the path it had slowly traveled down his forehead. Resting at the bottom of his forehead for a moment or two, it then slowly traveled down the bridge of his nose. At last, arriving at that pinnacle, it dangled itself precariously right at the tip of his nose.

Like Kev and his crew, the little pearl of perspiration was tenuously suspended between having an existence of its own and falling to the ground. If it fell to the ground, the hungry earth would absorb it and it would no longer live.

The bead's pantomime of his life fascinated Kev. Caught up in a life and death drama, he intensely stared at the glistening little bead of sweat. Existing for the moment, circumstance precariously suspended it between a life of its own and an absorption back into the absorbent earth. The power of the moment and drama of the little pearl of sweat strangely moved him as it reflected his own momentary existence.

Initially unaware of it, he began his first truly selfish prayer since he had been in Vietnam. Unashamed of his fear, he prayed.

"Dear God, if it come to it, please let them kill me and not capture me. Please give me enough courage to go down fighting rather than to meekly surrender."

His fearful prayer grew out of the knowledge that there was a substantial bounty on his head. A couple, maybe three months previous, Division Intelligence people had told him that the NVA had placed a five-thousand gold bounty on his head. Prior to watching the endless journey of the bead of sweat, he had repeatedly joked about the large bounty which had been placed upon his head. With a Scout pilot's black humor, he had thought it was funny and somehow demeaning that the claimant need not include the body with the head to receive the bounty.

Discovering that he himself was precariously balanced between life and death, his black joke had suddenly lost any semblance of humor! Always given to flights of fancy, He knew that ole Kev had become a timeless legend in his own very colorful imagination. However, he found it hard to believe that he had been effective enough, as a Red Bird, to merit such a large bounty. The young man knew that, on the larger scale of life, he was not worth that much. While waiting for the sweep second hand to make another click, he tried to imagine what five-thousand dollars' gold would mean to a poor Vietnamese peasant.

Young Kev quickly gave up his heavy intellectual quest. With a shake of his head, he regretfully decided that death was preferable. He knew that a quick death was better than the gentle mercies his fertile imagination had concocted, and were continuing to concoct for him, should the bad guys capture him.

Crouching fearfully blind in their little hole in the rocks and brush, they anxiously waited to see what their future might be, or if they were going to have a future. Three sets of anxious ears were carefully following the slow advance of the Blues. Listening to the flat crack of rifles and the sharp chattering of machine guns, they tried to follow the progress of the fighting. From the increasing volume, it seemed to be coming closer and closer to them. Somehow, they knew that the fighting would eventually decide their fate.

With their future still hanging in the immeasurable balance of blind luck, the three little boys watched the sweep second hand of the clock eventually begin to speed up. Listening carefully, they became convinced that their own troops were steadily advancing toward them. The sound of rifles and machine guns filled the air with the sharp barking of human death and bodily destruction. Yet, as the weapons of war barked and bayed their death and destruction, the three young men also heard, within them, the bells of their freedom loudly peeling.

That blessed saving event, suddenly and almost unexpectedly occurred. They had alternately prayed for, despaired about, hoped for, and given up all hope as they crouched fearfully. With a soft movement of the brush about fifteen feet away from them, the bright sun of a new day's dawning warmed their chilled souls.

As they watched, an American soldier slowly and very very cautiously came into view. This brave trooper was walking the "point." As Kev continued to cower in his hole, he slowly shook his head. The courageous example of the man walking the point deeply moved the scared pilot. It was common knowledge, even to pilots, that the man walking the point, takes on the most exposed and dangerous position on the ground. He saw walking the "point" as true leadership in action. Gravely shaking his head, he could not imagine ever walking the point himself. The thought of walking the point caused him to mutter to himself.

"I don't have that brand of courage."

Uncomfortably accepting his forced role as a passive observer, Kev was watching the man as he slowly and cautiously emerged from the bush. Suddenly, he realized that something was strangely familiar about the point man's face.

362

"I don't understand. I don't know any of the blues well enough to recognize an individual face at that distance."

Nevertheless, he did recognize the face of the point man as he emerged. Kev could not believe what his eyes were showing him. He was completely convinced that the visual message his brain was receiving was not possible. The man his eyes saw was supposed to be somewhere else. Muttering quietly to himself, he said.

"NO way, Jose!"

Nevertheless, his befuddled brain insisted that his eyes were feasting upon the face of the Captain! Shocked and speechless, he found himself looking directly at, none other than, his old round-ball partner.

The sight of the Captain's familiar and friendly face emotionally overwhelmed him. It was the last face in the world that he expected to see coming out of the bush!

An enlisted man "always" walked the point. Furthermore, the Captain was supposed to be in the C&C bird! Yes, the friendly face of one of the enlisted grunts would have caused him to jump for joy. However, he was not, in the least bit, prepared for the Captain's face. Like most young men his age, Kev had falsely prided himself on being a full-grown and completely matured man. He had worked hard to get where he was as a military pilot, Warrant Officer, and Gentleman. Yet, when he recognized the friendly face of his old round-ball partner, the little boy within broke the tenuous grip of the would-be adult.

Staring at the deeply concerned face of his old round-ball partner, The unexpected sight abruptly turned Kev's self-ordained world order upside down. In the passing of a brief instant, all his presuppositions and prejudices about life, the Army, and Commissioned Officers were dashed upon the ragged rocks of reality. Overloaded, his emotional dam burst. Bewildered by what he did not understand he stood quietly.

The Captain looked on as the young pilot slowly stood with a flood of tears running down his cheeks like those of a lost little child. Overwhelmed by the moment, Kev felt like he was a little lost three-year-old at the shopping mall. For Kev, it was like his mother and father had suddenly rescued him. At last, he was freed from the trepidation of the smothering presence of countless strangers. The little boy was no longer in the grasp of an indifferent crowd. Scared little Kev's mommy and daddy had come to save him and he cried in joy!

Kev was feeling so excited, relieved, and hopeful that he again found himself, once again, at the point of total emotional overload. Taking a deep breath, he knew that he had to discipline himself. And, he knew that he had to do it quickly. Calming himself, the young man quickly reminded himself that they were hardly out of the woods. Yet . . .

"Yes . . . ! Yes . . . !"

He joyfully screamed, as loud as he could, that simple word repeatedly within the private confines of his head. Emotional discipline or not, things were definitely looking a whole big bunch better than they had for the proceeding couple of hours!

Cautiously, Kev knelt down and carefully looked about to see where the bad guys had gone. Feeling that it was momentarily safe, he quickly scrambled the rest of the way out of his concealment. Barely containing himself, he half ran and half scrambled toward the Captain His excitement was so overwhelming that he wanted to hug and kiss the man. He wanted to laugh and cry. He wanted to emotionally explode with joy.

Yet, he was torn between the two extremes of the moment. Part of him was a lost little boy who had just been saved. However, the other part was as the only other officer on the ground. Emotionally gathering himself and barely containing his excitement, Kev softly reported to the Captain. It only took a moment for Kev to bring the Captain up to date. Like any good commander, the Captain's first concern and question was about the welfare of Kev's observers.

"How are you and your guys, Kev?"

"Well Sir, we're a little bit banged up and scared as heck. I'm afraid that my observers will not be able to walk out and we'll probably need to call Dust Off. They both have strained or dislocated knees. But, now we are going to be OK!"

With his first concern satisfied, he then told Kev to stay put.

Mindful of the danger which surrounded them, the Captain quickly set up a defensive perimeter. He used the Blues who had followed him in the rescue attempt. After a couple minutes of quick and quiet orders, he was satisfied with the perimeter which the Blues had established. When he was finally satisfied, he gave Kev responsibility for the Air Evacuation of his observers. The Captain agreed with Kev that with their banged up and possibly dislocated knees, Kev's crewmen could not walk back to the LZ. It was more than four hundred meters to the LZ the Blues had landed in!

"Kev, call C&C and tell them to send in Dust Off for your crew."

Prompt, as always, Dust-Off arrived within ten minutes. Like all of its sister heli-born ambulances, it was unarmed and sporting big bright red crosses proclaiming its mission of mercy. With the RTO, Radio Telephone Operator/Radioman, crouched down at his side, Kev felt useful again. Speaking to the pilot, he began to guide Dust-Off Three-Three into position for the evacuation.

Poor Ole Rocinante had met her abrupt end broken, smoking, and scattered over the side of a very steep hill. Choosing to be unfriendly, Mother Nature had capriciously covered the hillside with huge boulders and tall trees. Kev did not have to survey the lay of the land. Having seen it before he crashed, he already knew that the Dust-Off helicopter could not land at such a rough site. Therefore, it was going to be a tough extraction. Because of this, the medical rescue helicopter would be forced to hover about one hundred feet off the ground. Once Dust-Off was in a stable hover, he would have to use a jungle penetrator to pick up the crew chief and observer. It would take two trips with the penetrator to recover them, one man at a time.

"Dust-Off Three-Three you are going to have use the winch to lift my two observers who cannot walk. They are not wounded or in immediate need of medical attention. However, they are hurt from the crash and cannot walk."

Dust-Off's problems with the extraction gave Kev much to be concerned about. However, While Kev was waiting for Dust-Off to arrive overhead, he had a growing, gnawing, and very uneasy feeling about things. When the Blues had found the three young men, all contact, that is combat, shooting, fighting, and that sort of thing, with the NVA had abruptly ceased. As far as Kev was concerned, his world had become unnaturally calm. It felt like he was temporarily safe in the eye of the hurricane.

However, if that were true, Kev knew that they would have to survive the backside of the hurricane. The backside, he knew, was the worst part of the storm.

"Dust-Off Three-Three, your Pick Up Zone is currently cold. Be advised . . . I'd be ready for a warm reception. We already have one Loach down and a couple of our slicks have been shot up. I fear that the bad guys are holding back and waiting for you."

Try as he might, Kev could not control his active and sometimes overly vivid imagination. He became increasingly concerned as he silently wondered what the bad guys were up to. The silence did not follow the events of the day. All day long they had held the upper hand. Looking about, Kev saw no reason for them, at this stage of the game, to crawl away with their tails between their legs.

"Most likely," Kev thought, "things are going to get terribly busy sometime soon. I may not like it. However, I am still afraid that my crew and I remain the bait in the helicopter trap. How strange, suddenly the three of us are no different from the blond kid lying on the rocks. Except, for the moment, we're still breathing."

The Captain and the Blues had formed a solid defensive perimeter offering Kev a little peace of mind. He was happy that they were protecting, ole Kev, crew, and extraction site. Wisely they had all "gone to ground" out of Kev's sight. Muttering to himself in concern, Kev gave voice to his fears over the Captain and grunts.

"Hopefully, they are all well hidden from the NVA."

Kev's own position was different.

Much to his personal dismay, he and the RTO were forced to remain fully visible so that they could direct Dust Off's rescue attempt. The still of the moment found the two of them lying flat upon the surface a large rock. Their position exposed the two young men to every prying eyeball in the area. However, as best Kev could tell, this was the only way that they could see and direct Dust Off in the upcoming rescue attempt. Not wishing to feed his growing anxieties, Kev gave no voice to his concern about his own safety and told his, always colorful, imagination to stay put. For once, his imagination followed orders.

After all that they had been through, the absence of the constant hammering of rifles and machine guns created a strange and foreboding silence. Flying into this stillness of shooting, Dust Off Three-Three came to a completely stationary hover about 100 feet directly over their heads. It was a strange sight to be looking up at the exposed oil-streaked underbelly of the big Huey. As Kev looked up he was surprised, but not surprised, by the bravery of the crew.

The pilots, while wrapped in armored seats sat exposed and vulnerable. Lying on his belly with his head and shoulders exposed was the medic as he controlled the jungle peretrator. Like a good observer, the crew chief was standing on the opposite skid to help balance the weight when the hoist started to lift the wounded. Shaking his head, Kev marveled at their "coolness."

As Dust Off stabilized, the medic immediately lowered the jungle penetrator. Collectively holding their breath, everyone feared that this strange tranquil hush was only the temporary. No one dared to believe that the absence of the weapons of war speaking their harsh tones was going to last. In turn, it was anything but quiet directly under a hovering Huey. Lying upon the exposed rock, Kev and the RTO found themselves engulfed in a deafening tumult of wind, dust, flying trash, and screaming mechanical noise.

After what was a forever wait, the jungle penetrator touched the rocks. Gratefully accepting the respite from enemy fire, Kev's observer quickly lowered the seat on the penetrator and strapped in the crewchief. Feeling as if Dust Off had lifted the weight of the world from his shoulders, Kev keyed the microphone and sent his first happy message in two hours.

"Dust-Off Three-Three, you have got the first fish on your hook. Haul away!"

With that simple command, the medic started the winch. Lying on their backs, Kev and the RTO were looking up at the bloated, oil streaked, belly of the Medivac helicopter. With silent prayer on their lips, they watched the injured crewchief twirling round about in the rotor down-wash during his ascent up the long metallic lifeline. Kev also knew that the Medic had a "cut-off switch" that he could cut the cable if they got in bad trouble.

"Dear God," he prayed. "Don't make the medic use it to save the crew and craft."

Despite the fact the evacuation was going well, Kev's disquieted internal warning system continued to send him strident messages. As usual, it had been correct in its warnings!

Without a preamble, a full scale fusillade of automatic weapons shouted out with revenge. The Cav was stealing the bait from the bad guys. The hammering AK-47's abruptly terminated the strange, foreboding, stillness and silence which the Cav had been enjoying. At the sound of the weapons, Kev cried out in rage, frustration, and despair that it wasn't fair. He knew that his words were wasted. Yet, he felt that he had earned the right to bitterly complain.

"D-----, we can't harm anyone. Look at us. Take a good look. We're out of the game and heading for the training room to get our wounds bandaged up. Furthermore, we will obviously not be returning to today's game. You won this time. Leave us alone!"

The situation was playing out just as Kev had feared. Like the dead blond kid sprawled out on the rocks, Red One-Five and his crew had become the bait for an even larger trap. First, they were the bait to try and trap and destroy a rescue team. Now, we were the bait to try and shoot down the unarmed Medivac helicopter. As was becoming the unacceptable norm for Kev, the events of the day were moving much faster than he felt comfortable handling.

With the sudden explosion of ground fire from farther up the hill, the smooth teamwork of the moment came under severe stress. Kev was powerless and the rescue attempt was in immediate danger of falling apart. For a brief part of a moment, Kev froze in deadly cold fear. He was naked, exposed, and completely vulnerable on the big rock. Unexpectedly, the heavy gunfire showered Kev and the RTO with bits and pieces of plexiglass. This rain of parts constituted the remains of Dust Off Three-Three's exploding windshield.

The unfriendly rain of helicopter bits and pieces reminded Kev that he wasn't the target, only the trap's bait. He wasn't sure how to feel about that! Part of him rejoiced at not being the target. Another part of him despaired at being the bate drawing Dust Off Three-Three into the trap. Looking up through the shower of plexiglass, they saw a dozen more holes magically appear in the metal skin of Dust Off Three-Three. The bad guys centered most of the holes in the big Red Crosses. This was not an isolated incident. Several Dust-Off pilots had repeatedly told Kev that the NVA liked using the bright red as their aiming point.

"Well . . ., so much for the Gevena Convention." Kev bitterly thought to himself.

When his windshield exploded, it was only inches from his face. As a result, the explosion showered the pilot in a rainbow colored spray of sparkling shards of plexiglass. Understandably, the pilot of Dust-Off Three-Three reflexively jerked at the flight controls. However, just as quickly, the pilot showed just what kind of a man he was. Apparently equipped with nerves carefully constructed out of the purest carbon steel, he immediately stabilized his hover. From Kev's point of view, it appeared that the iron-nerved Dust Off pilot acted as if nothing out of the ordinary had happened.

Angry and not waiting to be told to do so, the Blues immediately responded in kind with a torrent of M-16, M-60, and M-79 fire. In the midst of this chaos, the Medivac crewchief and the medic quickly dragged Kev's crewchief safely into the helicopter. The calmness of the crew of Dust Off Three-Three made it appear as if it were a normal training exercise at Ft. Rucker or Ft. Sam Houston in Texas. With the Dust-Off crew seeming unconcerned with all the gunfire, the medic lowered the jungle penetrator to pick up Kev's observer.

A few days later Kev wrote a brutally honest account of the encounter in his journal.

Would that I could spin a wondrous tale of heroic valor about myself. Oh I wish that I could lie convincingly about my strength of character and abundant courage. If so, I would stand up and proclaim to all who would listen of my righteous response. This unprincipled incident of firing upon the unarmed Medivac plastered with large Red Crosses was the final straw, and I would take no more. Continuing, I would dramatically proclaim that I was fighting mad and filled with a Holy rage. Having made my proclamation, I would artfully tell my listener how I sprang into decisive, life saving, action! Would that I could make such heroic statements about myself. In contrast to that wished for dramatic picture of myself, sadly the truth about Kevin is quite different. I felt panic-like surges of fear, a death-like despair, and endless waves of hopelessness flow through me.

I silently cried out and berated myself mercilessly.

"Oh God, now what had I gotten everybody into? How many people are going to have to die because of me?"

In desperate fear for my crew and Dust Off Three-Three, I grabbed the radio handset from the RTO. Mashing down on the transmitter button, I called up to White Two-One the lead Snake. Almost reduced to tears, I cried, screamed, and sobbed into the radio.

"Roll in one-hundred and fifty meters up the hill from us! Nail the SOB's!"

It is hard to believe that White Two-One could understand me. I was neither calm nor was I rational. Rather, I was filled with a berserker's rage.

When I said "nail the SOB's," **I meant it!** I wanted both flechette and high explosive rockets to kill every living thing up the hill from us! My only interest was to kill. The last layer of civilization had become a casualty to my fear and rage. Seeing the muzzle flashes, I had pretty much pinpointed where the enemy fire was coming from. Best of all, I knew that we had no friendlies that far up the hill. In almost the same breath, as we were all on the same radio frequency, I called Dust Off Three-Three.

"Dust Off Three-Three break outa here. Please stand by till my Snakes fix those SOB's . I call you when things cool down. We can wait this out if you can."

While renewed enemy fire was exploding onto the scene, Kev and the RTO remained nakedly exposed upon the large rocks. Afraid to move and draw unwanted attention upon themselves, they continued lying upon their backs. Angry and concerned for the safety of the Medivac ship, they carefully directed the fire support from the Snakes. Looking up, a sight that very few Army Pilots have ever seen warmly greeted Kev's eyes.

From his new perspective on close air support, the vision before his eyes was strangely elegant and beautiful in its purposeful deadliness. Almost gleefully, he called for repeated gun runs by his friends in the Snakes. Creeping upon him with silent and unseen paws, something new was happening to Kev. He began to have some of the feelings of fear that this sight must have generated in hearts of the Viet Cong and the NVA. Never before had he been afraid of a friendly aircraft. However, in the confusion of the moment, his target's view of an avenging Snake froze his blood.

As the two stiletto-slim silhouettes, with only thirty-six inches of body width, began their diving attack, the sight of plunging death moved Kev with awe. His mouth slowly fell silently open. Slack-jawed, he discovered a new respect for the friendly and ever-present Snakes. Ever-present and underappreciated, these were his friends who had covered him on every combat mission he had flown. The Cav's flying rapiers, burdened with deadly ordinance hanging off their stub wings were presenting him with a startling view. The frightful and "business-end" sight of an avenging Snake was something that he had never expected to witness. It was like looking up at the downward sweep of an avenger's sword with death and destruction aimed for his head.

Just before the Snakes began firing their rockets for their first gun run, White Two-One called to Kev.

"One-Five, you guys had better dig a really deep hole. It's going to get very unhealthy for all the bad guys in your neighborhood. On our first pass, we are going to fill the area just above you with all the nails we've got."

Kev knew exactly what the gun pilot was talking about. He should know. He had begged and screamed for it. Each flechette rocket contained thousands of little arrows like flechette darts. When the warhead exploded, about halfway to the target, the explosion dispersed the flechettes over a wide area. When the rockets worked as advertised, they killed anyone unlucky enough not to be under cover. Understandably, Kev found himself disquieted by the gruesome thought of also being nailed by hundreds of those little darts.

The Snake driver had carefully warned him on the radio. For months he had been part of the Cav team. Yet, when the firing of the rockets actually happened, it startled him. With an explosive crack, the first pair of rockets left the stub wings of the snake. Following their rapidly accelerating path, the dramatic sight enthralled him. Their thin trail of exhaust smoke made it easy for the Kev and the RTO to keep track of the rockets.

Abruptly, a second explosive retort surprised Kev. It was a loud retort which he had not expected. He had never stopped to think about the retort of the warhead when it released the flechettes. The second explosive crack, marked by a puff of red marking smoke, was the explosion of the warhead. This second explosive report also marked the release of the deadly blizzard of sharp flechettes. Both loud retorts sharply punctuated the Cav's quest for vengeance for the shooting at, and the shooting up of, the unarmed medical evacuation helicopter. The Snakes were determined to fix the bad guys, Cav style, while Kev silently cheered.

Kev continued his brutal self-description and self-depreciation in his journal.

As before, the picture I would like to paint for my reader is of ole Kev standing boldly upon his large rock. Of course, he is standing defiantly in full view of everyone. Kevin Paul Johnson is the man who is setting the example of bravery. Standing proudly, his radio hand set would be at his mouth showing that he was fully in control of himself and the situation. Being the man in charge, all the Blues and the NVA would witness him calling the Snakes to the rescue.

If I had my druthers, he would look something like a young Eril Flynn. The fearless man standing upon the exposed rock would be strikingly handsome, suave, and brave. Grandly, he would be waving his shiny silver sword over his head. Possibly, I would want him to be astride his magnificent black stallion. All would see him at the front of the troops leading the Cavalry charge against the godless hoard that threatened all that was decent and good about humanity. Well . . . once again, Ole Kev has discovered that reality looked a little bit different than the artificial glories of the silver screen.

The true picture that must be carefully painted of ole Kev that exciting afternoon looks far different than my vivid imagination would have liked. While looking directly at the slim business end of the first diving snake, I heard the flat crack of the first pair of rockets as they fired them. With the sharp sound of that retort, I suddenly felt like I had my head stuck directly into the maw of the world's largest canon! As distasteful as the admission is, it terrified me to be looking at the business end of a Snake!

I might add. It was a Snake that meant business. Without a single conscious thought of what I was doing, I acted like the craven coward I had suddenly become. Reaching into an adrenalin boosted reserve of strength, I bodily lifted up the RTO and his radio. In my wordless fear, he felt as if he were weightless. Then, being only concerned with my safety, I placed him squarely on top of myself as the two of us lay upon our exposed rock.

Apparently, somewhere deep inside me, I came to a coward's logical decision. If one of those flechettes, or an NVA bullet, were to get me, it would have to penetrate the RTO and then his radio. It was from that, selfishly created, protected position that I directed the remaining gun runs of the diving Snakes. Later that day, suddenly the uncomfortable reality of what I had done to the poor RTO struck me like a ton of bricks. Truthfully, while the Snakes were making their gun runs, I was not aware of what I had done! With the Snakes diving and shooting, ole Kev was too terrorized to think clearly. Eating a large helping of tough old crow, I quickly and humbly apologized to the RTO. He laughed and said to me.

"Next time, Sir, I get the bottom of the pile, and you get the top."

Mind you, I don't want a next time, but the RTO's solution seems fair enough to me.

When the Snakes were finished with their gun runs, until the bad guys were to fire again, Kev called Dust Off Three-Three. Since the bad guys had quieted down, Kev asked him if he would be willing to come back in and pick up the rest of his cargo.

"No problem, One-Five. That's what good ole Uncle Sam pays me to do. Nevertheless, this one is going to cost you an awful lot of cold beer and a good rare steak one of these days when I catch you at the club."

Curiosity was killing poor Kev. Within seconds, it got the best of him and he asked Three-Three how he had faired when the NVA opened fire on him. His response was in the finest traditions of Army Aviation.

"I am almost afraid to check One-Five. However, given the putrid odorifious emanations drifting up from my seat, I'm pretty darn sure that I REALLY messed my britches when the windshield disappeared."

Following his descriptive comment to Kev, Dust Off Three-Three quickly and carefully maneuvered back into his position directly above them. Acting as if he didn't have a care in the world, the medic quickly and efficiently winched out the observer without incident. As Kev was watching his observer ride the metallic lifeline to safety, he thought about the pilot of Dust Off Three-Three. Without realizing that he was speaking aloud, the RTO later told Kev what he had said while looking up at the big Medivac ship.

371

"After what just happened to him, this man had either nerves of steel, or he is a bleeding fool. Shoot, we ought to make him an honorary Scout."

Some things about himself will always remain beyond Kev's understanding. His many unrequested forays into the surreal world of his fertile imagination are among those things. To the background music of the flat crack of rockets igniting and ripping sound of mini-guns firing, he found his overwrought mind drifting. The young man was again traveling to the mystic land of his over-active imagination. Closing his eyes, he tried to place himself in Dust Off Three-Three's seat. He quickly gave up. For all his experience, he could not place himself in that pilot's seat. Kev decided that he admired him. However, he doubted that he could emulate him.

Thinking for a moment, try as he might, he couldn't envision himself playing target and not being able to shoot back. Shaking his head in disbelief, he sighed deeply. However, he silently admitted that he had found himself in some strange places while flying his Red Bird. Yes, there was the time that he and Johnny went down into the hole to provide both protection and support for the Pioneer troops. However, they did their share of shooting that day and had expended all their ammunition. The closest thing he could remember was the time he stripped all his armorments and extracted that LRRP team. Even then, he didn't have to hold a hover while under fire.

Unable to get a handle on things, he tried to imagine what it would be like to see his front windshield explode before his eyes. He'd seen bullet holes appear. Yet, that wasn't the same. It didn't have the same shock value. Then, he tried to imagine remaining where he was as a big fat stationary target. Try as he might, he couldn't do that either. Regretfully, Kev admitted his own limitations within the privacy of his head.

"I might be the world's greatest romantic hero in my own fertile, colorful, and free-running imagination. However, the painful fact is that I can't hold a flickering candle to Dust-Off Three-Three in the guts department."

From an emotional distance, the RTO's radio crackle broke into Kev's private musings.

"One-Five, are you ready to come up?"

It took him far less than half an instant to respond to the invitation for a ride.

"No way Jose! This ole boy is going to walk out with the Blues. Thanks anyway."

Feeling like he owed Three-Three an explanation, Kev continued.

"I've been playing big fat juicy target far too often today. I do not plan on ending my day or my career dangling on the end of a rope. You

372

get my boys to the hospital and I'll owe you a tall cold one, or three, and the biggest, rarest steak this side of Nebraska."

Overall, it had been a strange and humbling day of discovery for Kev. At last, he was well aware that he was human and capable of paralyzing fear. The thing that he was most afraid of had almost beat him. Not by choice, he had met fear face to face. Yet, he knew that it was his friend the Captain, coming off the bench, who had made the difference. However, the recent terror he had experienced had deeply rattled him. Previously, he had told people that a trip up a jungle penetrator might have been fun. Looking back, a few days later, he realized that he had been more afraid of falling off the jungle penetrator than being shot at on the way up.

Wanting to salvage a little of his pride, he never told anyone that nasty little secret. He was a pilot at heart and was most comfortable when strapped into his beloved little Red Bird. However, he was deathly afraid of heights in any shape or form if he wasn't strapped into his little bird. While he was watching the jungle penetrator ascend, he had a painful memory. His frightful memory came complete with the sweats and shakes. He clearly remembered his instance of blind, mind-numbing, terror atop a twenty-foot ladder while helping his dad paint the house.

When Kev refused the gracious offer of a ride from the Medivac helicopter, it dipped its nose and quickly scooted away with its precious cargo. For Dust Off, it was all in a days work and Kev couldn't believe what he had just witnessed.

With the heavy beat of its rotors fading, the surrounding countryside became deathly quiet. One point for the good guys! The easy target had clearly escaped with most of the bait. Taking advantage of the lull in enemy activity, the Captain quickly organized the Blue platoon for their withdrawal. Using hand signals only, they began their withdrawal back down the hill. Carefully and cautiously the troopers began picking their way down the hill to the original LZ. While enroute, the Captain came up to Kev and gave the young pilot his instructions.

"Now that you have gotten Dust-Off on his way, I want you to stay in the middle of the pack. These boys are professionals. Do as they say, and they will get you safely down the hill and headed back home. However, if you try to do anything other than what they tell you to do, you will only become an unneeded liability."

He continued with a silly grin.

"If you do that, I'll probably have to shoot you to protect the troops."

Well aware that he was a gross liability on the ground, Kev willingly did exactly what his old round-ball buddy asked him to do.

"After all," he thought to himself, "the Captain is right about one thing. I've been nothing but a liability all day."

Liability or not, Kev found that it was a wonderful experience being protected by and escorted by the Blues. Adding the frosting to Kev's cake, upon approaching the LZ, the Captain had requested a transport Huey just for him. He was thrilled that Uncle Sam was providing a quarter of a million-dollar helicopter just for his safety! The troops that would have gone in that aircraft were going to go out with the Captain in his C&C helicopter.

When everyone arrived at the edge of the LZ, the Blues, as always efficient and cautious, carefully secured the LZ. That is, they set up a defensive perimeter around it to assure the safety of the landing helicopters. Keeping their backs to the LZ, they were prepared for trouble. When the first helicopter landed in the LZ, it was Kev's personal taxi. Before the dust had begun to settle, the Captain gently patted him on the back and sent him on his way.

"There's your taxi Kev."

With the way Kev's day had been going, dignity was not his most pressing issue.

Given the reality of his eventful day, ole Kev did not leisurely walk out to the helicopter and calmly climb into his personal taxi. Being sorely tired of being a scared sitting duck target all day, ole Kev threw his carefully crafted stoic warrior dignity to the wind. For understandable reasons, Kev felt that the day was not over until he fell asleep in his bunk. After all that had happened, he greatly feared that the NVA might still be waiting to take another crack at him. The little boy in him wanted to return home safe and sound!

No one in the LZ had a stop watch. With a laugh, some of the Blues said that it was a crying shame. Therefore, no one will ever know the absolute numbers. However, Kev deeply impressed those who witnessed the sprint. They were convinced that Kev set a record with his twenty-five-foot sprint from the tree line to the helicopter. Capping off his totally undignified retreat from the field of battle, Kev dove head first into the cargo compartment of the helicopter. The crew-chief later said that he dove in with such force that he almost slid out the other door and would have if he hadn't grabbed him as Kev slid along the floor.

As the Huey, with its characteristic thumping sound, made its graceful, yet ponderous, way out of the LZ, Kev clambered up to the cockpit area. Immediately, upon his arrival in the helicopter's main office, he planted big kisses on the flight helmets of his good friends, the two pilots. Kev later told Sven.

"Had I been able to, I would have done more. I am sure that I would have planted great big wet sloppy kisses smack dab on their lips!"

Then, with the renewed dignity of one who has just discovered that he is indeed a very wealthy man he made a small request of the command pilot.

"Home James."

Much to his surprise, his government issue, olive drab taxi did not take him directly home. Unknown to Kev, the Captain had ordered the pilots to take the shaken young pilot to the field hospital for examination and overnight observation. It didn't seem necessary to Kev for he was neither broken nor bleeding.

"Maybe," he thought, shrugging his shoulders, "I looked much worse than I felt?"

The Captain had his own motivations and the authority of rank. Therefore, ole Kev didn't have anything to say about where his military issue body was going. He was along strictly for the ride as olive drab cargo.

As the thumping Huey made its approach to the landing pad of the aid station, old, yet fresh, memories suddenly saddened Kev. The exuberance of his recent adventures and rescue had a somber damper placed upon them. Looking at that landing pad reminded him that this aid station was the last place that he had seen his old friend Johnny.

Feeling much older than his chronological clock said he was, Kev had forgotten that war is a young man's game. Like himself and most of his friends, the vast majority of the medical people in Vietnam were all very young. As the doctor was examining him, Kev looked closely at his face. The face that looked back at him was not like the face of his old family Doc back home. To Kev's young eyes, his family Doc has been around for roughly a million years. Those years showed in a deeply-lined face which had years and years of human and medical experience artfully etched onto it.

The Doc before Kev's face looked so young that ole Kev began to wonder if the Doc who was examining him had begun to shave yet. Yet, he had no complaints about his competence. When the Doc walked into the examining area, Kev immediately recognized him as the Doc who had kept Johnny alive. As far as Kev could tell, he was doing a good job on him. In the end, the young Doc proclaimed that Kev seemed fit, except some minor bumps, bruises, and burns. When he left, the enlisted medics treated these. and they put him to bed in a ward.

Arriving at the ward, the soothing sight that greeted him pleased Kev. Thankfully, the strange God's of Aviation and War had finally smiled upon him. He had fresh clean sheets to sleep on in a wonderfully air-conditioned hospital ward.

"Shoot," he said to himself. "This is a far sight better than the smelly sweat soaked bunk in my hooch. I think that I'll just lean back and enjoy the ride."

Thankfully, combat speaking, it had been a quiet day in his little part of the world. All of the beds in the ward were empty and he was the sole occupant. Keeping with his new status as a patient, he had lots of people taking care of him. Two enlisted orderlies were assigned to the ward and Kev was their lone patient.

Yet, try as he might, the wound-up young man was having trouble going to sleep. This sleeplessness surprised him, as his recent adventures had completely exhausted him. What he didn't realize or understand was that he was still operating on several buckets-full of adrenalin. For the better part of an hour, he tossed and he turned. In frustration, he reached over to the bed beside his and grabbed its pillow for himself.

Lying on his side and wrapping his arms around it, he began to slowly drift off to sleep. Hearing the orderlies whispering to each other, Kev cracked open one eyelid. When his eye focused, he saw them chuckling and pointing out that he was cuddling the second pillow. After the tumult of the day he slowly sighed. The little boy continued to cuddle his purloined pillow like a teddy bear or a security blanket. Relaxing his baby face, young Kev drifted off to sleep. The snickering thoughts, of the orderlies, didn't matter to him in the least. He was safe. At the moment, for Kevin Paul Johnson, being safe was all that mattered.

It was a day later when they released Kev from observation at the field hospital. Much to his surprise, the Army did not park his personal taxi outside. Anxious to return, he walked over to the heliport as he tried to figure out how to get home. Eventually, he managed to hitch a ride back to his Cav Troop in a passing Huey. Hopping into the cargo compartment, a gruesome reminder of Army life in Vietnam greeted Kev.

The cargo bay was loaded with several body bags containing young soldiers killed in battle. He had not planned to keep the company of the recent dead. However, this flight was his only way home, so he carefully strapped into a seat. Sitting uncomfortably, Kev did his very best not to rest his feet on the body bags. Unplanned, the short flight, became a very long flight of thinking, pondering, and reflecting on his own mortality. Looking down upon the olive-drab body bags which were exactly like the one which he had placed TK's remains in, was an unsettling experience. That sight was a grim reminder, to the young man who had been shot down the previous day.

After making two bus transfers, on the Army's ever-present Huey bus line, Kev finally arrived back at home base. Upon his arrival, Kev was a man with a mission. Without waiting to pass "GO," and without waiting to collect his two-hundred dollars, he marched straight forward into the Captain's office. Kev was going to have his say and nothing was going to stop him.

The grim faced, determined young man was a sight. He hadn't changed his flight suit since he had been shot down. All that he had done was clean up the first layer of soot and dirt at the aid station. His flight suit was muddy, torn and smelled of fire and death. His boots looked like he had walked through five hundred feed lots full of mud and sticky cow droppings. His hair was wild and dirty and he had lost his cap to the fire. Kev didn't know how he looked. However, he knew how he felt.

Any resemblance between a solidly stoic John Wayne type character, and Kev was strictly accidental. The young man's emotional damn broke when he entered the Captain's office. A very grateful, to be alive, Kev immediately began babbling foolishly. Some might say that he was babbling almost childishly! Whatever the case might have been, he was carrying on and on. The Captain understood that Kev needed to try to express his admiration of the Captain's leadership and for saving his life. Nevertheless, much of what Kev said made little sense.

He was attempting to express all his jumbled up emotional overloads with jumbled together words. How could he tell of believing himself to be dead and unexpectedly finding himself resurrected? Eventually, he was forced to pause for breath. When he had caught his wind, Kev asked the Captain why he had disobeyed standing orders and left the Command and Control helicopter. Kev asked specifically why he had left Command and Control to rescue him. He also asked why he had left his aircraft with only one pilot.

The whole time Kev was babbling on and on at the Captain, he saw no reason to mention the Captain's risking a courts martial. Nor, did he mention the risk to his own life and limb. In Kev's highly emotional understanding of the conversation, both simply assumed that part in the general flow of conversation. When Kev finally wound down, the Captain's response was a surprisingly simple statement as was his custom.

"At the moment, it seemed the right thing to do!"

Pausing himself, but not long enough for Kev to begin babbling again, the Captain continued.

"Anyway," he added, with his delightfully boyish grin, "who would I play round-ball with if I did not come and bring you back."

Embarrassed, and needing to lighten up the whole conversation, he spoke again.

"Now if I remember correctly from the last time we played, I am up on you five games to three."

Kev wrote about his emotional day and the Captain extensively in his journal.

Sitting back with a pen in hand, I do a lot thinking about my life in the Red Birds. However, I keep that deep part of me carefully hidden.

377

I am coming to believe, despite my best efforts not to, that I have matured during these past months of combat.

Well, maybe I need to back track a little bit. I did use that poor RTO as cover when the Snakes were making their run with the nails. I guess that I might be maturing a bit. However, I still have my childish moments. Hopefully, they just don't happen as often.

Somewhat to my surprise, I have discovered that something very meaningful is happening here. It concerns the Captain and how he responded to my distress and near demise. Whatever it is I am talking about, it should not be limited to the fact that he saved my life. What I am discovering is so important that Hollywood and the publishers of popular literature should take careful note. They should share it with future generations so that they are better prepared than I was for the task of leadership.

Unlike so many of us taking part in the war, the Captain marches to a far superior drummer. Self-aggrandizement is not a part of his make up. He is both quiet and intense. Unlike popular heros, boasting and heroic speeches do not pass his lips. This gentle quiet man, who was and is, at least my secular understanding, "Poor in Spirit," could not be picked out of a crowd. I would have never guessed that one who was so very unassuming, contained the things of courage and true and honest heros! Maybe, it can only be seen by those of us who were there, who have experienced his internal power. Maybe, only those who have served under him could possibly begin to understand what it means to be a true leader. In a outlandish way, I am glad I was shot down that day. Without that day, I fear I lacked the wisdom to ever recognize him for whom he was. I can only pray that sometime in the future God will help me craft myself into a reflection of his courage.

Over the last few months I have struggled with my writing. In turn, I have come to believe that if you are going to try and write, you also have to be a wee little bit of a people watcher. For what it may be worth, from that point on, I have made it my business to carefully observe my friend, the Captain. Interestingly, I have seen something I greatly admire. My Captain would be one to go to Chapel any time that it was possible. Without show, or even notice, you would frequently find him sitting alone with his quiet reverence. I am beginning to wonder? Is it possible that when he is in Chapel communing his God, he finds his quiet confidence? Is that the quiet place where he finds his humility, and his loyalty to his troops? Personally, I have become convinced that it is so!

378

BATTALION COMMANDER?

War makes for strange happenings and stranger bed-fellows. The young man was only twenty years old. Yet, Kevin Paul Johnson was at the absolute top of his chosen craft. Good ole Red One-Five was unarguably the best scout in the troop, maybe in the squadron. To be sure, he continued to make his share of bone-head mistakes. Upon occasion, he convinced himself that he made total and complete use of someone else's allotment of stupid errors. He did this, of course, in addition to using his own generous allotment. However, in the end, no one knew their area of operations and the tricks of the trade any better than he did.

Well . . . , that is what Kev would have liked to have eloquently written about himself if someone asked him to do so. Not completely unjustified, Kev honestly believed that he was very good at what he did. Everyone who worked with him told him that he was the very best that they had ever seen. Like any normal young man, he desired to believe what they said. Occasionally, if he had a few beers in his belly, he might confidently suggest that he was the best Scout pilot in Vietnam. That was one of the reasons he stayed beyond his normal tour of duty. Better, he thought, that he did the job than someone who was not as skilled. However, by this time, he was not as concerned with the progress of the war as with someone inexperienced getting needlessly killed. This might not have been proper military or political thinking. However, it was how he felt.

Much to his discomfort, even after TK's death, the Major continued to require him to take on the unit's new wingmen and show them the ropes. Every time that a new wingman was assigned to him, he argued passionately with his platoon commander, Red Six. Kev argued passionately not because he was worried about a new wingman protecting him and keeping him alive. No, he was terrified of not properly protecting the new wingman and repeating or adding to his endless nightmare experience with TK. Try as he would, Kev never won his arguments. Unfortunately for him, both the Major and Red Six were convinced that he was the best pilot for the job. Though he was complimented, he did not want the job or the responsibility. Given his preference, he would fly without a wingman rather than experience the loss of another.

However, in the quiet of the night, alone in his bunk, his private thoughts about himself were a little different. Casually strolling around deep within the private confines of his personal and hidden thoughts, he was not as sure of himself as others were. In fact, he was not as sure of himself as he implied with his occasional bold swagger and loud talk at the club. Privately, the young man was painfully aware that he was only twenty years old. One night, while laughing a little bitterly in the privacy of his bunk, he said to himself.

"Heck, Kev old boy, you only shave every third day because someone, with nothing better to do, might be offended by your peach fuzz. Goodness gracious, son, you scrape your face like a crusty old soldier whether you need to or not. Before all this goes to your head remember. If you were back in the world, you couldn't buy a beer! You're not a man in the eyes of the law. You're only old enough to die for your country."

The strange and constantly changing, yet never changing, world of a twenty-year-old man in Vietnam is full of surprises. As usual, another of his surprising days started out innocent enough. Kev went through all of his usual morning rituals and then flew on out to the area of operations. He relaxed, while enrout, because it was a nice slow paced flight. Sven's team was assigned to fly the first shift of the day and Kev was to stand down until he was called. While he was loafing, Command and Control sent his ole friend Sven out into the valley across the ridge from Happy Valley. As far as the two of them knew, all that they were supposed to do was poke around the jungle for a bit. It was a straightforward and simple enough mission. Just do their usual thing and see if any of the bad guys wanted to come out and play.

Later, at the club, using his carefully cultivated cynical experienced Cav pilot voice, Kev climbed upon his pulpit and pontificated for the benefit of his listeners. As usual, he was speaking over a cold beer which he couldn't have purchased back in the world.

"If I remember correctly, today was only supposed to be another day and another dollar of Uncle Sam's flight pay earned in good old South East Asia."

Following Sven's first mission, Kev's team flew on out to their assigned area of operations. When he arrived, the boss gave him the usual informational call to begin the mission.

Unexpectedly, the Major told him to pick an LZ large enough for a rapid, battalion-sized, insertion. Kev immediately choked back a low moan of dismay. A battalion sized insertion meant a lot of strange metal and strange pilots flying around him of which he did not control. Closing his eyes, he could visualize the sky filled with other people's darting, climbing, descending, turning, and uncontrolled by him helicopters. Terrified of midair collisions, he much preferred to keep the air all to himself and within his tight control. When the Blue Six finished his briefing, White Horse Six immediately came on the horn. He wanted to talk directly to Kev.

"Red One-Five, this is White Horse Six."

Kev quickly responded to his call.

"You've got One-Five, White Horse Six. Please send your message."

Without a preamble, White Horse Six immediately knocked ole Kev's dirty olive drab socks clear off his two smelly feet.

"One-Five, your Six tells me that you are the best scout that he has ever seen. In fact, he tells me that you might know all of Two Corps better than our longtime friend, good ole Victor Charles. However, in my case, I'm a little new to this neck of the woods. Don't tell the troops. But, if I don't have a map in my lap, I'm lost. So, . . . here is what I am going to do."

Whoever White Horse Six was, based on his self-depreciation, Kev liked him immediately. White Horse paused for a moment and Kev braced himself for an unpleasant request, which always translated into an order. While he waited, he wanted to tell White Horse Six that if he himself were stuck on the ground with a map he would still be lost. Kev quickly thought better of assuming he could joke with the man.

"Because I've got a pair of silver eagles pinned on my shoulders, I am going to slightly change your current job description. Here is the basic situation. My whole battalion is about fifteen/twenty minutes out from this location and needs a place to land. Given your expertise, experience, and lengthy, military career, I'm giving you a promotion. You just became the lowest ranking Battalion Commander in the United States Army!"

When Kev heard White Horse Six's mike click off, he readily responded with the total current content of his startled brain. His profound and carefully reasoned out response was a stony, stunned, and stupefied, silence.

Assuming that Kev's polite silence was an invitation for him to continue, White Horse Six continued with his briefing.

"Your Six tells me that you have Air Mobile and Air Cav operations down to a science. Therefore Son, I want you to pick the LZ and control everything that has to do with the insertion." Kev got a sick feeling in his stomach as White Horse continued. "In simple language, this means that I want you to run the whole show. I want you to assign the flight paths in and out. You are going to control the arty and the gunship prep. Just to make sure that you have enough firepower, I'm giving you the two pairs of Fox Fours who are arriving on station in about one-zero."

White Horse was not finished with his request. However, Kev's head was spinning.

"When the troops hit the ground, you will assume tactical control of them until I get my bearings and CP set up. One-Five, this means that I want you to get them on the ground. Get them moving and make sure that they set up a good perimeter. Finally, it's your responsibility to make sure that they don't run into any unpleasant surprises. I'll give you a call from the ground when my CP is set up. Can you handle that One-Five?"

Floundering in rough water well over his head, as trained, Kev stuttered out the only proper and allowed military response to the good Colonel.

"Yes sir."

Maybe, for the first time, if not the first time, clearly one of the few times, in his tour of duty, Kev was struck honest to goodnessly speechless. In times past he wasn't sure what to say. Upon occasion, he had made a complete fool of himself by saying too much. A few times, he had wisely chosen to remain quiet and thereby not demonstrate his profound ignorance. This time, he was completely, totally, and absolutely speechless! The only thing that came from his mouth was abject silence. Right then and there, he almost died of fright. The coming insertion was scarring him spitless. And, he had little interest in being his typical wise mouth self!

Deep inside, he was awash and floundering in his own frothy sea of personal insecurities. When he absorbed all that White Horse had said to him, the young Scout was fearful. However, he was not fearful for himself. For the most part, the passing months had made him numb to personal fear. Yet, he questioned if he had what was necessary to carry the weight of responsibility unexpectedly placed upon his young shoulders. Young Kev, with not yet two years in the Army, was taking the place of a Bull Colonel with twenty years of experience. White Horse Six was faithfully placing more than a thousand men under his direct command and responsibility. As far as Kev was concerned, this was scary stuff. The responsibility was rapidly becoming intensely intimidating for the cocky young Aero Scout. At that moment, he would rather have been asked to take part in a suicide attack upon the North Vietnamese Parliament or whatever they called their government.

Ruefully, he shook his head as if to clear it. In many ways, the Colonel was not asking Kev to do anything that he hadn't done many times before. He had done every one of the assigned tasks at one time or another. Ole Kev had called arty in support of people on the ground. Countless times, he had directed gun-ship fire. Controlling a helicopter insertion of a platoon or two had become "run of the mill" stuff for him. Several times in the past, he had successfully controlled and directed the Cav's own Blue Platoon when they were on the ground. He knew that he loved to call air strikes by the big fast-movers. Individually, as noted, none of the assigned tasks was new to him.

However, to successfully accomplish all those tasks, all at the same time, was a very tall order! Controlling and commanding, roughly a thousand, combat troops on the ground felt like a very foreboding task to the young Aero Scout. The young man's natural instincts and honest self-knowledge demanded that he smash the mike button with his thumb in justified and vigorous protest.

"But sir, I'm just a twenty-year-old Warrant Officer."

Just before Kev bit his tongue off in indecision, his carefully groomed ego kicked in. He decided if that Bull Colonel and his boss said that he could handle it, who was he to argue with them? He then remembered that Kevin Paul Johnson was Red One-Five and that he was the best of the best. At least, he liked to believe that he was the best of the best!

"Red One-Five copies. White Horse Six, please give me one-zero to talk to my observers and I'll get back to you."

Switching his thumb from the radio side of the mike to the intercom side of the button, Kev continued with his conversation.

"Well guys, let's go back about three klicks and take a good look at that clearing we just passed over. I'm not sure, but it just might be what the doctor ordered for ole White Horse."

Gently wheeling his little bird into an easy wide right turn, Kev accelerated toward the other clearing. Slowly passing over the clearing, the three of them agreed that it was large enough to handle an eight-ship insertion.

Doing the math quickly in his head, Kev figured that using eight ships on the first lift would put a sufficiently large force on the ground to be self-sustaining in the event of trouble. Muttering to himself, Kev said.

"Let's see. Six times eight makes forty-eight. That's almost fifty rifles on the ground with the first lift. With proper gun support, they should be able to fend for themselves till I get the second lift on the ground. Furthermore, if these guys in the slicks are good, they should be in and out in less than a minute."

As he continued to quietly mutter to himself, Kev realized that he was in a strange, for him, position. Usually, he only had to keep his own counsel and answer to the Major or whoever else was flying C&C. However, like it or not, this mission made him responsible for far more than himself and his little team. Slowly shaking his head, the young Warrant Officer was not sure that he liked the additional responsibilities. He already had sufficient nightmares to last a lifetime. Speaking to no one, he muttered to himself half aloud.

"D--- it, ole Kev joined the Army just to drive helicopters! That's why I am a Warrant and not Commissioned."

Mindful of the people who were waiting for him to begin the operation, taking a deep breath, he keyed his mike.

"White Horse Six, this is Red One-Five. I'm confident that we can use this clearing directly below me as an eight-ship LZ. However, it is still your battalion and I'd like you to meter-meter things from your altitude and give me your opinion. While you are doing that, we'll take a closer look to make sure that there are no nasty surprises waiting for us that would ruin our whole day."

Finishing his radio call, Kev started a very slow flight across the proposed LZ. Almost brushing the top of the grass with his skids, Kev instructed his crew.

"OK guys, you keep a close eye on the tree lines and make sure that our little friends are not waiting for us. While you do that, I'll look for any booby traps in the field."

Almost fatal experience had made Kev was very mindful of booby traps which had be set in LZs. Several months earlier he had been looking over a proposed landing zone and had gotten a nasty little surprise. Just as he had been about to settle into a grass skimming hover Johnny had spotted a trip wire being depressed by their skid. Had they dropped the little bird any lower, Kev would have ended his tour of duty prematurely and with a big bang.

The startling sight of that hidden trip wire had convinced Kev to look for another LZ. However, before they left the neighborhood, he had the gun birds lob a few rockets into the field just to see what would happen. Whatever had been wired to the booby trap must have been huge. The LZ exploded with a thunderous explosion when the rockets hit. Kev still had an occasional nightmare about that scary incident. Sometimes, when he slept, he would watch his skid depress the wire. Each time, before he could stop his descent, the world would explode and he would wake violently with a start, soaking wet with nightmare sweats.

As he slowly flew along his proposed LZ, he could not see any trip wires nor any suspicious mounds indicating recently planted land mines. Satisfied, he grabbed an armload of collective and zoomed out of the clearing.

"Did you guys see anything in the tree lines?"

Both of the observers gave negative answers. The three young men agreed that the LZ appeared to be safe. If any bad guys were present, they were doing an excellent job of staying hidden. Kev figured that a good prep of the LZ by the gun-birds would make for an acceptable LZ.

Not wasting time, Kev was flying slow and irregular circles around and about the proposed LZ. Nervous and uncomfortable, the three young men in the little helicopter knew what was riding on their shoulders. If they missed something during their recon, their oversight could mean the deaths of many young GI's! They might not have liked the depth of their responsibility. However unwelcomed, they accepted that this time, more than their own butts were on the line. If it were possible, they were more cautious and careful than usual.

Grabbing a deep lung-full of air, Kev, trying to convince himself that he was in control of himself and of the situation, keyed his mike.

"White Horse Six, this is Red One-Five."

In a seemingly calm and unconcerned voice White Horse responded. Kev then decided to expand the call, thereby keeping all the players in the game..

"Blue Six, are you monitoring?"

To this, he also received a reassuring positive response. It was time to bite the bullet, grab the bull by the horns, keep his fingers crossed, and try to sneak in a quick prayer or two. Or, maybe a third prayer would help more.

"White Horse Six, if you are happy with this LZ, we'll use it. It looks clean and it is level enough that the troops will have good fields of fire in all directions. Break. Break. Blue Six, can you see that field about ten klicks to the west of our present position? It is the one that I had just taken a look into when White Horse came on the line."

After a couple of seconds pause, Blue Six came on line.

"That's affirmative One-Five."

Concerned about the depth of his responsibility and that they were deep in Indian country, Kev had a deceptive plan up his sleeve. If car dealerships could play "switch and bait," Kev felt that it was OK for him to do the same.

Keying his mike, Kev began to put his plan of deception into action.

"Blue Six, if you could do me a favor, I've got an idea that might gain us some time. It is no great military secret that we both know that I can't call arty to save my butt. The last time that I tried to call down some, I couldn't hit the right map-sheet. Also, to be honest with you, at the moment I have too many pots in the fire to try and call arty. If you would please, call an arty strike on that field I just mentioned. Begin the strike when the slicks are about zero-five from our location. Keep pounding it until the first lift is on short-short final. Have you got a good copy, Blue Six?"

Within a moment, the Major came on line.

"Roger, One-Five. I'll have the other LZ well prepped by the arty boys till the slicks are on short-short. I assume that you want the slicks to come in south and then break west on take off. If you do that, you'll keep them out of the arty's line of fire. Also, if you like, I'll set them up and give you a call when they are about zero three out of your location."

385

The new Major was quickly learning the ropes. Keeping the spirit of teamwork, he made his suggestions couched as questions and was very supportive of Kev's efforts and his ego. Thankful for the help, Kev heaved a sigh of relief. The Major would take a big part of the heavy load off his hands. Though his suggestion was appropriate and Kev had yet to think about those issues, he was not undercutting Kev's responsibility. Rather, Kev felt well backed-up by his boss. Life was good and the Cav was clicking along on all eight cylinders.

"Roger that, Blue Six. I have an excellent copy of your last transmission. When you have contact with their escorting gun-birds, would you please pass them off to me. I'll use them to prep the LZ and cover the insertion. That way, we'll be able to hold our Snakes in reserve. About those gun-birds, would you please brief them before you pass them off. Break. Break."

"White Horse Six, do you have any suggestions or questions? I'm open to any help that you might have to offer."

White Horse didn't have any for Kev so he continued.

"White Horse, what is the status of the Fox-Fours you said were on standby?"

Kev always enjoyed having the big heavy fast-movers at his beck and call. It made him feel like he could comfortably play the mouthy little guy at the bar. He could start the fight and when he got in over his head, his friends would finish it for him. However, his big friends did not usually have much loiter time when they joined him. With their fuel status always questionable, he didn't want to send them home without making very good use of them.

"Red One-Five, I've got a pair on station who have one-five mikes of fuel left. Another pair will arrive shortly with thirty mikes of loitering time."

Kev then re-keyed his mike.

"White Horse Six, wait one please."

Keying up the intercom, Kev asked the back-seater if he remembered the small ridge that was between the two LZs.

"Roger that, boss. We've seen the bad guys in that neighborhood more than once. Come to think about it, boss, they've greeted us rather warmly a couple of times. If they are around, I'd bet a month's pay that is the neighborhood where we'll find them."

Kev continued.

"What do you say we have the first pair of fast-movers put their stuff on that ridge? That'll keep the bad guys guessing which LZ we are going to use, shake them up a bit. With a little lick we might fix a couple of them before the grunts have to deal with them?"

The back-seater gave a double click on his mike to the affirmative.

386

"White Horse Six, this is Red One-Five. With your permission, I'd like the first pair of Fox-Fours to dump their heavy ordinance on the ridge between this LZ and the one my Six is shooting up with the arty."

White Horse immediately responded.

"I copy One-Five. I assume that is where you think that the bad guys live and play, and that you want to keep them guessing. The fast-movers are now up this push. I'll get out of the way let them talk to you."

When White Horse finished, the leader of the Fox-4 flight came on the line.

"Red One-Five, this is Red Cloud Two-Niner and One-Seven we have been monitoring your transmissions for the last one-zero. As usual, we're running a little low on go juice. So, get cracking little helicopter and put us to work."

The ever-present little boy and military historian in Kev couldn't miss the opportunity for a word play on their respective call signs. Chuckling to himself as he keyed the mike, Kev called upstairs to the fast-movers.

"Red Cloud, speaking for the rest of the Cav, having the great Sioux war-chief working with us for a change is much nicer. I'm sure that things are going to work out much better than the last time we met on the field of battle."

Not missing a beat, Red Cloud Two-Niner responded.

"Now you mind your manners', White Man. If you don't behave, I promise you that it will be Little Big Horn all over again! I'm pretty sure that I know where you want the heavy stuff. If you give us a mark, we're ready to go to work."

Up to this point, Kev was feeling pretty darned good the whole operation. He was surrounded by excellent professionals who knew exactly what they were doing. If he missed something, he was confidant that someone would note it and pick up the slack for him. However, he wanted to be careful so that no one was hurt unnecessarily because he missed something important. Concerned about everyone and everything, he touched base with Red Cloud before he began his attack.

"Red Cloud Two-Niner, we've got arty coming in. If you monitored and can stay clear of it, I'd like you to make your runs south to north with a west break."

Kev paused and waited for Red Cloud to respond. However, it wasn't Red Cloud who broke in. It was his lead Snake driver who was also on top of the situation.

"Red One-Five, this is White Two-Seven. If you like, I've got some Willie Pete on board and can make the mark for the fast movers. If I understand you correctly, you want the mark on the ridge where your got your butt shot up a couple of months ago."

Kev both grimaced and smiled. He grimaced painfully because it had been a hairy afternoon that his gun-bird was referring to that sent him home with some new holes in his bird. However, he smiled because, as usual, the Snake drivers had and were also taking good care of him.

"That's affirmative Two-Seven. It's pay back time. Break. Break. Red Cloud Two-Niner, if you are clear of the arty and as soon as you have the Willie Pete mark registered on your U.S. Air Force issued 'mark-one eyeball,' you are cleared to roll in. Also. If you have some pistol, please save it for me. I want to use it on the LZ."

He released his mike key and drew in a deep breath.

Quarterbacking the Air Mobil insertion of an infantry battalion was keeping Kev much busier than a standard recon. The young man felt like the proverbial one-handed paperhanger working in a windstorm. He had to fly his little bird, continue to recon the LZ area, talk to everybody and their brother-in-law, and somehow keep the big picture sharply in focus. Shaking his head, he came to the realization that command was a more difficult task that he had expected. As he was carefully sorting through his mental picture, the radio came on.

"Red Cloud One-Niner has a good ID on the Willie Pete mark and is inbound, hot. Friends, this war party is hot and ready to trot. Also. Red One-Five, we're both packing loaded pistols. But, you better use it quickly we're running low on go juice. Number two, cover my break and salvo your load along the length of the ridge line."

Pitching his voice a little higher than normal while staying in character the F-4 driver made his own war cry.

"Good morning Charley. Chief Red Cloud has arrived and its now pay back time!"

Poor Kev couldn't help himself. Without keying up his mike, he began laughing with a primal and savage joy. Some of the Fox Four drivers were totally outrageous. In fact, they were usually as much fun to work with as his buddies in the Cav. Sobering his soaring spirits for a moment, he reminded himself that war was not a game or fun. Be that as it may, the fierce competitor within him always loved the intense spirit of the contest. As he had told Pastor Bill, he was involved in the ultimate contest and the ultimate hunt. He liked a game where it was winner take all. That is why he always played ball to win. If he didn't bang bodies and if he didn't hurt when the game was finished, he was deeply disappointed.

Swinging his little bird's nose about so that he could easily see the ridge, Kev enjoyed watching the unfolding show. However, the fast-movers were going so fast that Kev almost missed the show. Yet, he was well pleased with what he saw. They plastered the length of the ridge with good ole Uncle Sam's finest high explosives. Kev keyed his mike.

"Red Cloud Two-Niner, this is Red One-Five. That's real nice shooting, guys. It appears, to me, that you two guys have some experience playing our game with the little people. I'm now marking the LZ with colored smoke. When you have a good ID on the smoke, I'd greatly appreciate it if you guys put a little pistol on the east and west sides. Please, use the same approach and departure as before. When you're finished shooting the place up, you're released back to your teepee for a sip of fire water. One-Five is clear of the area."

Red Cloud immediately responded to the invitation to play in Kev's ball-yard.

"Red Cloud Two-Niner has raspberry red smoke and is inbound with my pistol primed and loaded for bear."

As always, Kev shook his head at the Air Force's use of the term "pistol." He would never get used to the idea of a twenty-millimeter Vulcan cannon being called, "pistol." He only wished that he could carry such a wonderful and powerful "pistol." Enjoying all the firepower at his disposal, Kev watched the two fast movers tear up the foliage surrounding the LZ. At the same time, he was aware of the arty tearing up the decoy LZ. It was a lot of firepower for a twenty-year-old boy to have at his beck and call. And, he knew it.

When the "show" had finished, Red Cloud and his sidekick rode off into the sunset.

"Red Cloud Two-Niner and One-Seven are clear of the area. Good luck guys, and good hunting. Hey, you guys get a few scalps for me."

The dust had yet to settle from the twenty millimeter strafing when his radio, once again, came to life. This time, it was the Major calling Kev.

"Red One-Five, this is Blue Six. I have four Charley model gun-birds for you. They are up on our push and their call sign is Outlaw Two-Three. Give them a call whenever you want them to come on over and play with you."

Before Kev could respond, White Horse Six also came up on the horn.

"Red One-Five, this is White Horse Six."

Kev quickly acknowledged his call and White Horse Six continued.

"Red One-Five, if you have not received any ground fire, I'd like to hold two of the gun birds in reserve with your two Snakes."

Kev paused a moment, thought, and then responded.

"Roger that White Horse. We haven't seen any recent activity from the bad guys which should concern us. It appears, to us that a two bird prep will be sufficient for our needs. However, I'd like to be able to call on the second pair of gun birds without going through you first. Also. If my Six clears it, we have a second team of Loachs and Snakes available to you."

White Horse Six did not have a problem with that arrangement and gave Kev permission to call the second fire team if and when he needed them.

Refocusing on the LZ prep, Kev keyed his mike.

"Blue Six, how far away is my first lift? If I forgot to say so, I'd call this a comfortable eight bird LZ. That being the case, would you please have them set up for eight birds at a time?"

Kev was surprised by the amount of time which had passed when the Major told him that the first lift was five minutes away.

"Roger that, Blue Six. Break. Break. Outlaw two-Three, this is Red One-Five. Do you have a good copy on me?"

Kev had barely lifted his thumb from the mike button when Outlaw Two-Three responded.

"Roger that, I have you lima charley, Red One-Five. We're about zero one from you location and I understand that you are planning to put me to work. For your information, I'm in a heavy hog and my wingman is flying a standard package. Your slightest wish is my command. As you know, we little peons in Army Aviation live to serve the mighty slick driver."

With the lift ships "just over the horizon" preparing to land and the background music rising in volume, Kev was pleased that the gun-bird driver was ready to go to work.

"Roger that, Two-Three. I've marked the LZ and when you have a positive ID on the smoke, I'd like you to prep it on all three-hundred and sixty degrees. Also. I'd like your gunner to put some thumper into the LZ itself. I want to make sure that nothing that goes bang is buried in the middle of our LZ. The slick drivers would never forgive me if I missed that. Red One-Five is clear of the area."

As Kev pulled a couple of klicks away from the area, Outlaw Two-Three responded.

"Outlaw Two-Three has a positive ID on passionate purple smoke and is inbound hot."

Keying the mike, Kev acknowledged the call.

"You're cleared in hot, Outlaw. Break. Break."

"Blue Six, this is Red One-Five. The arty should be finishing soon on the other LZ. Before you have them quit for the day, would have them lob in a couple/three Willie Pete marks just to keep the bad guys guessing?"

As he released the mike key, Kev had another unnerving thought while he watched Outlaw Two-Three and his wingman prep the LZ. He couldn't believe it, he was sweating like he was running with a sixty-pound pack, rifle, and boots caked with mud. Yet, he was tooling around in a nice breezy helicopter getting paid for doing what he would have done for free.

"Outlaw Two-Three, this is Red One-Five. Please, don't expend everything on the prep. My grandmother was Scotch and I want to get my money's worth out of you. When the lift birds are zero two out, I'd like you to swing out and join them. Then, as they are on short-short, hit both the east and west sides of the LZ with whatever you have left. If I missed any bad guys, I want you to keep their heads down till the first group of grunts is ready to go to work."

Kev was pleased to discover that Outlaw knew his job and knew it well, when he made his next request. He had escorted a lot of slicks into a lot of LZs and knew the drill better than Kev did. Though he knew that these gun-birds were a part of an Assault Helicopter Company, he had forgotten that they were just as good a team as the Cav.

"I have good copy, Red One-Five. My lead slick just called on Fox Mike radio and said that he is zero three out. We are breaking back to join the slicks now."

If Kev's plan was working, his world would be wonderful and blessed. Under fire and shaken up, the bad guys would be unable to respond for, at least, another five minutes. With two LZs being prepped at the same time they would be forced to wait to see which one was going to be used before they could respond in force. Even when they saw the first lift on short final, they would not be sure that it wasn't a feint. The little people knew that the slicks could easily pull in power and go to the other LZ to drop off the troops. At least, that was how Kev planned it. It was an old trick, like the prepping of two LZs, that was used when dropping off and picking up LRRPs. He felt confident that it would work again. Suddenly startling him, his radio crackled.

"Red One-Five, this is Cowboy Six. We are on final approach to the LZ. I have a positive ID on thin purple smoke and my gun-driver Outlaw Two-Three confirms the LZ."

Just as the lead slick finished his call, Outlaw broke in.

"Outlaw Two-Three is inbound hot. I'll take the east side. Number two, you take the west side. Let's expend everything on this pass. Remember, our friends have got other gun-birds and Snakes if they are needed."

As the big Hueys began to slow for landing, no longer surprising him a new concern came to Kev. With that, he decided that command was nothing more than a never-ending string of concerns multiplied by worries beyond counting.

"Attention all gun-birds and Snakes. This is Red One-Five. Once the first lift unloads, no one is to shoot within two-hundred meters of the

LZ without my personal clearance. Hey guys, for the moment everything is going like clockwork and I don't want any last minute screw-ups."

Continuing to admire the teamwork, he was watching the big Hueys touch down and off-load their troops. With all going well, Kev decided that it was time for him to tighten up his scope of concern. Everything and everyone would be at its most vulnerable for the next few minutes. It was time for him to pass one of the many footballs that he had been juggling. A little unnerved, he had discovered that juggling that many footballs was very tiring and had caused him to break out in a serious sweat. Keying up the radio, he began to lighten up his load.

"Blue Six, this is Red One-Five. I think that it is time for me to start working with the grunts. Would you take over as the tower operator? Break. Break."

"White Horse Six, would you please give me the radio push and call sign for your folks who are on the ground?"

As Kev watched, the first lift of slicks were quickly lifting off and the grunts were rapidly spreading out to form a defensive perimeter about the LZ. He also knew that another eight ship lift was about thirty seconds away from touchdown. This was as it was supposed to be. The quicker that they got a large body of troops on the ground, the safer everyone would be. Also being concerned with his team's safety, he keyed his mike. It wasn't quite a public service announcement. It was more like a taking care of Kev service announcement. Nevertheless, he felt that it was important enough that every bird in the air should hear it.

"Attention all lift ships. Be aware. You have a pair of Loachs just east of the LZ. Please maintain your north-south approach and departure. That way, you will remain clear of them."

Believing that he had covered all of his bases, Kev set to begin working with the grunts as soon as he got their call sign.

Just as he was about to repeat his call to White Horse Six, Kev's radio impatiently crackled. White Horse Six gave him the call sign and radio frequency for the grunts. Dialing up his FM radio, Kev gave them a call.

"White Horse Five, this is Red One-Five. How do you read me?"

Slightly surprising him, White Horse Five responded immediately.

"Red One-Five, this is White Horse Five. I read you five by five."

From the nature of his response, Kev decided that White Horse Five was an old timer. Surprisingly, the unit XO used the old "five by five" rather than the NATO "lima charley" to indicate that he had clear reception.

"White Horse Five, I'm the little Loach working just east of the LZ. Your Six has asked me to advise and assist you. Wait one."

Wild Bill, Kev's back-seater had interrupted him.

"Sorry to break in, Boss. I can't tell you why. But, something bad is bothering my gut. It tells me that there are some bad guys close by."

Distracted and concerned, Kev told him to keep on his toes and to keep him informed.

"White Horse Five, this is Red One-Five coming back at you. My back-seater thinks that there are some bad guys over here on the east side of the LZ. I'd advise you to tighten up your security on the east side. Please. I repeat. Please inform me in any of your people move past the tree line on the east side. God forbid. I don't want to shoot them up by mistake. Break. Break."

"White Two-Seven, are you up this push?"

White Two-Seven immediately confirmed that he was monitoring the FM radio. That knowledge pleased Kev. It meant that if things fell apart and he needed his big friends, they would know the score and be able to respond quickly.

"White Horse Five, did you copy my last transmission?"

That radio crackled and the sounds of landing helicopters' and shouted orders were loud in the background.

"Roger that, Red One-Five. I understand that my Six wants you to control the troops from your vantage point. What do you suggest?"

Kev paused and thought for a moment.

"I tell you what White Horse Five. Why don't you form a strong skirmish line on the east side of the LZ? However, I'd strongly advise that you hold position until I get a little better look at the area. Anyway, you will need to move east toward the bad guys if you want to engage them. Please hold and I'll get back to you in a couple of mikes."

Mentally preparing himself, Kev keyed the intercom.

"OK guys. I'm going to start opening up the trees with my rotor wash. Keith, keep your eyes peeled wide open. If the bad guys are in the neighborhood, let's find them before they find the grunts. Better that they shoot at us early in the game. That way, we can use all these gun-birds without worrying about hitting any of the grunts."

Switching to his UHF radio, Kev called up the Snakes.

"White Two-Seven, thanks for monitoring Fox Mike radio. I'd like you to contact the second team of Charley Model gun-birds and coordinate with them. I agree with my back-seater. Something in the air doesn't feel right. Somehow, I have the feeling that lots of defecation is going to be splashing all over the oscillating air device any minute now."

Kev had barely released his mike switch when White Horse Six came on the air.

"Red One-Five, this is White Horse Six. I've been monitoring you on both radios. As far as I can see, you're doing some darned good work today. I tell you what, son. I'm going down after the next lift and set up my CP. Until that time, if you sniff out any bad guys, feel free to use the fast-movers on them. We need to use them as they are running low on fuel. When they finish, use the Charley Models. They are also running low on fuel. White Horse Six, out."

When White Horse Six finished with his message, Kev returned all of his concentration to the recon. At least, he tried to center his concentration though he found himself listening in of the radio chatter. In the background, he could hear White Two-Seven talking with Outlaw Four who was flying the lead Charley Model gun-bird. They were making plans about what to do if Kev found some bad guys. He could also hear Blue Six acting as the tower operator as he was getting the eight ship lifts in and out in record time. If Kev counted correctly, the fifth lift was on short final. That would be the last lift for a few minutes. The Hueys had to return and pick up some more grunts.

Tense, yet feeling like he was accomplishing something positive, Kev found himself pleased. Muttering to himself, he said.

"So far, so good!"

Suddenly, it was as if he had spoken a bad omen.

"D---, I should have kept my mouth shut."

Angry, he feared that he had just jinxed himself. A cold shiver slowly ran up and down his spine. As he shook it off, Kev decided that he had been in Vietnam too long. He was getting jumpy.

"Yet, . . . He said to himself."

As he was growing increasingly uncomfortable, a long burst of AK-47 fire confirmed his growing fears. Apparently someone on the ground had become as uptight as he was. They hadn't seen the bad guys. Nevertheless, the bad guys had just given themselves away. This was a serious mistake that Kev was going to use to his advantage.

The long burst of gunfire was close enough to scare Kev as well as to get his undivided attention. However, no physical damage was done. They didn't take any hits from the sustained burst of fire. Mashing down his mike, he called out in the excited, high-pitched, voice that he used in these situations.

"Taking fire! Taking fire!"

"We have marked with Willie Pete."

At the same time, Kev heard his wingman rip off a long burst of minigun fore directly under his turning bird as he broke away. Also at the same time, White Two-Seven called inbound, hot. Pumped full with nature's chemicals of fear, he was surprised how calm everyone else seemed. Very bad people were trying to kill him, and they were acting as if it were a training exercise. When White One-Seven finished his call, White Horse Six called.

"Red One-Five, I suggest that you use the fast-movers. Their call sign is Red Cloud Niner and they are up this push."

Passing over the LZ and struggling to gather a little speed, Kev was about to call the fast-movers. However, Red Cloud Niner beat him to the punch. Not only did he fly a big fast-mover. He was moving fast in response to Kev's call of taking fire. He spoke without a preamble.

"All helicopters clear the area immediately. Red Cloud Niner and Red Cloud Three-Niner are inbound, hot. We have a positive ID on the Willie Pete and the two Snakes who are breaking away. Are we clear to release, One-Five?"

Kev responded immediately.

"Roger that Red Cloud. You're clear, north to south. If possible, I'd like you guys to spread your load the along the full length of the LZ. Also, be advised. All friendly personnel remain within the LZ."

Just as he finished his radio call, the most horrifying flash of fear that he had experienced in his whole tour passed through Kev. With it, a massive vice clamped down upon his chest and he couldn't breathe. Breathless, his heart stopped beating and his blood froze solid in his veins. He knew that he was too young to have a heart attack. However, if felt like he was suffering from a very serious one which was about to kill him. Almost in an advance state of panic, he quickly switched to FM and mashed down on the mike.

"White Horse Five, please confirm that your people have not moved beyond the tree line? Also. Go to ground. You guys give ole Mother earth your biggest, fattest, and juiciest kiss. Fast-movers are inbound, hot."

Thankfully, White Horse confirmed that he people were clear of the aiming point and safe withing the friendly confines of the LZ. He added as postscript.

"Give the little buggers h---!"

Kev hadn't had the opportunity to ask the fast-movers what kind of ordnance that they were carrying. He was about to ask when he saw the two Fox 4's bearing done on the target area. Afraid that he would spoil their concentration with the troops so close, he quickly stopped himself. Watching the four elongated canisters tumbling from the wings of Red Cloud Niner, he immediately knew what variety of death and destruction that they were carrying. From about two-hundred feet in the air, the shiny canisters slowly tumbled end over end as they journeyed toward the earth below. When they struck, a fiery, man-made hell, of which the great Biblical prophets would have been jealous, burst upon and in the trees. Dante, for all his poetic effort could not have envisioned such horror. When the number two bird released his load, it served as an exclamation point.

Though he had seen it several times before, Kev was again awed by the inhuman power unfolding before his eyes. With the brutal stupidity of war slapping him on the face, he was slowly shaking his head. Pondering it all, he wondered if it was stupidity or courage that allowed the bad guys to repeatedly bring such hellfire upon themselves. With a strange admiration, he noted that they never gave up. They just kept on coming. He keyed up the mike.

"Red Cloud Niner, the is Red One-Five. Are you guys packing any pistol today?"

Red Cloud Niner quickly answered to the affirmative. Chuckling to himself, Kev knew that he shouldn't ask a fighter jock how good he was. If he was a fighter jock worth his salt, his ego was as big as Kev's own was. Therefore, he would tell Kev that he was the best of the very best. However, he wanted to get a feel for this guy before he made his next request.

"Red Cloud Niner, how confident are you in that six-shooter of yours?"

After a short pause, Red Cloud Niner responded.

"Sonny, you just give me a gnat on the fly and I can put all six rounds up his butt without bothering his hemorrhoids!"

Laughing openly, Kev believed him.

"OK, Red Cloud Niner, it's time to put your money where your mouth is. I'd like you guys to make another pass with your pistols. One of you put it between the napalm and the LZ and the other one put it on the west side of the LZ."

As Kev looked up, he watched the two big birds reverse their direction and begin to return. At the same time, the radio came to life.

"Red One-Five, be advised, Red Cloud niner and his friend are inbound, and this time we're going to count coup."

Again laughing to himself, Kev wondered how many people who were listening in knew what counting coup was. He almost keyed up his mike to make sure that everyone knew what Red Cloud meant. Counting coup meant that he was going to physically touch his enemy. In this case, killing his enemy meant less than having the courage to touch him while in battle. Red Cloud Niner was planning to go in low and slow.

"Heck," Kev thought to himself.

"With a little training, this guy might make a good scout pilot. After all, he's obviously got the 'proper' attitude!"

If his intentions hadn't been clear enough, the Fox-four driver keyed up his mike and announced his intentions.

"Three Niner, let's throttle back to about two-fifty so we can keep our six-shooters on target as long as possible. You take the west side and I'll shoot between the nape and the LZ. However, I want you to be very clear about one thing. If your set-up is not perfect, DON'T SHOOT! Remember, we have friendlies in the LZ."

Knowing that his confidence was well-placed, Kev let out his breath and prepared to watch the unfolding show. As he expected, he was not disappointed. Bright tongues of flame erupted from both aircraft and pointed purposefully to the ground below. Gracefully, the two big birds leveled out and filled the heavy jungle growth with a man-made inferno of deadly twenty-millimeter slugs. When they finished, Kev bid them farewell with everyone's heartfelt thanks.

"Red Cloud Niner, I confirm that you counted coup. However, be advised. When you land, your crewchief is going to bitterly complain about cleaning up the green stains running down your big a–ed bird's belly. You're released with a big thank you. I hope we get to play together again. Bt the way, you're my kinda playmate, Chief."

Though he was confident that the grunts could now walk through that little piece of real estate as if they were on their way to Sunday School, he believed in overkill. In his months in-country, Kev had been repeatedly surprised by the courage and resilience of the bad guys. He knew that he was spending thousands and thousands of the taxpayer's dollars by using everything that he had at hand. However, spending all that money didn't bother him in the slightest. He was responsible for the taxpayer's children. With the passing of the months, he had come to value each individual GI far more than the taxpayer's pocketbook.

"Outlaw Four, this is Red One-Five. If you guys have the time and the fuel, I'd like to you to do a little work today."

With a brief crackle of the radio, Outlaw Four came on the air in response to Kev's call.

"Red One-Five, this is Outlaw Four. We've got about one-zero mikes of fuel left. Tell Ya what, though, if we unload all these rockets and bullets, it will make it much easier for us to get home. All that extra weight burns fuel, don't Ya know."

As Outlaw Four was speaking, Kev made a quick glance at his own fuel gauge. Much to his surprise, it told him that his own fuel situation was getting a little low. He didn't realize that he had been working so long.

"OK Outlaw Four, you know how all these Air Force pukes are. They're all smoke, flames, and noise. Then they high tail it home to cold beer and clean sheets leaving us to finish the job. I'd like you guys to work over the same area so that all that the grunts have to do is to stroll around looking for little pieces to pick up. Let me know when you are expended."

While the Charley Models went to work with their rockets and bullets, Kev went back to work on the FM radio.

"White Horse Five, this is Red One-Five. If you like, why don't you get your boys ready to move out? I've got a couple of gun-birds working over the area and I'll zoom in as soon as they finish playing."

Kev was surprised by the voice that responded on the radio.

"Red One-Five, this is White Horse Six."

His response surprised Kev. Apparently, White Horse had landed between the Fox Four and the Charley Model strikes.

"I'm on the ground and we are preparing to move out. Just give the word, son, and we'll go pick up the pieces if they're any big enough to pick up. By the way, I just got through talking to your Six and I told him that you ran the best Air Mobil insertion that I have ever seen. We might give you a teaching job back in the world."

Kev was pleased by the compliment.

"Thank you Six, it has been our good and great pleasure to work with you and your people. Tell them that I think they are top notch."

Switching radios, Kev was becoming concerned by his own low fuel situation.

"All Cav aircraft, what's your fuel situation? Red One-Five is down to about one zero left on station."

Blue Six was the first to respond.

"Red One-Five, this is Blue Six. Your relief is zero one from our location. I suggest that you pull up stakes and head for the Texaco station. They have been briefed and Red One-Four is contacting White Horse now. He'll get the grunts heading toward the bad guys. Also. You did a darn fine job today."

With a chuckle, the Boss continued.

"Now, if we can ever manage to teach a dumb Wobblie One how to properly call arty, I can stay in the office and fly my desk."

Wringing wet and exhausted, Kev was not disappointed to be leaving station. He had never worked harder on a recon and began to wonder about the wisdom some Warrants were showing by accepting direct commissions. Commanding a large unit, if only for a few minutes, was a very demanding task. The only thing that would make Kev happier than going to visit Mr. Texaco was to head for the club and have a few cold ones. Just before Kev landed to refuel, the Major called and made him happy. A weather front had moved in and White Horse Six had released the Cav. They would go home early because they could no longer support White Horse in the mountains and Division didn't have any new task for them.

Somewhere on the edges of his consciousness Kev was aware of the social tumult taking place back in the States. Like most of his friends, he took most of it to be the mindless rantings of a small minority. Again, like most of his friends, he comfortably assumed that the, so called, "Silent Majority" was backing the troops. They might legitimately question war and its goals. Yet, he was sure that they recognized that the troops do not make government policy. Kev's friend and mentor had his own questions and Kev respected them. However, he was sure that Pastor Bill could separate his "geopolitical" questions from Kev's personhood. Working within this background, Kev continued to struggle to do his best in a difficult and unappreciated job. Then, he opened a deeply distressing letter from Pastor Bill.

The shocking letter which he received, complete with damning and condemning quotes from the political activist, was one of the most painful things that had happened to Kev since he came to Vietnam. The part of him which had trusted Bill's friendship, wanted to cry. However, another part of him exploded in hurt rage. When he eventually cooled down and finished his own ranting and raving, he fired off a response to his old friend. Because he had so much to say, it was a very lengthy letter that took him several nights to finish. He was so emotionally upset that he didn't want to write to Pastor Bill. Yet, he felt that someone had to speak for all the nameless GI-Joes & Janes in Vietnam and he accepted the job.

Dear Pastor Bill,

I just finished reading your last letter. Leaning back and digesting it, I am debating the worth of writing to my "old friend." Yes, I found it very interesting. Maybe I should say fascinating, with its information about the so-called atrocities being committed upon the helpless people of Vietnam by us, the psychopathic criminal military types. I think one of the nasty quotes that you share with me was about people like me being "Baby-Killers." To be honest with you, Pastor Bill, I am not completely convinced that I want to respond or ever talk to you again. I think that you are sharing foul trash spouted from the mouths of ignorant fools.

The "criminal" war and psychopathic people that you have written about are so far outside of my own experience that your letter is both laughable and absolutely obscene. The vile garbage, which was in your last letter, leaves me nothing less than sputtering, speechless, and stupefied. Nevertheless, I assure you, speechless or not, that such baseless propaganda makes me furious beyond measure. In truth, I find it hard to believe that such baseless filth is in circulation and that some people believe it. However, what has disappointed me beyond measure is that apparently you are inclined to believing it. What has lead you to have such limited faith in your own people? You know me and you know others who are over here.

Yes, my friend, I fully acknowledge that warfare, by its very nature, is brutal and inhumane. Over the passing months I have seen more brutality and inhumane behavior than I ever wish to see again. People and governments try to take what belongs to other people. Mistakes happen and innocent people get hurt. Children die and adults get maimed. The potential of twentieth century technological war is horrible beyond human description. However, that does not mean that I and my friends hurt innocent people on purpose or even by accident. If a woman, child, or doctor shoots at you, by definition, they become a combatant. Yet, if they should get hurt while trying to kill us, the propaganda machine goes into high gear and labels us as murders or worse. On the other hand, Jane Fonda poses at a North Vietnamese anti-aircraft gun pretending to shoot at Americans _and she is a hero!_ Please let me suggest to you one easily forgotten fact. If the North Vietnamese Army took its ten divisions home, I am sure we too would go home. At that point, there would be no war and no innocents getting hurt. However, I suppose that part of the conflict is irrelevant to you and your friends.

My dear friend, let me ask you a deadly serious question about me. Do you honestly think that "little Kev" whom you watched grow through the Sunday School commits the criminal activities you write about? Do you believe that "little Kev" who was in your confirmation class is also to be listed amongst the committers of mindless atrocities? Do you honestly think that I could act like you have suggested? Or, is it possible that another explanation fits the situation?

Maybe these poor innocents who just happened to wander in a southern direction with gifts of chocolates and flowers from North Vietnam are the bad guys? Oh, I'm sorry, I keep forgetting. I'm not using the proper language. These are wonderfully benign liberators who came south! I have previously told you what I have seen these so called "liberators" do! Or, do you believe that I was lying to you about the simple villagers I saw slaughtered? Honestly Pastor Bill, if you think such a thing of me and of my friends and comrades, it gives me reason to pause and reconsider our friendship. Maybe you and I are wasting out time struggling to sort out our divergent feelings with our letters.

Well . . . That's enough of my anger and feelings of betrayal! If I go any farther, my ever growing rage will reduce me to name calling. When people aren't calling me unjustified names, I honestly admit that there is sufficient confusion here in Viet Nam to go around. Please believe me about this one little thing. Nothing in this crazy place is as black and white as people on either end of the political spectrum would have us believe. In fact, I suspect that even the writers of pulp novels will quickly bypass our delightful little war in lovely Southeast Asia. I doubt that in thirty years that they will be able to figure out what was going on.

I honestly believe that most will be afraid to tackle it because of the general confusion that overshadows everything about it. In response, it seems that your friends sitting safely back home in their insulated and isolated judgement seats, have other ideas. They see none of the confusion, called war, that the rest of us experience. Apparently they have access to the perfect crystal ball. Furthermore, they seem to have all the clear and simple answers while the rest of us wallow in our terminal stupidness.

If you will allow, as a heartfelt response of sorts to your accusations, I want to tell you about one of my enlisted men. Maybe by reading his story, you will come to a better understanding about who we are and what it is that we are going through. Before I go any farther, let me make a confession. I love him for his honest humanness. In describing him, I suspect that he is not to be confused with a typical GI, but neither is he totally atypical. Unlike the misinformation someone has fed you about him and his comrades, this young man is one of the few true heros of my life. I say this because he is so typically atypical. Delightfully so, he is honestly terrified, yet he is also very brave. All of which is wrapped up in a simple yet also complex package. He's just another guy doing the best he can to with a difficult and dangerous job. Come to think about it, I don't know if he was drafted or if he volunteered.

Let me start by saying in describing his typical a-typicalness, you have met "The Bill," as we now call him. He is your brother, he is your father, he is your Uncle George and he is your beloved son. In fact, he is probably the noisy disruptive student in Pastor Bill's confirmation class. This kid would not be a bad kid. Rather, he would just be another normal kid with normal adjustment problems. Strangely enough, above and beyond all the many and diverse people I have met in lovely Southeast Asia, he's unique. The Bill stands head and shoulders above the milling crowd. Yet, few would recognize him for who he is.

In many ways, The Bill is most real human being that I have ever had the pleasure of knowing. I honestly believe that he is the type of person that has brought us this far as a nation and as a people. Furthermore, he is the type of person that will continue to aid us. If necessary, God forbid, that we need to call upon him when he finishes his job here, he will answer the call. While I readily admit that he might not impress any of the kids back in the world, today this special guy impresses me very deeply. True, I know that back in the world he would not have impressed me. Nevertheless, The Bill is real people. He is not the product of a propaganda machine. He is a humble man without any grand pretensions of greatness. In this man's Army, he is a lowly Specialist four, faceless, and one of thousands and thousands of lonely soldiers.

"Billy" was what he had become known to us one and all. When he came to us, the poor kid was sort of a strange duck who could effortlessly mess-up a one man parade. One day, out of the blue, came up to Johnny and me with a surprising request. Obviously this incident happened before Johnny was killed. Let me continue.

Late one afternoon, while we were down at the Red Bird line, he casually walked up to us. His request surprised us. Well . . . his straightforward request did surprise me. We hadn't spoken much to each other and I hadn't expected it of him. Billy asked Johnny and me if he could join our crew and become our left seat observer. Let me explain what made this simple request so surprising. My friend Billy's problem was brutally straightforward. None of the Red Bird pilots in our unit was inordinately anxious to have Billy along as a part of his crew. He had an honestly earned reputation among us as a major league, big time, "goof-ball." Before I go any farther, let me clarify something. Even as a first class goof-ball, Billy was a good kid. He wasn't a jerk or the south end of a north bound donkey.

Because of his earned reputation as a goof-ball, he had become known derisively to one and all by the diminutive Billy. By the time he spoke to me, he was, to use your Biblical language and imagery, the unit Leper/Samaritan. Not only did the Officers and Pilots not trust him as far as they could throw him, he also had very few friends among the enlisted men. No doubt about it, he was the Leper/Samaritan. At the time, he led a very lonely existence. He had many acquaintances and few, if any, friends.

We kind of cared for him like a retarded cousin. Mind you, no one wanted to see anything bad happen to him. However, we didn't want to be forced to depend upon him in a fight. Thinking about it, I suspect this condition came about mainly because he did not play any of our soldier hero games. Nor, for that matter, did he play any of our stupid little military games. Billy, being much different from the rest of us, was fully contented simply to be the happy-go-lucky kid that God had apparently created him to be. Obviously, this childlike behavior did not totally endear him to all of us more serious "killer types" of the Cav.

It takes no great effort for me to remember his simple request and our/my surprise at what happened next.

"Mr. J., I would like to fly the front seat with you and Johnny."

He paused uncomfortably, fidgeted for a moment or two, slowly gathered his breath, and then he continued.

"That is, I'd like to fly with you if the two of you will accept me."

On the surface, there was nothing really unusual about this request. It is custom for both pilots and enlisted people to pass judgement upon who would and who would not fly with the Red Birds. Whenever it is possible, it is also custom to decide among ourselves who would fly with whom. I've told you before, but let me reinforce my point. The Red Birds are a strictly volunteer platoon. As far as I am concerned, we are the most democratic outfit in the whole of the U.S. Army. With this democratic ideal in the forefront of my mind, I looked to Johnny to see what he thought about the idea of working with Billy.

To be completely fair, it was Johnny's butt on the line just as much as mine was should the Bill goof up. He smiled softly as I looked at him. When he smiled like that, I should have immediately known that I was being had! Then, after he had spoken, I could have punched him square in the nose for his laughing response to the Bill's request.

"Think about it for a moment Boss. I let you fly as my pilot!"

Well . . . Johnny's twinkling eyes and his artfully chosen words had now carefully tied my hands. We both knew that he had me dead to rights. The creative inventor of the $100,000 vegamatic was not in a position to pass judgement on a goof-ball.

Looking back at my early months, I like to think I wasn't a total goof-up when I started with the Red Birds. Yet, on the other hand, I had to be honest with myself. I had suffered my own share of brain cramps followed by complete brain failures. Some evenings, at the club, I was the butt of re-told stories of flying wonder. Therefore, I was forced to admit I was not a great prize either on that fateful day when Johnny took up residence in my back seat. The fact that we were still alive and were a great team had everything do with Johnny's skill and knowledge as a Scout. It had little to do with ole Kev's skill and knowledge as either a Scout or a helicopter pilot.

When Johnny finished speaking, I had a sneaky suspicion about this little encounter between Billy and myself. I decided that the two of them had prearranged it back in the EM barracks. Not wanting to find out how limited my authority was, I "wisely" kept my peace by keeping my mouth shut. Ole Kev was not about to trouble himself in finding out if they had prearranged the little encounter. If such arrangements were so, I suppose I had been had once again. It would not have been the first time Johnny put one over on me.

Later, when I thought about being had once again, I honestly could not see any harm in it. For in truth, the smoother the two observers worked together, the better it was for all parties involved. This close harmony of observers meant an improved chance for all of us to returning home safe, sound, and in one working piece. Anyway, I think that the EM's need to pull one off over the Officer types occasionally. It is just like children need to do it to their parents. Heck, we all need an occasional victory over the overlords.

Convinced that I had been very carefully set up, I slowly turned to Billy. It was time to stage my own little drama. Doing my best to keep the twinkling laughter out of my own eye, I proclaimed my judgement using my sternest command presence.

"BUT, just remember one little thing, Johnny and I are putting our lilly white butts in your useless hands. Billy, my friend, I want you to understand your role in the crew very clearly. It is your sole job to keep the two us alive. Now, if you should happen to see something useful while we are out on the reconnaissance, between you and me, we will just call that an unexpected bonus. On the other hand, if you turn out to be a goof-ball, the three of us will all die together. I'll be quite upset if you, me, and Johnny, who appears to be your partner in this crime against my common sense and good judgement, die because you screw up."

(In my fertile imagination, I like to think that I sounded just as gruff and mean as Lt. Simmonds did during my first mission with him!)

A little later that afternoon when he had heard about the apparent foolishness which I had just agreed to, Sven, ole Red One-Four took me aside. I knew that he was going to accuse me of another of my famous brain cramps. Failing that, he then carefully assured me that I was, at the very least, a little bit crazy!

"Most likely," he continued. "We should quietly put you away in a padded room wearing a jacket with its sleeves tied tightly about your body. In fact, I might recommend that the Major quietly put you away for both your and Johnny's safety!"

Thinking about it today, I know what I responded to when I gave my approval to their little game. I saw something unique in ole Billy that I liked. After all, most of us "Killer types" in the Cav were, in more honest fact, just little boys stuck in a strange place. All of us are trying to grow up and survive in a situation which is not of our own making.

For some unknown reason, when dealing with Billy, I found myself acting in genuine human faith and trust. Apparently, Johnny was also acting in a similar unseen instinct of human faith. And so, my story to you continues. Johnny and I gave Billy his chance to become a member of the team. Writing to you now, I clearly understand that I saw much of myself in ole Billy. The great difference between Billy and me was that he was just more honest than I was about how he felt when things got hot and heavy. I, on the other hand, always remained deeply concerned about my carefully crafted self-image as the fearless Aero Scout.

Weeks and months had (quietly?) passed since Billy had asked to become a part of the best crew in the Cav. Surprisingly to everyone except Johnny, as that time passed by, Billy had become a critical member of the team. Yet, some basic things had not changed for ole Billy. I remember well the day he managed to shoot up our rotor system while returning ground fire. When I steeply banked ole Rocinante, he never took note of the rotor disk dipping down. The only thing that he could see was the spot he was firing on.

That little incident took me a long time to clear up. Eventually I convinced maintenance that the damage was from enemy ground fire. Looking back, I doubt very much that they ever really believed me. However, maintenance wrote off the damage as ground fire all the same. I didn't have as much luck with maintenance the time that he put two holes in the skids. Thankfully, the folks in maintenance didn't too upset about that one as he was shooting downward.

In time, the three of us became a wonderful team. Somehow, we communicated without saying anything. We became pros. As I have told you, time brought about a tragic change. Johnny was killed. After a few weeks and trying several back-seaters, Billy became my normal back seat observer. We were and are happy working together. Who knows, maybe we are two misfits who belong together?

In the so-called annals and saga of Red One-Five at war in South East Asia, there is one specific day about which I want to tell you. Typically, in the middle of our normal recon, we had gotten a cry for help. Higher-higher told us that at a distance of not more than ten klicks away, a long range reconnaissance patrol, had become pinned down. The LRRP team was in deep trouble and they were in immediate danger of being overrun. Their situation was grim and no heavy air support was available to come to their aid. There were no F-4 Phantoms, no A-4's, not even old A-1 prop aircraft on call at the moment and it was doubtful that any could arrive on time.

That meant that only the Cav was available to help these guys get out of trouble. To further complicate the issue, we did not know exactly where the LRRPs were on the ground. Until we knew where they were, we could not even call in the devastating rocket and gun fire of our own Snakes. We had discovered that many times gun support was all that we needed to do for these people. Most of the time, the Snakes accurate and heavy fire would give the LRRPs a chance to disengage and run for an LZ.

After listening to our briefing on the radio, without a single word spoken by me, Billy calmly spoke up on the intercom. Surprising me, he spoke as calmly as if he were discussing the weather.

"We got no choice Boss. Let's get this show on the road."

Ole Billy knew the score of the game. For our friends on the ground, it was the bottom of the ninth inning and the seventh game in the World Series. They were several runs behind and in deep danger of losing it all. Unlike the countless baseball games we played in our youth, if they lost today's game, no one would schedule a rematch for tomorrow. It was time for Red One-Five and team to pinch-hit. In truth, we enjoy taking the big swing and going for the fences!

(Let me make a side note concerning my last sentence. Those of us in the Red Birds are proud of what we do. We fight hard and we do our best to put a hurt on the bad guys. However, we are prouder of being able to step up and take a might swing for the fences. Every time we hit a home run and another GI survives the day, we walk just a little bit taller. If that means that we have to kill bad guys to accomplish that we'll kill them with a burning passion. If you believe that makes us war criminals and "baby killers," then so be it. We'd rather wear that cloak proudly than see another GI go home in an olive-drab body bag!)

As I just pointed out, not having pinpointed the exact position of the LRRPs on the ground made our problems manifestly more difficult. Before we could give them gun support, we had to find the LRRPs. All we knew was that they were somewhere below us in the double and triple canopy jungle. Because of this, we had to put ourselves at a greater risk than normal by immediately going in very low and very slow. It was clear to us that we didn't have time to be cautious. We didn't question the need to do such.

Everyone accepted these higher initial risks, because we needed to find the LRRPs as quickly as possible. The deadly reality of their plight was that we couldn't help them if we couldn't find them. This mission was no different than many others we had flown. Your friends in their safe environment may not care about five or six LRRPs in danger of dying. However, we care enough to die for them, should it prove to be necessary!

After searching a couple of minutes in the general area we knew them to be in, the LRRPs said that they could hear us.

"Red One-Five you just passed directly over head."

When they said this, we asked them to pop colored smoke. As the smoke eventually came wafting through the trees, we quickly identified it as goofy grape. Things were going well because they gave us an affirmative to our identification. When they spoke to us, I could hear them huffing and puffing on the radio. Like the tragic drama it was, they were running for their lives. This was not poetic running of which I speak. No, this running was brutal and deadly reality. If they didn't run, they died! Bill could distinctly hear the sounds of the M-16's and the AK-47's constantly exchanging fire during this most deadly chase scene. Having been told that they were traveling north to a prearranged LZ, we started to move to their south. We surmised and hoped that the NVA troops were mostly to the south of their position.

Suddenly, our rotor wash opened another break in the trees and Billy spotted the fighting and running LRRPs. Thanks to the gods of war, it was finally our turn at bat. In some ways this was the easiest part of our mission. Having spotted the bad guys, our job became very straight forward. We were to give the people on the ground covering fire. In turn, we wanted to draw return fire from the bad guys. It was a logical strategy. If the bad guys stopped, to shoot at us, that would allow the ground troops disengage.

The situation was tense and the NVA troops were extremely close to the LRRPs. That meant that we could not call in the Snakes greater firepower for fear of shooting up the friendlies as well. Fully understanding the score and situation, we cinched up our pants, hefted out bats, and charged right in. Our little Red Bird was literally on top of the ground troops. In fact, our skids were gently brushing the tops of the tallest trees as we slowly hovered over them. While we were covering the LRRPs, we could move no faster that a slow walk. Exposed, vulnerable, and a choicer target, could we did our best and hoped to rescue the people on the ground.

Without a spoken word or apparently any thought of his own safety, Billy then jumped out onto the landing skid. Armed with his M-60 machine gun, he went to work. My young friend was a completely exposed target fat dumb and happy just at the tree tops almost directly above the NVA. Without any apparent consideration for his personal safety he vigorously engaged the enemy. He didn't speak. Grimly setting himself to his task, he allowed his M-60 to do all his speaking for him. In all my months in country and all my contacts with the enemy, I had never heard such a volume of ground fire directed at us from a small unit before. Green tracers were ever where. (The NVA normally used green tracers.)They were passing over, under, and I swear to you even through the aircraft. I'm sure that some when in one door and out the other.

Green tracers were lighting up the skies and Billy continually hammered away with his machine gun sending his own Red tracers downward an angry reply. The NVA fired away at him with their AK-47's and SKS rifles as fast as they could. The situation was getting tense and we were in great danger. We were taking hits faster than I could count them. Unfortunately, a little Red Bird is not armored and cannot take much abuse. I was sure that it was just a matter of seconds before we ourselves were shot down!

Through it all, Billy unflinchingly fought like a man possessed. He was determined to save those LRRPs by forcing the NVA to go to ground for their own protection from his anger. His selfless action was forcing them to seek cover and protection from his withering fire. At the same time he was demanding that they return fire at himself to protect the LRRPs lives. Setting in my armored chair, I was trying to make as small a target of myself as possible. Nevertheless, I could very uncomfortably tell that his strategy was working by the number of small arms hits we were taking. Eventually, because of Billy's selfless action the LRRPs were able to disengage. Within a couple of minutes they were able to put some distance between themselves and the pursuing NVA. In that dense jungle a hundred yards can be the difference between life and death.

"Truly, truly I say unto you," the picture of our little Red Bird, motionless hovering in full view the enemy was something else. I am sure that a Hollywood director would have fallen in love with it. Billy, for all intensive purposes, was standing completely exposed and literally naked. He was firing his M-60 from the hip like a man possessed by a demanding demon. To add color, the whole scene was lit by a backdrop of red tracer slashing downward from Billy's M-60 and green tracer streaking up from the ground. Make Billy about ten years' older. Put a stubble of hoary whiskers on his wizened cheeks. Have him swearing like a mule-skinner and the people from Hollywood would fill the theaters and make a million dollars. Fortunately for all of us, reality struck down the craziness of the moment. Reality meant that realistic fear remained to keep our so-called romantic and dramatic feelings carefully in check.

Lest you forgot the danger of it all, in the midst of this colorful picture of Billy and crew that I have just painted for you, I had heard a number hits on the aircraft. In my heart of hearts, I knew that it was all over and we were about to be shot down. In my honest opinion, our time as a flying combat unit could be counted with but a few ticks of the eternal clock's second had. While I was waiting for the final hit which would cause the ultimate demise of Red One-Five and crew, Billy cried out. He cried on the intercom with a voice tinged with terror and deep anguish.

"Oh God, Boss, I did it again!"

Not knowing what to think, I tried to patiently wait for a clarification. Immediately my vivid, full color, and highly graphic imagination went into overdrive. First, I feared that Billy, like Johnny before him, had been fatally hit by the massive volume of NVA fire. On the other hand, maybe he shot up the rotor blades with his machine gun. That was a real possibility. Much to my dismay, I well remembered that he had also done that before. Maybe, I dismally thought, Billy had actually managed to shoot himself in the foot or something even worse. Though, as far as I knew, he hadn't done that one before.

Only with Billy, you understand, would I think of such strange and unbelievable things. As far as I knew, only Billy could manage to accidently shoot himself in the midst of a life and death firefight. After the slightest pause when he hadn't offered me any clarification, I fearfully keyed the intercom.

"Dear God, what did you do again, BILLY?"

"J---- C-----, I wet myself, Sir" was his hesitant response!

His M-60 continued to hammer away as he restated himself to make sure that I had misunderstood him.

"D----- Boss, I p----- all over myself!"

Well . . . I am afraid that I am forced to tell on him. Ole Billy had done that before when we were in the midst of a firefight. Unfortunately, this was not the first time that the poor guy's bladder let loose in fear.

Spontaneously laughing like three totally insane fools who had just escaped from the state-run funny farm, we broke away from the heavy fire. For by this time the LRRPs, traveling at a dead run, had gotten far enough away to be safe. Looking to the north, I could sew a big fat Huey was on short final to pick them up out of their LZ. It was now time for the Snakes to do their own heavy duty pinch hitting. We Scouts are really "punch and Judy singles hitters. Whereas, the Snakes can drive the ball out of the park at will. Their job was to keep the NVA pinned to the ground till the Huey lifted its precious human cargo to safety.

As for the three of us flying Red One-Five that day, I am sure that everybody on the radio net knew we were shell-shocked or worse. Undoubtedly, they thought and that we would have to be removed from combat status. Not wanting to upset us any further, no one said anything. Yet, I suspect that the Major discussed institutionalizing us for eternity if not a little longer. Everyone knew something was wrong. For when I called the Snakes' gun runs I couldn't control the gales of laughter that burst forth as I gave them their directions.

I suppose all is not lost in my adventure and journey through Viet Nam. I am learning much about life. For starters, I have discovered for as much as some things change, other things change not in the slightest bit. Honest human fear and the terror still took their personally expensive toll on my young observer's dignity. In the case of the Bill, the clowning around and being a goof-ball remained in place. Wiser, I now believe that his foolishness serves as an efficient cover for the fear, terror, and greatly bruised dignity that he suffers. (He shouldn't feel that way. In combat, we all suffer from those things.) However, what is most important, I am coming to a new understanding and appreciation of him as a man and as my brother. Billy was still being just a little more honest than the rest of us about his feelings of being on the firing line.

I have delighted in the discovery that other important things had changed during our time together. Ole Billy's eyes have been getting pretty darn good as of late. That change has been well matched by his growing wisdom and countless timely warnings. We are still alive and becoming a pretty decent Red Bird team. In this world, that speaks volumes. He is becoming almost as good as our shared mentor, good ole Johnny. I suspect that to those who had not been watching Billy's developing maturity into a top notch observer this wondrous change seemed to come from somewhere deep in right field. This change was miraculous to say the least. Suddenly it was Billy that the other pilots were asking for when I wasn't flying.

Honestly, I would have never had believed it had you told me this transformation (resurrection into adulthood) would happen. Strangely enough, it has now become standard practice to place Billy with the new pilots as they break into the Scout game. (Mind you, I hate to give him up for those few days.) Most of the pilots now feel, like we felt about Johnny before him, that he can show these new pilots the ropes. We trust him to and keep them alive till they begin to learn their craft. It is Billy who had now become my personal trusted friend. At least as much as the Army allows an officer and enlisted man to become friends, we have become friends. (Though, I doubt I'll ever get as close to him as I did Johnny.)

Today, Billy is no longer the unit leper and Samaritan. We gratefully accept him, one of the team. He is now on the first string. In fact, he has a new name. No longer is he "Billy." Now we call him "The Bill." Today, The Bill is no longer the unit goof-ball. Though he is different from most, he has matured into a true leader. He has become a leader for two very powerful reasons. First of all, although he remains a bit of a clown, he now knows his craft better than anyone else in our little unit. Around our neighborhood, this is what counts because most of us respected skill in the craft above all other things. Secondly, he had the guts and most of all the brains to be scared enough to "wet himself" when under fire. Remaining silent about the incidents, most of us admired those guts in the face of his almost crippling fear above everything else.

I guess what I want to say to you Pastor Bill is that you may not be getting the whole story from your friends. No matter what propaganda might be fed to you by the so called arm chair experts, they do not understand this world and they never can. In the safety of their warm cozy studies and their historic ivy-covered walls, they can say what they like. However, we are not a demented bunch of crazed baby killers. I believe that when we are as honest as my friend The Bill has managed to be, we are all essentially the same. We are just a bunch of scared kids trying to do a job and at the same time stay alive.

Sometimes we even loose control of our bladders when we are trying to make sure some nameless kid from somewhere America returns home.

We are your war criminals and baby-killers.

Just Kev

Since time began, serving as a soldier and fighting in a far away land has always been a difficult task. It was in the time of the ancient Greeks and Persians and it continues to be in the letter half of the Twentieth Century. Sometimes, the task of being a soldier is more difficult than other times. As he became aware of what was going on about him, Kev found himself fighting in one of the more difficult times. The recent letter that he had received from Pastor Bill added to his difficulties. It stripped the remainder of the romance from his war. If it had been an option open to him, he would have sat and cried in pure frustration.

Nevertheless, a good soldier can suffer great physical and emotional hardship if he is fighting for something beyond himself. In the end, this beyondness is not necessarily a high ideal or an overarching "ism." If the soldier is a mercenary, at the very least, he has the comfort of knowing that he is fighting for his pay check. Fighting, killing, and dying is the way the soldier of fortune earns his meager livelihood. It is as normal for him as going to the factory or the office is normal for someone else. People may not like or respect him for what he does. Yet, mercenary generally understands why he is suffering and why his friends are dying. It is who he is and it is how he and his friends make their way in a generally uncaring world. Knowing this offered the troubled young man any solace. Kev did not consider himself a mercenary.

Kev's place in his world was a strange situation shared by many others. Back in the real "world," he was too young to go to the local tavern and order a cold beer. He also was too young to vote for the people who had sent him to Vietnam. Yet, he gladly volunteered for the army and flight school. Like so many others, Kevin Paul Johnson believed in his country and had believed in the people who committed him to the war in Vietnam. However, during the passage of the previous year, he began to have his deep inner doubts about the war and its apparent lack of progress. Nevertheless, deep within his private person, he believed that he was involved in an honorable crusade on behalf of a heavily oppressed people. Yet, as he looked about, he saw no progress in the war and was becoming tired of the ever spinning merry-go-round constantly spitting out dead GI's.

Someone once said that when the romance of war wears off, a soldier must find a good and powerful internal reason to keep on fighting. When the "Butcher's Bill" comes due and a soldier's life is reduced to smoke, blood, and mud, the waving of brightly colored flags and the oratory of great speeches are insufficient to carry the day. When that time comes, he must find a far better reason than the politician's rhetoric. The simple soldier quickly grows weary of the suffering and dying for abstract causes. Only those who do not pay the price of war find the strength to carry on with the flags and speeches. Kev had become weary and Pastor Bill's letter only added to his burden. He had made a commitment and would continue to honor it as long as he was asked to. Yet . . . Yet . . ., Kev's Vietnam was not turning out to be what he expected.

While he couldn't buy a beer and he couldn't vote, he wasn't ignorant. Nor had he remained a simple-minded child. Somehow and in someway, deep within, he understood that it was Pastor Bill, and people like him, who were fueling the vicious merry-go-round that he was riding. Hopefully, from Kev's point of view, unaware of what they were doing. For it was clear to him that they were encouraging the bad guys to keep fighting and breaking down the determination of his own people. And, this tragic lack of support was causing the deaths of his friends. Frustrated, he also knew that he could do nothing about the situation back home. Unlike many, Kev had extended his tour beyond the normal year because he was good at what he did. He also felt that by using his experience lives would be saved. After careful and prayerful thought, he did not extend his tour because he thought he would make a difference in the bigger picture of things. Unhappily, he had moved past that hopefulness.

For Kev, the hardest part was accepting the political reality of the war. He never said it. Being who he was, he couldn't share the tragic truth that his heart was feeling. Yet, in his heart, soul, and spirit he knew what the bitter truth had become. Ultimately, the war was going to bee lost. Shamefully, it had not been, nor was it being, lost on the field of battle. Unfortunately, Kev knew that it had been lost or given away somewhere else. Most likely, it had been lost in the hearts and minds of the American people.

Pastor Bill had made that situation clear to him. As a result, Kevin Paul Johnson's romantic crusade had run out of fuel and slowly sputtered to a hesitant stop. Powers and people beyond his control would assure that the war would eventually be lost or walked away from. The fact that they were still winning, and winning powerfully, on the field of battle only made that knowledge more difficult and bitter. Yet, the merry-go-round of death continued to no apparent purpose.

As an individual, Kev knew very clearly why he was fighting. However, ever more, the fighting only served to break his heart. The flags and speeches could no longer carry his day in the face of the "Butcher's Bill." Accepting his new ugly reality, he now fought for one special thing. That which Kevin fought for was the mystical thing that has sustained soldiers in losing battles since Og and Ug began the long retreat from their outer caves. Committed to his friends, he fought for and with his buddies. Protecting other soldiers was the only reason he continued to fight. Isolated and unwanted in Vietnam, Uncle Sam's finest fought for each other. And the war continued while the world and the promises of elected officials crumbled down upon them.

When Johnny died, Sven challenged Kev to take his writing seriously. Wrapped up in his own grief and feelings of guilt, Kev did not immediately see the importance of Sven's challenge to keep writing. However, by the time that Pastor Bill's letter arrived, a small light had begun to dimly glow. Pastor Bill's letter served to fan its flames into brighter light. Stunned by what had suddenly become so clear, Kev knew what he would have to do.

When he finished the letter, Kev knew that history would have to blame someone for the coming defeat. He also knew that the political animal would never take responsibility for any failure, let alone the war's ultimate failure. Kev also knew that recognizing its own failings would also be impossible for society and culture. Therefore Kev reasoned.

"Eventually, me and my friends will be forced to shoulder most of the blame. Those in power and those who write the histories, will charge the Army that continually won the field of battle with the political defeat which was beyond our control."

When Kev came to this sad realization, he took it as his task to tell Johnny's story. In the broader sense Kev struggled to do the same for his friends.

Turning to his diary in solace, he spent his nights examining his own experience and struggling to tell a different story.

"Maybe," he thought to himself. "I am only tilting at another wispy windmill. I fear that Pastor Bill and all the others will not be able to understand this story. However, what choice do I have?"

So he wrote, and he wrote, and he continued to write. Sometimes, like the writing that follows, it broke his heart to relive his experiences and to write about them. Yet, broken heart and all, he kept writing.

Completely powerless, I listened to a man . . . NO! . . . Impotent, restrained, held back, and weeping with rage I listened to a boy die today! From a safe distance, I listened on the radio. Unable to see him, I could not find him. Unable to help him, I could not bring him home. Unable to find him, I could not defend him. Unable to hold his hand, comfort, and stand by his side, I listened to a boy die.

*Try as I might . . . Try as I would . . . **I COULD DO NOTHING!***

Like countless previous nights, I sit here tonight. Alone and deeply tormented I sit silently at my wonderful "Viet Nam war rustic" desk. Made from the soft pine wood used to crate the numberless 2.75 rockets fired by the Snakes, it is temporary. I suppose that it is like everything else in my life. If the ravages of time wouldn't rot it all away, possibly in ten-thousand years some future archaeologist and anthropologist will excavate the ancient sites of the Viet Nam war. When they eventually complete this scientific excavation, what they discover will surprise them. For them will discover that the most useful building material available to the soldiers would be the soft pine rocket and artillery boxes. We build everything out of this useful left over wood. We build our living spaces, our bunkers, and our offices. Shoot. I even used it to make this crude desk where I make my pathetic attempts of writing. It seems that we build our exiled and forgotten little world upon out of the trash of war.

As always, legal pads, rocket boxes, cheap ball point pens, and exceptionally painful memories are the tools of my musings tonight.

However, tonight I sit here and I am stalling. If I really knew how to write about this place, I would say that I had writers' block. Whatever the case may be, I am studiously avoiding my task. Despairing for meaning, I am purposely seeking to escape the pain of trying to understand today's events.

"Maybe," I think to myself, "I am just not old enough and wise enough to understand."

Or, I wonder.

"Maybe there are just no understandable answers to the many, strange, different, and ancient questions of life. Maybe the task of telling this sad story is too daunting for a simple boy, like me, who comes out of a blue collar background. I suppose my problem is not new. These timeless questions are what has kept all the worlds' philosophers and theologians in work while the sands of time have run down the narrow neck of glass."

Why am I bothered? After all these many months in Viet Nam, death is not a new experience for me. The cruelly brutal presence death itself has become a constant companion in my life's travels over the last year. Looking back through the slippery sands of time, I have moved into a new existence. When I arrived in country, I was so green that a lawn mower could have attacked me the day that I experienced my first death of a Red Bird crew.

In the last year, I myself have killed a number of young boys and men from both the NVA and from the Viet Cong. Physically acknowledging the factiticty of death, I continue to wear the flight helmet that I wore the day Johnny was fatally wounded. I am not sure why, but I have yet to clean his dried blood from it. Furthermore, I do not plan to do so in the future. I have seen a lifetime's worth of bloodied, battered, and broken bodies. They have been both American and Vietnamese. Bodies and more bodies have littered my scattered fields of "valor." I speak truly when I say that I have seen enough pain, suffering, and death to last several lifetimes.

This is what I do not understand. What is so different about today?

Here we go again, its "another day and another dollar." Good grief, I could start 90% of my days over the last year or more with exactly these same words. Let's mount up. It's time for "another day and another dollar." The days are completely indistinguishable in their sameness. Get up. Preflight my aircraft. Take off and fly to our assigned area of operations. Do my recon. Maybe get shot-up or maybe shoot up someone else. If a little excitement is called for, that can happen too. We could get called out for ready reaction for some unit in contact. Then we could play a little John Wayne shoot em up on the bad guys and save the day for the good guys. Nothing seems to change and we wonder if our living and dying matters to anyone but us.

Like every other day, eventually, we will finish our deadly business and then go back to home base. Arriving home we shut down the aircraft and get a bite to eat at the club. With nothing better to do I may stay at the club for a couple of hours. If it's a normal night, I might drink a beer or two and spend my time swapping outrageous lies with the guys. Finally, I go back to the hooch. If I'm in the mood, maybe write a word or three and then grab some sleep. If repetition is a good teacher, I'll have the daily drill down to a science.

But today? I don't understand anything about it. I wish that someone would explain what was so shockingly different about today?

Pausing and thinking about my life as it stands, I can't really complain. I'm doing, essentially, what I want to do. For reasons of my own, I extended my tour of duty for an extra six months. True, I could just as easily have gone back to the safety of Ft. Wolters and become a flight instructor. If I were smart, with this extension, I could have gone to fly with a VIP unit. Then I could have flown the nicest and newest equipment flying generals and other VIPs all over the country. Even better, I could have been tooling all over the country-side at a nice safe altitude away from the nastiness of the war below.

However, I like being a Red Bird driver. Everyone knows that I like being in the middle of things. Being a proactive person, I also like calling the shots and quarter-backing the Cav team when it is in the field. Lastly, in case I have forgotten, flying the Red Birds is still a volunteer mission which means we have chosen to be flying here. If I'm honest, I have no basis for complaint. I freely chose my options and my lot. Unlike the majority of the troops, I wasn't drafted.

Still, today something, the same as it always has been, yet, quite different grabbed my gut. Moreso than usual, it hurts like hell!

Like I said, it was "another day and another dollar of flight pay." Got as usual up this featureless morning. Groggy-eyed and sleep-stupid, I grabbed the mandatory cup of bitter army coffee and went down to the flight line. Acting by long since established rote, I casually counted the four rotor blades. Satisfied they were all where they belonged, I checked the fluid levels of my bird, kicked the tire and lit the fire. Nothing new was happening in my strange little world. We followed our well-worn drill. Higher-higher, having nothing better for us to do, had us poke around an area we had looked over seemingly a hundred times.

Two shifts into the day, and we continue to fly our fruitless recon. Four hours of flight time and my bird alone has burned up over one-hundred gallons of JP4 fuel. For the day, we had nothing of merit or note to show for our effort. I was just starting my third flight of the day.

Uninspired, I was heading back into the same empty area to continue to keep snooping around for the bad guys who apparently weren't home. We hadn't let down from our transient altitude when division called the boss in command and control. When the call came in, I thought that Higher-higher was doing me a favor. I was so bored that I was afraid I would begin screaming. He told the Major that an LRRP team was in deep trouble and needed our help. The thought of helping the LRRPs was a bright ray in an otherwise dreary day. At last, we were going to be doing something that was of value and meaning.

Two Red birds, two Snakes and C&C immediately changed course and pulled in max power. With our noses lowered and engine instruments touching their red lines, we checked guns and rockets, and prepared to give whatever assistance we could. While we were speeding along, C&C quickly filled us in. Division said that this group of LRRPs had been on the run for two days. While running, these poor guys had been in sporadic contact with as much as two reinforced companies of NVA. Their situation was precarious, to say the least. I had been around long enough to know that they were exhausted. Division said that they were lost. Adding to their misery, they had already suffered two KIA. Only three of the original team of five were left alive. Each of the three was lightly wounded, and to top things off, they had very little ammunition. If we couldn't find them and extract them immediately. . . .

I pushed a painfully nagging thought out of my mind. The politicians in Washington had announced another troop withdrawal. It was aimed at removing all the American troops and giving the country to the folks from the North. Yes, they said that the South could probably stand on its own two feet. I knew better. However, most politicians honestly don't care about the Butchers Bill. Their only concern was and is next year's election. Kev commented bitterly upon his observation.

"If saving lives were their goal, why were three kids running from two reinforced NVA companies?"

Well, . . . I had been in country a long time and well knew what the score was on this ball game. As we rushed to the rescue, I wondered if the LRRPs' recon had any more meaning than our own recon seemed to have had earlier. Were these troops out there dying just because some staff weenie wanted to place pretty colored pins on his map? Bitterness and bile filled my stomach. The situation made me wonder about the wisdom and humaneness of staff weinies. Higher-higher didn't have a slick available to extract them if we found them. Yet, these poor, scared, and worn out LRRPS had been on the run for two days.

When the Major found that out, he was madder than hell. We heard him call the staging area. He needed one of our own Blue Birds to leave its grunts on the ground, head on out to our area, and stand by.

"I need an empty slick. Those G-- D--- jackasses at Division seem to have forgotten they have an LRRP team running for their lives. I want him fully fueled. I want him to red line it all the way out here, and, I want *him here yesterday. When he begins to run low on fuel, I want another on in route."*

The Major put the Blue Bird in the air in the hope that we could first find the LRRPS. If we found them, we needed to help them disengage from the bed guys, and then I needed to find an LZ from which we could extract them.

Flying flat out, I crested the last ridge separating us from the ten-mile long valley. In my mind, this was "The Valley of Death" in which these exhausted hunted young men were running trying to preserve their very lives. Silently praying that I could find them, I immediately tuned my FM radio to the LRRPs radio frequency.

"Groundhog Three-Five, groundhog Three-Five, this is Red One-Five. Do you copy?"

They made no response to my first call. So, I tried again.

"Groundhog Three-Five, groundhog Three-Five, this is Red One-Five. Do you copy?"

Turning up the gain on my radio, I heard him faintly. The poor guy was winded and apparently still running. Gasping for air he had trouble speaking.

"Red One-Five this is Groundhog."

His heavy and deeply labored gasping told me he was in very bad trouble.

"Just Tom and I are left."

In the background, I could clearly hear the pounding of his feet and his laboring to breathe.

"We have less than one clip of ammo each."

As he vainly struggled for each desperate breath , I believed that I could hear his heart urgently pounding. His next words broke my heart and stiffened my spine.

"O God, please help us."

C&C cut in on the UHF radio when Groundhog finished.

"You handle Groundhog, One-Five. We'll give you all the back up you need."

Deeply concerned, (That's not a strong enough word or feeling. Terrified! No. I was scared to tears for this poor kid!) Almost emotionally overwrought myself, I was grimly determined to be cool, calm, and controlled. I key the mike.

"Groundhog Three-Five, state you position please."

As I write this, with tears running down my cheeks, I remain convinced that a better writer than I might be able to catch the terror and desperation in Groundhog's voice. My stomach turns acidic and my eyes water just remembering those few words.

"Red,"

more heavily labored breathing --

"don't know"

-- painful gasping –

"running west."

416

He can't speak for a moment. I hear the pounding of his feet and the sound of him crashing through the underbrush.

"Tom's badly wounded."

He continues, with what, despite the unclearness of the radio sounds like resignation.

"We're going to die!"

Congress, being deeply concerned for the taxpayers and the upcoming elections, decided that nothing is too good for Uncle Sam's fighting men. So, of course, the navigational directional finding gear doesn't work in the battered old bird that I am flying. (Lately, maintenance has been bitterly complaining that it is getting harder and harder to get any spare parts. Stupidly, in my opinion, some units are having their flying hours cut . I suppose this is to save some more of the tax payer's money. **Maybe that is why Groundhog was running for his life toward a nonexisting Huey.**

Flying around in circles and waiting for these insignificant grunts would be an expensive waste of airframe time!) Given the wonderful state of my equipment, I call C&C on the UHF and asked if they can get a DF fix on the next transmission from Groundhog. Before keying my mike, I give myself a positive pep talk.

"This poor kid is rightly scared to death. Kev, it's time for Red One-Five to be the seasoned old pro that he pretends to be. It looks like Groundhog's his fate is resting in my hands. Kev, maybe this is why you are here."

Keying my FM radio, I begin as calmly as I possibly can.

"Groundhog, this is your ole buddy, Red One-Five."

Gathering an additional handful of calmness. I continue.

"Just listen to me for a moment son. I got two heavily armed LOACHS, and two very mean Snakes, waiting to go to work for you. Best of all, I got me a big ole empty slick just waiting to take you home. They are all here, right now, with me. We're all here because we are going to get you home in one piece. Now, when I finish talking son, I want you to key your mike and talk to be for a minute or so. If you can't talk, just keep the key mashed down. I want you to do this because we are going to follow your radio signal right to you. OK, now talk to me son."

A pause, which seemed to take forever, filled the airways. Just as I prepared to call down to him again, Groundhog came on the radio. As before, he was panting heavily and running as he gasps out his frantic words.

"Red, can't talk."

The mike remained keyed as I listened to his labored breathing.

"Running."

Though he wasn't speaking, the mike remained keyed. That was all we needed to find him.

"Help me!"

Then he ended his transmission. I immediately called C&C on the UHF and asked him if he got a fix on Groundhog's transmission.

"One Five, sorry. My unit isn't working very well. The best that I got was a quick swing to the west. I recommend that we head to the west and pray.

At last, I had a little bit with which to work. Kicking a pedal and pulling in an arm-load of power, I headed westward. Good Ole Bill was standing on the skid looking deeply into the jungle. No one said anything. However, I know that everyone in the Cav was praying for all he was worth. We were not going to give up on him. We owed him that much. Groundhog and his friend was far more to us than a colored pin stuck in a staff weenies map.

"Son, you've got to talk to me so I take you home. Please son, talk to me."

Another forever pause.

At last, Groundhog came back on the radio. He was crying out with a voice which contained both terror and resignation.

"Dear God, they're all around us!"

In the background I heard a three or four round burst of M-16 fire. A sustained burst of AK-47 fire quickly follows it.

"Jesus God, Tom is down! He's dead."

Silence follows his words. Shocked by the abruptness of it, I key my mike.

"Talk to me son. Please, talk to me son! Please, keep talking so that I can find you. If you don't talk, I can't find you!"

Tears of rage, pain, frustration, and absolute powerlessness are steadily streaming down my face. I can't help him! God help me, I can't find him! Powerless to intervene, I'm listening to this team die. I can't . .
.

Groundhog keyed up for the last time. Resigned to his abandonment by those who no longer cared, he is somehow crying and calm at the same time.

"I'm down Red -- hurt bad -- thanks for trying."

(I am unashamedly crying as I write this.) Following my instructions as his last lifeline, he has kept his mike keyed. I heard him fire off his last couple of rounds from his M-16. Groundhog's last effort is quickly followed by a burst from an AK-47 and a grunt from him. In the background, I hear Vietnamese voices for the briefest of an instance. Then . .
. I hear nothing.

Crying, screaming, and begging, I mashed down on my radio button.

"Dear God. Talk to me son. Please . . . Talk to me son. We'll get you out!"

C----- J----, he doesn't talk to me. I can hear nothing. His radio has gone dead.

I've talked to him. The voice I heard on the radio belongs to Groundhog Three-Five. I knew that he was somewhere within a fifteen

418

square mile area. We frantically searched for him in rotation till the sun set and division demands that we withdraw. The Major strenuously objected. His heart-felt objection didn't matter to the powers to be. Division ordered us out to return to the barn. We all hated what was happening to us. Maybe, he wasn't dead. Maybe, the bad guys only left him for dead. We wanted to look all night. Maybe he had a flashlight and he could signal us in the dark. Division said that they would send in another LRRP team in the morning. We all hated what was happening to Groundhog Three-Five.

Both times I was out there looking for him, I prayed that we would get lucky . After we lost contact, we looked for him till we were almost out of fuel. Later, after the second team left, I called and called for him.

Call out as long and as loud as I might, he doesn't talk to me. He doesn't talk to me.

In the late night silence of his little private area, Kev had begun to quietly sob. Carrying the weight of Groundhog's death on his shoulders, he puts down his pen and stares into nothingness. Fingering Pastor Bill's letter, Kev was not sure why he was sobbing. Yet, he can't stop the tears. According to some, he's a baby killer. Another baby killer lies cold upon foreign soil. Neither can go home because home doesn't want them. For them, home no longer exist.

The only grace that Kev can find in the moment was his solitude. He was blessedly alone with his quiet sobs and freely flowing tears. Thankfully, his condition was hidden from his peers and his enlisted folk. He doubted that either group could understand. Possibly, he was underestimating them. With each passing day he found it increasingly difficult to get close to anyone. Gathering a cold coke from his little fridge, he tried to take a drink. Its coolness tastes good. Yet, it painfully reminds him of an age long gone past. Something terrible had happened and he no longer was Mrs. Johnson's little boy. He had not enjoyed a sweaty day of round-ball at the "Y." Tomorrow will probably be another repeat of today and he has responsibilities.

Struggling to regain his emotional control, he prepared to sleep.

"I've got to get some rest. Tomorrow I have to fly and I have two other lives to protect."

Kicking off his boots and flight suit, he reached over for his forty-five. After fussing sufficiently, he turned in the thirty-eight and got back his ole friend. Its heft and weight felt good in his hand. It was a substantial old friend who had never let him down. Releasing the magazine, he pulled the slide open and carefully inspected it as he wiped it down with an oily rag. When he was satisfied that it was clean, he snapped the loaded magazine back into the handle and placed it on the makeshift table beside his bunk. With a weary shrug, he turned his light off and climbed into his rack.

With the light off and surrounded by a curtain of darkness, his tears returned and they slowly soaked the pillow. Filled with sorrow because of what he had just experienced, he felt as if he were carrying the weight of the world upon his young shoulders. For a man so young, it was a crushing burden. With a shuddering sob and a drawn out sigh, he reaches over to his forty-five. Pausing, as if in deep thought, he pulled back the slide. After a moment, in which he had a puzzled look on his face, he released the slide. A loud metallic snap announced that he has chambered a round. Kev paused for a moment, and the puzzled look re-crossed his face. Then, he checks the safety. It is off. His trusty friend is set to kill. A light pull of his index finger and it would discharge.

Lowering his head back to his pillow, Kev allowed its softness to soak up a few additional silent tears. He then took his forty-five, who has been his protective companion for months, and slowly placed it under his pillow.

A few more troubled minutes passed and the capricious gods of war begrudgingly allowed him to slowly drift into an uncomfortable sleep. Unaware of the world, his hand slowly caressed his forty-five as if it had a mind of its own.

ANOTHER "ISM" – CAREERISM

Troops in contact! Quickly snapping his head to the upright position, Kev saw a young trooper from the Blue platoon running in his direction. Cupping his hands and yelling, his was the voice loudly sounding the alert. The high-pitched whine of his two Snakes lighting off their turbines added an urgent background to the, all too customary, cry for help. The combination of stridency and high-pitch turbine noise abruptly lifted the fog which was gently swaddling his sleep-addled brain. Steadily and softly cursing like a cranky old garrison soldier, he stiffly moved into action. With the practiced efficiency of an old pro, he quickly slipped into his chicken plate and threw himself into his pilot's seat.

All the wonderful thoughts contained within his delightful sun-sodden nap disappeared. These youthful delights of a far distant dreamland left with the strident urgency of the young trooper's message. It was time to return to the war. Strangely enough, he loved and hated every aspect and practiced movement of the drill. Kev didn't have to look about at the faces of the scrambling men about to know that he was the senior man. No, the young man was not senior in rank nor was he senior in chronological age. However, he had run through the drill more times than any other enlisted man or pilot on the staging field. That made him senior in experience.

Moving with a casual effort which carefully masked his urgency, Kev flipped the master electrical switch on. Appearing unconcerned, he then carefully set the throttle to the start position. Realizing that he had forgotten something, he slammed his battered old brain bucket on his head. Knowing that he had given his crew chief sufficient time to untie the main rotor, Kev stuck his head out the door and yelled.

"Clear!"

Instantly, the crewchief echoed Kev's "clear" with his own affirmation that all was well and that it was safe to begin startup. It was time to add the shrill song of his own little turbine to that of the Snakes deeper and more powerful song.

Pressing down the starter button, he listened to the familiar whine of the little engine as its compressor slowly came up to speed. The battery in his bird was in poor shape. He had to be careful as maintenance didn't have another one available. When the rapidly spinning compressor reached starting speed, Kev rewarded the popping ignitor with a rich meal of raw JP-4 fuel. Then, with an explosive pop, a rush, and a roar, the little engine lit off and rapidly began coming up to speed. Carefully adjusting the throttle, he made sure that the engine didn't over-heat and damage itself. Burning up an engine was always a concern on a scramble. It was a greater concern today because he had a soft battery.

Noting that the main rotor had begun to slowly turn, Kev closely checked his oil pressure gages with his free eye. The other eye, he had already specifically reserved to monitor the turbine outlet temperature gauge. Satisfied that the little engine was operating within normal parameters, he casually glanced about. Noting the quiet efficiency of his crew, Kev felt pleased. They were a couple of good guys and they had almost finished strapping in and preparing for the unknown. Yet, what he saw also gave birth to a sad little smile. Kev was comfortable that the two young men would do their job to the best of their ability. He could ask no more than that from them.

They were volunteers and he had extended his tour. By this stage of the war, this made this crew different from most of the troops in Viet Nam. Knowledge of the continuing pull out of American troops took the aggressive edge off most of them. Less and less people volunteered for the Army and Vietnam. Tragically, it had become a drafted and unwilling Army. Understandably, nobody wanted to be the last casualty in a lost war. Generally, morale among the troops had reached an all-time low. With a deep feeling of regret mixed with sadness, he also was well aware that ole Kev had changed over the past year plus. Today, he was just a guy who couldn't go home with the job undone. He had come a long way from the bright-eyed, eager, little puppy standing on the sidelines. What saddened him was that he wasn't sure that it was a good journey.

"You guys set?"

Both of his crewmen signaled their affirmative reply with the standard double-click of their intercom buttons. His crewchief softly interrupted Kev's solitude.

"Everything is in the green Mr. J."

Practiced effectiveness had allowed the greater part of his mind to drift about as they prepared for the unknown. Oceans of water had gone over the proverbial dam since the bright-eyed little pup had marveled at the competence of Captain Jack's crew.

"How strange," he thought to himself.

"A couple of words, a phrase or two, and little wasted effort and my little Rosy II is up to flight idle and ready for take off. I think that Captain Jack would be proud of me."

Pressing his own mike button, he called his wing man.

"You set to go, number two?"

Another soft double click sounded through Kev's headphones conveying the message that the team was ready for takeoff. Young Kev continued to muse.

"If this were a football game, the announcers would be marveling at the efficiency of the 'two minute drill.'"

With the gentle earnestness of a young mother lifting a new born baby, Kev applied subtle upward pressure on the collective stick. Laughing quietly within the private confines of his head, Kev poked some gentle fun at himself.

"Holy mackerel, I'm getting to be a dottering old man. Jimeney H. Christmas, I fly with the slow pain-reducing movements of an arthritic old man. Shoot, ole Gramps moves a lot faster than I do."

However, he knew more than his premature ageing was involved in his cautious movements. A year earlier, he would have immediately sucked in an armload of collective pitch and gone charging to the rescue.

Yes, he would readily charge to the rescue today as he had so many times before. Yet today, he knew better than to beat the horses to death before the enemy was engaged. Wiser, he also knew that the little Red Bird also had to get him home when the battle was finished. If he beat and abused his little bird unnecessarily, she might turn and in spite, severely bite him. Kev and crew could help no one if their helicopter broke. In a recent letter, Pastor Bill had said that he was showing aged wisdom and newfound maturity.

"Maybe I am, Kev thought."

Combat loaded his little bird reluctantly clawed her way to a low hover. Hundreds of flight hours in the heavy bird had given Kev a soft, gentle, and loving touch at the flight controls. Six months previously, he would have maxed out the power to achieve this low hover. For this mission, he had a little bit to spare. If he wanted to, he could have pulled his little bird to a slightly higher hover. However, he decided that was foolish. Kev's time for bravado and showmanship had long-since passed.

"Why force her work any harder than necessary?" This had become his all-important mechanical mantra of survival.

Continuing with his soft touch, Kev easily seduced the little bird into a graceful and willing flight. She was his and would give him everything if he asked her too. Rosy II was a good bird. Yet, she wasn't ole Rocinante. However, countless hours spent together had given the two of them the harmony of familiar lovers. Kev had learned that sometimes you can get from point 'A' to point 'B' just as fast as the old way. However, treating her gently caused much less wear and tear on the equipment. With his wingman trailing obediently behind, Kev called the lead Snake.

"White Two-Five, this is Red One-Five. Hey guy, what's the hot skinny today? Give me a holler when you got something for me. Hey, don't forget that I'm coming along."

The two Snakes had led to way to the west. Until he heard differently, Kev would silently follow the climbing Snakes. He managed to keep up because they had to climb to a higher altitude. Whereas, the two Scouts stayed low in preparation for the mission. Again, Kev smiled wryly to himself. He could have put a reel to reel tape on his room mate's machine and listened to the rote conversation that followed. It would be the same old story played out in endless and seemingly meaningless repeat.

"Red One-Five, this is White Two-Five. I'm talking to C&C now. It appears that a company of legs has gotten into some big time trouble. Division says they have taken some casualties and says that they are in serious danger of being over run."

If the sad plight of the ground troops wasn't so serious, Kev would have bitterly laughed. The recording tape continued to play on his room mate's machine. It was spuing out the same words it always did. The story would be another repeat of the sad irony of his time in Viet Nam. He had heard this story of troops in trouble countless times before. What made listening to the story so bitter was that he had repeatedly fought this battle over the same little piece real estate. Kev's Viet Nam was becoming like a bad movie on an endless replay. Sometimes, he felt that Vietnam trapped him in, what science fiction writers called a time loop. The eager puppy was beginning to feel like a disillusioned old mutt. Beaten too often and without provocation, the master's footsteps no longer caused his tail to wag vigorously.

"Roger, Two-Five, I have a good copy. Troops in contact. I'm at your low six and maintaining ninety knots. Let me know when you've gotten more info. With a little luck, we'll be able to give these guys a hand."

Sighing deeply, Kev returned to the continuous play tape.

"Number two, I assume that you copied One-Five. Be advised. We'll be test firing the M-60's. I suggest that you test fire your weapons also."

Over the passage of the last few months, Kev's radio procedure had become curt and militarily correct. Gone were most of the colorful calls and quips. While the "game" remained unchanged, the contest had become deadly.

Too many hurts and losses had cost Kev more dearly than he realized. Very much a loner, he preferred his own company and didn't get close to his wing pilots. He also had not allowed himself to get as close to "the Bill" as he had Johnny. Nonetheless, the Bill was OK by ole Kev. When he had monitored Kev's call to the wing bird, he fired off a quick burst on his M-60. Maintaining good team work and harmony, the crewchief did the same from the front seat. Red One-Seven, a very green wing pilot, called Kev.

"Number two is locked and loaded. Let's get it on boss. We're ready to rock and roll."

Sending a double-click on the radio in reply, Kev allowed himself an ironic smile.

"Was I ever that eager?"

In the middle of the question he checked himself.

"Dear God, NO, don't tell me. I'm afraid that I'll get sick to my stomach."

Fifty feet below, the ancient battleground continued to flash beneath the racing helicopters. If he wanted to, Kev could have gotten a little more speed out of the little bird. However, another of his painful memories kept his speed in check. As had become his custom, he wanted to save the engine by not pushing it to 103% power. More personally, he did not want to add to his growing list of bad dreams. Months ago, though it seemed like aeons to Kev, TK had been about as green as his current wing man. Bitterly, Kev remembered. It had been a "ground troops in contact" call much like this one. That particular call for help had cost TK his life. As a result, Kev had learned that green pilots and war weary helicopters was not a mix custom designed for a pilot's longevity. The White Birds would let him know when he needed to hang it all out. Until they called, he would conserve the birds and crew. More patient now, he could comfortably wait and see how things developed. Badly burnt once, Kev kept much closer track of his wingman.

"Hey Mr. William, how's our number two doing back there?"

"Red One-Five, this is White Two-Five."

As the tape continued, Kev knew that this was his wake-up call. He'd get his situation report and then prepare to go to work.

"Send your message, Two-Five."

Three sets of ears in Kev's aircraft and two sets of ears in number two's aircraft were fully attuned.

"Roger One-Five. Just over the next ridge line we've got a company of grunts pinned down on the east side of the valley. They have taken a couple of KIA's. They also have several seriously wounded that need to be evaced. From what I understand, they got their KIAs in hand to hand and they're still eyeball to eyeball with the bad guys. When you crest the hill, I'm going to ask for smoke. Once you get a fix on the smoke, I'll turn the operation over to you."

When White Two-Five finished his message, Red One-Seven immediately came on line.

"I've got a good copy lead. Where you go, I'll follow."

Cinching up his safety harness, Kev gently lifted the nose of his little helicopter to clear the upcoming ridge.

425

"Two-Five, I've just cleared the ridge and I have a good visual on the valley. Anytime that you want, the folks on the ground can give me a little smoke."

Kev quietly listened as White Two-Five told the troops on the ground to pop colored smoke. Less than a minute later, Kev's crewchief spotted the first plumes of yellow smoke. It was slowly wafting its yellow tentacles through the dense canopy of dark green trees. Keying his mike, Kev identified the smoke.

"Two-Five, I've got lovely, lemony yellow to my ten o'clock."

During his briefing, the lead Snake had given Kev the grunt's FM radio frequency.

"Two-Five, with your permission, I'll switch to the Fox Mike radio. When I get a hold of them, I'll talk to the grunts myself."

"Roger that, One-Five. Did you just copy C&C when he said that we have a pair of Navy F-4's due to arrive on station in about zero five?"

This was welcomed news to Kev. He always enjoyed having some big boys in the neighborhood when he went into a brawl.

"Roger that, Two-Five. I have a good copy on your last message."

"Mud Hen Five, this is Red One-Five. I have a good visual on lovely lemony yellow smoke. Do you confirm lemon smoke?"

Kev had learned that the bad guys tried to monitor the ground troops FM radios. He had been in country too long to be fooled by the bad guys popping their own smoke. Softly chuckling to himself, as he waited for Mud Hen's response, he remembered an interesting incident.

A few months back, they had asked a ground unit to pop smoke to identify their position. Listening in on the conversation, the bad guys had simultaneously set off their own smoke grenade. However, they had used a different color. When the color of the good guys had been confirmed, the Snakes plastered the area where the bad guys had released the bogus smoke. That time, his own trick had fooled ole Victor Charles. He didn't sucker a helicopter into a killing bag that day. No sir, that day he drew the strings on his own bag.

The FM radio clicked on and Kev heard a steady staccato background noise of small arms fire before a voice spoke to him. The M-16's and the AK-47's sounded equally loud and clear to his ears. This told Kev that the grunts had not been exaggerating. It sounded like the bad guys were sitting beside the RTO as they fired their AK's.

"Red One-Five, I don't know who you are. We got yellow smoke out. The bad guys are on top of us. Anything that you can put about twenty-five meters west, we'll gladly take."

Kev ruefully shook his head. That was extremely tight rocket support. Much tighter than he liked on a first gun run. However, the background noise emphasized their need for close-in support. As far as

Kev was concerned, the needed all the help that they could get. Furthermore, they needed it, quick-in-a-hurry!

Unbidden by conscious thought, Kev suddenly remembered how horrible it felt to be on the ground and needing gun support. He also remembered how vitally important it had been for him to hear a friendly and reassuring voice.

"I roger your last transmission, Mud Hen. I've got a couple of Snakes rolling in as we speak. They are going to use mini-gun and high explosive rockets. When they do their thing, it's going to get very loud in you neighborhood. I want you guys dig in deep. My friend, let me warn you, that's extremely close rocket support. But, not to worry, we'll take good care of you. You guys hang in there now. I've got lots more good news for you. Things are only going to get better for you in the next few minutes. I've also got a couple of fast movers about zero three from your location."

Kev had not finished his report to Mud Hen when White Two-Five made his call inbound.

"Two-Five is inbound with rockets and mini only. No flechettes!"

Confirming that he was not in the line of fire, by looking up, Kev admired the slim silhouette of the diving Snake. He had seen its stiletto shape diving a thousand times. Much to his dismay, he had also seen it from the ground. Nevertheless, he always found the deadly, and simple, eloquence of a Snake attack to be a thing of strange beauty. As Two-Five was beginning his run, Kev keyed his UHF radio and called his wing.

"Number two, let's you and I make sure that no one comes in the back door. These guys on the ground have all the problems that they need for today."

With that command, Bill expertly and easily stepped out on the skid. Always dependable, he began a careful search as Kev slowly skimmed the trees behind the ground troops.

Finishing his gun run, Two-Five broke away from Kev's position. His number two man was inbound and waiting for Two-Five to get out of the way. Mud Hen yelling exuberantly came up the FM radio.

"Great! Wonderful! Fantastic! You guys stopping them dead cold. You're making them dig in and leave us alone. We need more of the same. As soon as you finished, they began to move up again. We are still in immediate danger of being over run. Next time, bring it in fifteen meters closer."

Kev instantly responded in a semi-controlled panic.

"Negative, negative! That's too tight, Mud Hen! We'll hit your guys."

Mud Hen responded to Kev's fears with his own urgency.

"We're deeply dug in Red. Our problem is so simple that even you fly-boys can understand it. Either you hit them and hit them hard or they overrun us and we won't be bothering your guys any more."

White Two-Three came up the FM. "Mud Hen, the second Snake is inbound. Pull the covers and pillows over your heads. Rockets and mini are inbound within ten meters of your smoke."

The Snake pilot paused for an instant and then hesitantly continued.

"I pray to God that you guys know what you are asking for."

Kev mentally crossed his fingers as he saw the smoke puffs come from the stub wings of the Snake as they were firing the first pair of rockets.

Bill unexpectedly spoke up from the back seat. He spoke softly so that he didn't startle Kev into thinking that the bad guys were firing at them.

"Hey boss, I've got an idea. Johnny once told me about the time that you guys went into the pioneer's hole and sat right on top of the grunts. Why don't we do something like that?"

Thinking for an instant, Kev thought that Bill's idea was worth a shot. Having quickly come to his decision, he called to C&C to see if he would go along.

"White Six, this is Red One-Five."

C&C immediately responded.

"Six, my back seater suggested that we park ourselves on top of the friendlies. While we are parked on top of them, we can kill two birds with one stone. We can act as a good aiming point for the Snakes and use our 60's and my number two's mini to cover the grunts."

A short pause followed Kev's suggestion.

"Truthfully, I'm not very comfortable with that One-Five. However, if you're willing, it might just make the difference."

Knowing that the Snakes and his wing had been monitoring, Kev switched to FM and told Mud Hen Five what he was planning to do.

"Mud Hen, you are going to have a lot of hot brass raining down on your heads. Don't you guys worry. Just stay under cover."

Moving to where the last wisp of yellow marking smoke had dissipated, Kev spoke to his crew.

"OK guys. It's time to find our friends on the ground."

The Bill was right on top of things. In less than a minute, he had gotten a good eyeball on the trapped GI's. When Bill pointed them out, Kev could also see them. Ready to begin, he keyed his radio and spoke to Mud Hen.

"Mud Hen, this is Red One-Five. I'm the little Loach hovering directly over your head. From my position, I can see your RTO. Do you have any friendlies west of him?"

Mud Hen quickly responded.

"Negative Red, what's left of us is pulled in around the RTO."

Without being told, Bill knew that he was cleared to fire and began to engage some bad guys.

While Bill was keeping the bad guys busy, Kev hit the mike and called his wingman.

"Okay Number two, it's your turn. I want you to make a slow pass with your mini just to my west. Keep it just as tight on me as you can. Also, fire at two thousand to save ammo. I'm parked directly on top of the friendlies."

"Break, break. White Two-Five, when he finishes, I want you and your wing to make continuous passes using your mini-guns only. Remember, they've done some hand to hand stuff and the bad guys are about to overrun them. So, I want you guys to keep it tight on me also. Tell you what, if you don't shoot me down and keep the bad guys off the friendlies, I'll buy all the beer tonight."

"Roger that, One-Five. We're setting up now. The four of us have got a good copy on all the cold beer. You all take very good care of your wallet now. Ya hear. You've got four thirsty gun-bird drivers up here."

Unexpectedly, Bill yelled into the intercom scaring Kev half to death.

"D--- it, boss! I've got a jam. You better kick a pedal and give Joe his chance at them. In the mean time, I'll try to clear this stupid jam."

Not bothering responding, Kev viciously kicked a pedal to turn one-hundred and eighty degrees. His one-hundred and eighty degree turn was loudly accompanied ripping music of his wingman's mini chewing up the jungle just beyond his door. When he could see the grunts, Joe also began firing his M-60 in support. He was squeezing off short burst to conserve ammo, as the first Snake began its mini-gun run. All was normal in Kev's world. Radios and intercom screaming in his ears, bad guys shooting, and observers shooting punctuated his pounding pulse.

"White Two-Five is inbound. Mini-gun only."

When Two-Five finished his first gun-run, C&C called Kev.

"Red One-Five, I've got the two Navy F-4's arriving on station. They are setting up their orbit now. Give them a call on UHF and tell them what you need. Their call sign is 'Sea Gull.'"

Kev felt as if he were juggling six grenades, each with its pin pulled. However, he had faith that Joe was doing a good job. At the same time, he also knew that Bill had more experience and also had a better field of fire. With that in mind, he keyed the intercom.

"OK guys, here we go. We're going to do the ole flip-flop again."

Kicking a pedal, he returned his and Bill's side to the bad guys.

"So far, so good!"

He thought to himself.

"Sea Gull, this is Red One-Five. If you can follow the Snakes diving run, I'm the little bitty OH-6 helicopter just to the east of their firing point."

As he spoke, Kev found himself softly chuckling to himself. This time, however, it lacked its recently acquired bitter tone.

"These Navy pukes," he thought to himself, "are getting a good show."

He knew that they could hear Bill's M-60 hammering away with its short burst of fire. Most likely Sea Gull could also hear White Two-Three's minis ripping up the foliage just outside Kev's door.

Everything was going well and Kev was pleased to have White Two-Three on station. His Snake was in 'Scout' configuration with two minis mounted on the wing pods and two minis mounted in the nose turret. Watching the trees just outside his window, he saw the combined mini's shredding the leaves from them like a gale-force wind. Kev didn't know how anything could live under that awesome firepower. Yet, somehow a few of the bad guys always did.

"Red One-Five, this is Sea Gull One-Zero. I've got a pretty good idea where you are. We will need the target area marked with Willie Peter. Be advised, we are at 'bingo' fuel and can make one pass only."

Shaking his head, Kev angerly muttered to himself.

"Why am I not surprised that the Navy is calling out Bingo fuel?"

Fortunately, Kev's little bird had yet to take any hits from the bad guys. What pleased Kev more was that they had been holding the bad guys at bay. With his mental fingers crossed, Kev was hoping that their luck would continue to hold as Bill hammered away with short burst on his M-60. Simultaneously, White Two-Five was moving into position to hose down the area with his turret a second time. Quickly analyzing the situation, Kev came to a couple of decisions.

"White Two-Five, I want you to put your mini on the same spot. However, while you are doing that, I also want you to mark the target area with Willie Pete rockets. Put your rockets about ten meters farther west."

"Break, break. Sea Gull One-Zero, I understand you are bingo fuel. However, I've got some friendlies in danger of being overrun. They have already taken heavy causalities including KIAs. Please, I need you to stretch the envelope a little thin today. I must have multiple passes so they can break contact."

Pausing for breath, Kev mentally re-crossed his fingers and continued talking with Sea Gull One-Zero.

"Sea Gull One-Zero, I've got ten thousand feet of nice smooth Air Force concrete about twenty to twenty-five klicks directly south. I'm sure that if you ask nicely they will give you some gas. Those Air Force pukes can be all right guys. They've fueled me a couple of times and even offered to clean my windshield and give me green stamps."

He held his breath. Inter-service rivalries were always a touchy problem. Muttering under his breath, he said.

"Welcome to the wacky world according to Viet Nam."

Just as he knew they would, four Willie Pete rockets exploded exactly where Kev wanted them. It was an excellent mark.

"Red One-Five, Sea Gull One-Six and I have a good visual on the Willie Pete mark. Where are the friendlies in relation to the mark?"

Kev quickly told them that the friendlies were twenty-five meters east of the mark.

"That's too close for us, One-Five. Our pull out is thirty-five-hundred feet and we can't bomb closer than five hundred meters. Furthermore, we're still bingo fuel. You get one pass. We're salvoing everything on that pass."

Fury, multiplied by righteous rage, exploded within the private confines of Kev's head. Biting his tongue till he could taste his own salty blood, he savagely keyed his radio.

Determined to remain calm, Kev did his best to speak softly and slowly to the stubborn and proud Navy types.

"Sea Gull One-Zero maybe you don't understand the situation. D--- it man, I've got American troops dying down here! Please, can't you at least give me a couple of close passes with your pistol? I know that if you can land on a pitching carrier deck that you can land on ten-thousand feet of concrete! H---, those Air Force pump jocks have even given a dumb Army guy like me fuel. My credit card is good with them. I'm sure that yours is also. Why don't we just let the paper pushers can figure out who to bill later?"

Shaking with barely contained fury, Kev awaited Sea Gull's response.

"Sorry Red One-Five. However, I'm bingo fuel. One pass and negative pistol. I've got to get back to my carrier. Am I cleared in or not? If not, we'll just dump these bombs in the gulf."

Shaking his head at this stupidity called Viet Nam, Kev answered the absurd question.

"Sea Gull One-Zero and Sea Gull One-Six, you are cleared inbound."

Firmly clamping his jaw tightly shut, Kev was afraid to say another word. He knew that if he spoke that word to Sea Gull again that he would loose control and say something that he meant.

Hatefully watching the two Sea Gull birds waste tens of thousands of Uncle Sam's dollars making useless kindling, Kev keyed the intercom.

"I hope those jerks choke on their hot chow tonight and get a crotch rash from their clean sheets."

He then closed his mouth as C&C came on the radio.

"Red One-Five, your second team and its gun birds are coming over the ridge now. I'll brief them while you guys expend your ammo. Don't worry, while you were wasting your breath with those seaborne heros, I scrambled a couple pairs of Spads. Why don't you brief the grunts while I brief the new team?"

That was the best news that Kev had heard since he began helping the grunts. "Roger that Six. Those Spads are exactly what the doctor ordered. If anyone can do it. Those old dudes can get the patient back to health!"

He paused for a moment, and keyed the mike again.

"Ah . . . Sir, good work!"

If Kev had been on the ground, he would have danced. He had tried dancing a couple of times while flying. It didn't work! Over the months, he had worked with the Air Force Spads several times. Specifically, they called them A1-Es. The Navy had developed that big ole bird at the close of the Second World War as a ground attack/dive bomber. At first glance, the big ole bird seemed out of place in a world of jets and turbines. They looked like a huge prop driven WW II fighter aircraft. With their massive three-thousand horsepower radial engine, those big ugly birds could carry a bomb load greater than a WW Two B-17 bomber.

From a grunt's point of view, the Spad's greatest advantage was that they could loiter on station for about seven hours. If that wasn't good enough, old pros flew the grand old bird. They were superb airplane drivers who could make five meter corrections with five-hundred pound bombs. If the mark were good and someone urgently requested it, they could drop their bombs within ten meters of friendlies. With playmates like these and a fresh pair of Snakes, Kev was confident that ole Sven would get the friendlies home in time for evening mess. He did hope for their sake that their mess was better than his.

While Kev was simmering in slow rage, Sven called and said that he had an excellent fix on Kev's position. He added that he would take over when they expended their ammo. First keying the intercom, Kev told his crew that it was time for the ole flip-flop. He wanted Joe to expend his ammo first. As he did the one-hundred and eighty degree pedal turn, he called the Snakes.

"White Two-Five, I want you guys to expend on the next pass. Put all your rockets about ten to fifteen meters out. Please keep the mini as tight as possible. The bad guys aren't doing much shooting now and I want to keep it that way."

While the Snakes were making their final run, Kev brought Mud Hen Five up to date. Mud Hen had trouble hearing Kev through the increasing inferno of exploding rockets. Mud Hen might have had trouble hearing in the increased noise level. However, he didn't ask the Cav to stop shooting to make radio communication easier! When the din had settled, Kev repeated his message when he handed him off to Sven in Red One-Four.

Breaking clear of the action, Kev checked in with C&C.

"Red One-Five is clear of the area."

C&C then told him that both the Red and the White team were to refuel and rearm as quickly as possible. When they had completed both, they were to immediately return to station. What was left unsaid was the possibility that Sven's team would also be forced to expend their ammunition. Forty-five minutes later, the four helicopters were rapidly heading back to the spot where the friendly grunts had been in trouble.

Heavy with fuel and munitions, they were prepared and eager to continue helping the folk on the ground. Kev was pleased, but not surprised, when C&C called.

"Red One-Five, this is White Six. I want your team and the Snakes to return to the staging area. The folks on the ground were finally able to pull back and a leg company from division reinforced them."

He had been confident that Sven, with the help of the Spads, would accomplish the mission. Ole Kev had not misplaced that confidence, in Sven. However, the woeful performance of the Navy F-4's had left a sour and very bitter taste in his mouth.

Later that evening, unable to elude his feelings of frustration and sense of shame by association, Kev left the little Officers Club early. As a former jock, over the last several months, he had broken training. He had taken to smoking cigars. Placing the unopened beer he had been carrying in his pocket, he dug out a rum soaked crook. They were cheap, plentiful and he didn't have anybody to kiss. Much to his surprise, he had learned to enjoy them. Playing with it, he wet it down good. Kev found the act of preparing the cigar almost as enjoyable as smoking it. Lighting up, he strolled over to his place of meditation, his Loach's revetment.

He wanted to write about the events of the day. However, he needed to think. Kev was struggling to make sense out of the Navy pilot's behavior. While he was thinking, he noticed a very weary old man who wearily sat his young body upon the crumbling olive drab sandbags. Humbled, Kev realized that the weary old man was himself. Looking up, he silently gazed at the countless stars in the clear night air. He had stopped thinking. Blank faced and motionless, his mind was slowly drifting. As best he could tell, his destination was nowhere. Gazing up at the vast nothingness, he/himself felt adrift, alone, and serene in a sea of meaninglessness.

Five minutes later, a warning cough announced that someone was approaching his hiding place. Well . . . maybe it was an hour later. Lost in his own little world, Kev didn't have any idea, nor was he concerned about how long he had been in his timeless and lost place. He only knew that his other-dimensional hiding place gave him some comfort and quiet because he had no responsibility in that non-place and non-time. A familiar voice broke the remainder of Kev's emotional escape.

"Ah my good friend Kevin, you're so darn predictable. When troubled, ole Kev strolls down and communes with his beloved Red Birds. I guess that they are like you, old buddy. All that these little birds want to do is what they were made to do."

Kev immediately knew who had spoken. It was his cynical, sarcastic, well lubricated, and very tender friend. Rising to Sven's gentle baiting, Kev gave his own retort.

"Sven, you drunken fool, you keep stumbling around, down here on the flight line, some at night you'll get yourself into big time trouble. Someone is going to fill you ragged butt with about twenty M-16 sized holes. You're hopeless. But, I love ya anyway. Pull up a sandbag and a lukewarm one."

They had known each other for the better part of a year and then some. Kev would readily admit that Sven was the closest thing to a friend that he had in Vietnam. This wasn't the first time that they had quietly sat on a revetment and shared silent thoughts and warm beer. Sven eventually broke the serene spell of silence.

"You know, an old friend of mine spent a couple of weeks up at that place that the Spad drivers call home. While we were sharing a couple of beers, he was telling me that they are one heck of a bunch of strange and crazy guys."

Sven was fishing for a response. He wanted to see if Kev needed to talk or if he preferred to sit and brood. He wasn't the least bit surprised when Kev took the bait. Hopelessly addicted aviation lore, Kev would talk flying at his own funeral.

"Oh ya. What did he say?"

"Well . . . he told me that they are members of a very special kind of club. Most of them are some kind of, lower echelon, bad boys. By and large, they are passed over Majors or Light Colonels. I don't think that any of them have done anything that you or I would call bad. They just didn't play the career track game by the Air Force's carefully laid out rules."

Sven paused to take a sip of his beer. The conversation had perked Kev's interest.

434

"Sven, I'm not sure what the rules are. I guess that I have been too busy flying and doing this combat thing to learn the rules."

This caused Sven to chuckle ruefully.

"There you go, you bloody romantic. You just broke the first rule of survival in this man's Army. 'One's career is far more important than flying or the mission!' Heck, my friend told me that one of those Spad pilots guys got in trouble because he refused to say an aircraft was flyable. His boss wanted one-hundred percent aircraft availability to show what a good job he was doing as the CO. This guy was the maintenance officer. Determined to do his job correctly, he made his boss look bad by grounding an unsafe aircraft. His next Officer Efficiency Report took spiteful care of his military career!"

Kev laughed somewhat bitterly as he continued to think about the earlier incident with the Navy pilots. Well lubricated and on a roll, Sven gleefully continued.

"I don't care what anyone else might say. These guys might be terrible 'professional' officers. However, I think, they are the greatest airplane drivers I have ever seen. I'll be honest with you Kev, if it wasn't for them we would have left a lot more dead GI's on the ground today! Believe me or not, that's up to you. The truth is that I was giving those guys five meter corrections. It didn't even raise a comment from them. They rolled in spot on the money each time. Those old coots flying those Spads quickly sent the bad guys running, post haste. As far as I am concerned I'd rather work for any one of them than most of the so called, 'good' officers I have met!"

Still feeling bitter, but warming to the conversation, Kev laughed and asked Sven.

"Have you ever seen those guys on the taxiways heading out for a mission?" In the comforting darkness, Sven smiled at the memory of watching the Spads taxiing out for takeoff. The loping idle of those huge radial engines caused the ground to tremble and shake in fear."

"Ya. It's a sight to behold. Heck, most of those guys are as old as dirt and they are still Majors and LTCs. Honest to God Kev, I hadn't seen that much grey hair, or baldness, since the last time I visited my great-grandfather in the nursing home! They sit up there in those big a--- - birds like they are the kings of aviation. With big ole cigars hanging out of their mouths, they are straight out of central casting."

Both of the young men chuckled at their memories. Yet, no anger nor cynicism discolored their laugh. If anything, they were more than a little jealous.

"You know, Sven, I really envy those guys."

Kev's face lit up as he drew heavily upon his cigar.

"In fact, I have decided that when I grow up, if I ever grow up, I want to be just like those old farts. Let's be honest with each other. You and I think that we are some kind of hot shot pilots. What have we got, twelve hundred, maybe fifteen hundred flight hours each? I bet that any one of those guys has more time pre-flighting than the two of us combined have flown! As God is my witness, I'd rather have one of those crusty old dudes covering my backside than a thousand hot shot Navy pukes."

As he took a sip of his beer, Kev's anger rose to the boiling point.

"I don't give a good God d--- if those pretty Navy boys can land on an aircraft carrier! They can brag about their supposed flying skills all that they want. However, being able to land on a carrier didn't do a d--- bit of good for those kids on the ground today!"

Having vented his spleen and drained his emotional tumult, Kev took a slow draw on his lukewarm beer.

It was silent. The two young men were of quite different temperaments. Yet, when it came to protecting the troops on the ground, they were more like identical twins. From the way that they viewed their world protecting the crunchies on the ground was the reason that they were born. After a couple of minutes, Sven broke the silence.

"Kev, let me play the Devil's advocate for a moment. Mind you, I'm not at all sure that I believe what I am going to say. Yet, for reasons unknown and very strange to me, I do want to be fair. Hmmmm, it must be the beer."

After "testing" his beer's quality, Sven continued.

"Maybe these guys were on a first mission shake down. Or, maybe they were only following orders. What is more important is that maybe they were so bad at air to ground that this was their way of protecting the guys on the ground. Truthfully, neither of us has ever been impressed with the Navy F-4 guys bombing ability."

Kev didn't respond at first. He just kept playing with his cigar while he smoldered and silently pondered what he would do if he ever got up close and personal with the offending Navy pilots.

At last, he spoke.

"I don't know Sven, what they did still isn't right. H---, how often has either of us severely bent the rules to help the guys on the ground. It seems to me that they could have loitered about for a little while and used some pistol. I just don't understand. What's so hard about getting some Air Force fuel and then going home?"

Sven was ready.

"Kev, you forget one little thing. You and I are just a couple of know nothing nobody junior Warrant Officers. As far as I know, we have no plans of becoming Generals, Admirals, or what not. I can't speak for you. The bald-faced truth of the matter is if someone wants to give me a bad OER, I simply don't care."

Sven drew heavily upon his beer as if he were seeking sustenance.

"Kev my friend, I'm over here to drive helicopters. If I can help some American kids survive this cluster f---, all the better for my effort! On the other hand, if you want to be a General or an Admiral, that takes a different approach to this war. You've got to do what you're told, take no chances, and above and beyond everything else make no mistakes, no matter how little. I'll guarantee that there isn't a single General grade officer in any of the services who have a single bad OER. You won't find a questionable comment like, 'he disobeyed SOP or orders to save the lives of some unknown ground-pounders' in any of their OERs."

Standing firmly on his views, Kev repeated himself.

"I just don't know Sven, what they did still isn't right."

Occasionally, Sven would get frustrated with Kev's terminal romanticism and naivete. This was one of those times. Without thinking, he angrily and lovingly snapped at him.

"J---- H. C---- Kev! Grow up! What you saw today is simply the way it is. Most people, in this crummy little world of ours, only care about number one. We're taught that from day one in out little world. 'Get yours before someone else gets it.' Furthermore, most people usually only do things that are in their own self interest. Maybe, just maybe, and if it doesn't cost them anything, somewhere along the way, they'll help some other poor slob. However, if you want to make it big in this man's Army, you better stop caring about the troops or the mission. Someone somewhere has decided that we are not going to win this thing. So, stop caring about it. The only thing in the whole wide world that you should care about is your next OER! You may not like the current situation. BUT . . . that's the way it is!"

Sven could see that Kev was angry and wounded. He had accepted that he was a first class cynic. Yet, he deeply valued his friendship with the romantic young man who was his only friend in the unit. As much as he saw his duty to act as Kev's reality checker, he also saw in Kev a person who kept his hope alive. In his private moments, he wished that he could capture some of what drove Kev. Though he never said it, he greatly admired the basic goodness and nobility of his foolish young friend.

"Look Kev, its OK to be the person that you are. I doubt that you could find a flying enlisted man who would hesitate to risk his life for you. For that matter, ole Sven here and every Scout pilot and Gun pilot in the unit feels the same way. Why do people feel this way? It is because we know that you would do the same thing for us. In my opinion, that's good!"

437

Embarrassed by what he had been saying, Sven fiddled with his beer and lit another cigarette with trembling fingers.

"Look buddy, all that I'm saying is that this is not the way the military works anymore. It is possible that when this mess over here got started it wasn't that way. Today, things are different. We've gone too far and gotten nowhere fast. Circumstance, politics, and God only knows what else, has reduced the war effort, such as it is, to its lowest common denominator. No one, over here, is waving the flag for motherhood, apple pie, and the American way of life. God help us. This whole mess has become every man for himself. Three quarters of the career officers are just trying to get their tickets punched, not get fraged by some druggie, and survive with their careers' in one piece."

Sven was not accustomed to delivering lengthily orations. Kev could sense that he was becoming increasingly uncomfortable.

Nevertheless, he was on a roll. All Sven's built up frustration and cynicism came flowing out in one explosive sound.

"Let's face the grim facts my friend. I can see no reason why we couldn't win this little war in a heartbeat. That is, we could win it if we chose to do so. At the very least, we could shift the fighting to the north where it belongs. For whatever reasons, the big boys in Washington don't want us to change the status quo. Apparently, the political types like things just the way they are. Maybe, they are afraid of upsetting the folks back home. Possibly, they are afraid that the Chinese will come south like they did in Korea. We both know that Uncle Sam's Army has been in this s--- hole too many years for anyone to suggest that we are planning on winning. When you look at it like through the lenses of our experience, it has to be every man for himself. That, my good friend, is exactly what the big boys in Washington are doing. They are taking care of themselves and shifting the blame for this whole mess on us."

This last outburst, by Sven, was more than Kev could take. He was a mixed-up combination of angry, hurt, and upset. Had he been a little boy, he might have broken down into tears. It is always difficult for an idealist to discover that his ideals have human feet of clay. A part of him screamed at him to lash out at Sven for debunking his vision of Santa Claus and the Army. The other part of him, which had spent over a year in Viet Nam, knew that Sven was speaking a harsh and unpalatable, to him, truth. He had been refusing to face the dissolution of his dreams for a long time. Nevertheless, Sven's talking about it didn't make it any easier.

Much to his regret, the day's incident with the Navy pilots was not an isolated one. The Navy pukes would sleep comfortable knowing that they had carefully followed orders. Their next OER's would reflect that they were good officers and pilots. They had followed orders and returned safely with their birds undamaged. The way things were going, they were probably busy writing each other up for medals. For all Kev knew, one of them was destined to become "Chief of Naval Operations" in thirty years. Somewhere, someone had decreed that something larger was at stake than the lives of nameless draftees. Still, a voice within himself screamed at the injustice that had put careers before the mission and the troops.

A long silence followed Sven's observations. Both of the young men were comfortable with the canopy of silence. Sven had only spoken aloud a tragic truth both of them had reluctantly come to recognize and hate. Kev's romanticism had preferred not to acknowledge the devastating truth of Sven's pragmatism. Sighing with his premature weariness, Kev broke the silence.

"Sven, you really p--- me off. Every time that you are right, I just want to punch you in the mouth to shut you up! However, punching you out for speaking the truth wouldn't be right and it wouldn't change the truth of what you say."

"The way I see it, I've got two choices. Either I grow up or I go completely crazy! I am beginning to discover that the world, according to Viet Nam, is not going to change simply because I decree that it should change. I suppose that things here are the way they are because that is the way they are."

Kev paused for a moment and shook his head.

"Does that make any sense? Anyway, I'm just a little guy and the big guys somewhere want it to be the way they have created it. D----- though, I don't have to go along with it. Do I?"

With that last comment, Sven allowed himself a long bitter laugh. If someone had observed the conversation, they would have thought that it was the beer doing all the talking. However, it was anything but the beer speaking. Rather and tragically, it was the age, the time, and the troubles speaking its truth through these troubled young men. Like many other young officers in the Army, and other services, they had grown frustrated by the waste of human life coupled with the lack of a clearly defined and understood mission.

"No, Kev, you don't have go along with the every man for himself crowd. What you do have to do is accept the reality and the fact of its overwhelming presence. If you choose, you can keep doing what you do. As far as I am concerned, 'please do.' However, don't expect the 'Professional Army' or politicians to thank you for it. In fact, if it causes them any sort of career problem, they will gladly crucify you for your trouble. Remember on thing, though. It will be a very public crucifixion in which you will serve as an object lesson to other rebels."

Silence returned to the dark revetment.

Throwing his cigar butt away, Kev levered himself off his sandbag perch.

"Sven, I going to make a few notes and then try to get some sleep. Tomorrow I am going to fly and try to keep some poor slob from getting himself killed or getting me killed in this stupidity. I don't suppose that I will ever become an admiral or a general. Yet, I hope that I sleep better than those useless SOB's that the Navy sent me today."

CAN'T WALK AWAY FROM THIS ONE

For the lack of finding a better word, I will call this illegible scribbling my personal journal of my unexpected vacation.

DAY One:

Charles Dickens started a book something like this, "I was born." That task completed, I'll skip forward several chapters. It has not been a good day. This morning, much to my dismay, I was put to work. The folks at the administration shack gave me the dubious honor of flying mail to higher headquarters. Kevin Paul Johnson is a discouraged and tired Chief Warrant Officer. (Having served a year as a WO-1, I was promoted to CW-2.) Emotionally and physically worn out, the heroic Chief Warrant Officer didn't really want to squander his day off by flying the mail. Selfishly, I did not volunteer my day off for the good of humankind. However, in this man's Army, when the Executive Officer asks you to fly the mail on your day off, well . . . , you fly the mail. Military reality dictates that the XO outranks me and I do what he tells me to do. Complicating my life is the fact that he is my friend and I hate to say no to him. Oh well . . .

Reluctantly acknowledging the inevitable, I slowly shuffled down to the Red Bird line. If forced to fly, I had hoped to strap into my usual bird, good ole Rosy II. The maintenance guys had just installed a new engine. In turn, I had hoped to enjoy the power and reliability of the new engine. Just my luck, today's mission needs called for every available bird. Therefore, the maintenance officer asked me to fly tired ole 624. Poor old bird, I am afraid that she isn't worth much to anybody anymore. All that remains of her earthly remains is a crumpled pile of aluminum scrap and olive drab trash. Aw Shoot! Please forgive me, I'm getting a little ahead of myself.

There is nothing special about poor ole 624. In fact, she was just like most of our helicopters. The constant wear and tear of combat in Vietnam had reduced her to little more than a war weary wreck. This morning, when I arrived at the flightline, she was pretending that she was a viable military helicopter. In an ironic way, she reminded me of an elderly matron who was trying to be the sex symbol which she was some thirty years ago. The brutal realities of life have decided that those days are well past. She, much like the elderly matron, was well past her prime.

If we were a stateside unit, they would have immediately grounded 624 for weeks on end. Most likely, they would have sent the poor ole girl to the depot for a total rebuilding. However, the big boys in Washington have not given us that luxury here in lovely South East Asia. As I have bitterly repeated, to all who would listen, <u>nothing</u> is too good for our boys over-seas. Just patch these old birds up with duct tape and beer cans and they will be considered combat-ready. Furthermore, if the bean-counters allow maintenance to be truly extravagant, sometimes we get olive drab paint to cover the assorted, brightly colored, Budweiser and Coors patches.

Carefully reviewing the realities of American culture and life, I have come to an unhappy conclusion. It would be a crying shame if the tax payers had to give up a little money to keep the boys over seas in top-rate, life preserving, equipment. Political types know that a big spending action, unless it is in their home district, is not the way to win an election. It is a given fact that winning elections is the most important thing in the world to most of these folk. Obviously, political types do not get reelected if they have the gall to raise taxes for an increasingly unpopular war. Therefore, ole 624 did not get her well-deserved rebuild.

I suppose that, at the moment, I am being just a touch bitter. If I seem so, please forgive me. So far, it has not been one of my better days since I started this wondrous Oriental Vacation. So be it. What discourages me is that I don't know if my days are going to get better in the near future. One bright light shines on this depressingly dark picture. Feeling generous, I told the crew chief to take the day off. I told him to go into town, d rink a few cold beers for me, and just relax. I reasoned, why should both of us be miserable flying the mail? Irony upon irony, little did I know how miserable I was going to be today. Hopefully he isn't going to be too severely hung-over or have an unwelcomed social disease when he returns to his hooch.

Well . . . let me begin at the beginning. Dawn's bright red sun appeared and our little heliport roused itself to a busy mechanical military life. Though it was my day off, sleep was not coming easily. The piercing whine of turbine engines and the heavy thump of pounding rotors invaded the sanctity of my solitude. This morning's mechanical symphony was loudly declaring the run up and takeoff of fifty to a hundred helicopters. As always, the war was disturbing my plans. After tossing and turning because of the noise, I groaned in the overwrought pain of waking.

"Oh well," I muttered to myself, "I might as well get up and answer the call of nature."

My hopes of getting some extra sleep had turned out to be another exercise in futility. Wearing only the bottoms of my grungy nomex flight suit, I prepared to face the world. Then, I trudged out to the military correct "eight hole facility" located just behind my hootch. While leaving my hootch, I grabbed myself a well-read magazine. It was time to sit, read, and carefully meditate and ponder upon the state of the world.

Sitting proudly, I was enthroned in all the magnificent dignity I could muster. With my flight suit casually dropped down about my ankles, I began to gently laugh. Reviewing my life's situation, I decided that this officer and gentleman had undoubtably come a long way. More than miles separated me from the deep dark deprivations of my glorious high school days. It was unbelievable. Back in my high school days, at such times, I was forced to sit isolated. All by myself, I had no one with whom to pass the time of day. Furthermore, the folks back in the world had forced me to sit on a cold porcelain stool with ice cold water directly beneath my naked little butt.

It became amusingly clear that the quality of my life had skyrocketed. Today, I enjoyed the soft caress of splintery wood. If I turned out to be very lucky, I might share this wonderful facility with seven other dignified gentlemen of Uncle Sam's Officer Corps. Blessed by each other's company, we can gather together in our male bonding. What a wonderful intimate way for us to bond. Sharing our morning constitutionals, we have the delightful opportunity to discuss many important things. It would be stimulating to discuss current events, the latest novels which we have read, and the Off Broadway Shows we were going to see. Furthering the delight of a Vietnam morning, we could enjoy conversing while we savored the panoramic overview of the heliport.

Alas, this morning, such male bonded delights were not to be. A prolonged creak was quickly followed by a foreboding scraping sound of metal on wood. These dreadful sounds abruptly disturbed my humorous musing. So much for the rare and wonderful delights of my morning constitutional in lovely South East Asia. As pungent morning vapors slowly rose from below the seat level, I both felt and heard the slam of a trap door. Groaning silently and very deeply, I mentally set myself to enjoy another of the great wonders of Vietnam in the morning.

"Wonderful," I said to myself. "The sacred dance of the s---burner is about to begin for my sensuous enjoyment."

With the wind gently blowing through the screening and softly caressing my back, I prepared myself. I well knew that a defiantly disgusting assault upon the tender tissues of my nasal cavities was about to begin. Listening carefully and in unwilling expectation, I heard the telltale splash of five or more gallons of kerosene. It was being emptied into the bottom one-half of a fifty-five-gallon drum. The stage was set and the sacred dance was about to begin. Shivering in anticipation, I could hardly contain my joy.

Waiting for the coming assault, I sought to distract myself. I found myself and pondering and meditating deeply about the more important aspects of human life and existence. The baser parts on my life interrupted my finely honed philosophical journey. Gritting my teeth, I wondered which was a more disgusting sound? Was it the sound of my own gifts splashing down in the drum directly below me? Or, was it the sound of kerosene splashing into the drum? Please allow me to assure

443

you that only while seated in a military eight-holler does one have such deep thoughts so early in the morning.

Cringing and cursing military life in specific and in general, I sorrowfully awaited, the coming, billowing clouds of pungent black smoke. The funeral flames would mark the daily disposal of the latest collection of human excretion contained within the fifty-five-gallon drum. The quiet noise of a soft poof signaled the lighting of the barrel. As I expected, the clouds of pungent black smoke quickly began to fill the Officers elegant outhouse. This was the signal for me to quickly finish my business.

Well experienced, I had no burning desire to remain in that lovely atmosphere. Not only did I not wish to enjoy the fragrance, neither did I wish to have the soot and residue settle upon my body! Hastily, I beat a graceless retreat to my hootch. Upon my arrival, I found my sleeping quarters, my so-called home environment, was also receiving the early morning's tender blessings. The daily sacred dance of the s--- burner exempts no one. This is a dismal, disgusting, and degrading smell and ritual. I might add that I will not miss it when I return to the world.

Sardonically chuckling at the strange circumstances of my life, I began to slowly trudge up to the Officers Mess. It was time to jump-start myself with a cup of coffee, such as it is. The pages of the calendar flutter in the winds of time. As a result, I have discovered that one's tolerance for the absurd changes beyond human expectation. A little more than a year ago, this morning ritual would have made me nauseous for the day. The last thing in the world that I would have wanted would have been a cup of coffee. Well . . . things do change. Pondering deeply, as I walk, I have discovered that I am a strange being. My behavior must have convinced people that I was about five cans short of a six-pack as they watched me walking toward the open mess. Walking alone, I was quietly chuckling to myself. I was laughing as I was thinking about hot water and shaving.

The story that was bringing a twinkle to my eyes, a smile to my face, and the laughter to my lips was an old one. The incident went back to my very first week with the troop. Ancient history it has become. It was early morning and the whole troop was standing down for the day. If memory serves me correctly, it happened about nine in the morning. Given that I was a new guy who was useless and underfoot, I had quietly planted myself on top of a sandbag bunker. My plan of action was simple. Stay out from underfoot, keep my mouth shut, and try to figure out what was going on. Hopefully, by quietly observing the comings and goings of my new unit, I could learn what was going on. Suddenly the morning silence was abruptly broken. Without warning, the loud crump of exploding 122 millimeter rocket shattered the quiet.

Shoot, I'm getting a little bit ahead of myself again. Let me go back to the beginning of the story. Sitting on top of that bunker, I was emotionally reeling. Lovely Vietnam had just introduced me to the sacred dance of the s--- burners. In my worse days of training, I had always taken for granted a basic level of human sanitation, dignity, and privacy. That expectation seemed fair to me. Everyone knows that civilized people rightfully expect certain things while doing their bodily functions. We all want to maintain a minimum level of human dignity.

Though my folks had raised me in the midst of the, so called, poorer side of the tracks, I too felt the same way. Relieving oneself into a slimy stinky rock-filled pipe stuck into the ground lacked something vital and seems to rate very low on the human dignity scale. Furthermore, doing one's morning constitutional in an open communal outhouse to the lovely scent of burning human waste had not been part of my "previous" life's experience. Unknown to me, Mom and Dad had also raised me with some strongly held beliefs about human hygiene. One of these simple beliefs was that a man has the right to expect some hot water to occasionally bathe in and to scrape the morning stubble off his face! (Of course, morning stubble was not one of my greatest problems. However, I had great hopes that some day it would be a daily issue.)

However, I quickly discovered that such basic and civilized necessities were not available in my current home. First, steaming hot water for bathing or shaving was an unheard of luxury. As I have previously indicated, due to my relative youth and innocence, shaving remained only an occasional duty for me. I am also further blessed with a very fine beard which doesn't need softening with hot soapy water. However, others living in my neighborhood are not so blessed. To continue with my amusing story, the whole squadron was standing down for the day. Thoughtfully, some delightfully enterprising individual had rigged up a field kitchen water heater in a fifty-five-gallon drum. Wonder upon wonders, at last, the gods of war had smiled upon us. Thanks to a man who deftly combined the skills of a tinkerer and thief, hot water magically appeared. At last, a man could washup and shave his face like a civilized human being!

Hot shaving water was the beginning of another of Vietnam's incidents of black humor. This "black humor" is the strange humor which occasionally brightens up the life of a combat soldier far from home. That morning, some kind soul was distributing a rare and wonderful elixir of human dignity and comfort. I watched the unfolding drama from not more than one hundred fifty yards. Sitting upon my lofty perch on the bunker, I had a, high dollar, front row seat. The strangely sad show started when the first 122 rocket struck the camp with a startling crump.

Sometimes, when the unexpected does arrive in my, new to me then, neighborhood, things begin moving faster than a simple new guy can understand The dust had not begun to settle from the impact of the first rocket when a second rocket exploded. The second one was ten to fifteen yards closer to the blessed fountain of human comfort. The sacred and holy device, which was dispensing hot water for shaving, was in grave danger. A great human dilemma of near epic proportions was beginning to unfold before my eyes.

Before I go any farther with this little story, let me make an honest observation. It should be clear to the casual observer, that the explosion of the first, if not the explosion of the second rocket, should have caused me to react in normal and understandable self-preservation. An average level of human intelligence would have quickly dictated that the three or four of us newbes seated on the top of the bunker would have quickly scrambled inside seeking safety. However, with a life and death drama unfolding before us, we shelved our limited intelligence. We also placed our instinct of self preservation upon the same shelf.

Peering through the settling dust of the first explosion, we looked about. We then noted that the two or three young officers who were waiting to get hot water had scrambled to the safety of nearby bunkers. Lacking normal intelligence, we chose not to copy their good example of mature discernment and great wisdom. In truth, their's was not the drama which held our fascinated attention. We collectively riveted our eyes upon one Captain Holt. This fine gentleman was the young Administration Officer of our "A" Troop.

When the first rocket exploded, he had already carefully and jealously gathered his magic elixir of civilization and human comfort in a shallow basin. The good Captain was scantily dressed in a pair of rubber thongs and had but an olive drab towel safely wrapped about his waist. When the second rocket impacted, he suddenly faced a heart breaking decision. The NVA gunner had begun walking the deadly rockets in his direction. His difficult decision was based upon one of the few things which we were in universal agreement. The steaming hot water in his shallow basin was more valuable than gold and more comforting than a loving woman's embrace. What was a man to do? Oh, what to do was the question of the moment.

Looking back through the softening lenses of time, I am not sure that I clearly saw his face that morning. Today, more than a year later, I can plainly see the messages which were rapidly flashing across his features. Understandable confusion came first. Anger quickly followed it. Lastly, grim determination not to lose his priceless treasure was clearly written upon his young stubbly face. Within an instant, he came to his meticulously formed command decision. Captain Holt carefully spun about exactly one hundred and eighty degrees. Doing his best not to lose any of the contents of his precious container of hot water, he began to run directly away from the incoming rockets. Incidently, this meant that he was running directly toward us. This was also bringing the rain of rockets that much closer to us. As stupid as it seems in retrospect, this turn of events and his grisly determination kept us riveted in place. At a great risk and personal peril, heroically, we intently followed this, Vietnam style, life and death drama.

As we watched with eyes wide open and jaws agape, the good Captain expeditiously cast aside his personal safety and his Commissioned Officers' dignity. All, who were watching, understood that he did this for the noble purpose of shaving with hot water. Overall, he was moving out at a good clip. Though he was stepping out as quickly as he could without spilling an excess amount of his hot water, things were not going well for him. Much to his dismay, he was losing the race. Poor ole Captain Holt could tell that the long steps of the rockets, which were reaching out for his treasure, were rapidly gaining on him.

The rocket attack's basic inhumanity strengthened his grim determination to persevere in the face of growing difficulty. All was almost lost when the third rocket had destroyed the source of his magic elixir. Tragically, he would get no more if he lost what he had. Attempting to further pick up his pace, he sought to escape with that little morsel of civilization. He was determined that he would not be deprived of a little human comfort. As he carefully balanced need for speed and the contents of his basin, the poor man's towel loosened and fell off him. This only served to add further insult to injury. Nevertheless, the chase was on. It was a running gun battle of epic proportion. Captain Holt was a-running and the exploding rockets were a-gunning.

Well . . . I have already established my own complete lack of intelligence. My front row seat was far more important to me than my personal safety. With rockets raining down, we began to stand and cheer him on like some kind of damn fools. The whole black comedy was unfolding before us. We acted as if the bad guys staged the rocket attack for our enjoyment as it took on the demeaning personality of a Roman Circus. The contest had gathered for itself more importance than the trivial issues of human safety.

Caught up in the unfolding drama of the moment, the possibility of Captain Holt's death or our own deaths had become irrelevant. We were excited, breathless, and mindless spectators at the "Roman circus" of death. All that mattered was that he did not lose his shallow basin of hot water. Evil forces were threatening to deprive the poor man of his precious prize. As we cheered, we also found ourselves bursting into gales of uncontrollable laughter. At last, the absurdness of the whole situation came into a sharp focus for those of us on the bunker.

The situation had become comic, tragic, horrifying, and absurd all in the same breath. Dignity thrown to the wind, poor ole Captain Holt was running down the pathway between the bunkers stark raving naked. Well . . . he did have a pair of rubber thongs upon his pounding dusty feet. Clutching his, all but empty, basin of hot water, he ran with everything he owned flapping in the wind. For the moment, he was not exactly a John Wayne type character. Somehow, as the string of enemy rockets was chasing him, we were also aware that his death had now become a distinct possibility. Yet, despite the threat to his life and limb, he refused to relinquish his cherished, by now almost empty, basin of hot water. The dumb fools that we were, we were now cheering and laughing so hard that tears were freely flowing down our cheeks.

Suddenly, he stumbled. Then, with a muffled cry of fright mixed with raging fury, he fell. Crestfallen, we looked upon him, sprawled out and face down on the dusty earth. The horror of his failure was deeply scribed upon his face. Looking closer, we saw the remaining small portion of his precious elixir seeping into the red clay of the highlands. The sight of failure and defeat silenced our foolish cheering. With an abruptness startling us as much as the impact and explosion of the first rocket, all the parties present were shocked back to reality. Captain Holt was lying face down in the dirt, naked and finally defeated. We laughing fools were about ten or fifteen yards from him and exposed and vulnerable on the top of our bunker.

The logical progression of the explosions would place the impact point of the next rocket within a critical circle. At best guess, it would fall within the ten to fifteen yards separating the spectators and the prone Captain. An observer might have thought that we were taking part in a Greek tragedy or maybe a comical farce. In unison, as if taking a cue from an unseen director standing off stage, sanity made its dramatic entrance. All the actors upon the stage suddenly surged into frantic motion. Those of us who were sitting on the bunker, dove, face first, onto the sand bags. At the same instant, Captain Holt made a startled cry in recognition of his exposed nature/position. Poor ole Captain Holt then grabbed his empty tin basin. He took less than a second to come to his decision. At last, he placed it upon his head for protection as if it were an Army issue steel helmet.

The ending of the story leaves me wondering as do many other parts of my experience. Do the bad guys have a carefully crafted sense of the absurd? For what happened next was . . . well . . . nothing. No more rockets fell at the fleeing heels of poor ole Captain Holt! Little wonder that I was laughing and chuckling as I made my way to the Officers' Mess for a cup of their so-called coffee. For you see, I had asked myself what was the purpose of that whole drama a year ago? Had it only been to deny that poor Captain a basin of hot shaving water? If so, it must have been a flagrant violation of the Gevena Convention!

Well . . . I had stalled at the Officers' Mess for as long as I could. However, the time had come to finish my coffee and slowly make my way down to the flight line. Oh well . . . It was another day and it was time to make another dollar.

First things first! I did my mandatory weather check, such as it is in this part of the world. Aviation weather forecasting is a sad joke around here. We high-tech pilot types look up at the sky and scientifically forecast our flying weather. If the pilot can see the top of the flag pole that means that he can fly. Feeling frustrated and angry because I could see the top of the flag poll, I strolled down to the Red Bird line.

Childishly, I was wearing my grungiest, grimiest, and most grotesquely dirty flight suit. Ole Kev was wearing his scruffy flight suit, the one with no rank upon it, for a specific purpose. I was planning the perverse enjoyment of frustrating all the pretty little Remington Raiders who wandered about Squadron in their stiffly starched uniforms. At higher-higher they like to strut around and play pretty soldier boys. When we come in from the field and don't play their game, the sometimes get so upset that their faces turn purple. Therefore, I felt that it was my duty to turn a face or two purple. Reluctantly arriving at the flight line, I looked down to the far end of the Scout line.

She sat alone, dejected, and unloved while her friends had gone off to war. Pathetic ole 624 looked like a badly beaten pup. Yet, I knew that she was a good old girl in her own special way. The two of us had been through countless tough scrapes over the past sixteen months. No doubt about it, today, we were a well-matched pair. She was at least as grungy as her pilot. Yes indeed, the poor old bird was a sorry sight. From top to bottom abuse and neglect crusted her with mud, oil, and nonspecific crud. The old girl was covered with beer can patches and hundred-mile-an-hour tape held the bubble in place, reflecting her glory in battle. Forlorn and alone, she was sadly sitting in place with assorted oils and fluids slowly puddling under her. Perfectly reflecting the moment, she was kinda indifferently slumping down with her oleo struts half deflated. I guess, she just was feeling as war weary, frustrated, and sad as I was.

Well trained and occasionally cautions, I began my preflight inspection. I checked all of the fluid levels. Discovering sufficient oil in the engine and in the gearboxes, I continued. Checking the log book carefully, I found that it was up to date. Unable to honestly reject 624 for our coming admin flight, I did a slow walk around inspection. As best I could tell, most of the necessary parts were bolted on, taped on, glued on, or otherwise accounted for. Climbing up on the rotor head, I noted that all four blades were still properly fastened to the rotor head.

Looking at this pathetic wreck pretending to be a combat helicopter saddened me. No piece of fine machinery should be allowed to get so badly used up. I know, had I been stateside, I wouldn't have flown her on a bet. Yet, here in lovely South East Asia, the Cav needed every bird possible for their missions. Ergo, tired ole 624 and I got to fly the mail. Trying as hard as I could, I couldn't find any acceptable, in the weird and wacky world of Vietnam, maintenance reason to refuse flying the mail with her. Ready to go, I spoke to her.

"Well, old girl, . . . I guess that you and I are going to motor-motor our way up to Squadron and then come back home."

Sighing deeply with resignation at the unfairness of it all, I continued. Wearily climbing into the right seat, I carefully fastened my seat belt and shoulder harness. Sadly shaking my head, I gave it a good yank to make sure the inertia reel locked. Little did I know that later I would test my safety equipment on my next landing. Satisfied, I plugged my helmet into the radio jack, and placed the old brain bucket upon my empty little head. Chin strap tightened, I flipped the master electrical switch on. Following a slight delay, most of the gauges came on. When the needles settled into their respective places, I grumbled to myself.

"Like it or not, I guess I'll have to fly this poor old beast."

Sticking my head out the door, I made sure Ole Kev had untied the blades. After all my months in combat, I was still prone to committing an occasional bone head mistake. Yelling, "clear," I pressed the red starter button. The starter whined and the igniters popped. When the N1 turbine reached 13%, I gently twisted the throttle to flight idle and the little turbine willingly lit off with a satisfying whomp and roar.

I was stuck flying an ash and trash mission on my day off and I was frustrated. At least, it was turning out to be one of those nicer highlands mornings. A scattering of ground fog covered the low places and valleys. Flying above it, the ground fog looked soft, clean, and fluffy. It reminded me of an aspirin bottle's cotton trapped between the hills. I thought of it gently protecting the valleys. Adding to the enjoyment of the moment, the thermometer had not yet risen to an uncomfortable level.

"At least," I thought to myself, "it will be a very pleasant flight this morning."

Accepting the inevitable and trying to make the best of the situation, I was looking forward to flying all alone at five-thousand feet. Deciding to grin and bear it, I remembered an old saying.

"If rape is inevitable, one might as well lean back and enjoy it."

Therefore, I was going to enjoy the morning's solitude and put the war out of my mind for a few moments. Getting clearance from the control tower, I hover/taxied to the active takeoff lane. After a moment,

624 and I staggered sloppily off into the wild blue yonder. I was not in the mood to look professional.

If I believed in omens, I would have said that it was almost as if this were supposed to be my last flight. Ole 624 was a war weary wreck. Yet, after all those months of always flying combat overloaded aircraft, she felt responsive and even frolicsome. It seemed as if 624 almost leapt into the air with the incredible joy and freedom of flight. She was so light and so nimble feeling that I could have called the old girl sprightly. Unconsciously, I thought of her as a frisky colt out for a spring run across a field. It was time to put the war behind me.

During this flight, I planned to enjoy the solitude and an self-induced illusion of peace. Playing little mind games with myself, I opted not to wear my chicken plate or flack jacket. However, with my vulnerable and unprotected state of being in mind, I still wanted lots of space between me and the bad guys. As the man once said, I wanted it quick in a hurry. Ole Kev was getting very tired of getting repeatedly shot at in all the same places we had supposedly cleared out yesterday. So, I held sixty knots and pulled in the power. It was delightful. Ole 624 and I rapidly climbed, like a pair of homesick angels. We quickly ascended to five-thousand feet in the cool crisp and blessedly peaceful air.

After a bit, the old girl and I leveled off at five-thousand feet. Setting an easy cruse speed of eighty knots, I comfortably leaned back and enjoyed the cool air coming through the door. Coddling myself, I decided that it was time to enjoy a cigar. While looked down upon the lush green carpet covering the hills below I observed a different perspective on Vietnam.

"You know, Kev, It's not a bad war from this vantage point."

Pondering that recent discovery of mine, I continued to converse with myself.

"So, this is what flying all those starched brass hats from point 'A' to point 'B' is like? Maybe I ought to stop flying Red Birds and start flying VIPS for a living. Nah., they probably wouldn't like my cigars."

Being relatively free, casually strolling through my day dreams was a delightful experience. However, I also had to take care of business. Looking about, I noted that it was time to make a radio check for arty. It was all well and good to pretend that the war was far away. However, I didn't want a 105-millimeter hole from friendly artillery ventilating my fragile young body. Pondering the size of the hole, I did some quick arithmetic.

"Let's see now. One-hundred and five millimeters translates to about four-hundred caliber. Translating to good old-fashioned English, says it is about four inches. Ouch! Yep, a hole that large would cause me severe pain."

Not terribly surprised, I had no luck in contacting arty. Then, I tried a couple of other stations. I had no response from them. Not surprising, the way my day was going. Ole 624's radio wasn't working all that well. So what's new in Vietnam? Flying along at 5,000 feet, there was nothing much that I could do about the situation. Gaping holes in the radio panel told me that maintenance had stripped the other two radios out. Most likely they were placed in aircraft flying today's missions. Deciding to look at the bright side of things, I saw this as a positive sign. My solitude wouldn't be broken by mindless radio chatter about a war that I had decided to forget about for the moment.

Well . . . , let me begin this part of the story like all good aviation story tellers open their carefully crafted accounts.

"There I was, minding my own business and flying along fat, dumb, and happy. All alone ole Kev was content. With not even the littlest little care in the whole world, I relaxed. For a change, anxiety was a foreign word which held no meaning for me. For the moment, I was throughly enjoying playing the disinterested spectator to a distant war. There I was, about three-thousand feet over the death and destruction that defined Charlie's country."

Without proper and due warning, a terribly distressing quiet viciously assaulted my anxiety free state. My delightfully boring helicopter flight suddenly became deathly and terrifying quiet. It didn't take a PH.D. in aeronautical engineering to figure out the source of the assault of unnatural quietness. Ole 624 had inexorably decided to proclaim that this was the end to her last powered flight. For no apparent reason in all of God's green earth, the faithful little engine had gone south for the winter. My quiet little world had become much too quiet for my comfort. True, I was planning to enjoy some much needed solitude. However, that did not mean that I wanted the reassuring whine of the little turbine to leave my life!

For once, good Army training of constant repetition payed off. Carefully trained reflexes began flying the broken helicopter while my brain struggled to come up to speed. Without conscious thought, I lowered the collective pitch lever and entered an Autorotational glide. My head rapidly pivoting about, as if I had mounted it upon a swivel. I was looking for as a suitable place to land and or crash the tired old bird. Frantically looking about, all that I saw below me was wall to wall trees. Not a clearing was in sight. After as a moment's near panic, I noticed a little spot that appeared essentially level. It was close to one of the little blue lines. That's where I steered my broken little bird. That little spot of hope is where I tried my best to put both of us safely down.

While descending in an Autorotational glide, mentally crossing my fingers, I gave a couple of hopeful May Day's on the radio.

"Maybe," I thought despairing to myself, "the radio is transmitting OK."

"Possibly," I despaired, "it is just the receiver that had failed."

As I previously lamented, 624 only had one radio in her. Oh yes, give my heart-felt thanks to tight-fisted politicians for wanting us to fight a war without them raising taxes. The Army can't afford enough emergency radios to go around so I don't have one of those either.

I will not burden you, my hopefully future reader, with the dreary details on my so-called landing. We, 624 and I, didn't get down to ole mother earth in anything that resembled one piece. My old flight instructor at Fort Wolters had once suggested that this wasn't all bad. Laughing and having a good time, he had told me how to rate landings.

"Any landing which you can walk away from is a good one."

"Any landing where you can use the aircraft again is a great one."

Well . . . maybe it wasn't all that good. It surely wasn't a great landing. I don't remember how this one should be rated. However, this time, I can't walk away from the landing. Sometime during the crash and before the dust settled, I broke my leg. Furthermore, during the crash, I broke poor ole 624 into several pieces of assorted sizes and crumpled shapes. Ole 624 isn't going to fly in the morning and neither is ole Kev.

In time, the proverbial dust finally settled and I got my brain working properly. I came to the uncomfortable realization, that once again, Red One-Five was the Red Bird which was down. Unfortunately, this time down, I didn't have a friend flying my wing who was keeping as a careful eye on me. This time, my problems were multiplied. I was left wondering if the Cav even knew I was down and when or if they would come charging over the hill to rescue me. For the moment, I suppose I could ask John Wayne what he would do in this situation. Not that he has helped me much the last year. As for myself, at the moment, I was flat out of answers.

Please, don't think that I am whining and complaining like a spoiled brat. Things are not all that bad considering everything that has happened so far. I managed to put her down beside a small stream with lots of cool clean running water. Adding to my good fortune, I had three cases of "C" rations squirreled away in the back of the aircraft. These, I have managed to salvage. A wretched thought just struck me with gastro-horror as I write this.

"I pray to God that cruel fate does not reduce me to eating the ham and lima beans! Good Lord, I hate those things."

I also have my manuscript and pens and paper tucked in beside me. Stranded somewhere here in the Central Highlands, I am well off the so called beaten path. Therefore, it doesn't look like anyone is going to bother my solitude for a little while. So. . . . that's good . . . I guess.

While I'm enjoying the quiet, I can get a little creative writing done. I am sure that my writing will pass the time while I wait for my friends to come looking for me.

If you had not yet guessed, this has not been one of ole Red One-Five's better days while vacationing in lovely South East Asia. Right now, as I am writing this little tome, I am hurting pretty badly. A few moments ago, I made an emotionally shocking discovery. My head had known it for months. However, my gut didn't realize what it meant. It is disgraceful. The first aid kits in our helicopters don't have morphine in them. Can't leave it in the kit, you know? The druggies just steal them. All they care about is their need to escape from this unpleasant reality. Sven's right, it is time for me to grow up. Like it or not, I must accept that things have gone to hell in a handcart in the Army. The all-knowing Remington Raiders did not trust this officer and gentleman with morphine. But he can fly an expensive helicopter. They also expect him to order young boys to their deaths. However, he is not to be trusted with a morphine syrette.

It took some time and some heartfelt moaning and groaning, but, I finally have my leg fairly well bound up. Better yet, the bleeding has slowed to just a tiny seep. To be honest, it was tough going for an hour or so. It hurt so badly that I almost passed out several times. Forgive me if I am rambling, but apparently the pain has exhausted me and I have gone into the auto-babble mode of conversation. Goodness, it is getting cold and dark. It's time to try and wrap up in my flight jacket and let myself drift off into the land of pleasant dreams. As tired as I am, sleep will come easily. The Good Lord willing, with the coming of tomorrow's dawn, my world will begin to look a little bit brighter for the broken remains of ole Red One-Five.

DAY Two:

The sun has been up about two hours and I am already feeling exhausted. It seems that I have been beaten up a little worse than I thought. Dragging myself, backwards upon my big fat butt, the fifteen or so feet to the stream bank darn near did me in. All I wanted was to get a canteen cup of water to have with my C-ration breakfast. Come to think of it, I need to make myself a note about breakfast. When I get back, I think I am going to tell the cook to occasionally serve C's for breakfast. At least they don't pretend to be edible. That is unlike some of the "stuff" the cook has tried to foster off on us. When I finished my breakfast, I took careful stock of my situation.

The Department of the Army, for reasons unknown to me at the moment, has said that I am an intelligent, well-organized, officer and gentleman. Accepting their word for it, I took command of this isolated outpost and quickly decided to set up camp. It was immediately clear to me that it would be better if I set up on the banks of the stream. That way, I would not have to drag myself back and forth each time I wanted a drink. After I issued my commands to the troops at hand, the whole process of moving all my worldly goods took about four or five trips. When I had completed the move, I was bathed in a running sweat and my leg had begun bleeding again. However, I was snuggled comfortably in my new home. Well . . . as comfortably as possible considering that home was now a hollow in the roots of a big tree. Now within easy reach are my C's, the cool stream, my canteen cup, and my plastic pouch with all my writing stuff. Not much I can do now except wait and write.

It was time for one of my famous "pep" talks.

"Stop complaining. Kev! You have been looking for a chance to write. Now put it to good use as you may have a lot of it on hand."

This is turning out to be a heck of a sorry vacation. I just discovered another major problem. My broken leg has made voiding my bladder a very complicated and difficult task. After breakfast and a cup of water, I tried to roll over on my side and do my duties. To understate things, my effort wasn't very successful. The position hurt like bloody blue blazes and I got it all over myself. The next time I had to void, I just didn't even bother trying. When I get back, I'll have to tell The Bill. He'll love it. Shoot, I've just had another terrifying thought. If my mother finds out about this I am going to get a spanking and have my nose rubbed in it! Oh well. I'll avoid thinking about voiding my bowels for the moment. I'm discouraged enough as it is.

I wish I could remember exactly what happened during my less than spectacular landing. Considering poor results of my landing, I must have done something terribly wrong. It bothers me because I don't know what I did wrong. After all, I had put a wounded Red Bird into the trees before. Those times I had not damaged either the bird or myself nearly as much. Autorotational speed had been sixty knots right on the nose. Shoot, 624 was virtually unloaded. She floated down gently like I was in a sport glider. I flared properly to kill off the forward airspeed just at the tree tops and built up lots of rotor speed to use to cushion the fall. The last thing that I seem to remember was the tail boom settling into the trees. Then . . . well I woke up and we were both badly broken?

Sometime later, when I woke up in the midst of the helicopter's and my own wreckage. I looked down toward my legs before the pain made its presence known to my befuddled brain. It was a shock to see my leg bent at an angle at which God never intended the human leg to be bent. Fortunately, for me, this wasn't a check ride or I would have busted it big time. Any respectable check pilot would have ripped my wings off my breast. Following that, the Major would have reduced me to spending the rest of my tour in the boonies! Well . . . , maybe the big check pilot in the sky has passed judgement. I am stuck in the boonies.

Never in my whole life have I hurt so badly. Shoot, when I tore my knees up playing ball, it wasn't this bad. I am sweating, shaking, nauseous, and on the verge of vomiting if I try to move. This is no way for a genuine U.S. Army Aviator to spend a day off! If memory serves me correctly, I am supposed to be drinking cold beer and thinking about round-eyed girls. Lord, I have got to find something to distract me from this pain. Thank God. I brought my writing stuff with me. It has been helping keep my mind occupied so far. At least it worked yesterday.

Let me think back for a moment. If memory serves me correctly, the last time that I wet my pants was when I was something like four or five years old. To quote the Sacred poet.

"Oh how the mighty have fallen!"

I just sat here a moment ago and relieved myself in my pants, another time. This easy-going willingness to soil myself gives me reason to ponder. I have heard it said that when you get elderly that you revert to your childhood. If this is correct, then I must be getting rather elderly. The years sure have been flying by and the changes have been quite surprising. While I am contemplating the many changes in my life, I guess I'll dip a couple of canteen cups of water onto my lap to dilute the mess. Here's a very chilling thought. I'd be in big trouble if this were the arctic! I can just imagine my pants freezing to my private parts.

If delirium has not set in, and I am not old enough to be senile, I suppose that laughing at myself is OK because I just had another flash-back.

Mrs. Johnson's little boy has been enjoying a strange education. Benignly, baffled, befuddled and bewildered, I was marking time in the Repo-depot awaiting my assignment to the Cav. This young guy had never been more than fifty to one hundred miles from home till he entered the Army. I was not prepared for the "real world." My first "private" shower in Vietnam was quite the eye-opening experience.

Waking up alone in a strange transient barracks, I felt extremely out of place and terribly alone. I knew who I was and why I was there. However, I still felt slightly out of phase with the world I had known. For the moment, I was the only officer present in the barracks. Due to the wonders and mysteries of the Army way, I had to wait an extra day for transportation to the Cav. All those who had come with me had left the day we arrived. Apparently, they were well on their way to their new units. Being the Army way, the guys at the Repo-depot had assigned all the enlisted men busywork details. It was quiet and I needed a shower.

My strange new world consisted of temporary buildings which they built close to other temporary buildings. Slats and screening served to separate the buildings. They gave the illusion of privacy. However, none was present because there were no solid walls to offer separation. People were moving about outside the building and I easily heard their conversation through the screening. Heads and shoulders of unknown people were visible as they walked by. If I could see and hear them, then in turn, they could see and hear me. I wondered, did this mean that my morning shower was a public event? Nevertheless, I needed and wanted a shower.

Ole Kev, the former jock, was no stranger to a locker room. Showering with a bunch of guys and all the attendant horse play was normal for me. Targeting sensitive and private parts of my friends anatomy, I'd done my share of towel snapping. Yet, this situation felt a little strange to me. It was as if I were a little boy visiting a distant relative. I wanted to go. I needed to go and I was toilet trained. However, it was a strange toilet at the unknown relative's house. It would be much nicer if mommy would take my hand and lead me there. While such feelings may seem foolish for a newly minted Army Aviation Warrant Officer, I felt that timid. Shaking my head, I drove the inhibiting feelings of timidity away. It was hot and humid. I had yet to take a shower. My mid morning nap had left me sweaty and smelly. All of this drove me to the shower that I wanted and needed.

Need caused me to gird my loins and buckle on my armor. This loin girding stuff was not of the poetic variety. I removed my boots and socks, my stiff new jungle fatigues, and olive-drab boxer shorts. Placing them on my bed, I girded and armored myself with a towel. Attempting to control my vulnerable feelings of undue exposure, I marched down to the end of the barracks. While en route, I reassured myself that the unknown people walking by would only see my naked upper torso. Furthermore, they wouldn't care. Turning the corner into the shower, I was greatly disappointed and very shocked. The unexpected sight which greeted my shocked eyes dashed my thoughts of a soothing cleansing shower. It was as if I had dropped a fragile dish on the cement floor to the rough shower. My expectations had shattered into countless pieces. The pleasant thoughts about showering were broken beyond reconstruction. My disbelieving eyes saw an old woman on her hands and knees. She was scrubbing clothes the floor.

Shriveled, wrinkled, and dried up, this old woman looked to be about one-hundred and fifty years' old, if not more. Stuttering, I excused myself and started backing out of the shower. I was deeply embarrassed. Mom and Dad are modest and private people and I was not prepared for what came next. Ole momasan, in her broken English, urged me to take my shower.

"You take shower GI. It's OK."

She assured me that it was fine with her. Remembering this story makes me think of Sven and all the times he told me to grow up. I stammered, stuttered, and shuffled my feet. Coughing and choking on my near nakedness, I told her that I would come back later. Ole momasan only laughed and deepened the flush on my face with her broken English.

"What's the matter G.I.? You afraid old momasan will see how little you are?"

While I'm not a threat to Charles Atlas, I'm not ashamed of my body. A year of flight school and my former life as a jock had left it in quite good shape. I had seen worse.

"Aw h---," I said to myself.

"When in Rome . . ."

With the bold utterance of that profound cliche, I turned my back to the old woman and gracefully dropped my towel. My father would have been mortified and my mother would have spanked me for standing butt naked in front of the old woman. However, the old woman had made me angry and I wanted a shower. Praying that old momasan wouldn't know how embarrassed I was, I kept my back to her and showered.

Yes, my life has changed. Less than a month later, I would casually throw a towel over my shoulder and march through the compound to the shower. If momasan or some cleaning girls saw me in all my "glory," so be it. Now, I sit here wishing and praying that I could shower. Shoot, I would march through downtown Boston naked for a hot shower! The smell of my own diluted urine rising from my groin has removed just about the last of my inhibitions. Yet, that first "public" shower definitely made me uncomfortable!

So far, the day has passed well. I haven't heard any helicopters come close. Maybe tomorrow they will start a good search. If I don't move around much, the pain is almost tolerable and my leg doesn't bleed. However, I am becoming concerned about the wound. It is beginning to swell and look inflamed. I also think that I am beginning to run a fever. Yet, who can tell in this heat. The old flight jacket kept me warm last night so I believe I'll wrap it about me and go to sleep. I'm exhausted. Writing must be harder work than I thought.

Day Three:

Jumping, I wake with a horrifying start. Intuitively, I know that something is terribly wrong! Yet, my sleep befuddled mind can't quite come to grips with the problem. What is it? How come I woke with such a start? I look up and note that the sun hasn't been up long. I can't figure out why I feel the way that I do. Yet, suddenly, I feel terribly – terribly threatened. An uncontrolled shiver runs up and down my spine.

If the war is still going on, at the moment, I can't hear it. Neither jets nor helicopters are about to disturb the woodsy silence. That's it! That's the problem. It's the silence. There's too much of it and its not natural. No noise. The normal background hum of the jungle is strangely absent. Somebody is out there and the jungle is holding his breath. I listen. Is it one of the bad guys? Or, is it some friendlies looking for me?

I dare not make a sound that would give me away. It could be that I sense bad guys. Yet, if I sense friendlies, how can I tell them I'm here? D---! I wish that I had a survival radio. Suddenly, I hear the soft crack of a twig being stepped upon. Very slowly turning my head, I begin a careful search of the underbrush with my honed Scout sensibilities.

"Maybe," I hope to myself, "it is only my imagination run wild."

"Take it easy Kev. Your heart is pounding away like an M-60."

I listen carefully trying to hear whatever it is over the thundering noise of my own pounding heart. Tilting my head, I think that I hear a soft noise in the underbrush. If it is possible, this soft noise causes my anxiety level to rise further. If they are Americans, they should have recognized that I am a GI and already come out. They have to be the bad guys. Trembling, I am afraid to breathe.

I had thought about this situation for a very long time. In fact, I had even prayed about it. My mind was firmly made up months ago. No matter what the situation was, I wasn't going to allow myself to be captured. Several months ago I heard an intelligence report that said that a five-thousand dollar bounty had been placed on my head. It might not have been true. Nevertheless, if they wanted me that badly, I didn't want them to have me. The thought of being in the bad guys "tender mercies" causes me to blanch with fear. Years ago, in the cheap novels I had read, they spoke of a person's blood running cold. At last, I know exactly what that expression means. Truly, my blood runs cold at the thought of capture. It takes my breath away. For a moment, my head is spinning, I can't think, and I believe that I am going to faint.

Doing my best to appear casual, I slowly reach down toward my right side. I know that somewhere, down near my writing materials is my old pistol. Gritting my teeth, I have decided that I will force them to shoot me. I know who I am and I don't haven't the courage to face captivity. Nor do I have the courage to be dragged through the jungle with this mangled leg. With the bones sticking out, bleeding to death will be the final cure for the pain. It is better that I go quick and maybe take one or two with me!

Now, I'm sure of it! My nerves are humming with the feeling of being watched. Someone or someone is out there. Looking closely, I see a couple of leaves move in a bush. Again, a shiver runs up and down my spine. I can feel them watching me. Looking carefully into the brush, I see some more leaves move a little farther on. What the h--- are they waiting for? Why don't they just come on out and try to get me? I want to challenge them. Yet, I keep my mouth shut in my ever climbing fear.

"Oh my God!"

The bushes slowly part. Out walks the biggest tiger I have ever seen! He is less than twenty feet from me. Supremely confident of his mature strength and power, he arrogantly sits on his haunches. Staring intently at me, he twitches his nose testing the air. I'm sure that he can smell my blood. The beast knows that I am wounded. Turning his head a bit, he carefully yet casually studies me. It seems that I can read his mind. His question is not can he defeat me. No, his question is much more basic than that. He is studying how he can defeat me at the least cost to himself? Afraid for my life, I contemplate trying to shoot him with my forty-five. Just as quickly, I reject that idea. The cat is too big and powerful for me to kill with less than a dozen rounds of the forty-five. Twitching his nose, he can smell my fear as my bladder voids.

Dredging through the dark recessing of my fear laden mind, I suddenly remember that tigers are lone hunters. They do not hunt in packs. In the world of the tiger, it is every cat for him or herself. Survival of the fittest is the rule of the day. I am wounded, alone, and in his jungle. Between the two of us, the big cat and I know who is the fittest. My mind screams.

"Why doesn't he just get it over? Why does he wait?"
My inner questions continue.

"Is he like a house cat and enjoying playing with his food? Or, is this cat somehow sentient and celebrating his total power of life and death? Is he somehow human and delighting in deciding who should live and who should die?"

I hope and pray that maybe he isn't hungry. If I don't serve a purpose to him, maybe he will walk away and leave me alone.

Languidly, the big cat gets up and he slowly stretches showing his contempt. I have never seen any creature so functionally beautiful, powerful, and sleek. His languid stretch speaks of his deep self-satisfaction and great confidence. Savoring his lordship, his eyes never leave me. It is as if he is trying to decide if eating me will make his life better. Will I serve a useful purpose in his world? Am I valuable to him for what I can give him? I know that my life holds no meaning to him except in what it can give him. For the big cat, ole Kev is just something "out there" in his self-contained world. Unfortunately, the only thing that I can do for him is to be today's breakfast. I can only hope that he has already had breakfast.

"Oh s---!"
I've had many house cats. I know exactly what's happening. The big cat is tensing for a single quick bound to be followed by the kill. It seems that his threat warning radar has told him that I am not a threat.

One bound and he is on me. My mind blanks in the horror of his claws, teeth, and strength. I scream and scream and scream! I fire my pistol two, maybe three, shots. In the same instant, I futilely try to roll out of the path of those claws and fangs. Oh my God! The pain is overwhelming. I never knew that so much pain was possible. My mind is shutting down in disbelief and horror. As the welcoming blackness rolls over me like a tidal surge, I feel myself vomiting.

It was nearly noon when I finally came to. I have never smelt anything so foul in my whole life. Mercilessly, old urine, half-dried vomit, and something sweet smelling and rotting assaulted my nostrils. My God, it's I! Pain and fatigue terribly disoriented me. The last thing that I remembered was something about a huge tiger leaping at me. It didn't make much sense. Eventually, I decided that I must have been having a bad dream because a tiger had not eaten me.

Slowly and with great effort, I gathered my whits sufficient to note that I had my forty-five clenched in my hand. I wasn't strong enough to move yet, so I checked it out. Somehow, somewhere, and sometime I had fired two shots with it. That scares me. I give serious thought to throwing it away before I hurt myself.

It took me the better part of two hours to clean up the mess I had become. Copious quantities of water poured down my shirt front and in my groin poorly served the purpose. What I endured wasn't exactly a hot shower. However, when I had finished my tin pot shower, I smelled slightly better. Several times, as I struggled to clean myself, I thought that I was going to pass out. The pain of reaching into the stream for water was beyond belief. Each time that I had to stop and rest, I was soaked through with sweat. I can't tell if I have a fever or if it is the pain in my leg.

When I looked closely, my leg was a mess and it scared me terribly. I am afraid that if I don't get help in a day or two I am going to be in big time trouble. If I am correct, running out of food is not going to be a problem. When I awoke, I saw that my broken leg had begun to bleed again. Doing my best not to move it, I unbound some of my rough bandages and tried to clean it up. The pain may be more intense than yesterday. Previously the pain was centered on and in the bone. Today, all the flesh, near where the bone is sticking out, hurts. It doesn't look right. The skin is whitish with some blue marbling. Strangely enough, the skin is cool to the touch. It seems like it should be hot if it is infected. However, a whole bunch of nasty puss-like stuff is coming out of it. I also saw some frothy, foamy garbage mixed in with the wound. I have no idea what it is. Whatever it is, it has a sweet decay kind of smell.

I'm no doctor, but I am afraid that it is gangrene.

ALONE ---- ABANDONED?

Day Four:
 I my scribblings have a faithful reader, let me assure you that ole Kev woke up this morning feeling quite disheartened and discouraged. During the night, I slept fitfully while suffering terrible nightmares. Sometimes terrible, man-eating monsters were chasing me hither and yon and then slowly devouring me live. Other times, I was a child separated from my mom and dad. As I ran and cried seeking safety, it all seemed so real. I know that I am becoming quite sick because of this leg. As the days pass, it is becoming very difficult for me to separate dreams and delirium from reality. I fear that if they don't find me in another couple of days . . . ?

The confusion and images that are beginning to rule my mind make me feel deeply distressed. Broken and immobile, what can I do? I continuously feel thirsty. However, try as I might, I can't force myself to drink more than a few sips at a time. I don't need a thermometer to know that my fever is starting to rise. When combined with sweats and chills, it makes me weaker and weaker. I combat it, as best I can, by pouring cool water from the stream all over my body. Can't be sure of anything any more, but I think that it helps? Even if it doesn't help, it does feel refreshing.

God, I'm so frustrated and mad I could scream. My helicopter is broken and scattered about the terrain. I'm lying here broken and encrusted in my own stinking filth. It appears, to me, that my leg is starting to rot off me. The good news is that I'll die of the rot's poisoning before the leg falls off. Now, to add the frosting to Uncle Sam's C-ration cake, the local leaches have decided that I'm a warm and nourishing meal. If they'll stop feasting on my mortal remains long enough for me to speak with them, I have an important question for them.

"My dear bloodsucking leach friends, are you Democrats or Republicans? If neither, what is the all important 'ism' that drives you to suck the life's blood from me?"

A few moments ago, I found myself thinking about my old friend Sven. Strangely enough it was while I was washing the top layer of crud off my body. The smell of my urine and feces, strongly accented by day old vomit and decaying rot, had me feeling sorry for myself. Suddenly I heard his cynical, yet loving, voice growling at me.

"For God's sake, grow up Kev."

My good friend can yell at me if he chooses. Obviously, I would warmly welcome his voice and person. However, I'll continue to waffle between despair and hope. Sometimes, I slowly sink into my deep dark despair because within the depths of my soul I doubt that I'll be found in time. The jungle has frequently swallowed up helicopters and claimed them as her own. On the other hand, I'll hope because I know the Cav will move heaven and earth. At least, they will for a couple of days. Then . . . Well, we take care of that when and if it happens.

Yet, I have to be honest about what God has given me. My situation could be much worse. If I am not immediately found, God has given me the opportunity to close a few loose ends before someone writes "the end" on the last page of the dull novel of my life. Very few people get the privilege and opportunity to have some parting words as the story of their life slowly closes out. Before I get any weaker or lose all track of reality, I've got a couple/three letters to write. Today, I will write to ole Sven and Pastor Bill. The good Lord willing, I'll write to the folks tomorrow. That one will be the hardest one to write. What can I say that will lessen their pain?

Dear Sven,

As you can imagine, I've got lots of time on my hands. Consequently, I would like to tell you about an experience that I had a long, a very long time ago. Obviously I was a much younger man when this happened. Yep, this happened so long ago that I shaved no more than once a week whether I needed to or not. Of course, that was a long time ago! As you know, I now have reached the dottering old age of male maturity. Heck, I now shave two, sometimes even three times a week!

That is to say, this story is so old that it takes place when I was just a mere sapling of a lad at nineteen years. As I flip through the pages of the calender, it dawns on me that I had not been nineteen for more than a couple of months. Through the grace of God, not to mention a fair amount of inherited cussed stubbornness, I had managed to survive the joys and wonders of basic training in Louisiana. In turn, I also survived the torture of four weeks of pre-flight conditioning and training. All this was part of my highly anticipated pilgrimage toward becoming an honest, to goodness, United States Army pilot.

In my colorful imagination, I can hear you now as you take a deep draw on your ever present beer. Leaning back to light a cigarette you would say to me.

"By gosh and by golly, I think that I know this story! It seems very similar to a good tale I could tell. Go on Kev. You like to play with words and you can probably tell it better than I can. Remember, I'm the cynic and you are the story teller."

Whatever the case may be, please my friend, bear with me for this is a glorious story that deserves countless retellings.

Though at times I feared that it would never come. Finally, after all the heartache and pain, my long awaited day of glory arrived. I had waited for, and prayed for, and strove for this special day with all my human power. In fact, it was the day that had been years and years in its final maturation. This was the day for which I had prayed for, hoped for, and struggled for more than any other day in my short life.

463

This, otherwise nondescript day, was to be the glorious moment of my very first ride in the cockpit of a military aircraft. True, it wasn't a supersonic F-4 or an equally exotic fast mover. Nevertheless, my wondrous day had finally arrived. After all those years of praying, hoping, and dreaming, I was a student pilot seated in a military cockpit. At last, I would get to touch the controls of a military aircraft in a neophyte's first feeble attempt to fly. My goal was to master the mysterious black art of powered flight.

That morning, long ago when I arrived at the main heliport of good old Fort Wolters, my glorious adventure began.

Kev paused for a moment, smiled, and spoke to the surrounding jungle.

"Oh, I remember well."

My civilian flight instructor took great pains to walk me all around the old training helicopter. He was showing me all the complex intricacies and carefully written liturgies of a pre-flight inspection. Treating me as if I were terminally stupid, which I was, my instructor went slowly. He stressed to me that even the simplest helicopter was a very complex mechanism. Continuing the pre-flight, he pointed out that all the working parts had to be in perfect order. They had to be operating in perfect harmony or the helicopter would not fly. Laughing, he added.

"Even an antique like this Korean War relic has to be in harmony with itself!"

Though to me, this old, battered, and beaten up helicopter was not an antique. No, in my mind's eye, she was a very lovely creation of efficient mechanical beauty.

As we continued his walk around inspection, my instructor maintained his nonstop litany of careful description of the pre-flight inspection. He informed me that the Lycoming engine had to develop all of its possible power. Both spark plugs in each of the six cylinders had to be firing at the proper instant. The heavy wooden rotor blades, of the main rotor, had to be spinning along their proper plane of rotation. Tracking properly, they produced both lift and directional control. The tail rotor had to spin at the assigned speed. If it did this, when I stepped on the pedals it would produce enough thrust to overcome the torque of the main rotor. This, little high-speed rotor was as critical as the main rotor. Both, he said, allowed the helicopter to maintain the proper direction hovering or in flight.

Adding to my informational overload, he tirelessly marched on. The push-pull rods had to tilt the heavy rotating mass of the rotor properly. They also had to change the pitch of the main rotor and tail rotor blades. Giving me no respite, he emphatically told me that I was never to forget that all the nuts and bolts had to be properly safety wired. He surprised me by explaining that there was a right and the wrong way to safety wire a bolt. So on and so forth, he carefully continued with the litany. It was about how all the parts had to be very carefully inspected. He was continually reminding me that they had to be working together to create the sublime mystery of flight. I was learning that the functioning of all these parts called for a very complex harmony. Without the teamwork and harmony of parts, the sweet song of flight would not tantalize and fill my being/ soul/ spirit.

Completing the unbelievably complex pre-flight examination of the little helicopter, we moved on. The two of us had walked from the very front of the plexiglass bubble to the aft tip of the tail stinger. Finishing that, we climbed up onto the rotor system. We went from the "Jesus" nut on the very tip top of the rotor head to the two skids upon which the helicopter rested. I remember his words.

"This big nut secures the rotor blades to the helicopter. They so name it, because if it ever comes off in flight the last two words you ever utter will be 'Oh Jesus!'"

By then, I was suffering from what was a near terminal case of sensory overload. Or, at least, that was my belief. However, as you well remember, little did I know, the best was yet to come. Truly, in a few minutes I was going to experience a TOTAL SENSORY OVERLOAD!

Finally, after I was suffering a killer headache from all the input to which I was being subjected, we moved on. At his instruction, I climbed into that old Korean War vintage OH-13. The old girl was complete with a gun sight mount still attached to the bubble. She was a real war bird! At last, my moment of aviation glory had come. I dutifully strapped myself in, using the two shoulder straps and a seat belt. In awe of the whole experience, I looked about in fear and trepidation for the unknown ahead of me. Suddenly, my feeble little mind abruptly noted the absence of doors on this helicopter. With that thought pressing down upon me, I became very uncomfortable. Being moderately afraid of heights, I strapped in really well. I mean, I strapped in really good! Afraid and excited in the same breath, I was set for the unknown.

When I was finished strapping in, my instructor told me to simply sit still. He added another comment for his own safety.

"Mr. Johnson, do not touch anything and do not do anything. Just sit still and listen to me for this one flight."

My only freedom of action was to listen to him over the intercom. Though you flew the little TH-55's, if you stop and think about it, you can remember your feelings as essentially the same when it came time to start the helicopter. Amazingly Sven, I did just that, I sat there quietly. For the first time in my whole life, I had no smart comment to make. In fact, I had no smart comment for the enjoyment of the quiet confines of my brain or the world. The truth of the matter was that Kevin Paul Johnson was sitting there speechlessly in awe of the whole process.

With the characteristic chugging sound of the Lycoming starter motor, my process of liberation began. The engine started with the unique noisy uneven rattle that marked the firing of every air-cooled aircraft engine ever built. With the starting of the engine, the rotor blades over my head began to slowly wake and begin turning. They continued to turn faster, and faster. Even faster yet, the big wooden blades turned. Eventually the rotors were at full operating speed. I was amazed. The two big wooden rotors were blurring themselves into a beautiful silvery disk glistening in the bright Texas sunlight.

At last, my instructor keyed the radio and called the control tower at the Main Heliport at good ole Fort Wolters. In turn, we received our hover-taxi instructions to go to a takeoff spot. Given that we are old friends, I can comfortably be honest with you. At that point, I sat in that old H-13 completely spellbound. I'm sure that it appeared as if I were trying to catch assorted flies with my mouth hanging wildly agape. I sat silently, almost in reverential awe, in the midst of it all. Do you still remember your first real sight of that helicopter ballet? It strained the imagination to believe that the hot tar and cement of the Main Heliport would become the dance floor of a delightful and graceful ballet. However ...

I vividly remember the ballet surrounding me for its incredibly beautiful harmonious dance. From their lofty control tower, the controllers magically choreographed the performance. Seemingly numberless helicopters were hovering across the black shimmering expanse of the main heliport. Each of the little machines was gently bobbing and weaving. In turn, they were taking off from their assigned spots. Looking through the bubble, I watched them climbing away in long snakelike lines to their unknown destinations. Low and behold, with the numberless helicopters filling the air like an undisciplined swarm of gnats. Yet, an orderly movement towards flight was taking place before my unbelieving eyes.

I will never forget that sacred moment for as long as I live. (Yuck! That expression has just taken on a personally uncomfortable meaning.) Finally, after waiting all my life, it was our turn to soar into the unknown. We approached the takeoff spot and got our take off clearance. My instructor, suddenly surprised me with an act of kindness previously unknown in the history and annals of military aviation. My civilian instructor, who had previously been an Aviation Warrant himself, turned to me and gently said.

"Just relax Kev. You, my friend, are really going to enjoy this. Today's ride is an honest, to goodness, freebie. It is probably the first and last freebie ride you will ever have in an United States of America Army helicopter."

Raising the collective pitch lever ever so slightly and twisting the throttle he matched the demands of the main rotor's increasing pitch. In preparation for flight, he gently pulled in the aircraft's power with his left arm. The throb of the engine became deeper, richer, and more resonant with its mysteriously appropriate labor. With these, almost unseen, actions, my instructor increased the pitch of the main rotor. To my awe-struck ears, their deep, throbbing base beat began to gently pound out a strange hypnotic and wonderfully harmonious music. This magical music was seeping deeply into the recesses of my soul. Mine was, and still is, a little boy's soul which had been yearning for flight since before I could remember.

That single, stark, fleeting moment was a blessing and a gift like none I had previously received. During the passing of that moment, my life was uniquely sacred. I have duplicated the event of a helicopter takeoff numberless times in the last couple/three years. However, no duplication or subsequent repetition has ever been the same.

Though I love to write, I don't have the words adequate to describe the moment. Yet, I think you can listen to my words and easily tap your own rich memories. I am convinced that those of us who have been there know what I am reliving with my paper, pen, and warm memories. I warmly remember, without having taken specific note of it, how the thrumming vibrating helicopter began to slide ever so gently and slowly forward.

Mysteriously, in the same almost motionless motion, my golden chariot began to gently elevate itself into the previously unknown heavens. The transition into helicopter flight was so subtle that I could scarcely notice the wondrous change. Ah, but I did notice, the mundane work a day world ever so slowly drifting away below my feet. Emotionally, I celebrated with an unfettered and previously unknown joy.

It was, well . . . , it was magic!

For the first time in my short life , I was riding the magic carpet of flight and freedom. As the ground slowly and magically drifted below my feet, we joined that weaving line of helicopters. Like all the others, we were following the line of colored telephone poles to my unknown destination of great romantic mystery. Moved beyond human expression, I silently savored and deeply cherished the experience of the wide-ranging panorama unfolding before me.

How can I ever forget that one special moment? Dare I say that even death's dark and dank doorway does not have the ability to blot out its transcendent power? As I sat transfigured in my seat, my personal magic carpet was lifting me to heights previously undreamed. With the black art of piloting being demonstrated by my instructor, I was soaring to unimagined zeniths, both physical and emotional. My deepest inner spirit was floating towards the heavens beyond my reach. Kevin Paul Johnson was lifted to new heights because of a carefully worked out symphonic arrangement. It consisted of all those whirling, twirling, rotating parts called a helicopter. Sitting in that hard helicopter seat/bench, I got the greatest thrill of my life. Deep within my heart, I know that the greater and lesser gods smiled as the ground was magically swept away beneath my no longer earth bound feet!

Ever the hopeless romantic, Kev gently set his pen aside. Emotionally caught up in his writing, he discovered that a big lump was forming in his throat. Somehow, the act of remembering his first flight in a helicopter softened the wretched loneliness of the moment. Though he was alone and no one could see him, he was suddenly embarrassed. As he reached up and wiped away a tear, he naturally looked about to see if anyone had seen him. Realizing just how silly that was, he laughed at himself. Laughing hurt. However, he found it cleansing.

467

Closing his eyes, he returned to his memories of the old H-13. Somehow, the simple act of remembering and relishing dampened the pain in his leg and heart. Almost smiling, he asked himself.

"Has it been worth it?"

Surprised, he found that he did not have to ponder his question. He answered it easily. Sliding his memory back a few months before his first flight, he reviewed his previous life. Assaulted by the picture of a dingy factory, endlessly repetitive work, and a lack of direction, he immediately had his answer.

"Yes. I have soared on the wings of the eagle and left a meaningless mundane world far below me. Occasionally, I have made a difference and a few kids have returned to mom, dad, and girlfriend. Yes, everything is OK. And, if I don't return, the big ledger sheet in the sky will show positive numbers as it tallies up my life's score."

Calmed, for the first time since 662's engine stopped, he smiled. Leaving his eyes closed, Kev allowed a spot of warm sun to bathe his face. It was day four and he was becoming very weak. With the warm sun in his face and the memory of the hypnotic beat of old wooden rotors in his heart, Kev slipped into a restful nap.

Forgive me Sven. I was so taken by my POSITIVELY WONDERFUL story telling that I quietly slipped off into nap time. I told you that I was getting old. Good ole Grandpa and I take naps whenever we stop moving. Anyway . . .

If someone like yourself wished, I suppose that he could accuse me of taking unfair advantage of my current, shall we say, most interesting situation. However, when one is quite sure he is dying, gently prodding friends doesn't seem so terribly abusive. It is not as if I am taking advantage of the situation for my own gain. I'll grant that you have not solicited my kind and loving words and advice. Because my "military" situation has become quite untenable, I feel that I can take a liberty or two.

It appears that the screaming hoards of the final and ultimate enemy are preparing to overrun my last lines of resistance. I get weaker by the day. However, the problem is not hunger. I still have plenty of "C's" left to eat and more than enough clean cool water to drink. Facing the truth, I fear that I am deathly ill. I seem to have a constant fever. Furthermore, part of the area where my shin bone broke through the skin is turning disgusting colors and is oozing a sweet smelly puss. That, in itself, pretty much tells the whole story.

Thankfully, my pain is not totally insufferable. That is, generally speaking, I can tolerate the pain. Of course, this is only if I don't try to move. Oh yes, do you remember how in the escape and evasion course all the "fun" we had hiding and getting caught? If you do, you also remember that they told us not to try to walk out from a crash scene because it would make it harder for our would-be rescuers to find us. No problem! For a change, ole Kev is being a very good boy. This time, like it or not, I have carefully followed my classroom instructions to the letter of the law. Ole Kev has run out of creative reconstructions of the rules.

At last, the Major will be pleased with my military behavior. Unfortunately, no free lancing or creative bending the rules is left in ole Red One-Five! As hard as I try, this time, I can't find a way to creatively rewrite the rules to my own advantage. Again unfortunately, I am more than adequately sure that I know exactly what is happening to me. Yet, I don't want to put the words on paper, at least not yet. Let it be sufficient to say that the stench from my leg smells as if a deadly and putrid rot is escaping from the core of my being! I fear that if I don't get some medical care soon, the point of my rescue will be moot. It really won't make much of a difference whether or not I name the source of the stench in my leg.

My dear friend Sven, I believe that I have discovered what keeps my life's hope alive for today and tomorrow. That hope is drawn from the experiential poetry of the ground slowly sweeping away beneath my feet. The awe and wonder of such a possibility happening in my life, when all the parts are working in beautiful harmony together, has touched the depths of my soul. The wonder of it all has moved my spirit in a way that I am just beginning to understand. I truly regret that I had to wait till I approached my current dottering old age to make this interesting discovery. Furthermore, when I remember that experience of a new possibility in my life when everything is in harmony, it always reminds me of the experience of the writer of Revelation.

If what I have to say offends, please excuse my previously carefully hidden religiosity. With your permission, I will share the reverential awe and wonder and the possibility for life which this creative and visionary writer's sublime poetry offers us.

"Then I saw a new heaven and a new earth; for the first heaven and the first earth had passed away, and the sea was no more. And I saw the holy city, new Jerusalem, coming down out of heaven from God, prepared as a bride adorned for her husband; and I heard a loud voice from the throne saying, 'Behold, the dwelling of God is with men. He will dwell with them, and they shall be his people, and God himself will be with them; he will wipe away every tear from their eyes, and death shall be no more, neither shall there be mourning nor crying nor pain any more, for the former things have passed away.' And he who sat upon the throne said, 'Behold, I make all things new.' Also he said, 'Write this, for these words are trustworthy and true.'" (Revelation 21: 1-5 RSV)

Now, wasn't that a surprise? I bet you didn't know that I also carried a little Bible in my sack of writing junk?

Please do me a small but meaningful favor. Humor ole Kev. I'll take but a minute more of your time my friend, and then I will leave you march on with your own life. We started, you and I, with such delightful dreams of doing something important that would count when the finally tally of our lives was taken.

Don't deny it. I know you too well. Sven, my friend, you also dreamed of making a meaningful difference in the world while we rode our magic carpets across the skies of lovely Southeast Asia. Why should we give up this dream? Why should we allow others to rip this glorious and meaningful dream from our grasp?

True, over the months, more than a year for me, we have mostly seen discord and disharmony in lovely Southeast Asia. The principalities and powers have told us that we should fight. Furthermore, they have said that we should die if necessary. You and I have shared our discouragement when they are obviously willing to do neither for us. It appears that they have gone out of their way to tie our hands to appease somebody/something. Maybe it has been to win their elections. Possibly it has been to get their "earned" promotions.

If my now cynical observations are correct, we have also "earned" our discouragement. In many ways it appears that we ourselves have been abandoned as an embarrassment. As I look about this Army, it seems to me that we, as he finest Army in the world, are dying a little bit every day from the inside out.

Having expressed my deep discouragement, I don't believe that these feelings are the end of the story. A good story should never end with discouragement! No matter how strong the temptation may be, don't give up. Sir Winston Churchill once led Great Britain during the darkest days of the Second World War. Looking the darkness full in the face, he defiantly and loudly spoke out.

"Never, Never, Never give up!"

You may not like this, but, I doubt that keeping your brain pickled and anesthetized, will change a thing. At this juncture of life, I hope that you have discovered that the world will be essentially the same the next morning. The only one suffering or effected from your self-administered anesthesia will be you. Believe me. I myself have discovered that a horrid hangover will not cure the ills of the world!

Like it or not, ole Sven is the lead scout now. I beg of you to carefully cause and create that beautiful harmony of all the whirring, twirling, spinning parts. With that harmony, and knowing you, convinces me that you will keep most of the kids given to your care alive. Furthermore, in time, under your leadership, you will send them home to their wives, girlfriends, and parents. I honestly did my best, though it wasn't good enough for TK and Johnny. (What else can we do, except to do our best to keep the kids alive?)

Please don't be angry about my comments. Look at it this way. If you can tell me to write, and to tell the story of these good people, in turn, I can ask you to dream once again. What's more, without shame, I can ask you to care for them. Please, dream again as we both once dreamt not so long ago. Further, I can ask you to, in your own way, recreate the harmony that we once shared. You remember, that was in those days before they sent us here to . . . do whatever they sent us here to do?

As for me, despite the occasionally overpowering temptation, I haven't given up yet. I'm still writing and editing my pathetic hen scratchings. *Not that I can read them by the time the ink dries. Realistically I suppose, by this stage of the game the United States Army has given me up for lost. To the movers and shakers, far more important geopolitical things are at stake. The life of one nobody Warrant Officer pilot doesn't begin register on their importance scale. Then on the other hand, maybe tomorrow, someone will accidently stumble upon me. Of course, if no one finds me, you will never have to read my little sermonic letter to you. (As if I, who of course, always remained sober and sane for the last year have a right to compose this letter to you!) See, everything is not lost, even at this stage of the game, I have not lost my sense of the ironic.*

Ah, my friend, I'm extremely tired right now. Not much energy left in ole Kev anymore. I'm going to nap and remember fondly how you were present for me the night Johnny died.

Love you like a brother, Kev!

p.s. If you do get to read this, don't be embarrassed by my love for you. Remember, I'll be long gone and no one but you will know what I said.

In terrible truth, Kev had blatantly lied to his friend Sven. The pain from his compound fracture was horrible to the extreme. The simple act of breathing seemed to cause subtle movements in his leg which only compounded his excruciating pain. However, he spoke the truth when he said that he was completely exhausted. After he had signed his letter to Sven, he carefully folded it. Pausing for a moment, he smiled at the thought of Sven's reading his sentimental letter. Grimacing in pain, Kev gently tucked it into his ever-present canvas sack of writing materials. Closing his eyes for a moment's peace, he quickly passed out and went to sleep. About three hours later he woke up and began his letter to Pastor Bill.

Dear Pastor Bill,

I have the time, I hope. Yet, I am not sure that I have the energy or the ability to concentrate on the task of expressing my inner thoughts to you. Nevertheless, I need to write this letter before it is too late. The last time we spoke face to face, I was on extension leave. We closed with some very harsh and unkind words. If you receive this letter, you will immediately understand my deeply personal reasons for writing it.

Carefully looking myself over, it appears to me that we may never again have the opportunity to share our heartfelt thoughts. If that is to be the unfortunate case, I don't want to end our long-time friendship on our last bitter notes. It is my heartfelt prayer that both of us can transcend our profound differences and remain friends. Your friendship has been much too important for me to give it up easily. I hope and pray that deep inside you feel the same way.

The last time we spoke, I matched you word for word and increasing volume for increased volume. Yet, in all that noise, I did listen to every word that you said. Combat experience has taught me not to let my anger rule. Yes, I was hurt. I was also very angry. However, when it comes to you, my anger can never completely rule my life. I suspect that if I am

471

found and this letter does not reach you, we will never agree on the meaning of Viet Nam. Then again, in twenty-five or thirty years, we should both be a wee little bit wiser than we are today.

Like with most things, I believe that we both have a part of the truth. I'll concede to you that this might be the wrong war in the wrong place and at the wrong time. In truth, I am not smart enough to make an absolute statement about the "rightness" or the "wrongness" of this war. Yet, my feelings and experience tell me that this war is not anywhere near as wrong as you would have me believe.

However, I will not budge an inch in my belief in and about the soldiers here. They are no worse and maybe a little better than the folks who are making their pretentious pronouncements while safely staying home. I have lived with these young men too long to think evil of them. Have they occasionally done wrong things? Yes. Yet, I also believe that rioting, disrespect for constitutional authority, and draft evasion for personal profit is also wrong. In your righteous anger, you suggested that God could not possibly be present in such a place. You further suggested that God would not be with such people as myself and my friends. In that statement, you have never been more wrong in your whole life!

OK, let me be brutally honest. Most likely, I am slowly dying. At this juncture, I have little or nothing to gain by denying death's bitter reality. Furthermore, if you are reading this, I am already dead. If I have any bitterness about my impending death, it is only because its specifics are going to be so futile and stupid.

Much to my surprise, and I suppose horror, it won't be a bullet which writes the opening line of my life's final chapter. Much to my regret, things are much worse than that. In the end, it will be a meaningless mechanical failure of a worn out piece of equipment that has ended my life! Though that is the case, I do not feel abandoned by God. Nor, have I ever felt that way.

However, and this is important, I do feel abandoned by you in particular and abandoned by the church in general. My good friend Sven and I suspect that the old adage still holds true.

"If you don't like the war, blame the warrior!"

That attitude, which so many back home hold, leaves me with a very bitter taste which continues to linger in my mouth.

When we last spoke/argued, the conversation became excessively harsh and angry on both our parts. Maybe it shouldn't have. However, for better or worse, we both strongly believe what we believe. In your passion you recommended that I read a book. That is, if I hadn't regressed so deeply into barbarism that I could no longer read.

You might be surprised to know that while it is true that I walk hunched over, drag my hairy knuckles, and carry a stone ax, a small part of my brain continues to function. I can still read. Yes, you were absolutely correct. The book you recommended is the most powerful expression of human evil that I have ever read. However, I believe that I have seen more evil committed by the "peaceful people" from the north than you will ever be willing to believe. I already know the face of evil. It is human and it is a horrifying available potential carried within each of us. Mysteriously to me, I'm not sure that you recognize the capability of evil that the "benefactors" from the north have continually displayed.

What you failed to tell me, when you sent me this little book, was the powerfully good news about this little piece of profound wisdom. You didn't tell me that I would also encounter the face of God in this little book. At the end of his fourth chapter, Elie Wiesel tells about the hanging of three people by the concentration camp guards. Those to be hung were two adults and one child. When I read and then reread the passage, I saw this incident as the title page. Clearly, what took place in that camp was the "dark night" of human depredation and degradation. I have copied the text so that you might read it again. Hopefully, sometime soon you will be able to read it with different eyes. Yes my friend. The evil which he speaks of is overwhelming. However, where does Wiesel see God? Strangely enough, he sees him in the middle of an extermination/concentration camp hanging on the gallows.

Some may not like what I have discovered over the last year and during the last few days.. I am sure that my discovery or observations do not fit nicely into a non-offensive white middle-class theology textbook. The God whom I have come to see is not an easy God of my nice little Sunday School. However, it is true. God is even in this "God forsaken" place. Today, I see God hanging on the gallows of war. He suffers with a young man from North Vietnam and a young man from the United States. Selfish, ambitious, a-moral old men, who are seated in the seats of power which they have coveted, have drafted both into their armies. Succinctly put, these ambitions old men have drafted simple young men to die on the gallows politic.

"The Three victims mounted together onto the chairs.
Three necks were placed at the same moment within the nooses.
'Long live liberty!' cried the two adults.
But the child was silent.
'Where is God? Where is He?' someone behind me asked.
At a sign from the head of the camp, the three chairs tipped over.
Total silence throughout the camp. On the horizon, the sun was setting.
'Bare your heads!' yelled the head of the camp. His voice was raucous. We were weeping.
'Cover your heads!'
Then the march past began. The two adults were no longer alive. Their tongues had swollen, blue tinged. But the third rope was still moving; being so light, the child was still alive . . .
For more than an hour he stayed there, struggling between life and death, dying in slow agony under our eyes. And we had to look him full in the face. He was still alive when I passed in front of him. His tongue was red, his eyes not yet glazed.

Behind me I heard the same man asking:
'Where is God now?'
And I hear a voice within me answer him:
'Where is He? Here He is-He is hanging on this gallows . . .'
That night the soup tasted of corpses."

<u>THE NIGHT</u> Elie Wiesel

Ah my friend, during the past year I have discovered that human existence is a massive coloring book of continual bitter, sad, and joyful irony. This ironic, and frequently dismally dark, turn of life always dismays the innocent romantic living within me. However, the comic absurdity of human life also brings gales of laughter to my dust dry lips. It causes me to laugh at myself as I continuously take myself too seriously.

However, what you and the church have forgotten is that my friends and I are but simple soldiers. We don't make grandiose geopolitical decisions. Difficult as it can be, we do our best to follow lawful orders. Condemning us is like killing the bearer of bad news. It doesn't change the reality of the larger human evil of greed.

Apparently, you wanted me to read "The Night" for something other than what I discovered within it. I believe that you hoped that I would see myself as one of the executioners/guards in a nation-sized concentration camp. I am sure that it was your hope that the power of this simple book would strike deep into my "now submerged" human decency. Hopefully, it would reach into my hardened heart and I would feel great guilt and restless remorse for the supposed atrocities that I am an integral part of.

Thinking about it, I see nothing wrong with your desire to convert me to your own world view. In my own strange way, I honor your noble quest for my conversion. However, I have seen far too much, and I have experienced too much horror to be that easily converted to your world view. Interestingly, I see another interestingly ironic twist in life when you ask me to read this book. Unexpectedly, you have become the glorious romantic, and I have become the cynical realist. Like it or not, the unavoidable fact remains that sufficient evil and guilt is available to paint all of humanity in the deepest possible shade of black.

Sometimes I think that in your exiles crusade, you forget the current history of our world. I assure you that Kevin Paul Johnson didn't start this war. Furthermore, I didn't send troops from either side into the mud, muck, and mire of combat. If I sinned in coming here, it was because I trusted my leaders and volunteered to do the best job that I could. Today, I lie dying and probably abandoned by my government as a political liability. Therefore, I believe that your condemnation of the soldier is poorly placed!

Therein lies yet another delicious irony in your quest to convert me. I can't thank you enough for challenging me to read Wiesel's little book. It wasn't a loss. Wonderfully enough, reading the text was a gift

474

beyond price. Granted, it didn't turn out as you expected it would. Yet, it is quite possible that God continues to work in strange and mysterious ways. Without meaning to, you have helped me to see God as my body slowly festers and rots away. I fear to tell you something that you may not want to hear. God is on neither side! Like any good parent, God doesn't take sides in childish squabbles between sibs. As always, the victim is not human. The ultimate victim is always Divine. Today, as I have all but run out of hope for my own life, I now see God hanging on the gallows between two young draftees.

In return, I want to offer you the questionable gift of my current thoughts. Please think of it as a small token for the words that you recommended. Please don't take offense because I intend no offense at this juncture of my life. Considering my tenuous situation, I'm not growling or continuing our argument. Lying here in my own filth and rot, I have moved past vindictive words. They would serve no useful purpose. In fact, I am sadly reflecting upon our last meeting and several encounters and conversations I have had over the past year.

Kev's head droops and his pen slowly slides down the paper leaving a trail. He has passed out from his pain and fatigue.

Forty-five minutes later he suddenly wakes with a startled cry of shock and pain. Thrashing about in near delirium, he has rolled onto his broken leg. The lancing pain and the resulting surge of adrenalin bring him to full wakefulness. Knowing that he must, he takes a sip of water. He also forces down a couple of spoonsfull of canned peaches. That is all he can eat from his C-rations. He laughs bitterly and ironically.

"Canned peaches are one of the few things from 'C's' that I enjoy. Yet, I have become too miserable to enjoy them!"

Glancing down at his pad he sees where the undirected pen left a wavering trail down the paper which well documented his condition. For a moment, he contemplates giving up trying to write to Pastor Bill. The wavering trail of ink cryptically tells his dimming story. Enjoying a moment of self pity, he despairs. Shaking his head in frustration and anger at his weakness, Kev knows that he must finish what he wants to say to his old friend Pastor Bill. If he continues to fail at his present rate, he probably will not be able to write tomorrow.

Sorry about the extraneous line running down the paper. It seems that I "fell asleep" for a little bit. Please overlook it like you would a messy confirmation paper from a twelve-year-old. As sick as I am becoming, I fear that I don't have the time to rewrite that page. I suppose, as dad would frequently accuse me, at the moment, I am being overly melodramatic. Yet, maybe I'm not. It is becoming increasing difficult for me to discern when I am conscious and or if I am delirious. Perhaps, this little epistle of mine is not going to make any sense at all. If it is garbled and rambled at times, please try to sort through all the wordy garbage. Shoot, that should be easy for you. You've done that with my writing before.

Bill, I speak from my heart. I am deeply concerned about the Viet Nam vet and his relationship with the church of tomorrow. Though believing it is difficult given my present condition. I am sure that this war is going to end someday. When that happens, I believe that many hundreds of thousands of young men are going to be looking to the church. This can be an important place for them to find new meaning in their life. Heck, if the papers are correct, there is in the neighborhood of two-hundred-and-fifty-thousand of us in Viet Nam right now. Add that to all the other years and we are talking about a lot of people. Then, if you add all their direct families we are talking about a sizable chunk of the population. The current stand of our denomination is troubling. It is going to make it difficult for any of us to look to our churches for support while rebuilding and making sense out the experience of this war.

Though you may not agree, I fear that most of the church's outspoken critics of this war have no conception of the devastating impact of their words. When denominational officials imply that the troops here are "baby killers," it sets us against our own church. When these same denominational officials, spokes-people, make draft dodgers and deserters heros, it only deeply alienates us. It appears, to me, that somewhere in their pious proclamations somebody forgot something both central and vital.

The young men who are over here remain human beings. We remain children of God and Christ's church.

As horrifying as I find this story to be, it is true. One young man who went home on compassionate leave, when one of his parents was reported to be very ill and possibly on death's bed, was asked to leave the worship service when he showed up in uniform. From the pulpit the minister insensitively proclaimed.

"We don't allow your kind in here!"

I know that this young man, of whom I just spoke, will never enter a church again. And, in all honesty, I don't blame him.

Allow me a more personal comment. When you say from the pulpit that freedom loving peasants are fighting the war here against American tyranny, you destroy your credibility with me. In well over a year in combat, I have never seen one of those so called Viet Cong freedom fighters. Truthfully, I have fought hard-core North Vietnamese Regulars almost every day that I have been here. To be honest, they happen to be magnificent, disciplined, and well-trained troops whom I hold in great respect.

Any resemblance that they might have to revolting peasants is purely accidental. Calling me a liar, in front of dozens of people in the narthex, did not help. Such insults further compounds your loss of credibility with me. You act as if you had spent a year here and not I. Were that not enough, you say that the Army has ruined me because I told the truth as I have experienced it every day for over a year.

Let me ask a couple of serious questions my friend. After those kinds of public comments, how can I come to you for the care of my spirit and my soul? Also, how can I respect you when, in turn, you offer my person and experience no respect? Please remember that I was taught to tell the truth and you were one of my teachers. How can you condemn me for that? While my truth drawn out of my experience may not match yours, is that grounds for condemnation?

The Good Lord well knows that I have never been a jump up and down Bible Thumper. However, I believe that we all need to look closely at the life of Jesus if we are to come to an understanding of God. Please don't misunderstand me. I have no pretensions of being a theologian. I couldn't split a theological hair if I had to. In brutal honesty, I am confident that I couldn't find a theological hair on me if it needed splitting. Yet, in my theological simplicity, I can look at the life of Jesus. I believe that a great many leaders of our church need to look a bit more closely at the life and ministry of Jesus. After they do so, then they can condemn me and my friends if it is appropriate. You taught me that our highest aim should be to imitate Christ. Please understand that I make no claims to be imitating Christ. However, I am not a denominational leader.

Let me illustrate what I am pointing to. Several incidents in Jesus' life stand out in my mind. The first interesting incident is the healing of the Centurion's slave. I hope that you remember that the Centurion was an officer in the occupying Roman army. Despite his being a soldier and officer, Jesus healed his slave and praised his faith for being superior to the children of Israel. Strangely enough, it was another Centurion who proclaimed that Jesus was Lord after the crucifixion. This observation leads me to wonder. Is there a place for soldiers in God's world as Jesus defined it? Ironically, these were Biblical soldiers of an occupying army. According to you, they are like me occupying another's home and oppressing them. Please, take some time and ponder and pray upon these little incidents from Jesus' life.

Let me suggest to you that if you are going to speak of God to a vet who has been out in the field you are going to have difficulties. What are you going to say to the guy whom the politicians in Washington have drafted and sent to this place? How are you going to talk to a man who has seen his buddies blown up and killed while he lies in the mud and muck of the battle field? Do you think that he is going to respond to a "kissie-face -- huggie-bear -- feel-good" easy God of Sunday School? I doubt that he will ever find the God of his salvation in that "safe antiseptic presentation." How is he going to make sense of his own suffering and the suffering that surrounds him while listening to platitudes and pretty words? Lastly, do you thank that making him a criminal and disowning him will bring him to a good end?

We all know that I'm not a trained theologian. However, I have learned that try as we might, we can't get to God. God is too different and too far away from the human chaos of our world. However, I have found a starting point in my own quest for the Holy. If Jesus is who you say he is, those of us thrust into and abandoned in this mess have a starting point. Today, I find nine words spoken from the gallows/cross of Jesus resonate with my life.

"My God, my God, why have you forsaken me?"

I remember the story. It was Friday and Jesus, whom you say is also God, felt abandoned. Sunday morning a stone was rolled away. God did not abandon him after all. If God is present and available for the Vietnam Vet, that is where we are going to find him. God will be at the place where we feel most abandoned.

Pastor Bill, I am getting so very weary. Once again, my head is starting to spin and I am afraid that I won't finish this letter if I don't end it right now. If you read this, obviously this is my goodby. Over the years you have meant too much to me and you have been too dear of a friend to close on a sour note. If I spoke, or have spoken today, out of turn and hurt you, I deeply apologize. Remember! Please – please remember that I have always had a very special love for my friend and pastor.

Just Kev.

Bathed in sweat and trembling in fatigue and pain, Kev slowly folded the letter. On each cheek, a forlorn tear was slowly marking its passage as it traveled through the grime of his face. He then carefully placed it, in his sack of writing materials, next to his letter to Sven. Suddenly he started to uncontrollably wretch. The spasmodic movement of his gut upsets his broken leg. Moaning in pain, he mercifully passed out. Feverish and thrashing about he was unaware of the excruciating pain which was wracking his battered body. The sun slowly slipped below the horizon.

THE RED BIRD IS DOWN, BUT NOT FORGOTTEN!

Day 5:
　　For young Kev, the simple and basic task of physical survival was becoming increasingly impossible. Somehow, he struggled, physically, spiritually, and emotionally to survive another agonizing and restless night. Finding neither rest nor peace, within or without, he continuously tossed and turned. The young man's distressed motions served to greatly amplify his pain and renew his bleeding. Occasionally, he would reluctantly come half awake. Aware that he was feverish and becoming dangerously dehydrated, he continued to fight his battle. Suffering and sweaty, Kev tried his best to drink something when he woke. Each time his pain woke him, disciplining himself, Kev drank a small sip of water or a little juice from the canned fruit. He drank a little water or juice because he knew that he must, not because he wanted to drink anything.

However, for the larger part of the night, he slept fitfully. Thankfully, when he made the torturous journey to the land of sleep, he wasn't aware of his pain. These few moments of oblivion were the only blessing which remained for the broken young man. Selfishly, yet understandably, he embraced each moment of sleep joyfully. His body was so damaged, sick, and fatigued that any time that the pain lessened, drifting off into oblivion was both easy for him and greatly welcomed. He did not know if he slept or passed out. The pain was so great that he didn't care what it was that he embraced the other side of wakefulness.

Following the long night which passed for a subjective eternity, a new morning renewed his conscious ordeal. The sun began to poke its first tentative rays through the jungle canopy and the land around him began to wake. To the east of him, the physical blackness representing his long night's suffering began to lift its leaden cloak. Stifling a low moan, the presence of morning's light in the east pleasantly surprised Kev. Deep within, he had not expected to survive the torturous night's agony. Yet, experiencing the light of another new day was a gift of mixed blessings. Kev was glad to see the sunrise and continue his fight for survival. However, the soft moan that tried to escape his parched lips acknowledged his suffering.

Deep within the private confines of his heart, he was a very frightened little boy. He wasn't a doctor. Yet, when he was rational, his weakness and fever convinced him that the coming day was going to be his last. Glancing at his stack of unopened C-rations and at the stream within his reach filled him with a twisted irony. Piercing his soul, he felt a disagreeable laugh rise in his throat. The foul gorge and the bitter bile of his cynical suppressed laughter gagged him. Despairing, he muttered to himself.

"D--- it, it seems that I can't win for losing! Look at this crazy situation! I have sufficient food for a couple of weeks. Better yet, I have plenty of water, and I am in a warm climate. With all this going for me, it is not going to do me a d--- bit of good! It appears that at best, I'm going to rot to death with a full belly."

Striving to maintain his last shard of human dignity, Kev attempted to clean the spreading foulness from his decaying body. Strain and struggle as he might, the simple task was far beyond his rapidly waning strength. Cries of deep anguish escaped his tightly compressed lips several times. Involuntarily, he cried out each time he shifted his bodily position. Quaking and exhausted, eventually he surrendered to the pain's overwhelming demands. His ineffectual effort to regain a small touch of his humanity had left him trembling, sweating, and gasping for breath.

The insecure little boy, who had always lived deep within Chief Warrant Officer Kevin Paul Johnson, wanted to cry in passionate rage at the world's unfairness. His dispirited spirit dearly needed a cleansing cry. Yet, no tears made their journey down his fevered cheeks. Dejected and despairing, he sat encrusted in his own filth. Dried blood, smelly stale urine, crusted vile vomit, foul feces, and the sweet smell of rot were his constant companions. These were not the companions he would have chosen for what he believed was his final journey. Nevertheless, he saw them as the fact and the proof that he was writing his final chapter in his personal saga.

It was now five days after his crash, and shedding tears required more strength than remained in his horribly corrupted and broken body. Of all his possible ending chapters, Mrs. Johnson's little boy had never envisioned this one for himself. In his current condition, Kev felt neither heroic nor valiant. He only felt dirty, discarded, and despicable. Looking down at himself and wearily shaking his head, he commented.

"God Kev, you're a pathetic sight. Shoot, your garbage eating dog would turn up his nose and walk away in total disgust."

Grimly, Kev came to the conclusion that he was waging his final epic battle within the intimacy of his own head.

His remaining shards of glory and romanticism found that internal battle site to be discouraging. Who would witness his final battle? When his last battle ended and the ultimate enemy defeated him, no report of his glory would be forwarded. Amused with his new concerns, he asked.

"Who will sing the wonderful folk songs and read the epic poems of my history-changing life and the great battles from which I emerged victorious?"

Yet, he was determined to fight on with the limited resources available to him. Surrender and retreat were not options that he was going to accept.

At last, he decided that if he were to die alone and in a far away place, so be it. Ruefully shaking his head, he decided that he would die facing his enemy eyeball to eyeball. His Swedish forebearers had taught him to accept the vaguenesses and various unjust varieties of life with a quiet stoicism. That task was very difficult because quiet stoicism was something that he had never done very well. Reluctantly embracing his heritage, Kev concluded that he would not cry out at the unfairness of life. In stoic defiance of his cruel fate, he was grimly determined to maintain his last shadow of human dignity. His tattered battle flag and personal colors were not going to be dipped in abject surrender to any outside force or further unexpected circumstance.

Pondering upon his emotions for a moment, Kev was quite surprised to discover that he was concerned with his dignity. This strange concern was as foreign to him as his decaying physical condition was. Like any other normal young man, he had his personal concerns and emotional concerns about himself and his life. However, he had never previously been interested in his personal dignity. Softly spoken, a string of letters hesitantly began to flow from Kev's parched lips.

"**D I G N I T Y**. Ha, I may not know exactly what it means or what it is. However, I can spell the word. I suppose that's a beginning"

From personal experience, Kev knew that strong young men don't need to be concerned about dignity. From his previous point of view, that foreign issue was a concern best left to the old and infirmed. Vital young men make their bold mark upon the world with the brashness and the endless strength of youthful maleness. Moving and shaking the stoutest and deepest foundations of the earth firmly establishes who they are. However, what bodily remained of Kevin Paul Johnson was neither strong nor was it physically powerful.

Looking down at the blood-soaked wrapping on his broken leg reinforced Kev's depressive feelings of dread and doom. With little else to do, he reviewed his short life. Smiling to himself, he remembered running a sub four-minute indoor mile while he was in High School. Proud of himself, he had told no one of his impressive run. He had done it as a personal training exercise. However, he had been greatly pleased at the wondrous strength of his wind and legs. Sadly, he knew that it was all gone and never to return. Like an elderly man lying in his final hospital bed, Kev could feel his life itself slowly slipping away between his fingers. The movement was like the countless dry grains of sand on the beach blowing in whatever direction they chose. Each blowing grain was like another drop of his blood slowly seeping through the crude bandages.

With a mournful shake of his head, he suddenly understood why he had become concerned with his dignity. Kevin Paul Johnson's dignity was the only part of his humanness that remained under his own control! A meaningless crash could, and did, destroy his leg. Faceless politicians could, and did, send him to war and leave him broken and dying. Blind fate could be, and was, the genesis of the internal physical rot which was slowly killing him. However, only Kevin Paul Johnson could give up his dignity. Gritting his teeth, he set himself to endure the unendurable.

Grimly hanging onto life, Kev struggled to gather sufficient strength to write one last letter. He wanted to write to his folks. There were so many things which he wanted and needed to say to them. Yet, he asked himself.

"How does one say goodby to Mom and Dad?"

Thinking about what he would write to his folks, his emotional control began to rapidly break down. Willing the loss of emotional control not to happen, was turning out to be a futile effort. Great sobs of angst and anguish formed in the pit of his stomach. Angry at his own weakness, he viciously fought to regain emotional control. From the depths of his memories and with warm feelings for his old and good friend Sven, he chided himself.

"D--- It Kev, Grow up!"

Suddenly, he thought that he heard a friendly sound in the distance. He wasn't sure that he heard it as he prayed that his ears had not betrayed him. Listening carefully, he thought it sounded like a Loach doing a slow recon. Though he was sure that had heard it, he didn't dare to hope for rescue. The brutal suffering and decomposition of his body had moved him past hoping for anything but release from his suffering. However, Kev had nothing left to hang onto, except hope. Within, he dared not ask if it was possible that the Cav was still looking for him. In his heart he knew that they would be. He was a downed Red Bird and the Cav took care of downed Red Birds. That is, if higher headquarters allowed them to do so.

Listening carefully, he was convinced that he could hear something that sounded like a little Red Bird flying a distance away. To his straining hopeful ears, it seemed to be slowly working its way in his general direction. Enduring the searing pain that was the result of movement, he gingerly changed position. The life-force, which remained within his diminished body, demanded that he look up to the open skies. Broken, buried, and mostly hidden under the towering trees, he could only see little patches of blue. Struggling to mate hope to sight and sound, he clearly remembered the little clearing he had been aiming for when he crashed.

With his hopes soaring toward the highest heavens, he started to move in the direction of the little clearing. Fully embracing the inhumane pain of movement, he struggled to move. With each incremental movement, the searing pain shot up and down his leg without mercy. Trembling and biting down upon his lip, he shifted position. Fatally weakened, Kev now lived only in the hope that he could catch a restricted glimpse of the clearing. His emotions were surging up and down like giant waves crashing upon a seawall. The fickle winds of fate had freely mingled hope and despair. Those opposing feelings of life and death were frantically intermixed like the wind-driven chop on his beloved Cape Cod Bay.

He knew it. He was convinced of that one elementary truth that had been his life for over a year. His friends in the Cav hadn't forgotten him! Kev's faith was well founded, and his spirits soared to heights he hadn't know in the last five days. His brothers were coming to his rescue! Things much more sacred than mundane political considerations drove the men and boys of his Cav! This wasn't the first time that they had disobeyed orders for the purposes of saving a life. His friends and comrades never disregarded the all important call.

"RED BIRD DOWN."

Just as suddenly, the fickle tide turned against him. Hope became deep, dark, and dreadful despair. He remembered that the crash had buried him and old 662 in the trees! Frantically looking about, he feared that they could never find him under the towering trees! His mood was changing as fast as the alternating current in a common house light. An outside observer, had one been present, could not have seen the emotional swings. However, like the common light bulb, he burned bright in alternating hope and dark in dreadful despair. Glowing, flushed, hot, and feverish, he feebly struggled to see the source of the reassuring buzz of an OH-6. Anguishing, because he could not see the little Red Bird, he searched the small patches of blue for the Snakes flying cover. Search as he might, he could neither see nor hear them.

As the sound of the searching Loach drew nearer, his prayerful anxiety about being found became dreadfully deep and dark panic. Instinctively, Kev knew that he had to help his friends find him. That was his obligation if the rescue mission was to succeed. With dry tears of anguish, rage, and frustration flowing down his face, he cried, cursed and frantically sought an answer. God, the Army, and the Congress were among the growing list of targets which his fumbling rage zeroed in upon. All of this emotional anguish was because he didn't have a survival radio to call for help.

Yesterday, he had faced his dwindling strength with sad resignation. Unwittingly, young Kev had given up the hope of rescue. However, he didn't know that he had given up the hope of being rescued when he had done so. Facing the possibility of being rescued, he suddenly realized, with great personal shame, that he had given up hope. In his current despair, he had forgotten the smoke grenades which he had so laboriously dragged over. When he had set up camp, he had placed the three grenades with his stash of C-rations. With his growing panic overpowering every thought and physical limitation, he reached down for a grenade. It was not there! During the night, when he had thrashed about, the three grenades had rolled out of his immediate reach. Lunging for them, for a brief moment, he was unaware of the intense waves of pain washing over him. Nothing in all of creation mattered to Kev but reaching the life saving smoke grenades.

The electric intensity of his physical anguish caused his field of vision to sharply constrict. What little information his eyes sent to his brain was swimming about in no apparent pattern. Overwhelmed by the pain stimulus, his stomach knotted and tried to empty itself. With his life force slipping away, nothing else mattered except reaching the marking grenades. Unable to see and unable to think, the reflex to sustain his life drove him without mercy. After a moment, or a lifetime of agony, his grasping hand found a grenade.

Blindly retching up a bitter bile-like nothing from an empty stomach, he managed to pull the pin. When the spoon snapped free of the grenade, the exploding grenade immediately filled Kev's world with billowing clouds of hot red smoke. Gasping to catch his breath and fighting to stay conscious, he was completely spent. Physical exhaustion and unbearable pain threw Kev prostrate upon the ground. The hot red swirling stuff obscured the world beyond Kev's tactile awareness. With a tragic poetry, it directly mirrored the burning world of pain and torment within Kev's inner awareness.

Long and agonizing minutes passed and the blood red smoke began to slowly dissipate through the trees. Eventually, the crashing and surging waves of nausea threatening Kev began to subside. Just as slowly, the young man's vision began to return. Panting as if he had run a marathon, he struggled to maintain his tenuous grip on an increasingly slippery consciousness. Thankfully, he could still hear the sweet mechanical music of one of his beloved Red Birds. However, his pain-hazed mind could not decide if it was getting closer or going away. A distant part of his brain was trying to tell him that his shattered leg was bleeding again. He ignored the message as totally irrelevant to the moment. Reaching deeper into his diminishing reserves, Kev managed to turn his head toward the clearing.

The approaching sight which greeted his eyes made his spirits soar on the wings of the mighty eagle. With all his remaining strength, Kev struggled to move. He wanted to wave, yell, or make himself conspicuous. However, any such physical effort was beyond his failing physical strength. Struggling to reach the scattered smoke grenades had used up the last of his reserves. Though he was physically spent, he stayed conscious to witness the arrival of his salvation.

"Thank God." He said to no one in particular.

At last, the previously silent gods of wayward Army helicopter pilots had kindly smiled upon him. **He had not been abandoned!**

Apparently, the little Loach, which he had been trying to attract, had seen his red smoke grenade. The wonderful little bird of all his dreams was on short final for landing in the clearing he had missed five days earlier. Half delirious, Kev couldn't see the little bird clearly. Still, he could see enough to know that his suffering was, at last, coming to an end! Continuing his fight against the surging waves of pain and the fuzzy warm allure of unconsciousness, he wondered whose bird it was. He couldn't see the tail number or even tell if it was from his troop. However, it didn't matter where it came from. Help was at hand.

Watching the little bird flare for landing, Kev noted that the back-seater was alertly standing upon the landing skid. He had his M-60 at the ready. Instantly and instinctively, Kev knew that this man was good. When the helmet-shrouded head swivelled, the M-60 seemed to be "mechanically" slaved to the observers eyes. It turned to the direction which he looked. Of course, Kev could not see his eyes. That window to the back-seater's soul was completely hidden behind the darkly smoked faceplate. To another, the equipment-laden man standing boldly on the skid might have looked like a hungry alien creature coming to devour him.

Nevertheless, Kev was undisturbed by not being able to see the eyes. Looking into the other's eyes was a luxury reserved for the peacetime world. He knew that the observer's eyes were looking out for his safety. After flying with the Scouts for over a year, the suffering young man did not need to make eye contact with the observer to feel safe and secure. He clearly understood the back-seater's job and responsibilities. The fact that the observer was paying strict attention to his job was what made Kev feel that his salvation was at hand.

"Discipline," Kev thought to himself.

"The observer has very good discipline. In turn, I also need the same discipline to hang on till they get me."

He/himself was of lesser interest to the observer than the possibility of trouble.

Unable to see the other observer, Kev was confident that he was just as focused and cautious as the back-seater. Kev knew that he/himself wouldn't have popped smoke if the bad guys were in the neighborhood. However, the people in the little Red Bird didn't have the comforting knowledge of Kev's intentions. As far as they knew, they could be landing in a cleverly designed helicopter trap. In this combat world of Vietnam, the wise Red Bird crew was ready for any unpleasant possibilities. Kev himself had stumbled into a helicopter trap or two over the last year. The caution that he observed was a good sign. It felt good to be in the hands of professionals.

Kev surprised himself with his professional concerns. Considering his dire straights, his pending rescue should have been his only concern. Yet, as an professional, he caught himself evaluating the pilot's flying skills. It was immediately obvious to him that the man driving the little Red Bird had a wonderfully soft touch. It appeared to Kev that he had been flying a Loach for thousands of hours. As he watched, the little bird was settling down, into a low hover.

To him, it looked as if the smoothly moving helicopter looked as if it were a carnival ride which invisible cables carefully guided. The pilot's control movements were so soft and light that Kev could not discern any of the pilot's hand motions as he gently guided the little bird. The pilot's mastery of the helicopter impressed him as he watched him lovingly caress the little Red Bird. It was as if the little bird was an extension of the pilot. Watching this, Kev felt confident that this pilot could handle the extra weight and take him to his destination.

Calm, yet ready for trouble, the pilot took a slow sweeping look about the area. He only briefly glanced at Kev. Satisfied that all was well, he gently set the little Loach on the ground. He seemed so calm that it could have been a training flight back at Ft. Wolters or Ft. Rucker. When the unknown pilot behind the dark face shield had looked his way, Kev tried to raise his arm in a wave. Well . . . , he knew that he had tried to raise his arm. However, he wasn't convinced that his hand and arm actually moved. At the end of his emotional rope and with his body rapidly failing him, Kev wept in a discordant stereo whimper. The sounds of joy and frustration were combined and intertwined in the soft sound that escaped his lips. He was thankful that his friends in the Cav had seen him. He knew that they would have to come to him for he was well beyond moving under his own power.

With the patience born of need and powerlessness, Kev watched as the unknown pilot slowly rolled the throttle back to flight idle. After a moment, the two observers cautiously stepped upon the ground. They had not removed their helmets and chicken plates nor had they disconnected their interphone cords. As he watched them, Kev could see the back-seater's lips moving, and he knew that he was talking to the pilot. When the front-seater got out, he had noted that both observers had armed themselves with M-60's. It made him feel good to note that it was exactly the same configuration that the lead scouts in his troop used.

By this time, he was sure that they were Cav troops and not some administrative unit using Loachs.. All the evidence pointed toward the Cav. However, the absence of another Red Bird flying wing deeply puzzled him. He thought to himself.

"Maybe this troop flies pink teams, one Scout and one Snake,"

Adding to his growing puzzlement, he had yet to hear or see any Snakes flying high cover over the little bird. Mentally shrugging his shoulders, he decided not to concern himself with the Snakes. The other bird, or birds, must be close by and he just couldn't see or hear them. Most likely his oversight was a clear reflection of his own weakness.

Continuing to confound a slightly bewildered Kev, the pilot of the Red Bird cut the throttle and shut down the engine. Kev couldn't understand why he would do this. Shutting down the engine of a helicopter when not at a heliport or staging area was very strange. Bewildered and befuddled, Kev watched the rotor blades as they slowly coasted to a stop. As the four rotor blades slowly windmilled their way to a stop, the pilot unstrapped his crash harness and stepped out of the little helicopter. Like his two observers, he kept his chicken plate and helmet on. When he stepped out, the three of them disconnected their intercom cords. Nodding to each other, they started cautiously walking line abreast toward Kev.

Lying upon the ground in his feverish state, Kev wasn't sure what he was looking at. Everything that was happening to him seemed so strange. Struggling to focus his eyes and keep his head clear, he had the feeling that he was watching a badly out of focus grade "B" movie. In focus or not, the three figures were slowly and steadily advancing in Kev's direction. The pilot was walking in the middle with his 45-cal. pistol drawn and at the ready. Like the observers, he had not bothered removing his olive drab nomex flight gloves. Flanking him, one on each side, were the two observers. Remaining alert and cautious, they carried their M-60's at the ready. Each M-60 had a belt of fifty to one hundred rounds of ammunition locked and loaded.

Advancing in a slow and steady cadence, the three olive drab figures continued to carefully walk in his direction. The only relief from the bland olive drab was the pale lower faces below the helmet visors and the bright brass of the belted M-60 ammo. Confused or not, Kev's battered and almost broken spirit wanted to jump up and down for joy. Yet, something strange and unnerving was holding him back. No one had spoken since they had landed. When the mechanical disturbance of the helicopter ended, the jungle seemed to pause and hold its breath.

The image before his eyes was grainy and almost washed out. Still, Kev watched the three olive drab figures as they continued their slow motion advance toward the feverish prone pilot. Kev silently watched, waited, and motionlessly celebrated. He was too weakened to do anything else. When the three figures got close enough to touch him, the pilot knelt down to speak to him. Unsure of himself, Kev began to sing in an ocean of feelings of deep dread and disease. Struggling to clear his head, he didn't understand why he had those feelings. However, those were his feelings. The faces of the hulking armored flight crew remained obscured by their dark face shields and microphones pressed upon their lips.

Just as Kev was sure that he would explode from the growing tension, the kneeling pilot spoke softly and gently.

"Boy, am I glad that we found you, Buddy. You may not know it, but we've been looking for you for a long time."

Kev's spirits soared because he had been right all along. The Cav doesn't forget its own, and the Cav didn't forget one of its own. Trying to say something to the faceless pilot, Kev's parched lips moved but no sound came out. Reaching deep within his meager reserves of strength, willing himself to lift his hand and arm, Kev struggled without success. He continued to lie helpless upon the earth looking up at the faceless pilot.

Everything that had happened during the morning continued to confuse and bewilder him. However, he accepted that he was sick enough to be confused and bewildered. Nevertheless, he couldn't understand their strange behavior. Why didn't any of these unknown men take off their flight helmets and gloves? Whenever he landed, Kev always removed his flight helmet and gloves. He hated the weight and heat of them in the steamy tropical stove that everyone called Viet Nam. Yet, they didn't. Kev wondered if they knew something that he didn't.

"Maybe," he thought to himself. "The bad guys are close and they want to be ready to run. No. If that were so, they wouldn't have shut-down the helicopter."

Looking down at Kev's mangled and bloody leg, the faceless pilot continued to speak kindly with a soft and surprisingly gentle voice.

"I don't know. That leg looks really bad, Bud. Tell you what I'm going to do. Before we go one step farther, I'm going to give you something for the pain. You've already suffered more than any man should be called upon to suffer. I've brought some good s--- with me."

Kev watched him as he took out a morphine surette. The kind faceless pilot continued to speak in his surprisingly soft voice.

"This is going to pinch a little. Then, all your troubles are going to come to an end."

Examining the kneeling pilot's hands as they worked compounded Kev's growing confusion. What the pilot was doing for him didn't make any sense. While it made no sense, he wasn't going to complain. However, it didn't fit in with his experience in Vietnam. Army pilots were not issued morphine. Kev already knew that! Somebody, safely protected by their military issue desk, had decided that they couldn't trust Officers and pilots with the drug. Nevertheless, when the needle punctured his exposed arm, Kev immediately felt the pain deadening warmth gently flowing through his body. He was grateful beyond words.

Slightly baffled by the strange and mysterious happenings, Kev finally began to feel a hopeful peace and contentment. The emotional warmth that Kev was experiencing complimented the chemical warmth of the drug as it spread through his battered body. Matching the slow ebb of the pain in his body was the ebb of the pain in his soul and spirit. However, all was well. Shortly, he would be going home. The Cav was standing by the broken young man. Bravely, someone with courage had broken the rules and supplied morphine to the searchers. Strengthened by the dissipating pain, Kev reached up and grasped the hand of the faceless pilot. Kev saw a small smile forming behind the mike pressed up to the man's lips. He spoke softly to the young pilot.

"You just take it easy Buddy. We're getting ready to go."

Looking about, he then spoke to the two observers.

"Is there any reason that we shouldn't take our friend home now?"

After a moment, the efficient back-seater spoke quietly.

"No sir. As far as I'm concerned, nothing is holding us here anymore. Our friend is going home. His job and our job is done"

When the observer finished speaking, the three young men removed their flight helmets. At last, Kev could see the faces of his rescuers. For some reason that he didn't understand, Kev felt that seeing the face of his saviors was important. However, the strange vision that his brain recorded didn't make any sense.

His immediate thought, in the midst of his confusion, was that the pilot must have given him a massive dose of morphine.

"Yes, that's it. He must have overdosed me. That has to be the reason I am seeing what I think that I am seeing."

Throughly baffled and completely bewildered, Kev thought that he recognized two of the three faces. Yet . . . , he knew that they couldn't be the people that he thought he recognized. Such a thing wasn't possible. Kev tried to say something. He couldn't. He was speechless. Sensing his confusion, the soothing voice of the pilot spoke to him.

"Hey lead, you just take it easy now."

With a loving smile he continued with a teasing tone in his voice.

"Don't get your panties all bunched up and get yourself all upset. There is nothing left for you to worry about. The three of us are here to take care of you."

Patting Kev's hand, he continued.

"Ole TK is here to take care of his old lead pilot. In case you forgot, a good wingman is forever. Anyway, we've got a lot more flying to do. Of course, you know the guy who was standing on the skid. This isn't the first time that Johnny has joined the effort to take your ragged butt home. Come to think of it, this is not the first time you saw him arrive standing on a skid. The front-seater, who you don't recognize, is called George. He used to fly with the Lieutenant who went down on your first mission. You remember. The day you flew as a sandbag on the C&C ship. When he heard that you were down, ole George asked to tag along with us. It seems that he remembers your first mission in country and wanted to return the favor."

It was all more than Kev could understand. His mind was numb. Convinced that the morphine was playing tricks on his overloaded mind, he was content to know that the Cav never forgot its own. What more could a man ask for than to be remembered by his brothers?

With that comforting thought on his mind, Kev watched the big back-seater slowly kneel down beside him. Possessively, carefully, and ever so gently, Johnny slipped his arms under Kev's battered body to lift him. As the broken young man was being lifted into the compassionate arms of his friend, the morphine finished its wondrous mission of mercy. Safe at last, young Kev drifted off into the blessed land of warm and fuzzy unconsciousness.

His face softened with his first gentle boyish smile in many months. All was well in his world. The Cav was taking him home just as he always knew that they would.